# SOLDIERS OF FREEDOM:

# THE WWII STORY OF PATTON'S PANTHERS AND THE EDELWEISS PIRATES

## VOLUME FIVE OF THE WORLD WAR TWO SERIES

# SAMUEL MARQUIS

## MOUNT SOPRIS PUBLISHING

# PRAISE FOR SAMUEL MARQUIS

**#1 *Denver Post* Bestselling Author**
**Kirkus Reviews Book of the Year Winner**
**Foreword Reviews Book of the Year Winner**
**Independent Publisher Book Awards Winner**
**Readers' Favorite Book Awards Winner**
**Beverly Hills Books Awards Winner**
**National Indie Excellence Book Awards Winner**
**Next Generation Indie Book Awards Winner**
**American Book Fest-USA Best Book Award-Winning Finalist**
**Colorado Book Awards Award-Winning Finalist**

"*The Coalition* has a lot of good action and suspense, an unusual female assassin, and the potential to be another *The Day After Tomorrow* [the runaway bestseller by Allan Folsom]."
—James Patterson, #1 *New York Times* Bestselling Author

"*Spies of the Midnight Sun* is not only a skillful, rapid-fire historical spy thriller, but also a fine source on one of the least-known and most heroic chapters of the Second World War."
—Kirkus Reviews

"Told through multiple viewpoints in a series of vivid scenes, *Lions of the Desert* is rather like a multi-character miniseries (a miniseries I'd love to see!)...Terrific storytelling."
—Historical Novel Society

"Marquis is a student of history, always creative, [and] never boring....A good comparison might be Tom Clancy."
—Military.com

"*Altar of Resistance* is a gripping and densely packed thriller dramatizing the Allied Italian campaign...reminiscent of Herman Wouk's *The Winds of War*."
—Kirkus Reviews

"Marquis grabs my attention right from the beginning and never lets go."
—Governor Roy R. Romer, 39th Governor of Colorado

"*The Coalition* starts with a bang, revs up its engines, and never stops until the explosive ending....Perfect for fans of James Patterson, David Baldacci, and Vince Flynn."
—Foreword Reviews

"Marquis writes quite well, but his real contribution with *Blackbeard: The Birth of America* is historical....An engrossing and historically grounded yarn."
—Kirkus Reviews

"In his novels *Blind Thrust* and *Cluster of Lies*, Samuel Marquis vividly combines the excitement of the best modern techno-thrillers, an education in geology, and a clarifying reminder that the choices each of us make have a profound impact on our precious planet."
—Ambassador Marc Grossman, Former U.S. Under Secretary of State and Co-Author of *Believers: Love and Death in Tehran*

"When I read a book about World War II these days, I look for something new...*Lions of the Desert* by Samuel Marquis delivered this in spectacular fashion. He has written another great book about the war that we should never forget."
—Ray Simmons for Readers' Favorite (5-Star Review)

"A simply riveting read from beginning to end, *Spies of the Midnight Sun* is impressively informed and informative, and a work of solidly researched history."
—Midwest Book Review

"In the richness of the texture of his material, Marquis far exceeds the stance of a mere raconteur and entertainer of the masses—he, in fact, becomes a public historian."
—Lois C. Henderson, Bookpleasures.com (Crime & Mystery) - 5-Star Review

"A combination of *The Great Escape*, *Public Enemies*, a genuine old-time Western, and a John Le Carré novel."
—BlueInk Review (for *Bodyguard of Deception*, Book 1 of WWII Series)

"*Cluster of Lies* has a twisty plot that grabs hold from the beginning and never let's go. A true page turner! I'm already looking forward to the next Joe Higheagle adventure."
—Robert Bailey, Author of *Legacy of Lies* and *The Final Reckoning*

"If you haven't tried a Samuel Marquis novel yet, *The Fourth Pularchek* is a good one to get introduced. The action is non-stop and gripping with no shortage of surprises. If you're already a fan of the award-winning novelist, this one won't disappoint."
—Dr. Wesley Britton, Bookpleasures.com (Crime & Mystery) - 5-Star Review

"Marquis is the new Follett, Silva, and Clancy rolled into one."
—Prof. J.R. Welch, Editor of *Dispatches from Fort Apache*

"Reminiscent of *The Day of the Jackal*...with a high level of authentic detail. Skyler is a convincing sniper, and also a nicely conflicted one."
—Donald Maass, Author of *The Emotional Craft of Fiction* (for *The Coalition*)

"Readers looking for an unapologetic historical action book should tear through this volume."
—Kirkus Reviews (for *Bodyguard of Deception*)

"Samuel Marquis picks up his World War II trilogy with *Altar of Resistance*, a well-researched and explosive ride through war-torn Rome with Nazis, booming battles, and intense cat-and-mouse chases....Grounded in historical fact but spiced up with thrilling imagination with the fate of the world in balance."
—Foreword Reviews

# BY SAMUEL MARQUIS

## WORLD WAR TWO SERIES

SOLDIERS OF FREEDOM
LIONS OF THE DESERT
SPIES OF THE MIDNIGHT SUN
ALTAR OF RESISTANCE
BODYGUARD OF DECEPTION

## NICK LASSITER-SKYLER INTERNATIONAL ESPIONAGE SERIES

THE FOURTH PULARCHEK
THE COALITION
THE DEVIL'S BRIGADE

## JOE HIGHEAGLE ENVIRONMENTAL SLEUTH SERIES

CLUSTER OF LIES
BLIND THRUST

## BLACKBEARD: THE BIRTH OF AMERICA

# SOLDIERS OF FREEDOM:

## THE WWII STORY OF PATTON'S PANTHERS AND THE EDELWEISS PIRATES

### VOLUME FIVE OF THE WORLD WAR TWO SERIES

# SAMUEL MARQUIS

MOUNT SOPRIS PUBLISHING

# SOLDIERS OF FREEDOM
## VOLUME FIVE OF THE WORLD WAR TWO SERIES



MOUNT SOPRIS PUBLISHING

Trade paper: ISBN 978-1-943593-27-9
Kindle eBook: ISBN 978-1-943593-28-6



First Mount Sopris Publishing premium printing: March 2020
Cover Design: Christian Fuenfhausen (http://cefdesign.com)
Formatting: Rik Hall (www.WildSeasFormatting.com)
Printed in the United States of America

**To Order Samuel Marquis Books and Contact Samuel:**

Visit Samuel Marquis's website, join his mailing list, learn about his forthcoming novels and book events, and order his books at www.samuelmarquisbooks.com. Please send all fan mail (including criticism) to samuelmarquisbooks@gmail.com. Thank you for your support!

**ATTENTION: ORGANIZATIONS AND CORPORATIONS**

Mount Sopris Publishing books may be purchased for educational, business, or sales promotional use. For information, please email the Special Markets Department at samuelmarquisbooks@gmail.com.

# Dedication

To the officers and enlisted men of the 761st Tank Battalion who triumphed on WWII European battlefields, and to the German youth of the Edelweiss Pirates who fought against Nazi tyranny. Both of these groups should have been properly recognized by the Allies immediately following the war for their bravery in the name of freedom—and for standing up to the intolerance and brutality of their own countrymen.

And to Coach Dave Rice (1927-2018)—Graland Country Day School athletic director, football and lacrosse coach, and legend—who was a great admirer of General George "Old Blood and Guts" Patton and who taught me more than a thing or two about sports and life.

# SOLDIERS OF FREEDOM:
# THE WWII STORY OF PATTON'S PANTHERS AND THE EDELWEISS PIRATES

*When you're young, you don't think you're going to die. Bullets don't mean anything. It's a cowboy thing. Then you see the blood and everything changes. We sacrificed—the camaraderie of the unit, that's what got me through it. We were the first blacks to fight in tanks. You can't say what a person can or can't do.*
—Sergeant William H. McBurney, Tank Main Gunner, U.S 761st "Black Panthers" Tank Battalion, and Winner of the Bronze Star for Valor

*What made Patton so remarkable was his willingness to take risks and to make crucial life-and-death decisions no one else would dare...[He had] that intangible, instinctive sense of what must be done in the heat and chaos of battle: in short, that special genius for war that has been granted to only a select few.*
—Carlo D'Este, *Patton: A Genius for War*

*Attack rapidly, ruthlessly, viciously, without rest. However tired and hungry you may be, the enemy will be more tired, more hungry. Keep punching.*

*Through the travail of the ages,*
*Midst the pomp and toil of war,*
*Have I fought and strove and perished*
*Countless times upon this star.*
*So forever in the future*
*Shall I battle as of yore,*
*Dying to be born a fighter*
*But to die again once more.*

—General George S. Patton, Jr., Commander of the U.S Third Army, quote and 1922 poem *Through a Glass Darkly*

*The story of the Edelweiss Pirates is slowly gaining its due acknowledgement. The very fact the Pirates cultivated their own ideology that was meaningful enough to spur them to action and strong enough to support them in withstanding the cruelties it entailed is more than impressive. Perhaps it was because of their youth that the atrocities of the Nazi regime were so clear and the choice to oppose it so absolute. Their decision was one of resistance and, consequently, was not without hardship, but it was also one of liberty, for, as one of their songs contends, "Our song is freedom, love and life—we're the Pirates of the Edelweiss."*
—Katie Kellerman, *The Edelweiss Pirates: A Story of Freedom, Love and Life*

# CAST OF HISTORICAL FIGURES

## AMERICANS: 761ST TANK BATTALION

**Sergeant William H. McBurney:** Twenty-year-old tank main gunner and later commander; native New Yorker and son of WWI veteran; fought in Northern France, Battle of the Bulge, Rhineland, and in the final conquest of Nazi Germany.

**Private Leonard Smith:** Nineteen-year-old tank loader and gunner; native New Yorker and close friend of William McBurney and Willie Devore; nickname Smitty.

**Lieutenant Colonel Paul Bates:** White commander of the U.S. 761st Tank Battalion; former All-American football star from Western Maryland College; worked for ten years as a high school teacher and coach before joining the Army; nickname Smooth.

**Sergeant Teddy Windsor:** Thirty-five-year-old tank commander from Cleveland, Ohio; brother-in-arms and father figure to McBurney.

**Lieutenant-Captain David Williams:** Twenty-three-year-old white commander of Able Company; Yale student and son of a prominent Pittsburgh industrialist.

**Lieutenant John Roosevelt Robinson:** Twenty-five-year-old tank platoon commander and later 761st morale officer; former All-American football player at UCLA and school's first athlete to win varsity letters in four sports: baseball, basketball, football, and track; nickname Jackie.

**Technician Fifth Grade Willie Devore:** Twenty-five-year-old tank driver; South Carolina farmer with a grammar school education; a favorite of the tankers.

**Private E.G. McConnell:** Eighteen-year-old tank bow gunner and friend of McBurney and Smith; fellow New Yorker from Queens born of Jamaican immigrant parents.

**Captain Charles Gates:** Thirty-three-year-old commander of the 761st's assault gun platoon of Headquarters Company; native of Kansas City, Missouri; graduate of Virginia's Hampton Institute who trained with the Buffalo Soldiers at Fort Riley, Kansas; nickname Pop.

**Sergeant-Lieutenant Warren Crecy:** Soft-spoken tank commander from Texas; known as the "Baddest Man of the 761st" for his fierceness and courage under fire.

## AMERICANS: U.S. ARMY OFFICERS AND THIRD ARMY STAFF

**Major General-General George S. Patton, Jr.:** Commander of Third Army; called Old Blood and Guts by his troops and the press.

**General of the Army Dwight Eisenhower:** Supreme Commander of Allied Expeditionary Force in Europe; nickname Ike.

**Lieutenant General Omar Bradley:** Commander of U.S. Twelfth Army Group.

**General Hobart Gay:** Patton's chief of staff and right-hand man; nickname Hap.

**Master Sergeant George Meeks:** Patton's African-American personal aide and confidant.

**Major-Colonel Charles Codman:** Patton's cultivated, French-speaking senior aide-de-camp.

**General Oscar Koch:** Patton's invaluable Jewish chief intelligence officer (G-2).

**Major Alexander Stiller:** Patton's junior aide-de-camp from Texas.
**Master Sergeant John Mims:** Patton's trusted African-American driver.

## GERMANS: COLOGNE EDELWEISS PIRATES, EHRENFELD GROUP MEMBERS, WEHRMACHT, AND GESTAPO

**Angela Lange (fictional):** Sixteen-year-old upper middle-class member of the Cologne Navajos branch of the Edelweiss Pirates; daughter of Colonel Günther Lange; native of Cologne; code name Mucki; based loosely upon real-life Edelweiss Pirate Gertrud Koch.

**Colonel Günther Lange (fictional):** Anti-Nazi Wehrmacht officer on convalescent leave and temporarily serving as commander of Cologne flak defenses; WWI-WWII hero; native of Cologne; served in Eastern Front and Tunisia under General Hasso von Manteuffel before being wounded multiple times; father of Angela Lange.

**Bartholomäus Schröder (fictional):** Sixteen-year-old member of the Cologne Navajos; nickname Barthel; based loosely upon real-life Edelweiss Pirate Bartholomäus "Barthel" Schink.

**Jean Hüber (fictional):** Sixteen-year-old guitar-playing member of the Cologne Navajos; based loosely upon real-life Edelweiss Pirate Jean Jülich.

**Günther Schwarz:** Sixteen-year-old, half-Jewish member of the Edelweiss Pirates; nickname Büb.

**Hans Steinbrück:** Twenty-three-year-old leader of Cologne's Ehrenfeld Group of escaped forced laborers, army deserters, and resistance fighters in the bombed-out district of Ehrenfeld; escaped from Buchenwald concentration camp and Cologne-Deutz work reeducation camp; nickname Bomber Hans.

**Marie Peukert (fictional):** Member of Cologne Navajos and friend of Angela Lange.

***Kriminalkommissar* Ferdinand Kütter:** Fifty-four-year-old criminal commissioner of the Cologne Gestapo, rabid Nazi, and commander of the *Sonderkommando Brauweiler* unit responsible for the arrest, interrogation, and punishment of fugitive forced laborers, army deserters, and political resisters; a World War I veteran who previously commanded the Bonn Gestapo's anti-Marxist office.

***Kriminalassistents* Josef Hoegen and Walter Hirschfeld:** Criminal investigators and interrogators with the Cologne Gestapo and Kütter's *Sonderkommando Brauweiler*; ruthlessly crushed German and non-German "enemies of the state" with savage violence, abuse, and torture.

# Soldiers of Freedom:
# The WWII Story of Patton's Panthers and the Edelweiss Pirates

## Volume Five of the World War Two Series

### To The Reader

SOLDIERS OF FREEDOM is the true story of the 1944-1945 War in Western Europe and the final Allied struggle to conquer Nazi Germany. The story is told through the eyes of William McBurney, a tank gunner in the 761st Tank Battalion, the first African-American tank unit in U.S. history; dynamic General George S. Patton, Jr., commander of the U.S. Third Army; and Angela Lange, a sixteen-year-old German resistance fighter with the anti-Nazi Edelweiss Pirates in Cologne. While Patton's forces liberate France and Belgium, fight in the grueling Battle of the Bulge, and cross the Rhine to conquer Germany, U.S. tanker William McBurney and his Black Panthers must fight two wars at once: one against the German army, the other against the racism of their fellow white soldiers. Meanwhile, as the Allies drive into Germany, Edelweiss Pirate Angela Lange must survive the Allied bombing of Cologne while she engages in fierce resistance against the Hitler Youth and Nazis and is hunted down by the Gestapo. The real-life heroism of the 761st Black Panthers and legendary "Old Blood and Guts" Patton to liberate Europe, and the Edelweiss Pirates to combat Nazism, are brought to life in this historically accurate tale of the final epic struggle in WWII Western Europe.

# PART 1

# THE OUTSIDERS

# CHAPTER 1



"NO NEGROES IN THE AIR CORPS, SON—IT JUST AIN'T DONE."

William Haywood McBurney looked at the U.S. Army recruiter with a confused expression on his face. The seventeen-year-old had been clamoring to join the Army for months, just like every other starry-eyed American boy did after watching the newsreels in the Saturday motion picture matinees across the country. But his father had warned him that war for a young black man would not be anything like in the moving pictures: "They are never going to let *us* fly, Billy," Thomas McBurney had cautioned him on more than one occasion. But how, William McBurney wondered, could black recruits not be needed for the Army Air Corps when he had—in his very pocket at this very moment—a *New York Times* article specifically requesting coloreds to fly airplanes for the war effort?

"No Negroes are gonna be flying airplanes. Not for the time being anyway," barked the recruiter again, as if McBurney was dumb or hard of hearing, or perhaps to underscore the futility of a black man even contemplating joining the United States Air Corps.

They were sitting in a cramped U.S. Army Recruitment Center office at 39 Whitehall Street, just east of Battery Park in Lower Manhattan. At a hair under six feet, McBurney looked tall and strapping in his one and only suit, which had grown a tad short in the arms. His high-waisted trousers he tugged towards the exposed rims of his worn leather shoes, and he donned a white dress shirt his father had loaned him, one of just three garments he had ever ironed. With only a month until graduating from New York Vocational High School, Billy, as his friends and family members called him, was studying aviation mechanics and had long dreamed of becoming a pilot. A female cousin was taking flying lessons at Floyd Bennet Field, and watching the planes take off and soar away into the wild blue yonder made the boy daydream of streaking through the skies as a fighter pilot, engaging in dogfights against Jap Zeros and dropping bombs on enemy aircraft carriers.

"Are you sure I can't join the Air Corps?" he asked, politely but with street-wise skepticism, as he had learned to do since an early age in the bustle of New York City's Hell's Kitchen and later Harlem.

The sergeant's sharply faceted visage tightened beneath his buzz cut and his agate eyes narrowed. "Yes, son, I'm quite sure. No Negroes." His voice was not from the Deep South, but from a border state to the north, maybe Maryland or West Virginia.

"But with all due respect, sir, I have the newspaper clipping right here." He pulled the aviation article from his pocket; he didn't need to read it for he had it practically memorized. "See, it says right here that the Army is creating Negro units in every branch of the armed service. That would be the Army, Navy, Marines, and—"

"I know what the branches of service are, son," the recruiter cut him off impatiently. "Now let's just concentrate on just how you can best serve your country. You can't be a flyer, so that's out of the question."

"I understand what you're telling me, but that's not what it says here in the *New York Times*." He pushed the newspaper clipping across the recruiter's desk. "According to the article, the army is requesting thirty-three officer pilots and four hundred ground crew, all colored, for the new squadron. I know I meet the qualifications. So if I meet the qualifications, are you telling me that the army has filled the spots already? Is that what you're telling me?"

The recruiter frowned. "No, I'm not saying that. You've got to listen better, son. I'm saying that you can't fly in the Air Corps because it is *not* an option. At all. Despite what your article there says."

"But don't you want to see it?"

"No, son, I do not." He pushed the scrap of paper back across the desk, as if disposing of a dead mouse.

Though still confused, McBurney decided not to push his case any further. Why the sergeant was insisting upon no Negroes in the Air Corps when the newspapers were clearly seeking colored airmen remained as baffling as it was irritating. Though McBurney longed to know the real reason he was being denied an opportunity, he knew he had better just move on. Arguing with the recruiter wasn't getting him anywhere. But if he couldn't fly fighters or bombers for the Army Air Corps, what was he going to do? He had no desire to be a sailor or infantryman. Though he agreed with the black leaders who maintained racial prejudice would have no place in the hearts and minds of comrades-in-arms who have fought, bled, and won together, shoulder to shoulder, in the name of freedom, he still wanted to be more than a navy deckhand or cannon fodder in the ground forces to achieve the equality he sought. His aspirations ran deeper.

"Look here, son. I'm going to give you a piece of advice."

"I would appreciate that, sir."

"In a word—tanks. That's my recommendation."

"Tanks?"

"Yessiree, the armored service is where you should be. You know what I'm talking about, right? Steel beasts from the Book of Revelations. Not only would you learn to drive them but you would get to shoot those big ole guns. Hell, it's like being behind the wheel of a snowplow but with a cannon. Now how would you feel about that?"

McBurney thought the sergeant seemed more like a huckster than a military recruiter. "With all due respect, sir," he said, keeping his tone polite and non-confrontational, "I don't know anything about tanks."

"Oh, but you will soon enough. Tanks are what this war is all about, son. You know about *blitzkrieg*, right?"

"Yeah, I've seen it in the newsreels. It's the German name for 'lightning war.'"

"Why that's right." The white recruiter looked surprised that a colored kid from Harlem would know such a thing, which irritated McBurney, but he said nothing. "That's because armored warfare is fast and furious—and you can be part of it. And I don't say that to just *any* old recruit. You have to qualify and receive a special invitation to be a tanker, son. Plus, you look like you would rather ride than walk.

Am I right?"

"I suppose so. If you don't mind my asking, what are the special qualifications I possess to be a tanker?"

The sergeant quickly scanned his file. "Well, for starters you scored well on the AGCT," he responded, referring to the Army General Classification Test that McBurney had taken and passed with flying colors. "But just as important, you're in fine physical condition. You're a football player, right?"

"Yeah, I play guard."

"There you have it. Now if you take my advice, I believe you will do right nicely fighting as a tanker."

McBurney had seen tanks and other armored transports in the newsreels, and he had seen the actual footage of Hitler's race across Europe in the giant behemoths that were rendering the trench warfare of his father's WWI generation an anachronism. He had to admit being a tanker sounded adventurous and exciting—a hell of a lot more than being a footslogging infantryman or sailor swabbing decks.

"All right, the armored service it is," said McBurney, smiling to expose two rows of perfectly stacked teeth the color of ivory. "Sign me up."

"Wise choice. Now because you're only seventeen, your pa, ma, or other legal guardian is going to have to sign this here certification of consent form."

The sergeant handed him the form.

"Congratulations, son." He stood up and held out his hand. "Welcome to the United States Army. Get that consent form signed and you'll be killing Japs before you know it. Or maybe Krauts. Now won't that be some fun?"

McBurney wasn't sure "fun" was the right word to describe killing other human beings, but he was looking forward to fighting for his country. He was also hoping to escape from being nothing but a menial laborer once he received his high school diploma. He knew from his high score on the AGCT that he had the potential to make something of himself, and he had no desire to end up in a gang like so many other kids from the neighborhood. He had already noticed the kinds of mischief young black men got into, especially with the police, and he intended to avoid going down that path himself.

He knew that with his air of watchfulness, his quiet intelligence, and his physical presence in standing up to the Italians and other Negroes who crossed him in the neighborhood, he stood out in his group of friends as the one you wanted watching your back. But he would have to do far more if he was to become a good soldier. Like many African-American youth, he had been pushed by his white teachers early on in his school career towards uninspiring shop and metal-working classes—despite his intelligence and academic success. But he wanted to be more than a janitor, longshoreman, garbage man, or street sweeper, which was why he had chosen to study aviation mechanics, dreaming of one day becoming a pilot. But as time went on, he began to realize that flying airplanes was a dream he seemed to have less and less hope of attaining—due solely to the color of his skin.

After school and on Saturdays he worked at a paintbrush factory for twenty-five cents an hour, helping his family to weather the Depression. Many of his buddies had taken similar menial jobs. As high school graduation approached, several more of his friends, with scant opportunity for advancement, were falling into selling hooch, gambling, and petty theft. McBurney saw himself and his buddies trending towards dead-end lives and he wanted out of Harlem. Serving as a tanker in the U.S. Army would take care of that. He saw the Army as a way of creating a new life for himself, especially if he could no longer realize his dream of flying.

But just as important a reason why he clamored to join the armed forces was to escape his past. Despite being only seventeen, he was the father of an unborn child with his girlfriend Sarah and a son with another Harlem girl—and he wasn't sure what the hell to do about the two teenage women. Though he and Sarah still had strong feelings for one another, he felt that he was too young to get married and support a family until he was on solid footing with a good-paying job. Sarah's pregnancy, and his infant son with the other girl, were just as important factors in his eagerness to enlist and leave New York as his patriotic fervor and lust for adventure. Though he felt guilty for his decision, he could see no other way until he could figure out his life. The war gave him his opportunity to do that. He loved Sarah and had decided that he would come back after the war and marry her if they still had feelings for one another. But he was not ready for marriage at this early stage of his life.

"Thank you, Sergeant," he said in closing. "I just want to tell you that I intend to do the armored service proud."

"I believe you will. Good luck to you, son."

After shaking hands, the dapperly dressed McBurney strutted out of the recruiter's office with his chest out like a game rooster and his head held high. Young and naïve in the ways of the world, he stepped out into a sunny and promising late April afternoon despite a world caught in the grips of a bloody conflagration, a world where grown men were dying by the thousands daily while crying out for their mamas. Though he had taken the train to the recruitment center on Whitehall Street, he felt like being outside and walking home. As he made his way north along Broadway, he caught a glimpse of himself smiling in each plate glass storefront he passed. He couldn't wait to get home and deliver the good news to his father, with whom he lived at their railroad flat at 117th Street and Madison Avenue in Harlem.

Though Thomas McBurney had made it clear he was skeptical of his son's chances of being accepted into the Air Corps, McBurney was sure that he would be proud of him for joining the Army's armored service. The old man had served proudly in the U.S. Army in Europe in the Great War, fighting as a member of the legendary 369th Infantry Regiment, known as the "Harlem Hellfighters." McBurney would be following in his father's footsteps by wearing the uniform and fighting overseas. But he knew that his mother, with whom his father was divorced and who lived only a few blocks away from their flat on Madison Avenue, would be proud of him too. While his father was a WWI combat veteran of African descent, his mother, Daisy, was a Seminole Indian born and raised on a Florida reservation. Proud of the Indian warrior blood coursing through his veins, McBurney often remembered back to when he was a boy staring up at the photo in the hallway of his great-grandfather in traditional Seminole battle dress with a musket in his hands and tomahawk in his belt. His Indian ancestor looked formidable—and McBurney was proud of his Native American warrior heritage.

Now he would be fighting just like his African-American father before him and his Seminole warrior ancestors.

*Hot damn!* he thought, as he sashayed merrily past the giant bronze equestrian statue of George Washington in Union Square. Feeling a sudden burst of patriotism, he came to a halt, looked up at the commander in chief of the Continental Army that had won victory in America's first epic struggle, and saluted.

"Good day to you, General," he said, standing ramrod straight. "I'm going to be a tanker in the United States Army!"

ΨΨΨ

"They may take you in, Billy, but they are never going to properly train you to fight in armor. The U.S. Army doesn't train coloreds."

Standing with his father in the creamy beige kitchen of their rented Madison Avenue railroad flat, young Billy McBurney tried not to let the hurt show on his face. He didn't much care for Thomas McBurney's blunt assessment of his situation. He had not expected his old man to uncork a bottle of champagne, but he had not expected to be openly dismissed either. He felt his face flushing with anger.

"I'm not trying to discourage you, son," his father continued. "I'm just trying to make sure you know what you're getting yourself into."

A methodical teenager not prone to rash judgment, McBurney took a moment to collect himself and gather his thoughts.

"I'm turning eighteen soon, Dad, and will be old enough to fight," he said after a moment. "I'm all grown now and I've made my decision. All I need from you is to give your permission and sign my consent form since I'm only seventeen. I want to be a tanker and this is the best way you can help me achieve that goal."

"So you just want me to sign? That's all you need from me?"

"Yep, Dad. That's about it."

His father's chestnut brown eyes narrowed. "You don't talk to me like that," he scolded him. "I'm your pop, remember? You had better listen to what I have to say or I'm not signing a damned thing. Because, unlike you, I've actually fought overseas in Uncle Sam's white-man army."

McBurney gulped and snapped silent. Now he understood what his father was really angry about. As a member of the 369th Infantry Regiment, the legendary Harlem Hellfighters, his dad had once harbored an idealism and patriotism just like him—only to have his hopes and dreams dashed by the cold hand of racism. Obviously, his father didn't want him to be treated like he had been by the U.S. Army in France, which was why his old man was urging caution and trying to temper his expectations.

Thomas McBurney had been shipped overseas in December 1917—but the Army quickly relegated the black soldiers to duty as manual laborers. Though he had come to Europe to fight, he was not allowed to for more than four months, when the Harlem Hellfighters were finally shifted to French control. The black doughboys swiftly went on the attack, fighting in Allied counteroffensives at the Marne, at Chateau-Thierry, and at the Meuse-Argonne in the final push against Germany, sustaining heavy losses. Thomas McBurney was one of the roughly 1,500 casualties suffered by the unit while grappling with the Kaiser's troops.

Though he had reveled in the camaraderie and the unit's fighting spirit, he had admitted to his son that he had been deeply conflicted. He was proud to have fought for his country under the French with open-minded American unit leaders who had little interest in race, but when he returned home to the U.S. following the armistice, he was disappointed not to find a similar brotherhood. In fact, instead of receiving a hero's welcome, he and his fellow Hellfighters had been treated no better than dogs, which McBurney knew had always been a source of extreme disappointment to his father. The 369th's well-documented bravery in Europe had not led to an opening for equality and respect back under American military control or at home—and McBurney knew that his father was worried that he would face the same frustration and disillusionment.

"I didn't mean to make you mad, Dad," he said, attempting to smooth things over. "I just want to fight."

His father shifted his weight as he often did when standing, still reeling from the enemy bullet that had torn a hole through his left thigh. "I know you do, and I also know I can't stop you," the decorated veteran said. "But you've got to know that even if they actually put you in tanks and let you fight, they're never going to treat you as an equal."

"Why not if I do my duty and am a good soldier?"

"Because they won't, son. Trust me, they just won't."

McBurney didn't like the certainty in his father's voice, but he didn't dare challenge him. Again, they fell into a strained silence. Now his father's initial dismissiveness about the Air Corps made sense. When the Hellfighters had returned from the war in 1919, they had marched up Fifth Avenue through Harlem in a victory parade to brass bands and the cheers of hundreds of thousands of people lining the streets screaming for their doughboys—and yet in the years that followed Thomas McBurney was unable to find steady work or advancement. Despite working his way through school to become a dental technician, he was unable to obtain a job as a professional and had no choice but to turn to manual labor, working on the docks as a longshoreman. Though he had made a pleasant life for his family well north of West 69th Street and 10th Avenue, occasionally even finding extra work as a dental technician, his weathered, full-time longshoreman's face told a story different than that of a comfortably respectable city-dweller.

"I just want to make a difference like you, Dad," said McBurney with quiet conviction. "What's wrong with that?"

"Nothing. I just know the reality of a colored man fighting for this country. It ain't a pretty sight, Billy, I can assure you."

"But me and the others signing up, we can change all that. We're going to have our own colored tank battalions."

"The first thing you need to learn is that the Army doesn't care a lick about you. Twenty-four years ago, they shipped me off to die and they're doing the same thing with you now."

"That was a long time ago. Are you sure you remember it right?"

"My memory is just fine, Billy. I admit I feel some bitterness. But you need to understand what it's like to be treated like you're invisible when you've fought and bled for your country. I served Uncle Sam. I did what I was told to do and killed a lot of Huns. A lot. But despite my honorable service, I returned to a nation that judged me not by my sacrifice on the field of battle, but by the color of my skin. I know what war is all about for a black man. But more importantly, I know first-hand the ugliness of America and the lies of the U.S. Army."

McBurney took a moment to digest what his father was telling him. "Dad, you're the wisest man I know. And I appreciate that you're always reminding me that war is nothing like how it's portrayed in the moving pictures."

"I feel a 'but' coming on."

"*But* I've got to do this."

"I know you do, son. I just want you to know what you're getting yourself into."

"I know what I'm getting myself into. I'm going to be a tanker in the United States Army. That's why I need you to sign my form. That's the only way I can be in the armored service. I want to fight in tanks, Dad. They say it's mostly going to be a tank war and that's where I want to be."

They stood in silence a long moment, father and son in a tenuous detente. More than a minute passed before either of them spoke.

"I know I said they are never going to let coloreds fly," said Thomas McBurney, "but I am going to be proud if they do let you fight in a tank. Damned proud."

His lip quivered as he took his son in an embrace. McBurney held the man he worshipped, the old Harlem Hellfighter wounded in the Great War, tight.

"I know that I can no longer delay the inevitable," the elder McBurney then admitted to his son. "I am just trying to protect you."

"I know you are, Dad. But everyone else is going so why not me?"

His father gently pulled away and looked him in the eye. "Is that the reason you're itching to fight? Because all your buddies are signing up and you don't want to be left out?"

"No, that's not it," said the teenager with conviction. "The reason I want to fight is because, this time around, we're not going to just *show* the world—we're going to *change* it."

# CHAPTER 2

## KILLEEN AND CAMP HOOD
## CENTRAL TEXAS

### TWO YEARS LATER - JUNE 9, 1944

THE CIVILIAN BUS was long and gray, with frayed seats, smudge marks on the windows, and a Hill Country redneck behind the wheel with a wad of Red Man chewing tobacco packed into his mouth like a chipmunk. On his hip was a loaded Colt .45 snub-nosed service pistol, which he carried to keep "uppity" and "back-talking" Negro troopers in line. The bus driver had been duly deputized by the local police, and in the backwater of Killeen, Texas, in the Year of Our Lord 1944 that made him as good as the law. In short, it gave him a license to kill—as long as he didn't shoot no white man.

From the rear of the bus where the colored were banished in a nod to Jim Crow, William McBurney of the U.S. 761st Tank Battalion stared out at the windswept Lone Star landscape rolling past in a slipstream of olive and drab brown. Wearing his neatly pressed sergeant's uniform and glossy black military shoes, McBurney never failed to salute a white officer smartly while privately thinking, "I am a Grade-A United States non-commissioned officer—and if you are a true soldier who respects the uniform then you *will* return my salute."

After two years of training, the twenty-year-old from New York City was certain a black man could drive and fire shells from a tank, storm an enemy outpost, and take a bullet as good as any white man. He believed in the power of the uniform and was convinced that, one day, the Army would prove to be a meritocracy for colored soldiers like himself. Some of his buddies in the 761st called him gullible and naïve. Like his father, they said he took what he saw in the Hollywood picture shows too literally. But he was intent on proving that a Negro could make just as fine a soldier as any white fellow—and he firmly believed that, some day in the not-too-distant future, people would be forced to acknowledge it. In the process, he would right the injustice inflicted upon his father, a hero who had served with distinction and deserved better treatment than what he had received from the country for which he had fought and nearly died.

But what McBurney didn't know—and would have refused to believe—was that the Army never intended the 761st to go overseas or see combat. The tank battalion was created on April 1, 1942 with no real intention of being committed to fighting on the war front. Negro fighting units were largely the brainchild of First Lady Eleanor Roosevelt, who used her bully pulpit along with her husband to advocate for the full and equal mobilization of African-American manpower. Her sentiments mirrored those of black leaders, who resented the restriction of Negroes in the military to noncombat roles. But every colored man who wore the uniform had to fight the stigma of being branded one of "Eleanor Roosevelt's Niggers." The 761st Tank Battalion, one of three experimental tank battalions activated to placate the First Lady, had no intended replacements to be trained and was not actually earmarked for overseas fighting—despite what its black soldiers were told.

The problem was the Army brass and most of the troops still viewed Negro fighting men as, at best, second-class citizens and, more often than not, as lazy and incompetent. Eleanor Roosevelt and her husband both were pushing to integrate the armed forces, but behind the scenes they were meeting resistance from the military brass and soldiers themselves, especially Southern officers, who had no intention of allowing black men to be on equal footing with their white counterparts. Unfortunately, if the 761st Tank Battalion was going to be deployed at all, it would likely be as a public relations stunt to appease the Roosevelts and maintain support from the black community for the war effort.

McBurney continued to stare out the bus window at the rolling hills. He was sitting next to a fellow New Yorker, Private Leonard Smith. Smitty had lived in Brooklyn and later Queens, and for the past two years had been one of McBurney's best buddies in the 761st. They had taken the bus into Temple for the day to shoot pool and toss back a few beers rather than go in the evening when the town was flooded with troops carrying weekend passes. The area of Wall Street in Temple—which the local whites dubbed "Nigger Town"—was one of only two spots near Camp Hood where blacks were allowed to set up their own businesses, congregate, and enjoy themselves socially. Wall Street had a colorful variety of cafés, juke joints playing blues and jazz, cinemas, barber shops, and pool halls along with a United Service Organization (USO), produce store, dentist, funeral home, and even a church down past the last juke joint. The street rocked with energy from early Friday evening through Sunday, with members of the 761st and other black armored and artillery units at Camp Hood adding significantly to the weekend revelry.

McBurney and Smith were something of an odd couple. Though they had both tested well on the AGCT, enabling them to receive special invitations to join the new black tanker units being formed in early 1942, they had different personalities. While McBurney was observant, composed, and cautious, Smith was an irreverent, rebellious, and adventuresome man of action, who, though he received high marks on most of the physical and technical challenges of training and was well liked by his superiors, couldn't help but get into frequent mischief. With regard to humor, McBurney's tended towards irony, Smith's towards open-hearted playfulness. Despite, or perhaps because of, their innate differences—Smith was the sort who jumped before looking, while McBurney was cautious and steady under pressure—the two had become fast friends upon first meeting at Camp Upton in New York shortly after signing up. They had remained close friends ever since.

When they had joined up, neither of them had any inkling of the size of the black tanker ranks or where the armored units might be deployed. Like the thousands of young men across the country enlisting every day, they were caught up in the wave of patriotism sweeping the country in the wake of the Japanese bombing of Pearl Harbor. They were just excited to be given the opportunity to fight in tanks.

The 761st had been activated on April Fool's Day 1942 at Camp Claiborne, Louisiana, where it spent the next year and a half training before moving on to Camp Hood in Central Texas. McBurney liked the 761st's new training post. In his view, Camp Hood was a hell of a lot better than Claiborne where he had begun his indoctrination as a U.S. tanker two years earlier. The sparsely wooded hills, valleys, and rolling grasslands were several notches above the swampy, flat, and densely vegetated terrain where he and his brothers-in-arms had been forced to spend half their time extracting their tanks from the mud.

What he liked most of all about his new home, though, was that the 761st had been converted from a light tank battalion to a medium tank battalion equipped with M4 Sherman medium tanks and 75-millimeter cannons instead of the lighter M5 Stuarts armed with mere 37mm guns. He and his fellow tankers had been undertaking constant maneuvers during the past several months with their Shermans, testing their skills against various tank destroyer units completing their Army Ground Forces Tests to see if they were ready for combat. Commanded by Lieutenant Colonel Paul Bates, a lanky former All-American college football player, the well-trained 761st had been beating the all-white tank-destroyer units so badly and so often that they had lost count of their victories.

But McBurney didn't like everything about Camp Hood. The thing that he hated most was that he felt like an outsider, both on the base and in town. The post was segregated, with separate officers clubs, bathrooms, special services clubs, movie theaters, and other post facilities for blacks and whites. But even worse was the open hostility between the white soldiers-military police and the colored personnel in the camp. When he and Smitty went to the exchange to get supplies, they were often shoved aside at the cashier if a white soldier happened to come in to make a purchase. Over the past two years of training, McBurney had learned to keep his mouth shut and just take it. He knew that if the members of the 761st were going to make a name for themselves and be treated as something close to equals, their only chance was to continue to outperform the all-white tank-destroyer units.

While Camp Hood had its challenges like Camp Claiborne, it was the transportation situation that remained the worst aspect for McBurney and the other tankers. As at Claiborne, buses were the primary means of transportation and no trip came without racial tension. Black soldiers were forced to sit in the rear of the bus and to stand if the bus was crowded. They were treated with suspicion by the white passengers and endured stares and insults. Armed bus drivers reigned over their routes like feudal lords, taking particular pleasure in inflicting cruelty on black soldiers on the last bus at night, which was always full of troops on temporary leave. When the bus was two or three miles from the post, the driver would claim the bus was overloaded and several black soldiers were forced to get out, sometimes at gunpoint. If they refused to give up their seat to a white soldier or get off the bus, or committed some other imaginary infraction, the driver would stop at the nearest MP station or law enforcement office, and the offender was dragged off in handcuffs. Drivers also often refused to pick up fewer than five black soldiers, or bypassed them altogether during their last run, forcing them to walk alone back to the post.

Bates, as commander of the 761st, refused to fall victim to a few local rednecks abusing their power, as it could impact the training of his men and their combat readiness. He thought it best if the 761st bypassed the bus system. He checked with his superiors to see if his men could use the battalion's military vehicles from its own motor pool to circumvent the ongoing abuse from the racist locals. Approval was granted, but vehicles were rarely available for the black troops for trips to Austin, Temple, Killeen, and the other off-base destinations where the tankers gathered to socialize when not on duty.

McBurney stared out at the world outside the bus window. It was not his world, of course. They were passing through the small town of Killeen a few miles from Camp Hood. A large metal sign on the road read "Niggers have to leave this town by 9 pm!" Smitty saw it, too, and they both shook their heads in disgust. McBurney looked around the bus. A pair of locals, a man and woman with yellow teeth, looked back from the middle section and scowled at them, as if they were vagrants or criminals. But he and Smith ignored them. They had become so used to the hostile glares from white folks that they scarcely even noticed such incivility any longer.

He thought back to Colonel Bates's visit the other day to the tank shed where the companies conducted equipment maintenance following weekly maneuvers. McBurney, Smith, and several others were all laughing around one of the tanks they were working on. The colonel asked them what was so funny and one of the men, McBurney couldn't remember exactly who, had grinned and said, "Sir, the tank destroyers have this logo: *Seek, Strike, and Destroy*. But it don't work when we're around. That's when it becomes *Sneak, Peek, and Retreat*." Everyone burst into laughter and Bates smiled and chuckled right along with them. McBurney knew how proud the colonel—whose nickname was "Smooth" but whom the black tankers sometimes called the "Great White Father"—was that his unit was kicking butt on all the white tank-destroyer units.

Smith said, "Now that we've invaded France and the Japs are in retreat, do you think they'll let us fight?"

McBurney thought for a moment. Though the high marks the 761st had earned in training and on maneuvers at Camp Hood had caught the eye of the Army's higher echelons, there had been no word that the unit would be deployed overseas anytime soon. Some of the skeptics in the outfit wondered if they would even get the opportunity to fight. The possibility they might not was a great source of frustration to both Colonel Bates and the men, but they continued to train hard and keep their fingers crossed.

"I got to believe they will," replied McBurney.

"We've been training going on two years now. If they don't let us have a go at the Krauts or Japs now, then when?"

"I don't know. But I got a feeling our luck is about to turn."

"You always look on the bright side of things, don't you?"

"I have to. Otherwise, I'd go crazy."

The bus slowed to a halt to allow six new white soldiers to board. It was now standing room only. The corpulent driver stood up, with his Colt on his hip and wad of Red Man packed into his cheek, and announced, "All right, you niggers, this bus has gotten too crowded. I can't take y'all to the post so six of you's gotta get off."

The colored soldiers on the bus just sat there, no one making a move.

"Goddamn niggers, didn't you hear what I said? Do as you're told, unless you want me to sick the MPs on you! Now six of you get off and I mean right quick!"

"Jesus Christ," grumbled Smith in a low, angry whisper. "I don't believe this shit. Not again."

"Keep your mouth shut, man," said McBurney. "There's nothing that can be done—unless you want a court-martial."

"But we only just passed Killeen. We're still more than three miles from camp."

"So we'll hump it and be back in an hour, just in time for dinner. We got plenty of daylight still left."

"Don't Uncle Tom me. This ain't right and you know it."

"You know the drill, man. My country tis of thee, sweet land of bigotry. You want to get yourself lynched over a seat on a bus?"

"But this is bullshit."

The driver stood up, angrily waving his Colt. "I want six niggers off this bus in the next ten seconds, or I become John Wesley Hardin!"

"That redneck mother is just crazy enough to do it, man," McBurney whispered to Smitty. "Now let's go."

They rose cautiously from their seats along with four other wary and outraged black soldiers. With lips pursed taut, they threaded their way through the crowd towards the front of the bus, keeping a steady eye on the driver, who chewed his cud of tobacco, menacingly tapped the handle of his pistol, and smirked at them as they shuffled towards the front exit.

"Bye-bye boys," he gloated as they passed. "Enjoy your *ex-er-cise*."

As they stepped off the bus, a cackle of disdainful laughter rose up from the driver and passengers, with the white soldiers from Camp Hood sniggering the loudest. McBurney shuddered inside with anger but said nothing. The bus door snapped shut. The six black men stood by the side of the road, watching powerlessly as the bus drove away and they were engulfed in a noxious cloud of diesel fumes. McBurney and Smith looked at one another, shaking their heads in disgust.

The group began the long walk back to the base. For the first mile, the men were still livid and grumbled with frustration, especially Smitty. But by the last two miles they had put it all behind them and were talking cheerfully about the fine-looking ladies in the juke joints on Wall Street in Temple.

Unfortunately, as soon as they reached Camp Hood the familiar anger and resentment boiled up again when they came upon a group of German POWs.

"Well, well, if it isn't the Negroes out for their usual stroll," said their silver-haired leader. The sergeant was dressed in a blue one-piece prisoner of war outfit like his men, and though his German accent was strong his English was near-perfect. "You got dropped off early again, didn't you *kameraden*?"

The returning tankers had just stepped around the corner of a barracks to find the Germans sitting on a clump of hay bales smoking cigarettes. McBurney wanted to smack the insolent NCO and his smirking buddies, but restrained himself. Few army practices infuriated him and the other members of the 761st more than the preferential treatment accorded the more than 3,000 German prisoners of war at the camp. The captured enemy German soldiers, many of them from Field Marshal Erwin Rommel's vaunted *Afrika Korps*, were given only light work details, and the Germans officers and most enlisted men were allowed to roam through the camp unguarded. Even more insultingly, Hitler's finest were allowed to eat meals in the same cafeteria next to the white U.S. soldiers, whereas the black soldiers had to go around back to another location to eat.

By virtue of their whiteness, the Germans had full run of the camp. Even at the post exchange, or PX, they enjoyed the privilege of cutting line at the checkout ahead of any black American soldier. But the hardest thing for McBurney and his brothers-in-arms to endure were the dismissive sneers and racist badgering of the

Germans: the POWs knew how deep discrimination ran in the States and they considered all colored troops, even officers, beneath them. They rarely failed to show their open contempt for the members of the 761st.

"You talking to us, you Kraut piece of shit?" said Smith, who though diminutive in stature stepped forward aggressively with his fists balled up.

The silver-haired leader squinted and rose slowly from his hay bale. The rest of the Germans flicked away their cigarettes and followed suit.

They were a tough-looking lot.

"We were just welcoming you *Schwarze Soldaten* back to your camp," said the leader sarcastically, calling them by their German name, *Black Soldiers*. "You did not like our welcome?"

"Not really," said McBurney. "In fact, we didn't like it at all."

"That is too bad because we certainly meant no disrespect."

He underscored his insincerity with a broad smirk.

"You Nazi fuck, you have no right to talk to us like that!" grumbled one of the other black troopers, and he went up and shoved the leader, knocking him to the ground. A tussle quickly developed between the tankers and German POWs. Just as punches were about to be thrown, a voice slashed through the air.

"What the hell is going on here?"

McBurney turned to see a pair of MPs. "These Germans were shooting their mouth off at us and trying to pick a fight," he quickly explained.

But the MPs weren't listening. Ignoring him, they went up to the silver-haired leader, who was dusting himself off.

"Sergeant Steiner, are these niggers pestering you?" asked one of them.

"No, it's just a soldiers' quarrel," he said, to McBurney's surprise.

"Are you sure, Sergeant? You can press charges."

"No, it was just a simple misunderstanding," said the German.

"All right then," said the MP. "You niggers get on back to *your* barracks. We don't need you causing any more trouble with these *real* soldiers. Now get fucking moving!"

"But those damned Krauts are the ones that started it!" protested Smith. "Why don't you tell them to get their Nazi asses back to *their* goddamn barracks? We're the real soldiers!"

The military policemen pulled out their wooden riot batons. "I told you niggers to get moving!" snapped the one in charge. "Now you give me any more lip, I'll crack your fucking skull wide open, you hear me boy?"

McBurney took Smith by the arm. "We hear you loud and clear. We're on our way."

The group moved out again. When they were out of earshot, Smitty and two of the other tankers resumed their complaining about their mistreatment. The insolent bus driver and passengers had been bad enough, but now German POWS and even their own MPs were terrorizing them. Though McBurney knew he and his brothers were in the right, it had been a long day and he was tired of fighting battles with everyone they came into contact with. But what bothered him most of all was that goddamned Krauts were treated better than the members of the 761st at Camp Hood. German officers who died while interned were buried in their uniforms with full military honors and American rifle teams firing salutes over their graves. Their coffins were draped with the Nazi flag. For their work assignments, many of the Germans cleaned up around the base, but they refused to pick up in the colored area. McBurney and the others had to do that themselves.

"I'm tired of those Kraut bastards walking around just like any Tom, Dick, or Harry," bristled Smith, as if reading his mind. "They treat us like we're fucking garbage."

"I'm tired of it too," said McBurney. "But there's nothing we can do about it except be the best damned tank outfit in the whole army. We've just got to keep kicking the crap out of those white tank-destroyer units."

"What difference does it make? We're never going to get a chance to fight."

"Yes, we will."

"Maybe if they run out of white tankers. That's the only way we see action. Otherwise, the only enemy we're ever going to go up against is goddamn rattlesnakes."

"Come on, we're gonna see action. Why else would they put us in Shermans?"

"I don't know, but I can tell you that I am *dis-gusted*. That's all I know for sure. Those goddamned Kraut prisoners treat us like crap and no one does shit about it."

"You think your bitching is going to help?"

"It helps *me*, goddamnit. I mean just think about it. Here we are, first-class Americans, never been in prison, never broke the law. We ain't even prisoners of war or anything like that. And yet those Nazi fucks have the gall to look down at us? They know they can go to any PX on the post and buy whatever they want—while we lowly niggers can only stand outside and watch, or go to a special PX for second-class troops. Those Krauts don't step back for us like they do for the white boys. Hell, they'd step *on* us if they could get away with it!"

McBurney said nothing. He was too angry for words and wished he had not set foot outside his barracks today. To avoid confrontations, he usually chose to remain on the base in his free time, though there was plenty of injustice on the post to keep him simmering. But the fact that the German POWs were treated better than the black tankers and were permitted to walk in and out of the PX and special services clubs from which the members of the 761st were barred filled him with bitterness. It seemed inconceivable that the Krauts were given more freedom than the black American soldiers at Camp Hood, but that's exactly the way it was. When would his country change? he often asked himself. When would he be granted the chance to fight not as a Negro but as a man? His father had warned him that his country would reject him, but he had believed that given the opportunity, he could overcome the odds and earn the respect of white soldiers.

How foolish he had been.

As they neared the barracks, he saw Colonel Bates walking towards them along with Lieutenant Williams, a likable but inexperienced Pennsylvanian who had gone to Yale College and commanded Able Company. McBurney felt his body tense. He couldn't help but wonder if the MPs had radioed ahead to report to Bates about the confrontation with the Germans.

"Wouldn't that just be our luck? We're the ones under arrest instead of those Nazi motherfuckers," grumbled Smith, echoing McBurney's fears.

"God, I hope not," he replied as moans and groans of dissatisfaction rumbled through the group.

But the rangy white colonel and baby-faced white captain walked right up to them with friendly expressions on their faces and saluted smartly. McBurney and the others stood ramrod straight and snapped crisp salutes.

"At ease, men," said Bates. "I know you were in town for the day and wanted to let you know of my announcement to the battalion two hours ago. We have been put on full alert for movement overseas."

McBurney's eyes lit up along with the others. "We have, sir? We're really going to the show?"

"That is correct, Sergeant. All communications are now strictly monitored and censored, and all activities of the unit from this point forward are to be considered top secret."

"Hallelujah!" cried Smith. "We finally have the chance to show the world what we can do!"

"It appears that way, Private."

Lieutenant Williams nodded in vigorous agreement, his boyish face lighting up with a smile.

"Thanks for filling us in, Colonel," said McBurney. "How long do you think before they deploy us?"

"It could be as long as a month, but the important thing is we're going. Remember this day, men."

"June 9, 1944," said Smitty ebulliently. "I ain't never gonna forget it, sir."

"I don't think any of us will," said Bates. "Four days after the Allies took Rome and three days after the Normandy D-Day landings on the French coast, the 761st was put on alert for overseas deployment. It's about damned time, eh fellas?"

"Yessir," said McBurney.

The son of a Harlem Hellfighter brimmed with excitement and wondered what his father would think of him now. He had never been gripped with such anticipation in his life. Looking at Bates, he knew there was still much work to be done before they sailed off for distant shores, but he couldn't help but feel he and his fellow tankers were finally destined to reach out and snatch their moment of glory.

"We're ready, aren't we, sir?" asked one of the tankers timorously. "I mean, you do think we're ready to go toe to toe with them Krauts or Japs?"

Bates, more than a decade older than most of the men at age thirty-six, gave a reassuring, paternal smile. "The 761st has been in service and in constant training for two years," he said with the conviction of a man who knew his business. "In the last year, we've run circles around every tank-destroyer unit that we've gone toe to toe with. You're *damn* right we're ready."

"The men are going to be real glad to hear you said that, sir," said McBurney. "Real glad."

And with that, he saluted the colonel and captain once again, feeling a great soaring feeling inside.

Young William Haywood McBurney felt like a man.

# CHAPTER 3

## KÖNIGSFORST, EAST OF COLOGNE
## WESTERN GERMANY

### JUNE 17, 1944

AS THE ACOUSTIC GUITARS began lightly strumming and the singing voices rose up in the summer breeze, a sunbeam filtered through the overhead canopy of trees onto the group of German youth. The tune was *An Rhein und Ruhr Marschieren Wir*—We March on Ruhr and Rhine—a WWI military song of soldierly bonhomie that had been co-opted by the Nazis but was now, in the hands of the teenagers present, a vigorous protest song against the Hitler Youth and National Socialism. To Angela Lange, a sixteen-year-old assistant nurse at the Hospital of Augustinians in Cologne, the mellifluous voices and radiant sunshine slanting through the towering pine appeared to be a sign from above. She felt a powerful sense of possibility, a freedom unlike anything she had ever known.

There were nearly thirty singing along with her and the handful of guitar players, all 14 to 17 years old. They were a unique-looking troupe. In a spirit of unabashed pride and rebellion against Hitler, the members of both sexes brandished metal badges of the edelweiss flower—*Edelweissblume*, the emblem of the anti-Nazi resistance movement—on their hats or left lapel of their shirts or jackets, and they were all dressed alike though not in uniform. The boys wore their hair long and donned checked shirts, dark short trousers, white stockings, and windbreaker jackets, while the girls sported white pullovers or waistcoats with their skirts. Their common outfits ensured that like-minded individuals on outings in the industrial Rhine and Ruhr regions of Western Germany could recognize one another even if they had never met before, thereby striking up an instant friendship.

Their universal greeting was "Ahoy" or "*Heidewitzka*," the latter a subversive anti-Nazi substitute for "Heil Hitler" that the gang members particularly enjoyed. Despite the ravages of war all around, they liked to take weekend trips into the countryside, where groups from the surrounding region met up, pitched tents, sang, and talked about how much they loathed the Hitler Youth, food rationing, Goebbels's ludicrous propaganda, and the relentless Allied bombing that had killed and displaced millions of innocents while turning German cities into rubble.

They called themselves the Edelweiss Pirates.

For years, Angela had heard about the *Edelweisspiraten*—the Navajos of Cologne, the Kittelbach Pirates of Oberhausen and Düsseldorf, and the Roving Dudes of Essen—but it was only two weeks ago that she had been accepted into the secret group, and today was her first large gathering. The loose confederation of anti-Nazi rebels had emerged, in response to the strict regimentation of the *Hitler Jugend*, out of the Scout and Youth Movements that had been banned in 1933 by the Nazis—the *Pfadfinder* and *Bündische Jugend*. In contrast to the Hitler Youth, the Edelweiss Pirates came together spontaneously as neighbors, schoolmates, teammates in local sports groups, and coworkers. Most had finished their formal schooling but were not yet of draft age; many were apprentices and steady wage earners as unskilled workers due to the shortage of manpower in the Reich with the

Allies attacking on three fronts: Western France, Northern Italy, and the Russian Front. A large number of the boys had evaded the Hitler Youth by leaving school, which was allowed at 14, and were still young enough to avoid military conscription, which was only compulsory from the age of 17 onwards.

In refusing to participate in the activities organized by Nazi Party associations, the Pirates had sufficient free time to meet at nearby street corners, cafés, or parks and participate in weekend outings into the surrounding countryside, despite wartime restrictions on travel and tight Gestapo controls. Though the individual groups were associated with distinct regions, all members of the group remained identifiable and united by their distinctive edelweiss flower badges, their common style of dress, and their opposition to what they saw as the paramilitary cult of the Hitler Youth and adult Nazi population. Most importantly, unlike the gender-segregated *Hitler Jugend* and *Bund Deutscher Mädel*—the League of German Girls, the female wing of the Nazi Party youth movement—the Pirates contained both boys and girls, though males made up around three-quarters of the Rhineland groups. Companionship with the opposite sex gave members an opportunity for uninhibited romantic encounters—yet another reason for young people to join given the indecency and delinquency attributed to sexuality by the puritanical Nazis.

At first, Angela had been hesitant to join the resistance group. Though she was intrigued by the rebels and their romantic deeds she had heard so much about, she didn't know how to get in touch with the group's leaders and was afraid she wouldn't be accepted. But her growing hatred of Hitler and National Socialism for its monstrous injustices and incessant intrusion into her daily life, coupled with her desire for adventure, led her to want to rebel against the Hitler Youth, SS, and anything else that had to do with supporting a war she knew was lost.

And then, two weeks ago, fate intervened when she saw two boys her age painting "Hitler is a Liar" and "Down with Nazis" on a wall outside an air raid shelter. One of the boys she recognized as Bartholomäus "Barthel" Schröder, whom she had met before the war from her cousin Max who lived in Ehrenfeld. After surprising them by revealing her approval of their rebellious graffiti, she asked if they were Edelweiss Pirates and asked them if she might be able to pitch in a hand with the group to protest the Nazis. At first, they were wary and dismissive, but once Barthel realized she was his former friend Max's first cousin they were more receptive to the possibility of her joining the group. But first she would have to prove herself. They made arrangements to meet her the following day, where she learned that Barthel Schröder's soft-spoken friend's name was Jean Hüber. The two seemed like natural leaders to her despite their youth.

But even though they seemed genuinely nice and courageous boys, she was still a touch scared to join the group. The Edelweiss Pirates, and the Navajos of Cologne in particular, were known to be working-class toughs, social outcasts, misfits, and rebels from the battered streets of the city—and she was an upper middle-class girl from Braunsfeld whose father was a Wehrmacht officer on convalescent leave. But Schröder, his friend Jean Hüber, and the other members of the Navajos made her feel welcome from the beginning and she soon got over her initial misgivings.

In the past ten days alone, she had attended a pair of clandestine meetings, distributed anti-Nazi leaflets, and painted "The War Must End" on a wall only a block away from the Gestapo headquarters at El-De Haus in the city center. As she was performing the illicit act, her heart beat so fast that she thought it might explode. It was in that adrenaline-filled moment that she realized she had joined the Edelweiss Pirates as much to partake in risky adventure as to rebel against the Third Reich. But she also liked the sense of belonging to a group of like-minded individuals dedicated to something important. What united all of the Edelweiss Pirate bands was their rejection of Hitler and Nazism, and Angela was proud to rally to the cause even if only in a small way.

When the group finished singing the song, Angela and Barthel Schröder looked at one another and smiled. He was the one who had brought her here to the leafy Königsforst for a Saturday afternoon of music and relaxation with their fellow *Edelweisspiraten*—and she knew she had a crush on him. He was a handsome boy with a sweetness yet toughness about him. As he reached out and touched her hand, she felt a little tingle. The group then launched into another song, this one a fight song targeting their foremost enemy, the *Hitler Jugend*.

*Hark the hearty fellows sing!*
*Strum that banjo, pluck that string!*
*And the lasses all join in*
*We're going to get rid of Hitler,*
*And he can't do a thing.*

*Hitler's power may lay us low.*
*And keep us locked in chains,*
*But we will smash the chains one day,*
*We'll be free again.*
*We've got fists and we can fight*
*We've got knives and we'll get them out.*
*We want freedom, don't we boys?*
*We're the fighting Navajos.*

*We're Edelweiss Pirates, and we're on our way.*
*We march by banks of Ruhr and Rhine*
*And smash the Hitler Youth in twain,*
*Our song is freedom, love, and life*
*We're Pirates of the Edelweiss.*

When the song was finished, everyone gave a rousing cheer. Then Angela and Barthel Schröder took a stroll alone together in the woods.

ΨΨΨ

They walked along a game trail for several minutes until they reached an outcrop of granite beside a small brook. Sitting down on the lichen-covered rock, a knowing smile came to Schröder's lips, as if he was privy to a private joke.

"What's so funny?" she asked him.

He looked at her bashfully. "Nothing."

"Come on, what is it?"

His grin widened. "You," he said. "I was thinking about you."

"Is that so?"

"I was thinking about going skinny dipping in the brook with you. And kissing you—on the lips."

"Oh, you think I'm that kind of girl, do you?"

"No, of course not…I mean, I just know I like you. You are quite pretty. And you are smart and funny."

"So are you Bartholomäus Schröder. That's why, despite my better judgment, I'm going to do this."

She leaned forward and kissed him on the lips. When she pulled away, he looked surprised for a moment before nodding approvingly and breaking into a smile.

"You caught me off guard," he said. "I definitely didn't expect that."

"What, a girl can't kiss a boy? It has to be the other way around?"

"No, I suppose it doesn't." He studied her a moment. "You do not lack for confidence, do you? What is your story anyway?"

"I'm not sure what you mean."

"You haven't told me anything about yourself except that you work as a nurse at the Hospital of Augustinians and live in Braunsfeld."

"Go ahead and ask me what you want. But you will have to tell me about yourself. That's only fair."

"All right, we have a deal. But I get to start. Tell me about your family."

There had been death in her family, as with so many others in the war, and she instantly felt a flicker of sadness. But the moment passed quickly.

"I live with my father," she said. "My mother was killed in a British bombing raid in March. Along with my little brother."

"I'm sorry."

"I miss them terribly. I hate this war."

"I do too. Are your parents from Cologne?"

"My father is, but my mother was from Alsace-Lorraine."

"It is too bad about your mother and brother. There were a lot of people lost in those Mosquito raids at the end of the month. The BBC said that more than a hundred planes took part in the attacks."

She nodded. She often listened to BBC broadcasts with her papa. The Nazi authorities had made it illegal and punishable by death for Germans to listen to *feindsender*—foreign radio broadcasts by stations of the enemies of the Reich—but the rebellious Edelweiss Pirates and many German citizens regularly listened to such broadcasts in secret to keep informed about the war beyond the puffery spouted by Reich Minister of Propaganda Joseph Goebbels.

She remembered back to the roaring engines and clatter of machine-guns as the death planes swooped down upon her and her family. She, her father, mother, and younger brother were making their way to the air-raid shelter, but they hadn't made it a hundred feet before the British fighter-bombers veered hard left from the Cologne Cathedral Church of Saint Peter and roared down upon them. She remembered the antiaircraft searchlights arcing across the night sky and the bulging bomb bay doors opening up like a chasm and disgorging their bombs from no more than five hundred feet above the city. The ground shook, dust and smoke filled the air, and she was thrown to the ground and knocked unconscious. When she awoke, she found herself partially buried beneath a pile of rubble with her father grievously wounded and mother and younger brother dead. Thus far, it had been the worst day of her life.

Seeing her sad expression, he reached out and touched her hand. "Perhaps we shouldn't talk about such things," he said softly.

"No, it's all right. It is best to remember those we loved. That way we can pay tribute to them. I loved my mother dearly, and my younger brother too."

"What were their names?"

"Diane and Arne."

"So only you and your father survived. That must make you feel guilty."

"It does."

"I'm sorry. What does your father do?"

"He is a Wehrmacht colonel."

An eyebrow went up. "A Wehrmacht colonel? Is he a Party member?"

"No, Papa hates the Nazis. He was seriously wounded in North Africa in May 1943 just before the surrender and was invalided to Rome. Two months later, when he was close to fully healed, he was badly injured again in a British air raid. This time he was sent home to Cologne. Three months ago, he was again about to return to action when the air raid that killed my mother and brother happened. He lost his right arm and still has shrapnel lodged in his back and head."

"So he's still on convalescent leave from active military service?"

"*Ja*, he was released from the hospital just last week and we live together at home. Though he can't return yet to active duty, he insisted on doing something. So he was made commander of the Cologne flak defenses. It is not a full-time job. But his heart was broken when my mother and brother died and he is not the same. I take care of him when I am not working at the hospital. He is a good man, a loyal German, but his spirit is gone. He drinks himself to sleep every night."

"Again, I'm sorry."

"Don't be. And what about you? What heartbreaking story do you have to tell? With this war, everybody has one."

"It hasn't been easy for me and my family. Let's just say that."

"What do your father and mother do?"

"My father is a post office worker, my mother a homemaker. I have four brothers and sisters. Surprisingly, they are all still alive despite the constant bombing."

"You live in Ehrenfeld?"

"Yes, our apartment is still standing but it has been heavily damaged."

"Were you in the *Hitler Jugend* before you joined the Navajos?"

"Yes—it was dreadful. Once our playing fields and club buildings were bombed out and they stopped our hiking trips, the HJ was reduced to constant military drilling. All we did was march and perform mindless exercises in obedience. They were all the more irksome for being supervised by leaders who were scarcely older than me. And far stupider. Every order that was given contained a threat."

"Is that why the Edelweiss Pirates' slogan is 'Eternal War on the Hitler Youth?'"

He nodded. "They took away our sports and leisure activities and tried to turn us into obedient Nazis. They don't want us to be human beings—they want us to be soldiers marching to a single drum beat. The HJ took over our lives."

"And now you can strike back."

"Yes, and we are doing exactly that each and every—"

He stopped right there as she signalled him to stop talking.

"What is it?" he asked.

"I thought I heard something."

"Really, I didn't hear anything." He scanned the trees. "And I don't see anyone."

"Just hold on a moment. I know I heard something."

She strained her ears and scanned the woods. But she heard nothing and saw no unusual movement, nothing out of the ordinary. She took a deep breath to steel herself, suppressing a faint miasma of fear. She knew she had not imagined the noise. What she had heard was real and someone was out there. But she felt an even stronger presence than that: she felt like they were being watched.

"It's probably just a squirrel or rabbit." He gave a mischievous smile. "Or maybe it's the big bad wolf. Don't worry, I'll protect you—if you give me another kiss."

She shot him a withering glare. This was no time to joke around. While the forest was the cornerstone of the founding mythology of German culture and identity, it was also a source of deep uneasiness for her and the vast majority of her countrymen. The old fairy tales she had grown up with warning her of the dangers of the forest, of tempting houses fashioned of sweets and clever wolves in disguise, always made her feel a sense of foreboding whenever she was in the woods, particularly at night. But she didn't want to show fear in front of him.

And then she heard it again, only this time she knew exactly what it was: the sound of a snapping twig.

She looked at him. "Tell me you heard that?"

"Yes, that I heard. What do you want to do?"

"I think we should get going."

"All right, but if it's Jean and Marie playing tricks on us, we're going to feel awfully foolish," he said, referring to their fellow Edelweiss Pirates Jean Hüber and Marie Peukert.

They started back towards the camp. But before they had gone ten paces, they heard the noises again. They halted in their tracks. Whatever was out there, it didn't sound like a small animal.

"Hello?" Schröder called out, his voice unnaturally loud in the quiet woods. "Who is it?"

There was no answer.

"Somebody there?" asked Angela, trying to act casual despite the thumping inside her chest.

They peered into the stands of pine trees, blanketed in dark shadow. There was nothing more than faint smears of light coming through the roof of the forest. They paused to carefully listen. Again, her instinct told her they were being watched.

"I feel like we're Hansel and Gretel in the Black Forest," said Schröder. "Let's get out of here."

They started off again, this time at a brisk pace. They walked ten feet, twenty feet, without incident and then, quite distinctly, Angela heard a crunching of brush behind them. This time there was no mistaking: they were footsteps. But were they animal or human?

She stopped abruptly and wheeled around, taking her companion by the arm and halting him. The woods stretched empty behind them, bathed in a pool of faint eerie light.

"Who's there?" she demanded, her voice louder and carrying a note of anger.

Schröder reached into his belt and jerked out a pocket knife. "I've got a knife and I know how to use it!" he cried, his voice sounding more desperate than threatening.

"Do you really think that little thing is going to stop anybody?" she whispered. "Now let's go."

They started off again. She heard no further sound except the gurgle of the mountain brook. Still, she couldn't rid herself of the nagging feeling they were being stalked. It was as if one or more interlopers were masking the sound of their footsteps by keeping in rhythm with theirs. She fought against the instinct to run, reminding herself that there was no reason to panic, not until they knew what they were up against.

And then, suddenly, her worst fears were realized.

When she glanced over her shoulder, she saw, not more than fifty feet behind them, a dark form poke out from behind a tree and then shrink back from the light into the oblivion of the forest.

She looked at Schröder and saw that he had seen it too. "*Scheisse*, that can't be good!" he cried. "Let's get out of here!"

He grabbed her by the hand and they turned and ran like jackrabbits.

The sound of running feet picked up behind them. Angela felt her body seize with panic. *Are we being chased down?* They ran as fast as their legs would carry them, ripping through underbrush, stumbling, banging into branches, recovering, running on, their breaths coming in terrified gasps. Up ahead, she could make out faint smudges of light where the woods ended and opened up into a clearing.

They broke into the clearing. Halfway across, they stopped to look back at their pursuers. But the noise had stopped and no one was there.

She looked at her companion. "Who do you think it was?"

"I don't know."

"Do you think it could be Hitler Youth?"

"Way out here? I doubt it." Once again, the crunching of brush underfoot could be heard. "Wait, there's someone coming."

She kept her gaze fixed on the trees but nothing happened.

And then they saw a white-tailed buck, a doe, and pair of fawns trot out of the woods and cut across the clearing towards the thick woods to the east.

Looking at one another, they sighed with relief. "Just a family of deer," he said.

She nuzzled up to him. "Look at them. They don't even know there's a war going on."

"When I'm with you, neither do I," he said.

"I feel the same way." She gave him a little kiss on the cheek and they started off again, walking hand in hand with the afternoon sunlight on their faces and their edelweiss flowers pinned proudly to their chests. But when they reached the woods on the far side of the clearing, they heard the sound of a footfall again, this time to their right. They stopped, expecting someone to appear. But there was no one and the footsteps had stopped. Still, Angela felt a tickling sensation on the back of her neck, as if they were being pursued.

"I don't like this," she said.

"Neither do I," he agreed.

They resumed walking, faster now. The woods turned darker as they penetrated deeper and deeper into the thick pine, spruce, and beech trees. She tried to tell herself that there was a perfectly logical explanation for the noise. But she knew there wasn't.

Instinct told her they were being followed.

They picked up their pace. She gripped his hand tighter.

To her consternation, she heard a noise again. This time it was unmistakable: the sound of footsteps, several of them, coming at them fast from their left-rear.

They both turned. But they were too late.

Out of the corner of her eye, Angela saw a terrible, swift slash of movement as they were overtaken by a swarm of brown-uniformed bodies brandishing red Nazi armbands and military rifles. The next thing she knew she was knocked hard to the ground and Schröder was dealt a series of sharp blows to his face and body from several rifle butts. To her horror, Angela realized that their attackers were members of the *Hitler Jugend Streifendienst*, the special patrol service consisting of older members of the Hitler Youth.

The unit had originally been formed to police the HJ. But with the war going badly for Germany, it had transformed into an armed body of hard-core youth who assisted the Gestapo in hunting down escaped prisoners of war, downed Allied airmen, resistance groups like the Edelweiss Pirates, and anyone else suspected of evading the authorities or considered "enemies of the state" working against the National Socialist regime. Trained to use small arms and rifles, its members were distinguished from the regular Hitler Youth by the rifles they carried, the special cuffs bearing the words *HJ-Streifendienst* and white piping on their shoulder straps, and the special patrol service *Streifendienst* gorget they wore at their throats. To Angela and everyone else in the Pirates, they were the most loathed members of the HJ and the two groups often fought in open battle on the streets of Cologne.

"Stop it! Stop it!" cried Angela.

"Shut up, you sow!" shouted one of them, and he jabbed her in the ribs with the butt of his rifle.

"Ouch, that hurt! Now stop this at once! You'll kill him!"

"Shut up, you cunt!"

He ripped off her edelweiss badge, threw it on the ground, and spit on it. She tried to help Schröder, but was shoved aside.

"You can't do this! We haven't done anything wrong!" she pleaded.

The tallest and oldest-looking one, obviously their leader, turned away from beating the boy and glowered at her. "You're Edelweiss Pirates—you are *Volksfeinde* and must be punished!"

He shoved her to the ground. She tried to get up, but he and the one who had jabbed her in the ribs knocked her down again. As the blows against Schröder continued, she began to cry. She couldn't believe the world Hitler had created. His policy of Aryan purity pitted the *Volksgemeinschaft*—the People's community in which all Germans, regardless of class or religion, were *Volkskameraden* or People's comrades—against the *Volksfeinde*—the People's enemies. The latter consisted of Jews, Slavs, Gypsies, black Africans, and other undesirable races or groups of people along with Communists, trade unionists, and what the Nazis referred to as "asocials" like the Edelweiss Pirates and other resistance groups that defied the will of the People's community. Even for ordinary Germans, the crimes for scrounging for food in the rubble after air raids, listening to Allied radio broadcasts, possession of enemy or homegrown anti-Nazi leaflets, and other minor infractions now often resulted in stiff penalties, and sometimes even execution.

The beating stopped.

The leader jerked her to her feet and wagged a finger at her. "Get out of the King's Forest! You don't belong here!"

"What are you talking about?" she protested defiantly. "We are Germans and these woods belong to us as much as you!"

He shook his head. "No, they don't! They belong to *Volkskameraden* like us! Now get out of here before I shoot you both! I'm letting you go with a warning just this one time!"

Angela helped Schröder to his feet and half-dragged, half-carried him back to the camp. When they reached the edge of the pitched tents, Jean Hüber saw them limping in and rushed out to help them along with Angela's friend Marie Peukert.

"My God, what happened to you?" cried Hüber, putting an arm around Schröder so that there were two people giving him much-needed support.

"An HJ patrol stalked us and beat us up," explained Angela. "There were five of them and they jumped us in the woods."

"Bastards. We'll get the boys together and go after them."

Schröder shook his head. "No, Jean, they have guns."

"So do we, damnit."

"No, we don't. We have a single pistol and five bullets between all of us. And it happens to be a popgun that sometimes doesn't work."

"But there are more than two dozen of us."

"Against five *Streifendienst* armed with rifles. Give it a rest—we'll get them another time."

"All right, if that's the way you want to play it. But next time, we are going to make them pay dearly."

"Oh don't worry, we will," said Schröder through his bloodied mouth. "They made one big mistake."

"*Ja*, what is that?"

"They shouldn't have taken our Pirate badges. For that, they are going to get a severe beating. When the time is right, of course."

And with that, he smiled and Angela thought to herself: *You are my kind of boy, Bartholomäus Schröder. Together, we will wage eternal war on the Hitler Youth!*

# CHAPTER 4

## CAMP HOOD

### JULY 8, 1944

"THE BRASS ain't gonna let us fight—it's as simple as that," said Private Leonard Smith from his barrack's bunk. "They may let us shovel shit in France, but that's as much 'liberating' as they're gonna allow us *nigger boys* to do."

Hanging his feet over the edge of his own bunk, William McBurney didn't believe that for one minute. He couldn't *allow* himself to believe it. In his view, with the Allies having established a beachhead at Normandy, either America needed the 761st and would make proper use of it for a breakout in France; or, the Allies would destroy the Germans before they were deployed overseas and the war in Europe would draw to a close without the tank battalion ever getting in the mix. He couldn't imagine that after two years of training, and endless suffering at the hands of abusive MPs and Southern rednecks, the war might actually end without the 761st doing any fighting at all.

"Hell, I don't even know why we have a motto or an emblem," Smitty continued on with his rant. "We're nothing but a manual labor pool to the goddamn army brass. Shit, they ain't ever gonna give us a chance to *come out fighting.*"

*God, I hope you're wrong,* thought McBurney, feeling a twist of anger at the possibility. "Come Out Fighting" was the 761st's official motto, and the unit was known as the "Black Panther" Battalion for its distinctive uniform emblem bearing the motto along with a black panther superimposed upon a silver shield. McBurney couldn't bear the thought that the motto and emblem might all be for nought if the unit never saw combat. The motto came from a quotation by world heavyweight boxing champion Joe Louis in 1938 as he was preparing to fight German Max Schmeling for the second time. Asked about his fight plan, the Brown Bomber confidently proclaimed, "I'm going to come out fighting." He was as good as his word, knocking out Schmeling two minutes and four seconds into the first round and cracking several of his vertebrae. Many in the unit had spent time in the ring, and the quote from their hero was a source of pride for McBurney and the other men of the 761st, as was their black-panther logo. The fierce and stealthy native of African jungles symbolized the twin objectives of the battalion: to strike quickly and unexpectedly, and to carry out its mission decisively.

"Okay, I've heard enough of your whining, man," said McBurney. "Why would they put us on alert status if they weren't going to send us overseas?"

"I don't know—you'd have to ask them. All I know is we're probably gonna kill more rattlesnakes than Japs or Krauts during this damned war. I've told you that before, and now I'm telling you again."

"I can't believe that. I think it's just going to take some time."

"It's already been a goddamn month. And we're no closer to—"

He stopped right there as the door to the barracks opened up and in stepped the battalion's morale officer, the college football and baseball star Lieutenant Jackie Robinson. McBurney had heard that two nights ago Robinson had gotten into some trouble over a bus incident. The abuse meted out by white bus drivers, local crackers, and white soldiers on the civilian buses going to and from Camp Hood continued to be a huge source of frustration for the black members of the battalion.

Like most men of the 761st, McBurney liked Robinson. The lieutenant always had a smile on his face and the unit's morale was high on account of the pick-up football and baseball games he organized. When he had first arrived to Camp Hood back in April, McBurney had no inkling of Robinson's outstanding ability as an athlete, but he quickly learned. In an early football game, he caught a pass and was heading for the end zone when Robinson came out of nowhere, flew head and shoulders first, and knocked McBurney hard to the ground, forcing a fumble. Robinson scooped up the ball and scored while McBurney lay gasping for air and mouthing, "He broke my ribs!" After celebrating his touchdown, Robinson helped McBurney to his feet, smiled with an unspoken but understood "Sorry," and both young men resumed play. But McBurney had learned his lesson and kept a sharp eye out for Jack Roosevelt Robinson at all times on the sports fields after that.

"Hey fellas," said Robinson, and he was greeted heartily in return by the twenty or so men lounging around their bunks. Everyone at Camp Hood—black or white, officer or enlisted—had heard about the latest bus incident. "I know by now you've heard what happened the other night. But I wanted to fill you in on where things stand because I may not be posted here for long. It looks like they may court-martial me. It's not definite but it's looking that way."

A chorus of sympathetic and outraged moans and groans rose up through the barracks. "It ain't right, man—it just ain't right," cried Smitty, and he was echoed vociferously by several others.

Robinson waited a moment for the commotion to quiet down. "I know it ain't right, fellas," he said. "That's why I came here to tell you how it all went down. There's a lot of bullshit rumors flying around this camp, but I want you to know that I was within my rights as an officer."

"From what we heard, you were just minding your own business on your way to McCloskey Hospital in Temple," said Sergeant Warren Crecy. A soft-spoken former high school football star from Corpus Christi, Texas, Crecy had swiftly risen as a leader by showing particular fierceness in the training exercises against the white tank-destroyer units.

"You heard right." Robinson stepped forward to signal that he had the floor, and the men hopped off their bunks to gather around him. "I was doing some more tests on my ankle so I could get fit-for-duty status. When I boarded the bus, I took a seat next to Lieutenant Jones's wife, Virginia. She was sitting in the fourth row from the back and was heading back to her home in Belton. It's halfway between the base and the hospital. With her light skin, no one questioned where she chose to sit. But one of the white passengers complained about me, and the bus driver told me to move my ass to the rear of the bus. I told him in no uncertain terms that as a United States officer I would damn well sit where I pleased."

"What did he say to that?" asked Crecy.

"He didn't like it, of course. I recommended that he mind his own business and concentrate on his driving."

Heads bobbed and roars of approval went up in the barracks. McBurney liked that Robinson had been defiant towards the driver, who had no right to tell him where to sit.

"What happened after that, Jackie?" then asked McBurney.

"The argument continued all the way to the transfer station. That's when the driver jumped off the bus and quickly returned with the dispatcher and several drivers. He shouted, 'There's the nigger that's been causing me trouble.' I pointed my finger at him and said, 'Quit fucking with me.' A crowd gathered round and began shouting and bullying me. MPs soon arrived and asked me, as the senior officer present, to go with them to straighten out the matter."

"They didn't mess with you?" asked Lieutenant Charles Gates. Older than most of the men in the unit at thirty-three, "Pop" Gates, as his fellow tankers called him, was a tough, principled graduate of Virginia's Hampton Institute who had joined the service in April 1941, trained with the Buffalo Soldiers at Fort Riley, Kansas, and was now in charge of the assault gun platoon of Bates's Headquarters Company.

"No, the MPs were all right," replied Robinson. "They were enlisted men. They called me 'sir' and seemed only interested in doing their duty under the circumstances. So I agreed to go with them to the military guardroom at the Camp Hood provost marshal's office. That's when the situation went totally FUBAR."

Here he paused, and McBurney could see the anger in his eyes as he recalled the disturbing events from two nights ago. McBurney felt a burning outrage, too, at the injustice of it all. *If white folks can't respect the uniform, even that of an officer, what's the point of serving in this white man's army?*

"When we reached the guard room, I was met by a sergeant and a private. The private immediately asked one of the MPs if he had that 'nigger lieutenant' with him. I told him that if he called me a nigger again, I would break him in two. The MPs summoned the duty officer. He proceeded to ignore my version of the events on the bus and again referred to me as a 'nigger.' When I protested, I was ordered outside. A short time after that, Captain Bear, the head of the MPs, arrived and I followed him into the guard room to give my account of the incident. But Bear ordered me out. I informed him that it wasn't right for me to be excluded from a process that could have serious implications for my future. But Bear did not recognize me as an officer at all."

Here he paused again, shaking his head in disgust. His lip trembled, ever so slightly, and McBurney felt for him. He could see the pain on his face. Robinson then licked his lips, as if to collect himself and stem back the anger building inside him at recollecting his mistreatment at the hands of the white MPs.

"At this point, I was burning up inside. I gave several sloppy salutes and repeated several times, 'OK, suh! OK, suh!' in as sarcastic a tone as possible. From there things turned from bad to worse. The stenographer arrived to record my testimony on the bus incident. She was a white civilian woman and her scorn for me was instantly obvious. She did not simply write down my answers to Captain Bear's questions—she interrupted me at every turn and put forward her own thoughts."

"What did she say to you?" asked Pop Gates.

"She said, 'Don't you know, boy, you got no right sitting up there in the white part of the bus?'"

A murmur of bitter groans and curses echoed through the room.

"I told Captain Bear that I didn't think she was impartial enough to record my words accurately."

"What did Bear say that?" asked McBurney.

"He said I was uppity and that I had no right to speak to a white woman in that manner."

More clucks of outrage, followed by a string of curses from Smitty and two other enlisted men. McBurney just shook his head in dismay.

"Did they put you under arrest?" asked Sergeant Crecy.

"No, Captain Bear ordered the military police to escort me back to the hospital in Temple. I asked him if this meant I was under arrest, but he refused to answer. I informed him that I had a pass until 0800 the next morning and that unless I was under arrest, I should be allowed to go where I pleased. Bear then told me I was under 'arrest in quarters.' That meant I would not be detained at the base but could not leave the hospital. When I arrived back at McCloskey, a colonel there told me that he had been alerted to expect a black officer who was drunk and disorderly and had tried to start a riot, which was of course a load of crap. He advised me to take a blood test to prove there was no alcohol in my system. There wasn't any since I hadn't had anything to drink that night."

"What's going to happen now, Jackie?" asked Pop Gates.

"I don't know. Captain Bear has brought forward court-martial proceedings. But such charges require the permission of the commanding officer, and Colonel Bates refused to sign off."

"The colonel's a good man," said Crecy. "He's got our back."

Heads nodded and voices sounded in vigorous agreement. Not for the first time, McBurney was glad they had the fair-minded Paul Bates in charge of their outfit. The former high school teacher and All-American football star from Western Maryland College brought an integrity and intensity that had swiftly won over the soldiers under his command. But more importantly, he was fundamentally decent, honest, and compassionate. McBurney worshipped him. The colonel treated the men of the battalion with a simple, direct humanity, and they responded in kind. Unlike other commanders of the battalion, Bates lived on the post with his men. He went with them on marches and runs, listening to their comments and complaints. There was nothing he could do to change the deeply engrained attitudes of other white officers, but he forbade any mistreatment of his soldiers and insisted they be given nothing but the highest caliber of armored training.

"The problem," said Robinson, "is the brass could do an end run around the colonel and transfer me from Camp Hood to some other—"

He left the words unfinished as Lieutenant Williams stepped into the barracks. The men stood at attention.

"At ease, men," said Williams, his eyes searching the barracks.

McBurney held his breath. Like many men in the outfit, McBurney regarded the former Yale student and son of a prominent Pittsburgh industrialist favorably but still a touch warily. Sometimes, the men were not quite sure what to make of the scraggly looking twenty-three-year-old who was scarcely older than them. McBurney had heard that other white officers at Camp Hood often teased Williams, sniping that his rich father must have used his political influence to place him with the black battalion to ensure that he wouldn't be shipped overseas for combat. It was supposedly for this reason that Williams had resented his assignment with the 761st and had tried to join the Air Corps, although he had not been successful and had returned to the battalion.

It was clear to McBurney that Williams had been raised with an ethic of racial tolerance, but he had little experience interacting with blacks, which made him nervous and unsure of himself. Determined to appear confident and in control, he seemed to overcompensate for his lack of experience by being something of a martinet. At the same time, although the men regarded him with caution due to his strictness, they appreciated the fact that he was always fair with them and cared far more about their performance than their race. But as far as the battalion's white officers went, he was still a distant second to their "Great White Father," Lieutenant Colonel Bates, who was held in the highest esteem.

"Lieutenant Robinson," snapped Williams.

"Yes, sir, Lieutenant."

"The colonel wants to see you. He said right now."

Robinson saluted crisply. "Yes, sir."

As Williams walked out of the barracks with Jackie Robinson in tow, McBurney thought to himself: *This can't be good—this can't be good at all.*

ΨΨΨ

"I'm sorry, Jackie, but it looks like there *is* going to be a court-martial," said Paul Bates. He and Robinson were alone in the colonel's office with late afternoon sunlight bleeding through the window.

Robinson looked deeply dismayed and Bates felt for him. "So that's it then. I've been court-martialed."

The colonel nodded solemnly and pushed several sheets of paper across the desk. "That's the order. Captain Bear is the one who initiated the proceedings. The charges require the permission of the commanding officer of the accused's battalion, but as you know I refused to sign the order. Unfortunately, that wasn't enough to put the matter to rest."

"I appreciate what you did for me, sir."

"You know I have nothing but the highest regard for your character, Lieutenant. That's why I refused to give consent. But I'm afraid the top brass did what I feared they would do and circumvented me."

Robinson shook his head glumly as he looked over the order. "I can see that, sir. I've been transferred to the 758th Tank Battalion."

Bates felt a ripple of anger at the injustice and stupidity of it all. Why couldn't he and his men simply be left alone to do their goddamn jobs?

"The commander of the 758th immediately signed the court-martial order once your transfer went through today," he said. "Again, I'm sorry, Jackie. This should never have happened."

A heavy sigh. "I still can't believe it's come to this. But you did all you could, Colonel. I want to thank you again for that."

*Yeah, but it wasn't enough,* thought Bates. He wished he had found a way to stop the sham proceeding. He still couldn't believe the army had taken the drastic step of transferring one of his top officers out of the 761st so it could initiate a court-martial. It was clear, from what Robinson had told him, that the witness statements from the whites on board the bus were grossly exaggerated, if not outright false. They claimed that he had gone berserk, used obscene language in front of women, and threatened bodily harm to the driver and an MP corporal. But Bates knew better. No doubt Robinson had lost his temper at the driver, MPs, and Captain Bear during the course of the unfortunate events, but as an officer he had been fully within his rights and army regulations to refuse to give up his seat, as well as to demand to know why he was being arrested.

But what really stuck in Bates's craw was that the charges against Robinson had nothing to do with the heated verbal exchange on the bus. Instead, to avoid dealing with the politically explosive situation of the mistreatment of colored enlisted men and officers on civilian buses, the charges were limited to Robinson's interaction with the head of Camp Hood's MP detachment. It was clear to Bates that Captain Gerald M. Bear was out to destroy Jackie Robinson for the simple reason that he was a black officer who knew his rights and refused to be treated like a dog.

"Do I have a chance at beating this, sir? You know as well as I do that a guilty verdict and dishonorable discharge will ruin my life before it has even begun. And it would crush my mother."

"We're going to beat this thing, Jackie. I'll bring a dozen or more members of the 761st before the investigating officer. They'll testify to the rough and unfair treatment you and others have regularly received on the buses at Camp Hood. But I'm not going to lie to you—it's going to be a tough fight."

"I didn't think it was going to be easy, sir."

"Unfortunately, a general court-martial is more serious than a summary or a special court-martial. As you said, they can boot you out of the army if found guilty."

"I think what bothers me most is the charges don't even mention what happened on the bus. But that's how the whole thing got started."

"The army can't afford the outcry and close scrutiny of bus policy that trying these charges against you will bring. You're nationally known from your football and baseball career at UCLA. That's why the other side wants the case to be decided by what happened *after* the MPs arrived at the scene and not what happened on the bus. There's also a new directive."

"A new directive?"

"War Department Directive Number 97. The Army just released it. It states that no discrimination on the basis of race for transportation, recreational facilities, theaters, and the like will be tolerated."

"So that's why they want to sweep the bus incident under the rug. I suspected they were up to something."

"Well, they're not going to get away with it. Whoever represents you will make sure the bus incident remains central to the case."

"It's still going to be a tough road ahead." He looked down at the order. "It says here that the army's charging me with Articles 63 and 64 of the Articles of War—including showing disrespect towards a superior officer and failure to obey a direct command. A conviction will result at the very least in a dishonorable discharge."

"Which isn't right, and you and I both know it."

"The whole case is built on a series of lies, sir."

"I know that, Jackie. That's why we have to try and get inside the other side's head. They're going to try to make the case about only two things: first, that you behaved disrespectfully towards Captain Bear in the guard room, and second, that you disobeyed Bear's order to remain in the receiving area."

"I think I need to use the press to get my story out."

"The press is unpredictable, Lieutenant. If you're going to get them involved, make sure you can trust them."

"I'm talking about the Negro press, sir. Surely, I can trust *them*. I'm also going to contact the NAACP for a lawyer, and write Mr. Truman Gibson at the War Department. I'm going to make it clear that these are trumped-up charges and that my sole interest lies in justice."

"I understand that you've got to do what you've got to do. Whatever you choose, I'll be there for you."

"Will you be able to, sir? The battalion is on alert for deployment."

"I told you I'll be there for you, Jackie. That's a promise and I'm a man who keeps his promises."

# CHAPTER 5

## BRAUNSFELD, WEST COLOGNE

### JULY 18, 1944

"WHERE DO YOU THINK YOU'RE GOING? IT'S PAST CURFEW."

With her rucksack draped over her shoulder and her beret askew, Angela Lange looked insolently at her father, sitting on a plush couch nursing a *zwetschgenwasser* plum brandy. They were in the parlor of their house at Hültzstrasse 26. The stately abode was fashioned of the same trachyte stone as the iconic Cologne Cathedral by the banks of the Rhine, with a gray slate roof and carved window flourishes, polished wood floors, high ceilings, and clean white walls hung with idyllic oil paintings of the Fatherland's craggy mountains and rolling hills. Located three miles from the *Altstadt*, the historic city center, the Lange residence had miraculously suffered only light bomb damage from the recurring Allied air attacks that had turned Cologne into a honeycomb of bombed-out buildings, twisted steel, and mountains of rubble.

"I can go where I please," she fired back. "I'm sixteen years old—old enough to fight."

Her father shook his silver-maned head. "The conscription age is seventeen. But of course, you already knew that."

"Tell that to the boys two years younger than me building the bunkers and patrolling the defenses of the Westwall. How can they not be soldiers when they build fortifications, march about, and are posted for guard duty?"

Known as the Siegfried Line to the Allies, the Westwall was the massive German defensive line built during the 1930s opposite the French Maginot Line overrun during the 1940 *blitzkrieg*. The two lines—both of which now belonged to the Germans—consisted of a series of complex defensive fortifications that included concrete pillboxes, machine-gun emplacements, underground bunkers, and triangular concrete antitank barriers known as "dragon's teeth." In the 1940 *blitzkrieg*, the Germans had simply marched their forces around the formidable barrier of the Maginot Line, rendering it useless by pushing through Belgium and the Ardennes Forest into France.

"The war has become desperate," came her father's answer. "Everyone is a *Volkskameraden*."

"No, life has become a daily battle for simple survival."

"Which is precisely why I forbid you to go out with those hooligans tonight. You'll only get yourself into trouble."

"Hooligans? That's what you call my friends?"

"They're Edelweiss Pirates, Angela. Frau Steinert told me she has seen you with them. On more than one occasion."

She felt a jolt of anger. "Frau Steinert is a nosy old bag."

"She's been a good friend to this family for more than twenty years. I trust what she says. Those young rebels you've been running around with are going to get you sent to a reeducation camp if you don't watch yourself."

"I can look after myself."

"You should stay away from them. I know that many of them have left their construction posts at the Westwall and no longer even work. Which means they don't have ration cards. No ration cards means no food, which means they are hiding out in the rubble. Even the ones with jobs are working class with no prospects for the future. Not only are they hooligans but they are socially beneath you. But more importantly, it is not safe out there."

"I don't care. I have leaflets to deliver."

"Leaflets? What kind of leaflets?"

"Allied propaganda leaflets. The people must know that the bombings will never let up and the war is lost. But most importantly, they need to know that it is Hitler and his henchmen that have sealed our fate. I know you despise Hitler and what he has done to our country just as much as I do. So why do you go on pretending as if everything is all right with the Nazis in power?"

An irritated twitch crossed his face. "I don't go on pretending any—"

"Yes, you do."

He took a gulp of his *zwetschgenwasser* and pounded the fist of his only hand—his left hand—on the side table. "Damnit, I was fooled just like everyone else."

"Don't give me the same old tired excuse about how unfair the Treaty of Versailles was and how *der Führer* brought us a national revival."

"But it is the truth. And that's precisely why the little bastard was popular with virtually everyone, until the tide of war turned at Stalingrad and the Tunisian campaign where I fought in North Africa. It is only in the past year that many have come to realize that his policies are responsible for nothing but horror and misery."

"You were blind and only now that we're losing the war do you see? Is that it?"

"All I know is that I am a loyal soldier and can never confide my true feelings to anyone except you. Unless, of course, I want to be put before a firing squad."

"I think we should cut our losses and surrender to bring an end to the destruction. But the Führer and his SS pigs will never let us do that. They are determined to continue the struggle even if it leads to the total destruction of the Fatherland." She gritted her teeth. "Damn Hitler—I would kill him if I could!"

At this, her father's eyebrows flipped up. "That kind of talk is dangerous and you must not breathe a word of it outside this house. Do you understand me?"

"Why should I obey you? You just sit by while Hitler, Goebbels, and Himmler destroy us from within. Why doesn't the Army stop them?"

"You know perfectly well why. Publically standing up to the Nazis means certain death." He ran a hand across his forehead in exasperation. "Why am I even talking to you? You are nothing but a rebellious child."

"No, I am a nearly grown woman. And I've got a lot more courage than you!"

"How dare you talk to me that way! You, young lady, are not going anywhere tonight when you talk to your father like that!"

"Who's going to stop me? Not you, that's for sure! Why just look at you!"

Her father's face reddened with a combination of embarrassment and fury as he struggled to raise his war-crippled body from the couch. In that revealing moment, he looked old and infirm, a mere shadow of the man that she had idolized growing up. Despite his neatly pressed Wehrmacht officer's uniform bedecked with a pair of Iron Crosses—one First Class, the other Second—as well as a Pour le Mérite and four Wound Badges, he presented a broken and withered figure. He looked like a great statesman whose time has passed. With his right arm severed just above the elbow, he was forced to salute with his left hand in the company of his fellow German officers, and he moved in a stiff and awkward manner from his many wounds sustained during both the Great War and the current conflict. He was supposed to report back for active duty by the end of the summer once he had recovered fully from his wounds, but she didn't see how he could possibly do it. If Hitler was recalling one-armed old men like her father back to the front, Germany was *kaput* and would become a pauper state.

Since his release from the hospital a month earlier, he was recuperating at home and serving as commander of the five hundred antiaircraft guns and one hundred and fifty searchlights in and around Cologne. Despite the importance of his job, it was only a part-time responsibility. He had agreed to do it only until he was declared fit enough to return to full-time active duty on the staff of Baron General Hasso von Manteuffel, whom he had served with on the Eastern Front and in Tunisia prior to his being strafed by a British fighter. The baron, an elfin five-foot-two and 120 pounds, was an experienced and widely respected Wehrmacht Panzer commander who was regarded by Hitler as "a daredevil, a bold and dashing leader," despite being a Prussian aristocrat and not being a National Socialist.

In serving as commander of the Cologne air defenses until his full recovery, her father was simply making the best of a difficult situation. By 1942, when it had become apparent that the Luftwaffe, Wehrmacht, and traditional civil defense organizations lacked the numbers of personnel necessary to protect the German cities, the *Heimatflak*—the national homeland antiaircraft defense units—had been established. Old men, teenage boys and girls, and foreign volunteers who, in return for better rations, preferred to make war against British and American aircraft instead of serving as industrial slave laborers, were all the Reich had to operate the command and control equipment of the Air Force's flak units. With the Allies having gained footholds in France, Italy, and Eastern Poland and soon to be knocking on the door to Germany, it was all part of Hitler's *Endkampf*—the final desperate struggle for the Fatherland's survival.

"You cannot talk to me like that, Angela," her father bristled in response to her incisive words. "Show some respect."

"Why should I? Hitler's turned you into nothing but a cripple and a drunk—and yet you still support him by serving as commander of Cologne's flak defenses."

His face, already red from drink and embarrassment, now turned crimson. "I am a soldier. I have an allegiance to the Fatherland, especially when it is under attack. I have sworn an oath."

"I think you're just hiding behind your soldiers' code. Where's the honor in that when you know Hitler is dead wrong? Why you're just as bad as him."

"Your mother would be ashamed to hear you talk like this. Especially when the enemy marches closer to our borders every day and our cities lay in ruins. I have a duty, damn you—a duty which your mother understood, God rest her soul!"

"Don't bring Mother into this."

"She would be ashamed, *Bärchen*. It's as simple as that."

With the word *Bärchen* Angela froze. Her father had called her by her nickname:

Little Bear Cub. He had been calling her by the term of endearment since she was a little girl. My, how she had worshipped him back then. Looking at the physical wreck he had become, she wondered how she could have admired him so.

"I have to go now," she said sharply.

"Don't you realize, *Bärchen*," he said with emotion, "that I hate the Nazis as much as you. More even. After all, look what they've done to me." With his left hand, he pointed to his missing right arm and the heavy scars on his face and neck. "Go if you must, but remember that I only worry over you because I love you and cannot bear the thought of losing you. I have already lost your mother Diane and brother Arne. I don't want to lose you too."

Feeling a swell of emotion, her lower lip trembled. She stood there staring at him for a long moment before turning towards the bookcase. Her eye caught a leather-bound copy of *All Quiet on the Western Front*. She wasn't sure why she hadn't noticed the book before and wondered if he had put it there recently. The authentic bestselling German novel about WWI was banned in the Fatherland because it captured all too accurately the brutality of war and severe hardships faced by the front-line soldier.

*Good for you, Papa,* she thought. *You have a banned book on your shelf.*

Feeling a sudden burst of affection, she rushed forward and gave him a hug. "I am sorry, Papa. I didn't mean to be so cruel."

There were tears in his eyes. "I love you so much, *Bärchen*. I just don't want anything to happen to you out there. There is death and destruction everywhere."

"I know but I have to do this. We have to show the Americans and British that some of us are different. I am embarrassed to be a German."

"That makes two of us." He sighed wearily. "Look, I know I can't stop you. But I want you to promise me one thing. Actually, three things."

"Three things?"

"Three important things. And in return, I promise not to interfere with you about this Edelweiss Pirate business. The fact is, I admire you for what you are doing. Resistance in the face of evil is the highest form of patriotism. But I am a soldier, and I have an allegiance to the Fatherland, especially when it is about to be invaded."

"You really admire me?"

"More than you can imagine. But you must agree to my three conditions."

"Wait a second. I don't think you're in any position to—"

"I am a Wehrmacht colonel and this is non-negotiable. I could have you sent to a work farm in the country for the duration of the war with one phone call if I wanted to. You would toil like an ox but be safe. More importantly, you would be cut off from the bad company you have taken up with. You do understand I could do this?"

She felt a chill on the nape of her neck as she realized he wasn't bluffing. He may have appeared like an old man on his last legs with his war wounds, his defeated manner, and his heavy drinking, but he was still a high-ranking and well-connected German military officer with an outstanding service record and the medals to prove it. The most important of those connections was his old commanding officer Baron General Hasso von Manteuffel, who was reported to have the ear of the Führer himself despite being a non-Nazi like her father. In short, her father still wielded tremendous power and authority as a highly decorated and well-liked officer, especially in his hometown of Cologne.

"All right, what do I have to do?" she grudgingly relented.

"First, I want you to promise me to be vigilant at all times and to trust no one."

"Very well, I promise. And the second?"

"If you are caught by the Gestapo, you must tell them immediately that you are my daughter and give them this."

With trembling fingers, he set down his tumbler of *zwetschgenwasser*, removed a sealed envelope from his jacket pocket, and handed it to her.

She looked at it for a moment with puzzlement. "What is this?"

"A letter that will keep you from the hangman's noose or a labor camp. You must keep it on you at all times, Angela. That, too, is non-negotiable."

She flipped the envelope over, looking for written text or an emblem on the outside, but there was nothing except her father's type-written name: Colonel Günther Lange.

"Don't tell me—it's a note signed by Himmler."

"This is no joking matter. Do not open it and keep it on you at all times. You must promise me."

"But who is it from and what does it say?"

"You don't need to know that. Just keep the letter on you at all times. It is the only thing that will protect you from the Gestapo. Believe me, I don't want you running around with those damn Edelweiss Pirates, but you are stubborn like your mother and I know in my present state, I cannot stop you. So, you must promise me that you will keep the letter on you and give it to the authorities if arrested."

She had the feeling he was up to something and wanted desperately to open the envelope, but she wouldn't. She may have been stubborn like her mother, but she had her father's strict code of honor and would never break a vow.

"All right, I promise. What's the third thing?"

He reached into his holster and calmly removed his Mauser *Hahn Selbstspanner* pistol. "Here, you must take this for your protection. Keep it on you at all times."

"You're giving me your pistol?"

"I have two more just like it. With the safety off, you just point and shoot like I taught you before with Arne. Just remember, if the safety is off, the hammer stays cocked and you can either begin shooting or put the safety on."

He quickly showed her then handed her the pistol along with two spare magazines, which she placed in her rucksack. Throughout the exchange, she noticed he was eyeing her closely, as if sizing up her military preparedness.

"I don't know what I would do if I lost you, *Bärchen*," he said with a genuinely tender expression on his weathered, battle-scarred face. "That's why you must be vigilant at all times and carry this gun and the letter with you. When the time comes, they may very well save your life."

"I will do as you say, Papa." She leaned forward and gave him a peck on the cheek. "I know you care about me and I love you."

"And I love you, my Little Bear Cub. Never forget that."

# CHAPTER 6

## EHRENFELD AND ALTSTADT NORD, COLOGNE

### JULY 18, 1944

IN THE DARKNESS OF THE BLACKOUT, she made her way beneath a sliver of moon northeast along Hültzstrasse towards Ehrenfeld, passing through neighborhood after neighborhood of bomb-razed buildings and endless piles of rubble. The Queen City of Cologne had been thrashed beneath the shadows of Allied bombs since February 1942. Whenever she saw the devastation around her, Angela realized it was a miracle that her family's house had not suffered a direct hit during the countless aerial attacks. Though the kitchen, parlor, and her father's bedroom had been partially damaged, their nineteenth-century stone house in the once fashionable district of Braunsfeld stood mostly intact.

The British nighttime bombing raids—recently augmented by those of the U.S. Eighth Air Force in daytime assaults—had grown increasingly frequent and devastating in the past two years. In the last year alone, more than ten thousand German civilians had been killed and wounded by the swarms of roaring Wellingtons, Mosquitoes, Lancasters, Halifaxes, and Manchesters that descended upon the city like swooping vultures. The damage was so pervasive that Cologners often pointed out at the desolation and remarked to one another, *"Das sind die Ruinen von Pompeii!"* Those are the ruins of Pompeii!

From Hültzstrasse, Angela took Melatengürtel, which curved northward towards the train station. On her right, she passed the ghostly Melaten Cemetery, which in daylight would have presented a vast swath of luscious greenery, historic gravesites, and ornate monuments broken by giant blackened bomb craters. The sprawling grassy lawn had once been a hospital and yard for lepers and other sick Europeans in the 12th century, and the name "Melaten"—or Yard of the Malades—had stuck.

As she walked further north, past Weinsberg Strasse, she noted the large number of people out on the streets. With scavenging punishable by a labor camp or sometimes death, it was in the evenings that the remaining civilian population of Cologne, and especially those displaced by the incessant Allied bombing, poked about the rubble to obtain extra food, clothing, and items for barter. Under the cover of darkness, they were harder to monitor and track by the Gestapo and Hitler Youth that hunted them down like wolves.

She could see hunched-over men, women, and children picking through the wreckage of the beveled houses. She felt badly for them. Many of those who remained in the city were living illegally in impromptu shelters in parks, underground bunkers and cellars, or the basements of bombed-out houses and apartments. There were escaped Russian, Polish, Ukrainian, Italian, and French laborers; Wehrmacht deserters who didn't want to return to the war; fugitive Russian and French soldiers; hardened German and foreign criminals; impoverished citizens simply struggling to survive; and a smattering of Jews who had miraculously managed to evade the SS roundups. From the exhaustion on the faces of the people on the streets and the appalling destruction of the city in the past six months, the conclusion was inescapable: Germany was facing certain defeat in the war, and the aftermath would be even worse than the ignominy following the Great War.

In every direction she looked, houses, apartment buildings, and storefronts had been leveled to the ground. It was as if a giant had stomped in and squashed them underfoot, leaving only skeletal ruins and endless piles of rubble. Despite the destruction all around, she noticed that some structures were still standing or only lightly damaged. But they were few and far between.

Looking to the east at the great Gothic Cologne Cathedral in the city center, she prayed that somehow the enduring symbol along the Rhine would miraculously continue to withstand the onslaught of Allied bombers. Stretching inexorably towards the heavens, the twin-spired cathedral was a great source of pride for Angela and everyone else in the beleaguered city.

She met Barthel Schröder, Marie Peukert, and Jean Hüber south of the train station. After greeting one another with the universal "Ahoy" of the Cologne Navajos and other groups of the Edelweiss Pirates, they set out along Subbelrather Strasse towards the *Altstadt*. Though only one or two out of every five structures was still standing and less than a half million people still occupied the city, they made sure to drop Allied leaflets into the letter boxes of every surviving house or apartment. From the slivers of light visible at the edges of the blackout curtains, they could tell where people were still living.

Since the earliest days of the war, Allied propaganda units had dropped tons of leaflets on major Reich cities to demoralize the population and sway public support away from Hitler's policies. Although a decree forbidding Germans from reading enemy leaflets and listening to Allied broadcasts was enforced early in the war, the punishments were typically light. Given the Wehrmacht's success early in the war, any attempt by the Allies to persuade the German people that the war was lost was considered by the Nazis as ludicrous. But as the war progressed and the German situation deteriorated on the Eastern Front and in the West, the Allied propaganda campaign was pressed forward with increasing vigor and the regime began to understand the true danger of Allied propaganda. On February 4, 1944, Himmler issued an order making the collection, possession, or dissemination of enemy propaganda material a state crime; from that point on, it was a grave risk to read or keep a leaflet dropped by Allied aircraft in Germany and the occupied countries.

To combat the propaganda war, the Germans organized a service of leaflet collection immediately following air raids. The Gestapo was in charge of the collection and disposal of the propaganda material. Schoolchildren not yet in their teens were pressed into the service, as they were considered too young to be corrupted by the Allied documents they collected. The Nazi youth organizations, the *Hitler Jugend* and *Jungvolk*, were set to work combing the area and collecting any leaflets found. They were then destroyed by the local Gestapo authorities.

Keeping a sharp eye out for SS and Hitler Youth patrols, Angela and the others distributed two different Allied leaflets on this particular night. The first depicted the devastating 1,000-bomber raid on Cologne in May 1942 in which over 2,000 tons of ordnance were dropped, warning the German people that what they would experience going forward would only get worse now that the Allies had a foothold in France. The second leaflet showed an unflattering caricature of Hitler smiling casually as he surveyed the corpses of his soldiers littering the ground, a stream of war refugees, and the ruins of his bombed-out cities. It was an attempt to show the German people that their beloved Führer didn't care about them and had in fact abandoned them to homelessness, death, and destruction.

Early in the war, the German population had observed the leaflets with humor. But as the war progressed, they looked upon them with sobering stoicism, realizing they were closer to reality than propaganda. Despite the torrents of rhetoric from Goebbels, most Germans were well aware the war was lost as the Wehrmacht suffered defeats on every front, the enemy forces drew closer, and their homes were rendered piles of moldering ruins under fleets of bombers. Angela understood the goal of the Allied propaganda: to overthrow the Nazi Party, to depress the population, to sap the determination of the German armed forces, and to sow the seeds of suspicion and distrust. The leaflets served as a constant reminder that the bombing was not going to stop until Germany laid down its arms, and they continued to hint at an unpleasant increase in death and destruction in the future.

When they had distributed more than two hundred leaflets, they heard a vague roaring sound overhead.

"Oh *scheisse*," cursed Barthel Schröder. "Here they come."

Angela listened. It was indeed the drone of Allied bombers. She and the others scanned westward in the direction of the sound, but she couldn't see the planes yet. But there was no doubt they were coming: the sounds were growing louder.

It was then the air raid sirens sounded.

"Should we make for a shelter?" asked Marie Peukert.

"What's the point?" said Angela. "If our number is up, it's up."

"Well, let's at least get out of the middle of the street," said Jean Hüber.

They took cover beneath the edge of a partially demolished apartment building. The roar of the aircraft grew louder and mingled with the shrieking air-raid sirens.

Angela looked up again at the sky. Now, with swarms of yellow searchlights crisscrossing the darkness above, she could see the enemy planes.

To her surprise, there were only six of them, screaming in towards the Rhine like a swarm of angry hornets, skimming the tops of the battered buildings as they skirted the western edge of Cologne. And then she heard the sound of the antiaircraft batteries opening up on the new interlopers. Unbeknownst to her, the aircraft were the same planes that had killed her mother and brother: de Havilland Mosquito B Mark IV Series 2 DK338s, from the No. 105 Squadron of the British Royal Air Force. Called the "Wooden Wonder" since it was made almost entirely out of wood, the twin-engined light bomber required only a two-man crew and was extremely fast and maneuverable. The plane carried four thousand pounds of bombs, had an effective range of seven hundred miles, and clocked in at over four hundred miles per hour, fast enough to outrun most Luftwaffe fighters, which was why *Reichsmarschall* Göring had declared holy war on the British plane.

The six Mosquitos banked hard to the south towards the Cologne Cathedral in the city center and swooped in to attack. With the searchlights and green tracer fire lighting up the night sky, the bomb bay doors began opening up and dropping their deadly payloads above the devastated city. Angela and the others stood there breathlessly watching as the whistling bombs dropped and smashed into the blocks of apartment buildings to the east. And then suddenly, three German Focke-Wulf fighters appeared from the north and opened up on the Mosquitos. For a brief instant, it was like some great pageant as the bombs plummeted downward through the air and the machine guns crackled and the nine aircraft desperately engaged one another, dodging and darting across the flickering and pulsing night sky above the bomb-cratered city, the men inside the flying machines heavily engaged in combat. It was so visceral and violent that it seemed surreal to Angela.

She and the others covered their ears and braced themselves for the explosions. The bombs went off one right after the other, rocking the neighborhood like an earth tremor. Even from a distance, she felt wave upon wave of searing airborne heat from the successive blasts. Clouds of heavy smoke erupted from the nearby buildings as a great quantity of dust and debris enveloped the street.

The British bombers climbed to a higher altitude and banked southwest with the German Focke-Wulfs hot on their tail. She saw more tracer fire as the aircraft battled it out in a running dogfight. With their payloads dropped, the British bombers were racing back to the safety of England, while the Germans were intent on stopping them. They worked their way southwestward in the direction of Aachen until Angela saw one of the German fighters suddenly catch fire and break off from the chase.

As the smoke began to drift towards the Rhine, she looked back at the four buildings that had been hit. One had collapsed completely and the other three were reduced to mere skeletons. Flames blasted upward through the gaping holes in the structures, sending up clouds of billowy black smoke. Angela stared off at the blazes with a mixture of awe and despair.

"There's almost nothing left of our city," she observed. "They've destroyed virtually everything."

Barthel Schröder shook his head sadly, saying nothing.

"It's not the British or Americans that are at fault—it's Hitler," hissed Jean Hüber. "I wish someone would assassinate him."

"If only we could be so lucky," said Angela.

"It's our own fault for allowing him to seize power," said Marie Peukert. "We stood by and did nothing—and now look at what has become of our country."

"She's right," said Schröder. "We have only ourselves to blame."

They stood staring at their smoldering, ruined city. After a moment, Angela noticed the tears trickling down her friend Marie's cheeks. She took her in her arms and comforted her. For a moment, they both just clutched one another. When they pulled away, Angela stared off glumly to the east at the bomb-cratered streets and ghostly ruins of the buildings aglow with flames. The once-vibrant city had turned into a pockmarked, blackened world devoid of life. Or hope. Looking down Burgmauer Street, she saw only a smattering of buildings still standing mostly intact in the *Altstadt*. They looked like little islands in a vast sea of rubble.

The sight of her ruined city made her feel sad and lonely inside, and she wondered if Germany would ever become whole again. Did she even want to live in such a desolate place after the war? Maybe she could go to America where her Uncle Friedrich lived with his family and practiced as a doctor in the city of Philadelphia. Like her father and uncle, she spoke English fluently, and she knew a great deal about America and had visited on two occasions years ago, before the war shortly after her Uncle Friedrich had moved there. But would America even take her when she came from the country of the detested Nazis? It all seemed so hopeless. Was there not someone out there who could rescue the Fatherland from the maniac Führer who was destroying the country for his demented Thousand-Year Reich? Was there no way to get rid of Hitler? It sickened her to know the German people were trapped in a war killing thousands of her countrymen every day even though Allied victory was no longer in doubt.

They started off again. They had not gone more than two blocks when they spotted a marching column of SS *polizeiregiment* troops. There were more than a hundred footsoldiers in the procession, goose-stepping down the street, nearly all of them weather-beaten old men in their forties or older. They were singing *Hupf, Mein Mädel*—Skip, My Lassie—a sappy ditty that front-line soldiers had enjoyed singing since the invasion of Poland. Angela found the song insufferably annoying.

She and the others stared at them apprehensively. Their singing voices and clap of their jackboots carried up the bomb-blasted street as the troops, marching three abreast, wheeled right onto Tunisstrasse Street. Looking into the eyes of her three comrades, Angela saw hate. She realized that she hated the SS troops too. They were Nazi monsters not human beings. She studied them closely as they marched in lockstep, singing in unison, and she wished she and her *kameraden* had machine-guns and could mow them all down. The *polizeiregiment* soldiers filled the entire street, tramping rhythmically, and then they disappeared around the corner out of sight.

"We should get out of the city," said Hüber. "There is nothing left for us here."

"But this is our home," said Schröder. "Where would we go?"

"There is nowhere else to go," said Angela. "All of Germany is in ruins."

"When the war is over, will there be any hope for the Fatherland?" asked Marie rhetorically, staring out at the bomb-scorched city.

"I don't know," said Hüber. "All I know is the war is lost."

Angela nodded somberly. "All this madness has led to is our ruin. It has all been for nothing but the destruction of—"

"You there! What are you doing?"

She and the others turned around to see a pack of Hitler Youth, visible in the moonlight and flickering bomb-fires. They had closed in quietly on foot from the south, the opposite direction from the SS column. Even though the illumination from the thumbnail moon and fires was not strong, she could see they bore the brown uniforms, red Nazi armbands, and military rifles of the *Hitler Jugend Streifendienst*, the special patrol service consisting of older members of the HJ who were allowed to bear arms and could not be arrested by ordinary police. They were led by a beefy, red-haired boy that seemed vaguely familiar to her; he was the one who had yelled out to them.

"There's too many of them," said Schröder. "We've got to split up and make a run for it."

"All right, let's go," said Hüber. "We'll meet back at the train station."

They quickly scrambled down through the rubble and dashed off in four separate directions on the bomb-cratered street.

"Halt, or we'll shoot!"

Ignoring the dire warning, Angela and the others ran on. The Hitler Youth members up front opened fire with a volley, but luckily the shots missed and ricocheted off the walls of the apartment buildings, storefronts, and blocks of concrete rubble. Fearing for her life, Angela dashed down the street as fast as her legs would carry her, heading north. The Hitler Youth fired a second volley and two members of the patrol ran after her, the rest chasing after the others.

She darted down one street and then another before ducking into an alleyway. When she reached the next cross-street, she could hear the armed Youth members shouting and running after her, but she fought back the temptation to glance over her shoulder. Her eyes were fixed on a vacant building three blocks ahead where she believed she could safely hide. It was silhouetted against a thin ray of moonlight.

She passed a mass of rubble and spurred down a gentle bomb-dust slope, gobbling up ground as more blind shots echoed across the barren street. With adrenaline now coursing through her body, she forced herself to pick up her pace and run on. More shots rang out, but she was far enough away and it was dark enough that the HJ seemed to be firing blind.

Two blocks further west, she took cover in a pile of rubble and paused to catch her breath. She could hear shouting voices and shots still being fired but thankfully the enemy appeared not to have caught any of her fellow Edelweiss Pirates. The sounds quickly grew more distant and she started off again, this time at a steady jog. By the time she had covered another block, she appeared to have lost her pursuers. But she still had the vague feeling she was being followed.

Yet she saw nothing. Though with the shadows so dark around the skeletal buildings how could she be certain? The lingering fires from the British bombs were blocks away now and the light from the waning crescent moon cast only a thin dusky glow over the demolished remnants before pinching out into soot-black night. She scanned the area and pricked her ear alertly to listen.

Still, there was no one. She told herself that she was worrying over nothing and continued on, trying to steel her jangled nerves. But she couldn't help but feel a growing uneasiness. She took a deep steadying breath then another, but she couldn't shake the feeling that she was being followed.

And then she heard, or thought she heard, a noise from behind.

She came to a halt. Again, she searched the shadows and strained her ears to listen. Nothing except a faint rustling coming from one of the honeycombed buildings. Probably a hungry cat or a big rat.

She started off again. But she hadn't gone five paces when she heard it again. This time she swore she heard behind her the soft scrape of a boot across the bomb-dust-smeared and rubble-covered lane. Without stopping, she peered over her shoulder, expecting someone to appear, but there was no one.

She stopped, straining her ears to listen. "Who is it? Who's there?" she called out, her voice sounding unnaturally loud and panicky in the still of the night.

There was no answer except a whisper of wind. She scanned the rows of gutted buildings. Still nothing. The street stretched vast and empty behind her with only faint pools of light in the center and complete darkness near the buildings. Should she run? It was best not to panic, and yet the urge to flee was overwhelming.

Was the Hitler Youth patrol still following her, or perhaps waiting in ambush?

She resumed walking, a little faster now, telling herself not to be afraid, that there was a perfectly logical explanation for the noise.

But instinct told her she was being pursued.

She began to walk faster.

To her infinite horror, she heard a noise again. This time it was unmistakable: the sound of footsteps, coming from behind her.

She turned abruptly. As before the sound stopped.

Probing the shadows, she pulled the Mauser pistol her father had given her from her rucksack.

"Who's there? You should know I've got a gun and I know how to use it!"

But there was no reply. She continued searching the area but saw nothing. She still felt a jittery sensation, as if someone was stalking her. She wanted desperately to dash home to safety, but whoever was following her blocked the way. Was it Barthel, Jean, or Marie? But why would they be mysterious like this?

"Barthel, is that you? Marie? Jean?"

There was no answer.

Heart hammering in her chest, she called out again. "Who's there?"

There was a snorting sound to her right. Turning, she saw a crippled old draft horse standing next to a bomb crater. What in God's name was an unsaddled horse doing in the middle of the bombed-out city? It raised its ear, turned its head, and looked right at her. She went up to the horse and whispered in a soothing tone, as much for her own reassurance as to calm the animal.

She heard the footsteps behind her again. They were coming up faster now.

Fearing for her life, she dashed into a bombed-out building. Much of the roof had been blown apart, but the stairs leading to the second floor were intact. She took them and at the landing threaded her way down a corridor, past a row of battered and empty book shelves, until she reached a dead-end. There was nothing but a broken window and a wooden chair leaning against the wall.

*Why is there a chair here?*

She scoured the walls and ceiling. In the faint light, the outline of a trap door was just visible. Presumably, it led to some sort of crawlspace or attic. Maybe she could hide in the attic. She pulled out the chair, stepped up onto it, and tried to push open the trap door, but it wouldn't budge.

She tried again.

Still nothing.

She heard a creaking sound and what sounded like a light footfall down the corridor. She turned her head in the direction of the sound.

But in the deep shadows, she saw nothing.

Feeling a shudder of fear, she drove her shoulder into the trap door. This time she felt the door give way.

But the delivery of the blow made the chair teeter beneath her feet and she started to lose her balance. Feeling a wave of panic from the sound down the hallway and now the wobbly chair, she pushed aside the wooden plank of the trap door and started to pull herself up into what she could tell was a surprisingly large crawlspace.

A sudden burst of relief poured through her: it was a perfect hiding place.

All she had to do was climb up there and shut the trap door behind—

Suddenly, she felt her legs grabbed from below in a tight grip. She tried to kick her way free, but felt herself yanked down and then allowed to freefall to the floor.

Her back hit the floor hard, and the air left her lungs in a terrible whoosh. For a second, she was unable to breathe or see who had jerked her down. Then suddenly, she felt herself pulled to her feet and shoved up against the wall.

Now, up close, she could see her attacker's face.

It was the beefy, red-haired Hitler Youth leader that had seemed vaguely familiar to her. But where had she seen him before? Was he one of the ones who had beaten her and Barthel in the Königsforst?

Dazed and terrified, she couldn't believe how quickly her luck had turned.

"Ah, aren't you a pretty little thing," he said, slinging his rifle over his shoulder by its strap. "But didn't your mother and father tell you that you shouldn't be out at night running around with Edelweiss Pirates."

"I am not an Edelweiss Pirate," she said, still gasping for air. "I was just out foraging for food."

"That is illegal. You are a naughty girl and will have to be punished."

He drew closer. It was then she realized something was terribly wrong, something much worse than being caught by the HJ. There was a look in his eyes like a wild dog.

Kicking the chair towards the broken window, he slapped her face hard—harder than any blow she had ever been dealt before—and grabbed her in a bear hug. As she struggled to pull away, he spun her around so that she was facing away from him and clasped a meaty hand over her mouth. Then, using his powerful arms, he shoved her towards the chair beneath the window.

She tried to fight him off, but he was too strong, his grip like a vice.

Keeping his hand cupped over her mouth to keep her from crying out, he pulled her back hard at the waist and doubled her over the chair. A plump hand slid up her skirt and jerked down her undergarments, practically tearing them off her body.

"You are a wicked girl," he leered. "You are *Volksfeinde*, and as an enemy of the people you must be punished."

"No, no, I am *Volkskameraden*."

"You're a liar and are going to have to be punished. You're also a little whore and are going to have to be fucked like a whore."

"You can't do this! The Führer would not approve! He requires abstinence!"

He licked her ear and gave a sadistic chuckle. "Like you, I don't always obey my Führer. Now spread those legs!"

She started to scream, but he cupped his hand over her mouth and pulled her tight against him. Then he shoved his way inside her.

"Oh my, you're a wet one. If I didn't know better, I would say you were ripe and ready for me. Heil Hitler!"

Using all of her force, she jerked back and shoved him away.

But he overpowered her again, jammed his way inside, and doubled her over the chair, panting like a dog.

She tried to break free, but he pinned her against the chair, pushing down hard and nearly crumpling her with his weight.

In and out. In and out.

*God Almighty, help me! God, please!*

The backrest of the chair broke from the downward pressure.

Suddenly, he let out a bovine groan and she saw his face in the reflection of the pane of the broken window, grotesquely contorted in a rictus of pain and pleasure.

Desperate, she grabbed a piece of the broken backrest with her free hand, jabbed him in the eye over her shoulder, and jerked free from his clasp.

Wounded, he screamed in agony and retreated from her as he sprayed himself and the floor with fluid.

She picked up the broken chair and smashed him over the head.

He fell to a knee, throwing his hands up to protect himself.

She clubbed him twice more with the chair leg. Upon the second blow, he hit his head hard on the floor and didn't make a sound. She kicked him in the ribs several times for good measure, hearing a cracking sound on the last kick, before collapsing against the wall to catch her breath. The Nazi rapist lay on the floor unconscious with his pants at his ankles and cum all over his front and the floor.

She wanted to kill him.

God, did she want to kill him!

She leaned down, pulled his rifle from his shoulders, and raised the butt to bludgeon him to death.

"Angela, what are you doing?"

Giving an involuntary start, she turned to see Schröder standing behind her. A glimmer of moonlight from the broken window illuminated part of his face.

"What does it look like I'm doing," she responded coldly. "I'm going to kill this HJ bastard. He tried to rape me."

"Tried?"

"He didn't finish, thank God. But he deserves to die for taking me against my will."

He stepped forward. "Listen to me, Angela. If you kill him, the Nazis are going to retaliate savagely. No one in the neighborhood will be spared."

"I don't care. He deserves to die."

"There's no time for vengeance. We need to get out of here now."

She began to cry. Gently, he took the rifle from her and pulled her into a reassuring embrace. The tears streamed down her face onto his shoulder.

"I'm sorry, Angela. I know what you just went through is terrible," he said after a moment. "But we have to go. If they find us, they will beat us up and arrest us. Or something worse."

"I hate them. I want to kill them all," she sniffled.

"Don't worry, we'll get even. I mean it, we're going to make them pay for this."

"You promise?"

"Yes, I promise." He hugged her tightly. "Because I love you."

Despite her trauma, she felt herself brighten. "You do? Really?"

"Yes, I'm sure of it, though it is true I've never been in love before."

"Well then, I love you too, Bartholomäus Schröder. Now let's get out of here before the rest of those Nazi devils find us."

# CHAPTER 7

## CAMP HOOD

### AUGUST 2, 1944

THE COURTROOM WAS QUIET AS A TOMB. William McBurney licked his lips anxiously as the presiding judge, Lieutenant Colonel Richard E. Kyle, a Judge Advocate General officer, prepared to have the charges against Jackie Robinson read aloud. Sitting in judgment next to Kyle were eight stony-faced U.S. Army officers ranging in rank from captain to colonel, most from field artillery units and tank-destroyer battalions.

The one thing they had in common was they were all white.

McBurney shifted his gaze to his brother-in-arms seated in front of him. Though Robinson looked dapper, calm, and collected in his neatly creased officer's uniform, McBurney knew he had to be jittery inside. After all, his future looked bleak. It seemed unfathomable that less than a month ago, he was the 761st's popular morale officer and ready to embark for overseas duty with a medical clearance—and now he stood on the edge of a cliff. In all likelihood, he was about to be booted out of the army with a dishonorable discharge for having the temerity to refuse to move to the back of a civilian bus.

In McBurney's view it was a travesty, and he was here with several other members of the 761st for moral support.

Next to Robinson sat artillery officer William Cline, the white lawyer representing him in the case. McBurney could only hope that the Texan knew what he was doing and maybe even had a trick or two up his sleeve. But looking at the man, he wasn't optimistic. He looked far too young and not all that impressive. Robinson had told McBurney and the other troopers from the 761st that he had hoped to secure an NAACP attorney to represent him, and later, when that didn't materialize, that he was considering hiring outside counsel. But a few days later he had decided against it: the financial burden on his poor family was simply too great, he admitted, and he needed to continue to help support his mother living in California. So now the only thing standing between him and a dishonorable discharge was the young and inexperienced-looking Southerner Cline.

Colonel Richard E. Kyle pounded his gavel to bring order to the courtroom and the charges were promptly read aloud before the court. The formal case claimed that Robinson had shown disrespect and disobedience towards a superior officer. Specifically, he was charged with behaving disrespectfully towards Captain Gerald Bear in the guard room, and with disobeying Bear's order to remain in the receiving area.

As the charges were read, McBurney returned his attention to the all-white panel of military judges and the trial judge advocate serving as the prosecutor in the case, Second Lieutenant Milton Gordon from the 665th Tank Destroyer Battalion. They were an unsympathetic and solemn-looking lot. It worried him that they, along with the uninspiring Cline, would decide Robinson's fate. He noted the look of confidence on Gordon's face. The prosecuting lawyer looked as if the case was already won. How in the hell was Cline going to outlawyer a fellow like that?

He shook his head in dismay: the deck was definitely stacked against his brother Jackie.

Captain Bear, the senior MP and Robinson's accuser, was first to take the stand. McBurney held his breath in anticipation. Over the next few minutes, Gordon led the witness through a description of the night in question, focusing on Robinson's behavior in the guard shack after being removed from the bus.

"On several occasions," said Bear in his nasally drawl, "I told him to get away from the door. But each time I instructed him to go away, he bowed his head, saluted, and said 'Okay, sir' over and over in the same facetious manner."

"So, what you're saying is he mocked you?" said Gordon.

"Yes, sir. You might could say he mocked me and our very military system. He was sarcastic, with his sloppy salutes, bows from the waist, and repeated grimaces. Why I reckon I had no choice but to consider his actions disrespectful towards a senior officer."

"That seems beyond question. What happened next?"

"He continued to raise and lower his voice and to act in a contemptuous and disrespectful manner. In fact, I had lost control of this Negro lieutenant."

By the time Gordon was finished questioning Bear, McBurney couldn't help but feel that the situation looked bleak for the defendant. Clearly, Robinson had defied and shown disrespect for authority. But then to McBurney's surprise, Cline rose to his feet and put forward an objection.

That's when things began to get interesting.

Over the next few minutes, McBurney watched in fascination as the two opposing lawyers pleaded their cases before the panel. Having given the MP as much rope as he would take, Robinson's lawyer made it clear that he had had enough of Bear's opinions and objected to his litany of thoughts and descriptions, insisting instead upon solid facts. Surprisingly, the court agreed with Cline, following an objection by the prosecution, and then the crafty lawyer went to work like a surgeon in his cross-examination. He promptly separated the case's few facts from Bear's racially-motivated conjecture, in the process methodically demonstrating how the MP's personal opinions and biased interpretation of Robinson fueled his testimony.

William McBurney was absolutely mesmerized.

"You state, Captain," said Cline, "that you considered it improper for the accused to question why he was removed from the bus and was being confined to quarters at the hospital."

"I considered it improper in the way that he asked. He was downright *uppity*."

A raised eyebrow. "Uppity? In what way?"

"I meant to say he was argumentative. He asked if he had to answer certain questions and he openly questioned my judgment."

"And you saw that as a loss of control. Is that what you're telling us?"

"Yessir, I did—and I reckon rightly so, I might add."

"So the lieutenant's manner was problematic to you. And yet, you admitted just a few minutes ago that the accused asked reasonable questions."

"I suppose he did."

"Captain, do you recall if he asked if he was under arrest at that time?"

"Yes, I do recall."

"Did you give him an answer?"

For several minutes, Bear evaded the question. But Cline patiently probed him until he managed to pry loose an answer similar to what Robinson had received on the night in question. Robinson had never officially been put under arrest; instead, he had been told to remain "at ease" and then was transported back to McClosky Hospital in Temple, where he was to remain confined to quarters. It quickly became apparent to McBurney that Captain Bear had made a colossal blunder, and when Captain Wiggington, the Camp Hood laundry officer and duty officer on the night in question, was subsequently brought to the stand for cross-examination, he, too, was unable to give the court a yes or no answer as to whether Robinson had been placed under arrest. As Cline continued poking holes in the witnesses' stories, McBurney could feel the tension in the courtroom mounting.

The lawyer continued to attack the prosecution's case on two fronts: first, by arguing that Captain Bear had himself acted in an unbecoming manner, and second, by recounting in detail the unfair provocation that had led Robinson to lose his cool and act in a disrespectful manner towards a superior officer. Bear was forced to admit, again, that he had told Robinson he was "at ease" and that the MP, therefore, had no right to question the manner in which Robinson conducted himself in the receiving room. Cline then argued that Robinson was well within his rights to voice concern over the accuracy of Bear's and Wiggington's statements regarding his behavior, and fully within his rights, as well, to demand to know whether or not he was under arrest. It became clear that Bear had violated strict military procedure when he had sent Robinson—whom he had not placed under arrest—back to the hospital under guard.

McBurney smiled inwardly: he had underestimated Cline. The Texan was a crafty lawyer all right, and obviously a fair-minded man as he was working hard to exonerate his colored client.

But would the white officers sitting in judgment be swayed?

McBurney looked at them sitting solemnly at the table. He still did not have a good feeling about them.

Private Ben Mucklerath, the third MP on the night in question, was then called to the stand. Studying him, McBurney thought to himself: *Not the brightest penny in the piggy bank.*

Cline began his cross-examination by casually asking, "Private, during this incident did you ever refer to the defendant as 'nigger'?"

"Under no circumstances, sir," replied Mucklerath.

"Did you ever use the word?"

"No sir, I never done used it."

"Did any of the MPs ever use that word?"

"Nope. None of us ever did."

Cline nodded as though he had suspected as much but was compelled to ask as a matter of formality. "I want you to tell me, Private—and this is very, very important so that we can punish this man properly—I want you to tell me the exact words Lieutenant Robinson used when he threatened you."

"Yes, sir," replied Mucklerath with an aggrieved air, immediately and without thinking about it. "The defendant said to me, 'If you ever call me a *nigger* again, I will break you in two.'"

The stunned courtroom fell silent.

Cline couldn't help a little smile. "I have no further questions of this witness," he said.

Now McBurney could tell the tide had truly turned. In fact, Mucklerath's incriminating revelation proved just the beginning. Over the next hour, Cline was able to bring out additional inconsistencies with the witnesses' accounts that demonstrated their extreme prejudice towards the accused. To McBurney's surprise, Cline somehow managed to push all of the prosecution's witnesses against the wall. Biases were stripped and laid bare before the panel, rendering the disrespect shown towards Captain Bear and disobedience of orders as nothing more than the justifiable reactions of an upstanding military officer to unfair treatment. This left the accused the perfect opening to tell the panel his version of events.

"Lieutenant Robinson," said the presiding judge Lieutenant Colonel Kyle when the cross-examinations were finished. "Do you intend to take the stand? I ask this because it is my duty to instruct you that you are under no obligation to testify."

"I understand that, sir," replied Robinson. "But I want to describe what happened in my own words."

"Very well, Lieutenant. Please proceed and take the stand."

As Robinson was being sworn in, McBurney knew there was a risk, but thought it was still the right thing to do. To convince someone of the truth, it was best to tell them with conviction in one's own words, and the accused didn't disappoint. Though it was readily apparent that he was nervous, Jackie Robinson was eager to talk and for the first time the court got to hear his version of the events. He spoke quickly, his frustration and outrage at his treatment at the hands of the white MPs coming out in a torrent of thoughts. But he was so genuine and earnest that McBurney could tell everyone on the panel knew he was speaking the truth. Cline had to ask him on more than one occasion to slow down, a scenario similar to what Bear described, but it detracted little from his story.

Vicariously, McBurney felt the whole gamut of emotions the lieutenant had gone through as Robinson described the flashpoint of the night in question. It was when he had arrived at Camp Hood with the MPs and Private Mucklerath rushed up to the vehicle, peered in, and breathlessly asked, "Did you get that nigger lieutenant?" Robinson testified under oath that that was when he told Mucklerath, "If you ever call me a nigger again, I will break you in two."

When he was finished recounting the event, the courtroom fell silent. For a moment, even Robinson was too emotional to continue and needed time to collect himself. McBurney held his breath as he and the panel members waited for the defendant's next words. But the lawyer Cline put up a hand to stop his client.

"Let me interrupt you, Lieutenant," he said. "Do you know what a 'nigger' is?"

McBurney hadn't expected that and looked at Robinson. All eyes were fixed on the defendant, who seemed to have been taken off guard as well.

"My grandmother was a slave. She told me that a nigger meant a low, uncouth person and it applied to no one in particular. One day I looked it up in the dictionary."

"And what did you find?"

"That it meant someone of the 'Negroid' race. It also referred to a machine in a sawmill."

"Was the word used on the night of July 6?"

"Yes, it was. In fact, it was used several times that evening by both Captain Wiggington and Private Mucklerath."

"Each time directed at you?"

"Yes, sir," replied Robinson. He then proceeded to describe the white female stenographer who had walked out when he had asked questions and whom he had tried to get to correct his statement, which she had deliberately misrepresented in her transcription. To McBurney, it was obvious that she had considered him beneath herself due to the color of his skin and had left abruptly because of racial discomfort.

"I am a Negro but I, sir, am not a nigger," Robinson continued. "Captain Bear said I was insolent, but that is not really true either. The only crime I committed was to have the audacity to exercise rights that belong to me as an American and a soldier. If that is considered 'uppity' then I am guilty as charged. But in all honesty, I was merely making sure that my rights as a United States officer were not being unfairly stomped on. And I would do it again if confronted with the same kind of mindless bigotry."

In McBurney's eyes, the human degradation of his brother-in-arms seemed to stand as the only issue, and he figured the defense would rest. But instead, Cline continued to draw out Robinson's heartfelt testimony and force the panel to acknowledge what the case was really about. Exposing the bigoted atmosphere of that fateful evening, he showed beyond a reasonable doubt that Robinson was facing a general court-martial purely because he ran into some people who could not tolerate a black man in uniform.

The court then called Lieutenant Colonel Paul Bates. In his uniform, he presented a tall, commanding figure that in McBurney's view most certainly trumped that of a post laundry officer and a mere private. Cline opened by asking him what his title and role were at Camp Hood.

"I command the 761st Tank Battalion," he replied in a way that only Paul Bates could.

"And what is your relationship to the defendant?"

"Lieutenant Robinson served as my morale officer."

"What was his reputation among the officers and men in the battalion?"

"Lieutenant Robinson had an excellent reputation, especially among the enlisted men. He is an exceptional sportsman and was a four-sport athlete and All-American football player at UCLA. In his role as morale officer, he organized many sports events for the battalion that have gone a long way towards—"

"Objection!" snapped Gordon the prosecutor. "The defendant's athletic history has no relevance to the case!"

"Sustained!" said Kyle. "Colonel Bates, please confine your characterization of the defendant to his military career here on the base."

Bates nodded and Cline resumed the questioning. "How would you judge Lieutenant Robinson's performance at Camp Hood?"

"Lieutenant Robinson's ratings from me and my officers have all been 'excellent.' His abilities as a soldier in my view are outstanding, and in fact, I wanted to have him permanently assigned to the 761st."

"Objection! The lieutenant colonel's personal opinion with regard to—"

"Overruled!" He looked at Bates. "You may continue, Colonel."

"As I said, Lieutenant Robinson has an excellent reputation among both officers and enlisted men and his rating is 'excellent.'"

"Would you be satisfied," asked Kyle, "to go into combat with this officer under your command?"

"I would indeed," Bates replied. "Not only would I not hesitate to go into combat with him, as I said previously I actively sought to have him permanently assigned to the 761st. That's the kind of man and soldier Lieutenant Robinson is."

Captain James R. Lawson, the Baker Company commander for the 761st, then followed Bates to the stand and echoed his responses. Lawson also could only refer to the second lieutenant as an "excellent officer." Others followed and the defense rested, bringing an end to the general court-martial.

After some deliberation, and to McBurney's surprise, the nine white judges on the panel found him not guilty of all charges. Colonel Kyle and the rest of the court-martial board stood up. The colonel ordered the charges and specifications read. To each he announced in a stentorian voice, "Not guilty."

Afterwards, McBurney, Smith, and several of the other men met outside with Robinson and Colonel Bates.

"It's over, Jackie," said the colonel with visible relief. "You can go on now with peace of mind. What are your plans?"

"I'm going to request reassignment back to the 761st, sir. I'd like to get the chance to go overseas with you. When is the battalion scheduled to depart for the European Theater of Operations?"

"One week from now. I'm sorry, Lieutenant, but getting the order for your transfer from the 758th back to the battalion before we leave is going to be tough. But I wish you the best of luck."

"We all wish you luck, Lieutenant," said Smitty.

"You can say that again," echoed McBurney. "We're all going to miss you too. But just so you know, I'm not going to miss you knocking the wind out of me playing football."

They all laughed.

"Jackie, the truth is this should never have happened," said Bates. "This is an embarrassment to the Army and the court-martial board knows it."

"I'd be lying if I didn't admit I'm bitter," confessed Robinson. "But the Army needs soldiers, black and white, and I honestly believe that one day things are gonna change. Sir, take good care of the fellas when you get over there to France. They need you."

"Thanks, Lieutenant. Like Sergeant McBurney said, we're all going to miss you."

"I sure wish I could go with you."

"We wish you could too, Lieutenant," said Bates. "But the main thing is you've been acquitted of all charges and have got your life back."

"Yes, sir, thanks to you."

"And thanks to that lawyer of yours. Cline did one hell of a job."

"He sure did, sir."

"Once again, good luck to you, Jackie. I have a feeling you're going to go on to do great things."

"God, I hope so, sir. After this, God I hope so."

"Good luck to you, Jackie," said McBurney.

"And to you too, Billy," said Robinson, and the group of tankers bid a final farewell.

A moment later, as William McBurney watched Jackie Robinson walk off towards the barracks of the 758th, he couldn't help but feel badly for him. There had been no dignity in the courtroom proceedings he had just witnessed, and he knew the calm and composed Robinson had to be feeling much angrier inside than he showed outwardly after the horrendous treatment he had endured at the hands of the United States Army. Once Bates had refused to sign the court-martial document, the case should have been dismissed and there never should have been a trial. What made it even worse was that Robinson would now miss his chance to join the 761st to fight overseas. He had served the armed forces well, but that same army had failed him miserably. Instead of being given a chance to fight the Japs or Nazis, he had been forced to spend his brief time in uniform struggling to be treated like a human being. Though free, McBurney realized, Robinson would probably never find freedom in the U.S. Army, and he knew that his own odds and those of his buddy Smitty were just as long. It made him feel sad and deflated inside. And angry.

*What in the hell are we fighting for then?* he wondered.

He pondered the question over and over again all day long—but at the end of it he still didn't have an answer.

# CHAPTER 8

**EHRENFELD, WEST COLOGNE**

**AUGUST 6, 1944**

PEERING OUT AT THE ADVANCING HITLER YOUTH COLUMN, Angela Lange felt her throat go dry. The enemy was sweeping up the bomb-cratered street on foot, policing the neighborhood one last time before day turned to night. The Nazi armbands on their uniforms appeared blood red against the backdrop of summer sky and roofless buildings ravaged by high-explosive blasts from Allied bombing. The entire Ehrenfeld district had been reduced to a surreal scene of desolation: blackened knots of concrete, steel, and wire; clumps of rubble with twisted rebar; and puddles of broken glass.

She noticed that the HJ members weren't carrying rifles but rather police batons, indicating that they were regular *Hitler Jugend*, not *HJ-Streifendienst*. That made them vulnerable to attack. But they were still a dangerous force and might have concealed guns or knives.

"I count one shy of a dozen," observed Barthel Schröder. "It will be no picnic, but with seven of us I think we can take them."

Angela shook her head. "No, we have nine counting Marie and I."

"You two aren't fighting," said Schröder. "We can't risk you getting hurt."

"I can handle myself, thank you very much." Five-foot-seven, full figured, and as strong and athletic as many boys her age, Angela wasn't about to be left out just because she was a girl. She was anxious to fight the HJ, and had even worn a broad-rimmed cap and her brother's clothing, as well as smeared charcoal on her face, for tonight so she couldn't be identified as a girl and looked more masculine.

"I can handle myself too," said Marie, a defiant expression on her smooth, oval face. "But even with nine of us, they outnumber us by two."

"Those odds are as good as we're going to get," said Jean Hüber. "And since when have crappy odds stopped us? We're the Cologne Navajos—we're guided by Indian spirits and not afraid of anything. I don't care that you and Angela are girls. You're tougher than those Nazi hooligans on your worst day. Come on, let's go."

Schröder took Angela by the hand. "Just please be careful. I don't want anything to happen to you." His eyes shifted to Marie Peukert. "That goes for you as well. These bastards will turn you over to the Gestapo, who will torture you and ship you off to a reeducation camp without thinking twice about it. The Nazis don't care if you're a girl or not. Just remember that. Give no quarter and expect none in return."

"Don't worry, we will do what we have to do to win and to survive," said Angela. "I hate these 'Little Hitlers' with passion."

"Don't we all," said Schröder. "But still, please be careful."

"I promise I will."

She took a deep breath to calm her nerves. The group made a final weapons check and then started off with Jean and Barthel in the lead. They threaded their way down through a path notched into the blocky ruins, careful to keep out of sight of the enemy, until they reached a small mountain of rubble and pair of burnt-out *Kübelwagens* fifty yards ahead of the Hitler Youth patrol. Armed with clubs, knives,

53

hiking staffs, and two pistols, they waited in silence to ambush the column. The guns were only to be used as a last resort in self-defense to avoid capture. Angela felt her heart racing in her chest as she listened to the approaching voices and the chuff of boots on the road, counting down the seconds to the attack in her head.

And then suddenly they were there.

Hüber stepped forward, his jaw set in an intractable pose, and landed the first blow with a large club on the leader out front, a hatchet-faced boy close to draft age.

"What are you Nazi pigs doing in our neighborhood? Get the hell out of here!" he roared, and he brought his club down upon the head of the stunned boy. He followed up his first blow with a whack to the head of the second in line, underscoring his triumph with a Navajo-like war whoop.

"Let them have it!" cried Schröder, and he and the others quickly stepped forward to join in the attack.

Within a matter of second the two sides were fully engaged and Angela had squared off with one of the Hitler Youth. Though the boy was smaller than her, he was a wiry fellow with a mean look about him. She realized, in that precarious instant, that she would have to fight like a wild animal to beat him. But to her surprise, her body responded to the threat with atavistic ardor: she stepped forward to do combat as if she were being directed by some primitive inner force. Gripping her thick, gnarly hiking staff in her hand, she set herself in a defensive stance, a look of grim determination on her face.

*Give no quarter and expect none in return,* she reminded herself.

The boy came hard at her with his police baton raised in an attack position. She dodged the boy's wild thrust and drove her knotty hiking staff into his stomach, driving him to the ground in a pig-like squeal of pain.

Another quickly stepped in to fill the vacuum created by his fallen partner and came at her swinging and grinning wickedly, thinking she was an easy target he would easily pound into submission. But to her own surprise, she managed to knock the baton from his hand with a two-handed strike with her staff. She followed this up by driving the stick into his open mouth as he emitted a gasp of shock. The boy screamed and convulsed mightily as a little stream of blood gurgled from his mouth.

Shocked at what she had done, she suddenly felt sick to her stomach. Withdrawing to the edge of the violence, she vomited and took a moment to gather herself. She still had trouble believing what was happening was real. Had the Fatherland descended into absolute madness and that was why its people were fighting one another on the bomb-cratered streets of their cities?

She took in the field of battle: it was complete chaos. In the fading dusk were more than a dozen bodies charging, grappling, thrashing, screaming.

*My God,* she thought. *This truly is insanity.*

She saw Marie and Schröder both get knocked down in a tangle of bodies and rushed over to help them. But as she did, a blond, blue-eyed specimen of Aryan perfection came at her with a bloody police baton. The boy was bigger than the other two and she was terrified. But she forced herself to present an outward mask of strength and gripped her hiking staff tightly with both hands as she assumed a wide fighting stance to defend herself.

A jarring blow to her jaw sent her reeling to the ground. Shaking it off, she jumped to her feet, taking a vicious kick to the ribs. Falling back down, she felt the baton again hammer her face, then ducked a second blow before leaping to her feet.

She licked the blood from her split lip; it tasted metallic, iron-like.

Their eyes met. His were as blue and crystalline as winter ice.

"You little sow—I'm going to crack your skull wide open!"

The Hitler Youth charged, feet pounding across the battered street. He knocked her back down and swiped an elbow across her face, drawing blood from her right nostril. As she raised her staff to deflect a second blow, she was jabbed hard in the shoulder and the stomach with the baton. Groaning in agony, she felt a deep, sickening, burning sensation hit her like a sledgehammer and fell to the ground.

Putting away his baton, the boy grabbed a grapefruit-sized block of concrete in his right hand. He climbed on top of her, pinning her down with the full weight of his body, and raised the big, angular block high above his head. Through pinpoint stars, Angela could just make out the Little Hitler's gritted teeth, the gleam of animal rage in his blue eyes that were every bit as piercing as those of his beloved Führer. With the implement of death poised to swing down in a cruel arc, she was certain her head was about to be crushed to a bloody, brainy pulp.

And then a strange thing happened.

A shot rang out, seemingly out of nowhere.

Angela heard a bullet whiz past her ear and crash into the rubble. Then there was another shot and suddenly the ground around them came alive with bullets.

She looked at the Nazi boy. His face registered incomprehension and the concrete block above his head hovered in suspended motion.

The unexpected barrage was just what Angela needed to reclaim the initiative. She drove her staff into his balls, raised herself up from the ground, and smashed the boy again with the gnarly wooden weapon. The boy grunted in pain and rocked back on his knees. She delivered one more blow to his face and then Barthel and Jean were shouting, grabbing at her and Marie, and pushing them down the street as both sides were now fleeing in all directions to escape the unexpected gunshots.

Angela ran north towards the train station along with Jean, Marie, Barthel, and his younger friend Günther Schwarz, while the others struck northwest parallel to Venloer Strasse. Bullets whizzed past like swarming wasps, thudding into the skeletal buildings and rubble blanketing the streets.

And then, quite suddenly, the shooting stopped.

The group of Edelweiss Pirates came to a halt to catch their breath and survey the street. They stood behind a blown-up, abandoned Mercedes-Benz 770 W150. The massive, eight-cylinder, 7,655 cc-engine luxury car was a rarity in the Third Reich now but had once been favored by upper echelon members of the German High Command, the *Oberkommando der Wehrmacht*, as well as high-ranking Nazi Party officials, including Hitler himself.

"Who was that shooting at us?" asked Angela.

"They weren't shooting at us," said Schröder. "They were trying to help us by breaking up the fight."

"He's right," said Jean. "If they were trying to hit us, they would have done so."

"Was it them?" asked Marie, pointing down the street.

All eyes turned to the German staff car and pair of trucks that had pulled up to the reassembling group of Hitler Youth. From her rucksack, Angela pulled out her father's backup pair of Wehrmacht Zeiss Jena 8X30 field glasses to take a better look. The sleek officer's vehicle came to a halt and out stepped a commanding man in his mid-fifties wearing the jet-black uniform of an SS officer. He immediately began barking out orders to the troops disgorging from the two heavy trucks lined up behind him. There was something about the man, something in the way he—

"Good heavens, its *Kriminalkommissar* Kütter!" she cried.

"Who the hell is he?" asked Hüber.

"Yeah, what's so important about him?" wondered Günther Schwarz, whose nickname was Büb.

"My father pointed him out to me a few weeks ago," answered Angela. "He's a criminal investigator with the Cologne Gestapo based at Brauweiler Prison. He and his security unit hunt down Communists, escaped forced laborers, army deserters, and resistance members. The man is a monster."

Gulping hard, Jean Hüber grabbed her field glasses and strained for a better look. But the *Schutzstaffel kriminalkommissar* disappeared behind a mountain of rubble.

"It couldn't have been Kütter shooting at us," said Schröder. "He and his men just drove onto the scene."

"You're right, it wasn't him," announced a new voice, coming from their left. "It was me who saved your ass."

Angela turned to see a man in his mid-twenties wearing ragged civilian clothing and clutching what appeared to be a sniper rifle. At first, she couldn't place the accent, but after a moment she realized that it was a Düsseldorf inflection. Tall and lean, the man had a confident and mature air about him.

"Who are you?" asked Schröder.

"Like a said, I'm the son of a bitch who saved your ass. And now I'm telling you to get off the damned street and follow me, before that Nazi fuck Kütter hangs every one of us from a meat hook."

The group conferred and quickly decided it was worth the risk. "All right, we will go with you," said Hüber. "But you are going to have to tell us who you are."

The man gave a knowing, streetwise smile. "Very well, I am Hans Steinbrück," he said with a hint of arrogance. "But my friends—as well as my enemies—call me 'Bomber Hans.'"

"You're Bomber Hans?" gasped Angela. "Oh, I have heard of you."

There were nods and murmurs of excited approval all around. Bomber Hans's reputation had clearly preceded him. His cocksure grin widened and he gave a courtly bow befitting a prince.

"Of course you have heard of me. I have a knack for retrieving unexploded ordnance under the most dangerous conditions and am irresistible to the *fräuleins*. Now if there are no more questions, let's get the hell out of here. I have no desire to be locked up and tortured by Herr Fucking Kütter and his Gestapo thugs today."

And with that, the legendary Bomber Hans and the Edelweiss Pirates disappeared into the dusky night.

# PART 2

# OLD BLOOD AND GUTS AND BOMBER HANS

# CHAPTER 9

**NORTHWEST OF LE MANS
WESTERN FRANCE**

**AUGUST 7, 1944**

GAZING OUT at the war-torn Norman landscape from the back seat of his rumbling command vehicle, General George Smith Patton, Jr. felt the muscular power of the U.S. Third Army. In the past two weeks of the Allied breakout from the Normandy beachhead and hedgerow country, more than 5,000 tons of ordnance had been hurled at the Germans by American and British medium bombers, artillery, and tanks along with mountains of white phosphorus and a new lethal jellied-gasoline agent called napalm. The Allies' swift and well-equipped motorized army was making life a living hell for the Germans as it broke out of the bocage and reverse-*blitzkrieged* eastward across Occupied France. Hitler's finest were now reeling in disarray, and all around Patton as far as the eye could see he gazed upon smashed enemy tanks and half-tracks, smoldering fires, and scorched Kraut corpses.

He found it an awe-inspiring sight.

A believer in reincarnation, Old Blood and Guts, as his troops and war correspondents called him, was convinced that he had tasted combat many times before in previous lives. He had been a Roman legionnaire, Viking berserker, and a cavalier in Napoleon I's army, among a roster of other notable warriors.

The Norman battlefield he was passing through now made him think back to the Battle of Jena in 1806 when he had fought alongside, at least in his febrile imagination, the legendary Murat, Napoleon's top cavalry officer. He and the daring and flamboyantly-dressed Marshal of France and First Horseman of Europe were attacking the Prussians across a plateau west of the river Saale. He pictured it as if it had happened yesterday: a mad cavalry charge across a verdant field, riding crops slapping muscled rumps, cannons and smoothbore muskets exploding all around, colorfully-plumed heads bobbing in the saddle, and, of course, Murat himself with his gleaming sword and the wind flapping his colorful hussar's tunic.

With the unforgettable image in his head, Patton remembered back to a year earlier during the present conflict when the Allies sailed from North Africa to invade Sicily. British General Harold Alexander had exclaimed to Patton in complimentary fashion that if the tank commander had been alive in the 19th Century, Napoleon would have undoubtedly made him a marshal like Joachim Murat—to which Patton replied: "But I was one—I was there with Murat and Napoleon both!"

Tapping his riding crop against the side of his armored WC 57 Dodge command car, Patton's mind returned to the present as his mobile headquarters caravan rolled on. Riding along with him were Major Codman, one of his two fiercely loyal aides-de-camp; Master Sergeant John Mims, his trusted African-American driver; and Willie, his white English bull terrier named after William the Conqueror.

"Pull over, Sergeant!" he suddenly cried.

Mims hesitated. "What, General?"

"I command you to stop, John! Now goddamnit!"

"Yessir, General, sir!"

He noticed Codman was looking at him funny. "What is it, General?" asked the major. "Why are we stopping?"

"Because I want to see it all up close."

Mims pulled the command car to a halt. Squirming up from his seat to take a closer look with the vehicle's menacing .50-caliber heavy machine gun forming an appropriately bellicose backdrop, Patton stared out at a sea of dead Germans charred to a blackened crisp; destroyed tanks and half-tracks; farms reduced to rubble; and a grassy field in the distance blasted full of artillery shell craters like a lunar landscape. Fires were still burning all over the battlefield, which was strewn with swollen dead farm animals along with the fallen Germans. The French were calling the growing battlefield soon to extend from Mortain to Chartres *Le Couloir de la Mort*—The Corridor of Death. He was transfixed by the scene of carnage and devastation, as he took a deep breath of the cordite lingering in the light summer breeze above the dusty roadway.

"Just look at that, Codman," he said in his trademark high-pitched voice, feeling a tug deep within his soul. "Could anything be more magnificent?"

His aide looked at him uneasily. "Sir?"

"It's goddamn beautiful. In its own way, that is."

At that moment, a battery of heavy guns opened up nearby and the air filled with thunder.

Cupping his hands around his mouth so he could be heard, Patton then barked, "Compared to war all other forms of human endeavor shrink to insignificance!"

Now his voice shook with emotion.

"God, how I love it! God, how I love it so!"

The artillery opened up again, drowning out the voices of the troops and the mechanical groan of the vehicles passing by on the road. He had Codman light an American-made White Owl Invincible cigar for him, his favorite brand, and then, for a full minute, he stared out at the battlefield, oblivious to the danger, as his aide and driver, both well-versed in his eccentricities, looked on in silence.

Standing there amidst a backdrop of smoking tanks and half-tracks with a cigar clenched between his teeth, General George S. Patton, Jr. looked larger-than-life. He had long made it a point to dress with military spit and polish, and as he gazed out at the wreckage of war spread across the rolling French tableland, he appeared particularly colossal. He wore a gleaming helmet emblazoned with three gold stars and a non-regulation "Eisenhower" General Officer service blouse overflowing with medals. It had been cut down and re-tailored in the U.K. to be a European Theater of Operations jacket. The remainder of his uniform consisted of cavalry-style "pink" officers' riding breeches, leather cavalry leggings, tall service boots, a pair of gloves, and a leather gun belt of his own design, holstering a Colt single-action Army .45-caliber revolver and a 3.5-inch Smith and Wesson .357 magnum, both pistols equipped with special ivory grips.

Though the eloquence of his speech often matched the sartorial panache he displayed in his "Ike" jacket and jodhpurs, he was quite fond of cursing and took to using four letters words to the point where they, too, were almost eloquent as they rolled off his profane tongue. "When I want my men to remember something important, to really make it stick," he had once written a family member, "I give it to them double dirty. It may not sound nice to a bunch of little old ladies at an afternoon tea party, but it helps my soldiers to remember. You can't run an army without profanity, and it has to be eloquent profanity. An army without profanity couldn't fight its way out of a piss-soaked paper bag."

Two minutes later, the profane and garrulous Old Blood and Guts was on the move again, heading towards the Third Army forward command post—Lucky Forward. Sherman and Stuart tanks chugged alongside him with GIs riding "Russian style" on the hulls. The footsloggers leapt off every so often to spray the thickets next to the road with machine-gun fire to clear out remaining pockets of resistance. Their faces were smeared with gunpowder, their hair gray with chalk-like dust, and grenades hung from their uniform lapels like Cartier clips. After two weeks of heavy fighting—and tough tours in North Africa, Sicily, and Southern Italy under the belts of many of them—they looked and moved with the confidence of true veterans.

All along the road French farmers and their wives, sons, and daughters stripped shoes and tunics from the German dead. Patton couldn't blame them. He knew that such was the nature of war. But it bothered him that such a proud people as the French, who had fielded the world's largest army at the beginning of the conflict, had been so easily defeated by the Germans during the 1940 *blitzkrieg*. The French civilians rushed up to plead for Camel and Lucky Strike cigarettes from the passing infantrymen, with two fingers pressed to the lips in what the soldiers were calling the "French national salute." Others offered tricolor nosegays made from, red roses, white asters, and blue hydrangeas. "Heep, heep, whoo-ray!" Frenchmen roared when Patton and his Third Army cavalcade passed by, repeating phrases learned from American doughboys in the Great War a generation earlier. Some of the soldiers replied in schoolboy French or with handy phrases published in *Stars and Stripes* magazine, and shouts of "Vive la France!" from the doughs elicited bottles of wine or jugs of calvados, toasts to the spirit of Marquis de Lafayette, or scathing denunciations of the Boche, Kraut, Jerry, or Hun—depending on the preferred moniker for the hated German enemy.

Down the dirt road the long column of marching soldiers, tanks, jeeps, and deuce-and-a-half trucks pounded, sometimes spilling out through bullet-threshed fields and orchards burgeoning with fruit. MP motorcyclists darted in and out among the ranks, commanding dawdlers to keep moving east towards Paris and Berlin. Patton continued taking in the pageant of war with a feeling close to euphoria as he, Codman, and Mims drove past stone barns and mules hauling milk in copper urns, past shops that still peddled perfume and silk scarves, past collaborators with crude swastikas tattooed onto their shaved heads. He knew he was fortunate to be back in command of any army after being consigned to near anonymity for the past nine months. Despite his tactical brilliance in leading the U.S. II Corps and Seventh Army in 1943 to victory in Tunisia and Sicily, he had made a series of blunders that had landed him in the doghouse with the press and his superiors.

Slapping two hospitalized soldiers suffering from battle fatigue in Sicily, for what he falsely considered to be cowardice in the face of the enemy, nearly cost him his stars. Striking a subordinate was a court-martial offense, and on New Year's Day 1944 command of the Seventh Army was taken away from him. Only the intervention of his longtime supporters General Dwight Eisenhower, supreme commander of the Allied Expeditionary Force in Europe, and General George Marshall, chief of staff of the U.S. Army, saved him from having to resign. He was further denied an early role in the Normandy invasion and a chance to command the U.S. Twelfth Army Group now led by General Omar Bradley, his junior and former subordinate. A minor but foolish indiscretion in April, when he told a British social club that it was the destiny of the United States, Great Britain, and Russia to rule the post-war world almost lost him command of Third Army. Narrowly pardoned, he spent the spring and early summer as a conspicuous decoy of the fictitious FUSAG—First United States Army Group—created to deceive the Germans into thinking that the main Allied force would land at Pas de Calais for the invasion of Europe instead of Normandy.

A man of action like Patton—whose lifelong dream was to lead conquering armies into great and bloody battles—was not satisfied with being a mere decoy. For him, being sidelined in England for Overlord and its successful aftermath on the Norman beachhead was the lowest point of his military career. But now thankfully all that was behind him. All the same, he knew he was fortunate to have a second chance at a major field command and recognized that he was unlikely to be granted another if he screwed up again. This time around, he intended to keep his trap shut and do what Ike and Brad told him—even if that meant holding back from some of his instinctive aggressiveness and going along with his more timorous superiors if he disagreed with them. It was a price he was willing to pay to get out of the doghouse and fulfill his destiny. Commanding the U.S. Third Army to victory over the Axis forces would serve as his redemption, the linchpin and consolidation of his role in history that he had yearned for since he was a little boy. To his soldiers, he promised that the enemy would once again "raise up on their hind legs and howl, 'Jesus Christ, it's that goddamn Third Army and that son of a bitch Patton again!'"

As they neared the command post, they passed a stretch of road and rolling farmland so packed with corpses of Germans, farm animals, wrecked tanks, cannons, and trucks that he doubted his feet would be able to touch the ground if he walked through it. The stench filled his nostrils like a plague. *God, forgive us the sin of our belligerence, but better those Hun bastards than our boys,* he thought grimly. Five minutes later, they pulled into Lucky Forward.

The general's full complement of staff vehicles in addition to his command car were parked in two rows, including his Willys-Overland jeep, his GMC ST5 two-and-a-half-ton shop van that served as his living quarters and mobile headquarters, and his M20 armored car. Like his command car, his Willys and M20 were customized with his signature horns, general's stars, and flag, as well as additional armoring and a heavy machine gun to provide antiaircraft fire. Indeed, Patton had good reason to fear becoming a target for the Luftwaffe as the big Dodges tended to stand out when viewed from above and were often targeted by enemy aircraft.

Stepping from his command car, he went to the "War Room" in his HQ tent. His roving headquarters and staff vehicles were equipped with secure phone lines, battlefield maps, radio equipment, spare vehicle parts, weapons, food and clothing, and extra fuel cans. The War Room tent was where he held his 9 a.m. morning and 4 p.m. afternoon briefings. It was three minutes to four and General Hobart "Hap" Gay, his chief of staff, Colonel Halley Maddox, his chief operations officer, and

Major Alexander Stiller, another aide-de-camp who worked alongside Codman, were waiting for him along with Colonel Oscar W. Koch, his chief intelligence officer. The walls were lined with color-coded maps of Normandy, the Cotentin Peninsula, and the Falaise area of Western France. On the table in the middle of the tent were piles of papers, more maps, and a copy of Edward Augustus Freeman's six-volume *History of the Norman Conquest of England*, which Patton was studying to understand William the Conqueror's use of road networks in France.

Despite Patton's public image as the hell-for-leather cavalryman, he in fact valued precise and methodical staff work. He had handpicked the members of his staff and molded them into a smooth-functioning team that could practically read his mind and anticipate his intentions. His Jewish friend and top intelligence man, Oscar Koch, was the star of his close-knit team. Patton never made a move without first consulting the G-2, who had an important say in the Third Army's movements. It was because of the highly proficient Koch that Old Blood and Guts was never caught by surprise and why he was able to consistently smash through the most vulnerable sectors in the enemy lines, outflank the Germans, cause havoc, and destroy them in large numbers.

"What do you have for me, Oscar?" he said to his G-2, blowing out a cloud of cigar smoke. "What's the latest on the counteroffensive?"

Despite lacking the resources to prevent the Allied breakout from Normandy, the Germans had earlier that morning mounted a strong counterattack into the Allies in an attempt to split the British from the U.S. forces at Mortain. Hitler had refused to allow Field Marshal von Kluge, the commander of Army Group B, to withdraw his overmatched forces from Western France and instead ordered him to conduct a counteroffensive against the U.S. breakthrough.

Koch pointed to the large wall map as the other staff officers gathered around. "The German counteroffensive is petering out, General. Our troops have continued to press south near Vire on the right flank of the German attack. The 116th Panzer Division has been driven back. The 1st SS and 116th Panzer Divisions have renewed attacks, but the flanks of the Mortain positions have been sealed off. VII Corps has been able to contain the German advance."

"That's what I like to hear."

"As we speak, General Bradley is sending two armored combat commands against the German left flank."

Puffing his cigar, Patton traced a finger across the map. "The 2nd Armored will be able to hit the rear of the two SS Panzer divisions. Now that's what I call holding the Hun by the nose and kicking him in the ass. This means we can advance through the open country to the south and take Le Mans by lunchtime tomorrow."

His officers looked at one another. "That may be ambitious, General. There are strong reserves and at least one SS division between Falaise and Le Mans," pointed out Hap Gay. A farmer's son from Illinois, he was one of a handful of Patton's staff officers who was able to stand up to the general's often overpowering personality, usually through tactful persuasion. The two had much in common: both were accomplished horsemen who played polo and had an eye for horseflesh.

"Don't worry, Hap, we'll keep abreast of SS movements. Anything else?"

"Our flanks, sir. What about our flanks?" said his G-3 Maddox.

"I told you, gentlemen, when we first broke out of the hedgerow country that we will be advancing constantly. Nothing's changed. From here on out, until we win or die, we will always be audacious. *L'audace, l'audace, toujours l'audace.*"

"Even if it means driving through Occupied France with open flanks and a vulnerable rear?" asked General Gay.

"You've got to be more like me, Hap, and refuse to take counsel of your fears. I don't need to worry about my flanks—that's the goddamn enemy's problem. Besides, Oscar here and the Air Corps take care of my flanks and that's how come I can sleep at night."

His officers chuckled. Although his staff understood and appreciated his bold methods, their conventional infantry training had so indoctrinated some of them to the importance of flanks that they were still not comfortable with his aggressive approach to warfare. The notion of abandoning the doctrine of secure flanks was anathema to many of them, running counter to what they had been taught. Yet Patton's seemingly cavalier dismissal of his flanks was not as casual as it appeared. One reason was that he had access to decrypted German wireless communications obtained through Ultra, the official name of the top secret radio intercept system British intelligence had at its disposal. The Allies had cracked the German Enigma code in 1940 and were able to read all German radio traffic at Bletchley Park, the location of British decoding efforts in Europe. The Government Code and Cipher School was hidden deep in the Buckinghamshire countryside, monitoring and decoding German military radio traffic as if reading the enemy's mail. Thus, Patton and the other Allied generals knew virtually every move the Germans were planning to make in the European Theater of Operations, or ETO, before events happened.

But his true secret weapon was his use of aerial reconnaissance and the close air support of Brigadier General Otto Weyland's XIX Tactical Air Command. During the past week, Patton had become a true believer in the value of air support when he saw, over and over with his own eyes, the carnage wreaked by Weyland's fighter-bombers. They harassed the retreating Germans without letup. He had also heard the airmen's praises being sung by his own tankers. Most of Patton's spearheading armored columns were supported by P-47 fighter bombers of XIX TAC, which roamed the skies like eagles seeking prey. In Sicily, Patton had cursed the air forces; now, a year later, Weyland and his airmen could do no wrong. For Patton and his new best friend, Opie Weyland, air-ground cooperation had never worked better.

"All right, that's enough of a briefing," said Patton to conclude the meeting. "Let's get this ass-kicking show back on the road. We're heading for Le Mans— and I'm going to see the front for myself. General Bradley's staff may scorn me as a showman and consider my frequent visits to the front as self-serving, but I don't see it that way. If you want an army to fight and risk death, you've got to get your butt up there and lead it. An army is like spaghetti. You can't push a piece of spaghetti, you've got to pull it, goddamnit!"

"That's quite a metaphor, sir," observed Gay, ribbing him just a little. "Did you learn that in Sicily?"

"Nope. I learned it in the Great War when I got shot in the ass!"

The men laughed, and he felt the power of their brotherhood as officers. But most of all, he felt spectacularly alive now that he was out of the doghouse and back in the fight. With the Third Army advancing daily and adding glowing new statistics to its list of achievements, the adrenaline was flowing and he was on the greatest high of his life.

"This is turning out to be a damned fine war," he said. It was then the new pile of maps on the table caught his eye. "Are those the ones I ordered?"

"Yes, General," said Codman. "The battle maps are twenty inches each, with a scale of eight miles to the inch. We had them laminated just like the ones you had in Tunisia and Sicily."

He plucked one up from the table and snorted with shock. "Jesus Christ, it only goes as far east as Paris!" he complained. "I'm going to goddamn Berlin!"

Codman paled. "Don't worry, sir, I'll get new ones."

"Yes, see to it, Colonel. Now let's get moving."

As he started for the open tent flap, he heard the distant thrum of airplanes. Stepping out into the late afternoon sunlight, he looked to the sky. At first, the sound was barely perceptible but it quickly grew in decibel, until he realized what was coming. He could tell by the sound of the engines that they were a squadron of Focke-Wulf Fw 190s, lethal German single-engine fighter-bombers.

*Don't take counsel of your fears. Don't take counsel of your fears.*

"We need to take cover, sir," said Codman, and he was swiftly echoed by Stiller.

Patton shook his head stubbornly. "No, I'm not going anywhere."

"But they're coming right at us, sir," protested Codman.

The Focke-Wulf's swooped down from above like a swarm of locusts. There were eight of them, screaming in from the east, skimming the tops of the trees as they skirted the edge of the rolling green hills. Now he could make out the black swastikas and yellow trim on their tails. From their low approach and aggressive-looking formation, it did indeed seem as if they were gunning for his Lucky Forward command post. He wondered if perhaps he should heed his aide's advice and take cover, but then decided against it. If the word spread that he was not afraid, there would be no reason for his men fighting on the battlefields to be scared either.

"Those rotten sons of bitches! We'll get them!" he snarled at the Luftwaffe marauders, waving his smoldering cigar up at them like a saber.

"General, we really should take cover now!" warned the Texan Stiller.

"No, I will not hide like a jackrabbit!" he roared. "It's going to take more than a squadron of Focke-Wulf's to kill George Goddamn Patton!"

Suddenly, the menacing German planes banked right and headed in the direction of Saint-Hilaire-du-Harcouët.

"Why just look at that." He pointed his cigar up into the sky. "I stared the sons of bitches in the eye—and by thunder they blinked!"

"By God, it seems like you're right," exclaimed Gay, coming up from behind.

"Damn right I am, Hap." Giving a satisfied grunt, he realized that in the coming weeks and months, he was absolutely going to destroy these Nazi bastards. Feeling very much the conquering hero of his starry-eyed childhood dreams, he again recited Napoleon's maxim: *"L'audace, l'audace, toujours l'audace!"*

Audacity, audacity, always audacity!

# CHAPTER 10

## LUCKY FORWARD, THIRD ARMY MOBILE COMMAND POST
## OUEN-DES-TOITS
## WESTERN FRANCE

### AUGUST 13, 1944

SIX DAY'S LATER, PATTON WAS STILL FEELING AUDACIOUS. The man described by a reporter as "a warring, roaring comet" and by a West Point classmate as a "pure-bred gamecock with brains" stood over a map in his mobile command post showing the current Allied positions in relation to the German Army bottled-up in the Falaise Gap. The German counteroffensive at Mortain to halt the Allied breakout from Normandy had failed miserably, and Field Marshal von Kluge and his Army Group B were on the ropes. Four depleted Panzer divisions were not enough to defeat the Americans, and Hitler's ill-advised gamble had enabled the Allies to commence an envelopment of the Germans.

While British and Canadian forces were striking from the north, American troops were cutting off and attacking the enemy from the south from Le Mans to Argentan. The plan had called for the two Allied armies to join together and close off the remaining pocket of resistance, thereby surrounding the German Army and capturing it in a short hook between Argentan and Falaise. But at this point the pincers remained open and a vast stream of German fighting men had begun pouring through the Falaise Gap, much to Patton's consternation.

It was time to close the gap and bag the whole German Army.

He studied the color-coded arrows, circles, and hachure lines showing the disposition of the Allied and German forces in the area of Argentan and Falaise on the map. The U.S. Twelfth Army Group, commanded by General Omar Bradley and consisting of Patton's Third Army and Hodges' First Army, was hitting von Kluge from the west and south, while British General Bernard Montgomery and his Twenty-First Army Group consisting of Brits, Canadians, and Poles struck from the north. Yesterday, Bradley had, with Ike's and Monty's blessing, directed Patton to ignore the existing boundary between Bradley's Twelfth Army and Monty's forces, capture the town of Argentan, and then push slowly north towards Falaise to close off the gap. To accomplish the objective, Patton had dispatched General Wade Haislip and his XV Corps to block the east-west roads north of Argentan.

Patton and Monty both had argued for a long envelopment rather than a short hook at Argentan and Falaise proposed by Bradley. Patton maintained that if they were to encircle the Germans then why not envelop them all the way to the Seine. The river would provide a natural protection for his eastern flank, while creating a large pocket to surround more of the enemy forces. Patton and Monty were in agreement that if the Allies did not take Argentan, Alençon, and Falaise quickly, too many Germans would escape the gap. Believing he could always fall back on the original plan if necessary, Monty accepted the wishes of Bradley as the man on the spot, and the proposal was adopted. Patton was confident that his troops could seize Falaise and make contact with Monty's forces northwest of the town, while at the same time closing the gap the Germans were at this very moment escaping through in large numbers.

The whole point of the short hook was to bag the two armies inside the pocket, which Patton knew would not happen if he waited until all Allied forces had moved into position. By then, the Germans would be pulling out their bedrolls on the eastern bank of the Seine. So, earlier in the morning, he ordered Haislip to keep pushing his tanks to the front, imploring him to "Take Alençon, take Argentan! Hell, go to the English Channel if you have to—just bag those Germans!" With XV Corps sporting three hundred tanks, twenty-two artillery battalions, and complete air superiority, he was confident that Haislip could pound his way through the German blockade, then push on slowly until he contacted the Canadians near Falaise, thus completing the encirclement.

In fact, he was more than confident. He believed it was a fait accompli.

And then the whole damned thing fell apart.

ΨΨΨ

Patton looked at General Hugh Gaffey and couldn't believe what he had just heard. "You've got to be fucking kidding me," he snorted, standing on the balls of his feet like a panther. "Tell me this is a mistake."

Gaffey shook his head. "It's no mistake, sir. General Bradley has ordered you to halt on the army group boundary just below Argentan. If they are already beyond it, General Haislip and XV Corps are to stop immediately and pull back to the boundary."

He was still stumped. "Has Brad lost his mind? Who the hell did you talk to?"

"Lev Allen," replied Gaffey, referring to Bradley's chief of staff and his opposite number at Twelfth Army Group HQ, Eagle TAC.

"Well, I'll be a son of a bitch. Get Lev on the phone."

"Yessir, but I'm telling you he was quite clear."

"I don't doubt that, but I'm not going to allow a stupid, gutless decision to take place unless I have no choice. If this order stands, it will go down as one of the worst decisions of the war, goddamnit. Now get him on the phone!"

Two minutes later, Patton launched into General Allen on the scrambler without preamble. "Lev, what the hell is this stop order halting me at Argentan?"

"It comes directly from General Bradley and there's nothing ambiguous about it. You are to have XV Corps halt at the agreed-upon interarmy boundary along the south end of the village and instruct General Haislip to consolidate his forces."

"But Monty has already agreed we can move the boundary north," he pleaded like a jailhouse lawyer, feeling his face reddening. "The Krauts have been forced to cover a long perimeter against four Allied armies. The bastards don't have enough forces to stop us. What is it that's giving Brad cold feet?"

"The general doesn't have cold feet. He is operating on reliable intelligence."

"Well, tell me what it is and I'll tell you if it's goddamn reliable or not."

"Brad's worried about friendly fire between the converging ranks of Canadians and Americans. G-2 has forecast a big German attack towards Haislip. That would make any further advance a huge gamble."

"But the Germans are spread too thin and don't have the firepower. They're counteroffensive at Mortain sputtered out in less than two days. They have more horse carts than tanks, for Christ sake."

"Brad believes the Germans will make a lunge at the XV Corps flank if Haislip puts himself between more than one hundred thousand soldiers and their freedom. How can one overstretched corps hold off two desperate German armies?"

"I'm telling you the Krauts are weak and this is the time to go for the jugular."

"George, we know how you feel, but Brad believes—"

"Just listen to me, Lev," Patton cut him off. "Pushing Haislip forward is the surest way to close the bag on these Hun bastards. That's what Brad wants, isn't it, a goddamn double envelopment? Otherwise, the Germans are going to skip out the back door. Can you just ask General Bradley to reconsider?"

"I'll try, but I'm certain his mind is made up on this."

"Just give it a shot and get back to me. You can do that at least, right?"

"Yes, I can do that."

He hung up. An hour later, Allen phoned back. Neither Bradley or Monty, he said, was interested in having Haislip drive against Falaise. The army group boundaries would remain where they were, and Haislip's XV Corps would halt and consolidate its position. There would be no appeals. Patton cursed, slammed down the phone, and called Bradley. He had no luck. Forty minutes later, he managed to reach him over the scrambler phone. He reminded himself to be calm and composed, though he knew it wouldn't be easy. His blood was boiling.

"We now have elements in Argentan," he opened up with a flourish worthy of Murat, before changing his tone to one of coarse humor. "Shall we continue and drive the British into the sea for another Dunkirk?"

"That's not funny, George," said the humorless, by-the-book Missourian who had earned the nickname "the GI General" from war correspondent Ernie Pyle for his down-to-earth approach to warfare that seemed the opposite of the inveterate showman Patton. "Dunkirk was a terrible loss for the British."

"And the Battle of Falaise will be a disaster in the eyes of history if we don't allow Haislip to seal off this damned gap. Hell, I've reinforced him with a whole division of infantry. XV Corps now has three hundred tanks and twenty-two artillery battalions. And let's not forget that we control the skies."

"Has Haislip taken Argentan?"

"Not quite. A scratch collection of Krauts from two Panzer divisions is putting up resistance to his advance parties at the outskirts of the town. But his main force will be there soon. They'll make mincemeat of those bastards. I'm telling you, Brad, the Third Army is ready to snap the trap shut. With your blessing, those two German armies hanging on up there at Falaise are as good as done."

"Nothing doing. Don't go beyond Argentan. Stop where you are and build up on that shoulder."

"Come on, Brad. Surely—"

"I'm worried about friendly fire between the converging Canadians and your forces."

"But Crerar hasn't even gathered together his four divisions and started south yet," he protested, referring to General Harry D. G. Crerar, commander of the Canadian First Army, a plodding chain-smoker with a hacking cough and recurrent dysentery regarded with contempt by his boss Montgomery. "I can take Falaise and cut off the Germans before the goddamn Canadians are halfway there."

"You're not to go beyond Argentan," he said, obviously hoping to settle the argument once and for all. "Just stop where you are and build up that shoulder. Sibert tells me the Germans are beginning to pull from Hodges and First Army to the west in large numbers," he added, referring to Brigadier General Edwin L. Sibert, his G-2 senior intelligence officer. "You'd better button up and get ready for them."

But the pugnacious Patton was having none of it. "Brad, I've got to tell you, I think you're making a huge mistake," he said to his old friend, comrade in arms, and former subordinate, thinking it only fair to warn him of the historical implications of such unwarranted timidity.

"I don't see how. Intercepted radio communications reveal that at least nineteen German divisions have begun stampeding eastward to escape our trap. Haislip's corps risks destruction by pushing north with an exposed left flank."

His gut told him the intelligence report was inflated and that Bradley was overreacting. But he didn't want to make him mad so he refrained from speaking his mind. Then a thought occurred to him. "Have you talked with Monty about this? What does he say?"

A lengthy silence. "I have not consulted with Montgomery," he finally admitted. "The decision to stop at Argentan is mine and mine alone."

"But wasn't Monty's original objective to take Argentan?"

"Yes, but I'm not about to capture one of Monty's objectives just to help him reach his goal. If he wants help in closing the gap, he needs to ask for it."

That wasn't exactly being a team player, thought Patton. "What about Ike? I can't believe he agreed to this. Not when we have these Hun bastards right where we want them."

"We're done talking, George. Just follow orders like a good soldier."

He sensed Bradley wasn't telling him the whole story. Was he really the one behind the stop order, or were Ike or Monty, or perhaps both, behind it?

"Of course, I'll follow orders, Brad. But I would be remiss in my duty as a United States officer if I didn't implore you one last time to let me push on. I'm telling you you're making a big mistake. Haislip can easily advance to Falaise and completely close the gap well before the Canadians arrive."

"I'm going to tell you one last time, George. Halt and build up that shoulder. I much prefer a solid shoulder at Argentan to the possibility of a broken neck at Falaise." And then he was gone.

Patton slammed down the phone and looked at Gaffey, who was standing there shaking his head. "I don't know what the hell is going on," he fumed, "but I am sure of two things. First, this halt is a great mistake and will be condemned by history. Second, I am certain that the British will not close on Falaise."

"I can't argue with that, sir."

"Monty has never moved an army faster than a snail in his entire career—and that includes his one great victory at El Alamein. Hell, he was supposed to take Caen on D-Day and it took him seven weeks to liberate the goddamn city. And then he declared to the whole world that the American breakout from the hedgerow country three weeks ago was all his doing and had proceeded perfectly according to *his* master plan. The British are always too slow and cautious. They're too reliant on their supposedly foolproof plans and attrition to exploit advantages—and most of the blame falls on Monty. If Sir George Bernard Shaw were still alive, he would say that our dear First Viscount of Alamein is 'blessedly tottering'—and that's on a goddamn good day!"

"I'm sorry, sir," said Gaffey. "Monty is a headache for sure. And I don't know what's gotten into General Bradley. It's not clear whether he's getting pushed around by the British, but he does seem to be unduly cautious."

"Monty and his Twenty-First Army Group are the ones behind it, I just know it. I attribute the whole damned mess to either jealousy towards us Americans or to utter ignorance of the military situation, or to a combination of the two. In any case, I won't have my goddamn name attached to it. General Gaffey, I order you to put the stenographic record of my conversation with Lev Allen into the Third Army's historical files."

"Yes, sir. I'll see to it."

"Good. At least the world will know that the charge of timidity cannot be laid at doorstep of George Goddamn Patton!"

# CHAPTER 11

## LUCKY FORWARD, LA BAZOGE
## WESTERN FRANCE

### AUGUST 15-16, 1944

PEERING THROUGH HIS ZEISS 10X50 FIELD GLASSES, Patton gazed north in the direction of The Corridor of Death. Having just finished his 0900 briefing, he had climbed the little hill behind the Lucky Forward command vehicles with his devoted bullterrier Willie to catch a glimpse of the distant battlefield. Even as Ike, Monty, and Bradley seemed to be going to great lengths to bungle the entrapment of the German Army due to endless vacillation and political appeasement, the advancing Allied ground forces and swarms of Spitfires, Typhoons, Mustangs, Lightnings, and Thunderbolts were having a telling effect. The Allies were pressing in on the remaining pocket of resistance like a tightening vice, and the relentless bombing and strafing was decimating von Kluge's army as it conducted its rearguard action and retreat through the narrowing Falaise Gap.

Though smoke and dust obscured large portions of the rolling farmland and uplands, through the gaps Old Blood and Guts could see that the grass was littered with unburied dead, thousands of dead horses and cattle, and smashed and burning vehicles. Allied armor and airmen were wreaking murderous havoc on the German positions, blasting away what little remained of their 88-mm antitank and antiaircraft guns. The damage was immense: flaming vehicles, carts, and dead horses lay abandoned in the road while the worn-out troops pressed on afoot.

He saw little mushroom clouds all along the retreating German columns. Even from his distant vantage point, it was obvious that von Kluge was on the run and Western France was lost for the Reich. The fiercest fighting appeared to be mostly between Argentan and Falaise. But he could tell that, due to the rapidity of the German retreat and reduction of the pocket from the inward pressure from the south, west, and north, the villages of Trun, Saint-Lambert, and Chambois would soon be the focal points of the attack. All the same, the pincers remained open and a steady stream of enemy soldiers was funneling through the still-twenty-mile-wide gap between Crerar's slow-moving Canadians and the U.S. Third Army that had been Johnny-on-the-spot but had been ordered to hold at the Argentan line.

Still, it was a fine sight to see. A brilliant Allied victory was close at hand. Like Monty, he had never had much enthusiasm for Bradley's cautious short hook and had preferred a long envelopment—a drive to the Seine River by the Third Army, the Canadian First Army, and the British Second Army to establish blocking forces and prevent the main escape of Army Group B from Normandy. But he could now see firsthand the raw punishment and destruction being meted out to the Germans— and he wholeheartedly approved. At the same time, he was pleased that Brad had allowed him to cut lose two of Haislip's five divisions for a dash to the Seine along with the corps headquarters, while continuing to hold the Argentan shoulder temporarily with a smaller force.

His mobile divisions were slicing towards the Paris-Orléans gap. Le Mans had fallen and Orléans, Chartres, and Dreux were close to being taken by the Third

Army. Patton found it all tremendously exciting. This was heady warfare fought by divisions and corps rather than by platoons, companies, and battalions as in the Cotentin Peninsula. He knew he was the perfect commander in exactly the right place at precisely the right time to exploit the fast-moving and fast-changing situation—if only his superiors would get their act together and turn him lose to do what he did best: wage all-out *blitzkrieg*, American style.

The simple truth was that he was not happy with either Eisenhower or Bradley over Allied strategy. He knew that they had been less than forthcoming with him. In his war diary and in letters to his wife and daughter, he referred to Ike as "Divine Destiny" and Bradley as "Tent Maker" because Eisenhower had become too big for his britches in his view and he believed Bradley to be an appeaser who lacked the charisma and backbone to stand up to Ike or Monty. From his G-2 Oscar Koch, he had learned that the official stop order at Argentan had *actually* come from Brad because Ike had insisted on appeasing Monty and the British.

He couldn't fucking believe it.

When a call had been placed on the night of August 12 to Montgomery's headquarters trying to get permission for Third Army to go beyond Argentan, Monty's chief of staff, the highly capable General Freddie De Guingand, refused to grant permission per his boss's orders. Furious, Bradley drove straight to Shellburst, Eisenhower's headquarters, to seek Ike's help with their "Montgomery problem." Bradley told Eisenhower that the "halt order" was contrary to everything they had learned about military strategy and that if American reporters ever discovered Monty's chicanery, Ike could kiss his precious Anglo-American alliance goodbye. The supreme commander agreed. If the American press ever found out that the ranking British officer in Europe had ordered both Patton's Third Army and Hodges' First Army to halt on an arbitrary interarmy group boundary line—so that the British would look better and not be beaten to a military objective by their American allies that had led the successful breakout from Normandy—the Anglo-American alliance might be shaken to its core.

Based on Koch's analysis, the supreme commander knew it would be too risky and not withstand scrutiny to allow Monty's "halt order" to stand as a direct order from the senior British officer in France. Therefore, he convinced Bradley that it would be politically expedient for them to handle Monty's "halt order" within the U.S. Army's chain of command. To keep their fellow American generals at bay, as well as the politicians, reporters, and general public, Ike requested that Bradley issue the order in his name, taking Monty out of the controversy. He told Brad to make up any justification he pleased for issuing the order and promised him his full support in later explaining the order. Brad cringed, but in the end, he agreed to do what the supreme commander asked. He would issue the "halt order" to Patton in his name. In Patton's view, Ike had decided that the Anglo-American alliance was worth more than the lives of his own U.S. troops. After all, the German Army was being allowed to escape and regroup east of the Seine, thereby enabling it to live on and fight another day. Though Patton was steadfastly loyal to Ike, he considered the failure to close the Falaise pocket by catering to Monty and British pride yet another example of high-command gutlessness.

He paused a moment from viewing the unfolding battle to lean down and pet

Willie, who had just finished relieving himself. As usual, the bullterrier donned his special GI dog tags his master had fashioned for him and was on a leash. Two nights earlier, Willie had been driven into a panic by the roar of hundreds of falling bombs not far from the Lucky Forward base camp and he was still skittish. Now when the dog heard the distant thunder of airplanes, he hid quickly under a chair, table, or bed, or behind the closest tree. Lately, Patton had been sleeping with his little buddy named after William the Conqueror to comfort him. With his wife Beatrice three thousand miles away, the little English bull terrier was his most frequent companion.

He resumed peering through his binoculars at the unfolding battle. Germans in armored vehicles, in horse carts, and on foot were scrambling to get out of the way of Allied diving bombers and tanks, and he thought to himself: *This is a wonderful war—if only it could last forever.* He thought of Beatrice and his fiercely loyal sister Nita back home in the States and the recent letters he had written them. God, he loved his Patton women. Then he thought of yesterday's diary entry. It read:

### Diary, August 14, 1944

*In exactly two weeks the Third Army has advanced farther and faster than any Army in the history of war.*

*Today I went to visit Haislip whom we found quite pepped up. I told him of my plan to move the XX Corps on Dreux and the XII Corps on Chartres.*

*I then flew back to see Bradley and sell him the plan. He consented, and even permitted me to change it so as to move the XX Corps on Chartres, the XV Corps on Dreux, and the XII Corps on Orléans. He will also let me keep the 80th and give Middleton an infantry division from the First Army to replace the 6th Armored in Brittany.*

*It is really a great plan, wholly my own, and I made Bradley think he thought of it. Oh, what a tangled web we weave when first we practice to deceive.*

*I am very happy and elated.*

*I got all the corps moving by 2030 so that if Monty tries to be careful, it will be too late.*

Willie barked. Patton heard approaching footsteps. He turned to see his forty-eight-year-old, African-American personal aide, William George Meeks.

"George, how the hell are you this morning?" he said to the veteran of two world wars and Buffalo Soldier cavalryman who hailed from Georgia.

"Just fine, sir. And I can see that you are doing well."

He squinted into the sun and grinned his trademark bucktoothed grin. "How can you tell?"

"You've got your fighting face on. That's when you're happiest."

His grin widened. "I do love to kill Krauts—and I do love the smell of cordite in the morning. I can't deny it."

"That's when you feel the most alive, isn't it, sir?"

"Boy, you sure have me figured out, don't you?"

"I like to think so. But I also don't want to be presumptuous."

"You're never presumptuous, George—you know that." He smiled again. "Now what have you got for me? Don't tell me its bad news."

Meeks smiled reassuringly as he took Willie by the leash. He knew the general's temperamental moods better than anyone, and the two men were close enough now, after two years of war, that he often gave Patton advice when the general asked for his input. Sometimes, he was just an ear for Old Blood and Guts to vent to, which was something the often emotional and highly charged Patton needed and benefitted from.

"To be honest, I think it could go either way, sir, as far as good or bad," said the aide. "But General Bradley is here to see you. I offered to come fetch you myself instead of Major Stiller as I thought I'd take Willie off your hands."

Patton let his binoculars drop. "Brad's here? Oh God, I hope our Tent Maker hasn't let his nerves get the better of him again. All right, let's go."

"Whatever he's got on his mind, General, just remember, he's no match for you. Everyone thinks you should be the one running Twelfth Army Group, not General Bradley."

Again, Patton broke into big, bucktoothed grin. "Now that's why I like you so goddamn much, George—you always appeal to my oversized ego."

"No, sir, I just believe in you. The whole Third Army does."

"Okay, now you're just bucking for promotion."

He gave him a good-natured slap on the back, as if they were football players on the same team, and not a white major general whose ancestors had fought for the confederacy and his black orderly—during a period when lynchings were still commonplace in America and blacks and whites were still segregated in the military. But Patton was no ordinary general. He was the first general to overturn segregation in the U.S. Army on his own initiative by integrating his rifle companies. Though deep down he was still something of a bigot—as were Marshall, Eisenhower, Bradley, Monty, and virtually all of the principal commanders in the war except the late General Leslie McNair, who had been instrumental in ensuring that black Americans were allowed to fight—he was quite close to his two African-American aides, his driver Mims as well as his personal valet Meeks, and his Jewish senior intelligence officer, the G-2 Oscar Koch. He spent a great deal of time with all three men, regularly confiding in them, treating them respectfully, and listening to them closely when they gave their input. In short, he valued their opinions. Thus far during the war, he had spent more time with Meeks than anyone else, developing a relationship of mutual respect that transcended that of a general and his valet. He also insisted on the presence of black officers as judges of military tribunals involving black defendants, to ensure a degree of fairness. But most importantly, when it came to the men fighting under him, he admired the martial zeal and prowess of black units more than the vast majority of his contemporaries, telling them, "I don't give a damn who the man is. He can be a Negro or a Jew, but if he has the stuff and does his duty, he can have anything I've got. By God, I love him!"

"All right, you two—about face and let's head on back down the hill," he commanded Meeks and Willie.

"Lead the way, General."

With Willie pulling Meeks by his leash, they stumped down the hill, their leather boots kicking up puffs of dust dispersed by the brisk French wind. At the entrance to the War Room, his headquarters tent where he had held his briefings, sentries saluted as artillery batteries crackled in the distance and the massive generators for the signals trucks hummed in a steady mechanical rhythm. The flap to the tent was open. He stepped inside, finding General Bradley standing next to General Hobart Gay, his chief of staff, and Colonel Halley Maddox, his chief operations officer. They were swatting away a pack of mosquitos above the map table.

Descended from hardscrabble Missouri farmers, Omar Nelson Bradley was bespectacled, six-feet-tall, and fifty-one years of age. In contrast to the bellicose Patton, he gave more the impression of a certified public accountant than a three-star general co-commanding one of the largest ground forces in military history. He bore a high convex forehead, thin hair that had been graying since his cadet days, and a jaw that jutted out like a rock cliff. His projecting jaw was sometimes mistaken for a sign of pugnacity when in fact a boyhood ice skating accident had shattered his teeth and left him with a lifelong reluctance to smile in public lest people poke fun at him. He wore his customary weathered field jacket coated with a thin veneer of dust and canvas leggings that bespoke a certain humility, a quality valued highly by his principal promoter and former West Point classmate Eisenhower.

Like Patton, the "GI General" could be quick to the point and ruthless, but the similarities ended there. He was narrow-minded, underconfident, and far more intolerant of failure than his former superior, who took mistakes in his commanders in stride as long as their failures weren't due to lack of confidence or aggressiveness. Furthermore, unlike Patton, he rarely got out to see his troops in the field or hospitals, and consequently had failed to make much of an impression on them. Despite his mild-mannered facade, he also bore grudges longer and with far more vehemence than Patton. He never forgave Monty for trespassing on the II Corps boundary in Sicily, and he privately loathed the Englishman despite the fact he had to work closely with him. Due to his rigid Christian upbringing, in which alcohol and profanity were forbidden, he had little tolerance for the widespread profanity, heavy drinking, and unrestrained sexuality of officers and troopers liberally tolerated by Old Blood and Guts to maintain morale. And yet, despite the differences between the two men, he and Patton worked well together. They somehow managed to complement one another with their different leadership styles, though Bradley's staff looked scornfully upon Patton for his bravado and showmanship that was so different from their straitlaced commander.

When their eyes met, Patton could tell that Bradley had not come bearing good news. "General Bradley, what can I do for you, sir?" he said politely. As a general rule, he referred to Bradley formally as "sir" or "General Bradley" in public and when other officers were present, and "Brad" when they were alone or over the phone. "Please tell me Monty hasn't taken over Third Army."

"Very funny, George. I am, however, going to have to order you to halt your army again," he said in his flat, sodbuster twang.

"What is it now?"

"It's been decided at the highest level that the Third Army is not to advance beyond Dreux and Chartres, or any further towards the Seine."

"But I don't see why. We've got the Krauts on the run and are poised to bag them all."

"Because XV Corps alone likely won't be able to contain the Germans that have escaped from the pocket. There's more than a hundred thousand of them."

"But my advance elements have already reached the Seine. In fact, I pissed in the river this morning. What do you want me to do, pull back?"

"I'm ordering you to, George. And being the good soldier that you are, you're going to obey me whether you like it or not."

Patton pursed his lips, doing his best to control his vexation. He couldn't help but feel that the man who had earned the nickname the "GI General" from war correspondent Ernie Pyle had simply lost his nerve. The Missourian seemed to lack the drive, imagination, ability to improvise, and willingness to take risks that Patton felt were vital job requirements for the top commander of all U.S. troops in Western France. He couldn't believe Bradley was holding him back again, this time further east at the Seine. The question in Patton's mind was who was responsible for these new stop orders? Was it Monty or Ike, or perhaps both? Or was Bradley acting of his own accord, which he considered less likely?

"I may be a prima donna, but I know how to follow orders. All the same, you've got to tell me why we're doing this because this just doesn't add up."

"We have reports of five Panzer divisions between Argentan and Falaise. The Canadians have met stiff resistance and are still ten miles from Falaise."

"And Hodges?"

"The enemy is pulling away in large numbers and will be heading your way. That's why I need you to halt your move to the east, pull your vanguard back from the Seine, and reinforce that shoulder at Argentan."

Patton didn't respond. Instead, he thought: *All right, so today I'll comply with the order, but by tomorrow I'm going to persuade him to let me advance again. Goddamn, I wish I were supreme commander.*

"Just be a good soldier and follow orders, George. That's all I can tell you at this point."

"You came all the way down here just to tell me this?"

"Yes, I did. And I came in person to make sure there's no misunderstanding."

"There's no misunderstanding. You're asking me to halt Third Army at the Seine and at Dreux and Chartres, thereby killing our pursuit at the precise moment we should be exploiting the enemy's weakness. But I will follow my orders like the good soldier I am."

"That's what I want to hear. I'll be on my way then."

Patton turned to his staff, who did not look pleased. "You heard the man!" he snapped. "Recall the armor to the Argentan line! And see that it is done quickly, goddamnit!"

He looked back at Bradley. "That good enough for you, sir?"

The "GI General" allowed himself a rare smile. "Yes, General Patton, that will do just fine."

# CHAPTER 12

## LUCKY FORWARD, LA BAZOGE

### AUGUST 18-19, 1944

"CODMAN, I WANT YOU TO DO SOMETHING FOR ME."

"Yes, General."

"I just received word that my old friend, General J.L. Koechlin-Schwartz, my World War I instructor at the Staff School at Langres, is living in retirement at Vannes. That's up towards the end of the Brest peninsula. Tomorrow morning, I want you to go fetch him for me."

"Fetch him, sir?"

"I want you to take a plane…hell, take two planes…I don't care how you do it, but bring my old friend back here to me."

The next morning, August 19, the cultured aide and Francophile Major Codman took off in an L-5 observation, artillery spotting, and liaison aircraft with another one in tow, retrieved the French general, and returned to La Bazoge, where Meeks and the rest of Patton's staff had prepared a lunch spread befitting a king for his old teacher and comrade. From a long-locked trunk, Koechlin-Schwartz had unearthed his mothballed World War I uniform colored horizon blue and his oak-leaf-bordered kepi. As he entered the mess tent, Patton thought he looked, in full regalia, twenty years younger than his actual age. The two men saluted and hugged one another then sat down for lunch with Patton's good friend, Brigadier General Otto P. Weyland, commander of the XIX Tactical Air Command with whom he had been working seamlessly and synergistically to vanquish the Germans. A bottle of Châteauneuf-du-Pape was served. They quickly hoisted their glasses as Patton made a toast in exquisitely accented French.

"To my old comrade, General Koechlin-Schwartz, the bravest and sagest of the French generals who fought in the Great War."

"And to my gallant old pupil, who I always knew would go on to be a great and daring general."

"Here, here!" concurred Weyland, and they all smiled and drank.

"Do you remember in October 1918 when you were wounded in the hospital and I visited you?" the Frenchman then asked Patton.

He smiled. "Why of course I do, General. Though I was embarrassed to have been shot in the ass."

"I said to you, 'My dear Patton, I am so glad you were only wounded. For when you left, I said to my wife that is the end of Patton. He is one of those gallant fellows who always gets killed.'"

"Well, I'm still here, General. I suppose I'm just lucky."

"You know that Napoleon always preferred luck to greatness."

The military historian Patton nodded vigorously. "When he was criticized for winning battles simply because of luck, he famously retorted: 'I'd rather have lucky generals than good ones. They win battles!'"

"*Mais oui, bien sûr!*" cried the Frenchman.

They laughed and sipped their wine. Five minutes later, Codman, Meeks, and

Stiller brought them their lunch of marinated French pepper steak covered with brandy crème and served with pommes frites, capers, haricots verts, Nicoise olives, and grape tomatoes. Koechlin-Schwartz found the meal sumptuous, which pleased host Patton immensely. As they ate and drank, the French general continued to lavish unreserved praise upon his former pupil as they swapped old war stories.

"Had I taught twenty-five years ago, my dear Patton, what you are doing now in France, I should have been put in a mad house. But when I heard that an armored division was racing for Brest, I knew it was you."

"The times have changed. It's now all about mobility and air support. Why do you think the French Army did so poorly in 1940 during the *blitzkrieg*?"

"The Germans defeated us in 1940 because for more than a decade we taught, thought, and practiced defense, never attack. Everything we did was the complete opposite of what you are doing now in this fast-paced mobile warfare of yours."

"At Langres, you used to tell me, General, that the poorer the infantry, the more artillery it needs. Well, our American doughboys are damned good but they still need all the firepower they can get. But now we give it to them with planes, tanks, and cannons all at once."

"I have seen the results. Most impressive."

"All the same, I believe that you were correct in 1918 and you are again today."

"*Merci*. But it is I, your old teacher, who must congratulate you on your growing list of achievements. Your Major Codman has informed me that in the past two weeks alone, Third Army has taken Brittany, Nantes, Angers, Le Mans, Alençon, Chateaudun, Dreux, Chartres, and Orléans. That is quite a feat—even for a lucky general."

Patton chuckled. "I'm damn proud of my boys—and General Weyland's flyers. They've been making life miserable for the Krauts in the Falaise Gap."

"Congratulations to you too, General Weyland," said the Frenchman, holding up his glass in tribute. "The only good German is, of course, a dead one."

Tipping back their wine glasses, they talked some more about the comparisons between the two wars in France before Koechlin-Schwartz congratulated Patton on his promotion to major general in the Regular Army.

"Frankly, it took longer than I had hoped," replied Old Blood and Guts. "But at least they bumped me up two grades in the same day."

"It would seem that your slapping incidents in Sicily are behind you. You know, General, I certainly never taught you anything like that at Langres."

The former instructor's tone was more patriarchal than scolding, and Patton was not offended. He knew himself well enough to admit to his own weaknesses. "I know, General. It was a stupid mistake and I shouldn't have done it. I also have to learn to keep my mouth shut when it comes to reporters." He broke into a guilty grin. "And just to remind me that all of my past missteps are neither forgotten nor entirely forgiven, General Eisenhower recently passed an unflattering message to me through General Bradley's chief of staff, Lev Allen, regarding my promotion."

"What did Lev tell you?" asked Weyland, looking vaguely amused.

"He told me that Ike had phoned him and asked that he get a message to me. It said Congress has acted favorably on my promotion, and General Marshall requests that I do not spoil the record of a magnificent job by making public statements. Ike asked that I avoid making any such statements and keep out of photographs. Also, I am to make no remarks to the press unless approved by General Bradley. Why the bastards are keeping me on a shorter leash than I do my dog Willie!"

They chuckled and sipped more wine.

Burrowing the sterling silver tines of his fork into his steak, Koechlin-Schwartz said, "Well, at least now the public knows who is responsible for exploiting the successful breakout from the Cotentin. I must admit I was surprised to learn from your Major Codman that your name was only released to the newspapers three days ago as the commander of Third Army. You are the right arm that has encircled the two German armies in Normandy at Argentan and now is pursuing the defeated German forces. The immense area of France that has been liberated, from Brest in the west more than two hundred miles to the east—all this is your doing."

"Much of the credit goes to General Weyland here," said Patton, nodding towards the airman. "As I said before, his fighters and bombers have been making life a living hell for those Krauts on the ground."

"I'll drink to that," said Weyland good-naturedly, and they tipped back their wine glasses once again. Meeks quickly refilled their glasses with an approving nod and smile from Patton, who truly enjoyed the role of ingratiating host.

"What are your estimates of German casualties and POWs?" asked Koechlin-Schwartz.

"Over one hundred twenty thousand total and counting. That includes over fifteen thousand dead, more than fifty thousand wounded, and over fifty thousand captured. Not only that but Third Army has also captured or destroyed some four thousand German tanks, artillery pieces, and vehicles."

"And your losses?"

"Fifteen percent of the Germans or less across the board. The latest numbers are only two hundred tanks or so along with seventy guns and eight or nine hundred vehicles. My boys are giving the Krauts hell. They know that a pint of sweat saves a gallon of blood."

"Thanks to you, our people feel as if we have been reborn. As your Third Army advances, I see it cheered everywhere by my countrymen. They line the roads for miles, throwing kisses and apples and offering wine to our liberators. The people of France truly love you, General Patton."

"*Et j'adore les Français!*" he replied in his flawless French accent. And I adore the French!

"It is the British that give our people fits. We French are known for our excessive pride, but we pale in comparison to the bombastic British. How are you Americans getting along with Montgomery?"

"About as well as can be expected. Frankly, I admire the son of a bitch, but I don't trust him. And it's mostly his fault the Falaise Gap is still open and the Germans are escaping."

"The gap is still open? But Major Codman told me during our flight here that it was closed."

"Not quite. Von Kluge's replacement, Field Marshal Walter Model, is keeping it open with SS troops and his few remaining tanks. According to my G-2, some twenty to forty thousand soldiers are escaping as we speak. They're taking refuge beyond the Seine."

"So it is looking like an incomplete victory?"

"Or a partial failure, depending on how you want to look at it. At the moment, Bradley is blaming Montgomery."

"How so?"

"As ground commander until Ike took over on September 1, Monty should have made sure that our interarmy group boundaries were flexible. Friendly fire is a real problem, but it should never stop us from closing ranks with our allies to cut off a retreat and destroy an entire German field army. The bottom line is the gap *could* and *should* have been closed much earlier."

"I have to agree from the intelligence I've seen," said Weyland. "Despite having British divisions in reserve, Monty has not reinforced the Canadians sufficiently. Their current drive on Trun and Chambois is slow. Monty should have brought up veteran British divisions to take the lead, and both he and Crerar should have done more to light a fire under both the British and Canadians."

Koechlin-Schwartz nodded and looked at Patton. "Do you think you could have prevented the German escape had you not been ordered to stop at Argentan?"

"Absolutely—and history will prove me right!"

"Coming from my star pupil, I have no doubt," said the Frenchmen.

They regarded one another affectionately for a moment. Something about the exchange reminded Patton of the 1912 Summer Olympic Games in Stockholm. He had competed in the first of the five events in the inaugural modern pentathlon created by Baron Pierre de Coubertin: fencing, shooting, swimming, riding, and cross-country running. The competition was based upon the original pentathlon of ancient Greece that celebrated the skills of a soldier. Patton had not won a medal at the games—though he managed to finish fifth overall and first among the non-Swedish competitors—but the event had made a lasting impression on him for the great comradery that had developed between himself and the other participants.

Koechlin-Schwartz said, "It does appear Montgomery should have run his Canadians behind the Boche and trapped them in the pocket. From what I have heard, he pushed his main force up the middle, squeezing the Germans out of the pocket like toothpaste from a tube instead of destroying them."

Patton cut off a tender part of his French pepper steak, ate it, and gently daubed the remnants of brandy crème sauce from his mouth with his white linen napkin. "Yes, it goes without saying that Generals Eisenhower, Bradley, and I are all disgusted with the lack of urgency on the part of Monty in making his attack. But I'm just as mad at Ike and Brad for letting Monty dictate the terms of the Allied relationship. Monty's the real one running the show, you know."

"That's all true enough, George," said Weyland. "But whatever the flaws of the Falaise campaign, it hasn't exactly rung lemons. Like you said, we've killed or captured over a hundred thousand Krauts. Hell, they've already written off thousands of vehicles and artillery pieces as irreplaceable. Not only that, but German POWs are saying that Hitler may lack enough troops to man the Siegfried Line."

Patton nodded. "You're right, the numbers are good. But there's no need for excessive caution or complacency. We should be pushing across the Seine and onto the Rhine right now instead of sitting on our goddamn asses."

"I would still have to say that, all things considered, you have won a great victory," pointed out Koechlin-Schwartz. "The roads are literally littered with the corpses of the Fifth Panzer and Seventh Armies. To me, it looks like the Somme all over again. The carcasses of horses and humans lay thick as far as the eye can see, along with burned and abandoned equipment. You and General Weyland here have given the Boche a damned good whipping."

"I consider it poetic justice," said Patton, as Stiller and Meeks topped off their water glasses and the crackle of a pair of artillery rounds could be heard in the distance, like the rumbling of a storm.

"Under such conditions there are no supermen—all men become rabbits looking for a hole," said the Frenchman. "Having said that, I must say that this is an exceptionally fine wine."

"It's Châteauneuf-du-Pape. Only the best for my old friend and teacher."

"It is heavenly."

"One of my divisions overran a warehouse filled with it. The wine cases were carefully labeled *Verboten for sale, Reserved for Wehrmacht.* So I had my boys steal every goddamn bottle of the stuff."

"Well, George, if you have any spare cases you might want to give away," said Weyland, "I know my boys would be pleased as punch if you sent them some. It would sure buoy their spirits."

Patton pounded his fist on the table. "Why that is a damn fine idea, Opie! That's exactly what we're going to do!"

"Let's drink to it!"

Raising their glasses once again, they swiftly worked out a procedure. They decided that Weyland would dispatch twenty or thirty cases of wine to each of his air groups, as well to each of his supply and service units, with a note saying that such-and-such division or corps within Third Army was sending them wine with their compliments in appreciation for the help that the flyers had given them.

"My flyboys already *love* Third Army," said Weyland once they had worked it all out. "But now they're going to go *absolutely* bonkers over you bastards."

"As well they should," gushed Patton. "They're going to be drinking *beaucoup de vin* in the coming weeks. The Krauts have warehouses all over France."

"Do you think you can get us some captured Lugers and Iron Crosses as well?"

"You bet," said Patton. "Anything we've taken from the Krauts is fair game and will be delivered to the 29th Tactical Air Group."

"Now that's what I call close air-ground cooperation," said Koechlin-Schwartz.

"You're damn right," said Patton. "I love Opie here. The man can do no wrong. He takes care of my flanks and makes me feel invincible."

"Invincible? Now that is a powerful potion for a general. I must say that I wish my beloved France had possessed a similar elixir in 1940 when the Boche rampaged through our country in three weeks with their *blitzkrieg.*"

"Well, we're making those Hun bastards pay now, General. Plus interest!"

The gallant Frenchman's smile widened. "Yes, you most certainly are, my old friend. You most certainly are."

# CHAPTER 13



WITH HIS HEAVY BARRACKS BAG slung over his shoulder, William McBurney stood on the pier of New York Harbor, gawking at the ship that would take him and the other members of the 761st to the war for which they had trained to fight for two straight years now.

Though dwarfed by several of the seagoing vessels docked around her, the HMS *Esperance Bay* was still gargantuan. Constructed in London in 1922 as a passenger liner, the ship had been reoutfitted by the British Royal Navy on the outbreak of war and served a stint as an armed merchant cruiser before being converted to a troop transport in 1941. The bright cruise-line colors had been stripped away and painted a gunmetal gray. The vessel's crew knew its business too. They had crossed the Atlantic multiple times during the height of the German U-boat wolf pack attacks on merchant vessels and transports carrying combat-ready soldiers like McBurney.

"Ain't she a beauty," he said to his buddy Smitty standing next to him.

"I don't know. She looks old and worn out to me."

"Come on, man. That there is one hell of a ship."

"She's big enough, all right. But just wait until we step foot on her. It's going to be mighty cramped below them decks."

McBurney knew that was true. They had been forewarned that the quarters on the *Esperance Bay* would be extremely cramped, as were most troop transports sailing out of the harbor. Its original capacity as a passenger ship was 1,500, but as a transport it housed thousands more, packing the soldiers in like sardines.

"We'd better get on board," said McBurney. "We set sail in less than an hour."

They headed up to the gangplank, lugging their duffel bags over their shoulders. Lionel Hampton and his orchestra were on the pier as part of the USO, playing a final farewell to the thousands of troops boarding the ships of the large convoy. McBurney and Smitty smiled at one another when Hampton's band cut loose with one of their favorite tunes, *Flying Home*, as they stepped aboard the giant ship. Though they were eager to get to Europe, join the battle, and prove to Bates that they were worthy of his faith in them as combat soldiers, the song lent a bittersweet melancholy to the morning as they were leaving their homes and families behind.

Though the New York native McBurney had a father who had long worked the docks, he was not familiar with them himself, and he felt a sense of excitement and novelty boarding the vessel with his fellow tankers. Most of the members of the 761st had never set foot on a boat of any kind, let alone a British vessel that had previously served as a civilian passenger liner. Not only that, but few if any of the Panthers had ever crossed a body of water larger than a freshwater lake. With the Atlantic Ocean and the war looming over the horizon, McBurney could tell that many of those funneling up the gangplank with him were anxious and worried, knowing that they might never return to their sweethearts and families.

Once they boarded the ship, they were directed belowdecks to select a bunk.

McBurney quickly realized that he had underestimated how jam-packed and uncomfortable the living quarters would be on the journey. Like all military facilities at the time, the troop transports were segregated. The members of the 761st had been forced to ride in the back of Southern buses; now they were quartered near the crew in the hold at the bottom of the ship. White troops, by contrast, rode in the bow and midship areas, where the stomach-churning effects of the huge ocean swells would be felt to a much lesser degree.

The bunks were stacked four and five high, and each enlisted man was allotted a space approximately two feet wide, two feet high, and six feet long. Soldiers had to sleep in twelve-hour shifts and keep their barracks bags with them at all times, because they never knew if they'd be going back to the same bunk. McBurney chose a top swinging hammock on the port side next to a blacked-out porthole, which he had to climb a pegged pole to reach. His feet would have to hang over the end of his hammock since the men's sleeping spaces had to accommodate a soldier's 24-by-18-inch duffel containing all his personal gear.

They returned to the stern deck a few minutes before the HMS *Esperance Bay's* lines were pulled. At 1040 hours, she began steaming her way down the Hudson Channel with the other ships comprising the Allied convoy, heading towards the open Atlantic. It was a clear, hot summer morning and several hundred soldiers massed the deck to wave goodbye to loved ones and see the big ship cutting through the lapping waves of the channel. Soon the ship sounded its farewell whistle, entered the Upper Bay, and steamed past the Statue of Liberty. McBurney smiled to himself as the copper-green, adorned head grew larger and larger and then smaller and smaller before finally disappearing behind the shimmering New York skyline.

He looked around at the faces. The men were in high spirits. Few of them had traveled more than a hundred miles from their farms and city neighborhoods before they enlisted. Now here they were embarking on the greatest adventure not only of their lifetimes but also of the century.

When the ship passed through the narrow neck between Staten Island and Brooklyn, the ship began slicing through the compact, choppy waves of the Lower Bay, before turning due east and heading for the open sea south of Long Island. Escorted by several destroyers and a cruiser, the transports and tankers of the convoy strung out in combat formation across the sparkling blue water. The ships laden with troops and their equipment stretched as far as the eye could see, and would soon join a muscular convoy of hundreds of ships. McBurney found it an awesome sight: an armada of giant, gunmetal-gray vessels plowing through the wave-chopped sea; the sun hot and shimmering on the frothy wakes; the seagulls wheeling and shrieking overhead. He thought of his former girlfriend Sarah. She had written him a Dear John letter a while back ending their relationship, and as he stared out at the fleet of warships, he realized that it was probably for the best with him headed off to war.

From the starboard railing, he spotted a school of dolphins racing through the midnight blue water, swimming with astonishing speed. A dozen miracles of nature with bottle-nosed beaks and gray dorsal fins glinting in the sunlight. They moved alongside the vessel with disarming ease, leaping out of the water every so often, carefree smiles clinging to their snouts as if there was nothing they'd rather be doing than racing against a 14,000-ton ship-of-war. What McBurney liked most about them was their sense of freedom: they made the war seem far away.

"Just look at them," said Smitty. "Now aren't they the lucky ones."

"How's that?"

"They are free to do as they please and don't have to take orders from nobody."

McBurney nodded. "Yeah, they sure do look happy and free."

"Ain't nobody mistreating them, bossing them about, or telling them what to do. Why even the damn sharks don't mess with them."

They were making eleven knots now. McBurney liked the feel of the wind and summer sun on his face. He and Smith continued to watch the school of dolphins racing beside the boat and the flying fish scattering before her bow. Beyond the tip of Long Island, the eleven-mile-wide convoy began a zigzagging course to avoid the Nazi U-boats patrolling the North Atlantic shipping lanes.

"Before we set sail, I was talking with two of the British Navy boys," said McBurney, picking up the conversation again. "They told me the chance of us being attacked by a German U-boat during the crossing is real low."

"That's good," responded Smitty. "Because from what I saw below decks in our berthing area, if we were to be torpedoed by a Kraut sub, our whole battalion would be wiped out. It's so jam-packed down there, there's no way we're getting topside before she goes all the way to the bottom."

"I guess we'll just have to keep our fingers crossed. But at least now, we get a chance to fight."

"Personally, I'll believe it when I see it. But I have to admit I'm glad to be out of Texas. Between the rattlesnakes, Kraut POWs, townspeople, and our own MPs, I'm not sure I could have survived that viper's nest for another month."

"Me neither," agreed McBurney.

Like Smith and the other Black Panthers, he had shed no tears when he had departed a state that, like Louisiana before it, had been far from hospitable to colored soldiers. The 761st's advanced detachment had left Camp Hood August 1 for Camp Kilmer, New Jersey, while McBurney and the rest of the main body, some 700 men, had boarded a troop train the evening of August 9 bound for Camp Shanks, New York. Located twenty miles north of Manhattan on the west bank of the Hudson River in bucolic Orangeburg, Camp Shanks was one of the principal ports of embarkation for troops headed to the European Theater of Operations and "Last Stop, USA" for more than a million soldiers.

The cross-country journey to Camp Shanks took four days. During the journey, when McBurney complained to an MP about the lowering of the window shades, he was told brusquely that in some of the Southern towns through which they were traveling, people would shoot at cars containing black troops. Once he heard that, McBurney was even more relieved to be getting out of the South.

Camp Shanks proved to be strictly a staging area and was segregated, with women and blacks having their own designated areas separate from white male troops. At the camp, doctors performed final medical and dental checkups on McBurney and his fellow tankers to ensure fitness for combat. The men also received last-minute inoculations and immunizations, completed the paperwork for wills, watched training films about the enemy they soon would face, and waited for the arrangements for their transit overseas to be finalized. During his stay,

McBurney watched the Army's newsreels closely and was able to learn a few words of French and German that might help save his life or that of one of his comrades.

Throughout their time at Camp Shanks, Colonel Bates, the company commanders, and the platoon leaders ensured the men prepped their gear for the voyage. Bates insisted upon a tight hold on the reins: no joyriding, alcohol, or ladies were allowed on the base. The men made repairs, ridded themselves of unusable equipment, and received new items as needed. What lay on the other side of the Atlantic remained as unknown to Bates as it did to the men and he wanted to make sure they were ready to deploy overseas. Their final preparations stood as their primary mission, which was just fine with McBurney.

He was itching to fight the Germans.

At the same time, he found Camp Shanks a paradise compared to Camp Hood. The unit commanders tended to be liberal in handing out overnight passes, and he and his friend Preston McNeil spent time with friends and family in New York City with the Army's blessing. He also had time to take in a few picture shows. His buddy Leonard Smith, however, got into trouble for returning late to Camp Hood from a furlough, and as punishment was denied permission to leave the grounds. But Smitty and several others who were not given passes soon tested the perimeter fence and found a place where they could slip out undetected. Smith sneaked out almost every night, traveling to Queens to see his family and getting back before roll call at 0530 the next morning.

In the battalion's first week at Camp Shanks, McBurney and more than a dozen others took the bus across George Washington Bridge into Harlem, to the legendary Savoy Ballroom. The Savoy was host to all the greats of the swing era—Louis Armstrong, Count Basie, Lionel Hampton, Duke Ellington, and Ella Fitzgerald. McBurney, Smith, and their buddies drank and danced the night away on the ballroom's vast 50-by-250-foot hardwood dance floor with young working women who had the night off from their domestic duties. When one orchestra took a break, a second would take over, allowing for uninterrupted dancing. Whereas Smith, McBurney, and McNeil had been to the Savoy before they joined the service, some of the men from small towns had never seen anything like it. They were dazzled by the red and blue spotlights, the mirrors and chandeliers, and the hundreds of people pressed together and jitterbugging the night away.

After two weeks at Camp Shanks, the 761st was put on "Alert" status on August 27, which meant they would be shipping out within the next twelve hours. Numbers were chalked on their helmets, giving them the order in which they were to march to and board the transport train. Their Black Panther armored unit patches were removed from the shoulders of their uniforms to ensure that enemy spies could not track troop movements. When asked where they were going, Captain Ivan Harrison told the men cryptically, "You'll know when you get there."

McBurney continued to peer over the starboard railing. Staring out at the vast expanse of ocean, he couldn't help but have mixed feelings. After two grueling years of combat training, he was excited to finally be heading across the Atlantic. But it struck him as ironic that he and his fellow Negro tankers were about to cross the same ocean their African ancestors had crossed in chains; and that, in taking part in the struggle against Nazism, they were about to fight a war in the name of freedoms neither the men of the 761st nor their forbearers had ever enjoyed. He and his fellow tankers were on their way to join the "Big Show" and fight a war for a country that, over the course of the past three hundred years, had either actively promoted the slave trade or done everything in its power to keep the black man down.

And yet, they were still jacked up to fight.

The trans-Atlantic voyage would take McBurney and the other members of the 761st twelve days to reach its destination of Avonmouth, England, a small port town near Bristol. Wind, rain, fog, and choppy seas were their reliable companions once they were out of the Gulf Stream. Most of the time they spent belowdecks in their quarters next to the crewmembers at the bottom of the boat, and only a minority of the men ventured up to look around. They read, played cards, and shot dice, often with the crew, career merchant mariners who had enlisted en masse when the war broke out. There was always a crap shoot or poker game under way somewhere on a spread blanket, while MPs patrolled the decks to maintain order and break up the occasional scrap.

Throughout the voyage, the Black Panthers were on their best behavior. They got along so well with the crew that Captain Peter Jacoby, the transport commander, took the unusual step of giving Colonel Bates a letter of commendation before the ship reached port. The letter complimented the 761st for its discipline, military courtesy, soldierly conduct, and high morale. He signed off his report by saying, "My staff and I wish you Godspeed in your future missions, and the best of luck and success to final victory."

The food aboard the converted freighter was terrible. White officers not attached to the 761st had tucked away most of the edible rations and gave the battalion the leftover garbage. The bread they cooked on the ship was half raw, and when McBurney bit into a slice, he thought he was eating dough. He dealt with the ration situation in his own way. Unable to eat the horrible army food, he and McNeil broke into the PX late at night, made off with several boxes of candy, and ended up living on Baby Ruths, Mary Janes, and M&Ms during the twelve-day crossing. Many of the men, however, could not have cared less about chow. At least half the troops at any given time were seasick and busy throwing up over the gunnels into the sea. Leonard Smith ate next to nothing, as he became seasick from the moment the ship rounded Long Island and transitioned from the calm waters of the sound to the rolling swells of the open ocean.

When the ship reached port at Avonmouth, England, on September 8, 1944 and McBurney gathered up his gear and prepared to debark, he had no idea what lay ahead for him. Like the other 675 enlisted men considered well-trained, disciplined, and ready for combat, he knew that the war in Europe would not be like it was portrayed in the moving pictures. And yet, he still clung to the romantic notion that it would be a heroic affair. He would perform daring deeds in the service of his country to destroy Hitler and Nazism. At twenty years of age, he felt invincible and, despite all his training, he still had no idea what the war would truly entail.

But he knew he would soon find out.

# CHAPTER 14

## BRAUNSFELD, WEST COLOGNE

### SEPTEMBER 4, 1944

ANGELA LAY next to Barthel Schröder on the bed, tingling as their naked bodies touched. A pair of bombs had gone off a few blocks away, but the air was quiet now. Indeed, it was so peaceful that it seemed to her as if the war didn't exist at all. When she was alone with Barthel, she sometimes felt as if it had never existed and there was only love and beauty in the world instead of endless Allied terror from the skies, Nazi treachery, and death on both sides.

She moved her body so that she was astride him. Their lips touched softly. She felt desire flowing through her veins, and her head swam with euphoria.

"Oh, Barthel," she whispered in his ear.

They rolled over so that she was on top then they changed positions again and his tongue reached inside her mouth, softly, and she kissed him back. He began stroking her hair and rubbing against her. She felt a delightful shudder of excitement take hold of her entire body, but it was the emotional connection that truly gripped her. She knew she was tapping into something sacrosanct, something only true lovers felt, a sense of profound intimacy.

She would remember this moment.

It was the first time for them both and she wondered if Barthel was as nervous as she. He was a sweet boy—tough but gentle and caring—and their courtship the past two months had been one new romantic adventure after another. But now, for the first time, they would share the pleasure of each other's young bodies.

She kissed his mouth, nibbling his lips gently. A moment later, when he climbed back on top and entered her, it was like a perfect dream.

Everything about it felt right, natural.

As they began to move together in a gentle rhythm, she took more and more pleasure in his body, in his kisses and caresses and thrusts.

Her body was responding with a passion she didn't know she possessed.

She moved with him in a gentle rhythm. His hands squeezed her swelling nipples, and she gasped with delight.

She wondered if it were possible to go insane with pleasure.

He kissed her on the lips tenderly and she slid her tongue deep into his mouth, clasping his tight buttocks and pulling him deeper inside her. She moaned softly between kisses; she could tell the sound of her voice excited him all the more.

As the pace quickened, the air filled with desperation. She felt herself letting loose with excitement. She sensed that he too was about to let go of his seed.

"Look into my eyes," she gasped, pulling him still deeper.

He pulled his head up and his eyes locked onto hers. "I'm looking, I'm looking!"

She stared at him mesmerically, her eyes as wide as pebbles as the climax came. They held each other's gaze as their bodies shook fitfully and she felt his warmth flowing inside her. Then suddenly tears streamed from her eyes.

"Are you all right?" he asked, worriedly. "Did I hurt you?"

"No," she cried.

"Are you upset? What...what happened?"

"I'm overwhelmed. I'm overwhelmed with joy."

"I am too, Angela, because I am in love with you. I love you and don't want to die. I want us to be like this forever."

"Die? Why do you talk of dying?"

"The war, I guess. Thousands of people are dying every day."

"Don't talk about dying. We can be together for as long as we like."

"I know that, but there is still the war."

"We can't control that. But you still must not talk of dying. It is bad luck, and I love you and don't want anything to happen to you."

His eyes lit up. "You really love me? I thought it was maybe just me."

"No, it is not just you. I love you more and more each and every day we are together in this terrible war. That's why you must not talk of—"

She stopped right there as she heard a sound at the front door: the jingle of a set of keys followed by the scrape of a key being inserted into the lock.

They looked at one another with surprise.

"Oh dear, it must be my father!"

"But I thought he wasn't supposed to be back for another hour or two!"

"He's commander of the flak battalion—he works only part time and his schedule is never the same. Hurry, get your clothes back on!"

They leapt from the bed and began throwing on their clothes. "Damn, we're in for it now! He's going to kill us!" said Barthel fretfully.

"Not if we hurry! Now get your clothes on!"

She jerked on her blouse as he wrestled to squeeze into his trousers. "I'm hurrying, I'm hurrying. But what are we going to tell him? I mean, he hates me and won't believe anything we have to say."

"He doesn't hate you. He's just trying to protect—"

"Angela, are you home?"

Her father's voice was urgent and she felt her heart skip a beat. "*Scheisse*, we have to hurry!" she whispered as she threw on her shoes. "Yes, Papa, I'm coming!" she then called out towards the living room.

Schröder made an effort to comb back his tangled and messy hair with his hands. "What do we say?"

"I'll talk to him. You step into the bathroom. Quickly now!"

After pushing him down the hallway towards the lavatory, she walked hurriedly down the corridor to the living room, where she saw her father. He was dressed in his Wehrmacht uniform with his Iron Cross, First Class at his throat and the right arm of his jacket where his arm would have been dangling like a wilted flower. He looked at her crossly.

"Angela, what is going on?"

"Nothing."

"Nothing? Who were you talking to then? I heard voices."

"Oh, that was just Barthel. He's in the bathroom."

"I thought I told you not to see *that* boy."

"You did, but I happen to be quite fond of him."

His eyes narrowed on her disapprovingly. "Tell me you two were not having sex together in my house? Under my roof?"

She pretended to be shocked. "No, of course we weren't having sex—we are only sixteen. I can't believe you would say that. I was showing him Arne's toy soldier collection. I thought he would rather enjoy seeing it."

Her father's face saddened at the mention of his deceased son's name, and Angela felt badly for him, but then his skepticism returned. His gaze lingered on her suspiciously for several seconds before he appeared satisfied that she was telling the truth. He motioned her to sit down on the threadbare couch. He then took a seat in an upholstered leather side chair, groaning in pain from his many war wounds.

He appeared tired and agitated and took a moment to collect himself. "There's something I need to tell you—actually, the both of you," he said. "I've just been to see the Gestapo." At that moment, Schröder entered the room, hands in his pockets and looking a touch guilty. Her father's eyes bore through him like a knife. "Sit down, young man," he commanded him.

The Edelweiss Pirate hesitated. "Is there something wrong, Colonel Lange?"

"I said sit down, Bartholomäus. You need to hear this."

Angela could see the suppressed defiance on her boyfriend's face as he sat down next to her on the couch with his edelweiss flower pinned to his jacket. The sight of the resistance badge of honor and symbol of peace and protest against the Reich filled her with pride. Her father looked at them both sternly.

"As I said, I've just been to the Gestapo. I pretended I was there to lodge a complaint about the increased looting in the city, but was really there to gather information. I did it because I am worried about what is going to happen to us with the Allies already on our western border and driving closer every day. The SS is going to be ruthless against those they believe lend aid to the enemy or are opponents of the regime. That's why this crowd you two are running around with is—"

She cut him off abruptly. "As I've told you before, I can handle myself."

"You may think you can, but we are all powerless when it comes to the Gestapo." His eyes narrowed on the both of them. "Were you two aware that the Edelweiss Pirates are specifically wanted by the authorities? They no longer look upon your youth gang as a minor irritant. They are going to crack down on and make an example of you. This, of course, means they're going to do a lot more than just shave your heads, ship you to the front for work details on the Westwall, or stuff you into a reeducation camp. I'm telling you they will arrest you and hang you from the gallows if you continue what you're doing."

She looked at Schröder, whose eyes were fixed intently on her father. He had turned a shade paler.

"In fact," continued her father, "the Gestapo is said to be preparing for a sweep of the city to arrest undesirables as we speak. They are looking specifically for members of the Cologne Navajos, who they say have been hiding escaped foreign workers and army deserters. The Navajos, isn't that what you two are calling yourselves these days?"

Schröder didn't answer. Instead, he said defiantly, "The Nazis are liars and murderers. They should be put out of existence and—"

Her father cut him off, motioning fiercely with his good arm. "I can't believe I'm listening to such rubbish. Your little club is no match for the Gestapo, I can tell you that, young man. Now shut your mouth and listen—or I will turn you in at El-De Haus myself. Do you understand me?"

Now Schröder's eyes narrowed combatively. He leaned forward in his seat and started to protest, but Angela warned him that would not be a good idea and he sat back resignedly on the couch. Her father waited a moment for him to simmer down before launching into his speech.

"A few days ago, a gang that included a fugitive from the Köln-Deutz work reeducation camp and an army deserter broke into the cellar of a grocery store in Riehl. They stole eighty pounds of butter, along with a sack of sugar, and several wheels of cheese. The value of the loot is estimated at nearly five thousand Reichsmarks. Needless to say, the police have committed much of their resources to hunting down the guilty parties. They are calling the gang the *Ehrenfeld Gruppe*. When the perpetrators are caught, they will no doubt be executed, without trial, or sent to labor camps." He paused with a raised eyebrow. "You two wouldn't know anything about this criminal gang, would you?"

In the uncomfortable silence that followed, Angela glanced furtively at her boyfriend. Though she had not taken part in the robbery, Barthel had, and he had told her all about it. The leader of the gang was Hans Steinbrück, who had intervened to help her and her Edelweiss Pirate friends three weeks earlier in the attack on the Hitler Youth. The streetwise, twenty-three-year-old Düsseldorfian was a former bomb disposer and forced laborer who had escaped from the city's SS construction brigade a year earlier. In the past few weeks, Bomber Hans had formed a group comprised of German army deserters, Jews, war refugees, and other enemies of the state. The Ehrenfeld Group, as it was called by the Gestapo, frequently associated with the Edelweiss Pirates and other teenagers who had deserted from their posts building up the Westwall at the front, as well as fugitive foreign workers, including Russians, Ukrainians, and Poles. Since the robbery, Steinbrück had been fencing the stolen butter and other loot on Cologne's thriving black market. The sale of the butter alone had supposedly netted the gang over a thousand Reichsmarks so far, most of which Steinbrück and the army deserters seemed to be gambling away or spending on cigarettes and alcohol.

"Well, what do you have to say for yourselves?" demanded her father. "Do you two associate with this criminal gang or not?"

"No, of course not," said Angela, rolling her eyes as if such a thing were impossible. "But we have heard of them," she conceded. "Everyone has."

"I advise you to stay as far away from them as possible. They will do nothing but get you both killed."

Angela suspected her father was right. From what she had seen of the Steinbrück gang, they were far closer to armed robbers than resistance fighters, as were many of the gangs in Cologne now that the city was in ruins, food supplies were dwindling, work hours were getting longer, and the Allies were knocking on Germany's doorstep. Guns and butter were now the new coin of the realm in a world where gas, power, and telephone lines were often cut off and motorized transportation through the city was severely limited for days, and sometimes weeks, following Allied bombing attacks.

An important factor in the rise of gang activity was the growing number of weapons inside the city from retreating Wehrmacht units. Soldiers, especially deserters needing a swift infusion of cash or supplies, often sold their weapons and other equipment to civilians. Thieves like Steinbrück also stole guns and hand grenades from army supply depots, unguarded vehicles, and drunken soldiers. They often resold these weapons, with pistols alone fetching as much as a thousand Reichsmarks. Unsurprisingly, along with the weapons came a spike in violence, as gang members panicked and shot their victims during robberies or fought back against the security forces. Many of the city's law-abiding citizens had also recently begun to carry weapons for protection, increasing the risk of deadly encounters.

Most of the Queen City's criminal activity took place in the Edelweiss Pirates' home base of Ehrenfeld, now commonly referred to by the Gestapo as *Räuberfeld*—Robber Field—because of its notoriously high crime rate. But other sections of Cologne also appeared to be slipping into increasing chaos and violence. With so many people forced to go underground, the Allies approaching, and the understaffed Gestapo and other security forces struggling to maintain law and order, the city had turned into an increasingly volatile, ungovernable, and ruined wasteland.

"Who did you speak to at the Gestapo?" Schröder asked her father.

"Dr. Max Hoffmann, the commander of the department."

The boy's eyebrows flew up. "You spoke to Hoffmann?"

"I also spoke to Criminal Commissioner Ferdinand Kütter." He wrinkled his nose. "A most dangerous fellow."

Angela, too, was stunned at her father's ability to access such high officials in the Nazi hierarchy. But then again, he was a Wehrmacht colonel, decorated war hero, and commander of the Cologne air defense system so it shouldn't have come as a surprise. All the same, she didn't like that he was communicating with the likes of Hoffmann and Kütter. *Kriminaldirektor* Hoffmann and many of the SS officers on his staff were reputed to be coldblooded butchers, who had been transferred from the Eastern Front that her father and his more tempered Regular Army officers chillingly referred to as the "Bloodlands."

"Hoffmann and Kütter? But why would you speak to them at all, Papa?"

"I told you why—to get information—and believe me, I got plenty of it. They are on a mission."

"A mission? What kind of mission?"

"*Bandenkampf*. They want to secure the Rhineland from all forms of banditry and opposition to the regime. They want to eliminate all *Volksfeinde*, not just you and your Edelweiss Pirates. They want to root out every last Communist, Jew, army deserter, and escaped foreign laborer along with every supposed defeatist, criminal, and antisocial element in the city."

He paused a moment to let his words sink in.

"They came from the East—that is why they are so brutal," he continued. "Hoffmann and many of the other Rhineland security officers are veterans of anti-partisan operations in Poland and Ukraine. They have been weaned on *Bandensicherungsaufgaben*. It is like a mother's milk to them. *Bandenkampf* is their way to justify the murder of civilians in the name of protecting the Reich from so-called partisans, escaped foreign workers, and defeatists. They equate our Western home front with the lawless and violent Russian Front they encountered while stationed abroad in the occupied territories. As the Allies get closer and the war becomes more desperate, they will be lining up war-weary German citizens and shooting them down as if they are enemies of the state. Just watch, that's what will happen. Soon Germans will be shooting Germans on a scale we have not yet seen."

They fell into silence. Angela knew that her father wasn't exaggerating. But at the same time, she also knew that Gestapo officers were not as powerful as most people thought they were. Contrary to what many believed, the Gestapo did not have the authority to simply arrest German civilians and ship them off to labor or concentration camps; they had to have clear and irrefutable evidence of criminal activity and follow regimented policies and procedures, in order to preserve the loyalty of the *Volk*. The reality was that most cases ended up being dismissed, with no charge, or a surprisingly lenient punishment. The harshest forms of treatment were focused on those regarded by the Gestapo as key political, religious, or racial opponents: Communists, Jews, Jehovah's Witnesses, saboteurs, members of resistance movements, enemy agents, asocials, stockpilers of stolen goods, and Russian, Polish, Ukrainian, and Italian workers who left their job sites or refused to work. Except for these targeted groups, releases from custody at the end of investigations were the norm, not the exception for most German citizens.

At the same time, Hitler's secret police was not comprised of ordinary, reasonable men. Members of the Gestapo were almost invariably zealous Nazis, fanatical anti-Communists and anti-Semites, and violence-prone true believers who had volunteered for the security services and enjoyed wielding power over others. Angela had heard the horror stories from prisoners that had managed to survive Brauweiler Prison and El-De Haus. Gestapo officers like Hoffmann and Kütter, as well as the men that served under them, often skirted the law and relied on torture to extract confessions against those they suspected as being dangerous enemies of the state. They did not simply follow orders; they decided who would live and who would die. They tortured and murdered with surprising regularity, and were unrepentant, according to those that had managed to escape or be released.

The Gestapo performed its duties not through indiscriminate terror but by methodically singling out particular groups of victims and going after them with a pretense of legality. The flip side of the Gestapo's policy was that nontargeted Germans were for the most part left alone. Angela knew that most of her countrymen didn't fear the Gestapo, or even know anybody who had had a run-in with the state Secret Police—and not because laws weren't being broken. Low-level defiance was extremely common: people told Hitler jokes, they listened to BBC broadcasts, they read Allied propaganda leaflets without turning them in, and they listened and danced to decadent American Negro Jazz music. But the Gestapo looked the other way when petty crimes were being committed, just as ordinary Germans looked the other way when Jews were being rounded up and murdered. Angela knew that her own people had abetted Himmler and his SS in the killing of the Jews not through active collaboration but through passivity, denial, and indifference.

And it sickened her.

"The Nazis have destroyed Germany and rotted it from within," said Schröder, resuming the discussion. "Everything we see around us is on them. Hitler, Himmler, and the other monsters have created this nightmare for all Germans."

Her father shot him a glare. "I know you are a smart boy, but I don't particularly want to hear your political views."

"Boy?"

"Yes, that's what you are, a mere boy. You are, after all, sixteen years old—the same age as my daughter."

"I am almost seventeen, and there's more to a man than one's age. I know how to survive on the streets."

"That may be, but for how long?"

"Papa, you can't talk to him like—"

"I can talk to him any damn way I please. He thinks he's a bloody Navajo Indian for heaven's sake."

"I do not," protested Schröder. "It's just the name of our group. We happen to admire the American Indians and their warrior culture."

"Yes well, who doesn't? You're not the only one who has read Karl May," said her father, referring to the late nineteenth-century German writer of American Westerns. May was widely known in Germany for recounting, with a great deal of artistic embellishment, the adventurous exploits of noble chief Winnetou, leader of the Mescalero Apaches, and his scouting partner, blood brother, and loyal friend Old Shatterhand.

"I always loved those stories," said Schröder. "But one day I stopped enjoying them when I learned our so-called 'Führer' considers May his favorite author. He apparently worshipped the damned books growing up as a boy in Austria."

"As I said, I don't really want to hear your political views. What I want to know is whether you are going to bring harm to my daughter—inadvertently or not."

"I care deeply about your daughter. I would never bring harm to her."

"Not willingly perhaps, but you still strike me as dangerous…in these times especially. I'm sorry, Bartholomäus, but I don't think it's a good idea for you to come around here anymore."

Angela was up and on her feet. "But we're in love, Papa. Were you not in love with Mother when you were young? And with pretty Marie Bomblies before her?"

Her father shot her and Schröder a glare. "Don't speak as if you know anything about love. You two are but teenagers."

"That may be true, but I am still old enough to decide who I shall spend my time with." She motioned Schröder from the couch; quick to react, he was up and on his feet like a spry cat.

He bowed formally. "I thank you, Colonel, for sharing your wisdom and advice. And I promise to take care of Angela in these troubled times."

Her father gave a sarcastic roll of the eyes. "Oh, that makes me feel so much better." He wagged a finger at him. "I know I can't stop you two from seeing each other. But just so we're clear, if anything happens to my daughter, it won't be the Gestapo that hangs you from a meat hook—it will be me. Do you understand?"

"Yes, Colonel. I figured that part out when I first stepped into the room."

# CHAPTER 15



AS HANS STEINBRÜCK stepped forward to address his audience, Angela couldn't help but feel like a spy on a covert mission. In the presence of the charismatic former star of the Cologne bomb-clearing detail, she felt a thrill of excitement, an intoxicating element of danger. But she also feared that soon she would be in trouble with the Gestapo due to her newfound association with this wanted criminal and his subversive gang.

She stood next to Schröder and Jean Hüber along with a small group of military deserters, escaped foreign workers, German Jews, and other fugitives at the Ehrenfeld Group's hideout in the basement of a destroyed building. For security purposes, she was only known to Steinbrück and the other members of his *Ehrenfeld Gruppe* by her code name, Mucki. Located at Schönsteinstrasse Number 7 through 13 across the street from the Ehrenfeld train station, the gang's refuge consisted of a labyrinth of interconnected cellars that the members had created by knocking holes in the walls and tunneling into the adjoining rooms.

The Ehrenfeld Group was flush with Reichsmarks from the spate of recent robberies, and tucked inside the basement were stockpiles of stolen goods. The pilfered supplies included butter, margarine, liquor, meat, sugar, cheese, and chocolate as well as an abundance of military equipment, including Wehrmacht uniforms, boots, steel helmets, rifles, hand grenades, thousands of rounds of ammunition, a German *Maschinenpistole* 40 light submachine gun, and an American machine gun—all of which sold for high prices on the city's black market. If the Nazi authorities ever discovered the hideaway, Angela knew, they would arrest everyone present and hang them all. Looking at all the stolen goods, she couldn't help but feel it was just a matter of time before the Gestapo sniffed out the hideaway tucked away in the Ehrenfeld rubble.

Most of those present in the basement, she knew, didn't have ration cards and would be arrested if they were caught on the street by the authorities. Securing food and clothing in Cologne was exceedingly dangerous, but it was obvious to her that Steinbrück's gang had fared well in stockpiling not only basic necessities but luxury items like butter, cigarettes, and alcohol. In the past two months, the black market had grown in the city and even ordinary citizens pretended that food or goods had been stolen so they could get more rations or sell the items more expensively on the black market. Grocers would blame the crimes on the Edelweiss Pirates, since the Nazi propaganda said they were criminals. In Angela's estimation, a quarter of the people remaining in the city appeared to be engaged in something illegal in order to survive. And the situation was growing increasingly desperate every day the war dragged on.

There were two members of another youth resistance group present that had joined forces with the Ehrenfeld Group. Calling themselves the Committee for a Free Germany, they had recently begun putting up posters at prominent landmarks and high-traffic areas throughout the ruined city, encouraging soldiers to desert from the front by proclaiming, "We don't want a blood bath on German soil! We don't want the total destruction of our homeland! We don't want any more terror bombings! We want peace! We want freedom!" She had learned that, far from being a potent opposition force, the Committee for a Free Germany was in fact the work of a dozen of the city's residents rather than a large group of professional revolutionaries. But they were quite serious and dedicated.

The Committee, formed in the Klettenberg district in the southwestern outskirts of Cologne in late 1943, was composed of former members of Leftist political parties, along with a Jehovah Witness and several frustrated youths. They had not yet carried out resistance attacks, but rather spent much of their time posting flyers and meeting in private homes to discuss the future of Germany after the regime's defeat. Still, they represented another youth group disillusioned with the Nazis and willing to take direct action against them. Anticipating the quick arrival of the Allies who were now pressing eastward into northwestern France and Belgium, they had recently taken the bold step of reaching out to the Steinbrück gang and several groups of fugitive foreign workers to organize armed resistance. Angela had been told that the two youngest members of the Committee, who had escaped from the SS construction brigade based in the city, knew Steinbrück and were trying to recruit him to provide weapons for the workers.

She returned her gaze to Steinbrück. He was lean and sinewy, handsome and captivating—but what was most important about him was that he was utterly dangerous to the Reich. He was a daredevil who had already lived a risky and colorful life as a merchant seaman and bomb-defuser, but more than anything else he was a jack-of-all-trades. He could do seemingly anything: bricklaying, plumbing, electrical work, fixing cars—and now he was a professional thief, unlikely resistance fighter, and "antisocial element" who absolutely refused to fit into the order of the *Volksgemeinschaft*—Hitler's fanciful notion of a national community committed to war at all costs. That's precisely what gave him his charisma in Angela's eyes.

All the same, he was a dangerous man for her and the other Edelweiss Pirates to be running around with, given his criminal background. At twenty-three, he was several years older than any of the Navajos, and they tended to look upon him as a big brother and father figure. They were awed by his colorful stories of defusing dangerous bombs and his worldly travels as a sailor. Most of the Pirates were mere adolescent boys whose fathers were dead, had abandoned their families, or been killed in the war, and they were desperate to have authority figures they actually respected in their lives. They were already dead-set against the Nazis, and Angela knew they would be willing to take grave risks to do what the charismatic Bomber Hans suggested.

"We can do more, comrades," he began, surveying his audience with his piercing, azure-blue eyes. "In fact, if we want to take back the streets of this city, we will *have* to do more."

"What is there to take back?" asked Jean Hüber, looking around the room at the others. "The Allies have reduced our fair city to rubble."

"I'll tell you what there is to take back: our pride. The more we take from the Secret State Police, Party members, and their collaborators, the more we take back what has been lost and reclaim Germany for our own. They can call us thieves, but we all know what we really are: resistance fighters. Which means that we are on our own and have to look out for ourselves."

"What would you have us do?" asked Schröder. "We cannot fight the SS on anything close to equal terms. They will annihilate us. I am told that Hoffmann and Kütter already have a bounty out for the recent butter heist."

"There is too much crime in the city for the good Dr. Hoffmann and Herr Kütter to track everyone. That's why they still don't know *who* we are."

"Not yet maybe, but they will soon enough," said Hüber. "The Gestapo may be wrongheaded, but they are not stupid."

"Yes, we have to be careful. But now is the time to strike out. We have to steal as much as possible and get what we can for it while there is confusion and disorder."

"Or we could just wait until the Allies arrive," said a Wehrmacht deserter with a scar on his face dressed in a dirty *feldgrau* uniform. He took a swig from a bottle of Schnapps. "The Americans and British are closing in on the border as we speak."

"Be careful what you wish for, my friend. I doubt they will treat us any better than the Nazis," sniffed Bomber Hans. "They will consider us criminals hiding out in the rubble of Robber Field and stuff us into one of their POW camps. That's why we have to take matters into our own hands."

"The British might do that—but the Americans won't treat us that way," said Schröder. "They just need to know that we are fighting against Nazism. They will understand."

Angela wasn't so optimistic. When the war ended, Germany was likely to be paralyzed in a state of poverty and chaos for years, and the Allied occupiers would be bogged down in endless bureaucratic entanglements. Already the war had reduced the Rhineland to a state in crisis. Looting, robbery, black marketeering, and desertion were now commonplace, belying the Nazi propaganda's much-touted myth of a unified *Volk* selflessly sacrificing for the Fatherland's survival. By the end of the war, Angela knew, the situation was bound to be even worse.

She also recognized that at this late stage of the conflict, all most German civilians wanted was to survive and have their lives return to normal. They didn't care about *Volkskrieg*—the People's War; that was a fantasy of Hitler and his minions. The regime was naïve in believing that every person, regardless of age or sex, would fanatically resist the invasion, turning every German heart and every German house into a fortress, when in fact most people just wanted the war to end. Especially those living in the heavily bombed western portion of the country. The denizens of the Rhineland didn't care about putting up a determined fight along the border to halt the British and American advance into the Reich. They wanted stability and an end to the madness.

In fact, the high number of arrests in Cologne in recent weeks revealed that many Rhinelanders were flat-out refusing to do their part for Hitler's war. Hundreds of teenagers were leaving their work camps at the front daily and older men were openly rebuffing the Führer's call to join militia units. While the failure of citizens to report for labor and militia service vexed the authorities, they viewed the widespread crime taking place in the region as the most serious threat to the war effort. Cologne served as the important transportation hub linking the front with the interior of Germany, and the Gestapo was going to great lengths to ensure that an unruly and defeatist civilian population did not put the region at greater risk.

"I say we take the fight to the Nazis by taking out Party officials and security officers," proposed Steinbrück. "There are no longer enough of them to properly patrol the city, and now is the time to strike. It is true, we cannot take on the SS, but we can make hit and run attacks on individuals or small groups of the regime's loyalists."

"He's right—we have to fight back," said one of the young men from the Committee for a Free Germany.

"*Da*, this we must do," agreed a big, heavily bearded Russian forced laborer who spoke German. "We take it to the bastards!"

There were rumbles of support from a handful of the Navajos, several army deserters and forced foreign workers, and the two Committee members, but most of the audience stood there in silence, unprepared for such drastic measures. Angela had no problem distributing Allied propaganda leaflets, harassing Hitler Youth, hiding Jews, or supporting Allied airmen, German Army deserters, and foreigners, but she wanted no part of killing her countrymen, even if they were rabid Nazis who deserved to die. That was where she drew the line.

She noticed that the three Jews had been quiet and not said anything thus far during the meeting. With the Allies fast approaching, the city descending further and further into lawlessness, and the Gestapo becoming more violent with every passing day, they probably just wanted to lay low and wait for the arrival of the Westerners. But they didn't say anything to make their views known, probably not wanting to make waves when their long-awaited liberation was so close. She didn't know the Jewish contingent very well, but had learned their names. Ruth Kramer was two years older than her and half-Jewish, and she lived here at Schönstein Street No. 7 with her mother, Friedel, and a Jewish man named Paul Urbat. By a rare stroke of luck, they had managed to avoid deportation and inhabited the apartment above the basement with Steinbrück's pregnant girlfriend, Cäcilie "Cilly" Serve, a sweet and kindly young woman with a big heart who seemed to keep the risk-taking Bomber Hans somewhat in line.

Wanting to say something, Angela stepped forward to make her thoughts known. "If you start killing people, Hoffmann is going to order his pit bulls to search every nook and cranny in Robber Field. They'll arrest everyone they come across that they don't like, regardless of guilt or innocence. Everyone in this room will likely be arrested and strung from the gallows."

"No, the security forces are spread too thin and the Allies will be here by then," said the Wehrmacht deserter with the scar, taking another big swig from his bottle.

"I want no part of any killing," said Schröder.

"Me neither," agreed Jean Hüber.

"The boys are right. It is crazy to go after public officials," said Cäcilie Serve, speaking for the first time. She touched her bulging belly. "We must look to the future and lay low to survive. As you say, the Americans and British will be here soon and the war will be over for us, even if it continues to the east. Why stir up a hornet's nest and fight a battle you cannot win when the Allies are knocking on the door? We will be free in a month or two."

At the sight of his girlfriend rubbing her belly, pregnant with his unborn child, Bomber Hans's expression softened. "Cilly is right, it would be safer to wait out the Americans and British. But speaking for myself, I cannot stand by and do nothing. I want the war to end as quickly as possible, to the detriment of Germany. After all, that's why we have created this weapons' warehouse you see around you. So that we, too, can take part in the fight to defeat Nazism. It is a worthy goal."

"So what are you proposing?" asked Angela.

"I agree that maybe it is not a good idea to go Nazi hunting, at least not yet. But we need to continue to seize whatever foodstuffs and weapons we can so that when the Allies are near, we stand poised to blow up the important factories and railway facilities. We have to put our stamp on this war and let the world know that not all Germans were monsters like Hitler." He shifted his gaze to the Ukrainians, Poles, and Russians. "And as to our foreign friends, well, they get a bit of payback to their oppressors. What do you say, comrades, are you with me?"

"*Da*, we are with you," said the big Russian as several other foreigners nodded solemnly and murmured their approval.

"What we have before us is a war of ideas," continued Steinbrück with surprising sincerity, considering he, at times, seemed little more than a clever thief and greedy opportunist. "A war over culture and core values, humanity and freedom versus Nazism. In the past few weeks, the opening shot in our war for freedom was fired. Now it is time for us to form into battle lines and rise up against the enemy, even if we continue to do so quietly behind the scenes. I know we will not let each other down. For we are—all of us—true patriots to the notion of freedom."

The words hung there, giving a quiet urgency, a sense of history being made. Standing framed before a backdrop of stolen food and weapons, Bomber Hans looked like a larger-than-life statue. Taking in the resolute faces all around her, Angela felt a powerful sense of fellowship, even with the foreigners. She was still fearful of what might happen to her and the others if the Gestapo ever caught up with them, but at this epic moment in history, the little voice in her head seemed irrelevant. They were coming together as one to defy Hitler and his brutal regime— even if only in a small way—and that was what was most important.

"What we do," added Bomber Hans, "we do for the love of our homelands and in the name of freedom. And freedom does not come without a price."

"No, it doesn't," concurred Schröder, his voice ignited with quiet passion, the edelweiss flower pinned to his lapel sparkling in the light from the suspended bulb. "That's why we have to make a difference. That's why we have to take the fight to the Nazis who have poisoned our country and destroyed Europe. And we have to do it now!"

In that moment she would remember for the rest of her life, Angela was certain she was in love with Bartholomäus Schröder. And she was very proud of him.

# CHAPTER 16

**VERDUN, NORTHEASTERN FRANCE**

**SEPTEMBER 15, 1944**

THOUGH PATTON liked the feel of the breeze on his face as he sped past the small village of Belrupt-en-Verdunois, he was still in a foul mood. With Mims behind the wheel of the WC57 Dodge command car, Patton rode shotgun with his dog Willie on his lap and Lone Star State aide Al Stiller sitting in the back seat. He was in a cantankerous mood because his Third Army—through no fault of his own—had advanced less than fifty miles since the end of August.

His lightning-fast drive across France towards the Rhine had been halted near the Saar Basin in northeast France—not by stout German resistance but, once again, by Ike and the Allied high command. The stunning success of the Third Army's breakout from Normandy had created a logistical nightmare: the Allies had advanced to positions American and British planners had not expected them to reach until May 1945 and there was not enough fuel, supplies, or transportation infrastructure to keep both Bradley's Twelfth Army Group and Montgomery's Twenty-First Army Group in motion. At this stage of the war, the U.S. was accounting for over two-thirds of the men and matériel in the ETO and the British were providing less than one-third, including the Commonwealth troops from Great Britain's overstretched and dwindling colonial empire.

Patton's offensive had come to a halt in early September as the Third Army ran out of fuel at the Moselle River, just outside the French towns of Nancy and Metz. Old Blood and Guts had expected the supreme commander to keep fuel and supplies flowing to support the successful advance of both field armies, but Ike favored a "broad front" approach to the ground-war effort to keep the Germans spread thin and off-balance. With supplies low and priority given to Monty until the port of Antwerp could be opened, he gave Twenty-First Army Group a higher priority for available resources. Monty also needed the extra fuel and supplies for *Operation Market-Garden*, his planned airborne invasion of Holland to seize a bridgehead over the Rhine at Arnhem scheduled for September 17. The plan was for the British to push north through Belgium and Holland, across the Rhine, and into Germany's crucial Ruhr industrial region, thus ending the war swiftly. To achieve that end, Ike decreed that the priority of supply would go to Monty and to the U.S. First Army, whose drive on the British right flank was to screen the Twenty-First Army Group drive into Arnhem in support of the airborne operation.

Given the prodigious American contribution to the war effort compared to their British allies, Patton was justifiably incensed. Ike's only concession was to permit the Third Army to establish itself astride the Moselle, which would help anchor the right flank as the Allies pushed towards the Rhine along their broad front. Patton remained frustrated at being held back while the British received most of the supplies and stole the limelight, and by the lack of progress of his forces, whom he knew if turned loose might be able to penetrate the Siegfried Line and roll all the way to Berlin. But to resume the offensive east of the Moselle and mount a fresh drive towards the Siegfried Line and Frankfurt, at least 450,000 gallons of fuel per day would be required. That amount was not even close to forthcoming.

The reality was that Allied ground forces consumed more than 800,000 gallons of gasoline per day, and supply lines had already been stretched too far—over three hundred miles from the Normandy beachheads. The French railroads had been all but decimated by Allied and German bombing and could offer little aid to the effort. A special one-way trucking system was instituted to carry rations, ammunition, and gasoline inland from Normandy, including the "Red Ball Express," an African-American quartermaster regiment. But the trucks could not carry enough supplies to support offensives by two full army groups, and Monty was given priority.

All the same, Patton was far from idle. Whenever Third Army seemed about to run out of gasoline, he would find a clever way to get his hands on stashes of fuel and persuade Bradley to allow him to keep moving. But just three days earlier on September 12, Brad had reapplied the brakes, warning him that with the kickoff of Monty's *Operation Market-Garden* in five days' time, Third Army might well be stuck west of the Moselle for some time without ammunition or fuel. Patton pleaded: "Don't stop us now, Brad, but I'll make a deal with you. If I don't secure a couple of good bridgeheads east of the Moselle by the night of the 14th, I'll shut up and assume the mournful role of defender." Brad granted him two days, which proved ample time for Patton. And so it went. Whenever the fuel spigots seemed about to shut off, Patton would come up with some new scheme to continue to "edge" eastward in limited operations, justified by any reason he could conjure up to keep Third Army moving. But he wasn't happy about the situation and wrote his wife Beatrice that "The books will someday be written on that pause which did not refresh anyone but the Germans." Much to his dismay, the halt of the Third Army in September allowed the Germans to strengthen the massive fortress of Metz in northeast France and the entire Siegfried Line.

In making his case to Eisenhower to get his share of the fuel, Patton had declared that he didn't need a greater supply allocation than his rival Monty to rush on to the German frontier; he could get by if Ike would simply protect his existing tonnage.

"If you don't cut us back," he lobbied his old friend, "we can make it on what we're getting. I'll stake my reputation on it."

"Careful, George," Ike said in the friendly but incisive paternal tone that he used when he wanted to put his top field commander in his place. "That reputation of yours hasn't been worth very much."

To which, Old Blood and Guts—after having been the driving force behind the rapid Allied breakthrough in France—hitched up his belt, gave a toothy grin, and replied, "It's pretty good now!"

Though Patton bitched privately in his letters to his wife and to Codman, Stiller, Meeks, and the rest of his staff about his boss Ike, the two old friends remained on good working terms. The truth was Patton was fiercely loyal to the Supreme Commander of the Allied Expeditionary Force Europe. What vexed Patton about Ike was that he seemed to go out of his way to accommodate Monty and the British, while treating his own American generals under his command as if they were unwelcome relatives at Thanksgiving dinner. In Patton's view, Ike acquiesced to British demands and threats far more than what inter-Allied cooperation and diplomacy required. And he didn't just capitulate too readily to Monty. He seemed just as much of a doormat before Churchill and Sir Alan Brooke, George Marshall's equivalent as the British Chief of the Imperial General Staff. It also bothered Patton, as it did Bradley, that Ike had taken to Briticisms like "petrol" for gasoline and "tiffin" for tea with annoying regularity, and that he spent so much time with his driver and paramour, the beautiful 36-year-old Brit Kay Summersby. To Patton and Bradley, it was as if Ike secretly longed to be British. Though Patton respected him for his likable personality and diplomatic tact, he and Bradley both considered him overly conciliatory to the clubby, imperialistic Brits. But they weren't the only ones. Most American generals—not just Patton and Bradley—felt the Anglophile Ike had sold them out for America's former antagonist and current top ally.

After their decades-long relationship, as they slugged it out in France and Patton brought the Allies glory, Old Blood and Guts sometimes privately referred to Ike as "the best damn general the British have got." But in practice, he still remained fiercely loyal to Eisenhower, and to Bradley as well, despite his private venting in his letters home to his wife and to his sympathetic staff. Similarly, even though he sometimes complained about Monty, whose own British colleagues referred to as "an efficient little shit" and Patton sometimes called "the little monkey," he had great respect for the man as a military planner, field commander, and strategist— and the two were often in agreement in opposition to Ike and Bradley. He just didn't like playing second fiddle to the venerated British warrior in terms of resources when America was now the far dominant partner in the Allied war effort.

Commanding respect without an air of threat, Ike got along with the most difficult personalities the Allies could serve—with Monty and Patton at the top of the list. He was able to treat his peers and subordinates with equanimity, interceding only when necessary in squabbles over resources. In an operational as well as political move that had been agreed upon before D-Day, on September 1 Eisenhower had taken over the ground campaign from Montgomery. Though Monty received a "promotion" to field marshal, the highest rank he could reach in the British Army, on the same day by Churchill as a consolation, he remained embittered even though the move had been agreed upon before Normandy. Even more reprehensibly given the huge military stakes, Monty showed open disdain towards his superior Ike, whom he did not respect despite the clear chain of command. With the war at the point where America bled by far the most men and money of the Allies on the Western Front, FDR, Marshall, and Eisenhower understandably wanted the U.S. to have more say in the war's direction and an increased visibility of the American contribution to the war effort.

The Allies had hoped to end the war by Christmas 1944, but the American supply lines had been depleted nearly as much as those of the enemy. Both sides were fighting a war of attrition and the Allies could afford only one of its forces to move forward at a time. With *Operation Market-Garden* to start in two days, Ike's choice was Monty. But after the operation was completed, what then? The choice going forward lay between Patton-Bradley and Monty. With his broad front strategy, Ike had refused to make a choice of one field army over the other for the long-term, knowing that making such a choice could cause irreparable damage to the Allied coalition and to achieving its ultimate objective: the unconditional surrender of Nazi Germany. But in Patton's view, Ike also simply didn't want to deal with the overbearing Monty, nor did he want to deal with the equally exasperating Churchill. Both lobbied him incessantly to carve out more British control over ground operations and greater weight in the Allied partnership.

On the outskirts of Verdun, Patton and his staff pulled up to Bradley's Eagle TAC command post, a circus of tents, tangled phone lines, and narrow trailers ringed with barbed wire. Hopping out of the vehicle with Willie on his leash, he and Stiller sloshed through the mire that passed for walkways between tents and trailers and went inside the command vehicle. A converted truck half the size of a Pullman car, Bradley's headquarters trailer was rigged up with Plexiglas skylights, long fluorescent lamps, mahogany wall paneling, thick carpeting, and of course, a plethora of maps. Inside, a cherry-stained wooden bar resembling a communion rail separated Bradley's inner sanctum from the visitors' antechamber, and on his desk lay a red leather folder containing photographs of his wife Mary and his daughter Elizabeth. Scattered around his office were empty Coca-Cola bottles, legacies of Bradley's favorite drink. Asleep on the floor were two stray headquarters pups named Omaha and Utah, who passed their free time scampering up and down the camouflage netting that veiled the fleet of HQ vehicles.

To his surprise, Patton found Bradley in a heated argument with General Harold Bull, Eisenhower's stern-looking assistant chief of staff and head of operations at Supreme Headquarters Allied Expeditionary Force. SHAEF, commanded by Ike and filled out with a huge staff, was the final decider of which army got what supplies and when. As the SHAEF G-3, General Bull's unhappy duties included breaking bad news to the commander of Twelfth Army Group.

"…not going to do it, Harold," protested Bradley. "I'm not going to give any more to Monty—I've already given him half my army, fuel, and supplies. Ike can't honestly expect me to do this."

"There's no way around it," said Bull. "Those are Ike's orders."

Bradley shook his head in disgust. "So Monty does what he pleases and Ike just says yes sir. We're just supposed to play the role of second-stringers even though we're supplying most of the boots on the ground along with most of the tanks, planes, artillery, and fuel."

"You know that's not it—*Market-Garden* has to be the priority right now."

"But Monty always wants *more*. I'm going to tell you flat out that if he takes control of the XIX and VII Corps of First Army, I'm going to ask for a leave."

*Now that's telling him,* thought Patton, looking on with amusement along with Stiller from the map table. *I didn't think you had in you, Brad.*

Patton then stepped over to the two quarreling officers, taking position to Bradley's right along with Stiller. The Missourian was so ensconced in the argument over military resources that he appeared not to have noticed their presence.

"It just doesn't make sense, Harold," continued Bradley. "Monty wants all supplies sent to him and First Army and for Third Army to hold. But George here," he said, acknowledging Patton's presence for the first time, "is poised to take Nancy as we speak. What am I supposed to do, tell him to pull back?"

Stepping forward with a grin on his face, Patton for the first time spoke. "General Bradley's got you by the short hairs, Harold. If I were you I would surrender."

But the humorless Bull was in no joking mood and scowled at Patton. Then, to

Patton's surprise, his face softened.

"Ike feels," he began, almost apologetically, "that you two think he is selling you both out. But that is not the case at all. The truth is he has to hold you back and ask you to do the dirty work because Monty simply will not take orders at all."

"That shouldn't be our problem," said Patton. "Ike should put a dunce cap on that little British pecker and make him sit in a corner. Good God, Ike's treated me a hell of a lot worse."

Even Bradley cracked a smile at that. But then his granite jaw projected out like a sail taking wind. "All I can say to Monty not being able to take orders is that maybe it's time for a showdown."

"Come on, Brad," pleaded Bull. "You have to understand, Com-Z"—Communications Zone—"does not have the infrastructure to get additional supplies to Third Army. It's impossible."

Patton wasn't buying it. "That's a load of bull, Harold, and you know it."

"He's right," agreed Bradley. "Don't mess with us, Harold."

"All right then, let me put it to you this way," said Bull. "If Third Army can capture Nancy, you, George, can use the rail lines that lead there to disperse more ammunition, food, and gas. Cracking that nut, instead of complaining about SHAEF supply, is your best chance to get stocks rolling to the front."

Patton was skeptical. "Is that so? Well then, I suppose I'll just have to take Nancy, won't I?"

Bull smiled ingeniously. "If you do, your problems will be solved."

As if on cue, Bradley's dogs started barking, as did Willie, who had been sitting off in the corner chewing on a bone. Seconds later, Lev Allen, Bradley's chief of staff, walked into the room with a big smile on his face.

"Third Army has just taken Nancy!" he exclaimed to everyone in the room.

Patton couldn't believe what he had just heard. He turned to Bull, but the G-3 looked anything but happy. He appeared like a courtroom witness caught in a lie.

"Damn, how do you like that!" roared Old Blood and Guts, smiling from ear to ear. "Better congratulate me!"

Even the normally bland and dour Bradley cracked a smile. "There you have it, Harold. Mission accomplished. Now *when* are we going to get our supplies?"

"I've got to go," growled Bull, and he sullenly took his leave to head back to Versailles. The offer of supplies if Patton took Nancy was nothing but a fake carrot: he had never had any intention of making good on his promise to Third Army.

When he was gone, Patton slapped Bradley on the back like a teammate after winning a high school football game. "Goddammit Brad," he crowed, "you kept the flag waving! I'm goddamn proud of you!"

Bradley smiled bashfully. "Why thank you, George."

"And just so you know, once again I'll offer to resign with you to Ike if we don't get this supply situation fixed in a hurry. I love Monty—he's the best general the British have next to Ike—but this crap has got to stop."

"Come on, George. We can't threaten to resign and you know it."

"Why the hell not?"

"Because, it's not the right way to do things. Ike's hands are tied, and he's doing the best he can."

"For Monty, he is. But not for you and me, or for the American people whose boys are dying out there by the truckload."

"Come on, George, we can't blackmail Ike. And besides, regardless of who runs Twelfth Army Group, Ike has made up his mind. The great push is going forward in the north not in our sector."

"Yes well, in my humble opinion, Monty's *Operation Market-Garden* will prove not to be a 'dagger-thrust' into the heart of Germany, but a goddamn 'butter-knife thrust.' And you can quote me on that."

Bradley allowed himself a chuckle. Patton and Stiller laughed along with him. Though Patton was incensed about Ike's endless appeasement of Monty, the capture of Nancy still put him in high spirits. He and Brad talked another hour, hashing out several military matters before Patton wrapped up his business at Eagle TAC. After six weeks of fighting together, they and their staffs worked as a seamless team.

"Come on, Willie, let's go," he said.

It was then he noticed that Willie was sniffing at Omaha and Utah beneath the map table. He immediately plucked up his riding crop and leaned down to swat the bull terrier away, but Stiller already had the dog by his leash.

Patton erupted in laughter. "Goddamn Willie's a sodomitic son of a bitch," he chortled to Bradley. "Keep him away from the pups—or he'll jump 'em like a Mexican bandito at a tequila party."

To his astonishment, Willie then tried to do exactly that. Patton laughed even harder. "Goddammit Willie, you are one randy little fucker! We need to get you the hell out of here!"

"Bye, George," said Bradley. "I have to say it's been entertaining as usual."

They shook hands—the two rivals united by their mutual love of country and wariness of Monty, though they both respected the man militarily. Patton then marched out to his car with a grinning Stiller and the roving Willie in tow. By the time he had returned to his base camp, he had concluded he would be better off ignoring any threat posed to his northern flank and continuing to advance, with orders or without, on the assumption that once he was committed to battle, SHAEF wouldn't dare pull him back. He was so popular with the American press right now that few remembered his slapping incidents in the summer of 1943 in Sicily, or his verbal mishap at the British social club event in the spring of '44. Standing around his wall map, he told his staff as much. They agreed with his reading of the situation.

"Oh, to hell with Monty," he told them. "I must get so involved with the enemy at my front that the bastards can't stop me. That's the only way that Third Army can do what it was put on God's green earth to do."

"Yes, sir," said Hap Gay. "But we're going to need a hell of a lot more men to do it. Have you seen the latest casualty reports?"

"Yes, I have. Which is why I want you to get the War Office on the line—right now—so I can talk to them directly about my manpower shortage. See to it, will you, Hap?"

"I'm on it, General."

While he waited for the call to be connected, Patton looked over his map of Eastern France and Western Germany on the table. Having to support two Allied fronts and multiple army groups in Western Europe while simultaneously battling

Imperial Japan was proving to be a greater stretch on resources than anyone had anticipated, and he knew that already the U.S. had thrown nearly everything it had into both theaters, save for a handful of units still in the States. He was going to need a lot more men and tanks if he was going to drive to Berlin. Third Army had sustained heavy losses in its push across France in August and early September; Patton never failed to have his hands full whenever he managed to secure enough fuel to go on the offensive against the regrouped Germans. His two spearhead divisions, the 4th and 6th Armored, had lost more than 300 tanks since the Normandy breakout, and even though his operations along the Moselle were limited in scope, both infantry and armored units were taking heavy casualties when they did engage the enemy. In the coming weeks, he was going to need replacements badly—and what he needed more than anything else were trained Sherman crews.

Five minutes later, Patton was connected to the War Office. "I need tankers, the best you've got," he said to the voice on the other end. "What do you have for me?"

"There's only one fully trained tank unit not already in action—the 761st. But General, I've got to forewarn you, it's a Negro battalion."

"Who the fuck asked about color?" Patton shot back. "I asked for goddamn tankers!"

"Yes, General. Then the 761st is all yours."

"Where are they?"

"Let me see here. They shipped overseas last month. Arrived in Avonmouth, England, on September 8. They've been stationed at Wimborne in the south since that time, awaiting deployment."

"The 761st—I know that outfit. They call themselves the Black Panthers and their motto is 'Come Out Fighting.'"

"Yes, General, that is correct."

"I inspected those boys on maneuvers at Camp Claiborne, Louisiana, two years ago. I got a report there was a black tank battalion that looked pretty good. When I saw them firing their guns and hitting their targets, I was goddamn impressed. Who are they presently attached to?"

"Ninth Army."

"Well, now they're part of Third Army. Who's their commanding officer?"

"Lieutenant Colonel Paul Bates. Oh, and there's one other thing, General."

"What's that?"

"The 761st is a 'bastard' battalion," he said, which meant that the battalion was a self-sustained unit up for grabs to support any division to which it was assigned.

Patton scratched his chin thoughtfully. Since the 761st was a bastard battalion, this would allow him to commandeer and shift individual companies, platoons, and even tanks to and from various units within Third Army on an as-needed basis to get them up to full strength.

"All right, those Black Panthers are mine. You tell Colonel Bates that George Goddamn Patton specifically requested those colored boys of his. Also tell him they'd better be in top form when they get their butts over here to France—I accept only the finest in my goddamn army!"

# CHAPTER 17



ON THE LAST DAY OF SUMMER, William McBurney stared out at the lush farmland next to the 761st Tank Battalion's staging area and beyond at the jewel-green hills east of Wimborne. Standing alongside him puffing on Lucky Strikes were Privates Leonard Smith and E.G. McConnell. Dusk was settling over the gently rolling countryside of Dorset County twenty miles inland from the rocky southern coast. Wimborne had been a sleepy market town before the war; now it was overflowing with American soldiers, who were being billeted in every available bed-and-breakfast, house, abbey, estate, hotel, and makeshift barracks prior to their much-anticipated crossing of the English Channel to France.

Since arriving to Great Britain on September 8, the battalion had taken up residence in a sprawling country manor. But per U.S. Army policy, the 761st's six white officers were quartered apart from its thirty black officers in the rooms of the estate, while the enlisted men's barracks were set up in a barn and series of outbuildings on the estate grounds. After two weeks, the battalion had been told its ultimate destination was northeastern France, where the Germans had reformed their battle lines following the collapse of the Falaise pocket. Couriers had been sent to Southampton to make final preparations for the Channel crossing, which would take place around the first of October. McBurney and his cohorts were also informed they would indeed be fighting in tanks, although they hadn't yet received their new Shermans and Stuarts.

The Black Panthers' arrival in Britain did much for the battalion's morale. Most of the men spent more time drinking in pubs, dallying with the local ladies, and searching for extra food to supplement their rations than they did in preparing to fight the Germans. McBurney, Leonard Smith, and Preston McNeil took whatever opportunity they could to head to the nearby villages to go drinking, dancing, and carousing, while less rambunctious fellows like Warren Crecy spent most of their free time writing letters to loved ones back home. At first, McBurney and his cohorts found the people of Wimborne and the surrounding towns wary of them, but within a week they got along well and were regulars in the pubs. They discovered that the townspeople weren't prejudiced themselves, but that some of the white American soldiers stationed nearby had warned the British townspeople that they were dangerous and untrustworthy. Not wanting the English women to spend time with the Negro soldiers, the white soldiers told the locals that the tankers had tails, implying that the African-Americans were comparable to apes. They also claimed that they were dirty and ignorant and that the only reason they had tanks was because they were bringing them up to the front for the white troops.

Few British believed the tall tales, and in fact, most preferred the African-American soldiers to their white counterparts. In his private diary, political editor Cecil King of the British *Daily Mirror* newspaper noted, "The feeling is fairly common that Negroes are nicer and better behaved than the ordinary Yank. So there is some indignation when Negro soldiers are condemned to death for raping English girls. In the most recent case the evidence would surely have resulted in acquittal in an English court. In the far more numerous cases of rape or murder by white American soldiers, the punishment, if any, is of a wholly different order of severity."

Once he and his fellow tankers had dispelled the myths of the white soldiers, McBurney was pleased to find a place that rivaled his home town of New York. The British drinking establishments welcomed him and his buddies with open arms and the young Englishwomen proved unexpectedly friendly. It didn't take him long to discover why he and his cohorts were so popular with the local women: not only were they considered unique and exotic, but they were coveted for their dancing skills and considered more fun than their white American counterparts, who were also hugely popular for their novelty, though not as much as the Negro tankers.

On one evening in town, McBurney was surprised that some of the women in the pubs and dance halls actually believed the outlandish rumor that he and the other black tankers might have tails. A pair of British lovelies came up and patted him and several of his buddies on the rump to see if they had tails. In response, Smitty and some of the other fellows came up with a clever ploy that they instituted when on the pub circuit: "Yes, I have a tail," they would reply.

"Can I see it?" came the usual refrain.

"Well, my tail doesn't come out until late at night."

The women were so curious that they would drink and dance with the Black Panthers until late at night when the tail would eventually come out—but from the wrong end. McBurney and the other members of the 761st continued to have cozy relations with the British women, who liked to sing a racy sexual number that was hugely popular in England at the time: *Roll Me Over in the Clover*.

Though the members of the 761st were fortunate to be spared from the race-baiting tribulations suffered by many of their black compatriots in the U.K., the men still suffered from the occasional hostility of the white soldiers. Though their confrontations with white troopers were less frequent and virulent than what they had endured in Louisiana and Texas back home, they were still often treated badly by their own countrymen. The hostility came from their popularity with the white British women. While the young English women seemed to enjoy dancing and socializing with both white and black American soldiers, some of the white soldiers resented any contact between black troops and English women. They tried to impose American—particularly Southern—social mores in Britain, like forcing blacks to get off sidewalks to let white soldiers pass, and regulating which pubs and theaters blacks could attend. To their credit, the British citizens, especially women, protested at the ill treatment when packs of white soldiers, in mob fashion, spewed racial epithets or closed clown dance halls where black soldiers danced with local white girls. To many of the English people, the British phrase about the American GI— "He's overpaid, oversexed, and over here"—seemed to only apply to white soldiers.

McBurney resented the occasional bad treatment by the white Americans. Coming to England, he had hoped such behavior would be left behind in the bigoted backwaters of Louisiana and Texas. It bothered him that he was seen as dangerous, as less than human, simply because of the color of his skin. But it didn't change the reasons for which he had originally volunteered to fight. America was his country and he wanted to fight on its behalf. He also hoped—as did many of the battalion's members—that in doing his part and proving himself on the battlefield, he would help make life better in America for himself and other coloreds upon his return. That had not happened to his Harlem Hellfighter father when he had returned from overseas duty in WWI, and to this day his father was bitter about it. But McBurney was still hopeful that this time around, not just *some* but *all* doughboys would return to the U.S. as victorious heroes regardless of the color of their skin.

As he and the other men of the 761st prepared for combat, they learned to put aside their feelings of anger brought about by the ill-will they faced from their unenlightened white counterparts. They learned to put themselves into positive frames of mind that would allow them to perform what they had learned in their training, knowing the only thing that ultimately mattered was that Bates believed in them and they believed in themselves. Their ability to act as an effective fighting force, and their own survival as individuals, depended on it.

"Goddamn I'm hungry," exclaimed Smitty, staring out at the verdant farmlands next to the barracks. "What you say we sneak on over to that farm over yonder and get us some of them greens?"

"I know what Moms would tell me. She would say that's a bad idea, but I am so hungry I think I would disobey her even if she was standing right here," said eighteen-year-old Private E.G. McConnell—a scrappy, five-foot-seven-inch tall fellow New Yorker from Queens, who weighed no more than 145 pounds after a huge meal and had signed on with the 761st at the tender age of sixteen with his parents' consent. "I love these Brits—they're cheerful and open with no color-hate in them at all—but no soldier can live on half a sandwich from the PX for dinner. Even if it only costs half a penny. Back home we get a whole sandwich with two full slices of bread."

Smith nodded. "I hear you, man. Let's get on over there. Looks like there's corn and maybe spinach or lettuce. Look at those nice, neat rows."

"You're asking for trouble," said McBurney, shaking his head in warning. "You take from that farmer and you'll be stealing. That's a court-martial offense."

"I don't care. I'm so hungry I could eat a goddamn horse."

"The Good Lord does not want us to go hungry, I can promise you that," said McConnell, holding up his pocket Bible he kept on him at all times. "Let's grab our bayonets—we'll chop down plenty to eat in no time."

"I don't know," said McBurney. "We could get in trouble."

"Come on, it's getting near dark," said Smith. "No one will even see us."

McBurney looked over at the tidy rows of corn and green vegetables. They looked tempting as hell, he had to admit, and he could practically taste the fresh food in his mouth.

"All right," he said. "I'm too damned hungry to argue with you."

Smitty grinned naughtily at him. "What are we waiting for then? We can cook whatever we get on our stoves in the barracks."

"Yessir, the Lord works in mysterious ways," said McConnell, putting his Bible away.

After grabbing their rifles with their bayonets and a pair of haversacks, they crept over to the nearest field, cut down a huge batch of greens, and then began tucking into the corn. Smith proved the most enthusiastic harvester, hacking away with his bayonet. Once they had filled one of their haversacks with fresh produce, McBurney heard the sound of approaching footsteps.

"Someone's coming!" he whispered urgently to his two cohorts.

"Oh shit," hissed Smitty. "We be in trouble now."

The harvesters ducked into the corn with their booty, crawled on their bellies down one of the rows, and flattened themselves on the ground, hoping that with the fast-approaching darkness they could remain unobserved. For more than a minute they waited. Laying on his stomach, McBurney felt his heart thumping in his chest as he heard the sound of crunching feet on the ground a mere stone's throw away. The next thing he knew, an English voice cut through the dusk.

"Hi there, Yanks."

He looked up to see a farmer and his two adolescent sons. To his right, Smith and McConnell sat up, looking guilty.

"What are you lads doing on the ground?" asked the farmer.

It was McConnell, the son of Jamaican immigrant parents, who answered. "May the Good Lord have mercy on us, sir, but we were pilfering some greens and corn," he sheepishly admitted.

"What on earth for?" asked the farmer, a look of puzzlement on his face and that of his two sons.

McBurney rose to his feet along with the others. "We were mighty hungry, sir. All they feed us at the PX are half sandwiches with a single slice of bread. It's not enough food for us tankers."

"Oh, you're tank chaps, are you?"

"Yes, sir," said Smith proudly. "We're with the U.S. 761st Tank Battalion. We're supposed to be heading for France to fight the Krauts any day now."

"Why the poor lads are just hungry," said the farmer to his sons, and they smiled and gave a polite chuckle.

McBurney hadn't expected them to be so pleasant and carefree when their field had been invaded. "What's so funny?" he asked.

"Well, you see, chaps," said the farmer, almost apologetically, "we British don't actually eat our corn. We feed it to our livestock."

Smith burst out in a peal of laughter. "You mean you feed it to your pigs and cows? You don't say, mister?"

"It's the God's honest truth. You Yanks are welcome to come over and grab some corn, spinach, and the like whenever you want. Next time though, you don't have to crawl on your bellies and hide away in the corn stalks. You are welcome as our guests. By the way, do you by chance have a cigarette?"

Smith pulled out a pack of Lucky Strikes and held it out for the farmer. "Here, take as many as you want."

"Thank you, Yank," he replied, and he grabbed three cigarettes from the pack.

McBurney smiled and reached into his pocket, pulling out a pack of chewing gum. "How about something for your boys?" he said, and he handed them each a stick of gum. "There's more where that came from back at the barracks," he added.

The British boys thanked him so effusively that he, Smitty, and McConnell returned to the barracks and fetched them a pair of chocolate bars, which they swiftly and happily devoured, and several more packs of chewing gum. Once finished dispensing the gifts, they bid the farmer and his sons farewell and returned to the barracks with their haversacks filled with fresh corn and greens.

Twenty minutes later, Colonel Bates had the battalion's officers and enlisted men assemble on the well-lit lawn in front of the English country manor that had become the 761st's temporary home.

"Men," he began in a booming voice, "I have just learned that we will soon be relieved from the Ninth Army and assigned to a new army—an army that in the past six weeks has killed more Germans and conquered more territory than any other army in the Allied ranks. That army is General George S. Patton's U.S. Third Army. The order does not officially go into effect until October 5, and we will remain a 'bastard' battalion up for grabs by any division in the Third Army, but we are still under General Patton's command. Which means we're going to be in the thick of it. They don't call him 'Old Blood and Guts' for nothing. I know how long you men have trained for this fight and wanted you to know of this new development. We will be crossing over the Channel to Normandy shortly after we become operational, probably no more than a few days. I expect the battalion will assume its combat status in late October. We are in the game, gentlemen—we are in the game for real."

Here he paused a moment to let the men absorb the stunning new development. A murmur of excitement went through the ranks and there were nods of approval all around. McBurney felt a sudden jolt of electricity coursing through his veins, as if he had just downed a shot of whiskey. He was so proud, he determined there and then that he would go to hell and back for Bates and Patton both.

"I know many of you doubted this day would ever come. Sometimes, I myself never thought it would. But it has, and after your long, hard training I know you are itching for battle. You are about to be the first colored tank battalion in United States history to take the field of battle, and I can tell you I am damn proud of you. You men have the skills and training to succeed in any scenario. I am fully confident that you are going to give a good account of yourselves. I commend you all on the supreme sacrifices you have made leading up to this historic moment. I believe in you, and so does General Patton. You should know that he specifically requested you men. I know you will do a great job on behalf of Third Army and your country. You are Patton's Panthers now and I salute you all!"

He stood ramrod straight, his tall lanky frame like a flagpole, and gave a crisp salute before dismissing the men. The battalion went crazy: tankers threw their hats in the air, pumped their fists, celebrated in roaring exultation, and hugged one another as if the war had just been won. The more restrained McBurney just shook his head in euphoric amazement. A mere three months ago, the idea that the 761st Tank Battalion would be bound for combat had seemed unthinkable. But Old Blood and Guts Patton and his Third Army needed tanks—and, more than tanks, trained Sherman crews—so he himself had specifically requested the unit.

McBurney was thrilled that the battalion's future would be linked directly with that of the celebrated general. But even more importantly, he felt an enormous pride that Old Blood and Guts had specifically called for the 761st and that they would be the first African-American armored unit to be deployed in battle. But at the same time, he knew that the main reason Patton had asked for them was because he, like every Allied commander, was experiencing critical manpower shortages. To McBurney though, that didn't matter. The main thing was that Patton had asked for the 761st and now the battalion was finally being called up. Had anyone of less than his stature requested the tank outfit, he knew, the Black Panthers might never have been granted the opportunity to fight.

He thought of his father. The Harlem Hellfighter would be proud of him. Soon the tanks of the 761st would roll onto the shores of France and it would be a momentous day in the history of their people. For while Thomas McBurney and other black Americans had served as soldiers in France in World War I, this would be the first time in U.S. military history that Negro tankers would journey to foreign soil riding and fighting in tanks. And in making history, the members of the 761st would be grappling with the same enemy on the same soil where their fathers had fought twenty-six years earlier.

*This time around, Dad,* thought McBurney as he reflected back to two years earlier at their Madison Avenue railroad flat, *we're not going to just show the world, we're going to change it.*

# CHAPTER 18

## EHRENFELD, WEST COLOGNE

## SEPTEMBER 28-29, 1944

ANGELA PEERED THROUGH the dusk at the *Hitler Jugend Streifendienst* patrol, feeling the imminent danger of what she was about to do. Standing anxiously at her side, behind a mound of rubble, were two Jewish women she was attempting to deliver to Hans Steinbrück's *Ehrenfeld Gruppe* hideout in the basement of Schönsteinstrasse 7. The building in which the fugitive women had been hiding out in north Ehrenfeld had recently been bombed and, in desperation, they had been forced to move to a new location.

Angela crossed herself and prayed, appealing to the Holy Father, as she summoned all her courage and tried to exorcise her self-doubt. She had never hidden Jews before and hoped that she would not somehow be caught in the act of helping the two women, only to be interrogated, tortured, and hung by the Gestapo.

She reminded herself, once again, to patiently wait until the Hitler Youth patrol moved on and the coast was clear. But she couldn't wait too long; every minute she and the Jewish women remained out on the open street they were vulnerable. The two homeless women needed to be hidden as quickly as possible without drawing attention.

She didn't want to let her comrades in the Edelweiss Pirates or Steinbrück's Ehrenfeld Group down. She was part of the resistance now, and her cohorts had to know that they could rely upon her to carry out an assignment with no slip-ups to help those threatened by the Nazis. Steinbrück and his girlfriend Cäcilie Serve had asked her to deliver the two women safely to the network of cellars beneath the demolished building, where they would be hidden for the duration of the war if necessary. Angela was working alone, without either Barthel or Jean, since the chauvinistic Nazis would not be inclined to suspect a sixteen-year-old girl of clandestine resistance activities.

She looked down at her hands; to her dismay they were trembling. How would she be able to dash across Venloer Strasse and creep down into Steinbrück's lair when she was so nervous?

It was then she noticed that the two Jewish women were studying her, no doubt wondering if they could trust her to deliver them to safety. She was admittedly young and inexperienced and they seemed to have their doubts. Taking a deep breath to steel herself, she looked back at the patrol. There were three adolescent boys in all, each carrying a rifle and wearing the special *HJ-Streifendienst* cuffs with the white piping on the shoulder straps and the special patrol service gorget at the throat. They seemed to have their eyes on the train station. Repeated Allied bombings and fires had consumed most of the buildings around the station, but by some miracle the Ehrenfeld train station, its elevated train tracks, and the apartment buildings to the west along Schönsteinstrasse, were all still standing, though portions of the remaining structures were missing roofs and walls.

*Scheisse, why won't they move on? Why do they keep standing there?*

She scanned up and down Venloer Strasse and Schönsteinstrasse. Though most of Cologne's citizens had abandoned the city, there were a number of people on the streets. She saw an old man in clothing too big for his narrow frame walking with a young boy; two women with close-cropped hair crossing the street; a young man with a badly burnt face pushing a wooden cart filled with belongings; a group of dirty boys in rags playing in a pile of rubble with guns made out of sticks; and a corpulent Party member riding a bicycle to the northwest towards Bickendorf. Wearing a brown uniform and blood-red Nazi armband, he was pedaling casually.

At that moment, a young man in his mid-twenties came riding out on his bicycle from Ehrenfeldgürtel, turned northwest, and began peddling along Venloer Strasse in the same direction as the Party member. He was moving at a fast clip and Angela couldn't help but think to herself that he had a sense of purpose. And then, to her surprise, he quickly closed on the Nazi, withdrew a pistol, and pointed it at the man just as another male that somehow Angela had failed to see—this one a mere teenager—appeared walking his bicycle. He emerged from behind a collapsed building ahead on Venloer Strasse in the path of the Party member. As the fat Nazi slowed for the boy walking his bicycle, the man following in pursuit on the other bicycle opened fire with his pistol and shot him in the ribs.

Angela and the two Jewish women gasped with shock. It was a clever trap!

The Nazi screamed as he fell off the conveyance and tumbled to the ground. *"Mein Gott! Ich sterben! Helft mir!"* My God! I'm dying! Help me!

But the citizens on the streets didn't want to get involved and scrambled for cover in the rat's maze of rubble next to the street. Meanwhile, the older assailant on the bicycle, who wore a Luftwaffe blue-gray side cap, dashed up to the brownshirted Party member and shot him in the head to finish him off.

The Nazi's body went limp.

Angela and the two Jewish women covered their mouths in shock and horror at the swift and unexpected act of violence. Angela couldn't believe her eyes and felt a wave of revulsion. If this was what waging war against the Nazis was like, did she really want to be part of the resistance?

Alerted by the gunfire, the Hitler Youth patrol dashed from the train station along with a train constable towards the fallen Party officer and his attackers. The HJ raised their rifles, let loose with a volley, and chased after the assailants, who returned fire before swiftly disappearing on their bicycles between two partially collapsed buildings on the south side of Venloer Strasse. Their lightning-fast hit-and-run attack had been successful, and they seemed to have devised a plan of retreat. She suspected the older one in his mid-twenties with the Luftwaffe cap was an army deserter experienced in the ways of making war.

"Quick, this is our chance!" said Angela to the Jewish women. "Follow me!"

Moving briskly, they crossed the street. With voices shouting and rifles crackling behind them, they ducked down into the rubble-strewn entrance to the hideout at Schönsteinstrasse 7. Angela knocked on the door three times, which was the signal to enter, and a minute later the door opened. It was Steinbrück's pregnant girlfriend Cäcilie Serve. She let them in and led them through the bomb-damaged building and maze of interconnected rooms to her and Steinbrück's apartment on the first floor.

From their apartment, she then escorted them through a large hole in the wall to the apartment buildings next door at Schönsteinstrasse 9 through 13. Angela noticed a string that ran above them along their path. It was attached to a tinkling bell at the end of the line that was used to warn the people in the basement if the authorities were coming. Continuing through the adjacent first-floor apartment and then descending some broken stairs, they came to a heavy metal door that looked like it was from an air-raid shelter. Giving the designated three-knock sign to inform those hiding out that they were friendly, they climbed down into a series of interconnected basement apartments, where the string ended at the warning bell.

Here they found Steinbrück along with Barthel Schröder, Günther Schwarz, and three other Edelweiss Pirates as well as several Wehrmacht deserters and forced Russian and Polish laborers. Since Angela didn't see Ruth Kramer, her mother Friedel, or Paul Urbat anywhere, she concluded that the Jews must be hiding out somewhere else in the building as a safety precaution, since they couldn't venture outside under any circumstances. The labyrinth of interconnected cellars, created by knocking holes in the walls and tunneling into the adjoining rooms, looked like a gangster lair from a Hollywood movie set. One room was outfitted with bunk beds pilfered from an air-raid shelter; three were packed with stolen weapons, food, and other valuable black-market items from the gang's recent heists; and the fifth served as a training room containing weights and punching bags so the fugitives could stay in shape.

"Good, you have brought the women," said Steinbrück. "But what's all the shooting about?"

"Two men just ambushed a Nazi official riding his bicycle," replied Angela, who was still only known to Steinbrück and the other members of his Ehrenfeld Group by her code name, Mucki. "Three HJ took off after them and opened fire with their rifles, but the attackers escaped between a pair of buildings. They headed south."

"Is the Party official dead?"

"I think so. He wasn't moving."

Steinbrück weighed this new development. "Police will soon be crawling all over the neighborhood. We'd better all lay low for the night."

"That's a good idea. Hoffmann is bound to send out another patrol to scour the area," said Schröder.

He reached out and took Angela by the hand. Guiding her to a corner of the room, he whispered to her, "I was worried about you. I am glad you're okay."

She kissed him on the lips and they held one another close. "I was very scared," she admitted.

Cäcilie now addressed the two Jewish women, who were terribly frightened. "Everything will be all right. No one will find us here," she said reassuringly. "Can we get you something to eat?"

The two women, rail-thin and looking as if they hadn't eaten in days, nodded.

Bomber Hans gave them a welcoming smile. "Don't worry, you will be safe here. We will feed you now."

"Yes, thank you," said one of the women. She then turned to Angela. "And thank you for bringing us safely here."

"You are welcome," said Angela, still feeling her heart racing from the commotion on the street. "But to be honest, for a moment there I wasn't sure we were going to make it."

ΨΨΨ

Angela spent the night at the hideout with the others. She knew her father would be furious at her for not returning home, but it would be safer to remain in hiding until the Gestapo had finished searching the area, which they would no doubt do following the killing of the Party official. She and Schröder slept together on a spare mattress on the floor of the training room containing the weights and punching bags, while Steinbrück and Cilly slept in their apartment and Günther Schwarz and the other Pirates, the army deserters, and the foreigners spread out in different rooms. The two new Jewish women had been given a refuge in a more secluded portion of the building at Schönsteinstrasse 13 since they would have to remain in hiding indefinitely and would not be able to venture out onto the streets even at night.

The next morning, September 29, she was sleeping and in the midst of a strange dream when she thought she heard noises coming from the street outside the building. The sounds weren't particularly loud, but were enough to awaken her. Opening her eyes, she listened for a moment half-consciously, hoping the noise would stop so she could roll over and go back to sleep. She remained silent and motionless, casting an ear towards Schönsteinstrasse, trying to separate out the noise on the street from the natural sounds of the room.

Something didn't feel right. But when she didn't hear any further sound, she told herself that it was just her imagination.

Then she heard the tinkle of the warning bell, along with the chuff of boots across the rubble outside the building, a clink of stone or concrete, and whispering voices. She knew then that they were in trouble.

*Someone is trying to enter the building!*

She nudged Schröder. But all he did was change positions, grind his teeth together, and mumble some sleepy incoherence. She nudged him harder.

"Wake up! Someone's coming!" she whispered urgently.

He looked up at her groggily. "What? What is it?"

"Someone's here!" she said.

"Who?"

"I don't know. But I don't like the sound of it."

The warning bell tinkled again.

"Oh shit!" he gasped, the danger finally registering. "We have to hurry!"

Crawling quietly off the mattress, they grabbed their rucksacks and went into the adjoining bunk room where their Edelweiss Pirates comrades as well as the army deserters, the big bearded Russian, and three other forced laborers were fast asleep. The older men had gotten drunk last night and were snoring loudly.

She and Schröder went to wake them. But Günther Schwarz's eyes were open and he was already stirring.

"Someone's out there, aren't they?"

"Yes," replied Schröder. "Quickly, we have to hurry. We heard the bell."

While he and Schwarz woke the others, Angela went to the heavy steel door that led to Schönsteinstrasse No. 7 to listen. She moved stealthily, feeling her heart beating wildly in her chest.

That's when she heard a soft footfall on the other side of the door. Every sense was suddenly acute.

The noise outside the door stopped.

But just as she was about to turn and flee, three knocks sounded on the door and Steinbrück and Cäcilie Serve suddenly appeared.

"Shhh," whispered Bomber Hans, pressing his finger to his mouth to silence everyone.

He then gently closed the door. Angela heard the clinking sound of shifting rubble coming from above and a susurrus of voices again.

"They're doing a security check—it's got to be the Gestapo," whispered Steinbrück. "We're going to have to sneak out the back. It's our only chance."

He made his way into the bunk room and informed the others what was happening. The men quickly gathered their bags and rucksacks containing food, clothing, weapons, and other critical belongings. Angela put on her cap, tucked her hair underneath, and smeared charcoal on her face to conceal her identity and make herself look like a male. Now she could hear the sound of several voices and approaching footsteps, louder and closer than before. Her entire body froze as a tremor of fear lanced through her.

*Is the Gestapo coming for us?*

"Let's go, *kameraden*," commanded the leader Steinbrück. "We're dead if we stay here."

"Come, Mucki," said Schröder, calling her by her code name and taking her by the hand. "We have to leave now."

"What about the Jewish women?" she asked Bomber Hans and Cilly, feeling a taut knot of muscle squeezing her chest as the footsteps and voices grew louder. It sounded like a whole army was coming down the passageway.

"They know to stay hidden at Number 13," answered Steinbrück. "Hopefully, they won't be found. But we've got to go—there's no time to warn them."

With Bomber Hans in the lead, they began making their way through the labyrinth of interconnected cellars containing the stockpiles of stolen goods from the August and September raids. Before they had made it to the third room, Angela heard a crashing sound. When she looked back towards the heavy steel door, she saw a swarm of security officers pouring through the open doorway into the room. At the head of the raid team was the murderous *Kriminalkommissar* Ferdinand Kütter of the Cologne Gestapo.

"Halt!" he yelled as he spotted her and the others making their escape.

No one stopped.

"Halt, or you will be shot!" commanded Kütter a second time, and this time he took aim with his Mauser pistol and opened fire.

The bullet screamed past her ear, thudding into the wall and exploding concrete slivers and dust. Angela blew out a sigh of relief that the bullet had missed, but then realized they were about to be cornered unless they could slip outside through a basement window or one of the short tunnels that led to the street through the rubble.

More shots rang out. This time one of the foreign laborers went down. Angela and Schröder leaned down to help him, but Kütter and his men opened fire again and they were forced to take cover. But luckily, two of the man's comrades darted in, pulled him to his feet, and helped him down the passageway.

Dashing ahead, she, Schröder, Günther Schwarz, and the other Edelweiss Pirates scrambled through one of the partially collapsed tunnels leading to the outside. Along the way, she saw Steinbrück and Cäcilie making their escape through a cellar window.

Once outside, they took a hard right and scrambled down a small mountain of rubble, their eyes struggling to adjust to the sunlight after the darkness of the hideout. Steinbrück and the other members of the Ehrenfeld Group were running in different directions, struggling to escape. She and Schröder went north; Günther Schwarz and the three remaining Pirates went south. As she ran, behind her Angela heard shouting voices. She chanced a look over her shoulder once they were about to turn the corner to the north side of the partially demolished building.

"Halt!" cried Kütter, pointing his pistol at them.

"Don't stop! Run!" warned Schröder. "If they catch us, they're just going to torture and kill us!"

The Gestapo officer and his men opened fire on them, but the shots missed as she and Schröder managed to duck behind a pair of large concrete blocks. The clump of Gestapo officers and enlisted men then opened fire on Steinbrück's group. Bomber Hans, an army deserter, and the big bearded Russian returned fire. The Nazis let loose with another concentrated fusillade, the white-hot bullets kicking up shards of concrete and churning up puffs of bomb dust from the street.

To her dismay, Angela saw the pregnant Cäcilie Serve come under enemy fire as the fleeing group made a mad dash for Venloer Strasse. She threw up her hands in surrender, and Kütter and his men quickly engulfed her.

"Damn, they got Cilly!" cursed Schröder, and they ducked around the corner. From there, they made a mad dash for a narrow passageway that led between two buildings on the north side of the train station. If they could get in there, make their way north, turn east towards the Rhine, and then head south on Melatengürtel to her house in Braunsfeld, they would be safe.

They dashed across the street and into the opening between the buildings. As they entered the narrow corridor strewn with broken concrete blocks, Angela paused a moment to look back over her shoulder for their pursuers.

There was no one.

Feeling a wave of relief, she turned and dashed down the alleyway, weaving in and out of the rubble. Behind them as they ran, she could hear the sound of voices and the shuffle of boots, but the sounds quickly grew fainter.

When they reached Subbelrather Strasse, the city opened up before them and again there were people on the streets. They kept moving at a solid clip, but slowly and casually enough not to draw attention to themselves. At Ehrenfeldgürtel, they headed south.

It wasn't until they reached Aachener Strasse that Angela felt safe. "My father's going to kill me," she said as they neared her house in Braunsfeld.

"So is mine," said Schröder. "But at least we're alive."

"Yes, surprisingly. But for how long? The Gestapo caught Cäcilie and who knows who else. It's only a matter of time until they talk, don't you think?"

"Unfortunately. With the Gestapo everyone talks. We just have to hope we get lucky and no one comes asking around for us."

"I don't want to be caught by Kütter. He is said to be brutal during interrogation."

"He's nothing but a cold-blooded killer in a uniform. It's too bad he wasn't the one murdered instead of the Party official."

"I wonder what he'll do to Cilly."

"Whatever it is, it won't be pretty. Steinbrück knows that, and I imagine he will try and somehow rescue her."

"You think he would try and break her out of El-De Haus?" asked Angela. "Surely, he's not that crazy."

"I don't know. If the Gestapo were holding you, I'd try and save you. But then I'm madly in love with you."

She nuzzled up to him. "You would really do that for me?"

"The way I feel about you, I don't think I'd have a choice."

He leaned into her and softly kissed her. Then they French-kissed passionately before she gently pulled away, smiled at him, and said, "Maybe it's not such a crazy idea you wanting to rescue me. You are my knight in shining armor, you know."

He gave a winsome smile. "Yes, that's me," he said, proudly touching his edelweiss flower pinned to his lapel. "Your knight in shining armor."

And with that, they French-kissed again, feeling a youthful tingle of euphoria that they were both still alive and desperately in love.

# CHAPTER 19

## BRAUNSFELD, WEST COLOGNE

### OCTOBER 1, 1944

"I HAVE A SOURCE INSIDE THE GESTAPO."

Angela looked at her father, unsure if she had heard him correctly. "What?"

"The Gestapo—I have a source at El-De Haus," he said, his face already red from drink even though it was only early afternoon.

"Who is it?"

"For obvious reasons I can't tell you that. But I can tell you that this person has informed me that Hoffmann is planning to decisively crush all resistance—not only inside the city but in the surrounding areas. Ehrenfeld will be a primary target."

Now she understood what he was up to and frowned. "You're just trying to discourage me from seeing Barthel."

"No, that's not what this is about. It's true I don't want you seeing that boy any more because, in the end, all he is going to do is get you into trouble. But that is not why I am telling you this. I simply want you to know what's going on."

"I understand. Hoffmann will leave no stone unturned and show no mercy."

"It's going to be worse than that. He's going to turn his pit bull *Kriminalkommissar* Kütter and others loose like never before. No one will be safe. No one."

She looked at her father closely as he took a gulp from his tumbler of *kirschwasser*, a colorless fruit brandy with a subtle cherry flavor and hint of almond. He appeared as worried as she had ever seen him.

"Did you visit Gestapo headquarters again?" she asked him. "Is that why you're telling me this?"

"Yes, I paid Herr Hoffmann another visit, along with my informant."

"It seems to me you are playing a cat-and-mouse game far more dangerous than anything I am doing. Certainly, riskier than slipping Allied leaflets under doors and painting 'Down with Hitler' on walls."

"I do it to keep tabs on the goings-on here in the city and it is well worth the risk. Sun Tzu said, 'Keep your friends close, and your enemies closer' and I happen to subscribe to that notion. Cologne is being bombed by the Allies, but the true destruction does not come from the air—it comes from the Gestapo. They are hunting down and murdering our own people, Angela. That is the real tragedy. That is why we must know what they are planning to do as soon as they get their marching orders from Himmler and Gutenberger." Karl Gutenberger was the Higher SS and Police Leader, or HSSPF, in the western Rhineland, who reported directly to the Head of the SS Himmler.

"Are you sure you're not doing this to protect me?"

"Perhaps I am," he acknowledged. "But I wouldn't have to do it if you weren't taking such grave risks. As I told you, your current situation can only end one way for you and those criminal friends of yours. And that is badly."

"I don't like it when you call my friends criminals. And I can watch out for myself." Biting her anger, she thought for a moment. "I don't understand why

Hoffmann and his henchmen put up with your unannounced visits."

"Because I wear the uniform of a colonel and have won many medals. Nazis worship medals, ribbons, and the like. You know that."

"In other words, you are everything they want to be, but will never be."

"Something like that. They are nothing but mindless bureaucrats, torturers, and murderers who would be the dregs of Germany if the Nazis had never risen to power."

"What story did you feed them this time?"

"I told them I was robbed in broad daylight by three hoodlums and both my wallet and pistol were stolen from me."

"That was rather clever of you. Did you also manage to find out the name of that Nazi bigwig who was shot two nights ago?"

"*Ortsgruppenleiter* Heinrich Soentgen. He was Ehrenfeld's senior Party official. His assailant gunned him down on his bicycle, and now Hoffmann will task Kütter and others with sweeping through the district like a storm, knocking down doors to find him and his accomplice. In the coming weeks, dozens of innocent people will be rounded up and tortured at El-De Haus and Brauweiler Abbey. And then they will either be shipped off to labor camps or executed."

"But I thought the security forces were already stretched thin. It was my understanding that the police have been unable to control the resistance groups and criminal gangs in the district."

"That was the case a few days ago, but Hoffmann has now been given several companies of Order Police from the front to assist him."

In fact, the chief of the Cologne Gestapo, native of Silesia, and experienced *Bandenkämpfer* had formed four special task forces, or *Einsatzkommandos*, to violently hunt down and weed out *Volksfeinde* and other "defeatist elements" considered a potential threat to the Reich. Numbering eighty men each, these units were composed of Gestapo officers, as well as personnel from the Kripo and Border Police ordered to work under Hoffmann by Himmler. Their goal was to spread out behind the front to hunt down and arrest escaped foreign laborers, criminals, saboteurs, and deserters. Hoffmann stationed three of the *Einsatzkommandos* at the towns of Erkelenz, Düren, and Jülich, vital crossroads which controlled the main road arteries leading to and from the frontlines. He assigned a fourth unit to the town of Schleiden, in the Eifel Mountains, and stationed a fifth, *Sonderkommando* Mohr, in Cologne. Consisting of well-armed younger personnel led by Friedrich Mohr, a veteran of the Polish and French occupations, Hoffmann assigned the latter unit with stamping out gang activity inside the city. He supplemented the *Einsatzkommandos* with companies of Hitler Youth and *Volkssturm*, the German Home Guard, as well as four battalions of police reservists.

The clearance of the Left Bank Rhineland, now known as a "security zone," was planned by Hoffmann as a phased operation. He divided the region into two sectors: a high-priority "red" sector ten to fifteen kilometers behind the front that needed immediate clearance, and a secondary "green" sector east of the red zone prepared for future deportation. These security sectors remained flexible depending on the rate of the Allied advance, and the Gestapo viewed all civilians in the Left Bank area as potential threats. Since the Allies had begun pushing into northeastern

France, Belgium, Holland, and Germany in September, the Gestapo increasingly viewed Rhinelanders as suspect as they encountered the striking disconnect between the expectation of a *Volk* ready to sacrifice everything to achieve victory, and the reality of a war-weary population uninterested in fighting Hitler's *Endkampf* on their very doorsteps.

"Hoffmann has also formed a sixth *Einsatzkommando* headed by Kütter," said her father. "He's calling it *Sonderkommando Brauweiler*."

"What is its purpose?"

"To crack down on unruly Ehrenfeld."

"Don't you mean Räuberfeld?"

"Yes, that's what it's become: a nest of robbers. Hoffmann's new special unit found a *bandennest* in a series of linked cellars across the street from the Ehrenfeld train station. The bandit hideout happens to be not far from where the official was shot."

For a flicker of an instant, she thought about telling her father that she had narrowly escaped arrest at Steinbrück's basement. But the news would only mortify him, and he would likely strictly forbid her from seeing Barthel rather than merely discouraging her.

"I'm sure it's not really a 'bandit hideout,'" she said. "That's just the kind of thing the Gestapo calls it to make it sound more dangerous. People were probably only hiding out there so they wouldn't be harassed by the security forces. For most people these days, it's a matter of simple survival."

He looked at her pointedly. "It's a bit more complicated than that. As I told you before, the police are calling the gang the Ehrenfeld Group, and they say that the Edelweiss Pirates are associated with the gang."

"Is that so?"

"Don't pretend you don't know anything about this, Angela. You can make light of the situation, but your association with these street urchins is going to get you killed. Don't you realize that?"

"I don't know why you have to call my friends 'street urchins.' Or why you sound so angry. It is true that I have heard about this so-called Ehrenfeld Group. But my friends and I do not associate with them, I can promise you that."

"That is good to hear, but you should still not be running with this damned crowd of Edelweiss Pirates. The Gestapo uncovered stolen weapons and food in large quantities at the hideout, and they are mad as hell that people have turned to thievery and subversion when the enemy draws closer every day. You wouldn't believe all the black-market items they found in the hideout: meat, chocolate, liquor, complete Wehrmacht uniforms, machine pistols, rifles, hand grenades, and thousands of rounds of ammunition. Over the next few days, they will sweep across Ehrenfeld and make mass arrests."

"Hitler and the Reich should be resisted in my view. Where has your courage gone?"

"Don't talk to me like that."

"Did you lose it at the Somme in the Great War, or on the Eastern Front or Tunisia in this war? When did you think it was all right not to combat monsters like Hitler, Himmler, and Goebbels? You know perfectly well what they have done with the Communists and Jews. When they are shipped east, they never return. Never. Have you ever even considered lifting a finger to stop the madness?"

He took a hefty sip of *kirschwasser*, letting the fiery liquor sit in his mouth for a moment before turning his blazing eyes upon her. "Don't act holier than thou with me, young lady. Not when you have never taken the field in combat. Not when you have never shot at another human being and watched him bleed to death before your very eyes. You are too damned young to know what war is even about."

"That may be, but I am old enough to know what war is *not* about. It is not about murdering helpless women and children by putting a bullet to the back of their heads in the woods. I think you are too old and worn out to know right from wrong. When you were young, you would never have put up with something like this."

He tried to get up from his seat but fell back down as he was drunk and his legs gave out beneath him. "Damn you, you are a foolish girl if you do not listen to me," he snarled, waving an angry finger at her. "The leader of the *bandennest* is a man named Hans Steinbrück. Somehow, he managed to get away. But Hoffmann and Kütter will find him—and when they do, they will hang him. The police arrested several members of the gang and they will be singing like canaries soon enough."

Angela was stunned; she had no idea who all had been taken into custody besides Cäcilie. "Who was arrested?"

"I was told a pregnant woman, two fugitive foreign workers, and a pair of Jews."

Angela felt her heart skip a beat. "Two Jews you say?"

"The Gestapo captured two young Jewish women hiding out in a false closet in one of the apartments in the basement. My source told me all about the arrest."

She felt a sudden clot in her throat. He was obviously talking about the two women she had delivered to the hideout, not Ruth Kramer and the others hiding at Cilly's and Steinbrück's apartment. After all she had been through to deliver the two women to safety, they had in less than twenty-four hours been arrested by the Gestapo. She couldn't help but feel as if she had utterly failed.

"The Gestapo has been after this Steinbrück fellow for quite some time. I have to say he has led a rather colorful life for a criminal."

"Colorful? What did your source say about him exactly?"

"He said Steinbrück was assigned to the Cologne SS construction brigade two years ago after attempting to impersonate a Gestapo officer. Apparently, he quickly became a local legend and was nicknamed 'Bomber Hans' by his guards and admiring civilians due to his knack for retrieving unexploded bombs. He's originally from Düsseldorf. As a child, he repeatedly ran away from his orphanage in the city to the docks, and he later joined the merchant marine at the age of fourteen and traveled to Africa."

"He does sound like quite the adventurer."

"That's an understatement. After contracting malaria, Steinbrück's company discharged him. He returned to Düsseldorf where he worked odd jobs and tended bar before trying to join the city's Gestapo office. Although rejected due to his asocial background, this didn't stop him from trying to rent an apartment by claiming he worked for the Secret Police. His suspicious landlady tipped off the Gestapo, who arrested him for impersonating a security officer. The crime landed him in Buchenwald."

"Buchenwald? But how did he manage to survive?"

"He exploited his status as the star of the bomb-clearing detail to obtain extra food and clothing. He also used his assignment to plot his escape. In late 1943, he quietly slipped away from the Köln-Deutz work reeducation camp and fled to his former girlfriend's apartment in Berlin. Unfortunately, his bid for freedom was short-lived. The Gestapo quickly rearrested him after she telephoned the police. After they recaptured him, he managed to escape again while the train taking him back to prison stopped at a rail station. This time Steinbrück wisely made his way back to Cologne, where his work with the SS construction brigade had allowed him to familiarize himself with the city and its people. Upon his return, several sympathetic residents provided assistance and introduced him to the network of fugitives living in the city's rubble fields. But now it is the end of the line for him. Now that the Gestapo has located his hideout, his days are numbered."

"Whose days are numbered?" posed a voice.

They looked up to see Bartholomäus Schröder standing in front of the window, which Angela had opened to let in some air. Her father frowned.

"Don't you know it's not polite to sneak up on people," he bristled. "How long have you been standing there?"

"I just got here," said Schröder.

Angela could see that he looked on edge. *He must have some urgent news,* she thought.

"We were just leaving, Papa," she said in a matter-of-fact manner so as to not raise suspicion. "We're going for a walk."

"A walk? But it's dangerous out there. And besides, don't you have to get back to the hospital?"

"It's a Sunday, Papa. I don't work on Sundays. And it's dangerous every day."

He gave a disapproving sigh. "All right, but for God's sake be careful," he said, reaching for his tumbler.

"We will," she said, though inside she was worried. Schröder's visit was, in fact, unexpected and they had not made any plans to go on a stroll together. Which meant that something was up.

Something big.

# CHAPTER 20



## BLÜCHER PARK AND EHRENFELD, COLOGNE

### OCTOBER 1, 1944

"THE GESTAPO are holding Cilly as bait at the apartment. We need your help to rescue her."

Though Angela was both stunned and frightened at what Steinbrück was asking her and her fellow Edelweiss Pirates to do, she couldn't help but feel excited at the prospect of taking part in a daring rescue attempt. But still, it was risky. She scanned the faces of Barthel Schröder, Günther Schwarz, Gustav Bermel, Johann Müller, and the other Pirates gathered at the outdoor gazebo at Blücher Park. They seemed not to believe what they were hearing either.

She then shifted her gaze to the Luftwaffe deserter, Roland Lorent, and his teenage sidekick Hans Balzer, the two assailants that had taken down the Nazi official Heinrich Soentgen on his bicycle two days earlier. Despite having only met Steinbrück yesterday, they had already joined his gang and agreed to help him rescue his pregnant girlfriend. They were nodding vigorously and grinning drunkenly as they passed a stolen bottle of Austrian *marillenschnaps* between themselves. Looking at them, she couldn't help but feel that she was entering into treacherous waters through her association with these desperate criminals.

"The apartment is bound to be heavily guarded with HJ and Gestapo," said Schröder, injecting reason into the meeting. "Are you sure we can take them?"

"What choice do we have?" asked Bomber Hans, who in the past two months had become a full-fledged father figure to the young, impressionable Pirates. "We have to get Cäcilie back. We can't just leave her in the hands of those Nazi pigs."

"There's always a choice," said Angela, sounding more decisive than she felt inside. "There needs to be a good chance of success—otherwise, it's too risky."

"What the hell do you know? You're just a girl," snorted Roland Lorent, drunkenly slurring his words and glaring at her. The Luftwaffe deserter looked to be a little older than Steinbrück, in his mid-twenties, and several years older than his sidekick Hans Balzer. She had a bad feeling about the both of them, especially after having seen them shoot down *Ortsgruppenleiter* Soentgen in cold blood.

"This *girl* has got as much courage as any one of us," said Schröder in her defense. "She has stood shoulder to shoulder with us against these Nazis for the past three months, and never once wavered. So, you had better watch your tongue."

"He's right. Mucki is one of us," agreed Steinbrück, referring to Angela by her code name, the only name that anyone in the group but Schröder knew her by. "And besides, as leader of this outfit, I'll be the one to decide who is and who isn't up to snuff. Have I made myself clear?"

Lorent's eyes narrowed with defiance, but after a moment he backed down. "All right, I didn't mean anything by it. But if we're going to pull this off, we had better have a plan."

"I already have a plan," said Steinbrück. "We will set out in the two stolen cars loaded with weapons and make the rescue. I will take my car around the back, while you and Hans drive the other up to the front on Schönsteinstrasse. We will hit

Number 7 from two sides at once, storm the cellar, and free Cäcilie. With the element of surprise, we can be in and out in five minutes."

They all looked at one another. Angela thought the plan was too wildly fantastical and amateurish to possibly succeed. For a moment, she considered backing out, but as the only female in the group she didn't want to appear soft and weak, and privately she desperately wanted their approval. She was especially concerned since Schröder had told her that the level-headed Jean Hüber and two other Edelweiss Pirates had had a falling-out with Steinbrück recently, and were no longer willing to work with the group.

The deserter Lorent said, "Okay, I like the plan for its simplicity. But I want to add one thing. While Hans drives towards the front of the building, I will be on the front of the hood ready to shoot anyone who resists."

Steinbrück nodded approvingly. "I am fine with that. It's going to be one hell of a Nazi duck shoot, a real Nazi hunt." He laughed, slapped Lorent on the back, and took a pull from the bottle of *marillenschnaps*. "All right, that's it then—let's get going. With any luck, in an hour Cilly will be free."

*That's it?* thought Angela. *That's the plan?*

She looked at Schröder, Günther Schwarz, and the other Pirates, hoping someone would speak up and tell Steinbrück and Lorent they were crazy, or at least propose a better alternative, but no one said a word. They were all awestruck by the older and more experienced Bomber Hans, a legend in the neighborhood for his bomb-defusing and black-market skills. Every instinct told her to protest the harebrained scheme, but as she was about to speak, she felt herself freeze up and didn't utter a word. She didn't want to be the one to second-guess the plan or appear timid.

The next thing she knew they were all piling into the stolen cars, armed with handguns and a machine pistol, and her opportunity to bow out disappeared. She cursed herself because suddenly it was too late and her moment was gone.

They drove to Schönsteinstrasse 7, but the whole operation went badly from the beginning. They descended on the building at full speed before coming to a screeching halt and opening fire on the stakeout team. In the first fusillade, Lorent killed a Hitler Youth member and wounded a Gestapo officer, hitting him in the knee. The first shot was supposed to be the signal for the attack, but Balzer panicked and sped away, crashing into Steinbrück's car, which bore not only the gang leader but Angela, Schröder, and Günther Schwarz.

To Angela's dismay, the car stalled.

"What are you doing, you fool!" cried Bomber Hans to the panicky, drunken sixteen-year-old driver. "You have stalled my car!"

"There's too many of them!" cried Balzer. "We have to get out of here!"

"No, we can take them!" shouted Lorent, as the team of Gestapo and Hitler Youth returned fire.

"We *have* to take them!" bellowed Steinbrück. "I'm not leaving my beautiful Cäcilie in the hands of those pigs!"

On the fly, he quickly put together another plan. While Angela and the other Edelweiss Pirates kept up a steady fire on the enemy, Steinbrück and Lorent would flank the building by climbing up the side of the elevated train line. During the next few minutes, they executed the new plan, but it too was thwarted as Steinbrück and Lorent met stiff resistance. Realizing now that they were badly outnumbered, they were forced to give up, but not before they had shot and killed a brownshirted *Sturmabteilung* officer on his bicycle and drawn in more police and Hitler Youth to counter their flanking maneuver.

They quickly returned to the others.

"It's no good," said Steinbrück. "The place is too heavily guarded."

Angela felt an overwhelming sense of relief; she knew that they were in way over their heads, and felt not only guilty but physically sickened that they had shot and killed two of the opposition and wounded another. She had fired her pistol at the enemy several times, but had not actually hit anyone. Though she hated the Nazis, she had found her commitment to the enterprise wavering when she saw the enemy hit with bullets and heard their anguished screams in the night.

"Well, you can't say we didn't try!" said Schröder. "Now let's get out of here!"

"Damnit, we shouldn't be leaving Cilly behind!" snapped Steinbrück angrily.

"We have no choice unless we want to die," said Angela. "Is that what you want?"

"No, but I'm beside myself! We should have rescued her!"

Unfortunately, it took a minute to get Steinbrück's stalled car up and running again. In the meantime, Lorent and the Pirates continued firing out the car windows at the enemy to keep them at bay. Once Bomber Hans got his car running again, the whole group fled the scene and stopped to rob a nearby store before returning to their new hideout at Blücher Park. At this point, Angela and Schröder were whispering to one another that they should get away from the group, as their close friend Jean Hüber had wisely done. What had taken place tonight, they agreed, was not what they had envisioned when they had joined up to help Steinbrück and his *Ehrenfeld Gruppe*.

"I know what I'm going to do!" snorted Lorent as they gathered at the gazebo. "I'm going to get good and drunk!"

"Oh, that's just great!" snapped Steinbrück. "It's because of your drinking that the plan failed, you know!"

"No, it's because your plan stunk!" countered the inebriated Luftwaffe deserter.

As they continued arguing back and forth, Angela became exasperated. How had she managed to join up with this dangerous band of rebels, who were far closer to common criminals than resistance fighters? It seemed unbelievable that she had allowed herself to get caught up with such a disorganized gang. After Steinbrück and Lorent had downed another bottle of liquor, the group was told by an informant that the Gestapo had already removed Cilly from the apartment earlier in the day and, therefore, the rescue operation had been doomed from the start. Angela couldn't believe that the whole rescue and death of two men had been for nothing. Angered by their failure to free his pregnant girlfriend, Bomber Hans concocted a plan to steal explosives from a supply depot and car bomb the Gestapo's headquarters, an outlandish plan that proved the final straw for Angela and Schröder.

"Mucki and I are out," said Schröder once the two had spoken alone and made their decision. "We are not going with you and will find our own way home."

"That's your choice. We are not the Gestapo and there are no hard feelings," said Steinbrück with surprising equanimity. "Does anyone else want to call it quits?"

No one uttered a word.

"Good luck to you two then," said Bomber Hans. "Eternal war on the Nazis."

"Yes, eternal war on the Nazis," said Angela, and she and Schröder left the group and walked back to Braunsfeld.

As she would soon discover, the plot to steal explosives and car bomb El-De Haus was foiled by attentive guards at the weapons dump. After the guards at the dump chased them away, the remnants of Steinbrück's group returned to their hideout empty-handed. With the night fuelled by adrenaline and liquor behind them and nothing to show for it but failure, already frayed tempers reached their breaking point and the remainder of the group split up after Steinbrück again blamed their failures on Lorent's heavy drinking.

The next day, efforts to apprehend Bomber Hans and the other members of the Ehrenfeld Group and clear the city's rubble fields were begun in earnest. Gestapo officers and Order Police armed with machine pistols and hand grenades spread out all across Ehrenfeld and other parts of the city. Six companies of police reservists bolstered by Gestapo units led by *Kriminalkommissar* Kütter and *Hauptsturmführer* Friedrich Mohr hastened forth to purge the city of the resistance fighters and other subversives. The units established traffic stops to check for proper identification and weapons and swept the ruins and air-raid shelters for Steinbrück and his freedom fighters. The Gestapo's primary suspects were anyone remotely connected with the Ehrenfeld Group and their caches of weapons and black-market goods.

But as the security forces struck back with a vengeance, they were surprised to be met by bands of highly determined, well-armed, and cornered fugitives who had decided to put up stiff resistance rather than surrender. Firefights exploded throughout the city. Barricaded in cellars and armed with small arms and explosives, the suspects, mostly deserters and foreign workers, knew they likely faced execution if apprehended. Consequently, they were difficult to root out and fought tooth and nail to resist.

But with hundreds of security officers swarming the city streets, the Gestapo quickly arrested scores of men and women and re-established order. After his hideout had been betrayed, Roland Lorent was arrested on October 3. Bartholomäus Schröder was arrested a day later by Kütter and subsequently imprisoned and interrogated at the notorious Brauweiler Abbey Prison located on the city's outskirts. Within a week, the Gestapo would have most of the rest of the group, including Steinbrück and several Edelweiss Pirates that had taken part in the October 1 attack—but not Angela, codenamed Mucki. Security officers arrested Bomber Hans at the apartment of another girlfriend on October 11.

Steinbrück, Lorent, and the Edelweiss Pirates involved in the attack, with the exception of Angela, were not the only ones taken into custody. Over the next several weeks, the security forces continued their sweep of Ehrenfeld, rounding up two hundred German civilians and fugitive foreign workers who they brutally interrogated at El-De Haus and Brauweiler. One of the Cologne Navajos they managed to hunt down was Jean Hüber. The police and Gestapo personnel— ideologically committed, overworked, and fearing for their own safety—reacted with lethal force against anyone who resisted arrest, attempted to escape, or appeared on a black list of suspects. Those who did surrender were subjected to savage interrogations and pestilent conditions in both prisons, whose overcrowded nature helped to expand the extreme violence being directed at not only escaped foreign workers and criminals, but those ordinary German civilians who were deemed to lack sufficient commitment to the regime.

When Angela learned that Schröder had been arrested, she did two things: she cried until she ran out of tears, and she anxiously waited.

Waited for him to give up her real name under torture and for Criminal Commissioner Kütter to come hunting for her.

But by the first day of November 1944, he had not yet come.

# CHAPTER 21

**SAINT-NICHOLAS-DE-PORT
NORTHEASTERN FRANCE**

**NOVEMBER 2, 1944**

THE CAVALCADE SWEPT IN FROM THE NORTHWEST. Five quarter-ton jeeps bristling with MPs and .50-caliber machine guns, followed a moment later by a Dodge WC57 three-quarter-ton command car and armored scout car. McBurney watched with great anticipation as the fleet of jeeps rolled to a stop and took up strategic defensive positions that left a small gap for the command car to make a grand entrance.

The Dodge roared in to the head of the formation, with two large air horns and a siren blowing, and parked directly in front of the battalion's commander, Lieutenant Colonel Paul Bates. The command vehicle bore the insignia of the U.S. Third Army on the driver's side and the insignia of a three-star general on metal plates, painted red, with large silver stars on both the front passenger-side grille and rear of the vehicle.

Now McBurney understood why Bates had called the men into formation: some army big shot was here to make a review.

The 700-plus tankers of the 761st Battalion were assembled in a semicircle on a small hill in front of the tanker bivouac area, located southeast of Nancy. McBurney found the soggy and muddy ground reminiscent of Camp Claiborne in Louisiana. The company first sergeants and battalion command sergeants at the assembly point had the men turned out at attention and looking their best. They were less than twenty miles from the front lines, and the artillery in the distance rumbled like thunder. The thermometer hovered in the low forties and the tankers wore mackintoshes against the light drizzle; despite the cold, driving rain, they were in fine spirits.

Since arriving to France, McBurney had learned that the U.S. Third Army in which the Black Panthers would now fight was comprised of XII Corps under Major-General Manton Eddy, and XX Corps under Major-General Walton Walker. The 761st was specifically attached in a supporting role to the 26th Infantry Division of Eddy's XII Corps, commanded by Major General Willard S. Paul. Known as the "Yankee Division" because of its New England National Guard roots, the 26th had been in combat since mid-October. Despite the 761st's experiences at the Louisiana Maneuvers and Camp Claiborne and Hood exercises, the battalion had not supported an infantry outfit this large. But Bates had assured McBurney and the others that they would support regiments, battalions, and smaller units. They had the skills and training to succeed in any scenario, he reassured them. All the same, McBurney felt the Panthers were now in the big leagues and couldn't help but feel anxious as they prepared to fight for the first time in actual combat.

A black driver stepped from the command car, opened the passenger door, and stepped to the side, allowing the general, whoever he was, to hop out of the vehicle. The man was big and brawny, and he wore a brace of ivory-handled pistols, an "Ike" jacket, polished riding boots, fawn-colored Jodhpur riding breeches, and a large

128

brass buckle to hold up his gun belt. McBurney had read stories of General George S. Patton, Jr. in *Stars and Stripes* and other magazines and he had seen the news clips celebrating Patton's victories, so he knew as soon as he saw the two ivory-handled pistols holstered at the man's belt that he was staring at the legendary Old Blood and Guts himself.

At the sight of the man in the flesh, McBurney felt a ripple of excitement course through his system. He found Patton one of the most dashing figures he had ever laid eyes upon, standing next to his command vehicle with all his stars, his gunfighter's squint, and his brace of pistols. Like the other men in the outfit, McBurney stood mesmerized in ranks at attention, his eyes studying the Third Army commander's every move.

"Holy shit, that there's General Patton himself!" gasped Smitty, standing open-mouthed next to him a mere twenty feet away from the legendary general.

McBurney nodded approvingly. "You know what this means, don't you? We're going to be up to our ears in Krauts real soon."

"You think he's here to give us a pep talk?"

"I don't know, but whatever it is I'm sure glad he came on down to see us in person."

They watched as Patton received Bates's salute and then the two tall men—one lean and rangy, the other solid as a bull terrier—spoke together a moment, their aides hovering nearby. McBurney noticed that Patton wasn't wearing a raincoat. The man also seemed shorter than he remembered from the newsreel footage, and as he caught snippets of his voice it had a higher pitch than he had expected.

"What do you think they're saying?" asked Smith.

"I don't know," said McBurney. "But I sure would like to hear it."

"Me too," said Smitty. "It sure is something, him coming down all the way from his headquarters to visit little old us."

ΨΨΨ

As he received Paul Bates's salute, Patton found something impressive and admirable in the cut of the lanky colonel and former All-American football player from Maryland. All in all, he thought, the officer gave the appearance of a competent leader of men and straight-shooter. He felt comfortable in his presence and could tell that Bates reciprocated the feeling.

He had decided he would address the soldiers of the 761st in person because he had specifically requested the tanker battalion and wanted to impart to the men the importance of their mission. But before addressing the new outfit, he wanted to hear what Bates thought he should say to the Negro tankers to prepare them for the hard battles that he knew lay ahead.

"Colonel, is there anything specific you want me to say to your men?" he asked politely, wanting to make Bates and his men feel important and valued.

Bates thought for a moment. "Well General," he said, "the 761st stands well-trained with the best equipment the army has in its possession. But the men do need one thing from you."

"What is that, Colonel?"

"They are in need of the needle, so when the time comes they will kill the enemy."

Patton nodded. "I understand, Colonel. I will take care of it."

"They all know you and your reputation. They just need a little push."

"Give me five minutes and I'll make these boys of yours as good at killing Krauts as any outfit in Third Army."

"Thank you, sir."

With Bates's help, Patton stepped up onto the hood of a half-track that would serve as his podium. The sky above him was a dull pewter broken in places by white wedge-shaped clouds with silvery rims. Looking out over the assembled battalion, a sea of dark faces, he directed the men to stand at ease.

These were his tankers—Patton's Panthers—and he damn sure wanted them to wreak bloody hell upon the enemy, like something out of the Old Testament, which he read from and quoted almost daily. He and his fellow generals had on occasion expressed their doubts as to whether a colored soldier, even with extensive training, could think on his feet fast enough to fight in armor as effectively as a white one, but he earnestly hoped that these Negro tankers would prove the U.S. Army's doubts unfounded. Staring out at the men, he had to admit they made a very good first impression, but only time would tell if they would kill as many Krauts as possible for him and a few extra for their families back home. In any case, he had to inject some realism into the green battalion and get the men fired up.

But even if the jury was still out on the 761st's capabilities in his mind, since the men had yet to be blooded and see the elephant, he was absolutely counting on them. That was the reason he had driven all the way out here to address the battalion in person, something he did not do for every unit. He had seen the War Department reports—the Army had few even semi-trained tank units left in the States and he had been given little choice but the Black Panthers if he wanted an outfit with extensive combat training to fight under his command. But by a stroke of luck, he now had the well-honed 761st to support Third Army, and by God, he was banking on them to fulfill their motto and come out fighting. If an outfit killed Germans and did not sustain an unacceptable casualty rate, he cared little about color. At this point, he would even take slightly higher casualties as long as these Negro boys killed truckloads of Krauts, made the accompanying infantry feel more protected, and pushed themselves to the limit in the final victory over Nazi Germany.

"Men, you are the first Negro tankers ever to fight in the American Army," he began in his trademark high-pitched, almost squeaky voice. "I would never have asked for you if you weren't good. I have nothing but the best in my army. I don't care what color you are, so long as you go up there and kill those Kraut sons of bitches! Everyone has their eyes on you and is expecting great things from you. Most of all, your race is looking forward to you. Don't let them down and, damn you, don't let me down!"

Here he paused. He stood there with his feet spread apart, fists on his hips, and his eyes sharply surveying the ranks for several seconds before resuming.

"They say it is patriotic to die for your country. Well, let's see how many patriots we can make out of those German sons of bitches. You hear me?"

He again paused for effect, letting his words have their impact on the young, impressionable men before him. He noticed that they were unusually well-disciplined: every one of them stood erect as a flagpole and not one of them blinked or batted an eye. A little sliver of sunlight penetrated the clouds, and he found it a good sign. A damn good sign. He took an invisible deep breath. He felt a certain sacrosanct power in the moment with some 700 men standing before him, hanging on his every word in the land where the legendary Napoleon and Murat had once fought, and he wanted to soak it all in before making his final remarks, calmly basking in the adulation of his new starry-eyed tankers.

He knew this was history in the making.

"Killing Krauts, men—that is your goddamn job," he said in conclusion. "And know this. There is something important you all will be able to say when you make it safely back home. You may thank God that thirty or forty years from now when you are sitting with your grandson on your knee and he asks, 'Grandfather, what did you do in World War Two?' you won't have to say, 'I shoveled shit in Mississippi.' No, sir, instead you can tell him with pride that you won a great victory in the cause of freedom and democracy, by killing a hell of a lot of Germans for General George Goddamn Patton. Now good luck and Godspeed—and do your damn job and do it well. That's all I have to say."

ΨΨΨ

As Patton stepped down smartly from the half-track, McBurney did not think any moving picture could adequately portray what he had just witnessed. In that moment, he would have followed Old Blood and Guts to hell and back if called upon to do so. He was totally taken by the general's aura of command and colorful cursing. But he also noted a certain paternal affection beneath the Old Man's gruff exterior. It was for this latter quality that Patton reminded him of the "Great White Father" Paul Bates and his WWI veteran father Thomas McBurney, the two men he respected and trusted most in the world.

"Man, was that motherfucking something?" exclaimed Leonard Smith. "And on my twentieth birthday, no less. I'm telling you that's got to mean something."

"Today is my twenty-second birthday," said Preston McNeil, standing to their left. "You're right, it's got to mean something for the both of us. That son of a bitch is something else."

"I'm sure not going to be the one to let him own, I can tell you that," said McBurney with feeling.

"Me neither," said Smitty, shaking his head emphatically.

McBurney found that Patton's unexpected visit seemed to confirm his own boyhood notions of glory. The man just had a mystique. His bearing, his rugged features and piercing eyes, his very presence had mesmerized all the tankers and rendered them speechless. But he had to admit Old Blood and Guts also seemed a little fanatical and over the top. He was also still shocked to discover that the general had a high-pitched voice that sounded almost like a woman with a bad cold. He suspected Patton used profanity in order to be taken seriously and generate an esprit de corps amongst the men so they would be better fighters.

"Hey look, he's coming over to talk to us," said Private First Class E.G. McConnell.

Indeed, after the Old Man had climbed down from the half-track, he had conferred a moment with Bates, and he now seemed to be conducting a personal inspection of the battalion's tanks and crews. As McBurney's group was closest to Patton, the general stepped over to them first. They snapped to attention, ramrod straight. Putting them at ease and playfully joking with them a moment, he then proceeded to climb up onto their Sherman tank to inspect its new high-velocity gun.

The 761st was equipped with a full battery of fifty-six M4 Sherman and seventeen M5 Stuart tanks. The majority of the medium Shermans were the most recent model of the M4, the M4A3E8, known by tank crews as the "Easy Eight" because of its improved suspension and smoother ride. The Easy Eight, in addition to a better suspension system, had slightly thicker armor, safer stowage racks for ammunition, and—most important of all—a more powerful, higher-velocity cannon. Allied tankers still called them "Iron Coffins" since they were outgunned by the newer German Panzer Mark IVs, Panthers, and gigantic Tigers, which could blast a hole clean through a Sherman with an armor-piercing round, but they maneuvered well and had increased firepower over their predecessor. The original 75mm cannon of the M4s had a muzzle velocity of 2,050 feet per second; the new, longer-barreled 76mm main gun of the M4A3E8 had a muzzle velocity of 2,650 fps, an improvement of almost 30 percent.

"That is one hell of a gun, fellas," observed Patton, running his hand along the big 76mm cannon as if stroking a favorite horse.

He climbed down on the commander's side and looked the tankers in the eye.

"Like I said before, men, I want you to kill those Kraut sons of bitches, no matter what it takes. That means I want you to shoot every goddamn thing you see—church steeples, water towers, houses, little old ladies, children, haystacks. Every goddamn thing you see. This is war, goddamnit." Now he fixed his intense gaze upon E.G. McConnell. "You hear me, son? Shoot every damn thing in your sights and show no mercy! If you do, those Kraut bastards will kill you first!"

McConnell trembled in his combat boots. "Y-yes, sir, General, sir. I'll shoot everything in sight."

"And I will too, General," said McBurney. "I'm one of the best shots in the outfit. I'll kill plenty of Krauts for you, sir."

"Well goddamnit, that's what I like to hear. What's your name sergeant and where you from?"

"William H. McBurney, main gunner. I'm from New York City. They call me Billy."

"Well, give 'em hell, Billy, and do your country proud."

"Yes, sir, I will!"

Old Blood and Guts then headed on down the line, inspecting the men and their new tanks. A half hour later, he left in a procession of vehicles just as dramatically as he had arrived. When he drove off, McBurney and his buddies overheard Corporal Howard "Big Tit" Richardson talking to his Able Company commander, Captain David Williams, about Patton's visit.

"Sir, that old man is crazy as hell. Did you see the way his eyes roll around when he talks? No bullshit about the Hornet, that's for damn sure. I'm more afraid of the Old Man than I am of those damned Krauts. That soldier under his command in Sicily was lucky he just got slapped at that hospital. Patton could have had him shot!"

McBurney chuckled at the reference to the "Hornet." The unflattering nickname had been given to Patton by the press based on the garish green tankers' uniform he invented in the 1930s for the U.S. Army. The uniform, which included a leather Washington Redskins' football helmet for head protection, was never formally adopted by the armed forces and resembled the outfit worn by the "The Green Hornet" from the popular radio program and movie serials.

"He may be a little over the top," said McBurney to Smith, McConnell, and the others in his group. "But I'll follow that man to hell and back."

"Me too," echoed Smitty. "Because if there's one thing that son of a bitch knows how to do, it's wage war."

"Nothing but the best," said McBurney. "That goes for him *and* us."

A chorus went up from several of the tankers, who appreciated the moniker. "Nothing but the best! Nothing but the best!"

Others soon weighed in. While Patton's bloodthirsty bravado worried some, most had an overriding respect, indeed awe, for the legendary general. McBurney trusted the man implicitly and firmly believed he would lead them to victory. He found him tough and straightforward, the type of commander who would be up at the front and not playing armchair general in the rear. Yesterday, to even catch a glimpse of the three-star general in France would have been an absurd notion. But today they were officially Patton's Panthers and had met the man in person. He was proud that Old Blood and Guts had taken time to address their relatively small group, and the man's words made him proud to be part of Patton's ground forces. After the varied hardships of their training, the commander of the U.S. Third Army had acknowledged them, had specifically requested them, and they were now here in Europe—as they had long hoped to be—to fight on his winning team.

As if on cue, McBurney heard the rumble of guns to the east. The sound, though distant, seemed to take on a life and personality of its own. He knew that soon the 761st would be in the thick of it with bullets and shells flying all around.

They would see the elephant.

But for the time being, they would prepare their tanks for battle as they had trained to do at Claiborne and Hood: oiling and re-oiling the guns, testing equipment, making repairs, fitting their tanks out with new parts, and going on practice runs in the soggy French fields to get used to the feel of those new parts. One of which was the newly issued "Duckbill," a device attached to the M4's metal track-extender to distribute a tank's weight more evenly and prevent it from bogging down in the mud.

He looked to the east in the direction of the rumbling artillery fire, which was picking up in intensity. Patton's exhortation rang in his ears like the tolling of a bell.

*I don't care what color you are, so long as you go up there and kill those Kraut sons of bitches! Everyone has their eyes on you and is expecting great things from you. Most of all, your race is looking forward to you. Don't let them down and, damn you, don't let me down!*

# CHAPTER 22



## NOVEMBER 8, 1944

IN THE PREDAWN DARKNESS, the tanks of Baker, Charlie, Dog, and Headquarters Companies rolled towards the front as part of Patton's Saar Campaign. The Third Army's heavy artillery shells pummeling the German positions sounded to McBurney like lightning strikes multiplied a thousand-fold. The force of the percussions was astounding. The noise reverberated in his ears and jarred every nerve in his body—even though he was buttoned up inside his heavy steel M4 Sherman "Easy Eight" and his ears were partially covered with an A.G. Spalding & Bros. leather football-style tanker's helmet.

*This is no Hollywood moving picture show—this is the real thing,* he reminded himself as the tank column made its way slowly towards the line of departure, or LD, where it would transition from maneuver into attack formation. At long last, he was about to go toe to toe against the vaunted Wehrmacht, whose reputation in battle was on par with that of the Spartans, the Roman legions, and Napoleon's legendary *Grande Armée.* He knew damn well that he and his fellow Negro tankers were just as good as any white soldiers.

Today, they would get their chance to prove it.

The Germans expected an attack on Dieuze. But to deceive the enemy, the plan was for the Black Panthers and accompanying infantry to jump off in a two-pronged attack in the direction of the small French villages of Moyenvic and Vic-sur-Seille. The goal was to relieve the stress on Third Army as it struggled to take the large city of Metz, located fifty miles north of Patton's headquarters at Nancy, the Lorraine region's ruling city over the centuries.

For Old Blood and Guts, Metz had become an obsession. In early September, he had breezily told General Walker, head of his XX Corps and one of his personal favorite battlefield commanders, "See you in Metz." But Walker had attacked for ten days straight along the Moselle and failed to take the town in the face of stiff German resistance. The problem was the city was protected by a chain of thirty-five forts, anchored by the thus far impenetrable Fort Jeanne d'Arc and Fort Driant. Ringed by artillery, moat, and automatic weapons, Driant guarded the southern end of the approaches to the city and was last captured in the year 45 A.D by Attila the Hun. Since then, Metz had become an impregnable military objective and a career-destroying obstacle to any general bent on its seizure. Patton had originally hoped to outflank Metz and leave its defenders to wither for later mopping up, but the enforced delay in early September for Montgomery's ill-fated *Operation Market-Garden* to the north made that impossible.

The temperature was cold, the skies overcast, and a drizzling rain pattered down on the moving column. The tanks of the 761st smelled of oil, gunpowder, and locker-room-like sweat, but for McBurney the scent was familiar, even reassuring. Daylight was close to breaking, and the world outside visible through the periscopes and hatches remained little more than buttery gray shadows in the pre-dawn light.

Soon the Third Army artillery shelling stopped and the air turned eerily quiet. The only sounds were the steady rumble of the tank's 9-cylinder radial engine and the rolling squeak of the metal-and-rubber tank tracks. McBurney stifled a yawn. He and the other men had slept only fitfully last night in their tanks, hatches closed against the driving rain, and he was dog-tired.

The M4 Sherman carried a crew of five: commander, turret gunner, loader, driver, and co-driver/hull gunner. For firepower, the tank was equipped with a 75mm M3 or 76mm M1A high-velocity main cannon; and secondary armament consisting of a .50-caliber Browning M2HB rooftop machine gun, a .30-caliber Browning M1919A4 coaxial machine gun that moved with the main gun, and a .30-caliber bow-mounted machine gun. Collectively, the machine guns were for fending off enemy aircraft, buzz sawing through woods and walls, and taking out soft targets at close range when the main gun's potential collateral damage would be excessive, or to conserve its ammunition. The .50-caliber antiaircraft gun was highly effective against not only airplanes and troops but also trucks and wooden structures, and it could rotate on its ring mount on a 360-degree axis.

As turret gunner, McBurney handled his tank's lethal 76mm main cannon. As he had no hatch of his own, his periscopic gun sight—a five-inch-wide relay of glass prisms and a 3x telescopic gun sight—was his predominant window into the outside world. Behind McBurney was Teddy Windsor, the thirty-five-year-old tank commander, or TC, from Cleveland, Ohio, who gave orders to the crew and had been with McBurney since Camp Claiborne. From his turret vantage, Windsor ordered driving and attack maneuvers from both inside and outside the tank using his hand-held microphone, warning of hazardous terrain, tank obstacles, opposing forces, or other tanks. McBurney sat in the gunner's chair in front of Teddy Windsor, to the right of the gun breech, and to the left of the loader. In front and to the left of him was the tank's driver, Willie Devore, an easygoing, twenty-five-year-old South Carolina farmer with a grammar school education and knack for the ladies. He also happened to be one of the most popular fellows in the battalion. Devore's driver's seat was to the left of the bow gunner and co-driver, who manned the .30-caliber bow machine gun.

Virtually all the tanks had been given a name by the men, which was usually painted in thick white letters on the main gun or turret. The members of the 761st got a kick out of their vehicles sporting names, each rolling and grinding with its own distinctive personality. But it was more than that. They felt a deep sense of pride and proprietorship towards their Shermans and Stuarts, similar to a teenager's passionate feeling of ownership towards a first car.

In Headquarters Company, Windsor's and McBurney's tank served as Bates's battlefield command tank. It was named after the lieutenant colonel's girlfriend, a U.S. Army nurse named "Taffy." McBurney would have liked something a bit more edgy and tough-sounding, but he was okay with it. His friend Leonard Smith's tank was christened "Cool Stud," a name that was well known by everyone in the battalion. Cool Stud shared its name with a rooster once procured by Sergeant Dan Cardell for his Charlie Company tank, which served as the mascot for the battalion. Other tanks carried monikers like "Thunderbolt," "Kraut Killer," "Big Mamma," "Black Jack," "Hurricane," or "Widow Maker"—but the main thing was that most tanks had an individual name. The tankers had gotten to know Warren Crecy well, so it came as no surprise when the shy but hellacious fighter named his tank simply "Crecy."

The designers of the Sherman tank had emphasized speed and mobility, limiting the thickness of the armor and the size of the main gun, thereby compromising on firepower and survivability. The thirty-three-ton tank's squat, bulbous turret looked incongruous against the tall, sharp lines of its body, as if the components had been pieced together from salvage. The tank had a maximum speed of just under 30 miles per hour and a range of 150 miles. It was equipped with five periscopes for the crew and vision blocks on the commander's hatch with added rings of rectangular glass to help the crew see outside the tank when it was buttoned-up.

The cramped, tracked vehicle with its crew of five provided little room for a nearly six-foot-tall young man like McBurney. But he was skinny and could stretch his frame out through the narrow, upper steel split hatch on occasion and survey 360 degrees. With his height, he preferred the view from the turret and was glad he was not a driver or machine gunner seated in the bow of the contraption.

To enter the tank, the commander and gunner lowered themselves through the commander's split hatch, while the driver, loader, and co-driver/hull gunner used their own smaller individual hatches. There were no ladders and the tankers merely dropped down from the top, lowered the hatch covers, leaving just a crack for air in the commander's split hatch, and crammed themselves into their seats among the equipment and ammunition.

Everything had its place in the tank—spare tracks and wheels, fire extinguishers, repair tools, a tarp, ax and pick, radios, blackout lamps, water cans, food, gun-cleaning materials, first aid kits, extra periscopes, searchlights. Machine-gun ammo in a Sherman was stored in compartments in the side walls, while most of the high-explosive (HE) and armor-piercing (AP) shells for the 75mm main gun were tucked beneath the turret floor and for the 76mm main gun in vertical and horizontal racks on either side of the drive shaft enclosure and behind the bow gunner's seat. The M4 held seventy to ninety shells and around 170 gallons of gasoline—which made for a combustible combination if the tank took a direct hit by a dreaded German "Ripsaw" 88 or *Panzerfaust* hand-held rocket shell.

The tanks of the 761st had started out all together with Bates leading the way eastward in his jeep, and the vehicles were still in good maneuver formation. Directly ahead lay enemy fortifications, machine-gun nests, artillery, mortars, *Panzerfaust* tank destroyers, and enemy armor intent on halting their offensive in its tracks. Germany, the Siegfried Line, and meandering Rhine lay less than fifty miles away, but McBurney knew that the Germans, though their ranks were severely reduced after Falaise, would give up little ground between here and Berlin without a vicious fight. The advancing tank column was soon joined by the tank destroyers and trucked infantry of the 101st and 328th Regiments of the 26th Infantry Division.

McBurney was confident the 761st was ready to come out fighting in its first taste of combat. He and his brothers-in-arms had spent the past week checking and replacing parts, oiling guns, and stocking and positioning the full supply of 75mm and 76mm shells and .30- and .50-caliber ammunition for the machine guns. He had personally inspected every inch of his main 76mm gun, running his hand along the exterior like he did with the armor of each new tank. He checked the barrel and breech. He zeroed in the tank gun, put a cross on it, and lined up the sight. He checked and rechecked his M3 "grease gun"—an odd-shaped, compact, .45-caliber submachine gun that was standard issue for tankers forced to abandon their tanks and fight on foot. He also checked the .30- and .50-caliber onboard machine guns.

Though Taffy's commander Teddy Windsor hadn't actually told him so, he knew he was one of the best gunners in the battalion. He seldom missed his targets. But that had been in training exercises, not in battle. Now he would be trying to bring down real tanks and kill actual human beings. He knew that training alone, no matter how realistic, could not approach the horror and violence of true combat.

Soldiers had to get in the water and swim across the river. They might be dragged under a few times, but most would make it to the other side and become veterans. For McBurney, the briefings through which some dozed and the films they saw made combat no more real than in the moving pictures, and though their training exercises at Camps Claiborne and Hood had trained them well, they were still just exercises and not live combat with German 88s, mortars, and *Panzerfausts* firing at them and explosions all around.

Today, all that would change.

Two miles down the road, near the town of Arracourt, the tank and infantry column came to a halt. A French farmer had blocked the crossroads with a herd of cattle, causing a traffic pileup. Bates assumed he was a collaborator sent to disrupt American troop movements; he immediately placed the farmer under arrest and ordered several of the infantrymen accompanying the tanks to clear the road. The Alsace-Lorraine region had passed back and forth repeatedly between French and German hands in the past two centuries, and the Germans had maneuvered to increase their influence and create loyalty whenever they had control, shaping a population split between pro-French and pro-German factions.

The column continued crawling forward towards the LD where they would spread out into attack formation. The near-constant rain had produced the greatest flooding the region had witnessed in a generation: the roads and fields had turned to oceans of mud. The conditions reduced off-road travel to a minimum and rendered tanks more vulnerable to fire-covered roadblocks, tank traps, and artillery. But still the attack force pressed on through the molasses-like muck. White doughboys of the 26th Infantry splayed out behind the tanks, and more than a few climbed aboard the armored vehicles to hitch a ride and rest their weary feet.

The voice of Major Charles Wingo, riding in one of the other two tanks assigned to Headquarters Company, came in over the radio intercom. The white Southerner from Virginia, the battalion's executive officer and second-in-command to Bates, had always viewed the black members of the 761st with open contempt, frequently addressing the soldiers as "boy" and believing that the men would never perform well under fire, despite the battalion's outstanding record throughout training.

"I want absolute radio silence. Is that understood?" snapped Wingo in his shrill, condescending voice that the Black Panthers had always found irritating. "You boys keep quiet on those radios, you hear?"

A radio crackled. "Yo mama!"

McBurney and the others burst out with laughter. Only the tanks of a platoon leader and platoon sergeant could transmit over the radio, using the agreed-upon platoon frequency, so McBurney knew it had to be a platoon leader or sergeant making fun of Wingo. Everyone else in the battalion's Shermans could only listen over the airwaves.

"That's telling him," said Willie Devore, who coming from the South had encountered more than his fair share of Major Charles Wingos. "Man, that cracker is one serious asshole."

"You can say that again," agreed McBurney, who wore headphones sewn into his leather earflaps and a throat microphone clipped around his neck, which was plugged into the intercom. "Nothing we do is ever good enough for that S.O.B."

"Never has been," agreed Devore. "He's always considered us nothing but a bunch of dumb-ass niggers. I don't know why he never asked for a transfer—he ain't never believed in us."

"Well, today we get our chance to prove him wrong," said Teddy Windsor. The tank commander's head and shoulders stuck out of the turret like a groundhog, and he spoke into a hand-held microphone the crew had nicknamed the "pork chop" due to its unique shape. "We're going to come out fighting just like the Brown Bomber and show these Krauts how we spearchuckers wage war. Right fellas!"

McBurney and the others gave a rousing cheer. "Come out fighting! Come out fighting!"

The voices echoed over the intercom of the hollow metal tank, covering up the fears of the crew members with a youthful burst of bravado.

Just shy of the front, Bates hopped out of his jeep to direct the tank crews and make sure the assault elements were in order and heading in the right direction. The tank commanders had been told which way to go the day before, but a patrol returned and informed the colonel that much of the ground to the unit's front looked impassable due to flooding from incessant rainfall and the bursting of the Dieuze Dam. Bates quickly shifted the axis of approach by thirty degrees to take advantage of more favorable terrain.

It was now daybreak. As they passed the colonel, Windsor and the other TCs riding head and shoulders above their open hatches waved at him and flashed V-for-victory signs and thumbs-ups. The column kept moving towards the line of departure for the kickoff of the attack. As the tanks rumbled and squeaked past Bates in a long green line, he stood on the hood of his jeep, presenting a tall, imposing figure in his leather tanker's helmet and combat gear. Like Patton whom he greatly admired, he was out front and visible to his men, encouraging and firing them up for battle.

Suddenly, the early morning calm was shattered by a thunderous roar and bright illuminating flashes against the pewter sky, as German tank-killing 88s, mortars, and machine-guns opened fire. The doughs hit the muddy earth as green lances of tracer fire streaked towards the armored vehicles and infantrymen, crisscrossing the field. McBurney felt the heavy steel Sherman and muddy ground beneath his main gunner's seat quiver and tremble. The road was being targeted with concentrated enemy fire and the shells began exploding all around the column.

"Jesus Christ, they're coming in hot!" cried Windsor, his head still poking out the top of the turret. "Quick, battle stations!"

He buttoned up his commander's split hatch as the tanks of each platoon swiftly deployed into combat formation, with a spacing of thirty yards between tanks. Devore held Taffy's pace at ten miles per hour, the speed being engaged now by the other tanks in the advancing column. Peering through his periscope, McBurney scanned the low ground and rounded hills and ridges that stretched ahead. The drab olive-brown terrain was broken here and there by forests of trees, neat rows of farmland, grassy meadows, the spires and rooftops of Moyenvic and Vic-sur-Seille, and the meandering watercourse of the Seille River. Though he couldn't yet see the enemy, he knew the valley was filled with hidden Krauts in field gray and leopard-spotted camo.

Then, in the distance, he and Windsor both spotted a German Panzer Mark IV covered with underbrush at one o'clock. A puff of smoke erupted from the tank's cannon muzzle and an angry green bolt appeared to be heading straight for their M4 tank. Before they could tell Devore to make a hard turn and take evasive action, the round streaked past and missed, churning up muddy earth in a massive explosion behind the Sherman.

*Damn, that was a close call,* thought McBurney, breathing a sigh of relief. When two more German rounds screamed past and hit an armored vehicle with a wrenching metallic crash out of his field of view, he felt a watery feeling in the pit of his stomach. He had been a little jittery before going into battle this morning, but with the near-misses and deafening explosions all around he was now far more on edge. He could feel the battle adrenaline kicking in now.

*Hold it together,* he told himself. *Just follow your training and do your job and everything will be okay.*

Soon the voice of Captain Williams, commanding Able Company in a separate combat team advancing on Vic-sur-Seille with the 104th Infantry Regiment, broke through the radio intercom.

"Now, looky here, ya cats," he said to his tankers in his best cool-cat Harlemese. "We gotta hit it down the main drag and hip some of those unhepped cats on the other side. So let's roll on down ole Seventh Avenue and knock 'em, Jack."

McBurney and the other tankers laughed, the tension inside the tank easing momentarily. Unlike the uninspiring and bigoted Wingo, the rich Philadelphia white boy Williams had slowly but assuredly gained the trust of the men during their training at Camp Hood and in England. They knew he was fair and had their back, just like Bates. And he had a sense of humor to boot.

McBurney anxiously peered again through his sight at the growing battle to his front. Puffs of smoke now dotted the French countryside along with streaming green bolts of tracer fire. The sound of booming explosions, some close by, others more distant, assaulted his ears through the hollow echo chamber of the Sherman.

*Sweet Jesus, it's happening—this is really goddamn happening!*

The Black Panther's first major test had begun.

# CHAPTER 23

**VIC-SUR-SEILLE
NORTHEASTERN FRANCE**

**NOVEMBER 8, 1944**

"DRIVER, STOP!" cried Teddy Windsor over the intercom, his scratchy voice just loud enough to be heard over the groan of the engine and explosions reverberating outside Taffy's cramped interior.

Willie Devore, jammed into his driver's seat, instantly obeyed and brought the Sherman to a halt.

"Gunner, *Panzerfausts* at one o'clock! Take them out before they get into position to fire on us!" the tank commander then commanded McBurney.

"I see 'em, boss!" cried the wide-eyed kid from Harlem.

Peering into his telescopic gun sight, he zeroed in on the company of German infantrymen making their way along the treeline armed with the dreaded *Panzerfausts*—single-shot recoilless antitank rocket launchers that, with their high-explosive rounds, were already wreaking havoc on the advancing column of Shermans and Stuarts. Turning his handwheels, he fine-tuned his aim until he settled the reticle—the main gunsight's crosshairs—on the center of mass of the clump of enemy troops. His booted foot hovered over the trigger, a button on the footrest for the main 76mm turret cannon.

Now Windsor gave an order to the loader: "HE!" he cried, calling for a high-explosive shell, which was typically used for soft-skinned vehicles, buildings, and troops but not tanks.

"Coming right up!"

"Traverse a hair right…steady-on…range two hundred yards!" roared the TC.

McBurney made a final adjustment. "Ready!"

"Fire!"

Stomping the foot pedal and flipping the fire switch, he unleashed the tank's 76mm cannon on the German *Panzerfaust* company. Spotting the HQ tanks at the last second, the Germans hit the dirt. The shot sailed harmlessly over their heads, blasting away the conifers behind them in a Vesuvian eruption of flame and smoke.

"Damnit!" cursed McBurney, seeing that he had overshot the target. "Don't worry, Sarge, I got 'em now," he grumbled. It pissed him off that he had missed on the first shot, for the Third Army Standard Operating Procedure manual clearly stated that it was of the utmost importance that tank crews, particularly the commander and gunner, be trained to get a hit with the first shot against surprise targets such as antitank guns or enemy tanks.

He quickly adjusted the barrel until the clump of the closest Germans were centered on his reticle's crosshair. The spent shell popped out of the breech and the loader shoved in another round. When Windsor ordered, "Fire!" McBurney let loose with a second round before the Germans could escape or move to within the *Panzerfaust's* effective firing range of 200 feet.

A blinding flash filled his sight, the tank jumped like a startled horse, and this time he saw bodies fly in the air in an explosion of humanity, earth, and smoke.

"I got 'em! I got 'em!" he cried triumphantly as the smoke and dust from the two 76mm muzzle blasts filled the tank with a stinky cloud, which was quickly dissipated by the exhaust fan.

"First blood!" shouted Devore. "You be a Kraut-killer now, motherfucker!"

"Yessir, that's fine shooting, Billy!" roared Windsor. "Now do it again!"

But their Sherman and the other two tanks of the Headquarters Company came under heavy fire from German 88mm antitank guns. The enemy shells impacted nearby, shaking the ground so hard that the rippling shock waves penetrated the heavy steel tank. With the Germans trying to bracket them, they were forced to move to safety with the rest of the HQ Company. Drive sprockets churned and track links clacked forward in unison. But with the heavy smoke and dust all around, McBurney was no longer able to sight a target and couldn't help but feel claustrophobic, as if he was trapped in a tin can and at the mercy of the enemy.

The Shermans made it to the protective cover of a copse of trees on their right. The air continued to be shattered by a series of thunderous roars, green tracer bolts, and bright illuminating flashes against the wall of smoke. Now a pair of prowling German Mark IV Ausf F2 Panzers opened fire up ahead at ten o'clock and the Black Panthers exchanged fire with the German tanks.

The most-produced German armor and main rival of the M4 Sherman, the Panzer Mark IV medium tank was equipped with a long-barrelled 75mm gun, the KwK40 L/43, which was able to penetrate most Allied tanks with their high-velocity, armor-piercing rounds. The Sherman was equipped with two and a half inches of armor laid at a forty-seven-degree angle on the front glacis plate to deflect incoming rounds—but it was no match for a well-delivered armor-piercing round fired from a German 75mm gun, which packed 25 percent more punch than its American 75mm counterpart, or the lethal German 88mm cannon.

Peering through his periscopic gun sight, McBurney saw bright, fiery spumes erupt from one of the 761st's tanks in the spearhead of the advancing battalion. A pair of hatch covers blew open in a volcanic eruption of flame and smoke that reached twenty feet in the air. Three disoriented crew members scrambled out of the flaming Sherman, two of them with uniforms ablaze as "living torches."

*Lord have mercy!* he gasped inwardly, realizing it had to have been a direct hit into the 400-horsepower gasoline engine, fuel tank, or ammo stowed on board for fire to belch out of the hatches like that. American tank crews had given the Sherman the grim nicknames "Iron Coffin" and "Ronson," like the cigarette lighter, because when the tank was struck by German AP rounds "it lit up the first time, every time." In such cases, crew members often had only a few seconds to escape before being burned alive. McBurney noted grimly that the struck Sherman blazed like an inferno—his first glimpse of the horror of the Ronson effect—and only one of the crew members managed to escape the flaming tank without being torched.

*Damn, we are in the shit now!* he thought. *Is this what I really wanted?*

All he knew was he didn't want to burn alive like that. Sometimes, he had heard, it didn't even take a direct hit to blow up a Sherman; sometimes when the hull was penetrated, the electrical cables shorted out and sparked a fire of the onboard munitions, even if the gasoline failed to explode. Regardless, with a direct hull penetration the crew had to escape swiftly or be burned alive, which was why many

TCs left their top hatch open even during combat. Sometimes, the tank itself could still be salvaged if someone thought to pull the fire extinguisher switch on the way out. Otherwise, the tremendous heat softened the armor and destroyed the tank.

Even if a tank didn't light up like a Ronson, blisteringly hot shell fragments ricocheting around inside a tank could tear the guts out of a crew, spilling them all over the walls and floor of the tank. McBurney knew that there was little he could do if his tank got hit, except get the hell out through the TC's hatch if he was able to and run like hell. His personal weapons, a pistol and .45-caliber grease gun, would hopefully allow him to fight his way back to the rear if necessary.

The battle heated up as both sides were now exchanging heavy fire. The dreaded *Panzerfausts* took out vehicles, and MG-42 machine guns—called *knochensäge* or "bone saw" by the Germans, altered to "buzz saw" by GIs—wreaked carnage on the infantry. Bitter-tasting cordite fumes, palls of smoke, and mass confusion blanketed the field of battle. Up and down the column, Teddy Windsor and the other tank commanders gave firing orders, McBurney and the other main gunners followed the commands, and loaders yanked HE and AP shells from the "ready rounds" armored boxes and the vertical and horizontal racks on the turret walls, ramming them home into the breech. Meanwhile, Willie Devore and the other drivers struggled to keep moving forward, finding the Duckbills little help against the torrents of mud.

To McBurney, the 761st's baptism of fire was a chaos of noise and confusion. The groan of Taffy's engine, the thudding and recoil of his own cannon, the clink of the spent shells, the ear-splitting crashes of incoming German shells, and the radio squawking with the overexcited voices of men passing orders, shouting, confirming, questioning, and cursing all mingled together in a mad orchestra of sound.

Straining to see what little he could out of his periscope, he was astonished by the courage and resilience of the white doughs of the 26th Infantry Division. The infantrymen took countless hits in the open field but somehow still kept going. They had never fought with tanks before and at first stayed too close beside the vehicles, operating on the natural assumption that thirty-three tons of steel would provide them with protective cover. But the Sherman was essentially a big, wide, high-silhouetted target, drawing enemy small-arms, automatic, mortar, and artillery fire like a magnet, and the doughs quickly learned to spread out.

After what seemed to McBurney a long and intense time, the shelling on both sides slackened. He and Windsor climbed out of the top hatch to take a look. They quickly spotted a dead horse just off the road. It had been hit by an artillery shell with such force that it was turned inside out, the strange pale lines of its intestines fully exposed. Throughout the unit's trek across France, McBurney had seen various signs of death and devastation—German corpses, buildings reduced to rubble, bombed-out tanks and half-tracks, ruined fields—but for some reason the sight of the eviscerated horse disturbed him more than anything. It brought home the bitter reality of just how far away from home he was and the fierceness of the enemy.

*Good Lord,* he thought, *this is just the first day. Am I really going to be able to do this for another three or six months? What if the war takes longer?*

He looked at Windsor. The two just shook their heads and climbed back into their tank. Soon they received new orders to stand back and wait with Dog Company on the ridge overlooking the valley. There they were to guard the supply train, which had just arrived and was beginning to unload. Over the next few minutes, Devore ably navigated Taffy to a position just beyond the front up on high ground overlooking the tidy French villages of Moyenvic, Vic-sur-Seille, and Morville-lès-Vic. No longer pestered by artillery fire, the five crew members climbed out of the tank and stared out from the turret at the ongoing armored battle.

"Jesus, look at all that burning metal," said Windsor.

McBurney nodded. Not only did he see several smoldering tanks from both sides, he saw a company of infantrymen pinned down and taking heavy enemy fire. They had many wounded and he asked Windsor why their Headquarters Company wasn't being ordered to fire smoke down there to distract the Germans, so they could pull some of their own guys out. Sherman tanks were outfitted with British-invented M3 smoke mortar launchers, which the tank's loader fired like a flare gun from a hole in the turret. But the TC didn't know why the battalion wasn't laying down a smokescreen, so he went off to talk to Ivan Harrison, the HQ Company commanding officer, to see what could be done. Five minutes later he returned.

"Our orders are to stay put," Windsor informed the tank crew. "But you're not going to believe what else I learned."

"What?" asked McBurney, fearing the worst.

"Colonel Bates has been wounded and is no longer in command."

"He's out of the fight? What happened to him?"

"Once he finished directing us towards the LD and the column passed, a German patrol opened fire with a machine gun. Somehow, they were able to sneak behind our lines. They cut him down as he was about to make his way back to his jeep."

"Damn. But he's going to live, right?" asked Devore hopefully.

"Yeah, he's okay. The rounds broke his leg above the ankle and he was evacuated. But word is he's going to be out of commission for a month or two."

McBurney shook his head. This was disturbing news. The Black Panthers, to a man, had long trusted and admired Bates. He was the father figure who had built up and trained the outfit, who had helped the battalion develop a pride and belief in itself, and who had kept the men focused amidst the bigotry at Camps Claiborne and Hood. For their trusted leader to fall on the very first day of battle was more than just a setback—it was a disaster.

"Who's the new CO?" he asked Windsor. "Don't tell me it's Major Wingo."

"That's what I was about to tell you. Wingo will not be taking command of the battalion because the son of a bitch abandoned his post."

"What are you talking about?"

"An hour ago, he climbed out of his tank and drove off in a jeep towards the front. Not long afterwards, one of the tank crews saw him heading back the other way towards the rear."

The men were shaking their heads in disgust.

"What a chickenshit," said Devore.

"He must have gone nuts," concluded McBurney. "That's the only explanation I can come up with."

Devore shook his head. "Fuck that, he just skedaddled. I've seen crackers like that son of a bitch my whole life—all hat and no cattle. The crazy thing is they probably won't even court-martial his ass. The doctors will say he has 'battle fatigue' or some other such nonsense. That's how they do it for the white boys who can't cut it. If it had been one of us, they'd just throw us in the brig or line us up and shoot us without asking any questions. But not good ole white-boy Wingo."

Windsor just pursed his lips at the sheer inexcusability of the XO's actions when so many inexperienced men were counting him. "All I know is it looks like we're on our own until this gets sorted out. We'll make due, but I'd be lying to you if I told you I didn't already miss the colonel."

McBurney nodded in agreement. Bates had indeed been their undisputed leader. Most importantly, he was the one who had instilled in them the pride to keep going forward with their training and ignore all the naysayers back in the States as well as in England. That was why McBurney couldn't help but wonder if the battalion was now rudderless and would be unable to forge ahead without the commander that had molded them into what they were. But it was precisely because Bates had trained them so well, he realized, that they would make it on their own. They really had no choice. Either they would buck up and find a way to succeed—or they would end up as mistreated guests in some German prisoner-of-war camp.

He realized now what he was fighting for. It definitely wasn't for God or country, and it was only partly to rescue Europe from Nazism or for his Negro race. No, he fought mostly for himself and his brothers in the battalion—the guy next to him—and for Paul Bates. That was his primary motivation now that he had gone toe to toe against the legendary Wehrmacht. He swore to himself that he would never be a chickenshit like Major Charles Wingo from Virginia. A soldier, in time of war, was supposed to perform his duty and accept the possibility of death in battle. Wingo had let all the men of the 761st down—officers and enlisted men, white and black alike—with his selfish act of desertion. When the battalion was desperate for leadership following the wounding of Bates, Wingo had fled the field in cowardice, hanging the unit out to dry.

"Well, the good news is they can't say us nigger boys is the yellow ones," said Devore with a wry grin. "This is all on Wingo and nobody else."

McBurney chuckled inwardly. He liked that Devore always told it like it was. The farmer from Greenwood, South Carolina, was five years older than McBurney and Leonard Smith, and the two younger men had for the past year looked up to him like an older brother. Able to find humor in any situation, Devore possessed a rakish confidence and was quick on his feet, handsome, gregarious, and intensely loyal to his friends. During their time at Camp Hood with him, McBurney and Smith had learned that he had several different girlfriends writing him from home, and they were duly impressed. He also happened to be one of the most popular soldiers in the entire battalion.

"Old Wingo always said we would never fight and would only embarrass ourselves and the Army," continued Devore. "And yet, here that white boy is the one who run off at the first sign of the enemy. Now that's what I call *i-ro-ny*."

"You could call it a lot of things," said Windsor. "But the bottom line is the man let us all down."

"He sure as hell did," agreed McBurney.

By late afternoon, the 761st and 26th Infantry had captured Bezange-la-Petite, Vic-sur-Seille, and Hill 253. But the cost had been high for all units involved, with the infantry suffering casualties numbering in the hundreds. Two hours later at dusk, the fighting had slackened all across the front and Baker, Charlie, Dog, and Headquarters Companies set up defensive perimeters outside Bezange-la-Petite, bivouacked for the night, and continued to remove the casualties from the field. Streams of jeeps, trucks, and half-tracks poured back from the front with piles of bloodied and mangled bodies. The anguished moans and screams of the wounded rose plaintively into the frigid night as temperatures plummeted.

While the medics transported the injured to the rear, the tankers checked on friends, sat around shivering, and recounting today's baptism by fire and those wounded and killed in action. It was agreed Charlie Company had suffered the worst, losing Sergeant Harvey Woodard and many others in the hard fighting. Surprisingly, several men appeared not to have been hit by the enemy shelling or machine-gun fire, but rather had sustained internal injuries from high-explosive blasts or carbon monoxide poisoning in the confined space of their tanks. Some had been found in their tank seats staring into space with not a scratch on them.

McBurney was stunned to learn of Leonard Smith's tragic fate. His good friend had apparently died from carbon monoxide poisoning when his tank "Cool Stud" had been caught in an antitank trap. Apparently, the driver was unable to free the tank and the exhaust pipe had become blocked, allowing deadly gas to back up inside the turret. Smith, with his slight frame, was the canary in the coal mine. He immediately passed out, and the other crew members, realizing what had happened, switched off the engine, jumped out, and pulled Smith up onto the turret to see if fresh air would revive him. Unfortunately, it didn't. The crew couldn't see Smith breathing or feel any pulse, so leaving his dead body atop the turret they ran back to the supply train to inform the battalion's ordnance team, responsible for reclaiming damaged vehicles, of the tank's position. But with all the disabled tanks from the fighting, the ordnance team was too busy to recover Cool Stud.

The news hit both McBurney and Devore hard. The two both got teary-eyed upon hearing the unfortunate fate of their lively and entertaining brother, who, despite his wild and hellish ways, had proved to be a damned fine soldier. But their sorrow was mixed with feelings of relief and even joy that they themselves had survived. After an hour of mourning, McBurney forced himself to put his grief aside and carry on with his duties. He checked and prepared his main turret gun for what was likely to be an even bloodier day of fighting tomorrow. The one thing he had learned already was that the battlefields of France were going to be a slaughterhouse, and he would not have time to cry long over all the friends and comrades he lost along the way. At the same time, he couldn't believe this was only the first day.

He thought back to the fighting. He realized that he had stopped thinking after he had fired his first round. He had acted on instinct and his two years of training. By the time the sun had set, he had performed as well as could be expected considering that it was his first taste of battle. He knew he had Paul Bates to thank for that. But what he realized most of all was how lucky he was to be alive.

Climbing back out of the tank once he had finished his gun check, he saw Windsor coming up. The TC offered him a Lucky Strike. Lighting up, they stared up into the dark night sky.

"Sorry about Smitty," said the elder tanker as they puffed on their cigarettes. "I know you two were close."

"Only one day of action for him and the colonel both," lamented McBurney. "Seems like we're off to a rocky start. War really is hell after all."

"It ain't like the moving pictures, is it?"

He shook his head. "No, it sure ain't."

"Well, at least now we all know. We needed to get that hero shit out of our system. You enjoy that there smoke—the battalion can't have shaky hands for one of its top gunners."

Smiling, he gave McBurney a good-natured pat on the back. The young tanker found the friendly gesture from his superior officer and mentor reassuring as always. He took a deep drag from his cigarette; the tobacco was soothing and, given the mayhem and horror of today's battle, he was again grateful to be alive. He wondered if he had not rushed to judgment regarding war. It was a bloody and brutal human endeavor—that much was certain—but he had never felt such an adrenaline rush in his life. More importantly, he had no choice but to give it another chance.

*How much worse can it be than today?* he wondered.

*A whole hell of lot worse,* he realized.

In his first day of combat, he had already lost his commanding officer and his good friend and the task force had failed to execute its mission of taking the heavily fortified town of Morville-lès-Vic. But the Panthers had managed to take three other towns of strategic importance and one big hill, General Paul was apparently pleased, and the experience the outfit had gained would prove invaluable when even more furious fighting was in store. With the battalion finally seeing action, McBurney wagered that tomorrow, he and his fellow Black Panthers would be at least twice as good soldiers as they were today.

Windsor then quietly informed him about "the plan." Tomorrow, the script called for the five companies of the 761st to continue fighting towards the primary objective, Morville-lès-Vic, and this time take the town. To do that, tonight McBurney and his brothers-in-arms would finish oiling their guns, re-load their tanks with ammunition, and gas up. Come tomorrow, they would head back into battle, with many more miles ahead to be covered, and with fighting conditions becoming more and more muddy and nut-freezing cold.

The first battle—their baptism of fire—was over. He had seen the elephant and knew what to expect now. He knew what the enemy's much ballyhooed "Ripsaw" 88s and the dreaded *Panzerfausts* could do, for he had heard the projectiles screeching past and seen them crashing in orange-colored flame all around as they devoured his fellow Black Panthers and the doughs of the 26th. His initial fears of battle had been dealt with during the course of the day as he had fought against the German enemy that he now knew were not Supermen, and a feeling had settled in his mind that he could actually take it. Going forward, he vowed to carry on and do his duty without ever letting a single one of his buddies down.

Not one.

Compared to yesterday, William Haywood McBurney felt like a seasoned vet. But he badly missed his good buddy Smitty.

And he would never forget him.

# CHAPTER 24

**MORVILLE-LÈS-VIC
NORTHEASTERN FRANCE**

**NOVEMBER 9, 1944**

AT DAWN THE NEXT DAY, McBurney gazed through his binoculars at the slowly emerging red-tile rooftops and white spires of Morville-lès-Vic. Windsor stood next to him atop Taffy's rain-slicked, battle-scarred turret. The town was less than a mile square but of critical strategic value for the Third Army's offensive, along with the neighboring village of Château-Salins, an important rail and communications center. Morville, as the troops were calling it, was situated along the main road to the 26th Infantry Division's first two objectives of Patton's Saar Campaign: the towns of Rodalbe and Bénestroff located ten miles to the northeast. A new commanding officer, Lieutenant Colonel Hollis Hunt, had taken over control of the battalion from the wounded Colonel Bates and the cowardly Major Wingo.

At the tail end of the advancing column, the three tanks of Headquarters Company sat idling in preparation for striking out. The HQ tanks included a new "Cool Stud" tank; the moniker had been painted on a replacement tank only this morning by the surviving crew in honor of Leonard Smith. Headquarters Company's orders were to stand by in reserve along with the mortar and artillery platoons, while Companies A, B, C, and D took the town and other nearby objectives.

Williams's Able Company was to cover the west flank of the attack and seize the neighboring village of Château-Salins swiftly after dawn with the 101st Infantry Regiment. Baker Company was tasked with undertaking the frontal assault on Morville from the southwest via the main road, covering elements of the 26th Infantry Division in what was sure to be grueling house-to-house fighting. Dog Company was to guard the east flank, supporting the infantry in seizing the town of Salival and then screening the nearby woods to keep German relief forces from reaching Morville. Charlie Company was to press ahead through the woods, approaching the town from the east and north and thus completing its encirclement.

Waiting to welcome them, McBurney knew, were concealed German machine-gun emplacements, antitank guns, mortars, and artillery batteries. He found the enemy's powerful weapons terrifying, though he had not noticed his fear until late during yesterday's combat. Out of all the German antitank weapons, the *Panzerfaust* was the one he now feared the most. He had seen with his own eyes how surprisingly easy it was for a lone German to creep up on a Sherman or Stuart with one of the cheap, disposable rocket-launchers on his shoulder. The enemy tactic was to steal in like a stalking lion to within 60 yards of a tank and blast through the hull or disable the tracks with a preloaded 150mm high-explosive shaped charge. He couldn't believe that the weapon could penetrate nearly eight inches of armor with ease, more steel than U.S. tanks carried, but that's what the armored service field manual said.

Though the U.S. had invented the one-man antitank weapon, it was clear to McBurney that the enemy had won the contest with its improvements. The lethality of the *Panzerfaust* trumped the bazooka, which could only penetrate about four inches of armor. The only blessing in McBurney's estimation was that the

*Panzerfaust* had an effective range that averaged two to three times less than that of its American cousin.

He blew out a breath of cold air. The rain had frozen in places and snowflakes fluttered in the air. The only sounds were the idling and mechanical grinding of the tank engines, the squeaking of tracks and creaking of steel turrets, and the slosh of mud being swept aside by giant masses of steel.

He glanced at Windsor. The thirty-five-year-old was not only his commander and teacher, but surrogate father in the absence of his own WWI-veteran father, Thomas McBurney. Though Theodore W. Windsor came from Cleveland, Ohio, a hint of an Alabama lilt remained from his childhood. McBurney knew that he had graduated high school and lived an entire lifetime before he had joined the Army—but that like many of the other tankers he had found a steady living wage evasive. Before his thirtieth birthday, he had swapped his janitorial uniform for that of a U.S. soldier and, from then on, he hadn't looked back. If there was one thing Windsor understood, in McBurney's view, it was the United States Army and soldiering, and the younger man and understudy had been watching and learning from him for two years now. There was no one he trusted more in the 761st, with the exception of Paul Bates, who was now regrettably out of commission.

After a moment, Windsor broke the silence.

"You miss him, don't you?"

"Smitty? Yeah, I miss him."

The older man nodded. "I miss him too."

"I'll tell you what though," said McBurney. "We sure had us some good old times whooping it up at the Savoy." The legendary ballroom in Harlem, known for its Big Band roster and polished oak floors, had been their favorite watering hole and place for dancing. "After the war, we were planning on getting back there together. You know, with our uniforms covered with medals. We both agreed the ladies would find us irresistible."

"He was a character. Like I said, I miss him too," said Windsor wistfully. "But at the same time, we've got a job to do and we have to keep on keeping on."

"I know that, Sarge. You don't have to worry about—"

He stopped in midsentence as two figures appeared to their left, a hundred yards away, coming in from the woods on foot. Even from a distance and in the faint early morning light, he could tell by their uniforms that one of them was an American GI, the other a German. But there was something else: the American was a Negro soldier in a tanker's uniform.

He turned his binoculars on the approaching figures. His heart rate instantly jumped off scale. He couldn't believe his eyes.

*No way! That can't be him!*

"You are not going to believe this—take a look," he said to Windsor, handing him the binoculars.

The TC pointed them at the figures walking towards them. "My God, it's Lazarus risen from the dead," he cried. "Smitty escorting a Kraut prisoner—now that is an unexpected sight."

McBurney yelled down into the open hatch to Devore in his driver's seat warming up the tank. "Willie, you got to see this! It's Smitty!"

"What?"

"Smitty's alive! Get your butt up here, man!"

A moment later Devore clamored out of his driver's hatch. "What are you talking about?" he exclaimed. "They told us he was dead."

"If he was, he ain't no more! Looks like we got ourselves a modern-day Lazarus!" cried Windsor, pointing.

They waved Smith towards their tank, as did the crew of the second incarnation of Cool Stud directly behind them. Up and down the line, men began to cheer as they recognized that their fellow tanker who had been written off for dead was, in fact, very much alive. Smith dropped his German prisoner off with a group of MPs and then jogged up to the idling HQ tanks. McBurney and several other tankers stepped down gleefully from their Shermans to greet their friend and comrade as he came running up.

"Now look what the cat dragged in—man oh man, are we glad to see you!" cried McBurney.

"Lordy Lord, you can say that again!" echoed Willie Devore with tears of joy in his eyes. "Come here, my brother!"

"Man, I don't know how I made it, but I did!" exclaimed Smith with his trademark easygoing smile.

"Why you be just like that bluesman Robert Johnson!" said Devore. "You must have done a deal with the devil because you got some serious motherfucking mojo!"

The three good buddies embraced. The crowd of onlooking tankers gave a rousing cheer. A moment later, the trio broke apart and Smith gave an exaggerated bow before all the troopers, while Willie Devore did a little South Carolina jig.

The men hailed them even louder.

"Lord have mercy, where have you been, son?" asked Daniel Cardell, Smith's and Cool Stud's commander, once the cheering had quieted down. "We thought you were a goner, man!"

"I'm still not sure what happened. All I know is when I woke up late yesterday afternoon, I found myself laying on my tank. I still have no idea how I got there."

"It was the gas buildup inside the turret when we got stuck in an antitank ditch," said Cardell. "You passed out."

"Carbon monoxide poisoning—that's what it was," explained Cool Stud's driver Hollis Clark. "Once we realized what was going on, we switched off the engine and jumped out. We hauled you onto the turret to see if fresh air would revive you. But it didn't."

"You weren't breathing and we couldn't feel a pulse, so we assumed you were dead," said Cardell. "We left your body on the turret and ran back to the supply train to give the ordnance team the tank's position."

"But they were too damn busy to recover Cool Stud," said Clark. "So we got ourselves a new Cool Stud and named it in honor of you. Check it out, man!"

He pointed proudly to the words "Cool Stud Inc" emblazoned on the left side of his and Cardell's tank in big white letters. Smith gave a thumbs-up sign and the men applauded them again.

"What happened after you woke up?" asked McBurney.

"I heard the voices of German soldiers. Scared the crap out of me. I quickly realized an enemy patrol was approaching. So I pretended to be dead. Surprisingly, none of the patrol stopped to check if I was still alive. I stayed there, not moving, until dark. Then I climbed down into the turret, locked the hatch, and went to sleep. When I woke up a half hour ago, I got out of the tank and a Kraut soldier came walking up to me holding his rifle up in the air. It took me a minute to realize that he was trying to surrender. I took the rifle from him, signaled for him to start walking, and followed him. I figured he would know the way since I had no idea where I was or where the rest of the unit had gone. We reached a road and walked for a while before I heard the sound of tanks approaching. And now here we are."

"I am so glad you made it, man," said his good buddy Willie Devore, and the two men hugged again.

"Yeah, but you're going to have to be careful from here on out. You've only got eight lives left now," said McBurney, patting him on the back.

Suddenly, they were interrupted by a deep, booming voice. "Hey, you fellas, get back in your damn tanks! There's a war on and we're moving out!"

McBurney looked up to see Captain Harrison, commander of Headquarters Company, stomping towards the group.

"It's Private Smith! He's alive, sir!" explained Cardell.

"I reckon there is a God! Now mount up! We're rolling out!"

"Yes, sir, we're on our way!" said Windsor.

The men jumped back into their tanks and joined the departing column. The engines of their Shermans and Stuarts throbbed and puffed exhaust into the cold fall air. As they started off, a squadron of eight P-40-series fighter-bombers strafed the town of Château-Salins to soften up the defensives for Captain Williams's two platoons of Able Company and the 104th Infantry Regiment of the 26th. Black tankers and white infantrymen cheered them on all along the American line.

Following the bombardment, Able Company's tanks rolled forward with little opposition, encountering only sporadic machine-gun and mortar fire. The tanks were arrayed in standard combat formation, with a spacing of thirty yards between vehicles. The lead tank was out front setting the pace with its 76 mm main gun and .30-caliber coaxial machine gun aimed forward at twelve o'clock. The second tank shadowed the first, in case the company or platoon commander missed something. The third protected the right flank, and the fourth guarded the left, as the attacking formation chugged and squeaked its way forward towards the enemy positions.

When A Company reached the town, the tanks fanned out through streets filled with smoking rubble, covering the infantrymen as they cleared what was left of the town's buildings one at a time. With the rail and communications center of Château-Salins taken, the Black Panthers took up positions around Morville-lès-Vic with Able Company on the east, Charlie Company on the northwest, and Baker Company in the middle poised to seize the town. On the right flank, while Dog Company conducted screening operations from the direction of Salival, the Sherman tanks of McBurney's Headquarters Company, along with the 105mm assault gun and mortar platoons, moved towards the woods near Salival.

As the attack on Morville-lès-Vic was launched, Baker, Charlie, and Dog Companies were not as fortunate as Williams's Able Company. The units quickly met with stiff German resistance. As Baker Company and the footsoldiers reached the outskirts of the village, the Shermans fired high-explosive shells to clear a path, but with only limited effect. Realizing the importance of Morville as a passageway to the east, the Germans manned the vast majority of buildings. German machine-gun and *Panzerfaust* teams were strategically placed overlooking every intersection, cleverly positioned in upper-story rooms and around street corners throughout the town. The infantrymen fanned out with Baker's tanks in close support, firing their main guns and .30-caliber coaxials to eliminate positions as the German teams opened fire and revealed themselves. But the barricades and antitank fire held up the advance. When Baker Company finally overcame the barricades, a handful of tanks clanked into town only to be stopped dead in their tracks by a fury of antitank and machine-gun fire. It came from all directions and the doughs suffered heavy casualties.

While Baker Company pressed the enemy from the south, Charlie Company raced towards the northern end of Morville-lès-Vic. Charlie had such success in pushing through German-controlled terrain that it sped across a key bridge before the Germans had time to detonate it. But soon the company was slowed by a hailstorm of carefully directed artillery fire from a nearby German officer candidate school.

As Lieutenant Kenneth Coleman's platoon reached the outskirts of Morville, his lead Sherman took a direct hit and was immobilized. Though the five-man crew managed to evacuate safely, their M4 now blocked the road, leaving the remainder of the platoon exposed. This was a common German tactic: when American tanks were in column formation, the enemy often waited until they drew close, then with pinpoint accuracy fired to disable the first and last tanks in the line. This made it impossible for the other tanks to move forward or back out, enabling the Germans to take their time picking the tanks off one by one. In this instance however, Coleman reacted quickly, leading his crew on foot in an assault against the enemy artillery and small-arms positions overlooking the road. Though under fierce fire and armed with only grease guns, the tank crew succeeded in routing the German teams. Once the damaged tank was pushed off the road, Coleman took command of the next tank in line and led the platoon forward. But resistance was stiff.

Two other platoons of Charlie Company had to contend with a long ditch running in a field to the northeast of Morville. The tank trap had been dug deep and covered with brush. Fifty yards beyond the woods, the light snow helped to conceal German troops crouched in a series of concrete pillboxes, and Charlie's Shermans moved in formation downhill into the well-concealed trap. When the front ends of the thirty-three-ton Shermans pushed in, they lacked sufficient traction to back out with the steep slope and became stuck. German machine-gun, *Panzerfaust*, and antitank artillery teams opened fire, killing seven members of C Company in a matter of minutes.

In the forest near the town of Salival, Dog Company's "screening" operation had quickly devolved into a pitched battle. D Company's light M3 Stuart tanks had started by shelling Salival to clear the way for an infantry assault before taking position in the hills and woods around the town. Lacking full armor, the light tanks of the "mosquito fleet" weren't made for direct combat. But the situation dictated that they fight and soon the men were grappling for their lives.

By this time, McBurney and the tanks of Headquarters Company had moved up into the woods near Salival along with the 105mm assault gun and mortar platoons. In radio contact with the other companies, they could hear what was happening to Baker and Dog Companies and knew that Charlie was being decimated. When an American spotter plane sighted a relief column of two hundred German soldiers and thirty vehicles en route to destroy the beleaguered C Company, Captain Charles "Pop" Gates, the thirty-three-year-old former Buffalo Soldier, moved his five assault guns forward, trapping and destroying the enemy relief column with a well-executed indirect-fire mission. The pre-emptive attack prevented a horrific situation from becoming even worse.

With temperatures dropping and the snowfall picking up, the battle raged on until late afternoon. Morville-lès-Vic was taken by the 761st and the 101st Infantry only after the town was cleared in desperate house-to-house fighting. When the final tally was in, two officers and twelve enlisted men had been killed in the day's violent action, including seven members of Charlie alone, with many more severely wounded. The toll on the Black Panthers would have been much higher had it not been for the quick-thinking actions of Lieutenant Coleman and Sergeant Turley, both killed in action, and Sergeant Crecy of Texas, who had all distinguished themselves in the bitter fighting in the driving rain and snow. The soft-spoken Crecy had fought with such tenacity that some of the troopers were now calling him the "Baddest Man in the 761st."

As the men settled in and prepared to bed down in their vehicles for the night, McBurney and Smith shared a couple of C-ration cans of frankfurters and beans while standing watch outside their HQ tanks. They talked at length about the battle, but like always, they also covered the 761st's most recurring topics of discussion: life in their hometowns, football and baseball, and women. To the north and east, they could see the scattered flares and flashes of artillery over the trees. Nearby, medics busily removed the last casualties from the field and dressed the wounded. The ricochet effect of armor-piercing enemy shells inside the Shermans and Stuarts had been particularly brutal, causing severed limbs and horrific wounds that made McBurney cringe when he saw the tankers being carried back to the aid station. Other men in the battalion checked on their buddies from other companies and the technicians worked on fixing the tanks that were not beyond repair.

"I can't wait to get back in action tomorrow," said the excitable Smith as they watched a lobbed shell explode in the distance. "Unlike you, I haven't even gotten the chance to fire my gun yet in combat."

"Don't worry, you'll get your chance tomorrow," said McBurney. "But I don't know why you're in such a hurry. There's going to be plenty of fighting in the days ahead. Word is we're striking north tomorrow at dawn."

"I want to be a hero, man. I want me a Silver Star."

"I wouldn't be too gung-ho. You've already died once, remember?"

"Yeah, but I think I like this here war. I mean, it pains me to see what happened to Charlie and Dog today, but I've got to say that I think I was born to be a soldier."

McBurney shoveled a spoonful of C-ration frankfurters and beans into his mouth that the troops disdainfully called "fuckers and beans." "You may have been born for glory, but I sure as heck wasn't," he said while noisily chewing. "There's too much blood everywhere and too much dying for me. But I'll do my job."

"I need to check my equipment again and my supply of shells."

"Come on, man, you've already checked 'em both three times. Don't you think you've got it covered by now?"

"Yeah, I suppose you're right. I'm just restless is all. I want to go where the action is hot instead of this supporting role with HQ."

"Like I said, you'll get your chance. The Krauts aren't going anywhere anytime soon. These Nazi boys are fighters."

"That's why when tomorrow comes, I'm going to really come out fighting and make them wish they had never been born."

"I have no doubt you will, my brother," said McBurney, and they fell into silence and quietly ate their cold dinners.

McBurney thought about the past two days. He had taken out several of the enemy and seen enough maimed and killed human beings and farm animals to realize that France was not much different from a New York slaughterhouse. He had trained to be a tanker, but over the two days of fighting he had discovered that all those months at Camp Claiborne and Camp Hood now came down to a simple choice: kill or be killed. There was little margin for error. He was going up against a battle-hardened, fierce, and methodical enemy that had been fighting for five straight years. No longer could he reconcile what he saw here in Lorraine with what he had seen portrayed in the moving pictures he enjoyed so much. Whatever remaining notions about the glory of war he had harbored going into the fight were now gone after seeing the wounded being brought back to the aid stations the past two days. He was fully aware that a similarly tragic fate might very well await him.

It was funny but now his home in Harlem—against his WWI veteran father's wishes the place he had been so eager to escape to prove himself—seemed not such a bad place after all. But he was committed to continuing to do his job and take the fight to the Nazis, even though Lorraine was proving to be a far more gruesome blood bath than he had anticipated. He bought into the motto repeated with varying degrees of irony throughout the ranks of Patton's GIs: "The quickest way home is through Berlin."

He now understood why Bates had trained them so damn hard. Back in the States, he had thought the colonel worked them to keep them out of trouble. But the reality was that old Smooth had pushed them to the limit so they could act on instinct in order to survive. McBurney had learned thus far in his brief stint in combat that the countless days of monotonous drills took over his terrified and hesitant body when his mind went blank. He fought because that is what Bates had trained him to do, regardless of the adversity the battalion faced. The colonel had handpicked the company and tank commanders—men he was confident would hold their own under fire—and thus far only Major Wingo had not stood up to the test of combat and lost his nerve. Yet despite everything Bates had done to prepare the men, McBurney knew that no training in the world could have prepared him for the shocking carnage he had witnessed the past two days. He had seen sons, husbands, and fathers screaming in terror and scrambling from burning tanks, gun emplacements, and pill boxes, and he had seen infantrymen on both sides being mowed down like a scythe slicing across a wheat field.

Maybe, he thought, it was better that the battalion would be up early on the move again tomorrow and that he had no time to grieve for Coleman, Turley, and the others that had been lost. Though he felt sadness for his buddies that had crossed over to the other side, he knew that his first priority had to be to survive himself and defeat the enemy. Pride and honor were also at stake. The white military brass and civilians said colored units like the 761st were yellow and couldn't cut it. They said Negro soldiers couldn't think fast enough to fight in tanks or airplanes. But from everything he had witnessed firsthand or heard about during the past two days of combat, the only evidence of incompetence or cowardice was the white senior officer Major Wingo, who had abandoned the battalion. He and the other men had worked too hard not to succeed and were filled with resolve. They had no plans of quitting until the 761st completed its mission of defeating Hitler and Nazi Germany.

But at the same time, he knew that the past two days of bitter fighting had hit the battalion hard. In the process, the 761st had transformed into something new. Charlie Company had been decimated, and the new battalion commander, Hollis Hunt, was said to be scrambling to rebuild the outfit as well as Dog Company. McBurney knew that he had changed, too, over the past two days. He had grown as a man and was not the same as before. He had executed his assignments as tank gunner with the same steady hand that had distinguished him throughout training, but the actual experience of war had made him harder and tougher and his life simpler. His job now during every new day of fighting was reduced to zeroing his targets, not letting his brothers down, and making it back to camp in one piece.

Finishing his C-ration, McBurney lit a Lucky Strike. "I'm glad you made it, Smitty," he said earnestly to his friend. "I've got to confess, this old war just wouldn't be the same without your big ole smile."

The private nodded as a shell exploded in the distance. "I'm glad I made it too," he said. "Someone's got to keep you entertained. Might as well be me."

"When this is all over, we're going to sashay on down to the Savoy and have ourselves a real good time."

"We surely will. But until then, this is exactly the place I want to be."

"You're the hero of the war movie that's been playing in your own head since Pearl Harbor. That's why I love you, man—you're so predictable."

At that moment, Teddy Windsor came walking up. "Got new orders," he said without preamble. "All three Headquarters tanks and crews are being shifted over as replacements tomorrow to C Company. We're moving on."

McBurney was taken aback. "You're saying we belong to Charlie now?"

"Yes Sergeant, that's exactly what I'm saying. Is that a problem for either of you?"

"No sir, not at all. Private Smith and I both would like nothing better than to serve with the best."

"Damn right—nothing but the best for us, Sarge," echoed his buddy, grinning from ear to ear. "I'll be checking my equipment again then."

"You do that, Smitty," said Windsor. "Because tomorrow it's bound to get real hot again for Charlie."

# CHAPTER 25

## EHRENFELD, WEST COLOGNE

## NOVEMBER 10, 1944

ANGELA WATCHED WITH TEARS in her eyes as her love Bartholomäus Schröder and twelve other German prisoners were forced to mount the gallows where they would be publically hung. The condemned consisted of six teenage Edelweiss Pirates and seven adults, including the notorious Bomber Hans Steinbrück and several others from his broken-up Ehrenfeld Group. The heads of the prisoners were closely shaved, their bodies weak and thin, their faces covered with cuts and bruises, and several shambled as they walked from sustained injuries. "Intense interrogation" was the euphemistic term the Gestapo used for the brutal torture of prisoners to force them to confess, and it was immediately apparent that the thirteen prisoners had been subjected to savage treatment at the hands of their Nazi captors.

The prisoners had been hauled by truck from their overcrowded cells in the infamous Brauweiler Prison to the bomb-ravaged Ehrenfeld neighborhood, where a solemn crowd of war-worn citizens had assembled beneath the cold gaze of armed German security forces and Hitler Youth. With their hands manacled behind their backs, the six boys and seven grown men were poked and prodded by the Gestapo at machine-gun-point to the hanging platform beneath a mercury-colored sky. The heavy wooden structure specially constructed by the State Secret Police for today's violent spectacle stood in an abandoned concrete lot between the Ehrenfeld elevated train line and Steinbrück's recently uncovered hideout in the basement of Schönsteinstrasse 7-13.

The hanging site was in the heart of crime-ridden Ehrenfeld, and the Nazis had strongly "encouraged" everyone in the neighborhood to come down to the train station to witness the grisly event. The Gestapo called it *"Sonderbehandlung"*—special treatment—the term they used for executions carried out without the requirement of a court judgment. The timing and location of the public execution had been chosen with fastidious care by *Kriminaldirektor* Dr. Max Hoffmann, the ruthless head of the Cologne Gestapo and a veteran of anti-partisan operations in Poland and Ukraine. Angela saw him standing with a coterie of his senior officers to the left of the hanging scaffold. Today marked the day after the anniversary of Hitler's 1923 Munich Beer Hall Putsch, a date of historic importance to the Nazi regime which allowed its leaders to juxtapose the self-sacrifice and purity of those early National Socialist martyrs against today's German gang members set to be hanged. In the eyes of the Nazis, the condemned had betrayed their *Volk* by attacking Party members, stealing from their fellow loyal countrymen, and associating with so-called foreign "criminal elements."

The selection of the Ehrenfeld Hüttenstrasse as the killing site was doubly significant: the public humiliation and execution of the prisoners was set to take place directly across the street from Steinbrück's *Ehrenfeld Gruppe* hideout, allowing the Nazi authorities to engage in the symbolic reclamation of the neighborhood by carrying out the killings at the source of unrest. The execution site was also intended to terrorize the neighborhood's residents, who would have to pass the dead bodies on their way to and from the still-operating train station. The only question was how many days the Nazi leadership would leave the limp, decaying corpses hanging in the air to frighten the unruly neighborhood into submission.

Angela watched with a mixture of horror, dread, and sadness as the nooses dangling from the crossbeam of the wooden gallows were placed around the necks of each of the prisoners. The thirteen victims—six of whom were teenage Edelweiss Pirates that she personally knew—all stood in a row on a long narrow plank of wood that would be removed to allow them to hang and die by slow strangulation with their hands tied behind their backs. In a normal hanging, the drop between the surface where a prisoner stands and the end of the rope is usually four to six feet, which allows for sufficient force to result in immediate paralysis and death as the neck snaps from the fall. But the length of the drop at the scaffold Angela saw before her was less than three feet, which meant that the nooses would slowly tighten around the necks of the prisoners and they would strangle to death, a far more gruesome punishment favored by the Nazis. Instead of an instant and somewhat merciful death, execution by this method could take an excruciatingly long time and was grislier and more dehumanizing.

She stood in the front row with her father, who looked commanding in his neatly pressed Wehrmacht uniform and lengthy greatcoat with the pair of Iron Crosses and his other shiny medals proudly displayed. He had disapproved of her coming here today, but had insisted on accompanying her when she had stubbornly maintained that she was going despite his wishes. She knew she was taking a risk coming here today, as someone might recognize her and point her out to the authorities. But she had concealed herself by bundling herself up in the fall chill with heavy clothing and a thick wool scarf.

As the noose was tightened around Schröder's neck, their eyes met and tears poured from her eyes like a sudden cloudburst. His face was mottled yellowish-green from old bruises and purplish-black from fresh ones, as a result of the severe beatings he had sustained during the past week from *Kriminalkommissar* Kütter's Gestapo goons at Brauweiler. She shook her head in dismay, feeling a shortness of breath at the sheer tragedy of the situation. She couldn't believe that Schröder, Günther Schwarz, and four other of her Edelweiss Pirate friends, as well as Hans Steinbrück and Roland Lorent, were about to be hung without trial; and yet, at the same time, she couldn't help but feel guilty for having not even been brought in for questioning. Obviously, Schröder hadn't given up her real name, nor had any of the other arrested Edelweiss Pirates or members of Steinbrück's gang, though under extreme torture she knew that her code name Mucki must surely have been muttered by someone. But how long before the Gestapo discovered that she was Mucki? Surely, her luck wouldn't hold out indefinitely.

Wiping away her tears, she kept her gaze focussed on Schröder, who looked surprisingly calm and resilient despite the grim fate that awaited him. He seemed to have come to terms with his fate. Especially as he gave her a little nod of reassurance that seemed to say, "Please don't worry—I love you and will always treasure our time together." She would never forget this tragic but uplifting moment, the sight of him standing tall as an Edelweiss Pirate, an anti-Hitlerite, before their ruthless Nazi oppressors. Seeing the strength on his bruised face and the hint of a subversive smile on his lips—in her eyes, an unmistakable expression of resistance—she found a certain inner peace. But at the same time, she wanted desperately to jump onto the gallows and set him free, or at least tell him one last time that she had never loved anyone as she had loved him. But her father had warned her not to show any sign that she personally knew any of the prisoners, lest she get caught up in the police roundup that had already snared more than two hundred souls.

With the war going badly for Germany, the Gestapo had made it increasingly a point to make a public example of those deemed disloyal or that posed a potential threat to the Reich. Just two weeks earlier, on October 25, eleven foreign workers had been hung without trial at the same gallows where the thirteen German prisoners now stood. Angela had not attended the hanging but she had heard from Marie Peukert and several others of its gruesome details. In front of a crowd of assembled onlookers and police almost as large as today's throng, the accused had been executed for crimes ranging from petty looting to attacks on German civilians and police. The Gestapo had cataloged their handiwork by carefully photographing the execution from start to finish in a series of shocking pictures, supposedly to keep Himmler apprised of the punishment. The photos revealed that one prisoner proved too tall for the makeshift gallows, and that a plainclothed security officer was forced to tug down on his legs until he expired. Notably, the cameraman also took care to film the crowd's horrified reaction to the incident, and security personnel left the prisoners' bodies to hang throughout the day as a warning to other would-be lawbreakers.

But today, there was a difference. Today, they were hanging thirteen German citizens—six of whom were still legally children—without following the due process of law.

Now she saw Criminal Commissioner Kütter step onto a makeshift podium on the back of a heavy truck to address the crowd. She felt a shiver run down her spine as the commander of the Gestapo's *Sonderkommando Brauweiler* unit responsible for the arrest, interrogation, and punishment of fugitive forced laborers, army deserters, and political resisters began speaking, his voice coming over the loudspeaker. The fifty-four-year-old was corvine and ugly as sin—with a beak-like nose, blond hair smothered with brilliantine, and crush of fissures and pock marks lining his face to go with an oddly bookish quality due to his thick-framed glasses.

Kütter was often seen wearing plainclothes, but for today's grand spectacle he had chosen to wear a jet-black leather uniform with a peaked cap bearing a *Heer*-style eagle together with an SS-*Totenkopf*. In the death's-head holster at his hip, he carried a 1939 Walther PPK 7.65-mm SS officer's pistol. In 1942, Himmler had ordered most all of the black SS uniforms recalled, stripped of insignia, and replaced by grey-green *feldgrau* uniforms; but Kütter liked wearing black, so he had a National Socialist tailor make him a special black-leather outfit that borrowed equal parts from the Waffen-SS Panzer Troop double-breasted uniform and the Gestapo police unit uniform that was still allowed in the field.

Since the beginning of October, Kütter's *Sonderkommando Brauweiler* and several other special task forces housed at Brauweiler Prison had been relentless in their efforts to destroy alleged enemies of the state. In addition to hunting down members of the Edelweiss Pirates, the task forces had aggressively pursued members of the free youth movement *Bündische Jugend*, the National Committee for a Free Germany, the Ehrenfeld Group and other gangs hiding out in Cologne's rubble, and a resistance group of Polish officers. Due to manpower shortages, *Sonderkommando Brauweiler's* officers worked alongside the Hitler Youth and *Volkssturm* patrols searching the ruins of the city for gang members and fugitives. Because Kütter and his men took an active part in these sweeps, the suspects arrested and taken to Brauweiler were often questioned by the same officers who had apprehended them, sometimes after shoot outs or chases through the rubble, encouraging their abuse at the hands of angry and frustrated Gestapo officers.

"As has been made clear these past few weeks," he began, "we German patriots will no longer tolerate crime in our city. For the protection of German life, I have ordered that these thirteen terrorists you see before you be publicly hung in the same manner that the eleven foreign criminals were executed two weeks ago. We have arrested many other *Volksfeinde*, and pending the results of our ongoing investigations, those that are found to be criminal elements in our midst will not be spared either. Rather after their investigations, they will meet the same fate as what you are about to see here today."

Looking up at Kütter, Angela felt a burning hatred. The Nazi officer represented everything that the Edelweiss Pirates were rebelling against.

"There is no doubt who will win this war for the soul of our city—our beloved Führer and our loyal *Volksgemeinschaft*. Yes, it is the People's community that is the source of all that is good in the struggle against the Bolshevik menace. To the east lurk the blood-lusting monsters hell-bent on destroying our social order." Now he gestured to the prisoners. "And right here in our midst are criminals that are a bane not only towards we *Volkskameraden*, but to all of mankind. As these terrorists commit crimes against mercantile property and disrupt the social order, they need to be eradicated like rats. It is, therefore, the civic duty of every citizen here in Cologne, indeed throughout Germany and all our occupied territories, to protect property, to punish those who resist its law, to take vengeance against the *Volksfeinde* that is our mortal enemy, and to instill fear in those who might be tempted to selfishly break the law. This you should do in the name of our Führer."

In that instant, the wind picked up and Angela felt the crisp breeze cuffing her face. Though it was only mid-November, the wind felt wintry cold. She looked around at the faces. They were a worn-out lot: mostly older men and women of various ages in frayed wool sweaters, overcoats, and hats with fidgety children in ragamuffin clothing at their sides. Dozens of people had peddled here on bicycles; some stood gripping the handlebars, others had leaned the conveyances against the walls or piles of rubble. Gazing at the faces, Angela was hard-pressed to find anyone who seemed to look favorably upon Kütter's comments, with the exception of the uniformed Party members and Hitler Youth who were nodding vigorously. Most people appeared visibly frightened or just plain exhausted from the war.

"Again, I am here to warn you that we will not tolerate defeatism or revolt in the Reich. Desertion from the front, tuning in to enemy radio broadcasts, associating with foreign workers, stealing and black marketeering, making disparaging remarks about our Führer or the Party—all of these will be dealt with swiftly and harshly.

There will be no demoralization or insurrection like that which undermined Germany in the Great War. We will not allow a repeat of the stab in the back that occurred in 1918. Through our unity of purpose and loyalty to our Führer, final victory will be ours."

The crowd stood there in a silence of shock and disbelief. Angela looked at Schröder, Günther Schwarz, and Bomber Hans, who were all quietly shaking their heads in subtle resistance. When she made eye contact with them, her father shot her a warning glance and squeezed her hand.

*Do not give the Nazis a reason to arrest you,* his narrowed eyes warned her.

Kütter continued: "These terrorists that stand before you are guilty of looting, stockpiling weapons, making attacks on civilians and police, and planning the despicable bombing of Gestapo Headquarters at El-De Haus." Now he read from a list. "Hans Steinbrück, Roland Lorent, Günther Schwarz, Gustav Bermel, Johann Müller, Franz Rheinberger, Adolf Schütz, Barthel Schröder, Peter Hüppeler, Josef Moll, Wilhelm Kratz, Heinrich Kratina, and Johann Krausen—you are criminals who have ceased to have rights. The sentence that the law has appointed to pass upon you for your offenses, and which has been decided by the established powers of the state, is that you shall all be hung by the neck until you are dead. For your heinous crimes, there can be no mercy for your souls. Let us proceed with the execution." He clicked his heels together and raised his right hand high in the official, right-handed Führer salute. "Heil Hitler!"

"Heil Hitler!" less than half the crowd rejoindered, arms raised in the Nazi salute. But even then, some people, Angela could tell, were just going through the motions.

Kütter now gestured to the two Gestapo officers acting as hangmen. The crowd gave an audible murmur and several women who looked to be mothers or sisters of the victims began to cry. Though Angela had tried to prepare herself mentally for what was about to happen, she was still crestfallen. Once again, tears began to pour from her eyes uncontrollably. Sensing her discomfort, her father squeezed her hand to reassure her.

Slowly, the hangmen drew back the wooden plank the prisoners were standing on and, one by one, they began dropping. She saw several older men drop first; then Bomber Hans Steinbrück, who gazed out in proud defiance at his Nazi captors just before he went; then Roland Lorent, who had been especially badly beaten; and then several of the young Edelweiss Pirates, including Günther Schwarz, Gustav Bermel, and Johann Müller. With the fall to the ground insufficient to break their necks, the victims hung in mid-air suffocating and twitching as they struggled.

When Schröder's turn came, Angela thought she would faint. Her father clasped her hand tightly and tried to cover her eyes, but she pushed his hand away. Despite the macabre scene, she wanted to pay her final respects to the boy she loved. But the gruesome scene was too much for her to bear and she buried herself in her father's shoulder, averting her eyes and weeping uncontrollably.

*I love you, Barthel. I shall always love you and am sorry but I cannot look.*

When the kicking stopped and the grim spectacle was mercifully over, the people began to move off solemnly in small groups. Angela wiped the tears from her eyes with a handkerchief and blew her nose. It was then she saw her father tense.

"What? What is it?" she asked him.

"We need to get out of here," he whispered. "It's not safe."

"What do you mean?"

"Hoffmann and Kütter are staring at us. We need to go now."

Had Kütter recognized her from the raid upon Steinbrück's basement lair? Probably not, since she had wisely been wearing her cap with her hair tucked beneath it, and she had smeared charcoal on her face to conceal her identity. But still, it wasn't worth the risk and they should leave as quickly as possible.

"Don't look," said her father. "Just come with me."

He took her by the arm and started for the sidewalk across the street on Schönsteinstrasse. When they were halfway across the street, he said, "Kütter is following us but don't turn around. It could be nothing, so let's just keep walking to the car. And let me handle this."

The *kriminalkommissar* called out to them, his voice incisive like a knife. "Colonel Lange, where are you going in such a rush?"

Angela felt her heart pounding in her chest as her father turned around, still clutching her hand tightly. "I am afraid I am not feeling well—my war wounds are acting up," he said, faking a polite smile. "Commissioner Kütter, this is my daughter Angela."

Clicking his jackboots together, he raised his right hand in the Nazi salute. "Heil Hitler!"

Her father immediately returned the salute—with his good left hand—so she wouldn't have to. "Heil Hitler," he said perfunctorily. "If you'll excuse us, we have to get home. I'm afraid we are both feeling poorly in the cold winter weather."

"But it is not winter, Colonel."

"No, but it feels like it."

"Yes well, I will let you be on your way soon enough. But first, what did you think of the hanging. It was quite a good turnout, wasn't it?"

"Yes, I think it achieved its intended goal."

"And what is that, Colonel?"

"A simultaneous deterrent and calming effect to heal public anxiety over the rampant crime here in Robber Field and the surrounding communities. Your message came through quite clearly. Furthermore, after being robbed myself I am pleased to see that our security forces are making our streets safer from crime."

"And defeatists. There is no place in the Fatherland for defeatists."

"No, indeed there is not. Now if you'll excuse us, Commissioner, we have to get home now."

Angela noticed that Kütter was eyeing her closely. "Have you been crying, young lady?" he asked her.

"No…I mean yes. I guess the hanging made me sad."

His face scrunched up with displeasure. "Sad? But those men were common criminals and enemies of the state. How can you shed tears for those *Volksfeinde?*"

"*Volksfeinde?*" she blurted. "How can they be enemies of the people when half of them are boys who have barely reached puberty?"

"That's enough, Angela!" snapped her father, and he stepped between them and took her by the hand. "My apologies, Commissioner Kütter, but my daughter has never seen a public hanging before. I'm afraid it was a traumatic experience for her."

"Yes well, hopefully the next time she will have a more *favorable* reaction."

"Yes, I'm sure she will."

"I am sure she will too." He looked sternly at her for a moment before his face softened. "But all the same, I am sorry that today's events have upset you, my child. It is quite a lot to take in for someone of your tender age."

"Yes, it is," she said.

But then his sympathetic expression abruptly turned back to that of an interrogator. "Did you by chance personally know any of the young men that were executed?"

To her dismay, she hesitated.

Her father jumped in quickly, but Angela could see that even he was too late as a triumphant I've-caught-you-red-handed smile appeared at the corners of Kütter's reptilian mouth.

"No, of course my daughter doesn't know any of those criminals. The very idea is outrageous. Now we must go now. Good day to you, Commissioner."

"Yes, you should go. But first I have one final question."

Her father was shaking his head in exasperation. "Is this really the time to—?"

But the bloodhound Kütter cut him off. "Do you know a girl named Mucki?" he asked Angela.

Her jaw almost dropped, but at the last second her survival instinct kicked in and she looked at the Gestapo officer with feigned puzzlement. "No, I've never heard the name before. Who is Mucki?"

He smiled thinly. "I don't know," he said. "But it will not be long before I find out. Good day to you two."

"Good day to you, Commissioner," said her father between clenched teeth, and he practically crushed her hand as he escorted her to the car.

# CHAPTER 26



**CASERNE MOLIFOR**
**NANCY, NORTHEASTERN FRANCE**

**NOVEMBER 15, 1944**

"WHEN THIS WAR IS OVER, IKE, I say we make the Krauts keep Lorraine as part of the surrender terms. I can imagine no greater burden than to be the owner of this godforsaken country, where it rains every damn day and the entire wealth of the people consists of assorted manure piles."

"When the time comes, George," responded Eisenhower with an amused smile, "I will be pleased to tell that to the War Department. But for now, just concentrate on winning the war, will you?"

The two old friends shared a laugh and stared out at the rain-soaked Gallic landscape, as a column of jeeps and half-tracks sloshed through the mud towards the front. Eisenhower and his retinue—which included his young, attractive British paramour and aide Kay Summersby and his little dog Telek—had driven down this morning from the supreme commander's palatial estate northwest of Reims, which overlooked a golf course. Ike and his lover—whom he only fondled and kissed and did not actually have intercourse with despite British Chief of the Imperial Staff Alan Brooke's and Monty's excoriations to the contrary—were visiting Patton's end of the long, bloody line. Summersby had become something of a problem for Ike, Patton knew. Her commission as a Women's Army Corps lieutenant, her status as the supreme commander's official secretary instead of merely his driver, and her prominent role as one of his three constant traveling companions continued to raise eyebrows. Especially amongst conservative Brits like Brooke and Monty, who were always looking for ways to knock Eisenhower down a peg, or preferably two.

As always, Old Blood and Guts proved to be a convivial host as he escorted his boss hither and yon with artillery batteries thundering in the distance. Trudging around with his overcoat buttoned to the top, a smiling Eisenhower had been widely photographed standing in the mud talking to GIs and presenting decorations and medals to wounded soldiers at the 12th Evacuation Hospital in Nancy.

During Eisenhower's frontline visit, Patton informed his boss that trench foot was putting as many of his troops out of action as the damned Krauts. Ike, a fanatic just like Patton when it came to troop welfare, was especially pleased at how Third Army was combating the affliction by handing out liberal supplies of dry socks. Since the beginning of November, more than ten thousand cases of trench foot from the cold, wet weather had been reported in hospital units. Patton had issued orders that company commanders were to see to it personally that every man in every squad had a fresh, clean pair of socks each day and that they dried their feet and boots after a river crossing or rainy spell.

"George, you know I can't compliment you too often because it goes straight to that big, fat head of yours. But you are doing a damned fine job under difficult circumstances, and I must commend you."

There was no one in the world whose opinion mattered more to him than his old friend and comrade-in-arms from Abilene. "That means a lot to me, Ike, and is just the kind of thing that sets me to crying. You know that I am a big ole crybaby when it comes right down to it."

"I know you are, George. And that's why I love you. You wear your emotions on your sleeve—while I can't cry unless you put tear gas in my eyes."

"That's because you're a stoic German. Not like these Nazi bastards we're killing by the bushel, of course, but you've got Kraut blood flowing through those veins of yours."

"Which is funny because I hate the Germans."

"I don't much care for them either, though I loathe the Russians even more. But the Huns are damn good fighters, I've got to give the sons of bitches that. We aren't taking on the junior varsity in this war, that's for sure."

"Yes, but I can smell victory. Even in this rain-soaked morass we now find ourselves."

*I smell it too,* thought Patton, *but I've got to take Metz or I'm going to be out of a goddamn job!* Indeed, the Occupied French city with its network of forts continued to be a huge thorn in his side. Especially Forts Driant and Jeanne d'Arc on the west bank of the Moselle. The two hilltop *festen,* originally built by the Germans in the 1890s when they ruled Lorraine, were state-of-the-art with thick reinforced concrete positions, artillery in steel turrets, interconnecting underground tunnels, vast trenches, and thick belts of barbed wire. Patton had ordered multiple assaults on Driant and Jeanne d'Arc that included heavy artillery bombing, air strikes, and infantry attacks backed by tanks and flamethrowers to seize the various compounds and the underground labyrinth of tunnels connecting them. But the Germans had put up stout resistance and inflicted heavy casualties on Third Army, forcing Patton to call in yet more massive air strikes. But they, too, had little effect on the seemingly impregnable bastions designed to withstand 240mm shells. Since September, Patton's plan to race across the Rhine and be the first Allied general to storm Berlin had been frustrated by the old forts and rugged German defenders of Metz.

Eisenhower said, "The Germans are being attacked from all sides now. In their desperation, they are throwing their last reserves into the line. Old men and young boys are no recipe for winning a war. Even Hitler has to know that."

"Metz is still one hell of nut to crack. Quite frankly, I had no idea it was going to be this goddamn hard."

"I know it has been tough on you and your men. But surely it can't last much longer. Our intelligence indicates that the city's water system has been destroyed and that ammunition is short. I am also told that the reinforcements received in the past few weeks include constables armed with ancient French rifles and decrepit supernumeraries wearing brassards in lieu of uniforms."

"Yes, that is true."

"I'm also told that Nazi functionaries are fleeing the city in stolen Renaults and Citroens—even though Hitler has issued orders to fight to the last bullet and the last man."

"That paper-hanging son of a bitch is always ordering his generals to do that. Beats the hell out of me why they still obey him."

"Where are your forces now, George?"

"We've crossed the Moselle, both north and south of Metz, and are slowly encircling the city and its holdout forts. But the two wings of my army haven't met up yet."

"What about your artillery support?"

"I was planning to double the daily artillery allocation for XII Corps to twenty thousand rounds tomorrow. If we win now we will not need shells later—and if we do not use the shells now, we will not win the war. That's the way I look at it."

"The good news is that while the weather has been terrible for us, it has been far worse for the Germans."

"How do you figure that?"

"Because they have nothing but certain defeat in front of them."

"Now that's a goddamn fact."

"That's why going forward, every effort must be made to keep our troops comfortable. Because in the long run, the man in the front lines who feels he is better clothed and better equipped than the enemy is the man who will win."

"You're preaching to the choir there, old friend."

"I know I am. But I just want you to know that soon victory will be in our grasp all across our front if we keep our boys better equipped than the enemy."

Patton nodded. Yessir, he could almost taste the victory. First, take Metz. Then crash over the Saar and Rhine before taking the Big Prize—Berlin. He couldn't wait for his Third Army to press into Nazi Germany. But the only way to move his army there was for him to conquer a huge swath of French and German territory and then pull, like a piece of spaghetti, mind-bogglingly immense stockpiles of food, ammunition, and gasoline along with him. It was going to be a challenge, he knew now after the slow and painful Lorraine campaign. There was no question the war's end was in sight, but given the regrettable "October Pause" on the Western Front resulting from Monty's fantastical *Operation Market-Garden* in the north, he and Ike both had to tamp down their expectations of a quick victory.

The reality was that the fierce German resistance at Metz and miserable weather thus far in November precluded the type of swift and violent armored thrust for which Patton was most suited. Seven inches of rainfall had fallen in the last two weeks alone, swelling the Moselle River over its banks. Not only did it rain all the time, but a dense fog had descended over Lorraine and the swollen rivers had flooded the fields and roads, turning them into muddy quagmires through which Third Army was forced to slog. That wasn't all though. The Germans also left booby traps and mines everywhere to slow the advance, sometimes planting time bombs in buildings that did not go off until days or even weeks had passed. And then there was the alarming increase in trench foot cases and other nonbattle casualties due to the flu and other assorted lung, ear, nose, and throat ailments.

Patton couldn't help but fume at what he saw as a senseless waste of his men and a lost opportunity. If he had been allowed to charge eastward back in late August following the collapse at Falaise, he firmly believed that he would have crossed the Rhine by now, and might even be knocking on the gates of Berlin.

He looked at the square-jawed, friendly-eyed Ike. "I appreciate you taking the time to visit Third Army," he said. "But as I've indicated, Metz is going to be harder to take than I thought. I just want you to know that."

"How long, George? And don't bullshit me."

"A week."

"One week? That's November 22."

"I can do it."

"Can you? Weyland has been bombing the hell out of every one of those forts, and the Germans are still holding out. It's going to take more than a week, don't you think?"

*Goddamnit, he's probably right, but I'll be damned if I'll admit it.* "Nope," he said. "I guarantee to have Metz, and hopefully its remaining forts as well, in my hands in a week or less."

Ike gave his trademark grin. "That will be just fine, George. Now why don't we grab some lunch."

Patton assumed a mock British accent. "Right this way to my headquarters," he said, aping his rival Montgomery, "where we shall make a *dagger thrust* into some good cans of Spam."

"Sounds good to me, George. I'm quite partial to Spam."

A half hour later, they were back at Patton's Nancy headquarters. In deference to Eisenhower's mutt, Telek, the commander of Third Army had banished Willie from the mess room. But as the group dined, a boisterous racket broke out under the table as Willie and the SHAEF Scottie banged and tumbled against legs and chairs. To his mortification, Patton realized that Willie had crept back into the room to find Telek occupying his place of honor under the table between the two generals. War had suddenly broken out beneath their feet as Willie had launched a surprise counterattack, and the two dogs were going at it, heedless of the high-ranking company.

"Jesus Christ, Willie, you little cocksucker!" cried Patton in shock. "What the hell are you trying to do—get my ass fired?"

But Gay and Codman were already on top of the situation. With the startled guests, including six generals in all and Kay Summersby, looking on in shock, they yanked back their chairs and scrambled beneath the table on all fours like crocodiles to break up the dog fight.

"Goddamnit, lasso my pit bull before I am forced to relinquish him to the French!" he growled to his aides. "Willie," he then said, ducking his head below the table, "you have severely disappointed me, you little limey bastard!"

Now Gay and Codman emptied their water glasses at the snarling animals to separate them. It was then that Patton's batman Wally was able to coral the snapping Willie long enough to drag him out of the room.

"My God, Ike," apologized Patton profusely, "I am sorry to have caused such a terrible ruckus."

"No, no, no," insisted Eisenhower, equally embarrassed. "This is Willie's home—we should lock up Telek."

"No, sir!" Patton replied firmly. "Telek outranks Willie, so Telek stays right here. Willie is confined to quarters, under arrest. That's Army protocol."

Eisenhower smiled. "All right, George. That's fair enough."

"Good," said Patton. But then, unable to resist temptation, he added, "Fair is fair, Ike. But you've got to admit my little Willie was chewing the bejesus out of your goddamn Scottie—rank or no rank!"

Everyone laughed uproariously. That night, the two balding, past-middle-age generals had dinner together on the Rue Auxerre and stayed up until two thirty, reminiscing about their younger years in the Army and talking through the thorny problem of taking Metz and the Siegfried Line beyond. The friendship born in 1919 had weathered the repeated incursions of time, distance, army politics, a reversal of seniority, and the fortunes of war. Yet both had survived, and it was precisely these late-night visits between the two American lions that made them both realize how much history they shared and how deeply they cared about one another, despite their differences during the past year. Indeed, they had a special relationship. Unfortunately, that relationship was being increasingly tested by the supreme commander's inexplicable tolerance for the irrepressible Monty, who Patton knew was gunning for Ike's job and doing everything in his power to undermine him for his own, and Great Britain's, wounded pride at having to play second fiddle to the U.S. But not tonight. Tonight, they were two old friends staying up late swapping stories.

Ike left Nancy the next morning with one of his "Georgie Patton hangovers"—foggy-headed from drinking too much and not getting enough sleep, but satisfied that, with Old Blood and Guts once again turned loose, Nazi Germany was that much closer to defeat.

# CHAPTER 27

## METZ, NORTHEASTERN FRANCE

### NOVEMBER 22, 1944

"PULL OVER NEXT TO THAT TROOPER!" cried Patton. "I want to talk to him!"

His African-American driver, Master Sergeant John Mims, reflexively obeyed, navigating the Willys-Overland jeep up next to the muddy-uniformed GI walking along the road. Mims then brought the command vehicle to a halt. In the backseat sat Major Codman with Willie, who had been passing appreciable gas and was still a tad jittery from yesterday's massive artillery shelling.

"Hey there, son," said Patton, leaning out the jeep. "Why are you all alone? Is there something wrong?"

The infantryman recognized Patton instantly and saluted in the rainy drizzle. "My unit has lost most of its officers and NCOs and the Pfcs are now running things," he replied in a Texas twang. "I'll be catching up with them directly."

"So you have private first class's running the show? What's wrong with that?"

"Plenty! Why General, those sons of bitches are drunk with power!"

"Why I didn't know that. Thank you for keeping me informed, Private. Now you just keep walking towards the front, and if you see a Kraut, please get him to surrender without a fight, will you?"

"Yes General, I reckon I'll be more than happy to oblige."

Patton chuckled and, after an exchange of salutes, Mims drove off. Forty minutes later, they drove into Metz, which had formally surrendered at 1435 hours. At the head of his motorized cavalcade, Patton entered the city as a conquering hero with sirens wailing to announce his arrival, punctuated by the "steamboat trombone" on his Willys. The German stronghold had fallen only after heavy fighting to root out the defenders from their underground chambers room by room and tunnel by tunnel; however, Forts Driant and Jeanne d'Arc, as well as a number of other smaller forts ringing the city, were still holding out. They were being blasted with heavy shelling using the Germans' own captured guns. But after two months of failed frontal assaults and relentless bombardment from the air and artillery, Metz was finally back in Allied hands thanks to Third Army. Patton knew it was only a matter of time before the last German holdouts in the surrounding forts surrendered.

With an honor guard playing ruffles and flourishes for the victors in the city's central square, Patton reviewed the 5th Division, which had carried the brunt of the attacks on Metz and suffered heavy casualties. GIs in muddy boots and frayed uniforms stood at attention, as a military band with colors flying preceded French soldiers in black berets, white leggings, and Sam Browne belts, each man with two submachine guns slung over his shoulders. Patton awarded dozens of medals for valor to his men and officially returned the city, which had changed hands so often before, to French custody.

"I am very proud of you," he told his troops in a shrill voice steeped with genuine admiration. "Your country is proud of you. You are magnificent fighting men. Your deeds in the Battle of Metz will fill the pages of history for a thousand years, and in crossing the Moselle, you men have engaged in one of the epic river crossings of history..."

For ten minutes he lavished praise upon everyone from his top generals Walker and Eddy down to the cooks. But deep down, he knew that too many had died in taking the city, and he felt guilty for it. He had made more than his fair share of mistakes during his initial attacks on Metz and its network of forty-three forts, and ultimately the battle was largely a symbolic victory won at great cost by the brave men of his Third Army. In the midst of one of the worst European winters in nearly a century, the securing of the Moselle and siege of Metz had proved to be merely the longest and bloodiest battles of an ugly campaign. But at least it was over and Third Army was off to the Siegfried Line.

Following the victory ceremony, he drove to a nearby field hospital to visit the wounded. If he encountered any soldiers suffering from battle fatigue, he wasn't going to utter a word of protest, and he was certainly not going to slap them. He had learned his goddamn lesson in Sicily. Stopping by the bed of the first GI in line, he inquired if he was aware that the city had fallen.

"Metz is in the hands of the Third Army now," he said in a soothing voice to the heavily bandaged infantryman. "Were you aware of that, son?"

"Yes General, I was," replied the soldier, who had recognized him instantly.

Patton leaned down and gently took him by the hand. "Tomorrow, son, the headlines will read 'PATTON TOOK METZ!' which you know is a goddamn lie. You know why it's a lie?"

"No sir, I'm afraid I don't."

"Because you and your GI buddies are the ones who actually took Metz."

"Thanks, General. That means a lot. And so does your coming here to visit us."

His gaze turned to the left down the row to his wounded compatriots lying in their hospital beds. Following his gaze, Patton nodded in solemn tribute in their direction before turning back to the wounded soldier.

"Because you and your buddies are the ones who have won a great victory and suffered through heavy fighting, you know what I'm going to do?" he asked him.

"What, General?"

"I'm going to distribute fifty thousand cases of champagne I have been informed Third Army has just captured and hand it out to you troops. You men have fought bravely and you deserve a little celebration. What do you say to that?"

"I say it's going to be one hell of a party, sir."

"Goddamn right it is. Get well soon now, son, you hear? We need fighters like you in Third Army."

"I'll do my best, General."

Continuing down the neat row of medical cots, he spoke with a few more men before Hap Gay informed him that a German SS officer, General Anton Dunckern, had been taken into custody by a 5th Division patrol while trying to slink out of Metz with an aide. Patton insisted on interviewing Dunckern personally, and with Gay, Koch, an interpreter, and sentries present, he had the paunchy SS general and security commander for Lorraine brought to an interrogation room. To intimidate him, he wore his high-topped combat boots. He also commanded the immaculately dressed officer to stand at attention for the questioning and informed him that he would be questioned by a Jewish lieutenant serving as Patton's interpreter, which drew a frown from the bug-eyed SS man.

"You should know, Dunckern, that I always wear high boots when I talk to SS bastards," Patton hissed to the German in his native tongue. "You will stand at attention when I speak to you and you will preface every answer to me with 'sir' or 'general.' Is that understood?"

Looking anxious, Dunckern nodded and said in German, "Yes sir, General."

Now Patton turned away and made eye contact with his interpreter. "You can tell this bastard that, naturally in my position, I cannot demean myself to question him. But I can say this: that I have captured a great many German generals, and this is the first one who has been wholly untrue to everything...because he is not only a Nazi but he is untrue to the Nazis by surrendering. If he wants to say anything he can, and I will say that unless he opens up and talks, I will turn him over to the French. They know how to make people talk. Tell him that."

The Jewish interpreter smiled. "I'll be happy to, General." He then proceeded to relay the information in rapid-fire German, to which Dunckern replied, "I received orders to go in the Metz sector and defend a certain sector there, and the reason I did not perish was that I could not reach my weapons and fight back."

Patton shook his head in disgust. "Tell him he's a liar," he growled, understanding the Nazi's every word.

Once Old Blood and Guts's words were translated, Dunckern stiffened noticeably before responding. "There was no possibility to continue fighting!" he blubbered. "The door was opened, and they put a gun on me!"

Patton: "If he wanted to be a good Nazi, he could have died then and there. It would have been a pleasanter death than what he will get now. Tell him that."

Dunckern, pleading now: "It was useless to do anything about it under the circumstances! May I have permission to ask a question?"

Patton mulled it over a moment. "All right, I suppose the son of a bitch can ask a goddamn question."

Dunckern: "I was fighting against and captured by American troops. Therefore, I should be considered a prisoner of war of the American forces. Is this not correct?"

Patton: "Tell him he will be a prisoner of war of the French forces soon. They have a lot they want to ask him."

Dunckern, face contorted in panic: "I consider myself a prisoner of war of the American forces, and I have not been captured by the French forces! Please!"

Patton scowled at him and again addressed his interpreter. "When I am dealing with vipers, I do not have to be bothered by any foolish ideas. Tell him that."

Dunckern: "I consider myself a prisoner of war since I fought as a soldier and should be treated as a soldier!"

Patton: "Tell him he has also acted as a policeman—a low type of policeman."

Dunckern: "I acted as an officer of the police in an honorable and practical manner, and I have nothing to be ashamed of!"

Patton: "That is a matter of opinion. No one who is a Nazi policeman could act in an honorable manner. Tell him that."

Dunckern: "I can only say that during every day of my life I have been honest, rightful, respectful, and humanitarian!"

Patton: "If that's the case, ask him if he has anything he wants to say by way of giving me information that will change my opinion."

Dunckern, still panic-stricken: "No one will be able to stand up against me to testify that I did anything against the rules of humanity or human treatment!"

Patton: "As I've said, I understand German very well, but I will not demean myself by speaking the language of Nazis. I think before I turn the general over to the French, I will send him to the Army Group who may question him or have some special investigators question him. They can do things I can't. Tell him."

Dunckern, visibly pale now: "I am not worried about having myself investigated! Of course, there may be some mistakes I have made, which is only human, but I am not worried about inhuman acts charged against me!"

Patton: "Tell him he's full of shit. And also tell him I have great respect for German soldiers—they are gallant men—but not for Nazis. Have the guards take him outside and have his picture taken and then we'll see what we will do with him. Also tell him that those bayonets on the guards' guns are very sharp."

When the information was translated, the SS officer swallowed hard. Glowering at him, Patton spoke again in German, "I have captured a number of German generals but you are the most sordid son of a bitch of them all. I know you are guilty of war crimes and we are going to find out about them, mark my words." He turned to the sentries. "Take the dirty bastard away!"

Stepping back outside into the rain with Gay and Codman, he shook his head in disgust. "I need a fucking shower and a stiff drink. Nazi sons of bitches like that make me sick to my stomach."

Gay nodded. "I know how you feel, sir. But at least the SS are going to get what's coming to them."

"Damn right they are. That son of a bitch Dunckern was the most vicious-looking bastard I have ever seen—and after I got through talking to him, he was unquestionably one of the worst scared. I do believe, Hap, that he is the first man I have deliberately brow-beaten. I must admit I took real pleasure in doing it."

"General Gay and I could tell, sir," said Codman.

"Frankly, I believe we should line up every SS bastard and shoot the sons of bitches. I believe in the unwritten soldier's code that anything is fair in battle, but once captured, a soldier is entitled to be treated decently under the covenants of the Geneva Convention. But not these SS and Gestapo bastards. In my eyes, they are not soldiers at all and shouldn't be entitled to humane treatment. I know that sounds harsh, but that's the way I see it."

With that, he went to question Colonel Constantin Meyer, a German Regular Army officer also captured in the Metz area, to whom he was solicitous. Allowing him to sit down and offering him a cigar, he informed him about his little chat with Colonel Dunckern and told him that his treatment would much different.

Meyer was infinitely relieved. "Thank you, General Patton. I am very grateful that I do not have to stay with that SS officer," he said.

Old Blood and Guts gave an ingratiating smile. "I don't blame you, Colonel. He's a dirty, rotten scoundrel and will probably end up being hung for his crimes against civilization. I only wish I could goddamn do it myself!"

# CHAPTER 28



## ALTSTADT NORD, COLOGNE

### NOVEMBER 26, 1944

BUNDLED UP AGAINST THE CHILL, Angela stared up at the intricate stone façade, flying buttresses, and soaring twin towers of Cologne Cathedral. Taking over six hundred years to be built between 1248 and 1880 A.D., the Roman Catholic Cathedral Church of Saint Peter, as it was officially known, was the most prominent architectural achievement in all of Germany and a great source of pride for her and her countrymen. Late in the previous century, the cathedral's completion signified the alliance of several individual kingdoms and the unification of Germany. The cathedral also happened to be one of the tallest houses of worship in the world and the mother church of the archbishop of the Queen City. Gazing up at the impressive Gothic edifice with its five-hundred-foot-tall north and south towers, Angela couldn't help but feel the power of God.

Though the nearly seven-hundred-year-old *Kölner Dom* had been struck nearly a dozen times during air raids, temporarily transforming the church to a smoking hell on earth, the main structure remained standing and the colorful stained glass windows had been removed to a safe location. From a distance, the cathedral and its towering twin spires appeared unwavering to the global conflict. The historic edifice was made almost entirely of stone and thus, could not burn down, and the tall, open windows and hollow interior had helped funnel bomb blasts outside. The last attack on October 17 had been waged by more than 1,300 British bombers, which used the cathedral as an easily recognizable navigational landmark for Allied aircraft assaults. The sacred house of worship's resistance to destruction amidst the devastation of seventy percent of the city was observed with a mixture of relief and awe by the German people.

Locking her bicycle, Angela stepped up to the main entrance to the cathedral, opened the heavy oak double doors, and walked inside. Her leather shoes tapped lightly on the laminated, dark-blue slate stones. Inside the church, the stone mass seemed to rise, almost weightlessly, up to the nearly 150-foot-high baldachin-style arches. Along with the stained glass windows, most of the wooden pews had been removed, and the floor was covered with rubble. But still a dozen or so people were present in the church, kneeling in prayer or sitting gazing into space. Angela walked the length of the long central nave, angled around a pile of rubble, and took a seat in one of the remaining pews on the right, facing north.

It was impossible not to be inspired here. The vast interior seemed to dwarf all humanity that found its way inside. The lofty ceiling was vaulted in stone, the cross-ribs covered in shimmering gold paint. The columns separating the nave from the side aisles were exquisitely decorated, and the tracery of the remaining pews was lithe and graceful. Banks of guttering candles in the nave provided illumination. All in all, the faithful who came here to surrender themselves before God, or to contemplate the beauty of the damaged but still resplendent church, could feel closer, at least for a moment, to understanding the mystical power of the universe.

She pulled out her rosary, kneeled down, and began to pray.

*Hail Mary full of grace, the Lord is with thee...*

It was a simple prayer, as much a vestige of her Roman Catholic upbringing as a supplication to a higher authority. But Angela truly believed in the words as she recited them from long memory. She accepted Jesus as Lord and Savior and sought, in quiet moments like these, to draw closer to Him. She knew that all true believers endured to the end, that only through faith could a person remain in a state of grace.

But it wasn't a quest for God's acceptance that brought her here today. It had to do with the new sadness in her heart. She couldn't remember feeling this melancholy in her entire life. The death of Schröder and the twelve other victims of the public hanging—six of whom were her Edelweiss Pirates comrades aged seventeen or younger—had, along with the imprisonment of Jean Hüber and dozens of other Pirates, torn a hole in her heart.

As part of the October and November arrests that had snared her friends, the 800 officers comprising the Cologne security forces had rounded up more than 200 German civilians and fugitive foreign workers. She had learned that many of them had been and were still being brutally interrogated and tortured at El-De Haus in the *Altstadt* and Brauweiler Abbey located on the city's outskirts. She had also been informed that the members of the Committee for a Free Germany had been linked to Steinbrück's Ehrenfeld Group. The Committee's association with the gang had proved disastrous: the captured gang members cracked under torture and gave up the names and addresses of the Committee's members. In the past week, the entire group was reportedly in the Cologne Gestapo's custody. With the mass arrests, public hangings, and behind-the-scenes executions by the Gestapo, the regime was making an example of "asocials" and "subversive elements" as Hoffmann's mass civilian deportations in the Rhineland accelerated and violence increased.

But the Nazi authorities had in recent weeks also begun to lash out at ordinary, war-weary German citizens. Many were merely destitute people struggling to survive or those who no longer backed Hitler and his apocalyptic vision for the Fatherland with sufficient vigor. Despite their success at crushing these so-called "defeatist elements" lurking within the *Volk*, a huge gap remained between the regime's vision of the ideal German and the actuality of a frustrated, angry population unwilling, or simply unable, to adequately support the war effort. Distressed by Rhinelanders' purported lack of interest in defending their homes, Hoffmann, Kütter, and other officials began to describe civilians ready to sacrifice for the Reich as *deutschbewusst*, or conscious of their duty as Germans. In the eyes of the Gestapo, these people were "unconditionally German" and willing to carry out the regime's demands with discipline and cooperativeness against selfish civilians or traitors who "do not identify with the nation." This rigid definition of Germaness as an act of unconditional sacrifice demanded that civilians remain industrious, fiercely loyal, and willing to vigorously resist the enemy—even in the face of certain defeat and at grave risk to their own lives and that of their families.

These attempts to categorize civilians as either "Germans" willing to give one-hundred-percent support in defense of the Reich or selfish community outsiders created a rigid juxtaposition between the reliability the regime expected of its *Volksgenossen* and most war-weary Rhinelanders. The behavior of civilians that the security forces encountered in the field only reinforced this growing sense of frustration with everyday, law-abiding Germans. The resulting disparity between the expectation that the *Volk* would give up everything in their lives to defend the Reich, and the war weariness, apathy, and surliness they encountered on the streets generated deep suspicion. This shift in turn caused the Gestapo to draw upon their brutal and violent experiences in the "Bloodlands" of the Eastern Front, as they grappled to understand the motivation of the people of the Rhineland.

With Germany's war fortunes plummeting, her world seemingly collapsing around her, and her own people turning against one another, Angela was emotionally torn apart. She missed her first love immensely. Schröder had made her feel special and loved, and she had thrived in the dangerous world of the Edelweiss Pirates that he had introduced her to and that had taken his life. The intimacy they shared had made it all that much more exciting. She remembered back to the pleasurable sensations she had felt with the fun-loving boy. When he kissed her, she got goosebumps. When he looked her way, she lost her concentration. When she was alone with him, she felt a sense of inner peace. And when they made love, it had been tender yet explosive. The love and tenderness on the one hand and the wild risk-taking in combating the Hitler Youth and Nazis on the other were but different sides of the same coin. They both made her feel wonderfully alive.

Based upon the Gestapo's drastic response to the Cologne youth gangs, she realized what a thorn in the side her resistance work as a Navajo had been to the regime. Illegally distributing homegrown and Allied leaflets, terrorizing the HJ, painting anti-Nazi slogans on the walls of the city, lending aid to Jews, escaped forced laborers, and German deserters, and performing other covert acts of resistance—all of these had enraged the Nazis, which made her feel a deep sense of pride and accomplishment. And throughout it all, she had been in love. Now the question was would she ever *love* and *feel* again in such a desperate and exciting manner, where the stakes were high and she clearly held the moral high ground? How could she possibly ever have such a pure, innocent, and exciting love affair while fighting for a noble cause?

Rising from her kneeling position and sitting back down on the solid oak pew, she felt a powerful sense of irony. On the one hand, she felt inordinately blessed to have found Bartholomäus Schröder; on the other, the sadness she felt inside with his passing made her wonder if her life was still worth living, especially when his death was added to that of her beloved mother and brother. What had she done to deserve God's ire that she lost three loved ones in only seven months? Was God singling her out for punishment?

Knowing she might never find an answer to her questions, she again let her eyes drift around the church. With wonderment, she took in the sheer vastness and graceful artistry of the sanctuary; the pained, otherworldly expression of the savior nailed to the holy cross in humble surrender; the Shrine of the Three Kings rising up behind the high altar; the beautiful chancel pillar sculptures of Jesus, Mary, and the Twelve Apostles; the magnificent Gero Crucifix hanging in the crucifix chapel. Gradually, as the holiness of the place took hold inside her, as the sense of God's design and majesty permeated her soul, she said a prayer for Barthel and the other victims of the Gestapo and felt at peace with herself.

Fifteen minutes later, she was peddling her bike along Tankgassenwerft, the bomb-cratered promenade in the old part of Cologne next to the Rhine. She was headed to the Hospital of Augustinians, where she worked five days per week. Though the air was cold and the route heavily pock-marked from explosive blasts, the promenade was wide enough that she could navigate her way around the holes. There was only scattered snow on the ground and much of the rubble had been cleared away since the most recent mid-October air attack, so she made good time. Locking her bicycle, she walked through the front entrance to the second floor to her nurses' station.

It was then she met with a shock.

*Kriminalkommissar* Kütter and two other uniformed Gestapo officers rose up from the chairs they were sitting in to greet her. It was an ambush.

"*Fräulein* Lange—we have been waiting for you," snapped the SS Criminal Commissioner. "You will need to come with us."

She felt her heart race off scale. "B-But this is my hospital shift and I have to work," she stammered feebly. "There are many sick and wounded that require my attention."

She looked helplessly at her friend Marie Peukert and the other nurses at the station, but they all looked down meekly, not wanting to get involved.

"No," said Kütter firmly, "you are coming with us."

"Where are we going?"

"Gestapo headquarters at El-De Haus. We have some questions for you."

Fighting an overwhelming sense of panic, she forced herself to think clearly. The most important thing was to get in touch with her father and let him know that she was being detained. She leaned in close to Marie, who stood petrified along with the other nurses at the station, and whispered to her: "Contact my father and tell him what's happened. Tell him he needs to get to El-De Haus as fast as possible."

"Yes, of course," answered Marie. "I will take care of it."

"Thank you." Turning back towards Kütter, she said: "All right, I'm ready."

He smiled thinly. "No, I don't think you are, *Volksfeinde*. This is going to be a whole new experience for you. But, indeed, you have brought it upon yourself."

She tried to be brave. "I don't know what you're talking about."

"Oh, you don't? Then let me give you a little hint."

In a surprisingly crisp motion, he withdrew his wooden police baton and jabbed her in the stomach. He delivered the blow quickly, precisely, like a prizefighter throwing a well-timed jab. In the next instant, the other two Gestapo men jerked her arms back savagely, clicked handcuffs around her wrists, and locked them in place.

Angela gasped for air. But it would not come as they each grabbed an arm and, with brutal but methodical efficiency, escorted her out of the hospital with her friend Marie Peukert and the other nurses looking on in shock and horror.

# CHAPTER 29



AS THE BLACK OPEL P4 COMMAND CAR pulled up to the notorious El-De Haus, Angela felt her throat go dry. Going into the Cologne *Die Geheime Staatspolizei* headquarters located at Appellhofplatz 23–25 was not the hard part—it was coming back out alive that often proved daunting for those considered traitors or dissidents by the regime. What terrified her most of all was that in recent weeks ordinary German citizens who set foot inside the building were never seen alive again. Today, she could only pray that she wouldn't be among them.

The massive, drab-brown, five-story building looked like a law or civil servant office—and yet, despite its bureaucratic blandness, it still managed to carry an unmistakable aura of calmly efficient brutality and violence. The building was built in a neoclassical style, with an ornate tufa façade and rounded corners. The only indication that it was a National Socialist redoubt were the pair of blood-red Nazi flags fluttering from its rooftop and life-sized portrait of the Führer hanging in the lobby. The original door fronting the building bore the initials L and D for the building's owner, Leopold Dahmen, who had been forced to surrender the building to the Gestapo in 1935. By the beginning of the war, El-De Haus was swiftly converted into Cologne's primary SS police and counterintelligence headquarters, holding area, and interrogation center. It contained several offices, a house prison containing ten holding cells, a truck entrance, and a stone inner courtyard where mass executions were quietly carried out. In an ironic twist, the Gestapo headquarters had suffered only minimal bombing damage thus far during the war, while the surrounding city had been reduced to rubble.

During the last three years, the name El-De Haus had come to strike fear into the hearts of the local population as a place of unmitigated police brutality and torture. The German citizens of Cologne—but particularly anti-Fascists, Jews, Communists, army deserters, and those harboring fugitives wanted by the Nazis—were very much aware that terrible things were happening behind the closed doors of the basement torture rooms of El-De Haus. The cells and interrogation rooms were not soundproofed, which meant that the screams of prisoners undergoing torture could be heard on both Appellhofplatz and Elisenstrasse outside the building.

Angela shuddered as the staff command car came to a halt in the inner courtyard so that a lorry from the Municipal Rubbish Disposal carrying a pile of dead bodies could exit the prison. The victims, she knew, would be carted off and unceremoniously dumped to the *Westfriedhof*—West Cemetery—where the Gestapo had its own section, the "Gestapo Field." The recent executions had apparently been carried out by hanging, as a transportable gallows stood next to the south wall of the courtyard where seven people could be hanged simultaneously.

She couldn't believe she was about to become a prisoner inside this miserable place that had haunted her imagination for years, a place where civilization and the rule of law did not apply. With her palms now sweaty, she was pulled roughly from the command car and taken inside through the basement stairs by a pair of Gestapo guards in *feldgrau* uniforms, black jackboots, and steel coal-scuttle helmets, with *Schmeisser* light machine guns slung about their shoulders. At a desk on the second floor, an officer greeted Kütter.

"Commander Kütter, so nice of you to visit us from Brauweiler. What brings you here today?"

"I was in the area and wanted to have a word with *Hauptsturmführer* Matschke," he said, referring to the commander of the Cologne Gestapo counterintelligence section under Hoffmann. "Please have this prisoner fingerprinted, photographed, and brought to Interrogation Cell 4 for treatment."

"Yes, Commander."

Angela felt herself stiffen. *Treatment? What is that?* But she realized, to her mortification, that she already knew the answer: they were talking about torture during interrogation.

Kütter and his men walked off. The desk officer said to Angela, "So, why are you here? I'm sure you're innocent, too, right?"

"As a matter of fact I am. I have no idea what I am supposed to have done."

"No idea? Well then, let me tell you."

Rising from his desk, he shoved her down the stairs. She tumbled all the way down to the landing. Excruciating pain shot through her head and shoulders as she crashed down upon the descending concrete steps. When she got to her feet, she saw a man washing himself on the landing below with a rag. The prisoner was covered in blood and had apparently just undergone the Gestapo's "treatment." It was all like a horrible dream and she thought she would faint.

But to her surprise, she was not mistreated any further while being fingerprinted, photographed, escorted to Interrogation Cell 4 in the lower basement by a pair of sullen-faced armed guards, and stuffed into a chair in front of a small wooden desk. All the same, she was terrified out of her mind. She knew that the abuse she had endured thus far at the hands of *Kriminalkommissar* Kütter and his officers was only the beginning, a psychological "softening-up" before the real interrogation. A far more onerous fate awaited her once she was subjected to the full "treatment." After fifteen minutes of waiting, the door swung open again and Kütter stepped into the room with his two officers, who were now introduced as *Kriminalassistents* Josef Hoegen and Walter Hirschfeld. They stood implacably at the door, hands folded in front of them, as Kütter took a seat at the desk across from her.

Angela felt her heart sink. She was well aware of Kütter's reputation for cruelty, but Hoegen and Hirschfeld, too, were known as two of the most brutal and sadistic Gestapo interrogators in the city. Edelweiss Pirates and other prisoners who had been fortunate enough to be released from El-De Haus and Brauweiler described them as men who lacked even an ounce of compassion. The stern-faced, middle-aged Josef Hoegen was a former Kripo officer and veteran of the Great War who had worked in the Cologne Gestapo office's anti-Marxist section and *Einsatzgruppe B* on the Eastern Front, ruthlessly crushing German and non-German "enemies of the state" with savage violence, abuse, and torture. A decade younger and wearing wire-rim glasses, Walter Hirschfeld was nearly as violent and pitiless as Hoegen. He had joined the Aachen Kripo in 1934 after failing to establish a career selling musical instruments. Reassigned to the border city's Gestapo office in 1942, he had been sent to Cologne, where his career continued to plateau and he failed to achieve promotion despite an understaffed personnel situation. At the hospital when Angela had first laid eyes on Hoegen and Hirschfeld, she knew instantly what they were: mediocre, colorless, angry little bureaucrats who, like so many of the Nazis she had come across, had obtained their careers and identities—albeit both totally false and flawed—through the rise of Hitler's National Socialism.

But as frightening as his two sidekicks were, Kütter was the one that terrified Angela the most. Beneath his jet-black uniform and peaked cap, he too was a bland and humorless-looking bureaucrat like so many of the unimaginative, second-tier SS and SD men that had risen to positions of power in Hitler's Reich. True, he had a certain cultivation and intelligence behind his wintry blue eyes. But as he pulled out a pen and black notebook with a swastika on the cover, he was still mostly cold and terrifying. She could tell he was so indoctrinated with the tenants of Nazism that he was devoid of any sense of compassion. Involuntarily shrinking back in her seat, she reminded herself to remain calm and talk slowly to drag out the questioning while giving up no useful information.

At the same time, she prayed that her father would hurry.

"So, *Fräulein* Lange," he began in a brusque, no-nonsense voice, "how long have you been with the resistance?"

She pretended not to appear taken aback. "I am not with the resistance."

"You are not with the Edelweiss Pirates, specifically the Cologne Navajos?"

"No, but I have heard of them. They were hung outside the Ehrenfeld train station two weeks ago. I saw you there, remember, with my father? He is a Wehrmacht colonel and hero of Germany with two Iron Crosses to his credit—one in each war. He will be here any minute to protest your treatment of me."

"Your father is coming to El-De Haus?"

"Yes, he is. He will be here very soon."

"Your father does not concern me. It is you, young lady, who concerns me."

"Why is that?"

"You know perfectly well why: you are an enemy of the people. Oh yes, I know all about you."

"I beg to differ. I am a patriot just like my father, who has served his country faithfully in two world wars."

"Your father is a drunk and one-armed cripple. He is no hero of Germany and, if he is unable to join our forces in combat in the coming weeks, he is of little further value to the Reich. But what happens to him is not up to me."

She felt a jolt of anger. "You are a pig and not fit to tie my father's shoes."

"Is that so?" He signalled Hoegen standing at the door with a little nod—and Angela received a sharp crack to the back of her head with a truncheon.

She screamed in pain. Kütter waited patiently a moment for her to calm down before resuming the interrogation.

"You know about me, right? I mean, you know of my reputation?"

It was hard to think straight when her ears were ringing. She felt for blood, but there was none. Still, her head hurt like hell.

"I'll ask you again. Do you know of my reputation?"

"*Ja.*"

"Then you know I ask that my officers encourage inmates to speak the truth."

She decided that she had better not antagonize him any further; she just had to hold on until her father got here. "I understand," she said submissively.

"No, I don't think you do. That's why I'm going to tell you a little story. Last month, a Border Police officer was assigned to my *Sonderkommando Brauweiler* unit. When he reported for duty, I drew him in close and said to him, 'Welcome to Brauweiler. But you should know that here we carry out the hard work. When the prisoners don't sing, we go at them with truncheons until they confess.' When he refused to participate with the customary enthusiasm I like to see, I told him he was too weak for my unit and reassigned him to another department to transport prisoners. You see, that is what you are up against."

She gave as honest and forthcoming an expression as she could muster. "I understand and will tell you everything you want to know."

His face relaxed. "Good, how long have you been with the Edelweiss Pirates?"

"I am not with them or anyone else. The first time I laid eyes on them was when they were hung at the train station. Someone told me who they were."

"You are lying."

"No, I am not. Has anyone given my name up? No, because I have no association with the group."

"A girl matching your description has been seen with the terrorist gang on many occasions. I think it is you."

*Papa, where are you? Please hurry.* "It is not me, I can assure you."

"Have you ever heard of Mucki?"

"No, and you asked me that before. Who is she?"

"It is most likely a code name. Is it yours?"

"No, it is not. And as I told you before, I don't know anyone with that name."

He looked at her, trying to divine if she was telling the truth. After several tense seconds, the moment passed and she felt a sense of relief. Though someone matching her description had been seen in the presence of the Edelweiss Pirates and her code name had presumably been given up under torture, no one had given up her real name and Kütter did not know for certain that she was Mucki. All he had heard was a name, because the only ones who knew her real name were Schröder and Jean Hüber, and they had not said anything except to give up her code name Mucki. *God bless you, Barthel and Jean,* she thought.

But still she had to be careful. Though she was a reasonably good liar—she had extensive practice getting what she wanted from authority figures—she had no formal espionage training. Furthermore, this was the first time she had been detained and interrogated by the Gestapo. All the same, though she was young and inexperienced, she was a natural spy and she knew it.

"Why did you go to the train station to see the hangings that day?"

"Because my father wanted to see that justice was done to the robbers of Ehrenfeld. As you know, he was attacked at gunpoint in broad daylight."

"So you are a law-abiding citizen. Somehow, I find that hard to believe."

"I'm just a girl. Why would you think I would know about criminal gangs?"

"You think because you are young and female that you are above suspicion?"

That was precisely what she thought. Hans Steinbrück had told her that her femininity and innocence were her best bets to dupe the Gestapo in Cologne. Most Germans, especially those in the Secret Police, had a traditional view of females and their capabilities in war. They assumed that women couldn't possibly be actively engaged in underground activities other than sheltering resistance members, which Angela knew was absurd. Females in the rubble fields of Cologne, as well as those living outside the city, had developed countless ways to use their gender to outwit the Nazis and escape their control and intimidation. She was living proof.

"No, I would never presume that," she said. "But the truth is I am as afraid of these people as you are. As I said, they robbed my father at gunpoint."

He looked at her for a long moment before jotting down notes in his little black book. She thought: *Damnit, he doesn't believe me. Maybe he is not as gullible as the rest of his countrymen. Is he going to torture me after all?*

"You know what will happen to you if I think you've been lying to me?" he said, as if reading her thoughts.

She suppressed a gulp. "But I'm not lying to you."

"I will have to send you to Brauweiler. I know you have heard the stories."

Indeed, she had. The interrogations at the prison were said to exceed even El-De Haus. Regardless of age or sex, officers savagely beat the prisoners upon arrival to Brauweiler, repeatedly striking them in the face and body with fists, keys, pistol butts, and truncheons. They also used a thick wooden table leg to strike prisoners across the head or body; the weapon was nicknamed "Clock of the Rhine" because it left prisoners' "ears ringing." The Gestapo used the beatings as a form of "welcoming" detainees to the prison. Afterwards, officers tightly handcuffed bloodied prisoners' arms behind their backs and placed them in solitary confinement for periods ranging from a day to a week. The handcuffs caused the prisoners' hands to swell painfully like fat sausages, and the officers liked to rip them off, causing severe injuries to the inmates' arms. Guards also humiliated the inmates, forcing them to eat a watery soup like animals by lapping it out of a bowl. By all accounts, Brauweiler was a hell on earth that made El-De Haus pale in comparison.

"I'm going to tell you what I think. I think you knew Bartholomäus Schröder and Günther Schwarz, and your code name is Mucki. When I saw you at the train station that day with your father, I knew it was you. You matched the descriptions the boys gave perfectly. They tried to lie to me at first, but eventually they came clean. And the young girl they described was you. That's why I followed you."

*Damnit, Papa was right—I shouldn't have gone to the hanging that day. The Gestapo would never have found out about me if not for that.*

"You must know that if you are lying to me and really are with the underground," Kütter persisted, "I will find out and you will be dealt with harshly. Everyone ends up talking in the end. The only question is how long you can last before I break you and you tell me what I want to know. Now, tell me about your work for these Navajos. Were you a courier or did you fight with them? Girls your age have been observed on several occasions fighting in the streets with the Hitler Youth."

She pretended to be shocked at such an accusation.

"Just tell me. If you don't, I am going to have to instruct my men here to strike you in the head again. Then after that, we can really get on with the 'treatment.'"

*Papa, please hurry. I don't know how much longer I can hold out.* She tried not to look scared. But she couldn't help a little grimace at the thought of the tortures awaiting her if Kütter suspected she was lying. Not only would they hit her with blunt objects but they would dunk her in freezing cold water, stick her under hot lights, stick needles into her flesh, burn her with blow torches, place heated coils under her fingernails, and pull out her pubic hair with tweezers. She had heard that some prisoners had chosen to take their own lives by hanging themselves or jumping out windows rather than submit to further Gestapo torture.

"Just tell me what you know. For instance, how about the Committee for a Free Germany? They have been linked to Steinbrück's Ehrenfeld Group."

"I have never heard of them."

With a subtle nod of his head, he signalled one of his officers standing at the door. It was Hoegen again.

"No, please, I don't know any—"

*Thwack!*

The blow was so hard that Angela saw white stars.

"You control your fate," said Kütter. "If you tell the truth, no harm will come to you—or your family."

"My family? What do you mean my family?"

"Why I mean that crippled drunk of a father of yours, of course."

"That will be unnecessary, *Kriminalkommissar*," sounded a new voice.

Turning her head, Angela looked up to see Dr. Max Hoffmann and her father standing in the now-open doorway. Kütter jerked back in his chair and his two lackey officers stiffened to attention.

"This girl is to be released at once," declared Hoffmann in a voice that brooked no opposition. "And you had better hope not a hair on her head has been ruffled."

Kütter's face whitened. "But *Kriminaldirektor*, I believe this prisoner is lying and I was just about to—"

"Release her, damn you—that is an order! Colonel Lange has just uncovered the location of a *Bandennest* that will make the Steinbrück bandit hideout look like a cubby hole. Now I need this girl released and all troops made ready at once."

"But sir, do you think that wise when—"

"Shut up, Ferdinand. This is our chance to strike a great blow to the enemies of the Reich. We shall now give our best, in pride and honor, by exemplifying the struggle of National Socialism and fulfilling our obligations to *Volk* and Führer by leading the attack on the gang hideout."

"But, *Kriminaldirektor*, what if it's a trap?"

"It's not a trap, damn you! Now let's go!"

Angela looked at her father in disbelief. How had he pulled this off? Was she really getting a reprieve, or was this all a dream? But then he smiled that little smile of his when he knew he was devilishly cunning, the smile that her mother had adored—and she knew that he had come up with something real. Even in his weakened state, he was a clever, resourceful man that was not to be trifled with.

Somehow, her father—Wehrmacht colonel, cripple, and drunk—had fooled the Nazis.

# CHAPTER 30

**CASERNE MOLIFOR
NANCY, NORTHEASTERN FRANCE**

**DECEMBER 8, 1944**

PATTON DIRECTED James O'Neill, Third Army Chaplain, and Colonel Paul Harkins, his deputy chief of staff, to the two seats before his desk.

"Chaplain," he said without circumlocution, "I want you to publish a prayer for good weather. I'm tired of my soldiers having to fight mud and floods as well as Germans. See if we can't get God to work on our side."

"General, it's going to take a pretty thick rug for that kind of praying," said O'Neill.

"I don't care if it takes a flying carpet. I want the praying done. We must do something about these infernal rains if we are to win the war."

"Yes, sir. May I say, General, that it usually isn't customary among men of my profession to pray for clear weather to kill one's fellow man."

"Chaplain, are you trying to teach me theology or are you the chaplain of the Third Army? I want a prayer."

"Yes, General. I'll research the topic and report back to you within an hour."

"That's fine, Chaplain—I'll be waiting."

"I'll see you out," said Harkins, and the two men left. Outside with the pouring rain splashing down upon them, the chaplain said to the deputy chief of staff, "Whew, that's a tough one! What do you think he wants?"

"It's perfectly clear to me. The General wants his prayer—and mighty quick."

"Do you think he wants it submitted to the whole command?"

"That's what I'm thinking. He seems to want it published on some sort of index card or something, so the troops can carry it around with them."

"All right, let me see what I can come up with."

"Sounds good, Chaplain. In the meantime, I'll see what I can do about the card."

The two men went their separate ways. Returning to his own office, O'Neill searched his copy of the Old Testament along with two other prayer books, but he was unable to find any formal prayers pertaining to weather. Momentarily stumped, he stared out his window at the slashing rains that had plagued the Third Army's operations for the past two months—and was struck with an idea.

He would come up with his own prayer.

Meanwhile, Harkins met with the Army Engineer, who informed him that the Third Army's field topographical company could print the rain prayer on a three-by-five card, making enough copies for distribution to the troops.

An hour later, after conferring again with Harkins, O'Neill returned to Patton's office with an Old Testament-style prayer that walked the fine line between beseeching divine assistance and requesting dispensation to kill. The general read the prayer, typed out on a small card by the chaplain, over twice:

*Almighty and most merciful Father, we humbly beseech Thee, of Thy great goodness, to restrain these immoderate rains with which we have had to contend.*

181

*Grant us fair weather for Battle. Graciously hearken to us as soldiers who call upon Thee that, armed with Thy power, we may advance from victory to victory, and crush the oppression and wickedness of our enemies and establish Thy justice among men and nations.*

"What do you think, sir?" asked O'Neill.

Patton smiled. "Why I think it's goddamn great. If any prayer could get storm clouds off my front, this is it. Well done, Chaplain!"

O'Neill winced at the taking of the Lord's name in vain, but said nothing, knowing that the general tended to get overexcited and use colorful language on occasion despite being a devout Episcopalian and regular church attendee.

"As you can see, I also added a Christmas greeting," he then said to the general.

"Yes, I can see that," said Patton, and he proceeded to read it.

*To each officer and soldier in the Third United States Army, I wish a Merry Christmas. I have full confidence in your courage, devotion to duty, and skill in battle. May God's blessing rest upon each of you on this Christmas Day.*
*G. S. Patton, Jr.*
*Lieutenant General*
*Commanding, Third United States Army*

"If the general would sign the card above the Christmas greeting, it would add a personal touch that I am sure the men would greatly appreciate."

"Why that's a fine idea, Chaplain."

He took a pen, signed the card, and returned it to O'Neill. "Chaplain, sit down for a moment. I want to talk to you about this business of prayer."

As O'Neill took his seat, Patton rose up and walked to the high window of the office where he stood with his back to the chaplain, watching the falling rain. In his uniform, his powerfully built physique made an impressive silhouette against the window. Though he was excessively competitive with his peers, cursed like a stable boy, and was an admitted narcissist who envisioned himself as a bevy of conquering heroes reincarnated from the past, he was utterly authentic—and the chaplains, officers, and enlisted men of Third Army knew it. They had observed him on many occasions caring directly for his troops, as he considered the welfare of the men under him a matter of grave personal responsibility. Even in the heat of combat, he would often take time out to direct new methods to prevent trench foot, to see to it that dry socks went forward daily with the rations to troops on the line. More than once during the Lorraine campaign, he had been observed by his staff and others kneeling down in the mud administering morphine and caring for wounded soldiers until an ambulance arrived. He had also been seen quietly crying and praying over wounded men in the field hospitals. Unlike Monty and Bradley, Patton was truly beloved by his men because he spent a great deal of time with them out in the field rather than tucking himself away at an ivory-tower HQ conducting staff meetings and poring over maps all day. He covered so much territory in his command vehicles and L-5 Cub spotter plane that, at times, it seemed to his troops as if he was everywhere on the front lines at once.

"Chaplain, how much praying is being done in the Third Army?" he inquired from the window.

"Does the general mean by chaplains, or by the men?" asked O'Neill.

"By everybody," Patton replied.

"I am afraid to admit it, but I do not believe much praying is going on. When there is fighting, everyone prays. But now with this constant rain, when things are quiet, men just sit and wait for things to happen. Prayer out here is difficult since there are few churches that haven't been destroyed from shelling. Prayer to most of them is a formal, ritualized affair, involving special posture and a liturgical setting. So, to answer your question, I do not believe much praying is being done."

Leaving the window, Patton sat back at his desk and leaned back in his chair.

"Chaplain, I am a strong believer in prayer. There are three ways that men get what they want; by planning, by working, and by praying. Any great military operation takes careful planning, or thinking. Then you must have well-trained troops to carry it out: that's working. But between the plan and the operation there is always an unknown. That unknown spells defeat or victory, success or failure. It is the reaction of the actors to the ordeal when it actually comes. Some people call that getting the breaks; I call it God. God has His part, or margin, in everything. That's where prayer comes in."

Here he paused and began toying with a long lead pencil between his index fingers.

"Up to now, God has been very good to us here in the Third Army. We have never retreated. We have suffered no defeats, no famine, no epidemics. This is because a lot of people back home are praying for us. We were lucky in North Africa, in Sicily, in Italy, and in Western France. Simply because people prayed. But we have to pray for ourselves, too. A good soldier is not made merely by making him think and work. There is something in every soldier that goes deeper than thinking or working—it's his 'guts.' It is something that he has built in there: it is a world of truth and power that is higher than himself. Great living is not all output of thought and work. A man has to have intake as well. I don't know what you call it, but I call it religion, prayer, or God. I wish you would put out a training letter on this subject of prayer to all the chaplains. Write about nothing else, just the importance of prayer. Let me see it before you send it."

"I will do that, General."

"Good. We've got to get not only the chaplains but every man in the Third Army to pray. We must ask God to stop these rains. These rains are the margin that holds defeat or victory. If we all pray, it will be like what Dr. Carrel said. It will be like plugging in on a current whose source is in heaven. I believe that prayer completes that circuit. It is power."

With that he rose from his chair, indicating that the meeting was concluded. "Make it one hell of a training letter, Chaplain," he added with a smile. "In other words, hold nothing back—the outcome of the war may very well depend on it."

"Oh, I'll make sure of it, General. With the Good Lord's blessing, of course."

# CHAPTER 31

### WOELFLING-LÈS-SARREGUEMINES
### NORTHEASTERN FRANCE

### DECEMBER 9, 1944

IN A SLEET-FILLED MORNING, the Black Panthers crashed through the former French Maginot Line now controlled by the Germans. Yesterday, they had been ordered to roll forward to punch through the formidable antitank barriers and dragon's teeth and take out machine-gun positions. But when they opened fire, their 75mm and 76mm high-explosive shells simply bounced off the thick pillbox walls. The company commanders responded by calling in air support from Opie Weyland's XIX Air Tactical Command, and the German defenses were bombed for more than two hours.

McBurney had been awed by the sight of the powerful P-47s strafing and blasting the Kraut positions. Now he and his fellow tankers were glad they had been given the decisive edge of air power as they passed through, without receiving return fire, the path cleared through the rubble of the fortifications. Using the Maginot Line along the Third Army's front as a delaying screen, the Germans had apparently pulled back their forces towards the German border and to the Siegfried Line, the German equivalent to the French Maginot.

Outside the village of Woelfling-lès-Sarreguemines, Baker, Charlie, and Dog Companies reassembled briefly before pushing forward again. McBurney kept a sharp lookout as they began moving through territory more heavily mined and booby-trapped than any they had encountered since their first battle at Moyenvic. They were now just two miles from the German border and seven miles from the formidable barrier of the Siegfried Line. He had not failed to notice that the fighting had become more ferocious the closer they got to Nazi Germany.

Soon they came under heavy mortar fire and a bridge disintegrated before his eyes. The tankers of the 761st and infantrymen from the 26th Division, who had developed a comradery and synergism in combat after a solid month of fighting together, quickly dispersed and set up a defense. The Germans shelled direct fire every ten minutes, adding mortar fire every twenty minutes. Air support was called in again, but there was little the American task force could do because the area was heavily sown with mines and infested with booby traps. Eventually, the combat engineers were able to construct a bridge under heavy fire and the Black Panthers rolled across the Blies River north of the town.

The next stop was the vaunted Siegfried Line.

The 761st was now a veteran outfit. Since its first taste of combat on November 8, the unit had fought in more than a dozen engagements, suffered more than 125 casualties with 26 men killed in action, and seen more than 35 of its tanks damaged or destroyed in the fighting. Battling forward from town to town, the tank crews had long since mastered the rhythms of daily life inside their vehicles and learned how best to destroy the enemy. McBurney noted with satisfaction, as well as a sense of relief, that the jitters he had observed among the men early on had dissipated the same way the Germans seemed to melt away from the conquered villages.

The heart-racing terror experienced over the past month of virtually continuous combat had transformed McBurney and the other Black Panthers into sober war veterans with all the reverence, reflection, and cynicism that came with the honor. They lived day-to-day, minute-to-minute, mission-to-mission under fire, and there was no longer a single wide-eyed greenhorn remaining in the battalion. Rah-rah idealism and naiveté had been replaced by a gritty, battle-hardened realism.

They were truly Patton's Panthers.

In coming to terms with his new role, McBurney was convinced that the 761st was destined to fight at the front for the entire duration of the war. For the gunner, a glimpse of a German tank meant a deadly dragon to slay—and he understood with perfect clarity that his job was to kill the creature without hesitation before it gobbled him up. He grieved over the men they had lost, but found inspiration in Pop Gates, the new commander of Charlie Company, his mentor Teddy Windsor, and his buddies Smitty, McConnell, Willie Devore, Preston McNeil, and Warren Crecy that had thus far survived. He would see this war through *with* and *for* them—and to honor his father who had done his duty in France in the last world war.

At the same time though, he couldn't help but wonder why he continued to follow Pop Gates and Windsor into the line of fire. Charlie Company drew Krauts like a magnet, and McBurney's Sherman had taken several direct hits from enemy tank and antitank rounds. Up until now, the tank and crew had remained unharmed and they continued rolling to the front, but for how long would that continue? Though C Company's skills improved each day under the paternal eye of Pop Gates, where Charlie went, trouble seemed to follow the unit like a dark storm cloud. It had the highest casualty rate of any company in the battalion, and always seemed to be in the thick of the worst fighting.

In the past month, the battalion's M4s had also taken a terrific beating. Not just in combat but maneuvering through the mud and snow of the cratered roads of northeastern France. Thankfully, a workable maintenance-combat rotation had been developed, but the 761st still needed more working tanks and crews. To stave off down time for repairs, the company commanders quickly discovered it most effective for their maintenance sections to follow closely as the tanks maneuvered. And when a unit came back to the command post for maintenance, another unit swiftly took its place in support of infantry. Tank crews also attempted repairs under fire, though they usually left the task to the maintenance section. Once a repair crew had a tank back in action it moved to the next tank, then the next. Badly damaged tanks went to the rear if they could be salvaged. Suspension systems were most frequently hit due to the enemy's extensive mines, overtaxing maintenance crews.

After thirty-two unrelieved days on the front, McBurney was looking forward to the upcoming R and R the unit had been promised. He, Smitty, and McNeil had talked the past few days of hot baths, mattresses, a clean change of clothes—and nothing else. The 761st hadn't been given replacement uniforms, and the men had worn the same gear for the past month. The Red Cross brought mobile showers up whenever possible to give front-line troops a brief but welcome cleansing and fresh gear, but thus far the 761st had not received such a break. McBurney couldn't help but wonder whether this inequity had something to do with their race.

If they were in a town for more than a few hours, they would seize the opportunity to wash their dirty, smelly uniforms in a washbasin or creek—though they rarely had that chance. To bathe, they'd wash their faces, chests, and underarms with water gathered from streams in their helmets when they could, using the helmet like a birdbath. If there wasn't any water available, they'd use gasoline, pouring it into their helmets and rubbing it on. The tanker's steel GI helmet, McBurney and his cohorts swiftly discovered, served multiple purposes in the field. A helmet was a stove, a bathroom, and a bathtub. In the morning, they'd cook breakfast in it; when the tanks were rolling, they'd piss in it and empty it out the bottom of the tank; and before using it to wash their clothes, they'd clean the helmet and wash up in it.

Trench foot afflicted the battalion as much as it did the footslogging infantrymen they fought alongside. With Patton's insistence on combating the malady, McBurney was determined not to lose any of his toes to trench foot and was diligent in following the Third Army commander's advice. Every night he took off his socks to dry them out—but they were usually soaked through from the rain and the nights were so cold that the socks would simply freeze. In the morning, McBurney would wake to find them frozen solid, standing straight up at attention. But he always took off his boots and socks and did his best to dry them off along with his cold feet.

The month of fighting had brought the Black Panthers closer together. What McBurney enjoyed more than the adrenaline rush of combat was the time he spent with his brothers-in-arms. What kept him going day after day, he realized, was his closeness to them. At night, in bivouac, he, Smitty, and others would sit back, joke, and talk about things back home, the war, the ways of the world. McBurney was amazed at the sheer intellect of some of the officers and enlisted men. He learned more about everyone from George Washington to Frederick Douglass to Albert Einstein around the campfires than he had back in high school in Harlem.

In Bidestroff, Pop Gates held a dinner for the tattered remnants of C Company in a commandeered farmhouse. He served chicken from a barn they had raided, and red wine one of the men had found in a basement. Eating their meal in the dining room by candlelight, McBurney and the other survivors told stories about their fallen friends and comrades, made teary-eyed toasts to them, and, most importantly, promised to remember them. It was a vigil of sorts, but not entirely a grim one, with a curious, shifting admixture of sorrow beyond words and bittersweet laughter. The old Buffalo Soldier Gates himself didn't speak. Seated at the head of the table, he just smiled, nodded, and looked around at the faces of the men he'd grown to love, determined not to break down in front of them with a sorrowful speech.

On December 3, the Panthers and 104th Infantry had taken Sarre-Union after a desperate battle, providing Third Army with a crucial rail and communications junction east of the Sarre River. The city was home to the legendary Pomeroi champagne factory, and the victorious GIs couldn't resist indulging themselves. After the hard fighting the tankers had just endured, an all-out raid on the treasure trove seemed well within their rights. Lashing cases of champagne to their tanks, they climbed back inside their Shermans and Stuarts and rumbled forward towards the Siegfried Line, drinking the champagne straight from the bottles.

Though the 761st still badly missed the leadership of Paul Bates, three of Patton's Panthers in particular had helped fill the void and gain the respect of the outfit. Warren Crecy, who had joined McBurney and Smith in Charlie Company, had been made a tank commander and fought with such vengeance that he had already been recommended for a Silver Star for valor. Tank commanders were trained to wait until targets revealed themselves in order to conserve ammunition—but Patton advocated a tactic known as "reconnaissance by fire," raining shells any place where German teams might be hiding. Although the M4 tank contained storage space for up to a hundred 75mm or 76mm shells, Crecy frequently ran out of ammo and was often seen racing back for resupply and rushing to return to the front to take out more of the enemy. To McBurney and others, he appeared to be on a personal mission, attacking enemy positions with such ferocity and disregard for his own safety that he had been given not one but two nicknames. He was known as the "Baddest Man in the 761st" and "Iron Man."

Despite initially making some youthful mistakes as a company commander, the twenty-three-year-old white officer Dave Williams had won over the battalion by leading Able Company in several savage engagements and for his promotion of Sergeant Ruben Rivers for a posthumous Medal of Honor. In the early part of the Lorraine campaign, Rivers had shown conspicuous bravery while fighting enemy tanks and rescuing his men despite being severely wounded. On November 23, 1944, four days after the battle for Guebling and Bourgaltroff where Rivers had fought with what his fellow tankers believed was almost superhuman tenacity, Williams had handed paperwork to the battalion's acting white commander, Lieutenant Hollis Hunt, strongly recommending Rivers for the medal. But Hunt was indifferent, at best, to his request. The enlisted men had overheard the overheated exchange as Williams rebuffed Hunt's protests. The black members of the battalion knew what little regard the racist Hunt had for them as soldiers, and they respected Williams for standing up to Bates's replacement for one of their fiercest fighters.

McBurney's company commander, Captain Pop Gates, had won over the men by looking out for their safety, following Paul Bates's credo of "Don't sacrifice your men or tanks on situations better avoided." At the town of Honskirch in late November, Gates was ordered to attack with his tanks by the regimental commander of the 328th Infantry. The order came despite Gates's warning that it would be a suicide mission for both the tankers and the infantry accompanying them, due to the soggy conditions that made the tanks vulnerable and the strength of the German fortifications. But the regimental commander, a finance officer without battle experience, ignored Gates's detailed map of the entrenched enemy defenses and ordered the attack to proceed anyway. Given the military chain of command, Gates had no choice but to obey, knowing that if he refused, the incompetent white officer would simply relieve him, going down the line until he found someone willing to carry out the order. Charlie's tanks and the infantry were going to be sent down the road to fight no matter what, and Gates intended to fight beside his men.

When the tanks moved forward, the Germans unleashed their wrath, confirming Gates's fears by inflicting heavy infantry casualties. After the debacle, Gates, who had received shrapnel wounds, let loose on the derelict officer, whom he felt had allowed the men under his care to be slaughtered for nothing. Patton agreed. The Third Army commander, a frequent visitor to the front for both white and black troops, interviewed Gates personally and wanted to know why the 761st lost five tanks in such a short period of time. Once Gates filled him in on the details of the ill-conceived attack, Patton had the offending white regimental officer who had refused to listen to Gates shipped back to the States.

With dusk approaching, the 761st and the doughs from the 26th bivouacked for the night south of the Siegfried Line. As the tankers were climbing from their armored vehicles and stretching their legs, McBurney caught a glimpse of a new group of U.S. soldiers marching in from the west.

"Who the hell are they?" wondered Smitty, hopping down from Cool Stud.

"I don't know, man," said McBurney. "But they look like replacements."

"That's right, Sergeant," said a new voice, and they turned to see Captain Williams. "That there is the 87th Infantry Division—the Golden Acorns. It's a new outfit. They've never seen action. Colonel Palladino of the 104th Infantry Regiment informed me that they're going to be taking over for the 26th."

"What's going to happen to the 26th?" asked McBurney.

"They're slated for rotation out for several days of R and R. They'll be pulled off the line once the 87th has settled in. Word is they're pulling them back thirty miles to Metz, now that it's been taken."

"Wait a second—what about us?" asked Smitty. "We were supposed to get our R and R starting the day after tomorrow."

"I'm sorry, boys," said the Yalie, "but that's not going to happen. God, I guess, has another plan for us."

*God ain't got nothing to do with it,* thought McBurney, who couldn't believe what he was hearing. Hell, he and Smitty, along with Willie Devore and Preston McNeil, had been talking about hardly anything else but soaking in a hot tub of water, sleeping on a plush mattress, and getting a fresh change of clothes for the past three days. He liked Williams, but the white captain seemed a little too pleased that the unit would continue on fighting with no break, despite the fact that the men and equipment had already been pushed beyond their limits.

"Ain't no break for us niggers," grumbled Smith. "I should have known better."

"Hell, don't blame me, Private," said Williams. "I take my orders just like you fellas. But look at the bright side—we get to kill more Krauts."

"I agree," said Pop Gates as he came walking up. "Killing Krauts is what we do, so we might as well get right after it tomorrow."

Smith shook his head. "Well, I don't know if we're going to be doing it with those new doughs. Check these motherfuckers out. They look like they got out of basic just this morning."

For more than a minute, the four men studied the column. Indeed, McBurney saw at once that the 87th "Golden Acorn" Infantry column was marching to take up positions along the front with a jauntiness and eagerness of purpose that could only be attributed to those who had never experienced combat.

*Man oh man, what did we do to deserve these raw white boys?*

"They do look mighty green," admitted Gates.

"Where the hell are they from anyway?" asked Smith, not at all happy with the prospect of fighting with green troops and the 761st not getting its promised leave.

"They're Southern boys," said Williams. "From Arkansas, Mississippi, and Louisiana, I hear."

"Jesus Christ, just what we need—a bunch of dumb crackers who don't even know how to fight."

"Smitty's not just complaining for no reason, Captain," said McBurney. "You have to admit they look like babes in the woods."

"Yeah, I got eyes too," said Williams. "But if you remember, we looked like that too once. Though I have to admit it pains me to say it."

McBurney continued to study the boyish faces—most of them no older than him—as they shuffled past. But in his mind there was a big difference between them and him: while they had no more than three months of training under their belts and had never seen the elephant, he had undergone two solid years of training and had been fighting the Wehrmacht continuously for the past 32 days on the front lines.

These raw white boys were nothing like him.

"Does this mean that we're being switched over to the command of the 87th Division?" asked Smith, still sore.

"That appears to be the plan," answered Williams.

McBurney shivered in the cold air. It looked like another storm was coming, and he wished he had another blanket to cover him in his tank when he slept tonight.

Pop Gates was grinning. "Buck up, you two. Six weeks ago, all you wanted was a chance at action. Now you've gotten that chance. The brass is making up for all the damn time they wouldn't even let us fight."

"And then some," said Smith.

"Look at it this way, at least now we're getting the attention we deserve," said Williams. "Have you all seen this yet?"

From his jacket pocket, he pulled out a copy of *Stars and Stripes* and showed it to the group. It was the November 27, 1944 Paris edition of the popular GI magazine and the front page featured a group of tankers from the 761st mounted on their tanks at Guebling. The tankers shown were from Williams's own Able Company.

"Damn, that's really us on the front page!" gushed McBurney. "The Black Panthers come out fighting—now that is a sight to see!"

He pulled out two smokes and handed one to Smitty with a grin on his face. Pop Gates and Williams smiled at him. The one-time demure New York teen, who abhorred tobacco, now smoked and swore like a longshoreman, yet still fooled no one in the battalion with his new tough-guy persona.

"Yeah well, the whole battalion earned it," said Williams. "Hopefully, there will be a lot more like this. But we've got to keep fighting to do it."

"Okay, thanks for the pep talk, Captain," said Smith with amiable sarcasm. "But I think us hep cats would have enjoyed getting our promised R and R a little more than killing Krauts. For four or five days anyway."

"I get it, and on that note, we'll see you hep cats later on." He and Pop Gates grinned at one another and headed off to spread the word to the rest of the battalion.

McBurney and Smith went to look around the new bivouac as the fresh troops from the 87th kept marching in. They were still disappointed about not getting their promised upcoming rest after fighting nearly constantly for the past month. Their frustration, however, was soon eclipsed once again by mindless bigotry. The battalion members were forced to confront a harsh and tragic reality when they came face-to-face with the new infantry division they would be fighting beside and that was supposed to have their back like the 26th.

McBurney and the other tankers swiftly discovered that their victories, hard-fought miles, and terrible casualties meant little to the vast majority of the new white doughs from the 87th beside whom they'd been assigned to fight. They were seen not as soldiers or men but as no better than dogs. As they walked amongst the new men and met some of them, McBurney and Smith heard the phrase "nigger tankers" over and over—sometimes said directly to their faces, other times whispered under the newcomers' breaths, but always spoken in a tone that implied the very thought was ridiculous.

Even McBurney, who tended to be among the more watchful and reserved of the 76lst's members, was thoroughly pissed off at the blatant racism and rudeness displayed by the division for which they would be spearheading. In sharp contrast to the 26th "Yankee Division" consisting of mostly tolerant New Englanders that they were replacing, the newcomers refused to even acknowledge the members of the 761st. With most of the 87th personnel from the Deep South, the relationship between the two units was off to a rocky start.

After enduring as much abuse as they could stand, the two returned to their tank. As they were eating their C rations, E.G. McConnell came walking up.

"Man, have you seen these crackers?" he exclaimed. "I'm about to kill one of these motherfuckers!"

"Yeah, we met them. Charming fellows—if you fancy a good old-fashioned lynching on a Sunday afternoon," said McBurney.

"I overheard one of their officers," said McConnell. "He told his men, 'I don't want them niggers messing with no white women, and don't you even socialize with them.' Can you believe that shit?"

McBurney shook his head in disgust. *No, of course I can't. Here we are fighting for survival, and this is all these bastards have to say?*

But at the same time, he knew that not all of the soldiers in the 87th were ignorant or anxious to stir up trouble. And it wasn't as if he and the other tankers hadn't heard such slurs before. What had changed for him was that he and his brothers-in-arms had seen so many of their buddies killed. Samuel Turley, Ruben Rivers, Kenneth Coleman, among others. Then there was Colonel Bates, who was badly wounded and might not even return to the outfit. The men were all gravely risking their lives for their country and had all hoped—without consciously realizing they were doing so—that their valor and sacrifices were accomplishing gains beyond any measured in enemy casualties or miles.

"What rankles my ass the most is these bastards are green as shit," grumbled McConnell. "I mean, they haven't even fired a shot or seen a single German—and yet they act like we don't even exist."

"It's Killeen all over again," lamented Smitty.

"Except now we don't have to step aside for nobody," said McConnell. "I still can't believe these crackers are talking this crap. But believe you me—when it gets hot out there and they are deep in the shit, they're going to forget about the color of our skin. I promise you they won't give a damn whether we are black or white when the Krauts are pouring lead into them and they have a chance to jump to safety inside our armored tanks. Until that day comes, they won't even want to talk to us. But when the Germans are dropping all that shit on them, those backward crackers are gonna be begging us to let them inside. When that time comes, my brothers, *we* are going to be the ones with all the power."

"That's right," said Smitty. "I can't wait to see the look on their damn faces."

McBurney thought McConnell was probably right. But he also figured the 761st would continue to receive this kind of treatment as long as the war lasted. That was the main drawback of being a "bastard battalion" that could be shifted to and from various units within Third Army on an as-needed basis. The needle would have to be set again to zero every time they shifted divisions, and they would have to gain the respect of the infantry units by demonstrating their ability, as they had done with the New Englanders of the 26th. The initial wariness and hostility would change under fire to respect. Or at least he hoped it would.

"It's no big deal," he said. "We've been through this before. We just have to prove ourselves again, that's all. Back home, here in France—has it ever been any different? Don't matter which side of the Atlantic, it's still the same."

"I still think its FUBAR," said Smitty. "I'm sick of having to prove ourselves when we're not the ones who need to prove a damn thing."

"Amen to that," said McBurney. "But complaining isn't gonna change anything. All we can do is do our jobs better than any other outfit. Now let's get some shut-eye. It's going to be another cold one tonight."

"Yeah, it sure is," agreed Smitty, looking up into the lit-up sky as a German 88 lobbed a projectile towards the American lines. "Cold as a motherfucker."

ΨΨΨ

That evening, unbeknownst to McBurney, the commanding general of Patton's Third Army XII Corps wrote a letter of commendation for the Black Panthers:

*1. I consider the 761st Tank Battalion to have entered combat with such conspicuous courage and success as to warrant special commendation.*

*2. The speed with which they adapted themselves to the front line under most adverse weather conditions, the gallantry which with they faced some of Germany's finest troops, and the confident spirit with which they emerged from their recent engagements in the vicinity of Dieuze, Morville-les-Vic, and Guebling entitle them surely to consider themselves the Veteran 761st.*

*—Maj. General Manton S. Eddy*

On December 14, the commanding general of the 26th Infantry "Yankee" Division forwarded the above letter of commendation to the 761st Tank Battalion, and sent along a note of his own:

*It is with extreme gratification that the corps commander's commendation is forwarded to you. Your battalion has supported this division with great bravery under the most adverse weather and terrain conditions. You have my sincere wish that success may continue to follow your endeavors.*

*—Maj. General Willard S. Paul*

# CHAPTER 32

## DRACHENBURG CASTLE AND BRAUNSFELD
## WESTERN GERMANY

### DECEMBER 9, 1944

ANGELA SHIVERED AGAINST the bitter winter cold. She and her father were preparing to leave Drachenburg Castle, where the colonel had met briefly with General Hasso von Manteuffel, whose staff he had served upon in the Eastern Front and later in Tunisia prior to being severely wounded by a British fighter. The two men stood bidding farewell out front of the castle as Angela took one last look at the panoramic view over the Rhine.

Since the incident with Kütter and the Gestapo, her father had refused to let her out of his sight for her own safety. Having cut way back on his drinking the past two weeks, he had forced her to give up her nursing job to work under him at the flak command center as a *Luftwaffenhelfer*. Here she worked alongside foreign laborers, elderly men, and other fifteen- and sixteen-year old boys and girls—all that was left for air defense in Nazi Germany at this late stage of the war.

In his role as commander of the Cologne air defenses, her father was in charge of the five hundred heavy and light antiaircraft batteries and the hundred and fifty searchlights in and around Cologne. He worked in close co-ordination with the flak gunners to protect the city from air attacks. But she knew that he would soon give that job up, as he was here to speak with von Manteuffel about returning to his staff, now that his wounds were for the most part healed and he had been declared fit enough to return to active duty. With the serious manpower shortages across the country and the Allies knocking on the doorstep, every semi-able-bodied German was needed to fight for the Reich in Hitler's *Endkampf.*

Angela stared up at the massive Drachenburg Castle. Completed in 1884, it had only suffered minor damage from Allied bombings and was still one of the most significant castle buildings of the late 19th century in Germany. The neo-Gothic citadel glimmered like something out of a fairy tale, and was surrounded by extensive grounds with ancient trees and rhododendrons. Siegfried, the hero of the *Nibelungenlied*, was said to have slayed the dragon Fafnir here and bathed in its blood to become invulnerable. The rock of the mountain around which the castle was built was formed by an ancient volcano and mined from a trachyte quarry in Roman times; the stone was used to build the iconic Cologne Cathedral. But like all things in Hitler's Nazi Germany, the fairy tale castle carried a darker side: the *Adolf-Hitler-Schule*—a Nazi elite school—had been moved into the Schloss Drachenburg in 1942 and continued to feed "little Hitlers" into the Reich war machine.

A minute later, her father returned to their car and they started off on their return journey to Cologne.

"How did the meeting go?" she asked him as they drove down the icy road towards Bonn.

"It went well," he replied. "I will be returning to the general's staff in the new year. I will be with the Fifth Panzer Army."

"And what will happen to me?"

"You will serve as my personal assistant and nurse. You will be posted at the closest hospital behind the front. It is the best I could do."

"You're doing all this because of Kütter, aren't you?"

"Yes, the man worries me. I fear that, like Inspector Javert, he will not stop until he has taken you into custody."

Since her arrest a month earlier, Kütter had come by their house to question her on three separate occasions about her links to the Edelweiss Pirates. Thankfully, each time her father had been there to control the situation. He had thoroughly coached her not to reveal anything to the *kriminalkommissar*, maintaining via his Gestapo informant that the Nazi was on a fishing expedition and had no real evidence against her except that a girl matching her description codenamed "Mucki" had been seen with the group on several occasions. A teenager fitting her description had been observed by various Hitler Youth members in clashes with the group, but she had not been positively identified and the only known names of the female members of the group were "Mucki" and "Elsa," the code name used by her friend Marie Peukert. Furthermore, Kütter himself could not definitively identify her from the raid on Steinbrück's hideout since she had worn her broad-rimmed cap with her hair tucked beneath it and had smeared charcoal on her face. Because the Gestapo had only circumstantial evidence of her association with the Edelweiss Pirates and Steinbrück's Ehrenfeld Group, her father advised her to continue to deny everything and insisted that she remain with him at all times.

"Kütter is a monster," she said. "He is exactly what is wrong with our country."

"That is true. But you still should never have gotten involved with those damned Pirates. That is what has created this situation."

She thought of Schröder, and hoped that he had not died in vain. She missed him terribly and still often cried herself at night thinking about him.

"I have to do something to fight back against the Nazis," she said. "To stand by and do nothing is more wrong."

"I disagree. Given the current state of affairs with the roundups, you need to lay low until the war is over. They will kill you—in fact, they will kill us both if we aren't careful. Our legal system is barely able to contain the SS and Gestapo. To anyone they view as an enemy of the national community, their power remains unchecked. And the terror directed towards ordinary Germans is only going to increase as the Allies draw nearer."

"Is there no way to stop them?"

"No, not really. The only thing that has kept us both alive is my association with the baron and the fact that I have ingratiated myself with Dr. Hoffmann. I delivered that *bandennest* to him on a silver platter."

"It was not a bandit hideout. Those foreign workers were just trying to survive without being slaves to our war machine."

"And would you rather be dead? I did what I had to do to save you—and I will not apologize for that, *Bärchen*."

"And now innocent people are dead."

"More than likely, that is true. But at the same time, they were technically criminals and I will not apologize for doing what I had to do to spare your life. I warned you, when you first joined up with those Edelweiss Pirates, that only trouble would come from your actions. But you wouldn't listen to me."

Though she hated to admit it, she knew he was right. But she disagreed with him on one key point. Becoming a member of the Cologne Navajos and taking on the Nazis was the right thing to do; where she and her friends in the youth resistance movement had gotten themselves into trouble was in joining up with Steinbrück and his *Ehrenfeld Gruppe*. It was the gang of older army deserters and escaped foreign laborers who were actually the desperate criminals and sought-after targets of the regime. Things had only gone to hell when the two groups had joined forces. Once the lives of high-ranking Party members were taken in broad daylight, the Edelweiss Pirates, up until then treated as a minor irritant, transformed overnight from a pesky group of rebellious youth into a dangerous criminal element in the eyes of Gestapo Chief Dr. Max Hoffmann and his security forces.

"I understand why you did what you did," she allowed, "but now Hoffmann is gone and we are back to square one."

"Yes, I know. Hoffmann's death has complicated things and we are no longer safe at all."

They fell into silence. The only sound was the rattle of the *Kübelwagen's* engine as it negotiated the slippery, ice-crusted road. By a bizarre twist of fate, Hoffmann, shortly after her father had informed him of the bandit hideout to spare her life, had been killed while leading the raid himself on November 26. After exhorting his men "to give their best, in pride and honor, by exemplifying the struggle of National Socialism," Hoffmann had been mortally wounded in the ensuing skirmish as he led an entire company of heavily armed Gestapo officers and Order Police in the attack. Surrounded and outnumbered, the fugitives had resisted for more than twelve hours, and the fighting only ended when a squad of military engineers blasted them out of their fortified cellar. In the aftermath, Herr Hoffmann became a martyr to his men in his noble attempt to fulfill his obligations to *Volk* and Führer.

The Nazi leader's death stunned his security officers. But more importantly, it confirmed in their minds that they were fighting an anti-partisan war on the home front against ordinary German civilians. Richard Foltis, who replaced Hoffmann at El-De Haus as the Gestapo's temporary commander, Kütter, and the other heads of the *Einsatzkommandos* gathered in Cologne to pay tribute to their fallen leader. At the memorial ceremony, Foltis and the others vowed to stamp out the "terrorists." Indeed, since Hoffmann's passing, the special task forces had intensified their efforts, spreading out across the shattered city armed with *Schmeisser Maschinenpistole* 40s and hand grenades, showing no mercy to those who resisted.

Though the task of deporting German civilians and violently weeding out "defeatist elements" was initiated by Hoffmann back in mid-October, following the Steinbrück attacks and plot to blow up Gestapo headquarters, the Secret Police's reign of terror continued to intensify in Cologne and throughout the Rhineland. Kütter's *Sonderkommando Brauweiler* and the other security forces spread out behind the front to search out and destroy gang activity, hunt down escaped foreign workers, and clear the Left Bank Rhineland of so-called "defeatists." To pacify the area, the *Einsatzkommandos* used the techniques developed during earlier anti-partisan operations on the Eastern Front against non-Germans. The difference this time was they were using extreme violence against war-weary German citizens.

Over the course of the clearances, civilians became increasingly suspect to the Gestapo. Officers continued to be flummoxed by the huge gap between the regime's desire for a *Volk* willing to sacrifice everything to attain victory and the sober reality of a dispirited population that just wanted the damn war to end. Since the deportations and associated roundups had begun, more than 200 Germans and foreigners had been murdered by the Gestapo in Cologne. Eastern Europeans comprised the largest number of victims. Many of them were executed for crimes such as looting and petty theft, while most of the German prisoners were shot for treason. Which usually meant they were not supportive enough of the state, or showed the audacity to question whether the war could be won.

"Papa, I'm scared," said Angela when they were on the outskirts of Bonn.

"I know you are. But you must remain strong."

"I don't know how we can survive this war. And even if we do, what is the point? Our country will never be the same again. Hitler has ruined it forever."

The colonel gave a heavy, world-weary sigh. "Let's just focus on surviving the war, shall we? At this point, I honestly don't know what else can be done."

"So, you believe the war is lost then?"

"Yes, the war is lost. But that doesn't mean that I can stop fighting. To admit any sort of defeatism would jeopardize not only my life, but yours as well. You do understand that, don't you?"

"Yes, I understand that. But that doesn't mean I accept it."

"We have to survive, *Bärchen*. Everything else is secondary. I am not going to lose you in this war, as I have lost your mother and brother. That is not an option."

"But what if there is nothing to *survive* for?"

"We can't think about that. We just have to survive, *Bärchen*."

"But if there is nothing left of our cities and most of the decent people have been killed or died off, what is the point?"

"We just have to remain strong. Our belief in each other—and in what Germany could one day become if we stay true to what is morally right—is what must guide our every thought and action."

That made sense to her and they fell again into silence. Though she wanted to cry, she forced herself to be brave. They continued driving on towards Cologne. As darkness fell, they began to see more and more troop activity along the roads and rail lines. The amount of traffic was far more than what they had observed on the way down to Schloss Drachenburg. Angela wondered what was going on.

"It looks like we're going on the attack. Is that what's happening?"

Her father looked at her. "What makes you say that?"

"There are trucks and trains full of troops and military equipment everywhere. I've never seen anything like it."

"We're probably just reinforcing the front. The American and British armies are gigantic and we have to counter them wherever they are strong along the Westwall."

"But trains filled with tanks and troops are everywhere. And why did we not see any of them until we approached the Eifel and it turned dark?"

"I don't know. I am not attached at the moment to any Wehrmacht unit so I am out of the loop. To me, it just looks like regular troop movement."

She could tell he was withholding something from her, but she didn't press the issue. Something was going on, something big, that he couldn't discuss. Perhaps that was why he had met with General von Manteuffel. Based on what she was seeing, a big offensive was planned and the Panzer Baron would likely be part of it.

Soon they reached their small house in Braunsfeld. They had scarcely lugged their travel bags inside when a sharp knock was heard at the door. Her father removed his Mauser 7.65mm pistol. Angela did the same with her sidearm.

"Who is it?" asked the colonel, holding his gun in his left hand.

"It is Criminal Commissioner Kütter—we have some questions for your daughter. Open up immediately!"

Angela couldn't believe her bad luck. But Kütter's visit was hardly unexpected. Her father had said the man would not leave her alone until she was in his custody.

Cursing under his breath, her father put his pistol away in its leather holster and opened the door. Standing before them were Kütter and two of his men, Hoegen and Hirschfeld. The trio were dressed in dark civilian suits with winter coats instead of regulation SS uniforms.

"We are going to have to make this brief, *Kriminalkommissar*," said the colonel, his tone brusque, official, and befitting his high rank. "My daughter and I have just returned from a long journey and visit with General von Manteuffel."

"The general is a great hero to Germany and to National Socialism."

"I would remind the commissioner that the Baron General von Manteuffel is not a Party member, nor has he ever been one. You should also know that I will be returning to the general's staff soon—*with* my daughter. As a matter of fact, I have a letter from him right here stating that I am not to be interfered with in any way and that if I, or anyone in my family, is questioned or detained for any reason, the general is to be immediately notified and the investigating officer is to summoned for questioning." He smiled cordially. "Now, won't you please come inside?"

With the threat made that Gestapo overreach would be dealt with harshly at the highest levels of the Wehrmacht, he waved Kütter and his men into the house. Put in his place, the commissioner stepped cautiously into the lightly damaged front parlor with his two stone-faced underlings. Unable to conceal her triumph at her father's clever arrangement with von Manteuffel to protect them from the Secret Police, Angela's eyes narrowed upon the visitors as the group took off their heavy winter coats and sat down at the dining table between the kitchen and parlor.

"Now what is so important, Commissioner, that you have to invade my house at nine o'clock at night?" asked her father.

Kütter smiled a vulture's smile. "My apologies, Herr Colonel, but new evidence has come to light concerning your daughter's involvement with this criminal gang of Edelweiss Pirates."

Her father shook his head emphatically. "I am afraid you are mistaken. My daughter has no association to any such entity. Do you, my dear?"

"No," she said flatly, "I don't."

"Well then," said Kütter, "how do you explain this?"

He proceeded to produce a flyer, pushing it across the table towards them. She instantly recognized the resistance propaganda piece she had helped produce as she and her father began perusing the sheet of paper. She had distributed it on behalf of the Cologne Navajo branch of the Edelweiss Pirates all over the razed city. It read:

> *To the Subjugated German Youth*
> *German Youth:*
> *Think of the old, golden age of the Boy and Girl Scouts, think back to the sunny days of outings and camping. All of this is denied to us today. Why? Because today's Nazi Germany wants to stick you all in the "Hitler Youth." Where you will be trained militarily and technically in marching, shooting, map reading, and topography, etc. The goal of all that leads back to this: cannon fodder for Hitler's insatiable greed for power!*
>
> *German youth, rise up to fight for freedom and right, for your children and your children's children, for if Hitler wins this war, Europe will be in chaos; the world will be subjugated unto the Judgment Day. Make an end of this slavery before it is too late.*
>
> *Lord, make us free!*

When finished reading, her father looked up and stared at the Gestapo agent with an expression of befuddlement. "What does this have to do with my daughter?"

"Look at the small symbol drawn below the words. It is a heart with an arrow through it that says, 'Barthel & Angela.' It proves, Colonel, your daughter knew the criminal Bartholomäus 'Barthel' Schröder hung in mid-November. In fact, the two were boyfriend and girlfriend. That makes her, too, guilty of treason."

Angela felt her heart racing uncontrollably at the accusation, but forced herself to look as innocent as possible. Meanwhile, her father's face reddened with anger.

"Why this proves absolutely nothing, Commissioner," he snarled, wagging the finger of his good, left hand. "The 'Angela' indicated in the document could be anyone. And furthermore, you still haven't told us where you found this."

"It was found with Bartholomäus Schröder's belongings. I am certain that the Barthel and Angela referred to are the criminal Edelweiss Pirate terrorist and your daughter. *Hitler Jugend* members have observed the two together in Ehrenfeld after curfew." He now looked at Angela. "Are you ready to come clean and tell us about your participation with Schröder, Günther Schwarz, Hans Steinbrück, Roland Lorent, and the other terrorists, as well as your efforts to sabotage the Gestapo headquarters? We know you were there, Angela—or should I call you Mucki?"

Her father leapt up from his chair. "This is outrageous!" he roared before turning away from Kütter and his men to face her. "You don't need to say a word, Angela. *Kriminalkommissar* Kütter has lost his mind and was just leaving."

"We are not asking you to confess your crimes against the state, Angela," said Kütter in a falsely mollifying tone. "We just want you to give us a few names and to know where the other bandit hideouts are so that we can roll up the remaining gangs. You want to help us do our jobs, don't you?"

"Keep your mouth shut, Angela—I will handle this," commanded her father. Then to Kütter. "Please get out of my house. My daughter has nothing to do with this and you are on a fishing expedition. You have nothing—nothing!"

Kütter smiled malignantly. "Then why are you so angry, Colonel? Why would you behave in such an agitated manner if your daughter is innocent?"

"Because you, Herr Kütter, have grossly abused your power. Even the Gestapo has to follow the rule of law."

"Yes, that is true. But I would be careful about—"

"As German citizens, we have rights, and as a Wehrmacht colonel, I am not subject to civil court authority. So, you have absolutely no authority over me. I will be reporting your ill treatment towards me and my daughter through official channels and directly to General von Manteuffel. As I'm sure you are aware, he enjoys the favor of the Führer, with whom he meets with on a regular basis regarding the Fifth Panzer Army. If you continue to press this issue, I can guarantee that you will be looking for a new line of work."

At this, Kütter swallowed hard. He looked like a failed door-to-door salesman or mid-level accountant in his foppish suit with his receding blond hair slicked back with brilliantine. But then he seemed to gather himself in an effort to put on a bold front. He stood up from his chair with an air of authority and gave a slight nod to indicate that the meeting, interrogation, or whatever it was, was over.

"Excuse me, Colonel, but I don't think that given your daughter's predicament, you are in any position to—"

"I am a senior Wehrmacht officer and you will not talk to me that way in my own home! I can bring you up on charges, you know! Now shut up and sit down!"

Now the criminal commissioner's corvine face registered shock; he obviously had not expected to come under scrutiny himself or open himself up to attack from powerful men in the Wehrmacht by coming here tonight. He did as instructed, timorously taking his seat.

"You, Commissioner, have violated every shred of human decency in this witch hunt of yours to implicate my daughter in the activities of the criminal gangs of Cologne. By harassing me and my daughter now on five separate occasions without a shred of real proof, you have forced me to contact the remaining legal authorities here in Cologne to look into your professional conduct. As I have said, my daughter and I have legal rights as German citizens that you have wholly neglected in your efforts to play judge, jury, and executioner."

"But we are operating under the orders of Higher SS and Police Leader Gutenberger, the commander of the Rhineland's security—"

"That still doesn't give you the right to barge in here and threaten me and my daughter! As I said, I can have you brought up on charges for imperiling the war effort! I would be fully within my rights!"

Kütter retreated into his seat, looking more like a terrified schoolboy than an all-powerful Gestapo officer. Angela enjoyed watching him squirm in his seat. The simple truth was that, despite its fearsome reputation for intimidation, torture, and violence, the Gestapo was not the all-powerful entity many people built it up to be. Its officers were not authorized to arrest ordinary German civilians indiscriminately and ship them by rail to labor or concentration camps, or execute them; rather, its officers had to accumulate significant evidence of criminal activity and obtain detailed confessions to meet Himmler's requirement of not antagonizing the civilian population and maintaining the loyalty of the *Volk*. And in this case, the fanatical Kütter had only circumstantial evidence of wrongdoing, which was an important reason she and her father were able to keep him in check.

It was also a fact that with limited manpower and few paid informants, the Gestapo simply did not have the means at its disposal to hunt down every potential enemy of the state and had to rely heavily on the Hitler Youth and civilian population for tips. The dirty little secret of her beloved Fatherland was that far more German citizens collaborated and colluded with the Nazi regime than took part in resistance and true dissent, and that most Germans, therefore, had nothing to fear from the Gestapo. In fact, in terms of popular opposition and *Resisting*, Angela and the Edelweiss Pirates were the exception rather than the rule—and that bothered her. Most Germans, she recognized, were sheep that on a daily basis aided and abetted the Nazis and the Holocaust. Angry neighbors, bitter in-laws, and disgruntled work colleagues often gave information to the Gestapo to settle personal scores or personally profit. By means of political denunciations, common citizens typically served as the eyes and ears of the State Secret Police, with the end result that the passive and compliant population largely controlled itself.

"Though you have flagrantly abused your authority, *Kriminalkommissar*, I would be willing to let it go," her father now said, "if you and your men promise me right now that you will put the case against my daughter to rest and move on to other, more pressing investigations. Are we understanding one another?"

"Surely, the colonel is not asking me to stand by and allow Cologne to sink into open rebellion," he replied. "There are bandits, terrorists, and defeatists in our midst. They must be forcibly removed, executed, or at least punished in some manner for their treachery against our *Volk* and Führer. What we are engaged here is *bandensicherungsaufgaben*. We must secure Cologne and the rest of the Rhineland from the bandits."

"But you are talking about German citizens," protested Angela. "This is not the Eastern Front."

"Oh, but it is—in its own way—which is why we must purge the region of banditry and defeatism. We cannot have a repeat of what happened after the Great War. We never lost on the battlefield but were stabbed in the back by the defeatists."

"I have heard enough! Get out of my house!" cried her father.

Now Angela saw that he had pulled out his pistol and was pointing it at Kütter and his men.

"I said get out of my damn house!"

The three Gestapo officers cautiously rose from their chairs and backed towards the door. When they reached it, Kütter glowered at her father.

"This isn't over by a long shot," he said menacingly. "We will be continuing our investigation into your daughter's treasonous activities and soon, very soon, we will have her, or perhaps the both of you, as our guests at Brauweiler. It is not a pleasant place, I assure you."

"You're going to hang," spat Angela. "When this war is over, you're all going to hang for the innocent people you've tortured and murdered."

"No, hanging is too good for you, you bastard," snarled her father, keeping his gun pointed at them. "Now get out of my home and don't come back—unless you want a military tribunal headed by General von Manteuffel to pass judgment on your conduct!"

# PART 3

# THE BULGE

# CHAPTER 33

## CASERNE MOLIFOR
## NANCY, NORTHEASTERN FRANCE

### DECEMBER 9, 1944

FEELING GLUM, Patton looked over the letter he had just written to his wife Beatrice in his usual succinct prose:

*December 9, 1944*
*Dearest Beat:*
*It is still raining. The Saar usually 50 feet wide is now 300, but that won't stop us. As I've told you before, I have a sixth sense in war. I can put myself inside the enemy's head, and also I am willing to take chances.*
*Willie and I have two green leather chairs in my room where we sit of evenings. When he snores too much, I give him a nose drop.*
*I love you with all my heart.*
*—Your Loving Georgie*

With Willie snoring at his feet, the 1909 West Pointer who had graduated number 46 out of 103 cadets, and the Olympic decathlete at the 1912 Stockholm games who had excelled in fencing, horsemanship, and shooting, took the letter and sealed it into an envelope. Setting it on his desk for Meeks, he leaned back in his chair and stared out the window of his headquarters office at the rain coming down in sheets. After a moment, a smile came to his lips as he thought back fondly to his early courtship of Beatrice, to whom he had been married since before WWI.

The daughter of a wealthy Massachusetts industrialist and owner of a woolen mill, Beatrice Ayer Patton had always been there for him—and he knew he was lucky to have her. Raised in a world of privilege, she had attended prestigious finishing schools and was bilingual in French, an expert equestrian, a fine writer and lecturer, a more than competent sailor, and the devoted mother of their three children: George IV who had followed in his father's footsteps at West Point, Ruth Ellen, and Little Beatrice. She had faithfully covered the entire country during the war raising money for bond drives, in the process covering more territory than even her husband. In short, the Massachusetts heiress was perhaps the only woman in the world who was every bit as stubborn, resilient, and multitalented as her blueblood-warrior husband who hailed from California.

And yet, George S. Patton, Jr. had cheated on her and was continuing to surreptitiously do so even as he vanquished the German enemy. Her name was Jean Gordon, and he and the twenty-nine-year-old Red Cross nurse and daughter of his wife's half-sister, had been having an on-and-off affair for nearly a decade. The whole situation made him feel guilty as sin, but he had not been able to call it off completely. He knew he was weak. He knew he was a shit. He knew that his devoted yet tough Beat was the one and only woman for him in this—or any other—lifetime, and that he would never leave her and blow up his marriage. And yet, he couldn't stop. He wanted to, but he just couldn't.

Young Jean called him "Uncle Georgie."

It had all started in 1936, when he was fifty-one, stationed in Hawaii, and thought he would never get his chance at the kind of military greatness tasted by the Roman Legions, Napoleon, or British Vice-Admiral Horatio Nelson, whom he particularly admired. He and his half-niece Gordon, a close friend of his daughter Ruth Ellen, had engaged in a torrid affair that had nearly destroyed his marriage. By some miracle, Old Blood and Guts and Beatrice had survived the debacle, but years later when a second world war erupted, Patton and his former young lover from a well-to-do New England family found themselves together again when she was shipped overseas as a Red Cross nurse attached to Third Army. Patton had reunited for liaisons with Jean in July in London before the Normandy invasion and in western France shortly after her arrival in mid-August—and now she had been stationed near him in Lorraine. Though he felt guilty as hell, he just couldn't call it off. There was no one more important in the world to him than his female doppelgänger Beatrice, but it was lonely on the war's front lines and he had not seen his wife in two years.

But though he cared for Gordon, he didn't love her, or at least not anything like he loved his darling Beat. The simple truth was that, while he enjoyed climbing under the bedsheets with the lithe and effervescent socialite-nurse with whom he conversed in fluent French at parties so as to not be overheard, the young woman meant nothing to him compared to his wife, who was in every way his equal. In 1936 and now again in 1944, he was just feeling old and lonely, like a spent old war horse. He wanted—and needed—female companionship, at least once in a while. More than anything else, carrying on with the young and attractive Jean was a means of assuaging the anxieties of a middle-aged man troubled over his virility and a fear of aging. But no one *would* or *could* ever replace Beatrice, he knew with certainty. She was the light of his life and as central to his quest for glory as he was.

With unconditional love and support, but with a firmness that was distinctly Pattonesque, she accepted his frailties, put up with his peccadilloes, tirelessly nourished his self-esteem, and protected and reassured him as she rode alongside him in his quest for greatness—a greatness that she believed in even more than Old Blood and Guts himself. Extraordinary in her ability to play the charming hostess, she had always devoted herself fiercely to his military career. Patton's parents and a smattering of other influential people had implanted the seeds of his ambition in his head with their tales of Alexander the Great, King Arthur, William the Conqueror, Napoleon, and Robert E. Lee, but without Beatrice he probably would never have reached his goal.

And he damn well knew it.

Willie snorted and the sound, while not loud, startled him. He turned away from the window. The rain was now coming down in a Biblical torrent, and his mind turned from his women to the war—something that was rarely far from his mind. God, did he hate Lorraine and the Saar. The Third Army had crossed into Germany and had its sights on Frankfurt, an Allied offensive was planned for the week before Christmas, and the intelligence staffs were confident the end of the war drew near— and yet, at the moment, Patton found himself and his army stuck in a muddy quagmire along the western edge of the Siegfried Line.

The goddamn rain just wouldn't quit.

In fact, the whole Allied army was stuck in the mud. The three army groups commanded by Bradley, Devers, and Montgomery that had advanced to near the borders of the Reich three months earlier were virtually immobilized in the slop, snow, and harsh terrain not only in Lorraine and the Saar, but in the outer Ruhr, Ardennes Forest, and the Vosges. The stalemate of the past three months was the result of Eisenhower's broad-front strategy and poor logistical planning, which resulted in the Allies' greatest *blitzkrieg* commander being sidelined instead of turned loose to be the spearhead of the three army groups. The broad-front strategy was geared for the snail's pace of the Normandy hedgerow country and failed to embrace the concept of rapid, mobile warfare. The end result was a series of battles of attrition that gained little in the way of significant ground, which infuriated Patton.

He wished he could move up his attack, scheduled for December 19, so that he could get out of this rain-soaked hellhole that had claimed three months and 50,000 Third Army casualties—all to gain back a mere sixty miles of French territory. His Christmas present to Herr Hitler would consist of a huge ground assault along the Saar River. It would be preceded by squadron after squadron of his buddy Brigadier General Otto P. "Opie" Weyland's bomb-dropping Mustangs and Flying Jugs. For Patton, the stakes were enormous. With any luck, he would punch through the Siegfried Line and Third Army would be the first of the Allies over the Rhine.

Success would make him the hero he was in August, when his tankers had dashed to the Seine with dizzying speed. On the flip side, failure would consign him to a secondary theater again and more of the same bitter frustrations he had endured since September. More than likely, it would result in the loss of more divisions to other, less capable field generals to the north—especially his rival Montgomery.

But he wasn't worried about failure, not if he could finally get his army moving again. His spearheading armored columns would advance far into the Saar Basin, and before the Germans knew what hit them, he would be blasting through the Siegfried Line and taking village after village bearing German instead of French names. He had inflicted 180,000 German casualties in Lorraine and would double that number if he was turned loose to do what he did best. It had taken Metz for him to finally realize that his problems of supply and strategy were in the hands of others over whom he had little or no control. But now that he had a better handle on the logistical challenges he faced and had been greenlighted to return to the offensive, he couldn't get cracking soon enough.

At that moment, Oscar Koch dropped in to see him. Though they were scheduled to meet in the afternoon for a special intelligence briefing, for important cases sometimes the two met before meetings to go over things beforehand. Koch's job was to protect Third Army from being taken by surprise by the enemy, and Patton considered him the best senior intelligence officer on the Allied side. He depended heavily upon the man and trusted him implicitly. Which was why even though his mood was as foul as the weather, he greeted the G-2 pleasantly.

"What do you have for me, Oscar?" he said to his close Jewish colleague and friend.

"There's something I've been looking into, General. It may or may not be anything, but I wanted to run it by you before our meeting. I know you're planning to move east in a few days. An attack by German forces to the west, just north of the Moselle, would be out of Third Army's zone of advance, but it would pose a serious threat to your flank. So, with that in mind, I wanted to go over what the intelligence gathered to date seems to suggest."

Patton nodded. He had received the enemy unit and strength estimates the G-2 had been collecting and documenting in official reports for weeks. But Koch had yet to put all the facts together into a conceptual model of what the enemy's intentions might be based upon a composite analysis of the details.

"Despite the advances of all three Allied army groups along the Siegfried Line," Koch explained, "there is a large force of German strategic and tactical troops being held in reserve in the north across from the Ardennes. These troops include armored and mechanized infantry units, paratroopers, and SS troops."

"SS now?"

"Yes, General. The question is why are they not being called on to at least slow down the Allied advance? What's the purpose of holding them in reserve?"

"Are you suggesting that the Germans are preparing for a large-scale offensive?"

"That's what all the intel points to. Whatever it is, they're building up for *something* big."

He knew that Koch had been studying the German frontline and reserve activity in the north for months. In the process, the G-2 had confirmed the identities and locations of multiple armored and infantry units. He had also compiled information on large enemy ammunition and gasoline dumps, mines, and unassembled enemy artillery pieces, which he had posted to his various maps in the G-2 section. Now all of the pieces of the puzzle had been added together, and they told the intelligence officer one thing: the Germans were building up for an impending attack.

"From the air reconnaissance section," resumed Koch, "I've recently learned of enemy tanks being loaded onto trains in Frankfurt and heading west. That wouldn't be such a big deal if we were attacking across from that sector. But I've discovered that of the fifteen known tank divisions in the western part of Germany, only five are presently in contact with Allied forces. The status of the others is unknown."

"You're saying we don't know where in the hell the Krauts' armored divisions could be?"

"Yes, sir, that's exactly what I'm saying. We've stepped up our night photo reconnaissance missions. We've specifically requested railroad marshalling yards and important highway intersections deep behind enemy lines as targets of interest. Our photo interpreters have been poring over the images. They've been able to trace the progress of several hundred trains a day and to estimate the size of the units being transferred towards the front."

"What have they found?"

"The air reconnaissance teams have reported unprecedented rail activity with large numbers of troops on several separate days in the past week. But we've got other intel that's even more disturbing."

"What do you have, Oscar?"

"Under interrogation, an enemy prisoner recently told us about a secret order sending captured Allied uniforms and qualified English-speaking personnel to Osnabruck for training in reconnaissance, sabotage, and espionage."

"Could it be a trick? I mean, at this stage, the Krauts are desperate. After all, we are finally knocking on the door of the Fatherland after two years of heavy fighting."

"No, we think the order's real. Whatever the Germans are planning, it involves English-speaking troops."

"Taking all the information you've gathered then you're convinced the Germans are preparing to launch a major counteroffensive."

"Yes, General. Definitely bigger than Mortain."

"Hitler's a crazy son of a bitch and a natural gambler—so I wouldn't put it past him."

"Hitler's psychological profile fits the intelligence we've gathered too, yes."

"Okay, you've made a believer out of me. But just so you know, if *der Führer* actually goes through with this, it will be the last crazy thing that son of a bitch does. When he presses forward and overextends his lines, we'll be there to snip the cord."

Koch grinned. "I figured you'd say that." He then spent the next few minutes going over how the Germans might try and pull off their winter offensive based upon their known combat strength, and how under such a scenario the enemy was favored. To support his conclusion, he provided terrain analysis and a review of Allied strength. The U.S. had three infantry and two armored divisions available for immediate employment in the general area of the Ardennes. This still left the enemy with a two-to-one numerical advantage, not to mention the psychological advantage of a successful diversionary attack, if Koch was right.

"Oscar, I want to thank you for bringing this to me so I can chew on it before the meeting. Your intelligence-gathering and analysis will obviously have to be stepped-up. You be sure to get all the intel you need, and if you run into interference, you inform me directly."

"Yes, General."

"I want you to put together limited outline plans to deal with the threat to the north so that we're in a position to meet whatever happens. Meanwhile, plans for our offensive on Frankfurt kicking off December 19 will continue. But limited planning is all we can do for the northern sector until we know more. I want to be ready but I don't want to be distracted from our current objective here in the south. Until we have more definitive information, I have to be more concerned with what's going on in my front than I do to threats that are mostly theoretical and mostly Hodges's problem."

"I understand, General. I'll keep you updated and see you later today for the special briefing."

"I've got to say, Oscar, if this thing is as big as you say, we sure are going to have our goddamn hands full."

"Yes, sir—we most certainly are."

# CHAPTER 34

**WEST OF COLOGNE
WESTERN GERMANY**

**DECEMBER 15, 1944**

"HERE THEY COME—IT LOOKS LIKE ANOTHER MAY 31!"

Angela stared up anxiously at the night sky. Powerful yellow searchlights traversed back and forth as part of Cologne's antiaircraft defense system to seek out attacking enemy bombers. It was well after 2 a.m. She and her father stood in the flak defense command and control bunker west of the city center, where he was directing the city's flak defenses to break up the approaching British bomber formations.

The May 31 date to which Colonel Günther Lange referred took place in 1942. That spring night, 1,050 British Royal Air Force planes dropped more than 2,000 tons of bombs on Cologne in less than seventy-five minutes. The largest air raid of the war thus far destroyed 600 acres and 13,000 buildings along the banks of the Rhine, crippling industrial, chemical, and machine-tool facilities throughout the city. With high-explosive bombs bursting, on average, every two seconds, approximately 45,000 Germans were rendered homeless by the bombing raid, nearly 500 were killed, and more than 6,000 civilians were wounded.

"How long now, Papa?" she asked him as he handed her cotton to stuff into her ears. Everyone in the bunker wore hearing protection, or would put it on as soon as the bombers were visible in the sky.

"Ten minutes, maybe less," he replied. "The RAF is out in force tonight."

"How many?"

"More than five hundred planes."

She took a deep breath to steady her nerves. The massive armada of approaching bombers had been identified and reported over the coast of Holland an hour earlier, and her father had rushed here with her in tow. Since her arrest by Kütter, he refused to let her out of his sight and had forced her to give up her nursing job to work with him at the flak command center as a *Luftwaffenhelfer*. Though she didn't want to do anything to prolong the war or support the ignominious Reich, she considered being a flak helper purely self-defence against the Allies' morally dubious efforts to target civilians and undermine German morale. The air-raid sirens rang out as the streams of bombers, escorted by swarms of fighters, droned towards them from the west. The initial alarm had been passed to the central communications network, and the British formations were being tracked and recorded for distance, altitude, and number of aircraft in each incoming squadron.

The *Heimatflak*—the national homeland antiaircraft defense—had been established in 1942, when it had become apparent that the Luftwaffe and Wehrmacht lacked the numbers of personnel necessary to protect German cities. Now old men and teenage boys and girls like Angela were the ones who operated command and control equipment like the air force's flak units. The *Luftwaffenhelfer* ranks were further rounded out with foreign volunteers who preferred, in return for better rations, to make war against British and American aircraft instead of performing industrial slave labor. With the Allies knocking on the door to Germany, it was all part of Hitler's *Endkampf*—the final desperate struggle.

"Flak positions, take battle stations!" commanded her father into his microphone, calling out to the gun crews of the various flak defenses. "The enemy is now twenty kilometers out!"

"*Jawohl, Colonel!*"

Soon Angela could hear the droning engines and see the silhouettes of the bombers against the probing searchlights. She licked her lips and clenched her hands as the first *Christbäume*—Christmas trees—were dropped to mark the targets for the oncoming waves of bombers. The brightly burning flares hung over the city, serving as a threatening indicator to the populace below that they were about to be pummeled with bombs.

"Bomber altitude twenty-one thousand feet! Let them have it!"

The crews of the flak batteries sprang into action, manning the high-velocity 88mm, 105mm, and smaller 20mm caliber antiaircraft artillery pieces ringing the city. Teenage boys, old men, and foreign laborers set to work adjusting the fuses on the antiaircraft projectiles to detonate and scatter clouds of shrapnel at the reported altitude of the invaders. As the aircraft swooped in, they were intercepted by German night fighters that dove and punched their way through the ranks of bombers, attempting to shoot down individual aircraft and break up flight patterns. The powerful pillars of the yellow searchlights continued to traverse the sky and reveal the hundreds of planes. The young girls manning the battery switchboards in nearby bunkers reported the positions of the aircraft as the information was relayed to them.

Now all across the night sky, the twin-engined Hampden, Whitley, and Vickers Wellington bombers were met by brilliant bursts of flak unleashed from the rapid-firing ground batteries. But Angela knew that less than one in twenty of the aircraft would be sent to the earth, even with the five hundred antiaircraft batteries ringing the city. Now the terrific explosions of the five-hundred-pound bombs could be heard through the thumping of the heavy flak as the searchlights crossed the skies. The ground shook, the flak batteries and concrete shelters quivered, and retrofitted gas and water lines burst as the whistling bombs descended and exploded. Soon entire city blocks collapsed under the storm of glowing phosphorus.

Throughout the city, elderly men, women, and children clustered together within the confines of the air raid shelters. The subsurface pressure waves were so strong that it felt as if they were being tossed back and forth on a ship at sea. Screams filled the darkness with each explosion from the huddled masses in the shelters as carpets of bombs fell. Several of the bunkers took direct hits, with enormous I-beams and heavy iron fittings being blown in front of the entrances by the pressure waves of the exploding bombs.

The air-raid shelters quickly became stifling, asphyxiating tombs as the city blocks burned. Cologne's citizens stumbled through the darkness to escape suffocation in the shelters. Blinded by heat, smoke, and phosphorus fumes, they staggered from cellars onto streets that were rendered rivers of burning, molten asphalt. Some of the occupants were quickly asphyxiated, lying in heaps in shelters, where, panic-stricken, they had attempted to flee when robbed of oxygen by the sea of flames. In several of the larger public air raid shelters, mass hysteria and panic seized hold of the crowds, and in the darkness many of those who sought shelter were crushed under the feet of mobs attempting to escape.

Angela heard the rumble of the detonations over the wail of the air-raid sirens and dull roar of the bomber squadrons. She covered her ears and braced herself as the percussion from exploding ordnance passed through her body. The distant skyline of the city was illuminated by the eerie glow of flames, from which she could see searchlight beams reaching skyward into the blackness. The inferno would remain visible for miles around the city's center until first light came at dawn.

She wondered if the British were using the time-fuse detonators, as they had on previous bombing runs that had leveled her beloved city. Following one particularly violent raid a year earlier, twenty thousand Cologne inhabitants had been ordered to evacuate their homes, or what was left of them, as the ruins remained inundated with unexploded ordnance and time-fuse bombs. The latter did not explode on impact but buried themselves deep in the rubble, the fuses methodically ticking away until they detonated with murderous effect. The unexpected detonations typically occurred long after the sounds of the aircraft and flak had subsided, when firefighters and rescue workers were attempting to free civilians entombed in bunkers and cellars.

Though Angela loathed Hitler and the Nazis far more than the Allies, she wondered how the British could be so cruel as to deliberately murder and cripple thousands of women and children each month with time-fuse bombs. It seemed unusually cruel and violent for any civilized people.

An ominous lull settled briefly over the flaming city as the initial squadrons of RAF bombers departed the skies above the Rhine and were followed by another formation of bombers. In the illumination of the traversing searchlights, Angela could see the silvery underbellies of the massive British twin-engined bombers and the delicate strands of the 500-pound bombs as they dropped though the open bays beneath the fuselages. Her father barked out orders through his microphone to the crews of the remaining antiaircraft batteries that hadn't been hit in the first wave.

Fifty-three minutes later, it was mercifully over.

As the droning aircraft disappeared into the night, Cologne remained a field of ruins blanketed by a huge cloud of dust and debris. But surprisingly, Angela could see the twin spires of the nearly 700-year-old cathedral still standing like stolid sentinels in the fiery and smoky distance. Her father had been right; the raid, while not as big as the 1,000-bomber raid of May 1942, was as devastating as any other previously experienced by the benumbed inhabitants. With the planes now gone, all that was left were the whispers of the flames, sporadic detonations of time-delay fuses on high-explosive bombs, and the earth-shaking rumble of collapsing buildings as the flames devoured entire city blocks.

With dawn approaching, fire, rescue, and police teams descended upon the city to clear away the prominent pedestrian and traffic arteries and search the rubble for survivors. *Sprengkommandos*—explosive ordnance disposal teams—began combing through the smoking ruins in search of the dangerous time bombs as well as *blindganger*—duds—to disarm them and prepare them for subsequent removal.

The bombs destroyed most road surfaces and only large thoroughfares were able to be cleared, and then only enough for horse-drawn conveyances and small motorized vehicles to pass. The first task was to provide emergency medical aid to the injured and bring them to safety. First aid stations, complete with surgery capabilities, were set up in the areas deemed to have suffered the most casualties.

Angela drove with her father to the flak positions around the city and dutifully recorded the number of positions knocked out. A dozen had been destroyed in the attack and more than twenty *Luftwaffenhelfer* killed—one foreign worker, two elderly men, and the rest fifteen- and sixteen-year-old boys. But not all the casualties were in and the numbers could grow. It was well past dawn by the time they started back to their home in Braunsfeld, which was not as heavily bombed as the *Altstadt* or Ehrenfeld to the north but was still more than fifty percent decimated.

As they wound their way through the western edge of the battered city, they came across signs of devastation and a nightmarish moonscape. Massive steel girders, industrial machinery, rails, roofs—everything lay tossed together or bent, twisted, or melted in a ghastly display of violence. Survivors stumbled from cellars and air-raid shelters to stagger aimlessly through the ruins, speechless, shocked, and confused. Starving wild dogs roaming through the rubble were shot by soldiers and policemen. Angela could hardly blame the British for this disastrous mess—this, after all, was what Hitler had wrought. A part of her thought it was Germany's penance for backing National Socialism. All the same, she felt badly for the everyday people who were finished with their Führer and wanted only to survive.

She could see that the fire brigades, Red Cross and hospital representatives, utility personnel, and police units were hard at work. The groups were augmented by soldiers on leave, Nazi Party volunteers, foreign laborers, and prisoners of war. Entire city blocks were cordoned off to inhibit looting and limit access by unauthorized people. With Germanic efficiency, massive bulldozers had already started clearing paths through the ruins, pushing collapsed buildings, incinerated belongings, and corpses into piles along the roadways. Couriers, many of whom were Hitler Youth members, stood by to relay messages due to the disruption of the telephone lines. The squads of HJ, fire brigades, and foreign laborers worked side by side in digging through the rubble. Somehow even the "little Hitlers" seemed less cruel and barbaric amidst the wilderness of devastation all around. The inhabitants who had lost their homes combed through the ruins to gather whatever items of value they could scrounge from the rubble. They would be assigned to shelters or told to seek refuge with friends and relatives.

An eerie silence had settled over the city. In the distance, Angela saw rescue workers pulling bodies and even body parts from the wreckage, and she saw human limbs sticking up from some of the piles. But she had long ago grown accustomed to such macabre sights. The gruesome task of locating, identifying, and burying the dead was an important one, she knew. Rapid removal of the dead from the populated areas was essential in preventing outbreaks of disease, and relatives were anxious to learn the fate of missing family members.

"I'm sorry you had to see all this," said her father when they were halfway to their house.

"I'm not a child anymore," she said, more sternly than she had intended. "Not after what I've seen during the past three years."

"I know. I also want to thank you for coming with me tonight. I know you would rather still be working at the hospital, but you are a good help and I appreciate it."

"I just want it all to be over."

"I do too, *Bärchen*. I do too."

On their circuitous route home due to the bomb damage, they soon approached the small western outpost of Lövenich along the Cologne-Düren-Aachen rail line. Angela was struck by all of the soldiers, tanks, and artillery equipment being moved forward to the front along the westward-moving train corridor and network of roads west of the city. Clogging the roads were all sorts of supply wagons. Unlike the Allied ground forces, which were virtually completely motorized, the German Army still relied heavily on horse-drawn transport. Angela saw infantry soldiers trudging along beside horses, donkeys, and oxen pulling wagons stuffed with ammunition, food, and other supplies. Motorcycles, cars, and heavy trucks packed with men and equipment rolled down the centers of the roads. What she was witnessing was a mind-bogglingly huge mobilization of men and war matériel—and it was all happening late at night under cover of darkness to avoid detection by Allied aircraft.

She had heard about the heavy street fighting in Aachen and in the muddy forests to the south, but she had been led to believe that the situation along Germany's western border was more or less a stalemate. True, with the Americans approaching, the situation in the rear areas and cities along the Rhine remained chaotic, but she had not once considered in recent days that her country might boldly go on the offensive when it had its back against the wall. She was no military strategist like her father, but looking at all the nighttime traffic around her, one thing was perfectly clear: the German Army was not just readjusting its lines or plugging in holes, it was going on the offensive.

In a very, very big way.

The rail lines, marshalling yards, and roadways west of Cologne were jammed with such a large number of troops and so much equipment that she realized much of it must have been shifted over from the Eastern Front. And the massive movement of men and equipment wasn't just tonight. For the past 48 hours, the roads up and down the Rhine had been filled at night with convoys of troops and supplies. The military police were out in force, checking papers at hundreds of checkpoints in and around Cologne, Bonn, Trier, and perhaps further south. There was so much traffic that several times she and her father were forced to stop and wait for the traffic to pass, and they had to present papers to military security personnel at major traffic junctions. Train car after train car, trailer after trailer, and transport truck after transport truck rolled by along with the horse-drawn wagons, carrying thousands of soldiers and tons of equipment.

It was a massive, coordinated offensive movement.

Contingents of Wehrmacht soldiers and foreign forced laborers loaded arms and equipment, directed traffic, and drove vehicles—with all efforts directed towards the south and west. The assembly areas and transportation corridors were well lit by big floodlights. Angela could overhear snippets of conversation in mostly German, but there were other languages audible as well—French, Russian, Polish, and Italian—over the sound of the grinding machinery.

More than seven million foreign forced laborers from the occupied territories were working in the Third Reich, comprising fifty percent of the workforce in some critical sectors. Though the National Socialist state was based on the concept of racial purity, Hitler's Nazi Germany had faced a growing internal contradiction since conquering most of Europe. Millions of foreigners toiled away in the Reich's heavy industries, munitions plants, and farms, and they had become critical to the war effort. These people, particularly those from Eastern Europe, were considered by the regime to pose a security risk to the German people. Attempting to reconcile the situation, the Nazis implemented harsh regulations to limit social interaction between Germans and foreign laborers in an attempt to discourage any attempts at rebellion and ensure productivity. By late 1944, these controls had become increasingly draconian as the regime began to fear insurrection and sabotage as Germany's military situation became more precarious.

But tonight—on the eve of what Angela could tell would be a collision of epic proportions—the foreign workers moved quickly and efficiently, deploying their heavy equipment with the precision of an army conducting military maneuvers. It was obvious that they had performed this kind of work many times before under the threat of death or injury by Hitler's Third Reich.

All sense of time became lost as Angela and her father gazed mesmerically at the massive military operations going on all around them.

"What's going on, Papa? What is this all about?"

"I don't know."

"Don't lie to me. What is Hitler trying to pull off?"

"You don't need to know about it. It's nothing but a pipe dream."

"I am your daughter and you need to tell me what's happening."

"Only the biggest offensive on the Western Front since the *blitzkrieg* in 1940."

"General von Manteuffel—he's part of it, isn't he? Which means that you could have taken part in the offensive, but for some reason you chose not to."

"The general was already far along in his planning, *Bärchen*, and I had to get many things in order. He could not take me back onto his staff until the new year."

"So, you have known all along? This is a Wehrmacht offensive."

"A huge offensive."

"What will happen?"

"I don't know."

"But surely you don't think we can win the war. Not when our cities lay in ruins and the Allies press ever closer to our borders."

"I don't know what will happen. But I do know one thing."

"What is that?"

"In the end, all it is going to do is prolong the war and increase our suffering. Our defeat is certain and Germany cannot win. The best that the Führer can possibly gain is to buy the Reich an extra month or two of time. But it's going to place a heavier burden on the German people, who are already taxed to the limit."

"But won't a counterattack allow us to possibly obtain favorable peace terms?"

"Probably not," he said glumly. "I am sorry but that is just the way it is."

"If Germany is *kaput*, then why do you fight at all?"

"I don't know, *Bärchen*. At this point, I honestly don't know."

# CHAPTER 35

## OUR RIVER
## LUXEMBOURG AND BELGIUM

### DECEMBER 16, 1944

AT PRECISELY 0530 HOURS on a fog-filled morning, the east bank of the Our River exploded with sheets of flame from 1,600 artillery pieces across an 85-mile front. The opening salvo of Hitler's Ardennes Offensive—what in American lore would become known as the Battle of the Bulge—was launched through the densely forested Ardennes region of Wallonia in eastern Belgium, northeast France, and Luxembourg. Moments later, the west bank of the Our, occupied by U.S. troops, disappeared under a hail of steel as thousands of shells came screaming back down to earth.

The drumfire fell in crimson splashes as the German 88s and *Nebelwerfer* six-barrel rocket guns—called "Screaming Meemies" by the Allies—unleashed a reign of terror, churning up turned earth and burnt powder. Then the *rat-tat-tat* of the German machine guns added their sawmill racket to the din. Rounds with the heft of railroad spikes splintered pine and fir boughs and GI bones alike. The thrum of Panzer Mark IV, Panther, and Tiger engines along with other assorted armored vehicles now carried from the east. While the German armored columns rolled forward, the night sky was blasted with searchlights to blind the American defenders and provide illumination for the assault teams as they crossed the river into Luxembourg and Belgium. A portion of the attack force came in rubber boats, pulling themselves across the river using tow ropes and other improvised flotation devices, as salvo after salvo of high-explosive rounds roared over their heads into the vulnerable American positions. Within minutes, the first boat-delivered troops had crossed the Our and were charging up the steep riverbanks.

The opening barrage lasted a full ninety minutes, vaporizing U.S. Army pill boxes, troop assembly areas, artillery batteries, and machine-gun nests all along the front; setting fire to huge swaths of forest; and throwing up great clouds of smoke and dust that hung over the Ardennes. The initial German attack force consisted of over 400,000 men; over 1,400 tanks, tank destroyers, and assault guns; 1,600 antitank guns; and 2,600 artillery pieces, all of which were supported by over 1,000 combat aircraft and large numbers of other armored fighting vehicles. In the battle, the Germans sported two murderous pieces of technology being used for the first time: the new 70-ton Tiger II tank and the new speedy Messerschmitt Me 262 jet.

Along the thin American line, dazed doughboys awoke to waves of Germans pointing searchlights and guns at them. They dug in deeper, scratching furrows with helmets and mess tins in the snow as the rush of artillery slashed through the early morning darkness and the German tanks ground forward. The enemy overran some units, machine-gunning Americans by the score as they went, and circled behind others. The troops that withdrew did so haphazardly and without a plan. Hundreds scuttled to the rear without stopping, past the first corpses, who wore the usual deadpan expressions, their faces a deep claret color because blood in the capillaries beneath the skin had frozen so quickly. Only the living were surprised by the attack:

they felt fear, isolation, confusion, and panic.

In the opening phase of the battle, the Germans faced only some 80,000 Allied soldiers, less than 250 pieces of armor, and 400 artillery guns. The flimsy American line was held by the 4th, 28th, and 106th Infantry Divisions, supported by the inexperienced 9th Armored Division. Two of the three infantry divisions had between them suffered 9,000 casualties in the recent Hürtgen Forest battle and had been sent to the Ardennes to rest. The third, the 106th, was a green outfit entirely new to battle. Onto these poorly outfitted and wholly unprepared American defenders, the Germans fell like a whirlwind.

While many of the American troops were inexperienced, the German force included many battle-hardened veterans of tough fighting on the Eastern Front. But at this late stage of the war, Hitler's *Endkampf,* the Wehrmacht ranks, too, had to be filled with mere boys and grizzled men who normally would have been considered too old for military service. Though the attacking Germans had lived for the past week on sparse rations, little sleep, and ersatz coffee, they were a formidable fighting machine and carried with them the element of surprise.

A pearly dawn leaked down the slopes, augmented by hissing German flares that tinctured the snow with metallic glints of silver and crimson. Through the trees, German infantrymen and *fallschirmjager*s materialized as bent shadows. Some donned snow suits or white capes, others greatcoats of *feldgrau* with flanged helmets or duck-bill caps. They swept in bold and fast, shouting and singing above the whipcrack of rifle fire. Overall command of the offensive was in the hands of Field Marshal Gerd von Rundstedt, who had instructed his legions before striking out, "*Es geht um das Ganze*—Everything is at stake. Your great hour has struck. You bear in yourselves a divine duty to give everything and to achieve the superhuman for our Fatherland and our Führer."

The goal of the German offensive was two-fold: to drive a wedge between the American and British armies in France and the Low Countries, and to recapture the Belgian port of Antwerp, thereby denying the Allies use of the port facilities. By routing the American forces in their path and breaking through to Antwerp, the Germans hoped to cleave away the British Army group from American forces as well as from their supplies, and then crush the isolated British. The German code name for the buildup to the offensive was *Wacht am Rhine—Watch on the Rhine—* while the field offensive itself was codenamed *Unternehmen Herbstnebel— Operation Autumn Mist.* By splitting the British and American Allied line in half, capturing Antwerp, and then proceeding to encircle and destroy four Allied armies, the Germans hoped to force the Western Allies to negotiate a peace treaty in the Axis powers' favor.

The Fifth Panzer Army, led by Baron General von Manteuffel, was to break through the U.S. front in the Ardennes, swerve westward, and then wheel northward across the Meuse, past Namur to Antwerp. The Sixth Panzer Army under SS commander Sepp Dietrich, was to thrust northwestward past Liège to Antwerp, creating a strategic barrier astride the rear of the British and the more northerly American armies. To these two *Panzerarmees,* von Rundstedt gave the bulk of the tanks. The Seventh Army, under General Erich Brandenberger, was assigned to the southernmost sector in Luxembourg with the task of protecting the flank. This army was made up of four infantry divisions, with no large-scale armored formations to use as a spearhead unit.

By 0800, all three of the German armies had attacked through the Ardennes and *Operation Autumn Mist* was off to a resounding start. The green American forces crumbled and melted away under the weight of the well-planned German *blitzkrieg*. In the northern sector Dietrich's 6th SS Panzer Army assaulted Losheim Gap and the Elsenborn Ridge in an effort to break through to Liège. In the center, von Manteuffel's 5th Panzer Army attacked towards Bastogne and St. Vith, both road junctions of great strategic importance. In the south, Brandenberger's 7th Army pushed towards Luxembourg to secure the flank from Allied attacks.

By 1000 hours, the Germans had tens of thousands of men pouring across the west side of the river. The light resistance and early success of the river crossings all along the front revealed that they had surprised the American defenders throughout much of the Ardennes. Aided by surprise, the counteroffensive then created widespread alarm and confusion throughout the ranks. After the initial shock, some of the U.S. troops reacted and began to slow down the German advance at strategic points along the front. But the Germans wisely bypassed American strongholds rather than assaulting them head-on. Soon, an east-west "bulge" began to develop in the hilly and wooded country of the Ardennes, as the German Panzer and infantry forces drove a wedge into the Allied lines.

By an alignment of the stars, the Germans managed to achieve a total surprise attack. Later historians would attribute their success to a combination of Allied overconfidence, poor aerial reconnaissance due to bad weather, and an overreliance on Ultra to divine enemy intentions, through the reading of the Germans' secret radio messages rather than other intelligence-gathering activities. The Supreme Headquarters Allied Expeditionary Force—SHAEF—and in particular the Allies three highest ranking field commanders—Eisenhower, Bradley, and Montgomery— were caught flat-footed and completely bamboozled in what amounted to the worst U.S. intelligence failure since Pearl Harbor and the most disastrous for the Allies thus far in the war.

On December 15, Montgomery had written that Hitler's plight was so dire "that he cannot stage major offensive operations." That same day, the field marshal had written Eisenhower a note requesting leave to return to Britain for Christmas. Monty jovially included an invoice for a five-pound bet wagered in October 1943, when he had challenged Ike's prediction that the war would end by Christmas 1944. "I still have nine days," the supreme commander jokingly replied, "and while it seems almost certain that you will have an extra five pounds for Christmas, you will not get it until that day."

Colonel Monk Dickson, the U.S. First Army intelligence chief, and British Major General Kenneth W. D. Strong, Ike's intelligence chief, issued clear warnings to the higher-ups in early December of the strong possibility of a German attack on the Allied lines. But they were either disregarded or considered alarmist and the threat in the densely forested Ardennes was not considered serious. Even by the end of first day of the German *blitzkrieg*, Bradley had casually dismissed the biggest offensive on the Western Front since 1940 as "a spoiling attack, nothing serious." At the top, the Allies ignored the warning signs and were asleep at the wheel.

Only Patton's team had seen it coming all along—and developed plans to do something about it. Though the Ardennes was out of Third Army's sector, Oscar Koch had early on sensed what others did not: that a dangerous, desperate enemy remained capable of wreaking havoc and was poised to do just that. For some time, the G-2 had not only been keeping a close eye on German dispositions up north in Bradley's sector but reporting a buildup of Panzer and infantry divisions and ammunition and gasoline dumps west of the Rhine in the Eifel and Saar.

To his boss Patton, Koch insisted that the German reversal in recent months was not a rout or a mass collapse at all. Quite the contrary, his evidence demonstrated that the enemy was gathering in strength like an approaching storm directly in the northern portion of Twelfth Army Group's zone of advance, and especially in the areas opposite the First Army from Aachen to the southern extremity of the Ardennes Forest. He pointed out the vulnerability of the U.S. units in the Ardennes and solved the ongoing mystery over the location of at least fourteen German divisions, most of them armored, which together could spearhead a counteroffensive. He made Patton aware of the massive rail movements, of increasing frequency and size, north of the Moselle in the First Army sector.

As the buildup continued, the possible ramifications became a matter of concern to Patton. He couldn't believe that the Germans had a two-to-one numerical advantage in the Ardennes sector. Furthermore, as the enemy moved into final position to begin its offensive, Koch reported that the Germans were in a state of radio silence, which he insisted signaled an impending attack. "I believe the Germans are going to launch an attack, probably at Luxembourg," he predicted.

The intelligence that Koch used to predict the battle was available to the other American and British commands. The difference lay in the interpretation of the available intelligence. Because of Koch's willingness to warn his commander of the enemy's intentions rather than just his capability, and because of the deep trust that Patton had in his G-2, Old Blood and Guts was able to prepare in advance and react quickly. His major new offensive, set for December 19, to breach the Westwall and drive to the Rhine was scrapped—to be replaced, thanks to Koch, with one of three contingency plans his staff had developed over the past week based on his G-2's prescient forecast of German intentions. The Allied failure leading to the Ardennes was not due to a blindness to the enemy buildup, or a breakdown in the intelligence service's collection techniques—it was in the evaluation and application of the intel available to all of the Allied intelligence units and SHAEF.

While Eisenhower, Bradley, Montgomery, and SHAEF were surprised by the strength of the German assault force and by the fact that Hitler would use his reserves in an offensive manner, Patton and his team were not only not surprised at all but amply prepared to meet the threat.

"We'll be in a position to meet whatever happens," Patton had told his staff back on December 9—one week before the German's launched what would later become known as the Battle of the Bulge.

On December 19, three days after the battle had been joined, he had his chance to ante up and kick in—and turn a military debacle into an Allied triumph.

# CHAPTER 36

## EAGLE MAIN HEADQUARTERS, U.S. TWELFTH ARMY GROUP
## VERDUN, NORTHEASTERN FRANCE

### DECEMBER 19, 1944

BOUNCING DOWN A POT-HOLED ROAD in his command jeep, Patton excitedly puffed his American-made White Owl Invincible cigar, while reviewing his mental calculations for relieving his beleaguered comrades fighting for their lives up north in Belgium and Luxembourg. The morning was harsh and dark, with an icy wind ripping at the Willys' flimsy Plexiglas windows and 30-caliber machine gun mounted on its swivel. Codman was with him, as was Paul Harkins, his deputy operations officer, as they rumbled into Verdun, the old French city where so many young men had lost their lives in the trenches of the First World War.

*If Ike wants us at St. Vith,* he thought, studying the pocket-sized Michelin map with its arterial network of roads on his lap, *then Millikin moves here, Eddy here, Gaffey's division along this road, 35th up this road. If he wants Bastogne, Millikin goes to Arlon, 4th Armored takes this road, McBride goes here.... If he wants St. Hubert, then...*

By 1045 hours, his command vehicle pulled up to the slushy entrance of Eagle Main, Bradley's Verdun command post, located within an ancient French Army barracks in a muddy quadrangle. As he and his staff started inside, Eisenhower drove up in an armor-plated Cadillac sedan he had first used in North Africa. Ike's escort included MP jeeps armed with .30-caliber machine guns and Deputy Supreme Commander Air Marshal Arthur Tedder, his second in command at SHAEF and one of the Royal Air Force's best commanders.

"Well hello there, Ike," said Patton cheerfully, though he kept his war face firmly in place given the gravity of the situation.

"George," replied Eisenhower cordially, but Patton could see the strain he was under. He looked grave, almost ashen, though he seemed to brighten at the sight of his old friend.

Going inside, they met with the other members of the war council. Bradley was there along with General Bedell Smith, chief of staff at SHAEF under Ike, General Jacob Devers, commander of 6th Army, and a handful of staff officers. Montgomery was absent but had sent his able chief of staff, General Freddie de Guingand. Patton considered Monty's absence a calculated insult to Eisenhower and the other American generals.

At 1130, they climbed the stairs and shuffled into a dank, second-floor stone squad room with a single potbellied stove, a large table, and a map unfurled across a wall. Bradley—whom Patton could see was in a testy mood after being caught off guard and pushed around by the Germans—pointed to a red arrow labeled "20 German tanks" approaching Namur on the Meuse, farther west than previously reported.

"What the hell is this?"' the commander of Twelfth Army Group demanded.

An intelligence officer scurried to the map, snatched off the errant marker, and apologized for the error.

*Man, this is going to be interesting,* thought Patton, as he and Codman exchanged glances and the senior officers began to take their seats around the conference table. Very little warmth emanated from the small stove in the old French barracks, and most kept their winter coats on to ward off the chill as they settled into their seats. It was at that moment Eisenhower's G-2 Kenneth Strong and his G-3 Harold Bull arrived late to the meeting.

"Well," said Eisenhower unhappily, "I knew my staff would get here—it was only a question of when. But now that we're all here, I guess we can get started."

A tense, uncomfortable silence gripped the room—like a pall of death. The cold atmosphere of the Spartan meeting room seemed to accentuate the bleak attitude that many of the senior officers were feeling. Since the *Market-Garden* debacle, not only had the Allies been stalled on the borders of the Third Reich, but there had been increasing signs of plummeting morale. This was manifested by a rapidly rising desertion rate and increased bickering amongst officers, between officers and enlisted men, and between the Americans and the British—especially between the supreme commander and his fractious underling Monty.

With everyone fidgeting uncomfortably, Eisenhower made a fragile attempt at levity. "The present situation is to be regarded as one of opportunity for us and not of disaster," he said to the gloomy group. "There will be only cheerful faces at this conference table."

Nodding vigorously, Patton immediately chimed in: "Hell, let's have the guts to let the sons of bitches go all the way to Paris! Then we'll really cut 'em up and chew 'em up!"

At first, the smiles seemed forced. But then, as the positive words of the two old war horses seized hold of the room—amplified by Patton's authentic and infectious swagger—the mood lightened. Now Ike smiled that big "Aw shucks" smile of his, reaching out to all in the room with that special warmth and congeniality that was Ike's and Ike's alone—and Patton knew all would be well.

The supreme commander gestured for his intelligence officer, the Brit General Strong, to proceed with his presentation of the current situation in the Ardennes, which he did with the assistance of another staff officer. Over the next few minutes, the two men reviewed the battlefront in detail, presenting a picture of the situation that was even worse than Patton had imagined. In three days, the Germans had pushed to create a "bulge" in the American lines 50 miles wide and nearly 70 miles deep that stretched all the way to Bastogne, a highway center in southern Belgium just north of Luxembourg. At least seventeen German divisions had joined the attack already; the identities of most were now known. American resistance ranged from stalwart to panicked flight. Atrocities had been committed by the attacking divisions: on December 17, the Germans gunned down nearly 100 American prisoners of war at Malmedy. Rumors of the massacre of the American prisoners had already traveled through the U.S. units, causing significant alarm.

The heaviest fighting was now taking place at St.-Vith and Bastogne, two vital road centers. Trapped in Bastogne were one combat command from both the 9th and 10th Armored Divisions and the entire 101st Airborne Division, temporarily led by Brigadier General Anthony C. McAuliffe. Daily Luftwaffe sorties over St.-Vith had declined sharply from six hundred on Sunday, although the overcast skies had also grounded Allied planes. Seven French infantry battalions were helping defend the Meuse, along with half a dozen COMZ engineer regiments. American strength in the Ardennes had doubled since the start of the German offensive on Saturday December 16, to about 180,000 troops in ten infantry and three armored divisions. More would soon follow.

As the preliminary briefing continued, Patton wanted to bang his hand onto the table in disgust. But he refrained from doing so, forcing himself to keep upbeat as Ike had requested. All the same, this was damned embarrassing. What bothered him most was that the Germans had caught the Allies napping, though he was glad that the intelligence failure couldn't be laid at his doorstep.

As Strong continued to summarize the situation, Patton and the rest of the group learned that two formidable German officers who had previously been thorns in the Allied side were playing a big role in the attack: General Hasso von Manteuffel, the Prussian aristocrat and commander of the Fifth Panzer Army, and Waffen-SS Lieutenant Colonel Otto Skorzeny—who had daringly rescued Mussolini from captivity after his arrest and confinement by the Italian government when it switched sides and overthrew the Italian dictator in July 1943. Baron von Manteuffel and his *Panzerarmee* had given Patton fits in his defense of Lorraine in October and November, outwitting the Third Army commander more than once. Patton knew the cagey German had likely played a significant role in the planning of the ongoing Ardennes battle, and he was anxious to get revenge on an enemy whom he respected. Meanwhile, the able Skorzeny was reported to be leading a commando group dressed in American uniforms behind Allied lines to seize the bridges across the Meuse. A rumor that Skorzeny's real object was to assassinate Eisenhower had created unprecedented panic at SHAEF headquarters in Versailles. Since their insertion, Skorzeny's men had been roaming the Ardennes ambushing convoys, spreading alarm and confusion, altering or removing road signs, and generally raising hell as a guerrilla force. Patton couldn't help but admire Skorzeny's dash and daring, but he would personally like to shoot the scar-faced son of a bitch.

Eisenhower then spoke. The supreme commander quickly proposed halting offensive action in all Allied sectors and concentrating on blunting the German drive. To do so, his strategy was to draw a stop line at the Meuse, beyond which there would be no further retreat. The scattered U.S. forces would be pulled together to contain the German attacks and then the Allies would counterattack. Holding the high ground south of Lieg would keep supply depots outside enemy artillery range. By squeezing the shoulders of the German salient, shoring up the Meuse, thwarting the enemy advance, and creating "a supply desert" for the Germans," they could smash von Rundstedt's "bulge"—as everyone in the room was now calling the German offensive—with an American counterblow again aimed at the Rhine. Patton's Third Army, which currently held an eighty-mile front with three corps facing the Saar, would pivot north to knife into the exposed German left flank in a combined attack with Middleton's VIII Corps. After gutting the south side of the bulge, the Allied armies would turn east—together in a broad front, Ike emphasized—and the battle for the Rhine would begin.

Peering down the long table at Patton, Eisenhower asked in his booming voice, "George, I want you to command this move—under Brad's supervision—making a strong counterattack with at least six divisions. When can you start?"

"As soon as you're through with me. My staff has already worked out three alternatives for counterpunching the Germans and providing relief in the Ardennes. I left three sets of instructions with them, and by telephoning a given code word I can put any plan in motion in a matter of minutes."

"How soon can you attack?" Eisenhower then asked.

"The morning of December 21," Patton replied without blinking. "With three divisions—the 4th Armored, the 26th, and the 30th."

Any other commander would have held his breath and believed himself taking a chance on four days or 96 hours—but not Old Blood and Guts. There was a stirring, a shuffling of feet and squeaking of chairs, as those present straightened up in their seats. Two of the British officers snickered. They were used to seeing Monty moving at a snail's pace, especially since he had failed to open up Antwerp to Allied shipping until November 29 despite Eisenhower's order to make the port his top priority and capture it in September. The British officers—quite wrongly—believed the Third Army commander was an American cowboy making yet another smug prediction that was quite out of place in the somber war council of Verdun.

But the British weren't the only ones skeptical. Patton saw that several of the American faces were doubtful he could pull it off, too. After all, the prospect of relieving three divisions from the line, making a sharp left turn and pointing them north, and then moving nearly a hundred miles over icy winter roads to prepare for a major counterattack in less than seventy-two hours was astonishing, even to a unit as accustomed to lightning speed and flexibility as Patton's Third Army. But Old Blood and Guts knew he could pull it off, especially since he and his prescient team had already planned it all out.

He looked at Eisenhower. The supreme commander was leaning forward in his chair and seemed to be making a calculation of space, time, and divisions on his fingers—details Patton and his staff had already worked out. When Ike looked up, their eyes met and Patton could see that his boss was not amused, mistakenly assuming that his subordinate had once again picked a very inopportune moment to act publicly boastful.

"Don't be fatuous, George," he said in a scolding tone. "If you try to go that early, you won't have all three divisions ready and you'll go piecemeal. I'd even settle for the 23rd if it takes that long to get three full divisions."

"I'll make a meeting engagement in three days," Patton said, again without blinking, "and I'll give you a six-division coordinated attack in six days." Again, the British officers snickered and an uneasy shuffle of boots could be heard on the bare floor. After glancing at his operations officer Harkins for confirmation, Patton added, "We can do it, Ike. I'm telling you we can do it."

There was a lengthy silence. He kept his fingers crossed.

"All right, George," conceded Eisenhower after a moment's reflection. "But I'm giving you until the 22nd, to be safe, even though I know I can count on you for December 21."

So there it was. Slowly but inexorably, the skepticism on the faces was replaced with a stiffening resolve and sense of shared purpose. Patton could feel an electric tingle in the room, like he used to feel before a steeplechase. The current of excitement leapt like a flame, and even the overly cautious British now seemed on board with the bold plan for the counterattack and rescue of the embattled forces in the Ardennes. Of course, the senior officers around the table—including Ike—were dead wrong to have doubted him in the first place. But what they had misunderstood was that it was not Patton the boastful individualist they were dealing with here, the Patton of Sicily, but rather Patton the student of war and consummate team player—and Old Blood and Guts knew it and reveled in it. Where others at Verdun came with only vague ideas and without specific plans, Patton had devised three plans, each tailored to meet any contingency that his superiors might require. He had come to the meeting prepared and confident, and having accepted that his Saar offensive would be postponed indefinitely, he was itching to start the operation.

This was a sublime moment in his career, the kind he had been waiting for—indeed training and planning for—his whole life. It was as if destiny now called upon the old horse soldier who had chased down Pancho Villa for this single, defining moment to ride in like the cavalry and save the day. While near panic existed everywhere else, in Patton's mind this was the chance to deliver the knockout blow. While others debated or waffled, Patton understood the problem facing the Allies and had created a plan to counterattack the Germans and occupy Bastogne—which, although not yet surrounded, was clearly soon to be besieged.

Now the group thrashed out the final details. The plan was simple: cut the bulge off from both the northern and southern end by stopping the advance of the Panzers rolling west, surrounding Bastogne, and heading to the Meuse. To do so, Patton was to pull out and strike north with the 26th and 80th Infantry divisions and the 4th Armored Division, hitting the Germans' exposed left flank in a combined attack with Middleton's VIII Corps no earlier than December 22, but no later than the twenty-third. Meanwhile, Devers's 6th Army Group would assume the defensive in Alsace, taking over the American line south of Saarlautern on the Saar River. Patton would keep Walker's XX Corps at Saarlaurern to the south, and everyone in Devers's group would stretch left to cover Third Army's former territory while Old Blood and Guts stabbed north. Since Patton would assume command of Middleton's VIII Corps as he approached Bastogne, his Third Army would be larger than before the German offensive. Moreover, with Devers's Sixth Army Group securing Third Army's southern flank, Patton could now focus solely on rescuing Bastogne.

Lighting up a fresh cigar, he pointed to the bulge on the map in the Saint-Vith/Bastogne sector, where the thin blue lines showing the Allied troops dispositions had been penetrated. "Brad," he said, speaking directly to his former subordinate and current superior, "this time that Kraut bastard von Manteuffel has stuck his head in a meat grinder." Turning his fist in a grinding motion, he added: "And this time I've got hold of the handle."

"I don't think anyone in this room doubts that, George," said Ike, smiling broadly now that the team had a sound strategy in place and the right commanders to pull it off. "But remember, I want a sledgehammer to hit the German flank, not a pinprick. Make sure to have your whole corps in place. Your advance should be methodical and sure—and your attack anything but piecemeal."

"Copy that, Ike—I read you loud and clear. And I promise to kick that Prussian son of bitch von Manteuffel's ass!"

A ripple of confident laughter reverberated through the chilly briefing room—the snickers were long gone. With the team's spirits now raised, Patton quickly laid out his anticipated troop movements and then replied to a series of questions from the gathered collection of high-ranking officers, giving specific and well-rehearsed answers. Within a half hour, all of the remaining questions had been answered and everything had been thrashed out—the divisions to be employed, objectives, new Army boundaries, the amount of the Third Army front to be taken over by Devers's Sixth Army Group. Patton was delighted that, for the first time in months, he was able to get everything he wanted to perform the job at hand the way he wanted. He thanked his lucky stars the fussy Monty hadn't been there to wreak havoc and steal his army—or the glory. Satisfied with the final plan, the generals ended the meeting and left to communicate their orders to their respective staff sections. The war council had been brief, only two hours, yet those hours were critical.

Bradley, whose Twelfth Army Group had been caught with its pants down, said hardly a word during the two-hour conference. He seemed to realize that the only principal players were Patton and Ike. The Old Man knew his cohort was bitter about being caught flat-footed and felt badly for him, but there was no time now for consolation. All he could do at the moment was drive north and bail him out.

After the meeting and before leaving the barracks, Patton began snapping out various movement orders.

"Harkins," he said to his deputy operations officer, "I want you to telephone Gay. Give him the code name for the drive to Bastogne—NICKEL—and tell him to get started. You know what to do. And remember, everyone is a son of a bitch to someone. Be better sons of bitches than they are—that's all you can do."

Since his staff had already worked out the various plans, to execute the Bastogne operation he needed only to issue the brevity code: NICKEL. When Gay heard it, he would know the axis of advance would roll to Bastogne via Arlan, and leading the way would be the 4th Armored Division. XII Corps was to wheel towards Luxembourg in tandem with the III Corps' drive into Belgium.

"Codman, you come with me. Tell Mims we start in five minutes. Let's get this show on the road!"

Five minutes later, Patton, Eisenhower, and Bradley bid their farewells in the slush and mud outside their command vehicles. Declining Bradley's invitation to stay for lunch, Ike said he would eat a sandwich in the Cadillac on the way back to Versailles. Turning to Patton before slipping into his car, Ike said, "Funny thing George, every time I get a new star I get attacked."

"Yes, and every time you get attacked, Ike, I bail you out!"

The reference was to the 1943 disaster of Kasserine Pass in North Africa, when untested American forces commanded by General Lloyd Fredendall were routed by Rommel in their first tank battle. Eisenhower was promoted to attain his fourth star around the same time, and shortly afterwards Patton took over as field commander and won the important Battle of El Guettar.

The three men laughed and shook hands, Ike smiling broadly. To Patton, he seemed not only sanguine, but brimming with a new energy and confidence—and Patton felt the same. The meeting had shot a bolt of lightning through the American High Command. No longer merely reacting to the unexpected, they had settled on a plan that would, if successful, erase the bulge, destroy Hitler's finest, and leave the German border open to a final sledgehammer blow. Patton knew if ever there was justification for his old buddy Ike to have saved his career, it was now.

The task that lay before him was going to be a challenge, but he would find a way to get it done. Turning the Third Army ninety degrees to the north along icy roads in terrible winter weather, when its supply dumps were located to support the drive to the Siegfried Line, was a logistician's worst nightmare. But the months of hard training and experience in combat would now pay off handsomely. He had full confidence in his supply team and in the professional skill of his fighting divisions, and he knew they would embrace the opportunity to turn a potential military debacle into a triumph.

As he watched Ike drive off, he remembered back to a conversation they had had years earlier following the First World War. Patton had fought overseas as a young tank commander, while Eisenhower had trained tank crews in the U.S., showing great leadership but, to his dismay, never getting the chance to cross the Atlantic to fight before the armistice was signed.

Patton told him, "Ike, you will be the Robert E. Lee of the next war and I will be your Stonewall Jackson."

Now—with the outcome of the war at stake and the whole world holding its collective breath—this was his chance to prove it.

# CHAPTER 37

## WUISSE, FRANCE, TO OFFAGNE, BELGIUM

## DECEMBER 25, 1944 – JANUARY 1, 1945

"BASTOGNE, MAN, that's where all the fighting is—and I reckon that's where we'll be headed soon enough."

Shivering against the frigid cold, McBurney raised an eyebrow at his New York buddy Preston McNeil, wondering just how in the hell he knew where they might be going. It was Christmas Day of the coldest winter in Europe in thirty-five years, a cold beyond imagining, and he, Smith, McNeil, and Willie Devore stood outside a mobile field kitchen. With no winter gear given to the Black Panthers or any other armored units except a tanker's winter hood, they were garbed in regular combat fatigues, boots without lining, and standard-issue wool GI blankets draped over their shoulders.

The 761st had rolled southwest all day long, past Honskirch, Bourgaltroff, and Guebling, to Wuisse, where the company cooks had gone ahead to prepare a Christmas turkey dinner. Their mood was relaxed, even playful, as they were happy to be moving out of the bloody, muddy Saar. McBurney and the other men had learned by this point that the Germans had mounted an enormous offensive to the north in Belgium, and that was where the 761st was headed. But in typical military fashion, they were told nothing more about precisely what or where their objective was. McBurney and Smith had pestered Pop Gates with questions, but each time the Charlie Company CO had simply told them to try to get some sleep or check their guns and equipment.

"Now where did you hear we're headed to Bastogne?" Smitty asked McNeil, mimicking McBurney's thoughts.

"I overheard some officer in the 87th Infantry talking to Captain Williams. I wasn't snooping or nothing—I just happened to overhear 'em when we stopped in Guebling."

"So, where exactly is Bastogne?" asked McBurney.

"How the hell should I know?" said McNeil. "Somewhere up north in Belgium."

What the Black Panthers didn't know was that Hitler had set his sights on the sleepy market village with a pre-war population of fewer than 4,000 people. With no fewer than seven major, hard-surfaced roads converging on the Belgian town, Bastogne was an important crossroads deemed crucial by the Germans for the rapid deployment of armored vehicles, infantry trucks, and supply vehicles. It was the hub of a transportation wheel that could greatly aid or hinder the advance to the west to meet Hitler's goal of capturing the port of Antwerp.

At the beginning of the German attack on December 16, the battle-weary U.S. 28th Infantry Division, well below combat strength, had been resting in the area and was in no shape to repulse a major attack. The Germans surrounded their command post at Wiltz, Luxembourg, twelve miles from Bastogne and tore it apart in three days. The 101st Airborne was swiftly sent in to stem back the German tide, arriving on December 19, but the unit was low on cold-weather gear, food, ammunition, and other items crucial to survival let alone repulsing the new interlopers. The Germans wasted no time in attacking in the plunging temperatures and blinding snow.

General Hasso von Manteuffel's forces surrounded the town by December 21. In the face of intense enemy shelling and relentless infantry attacks, the American forces at Bastogne held out amid dwindling food, ammunition, and medical supplies. But between the horrific weather and strong Germans forces, the 101st found resupply from both the ground and air impossible. On December 22, German General Heinrich von Luttwitz delivered a surrender ultimatum to the 101st Airborne's General Anthony McAuliffe, to which McAuliffe answered dryly, "Nuts!" knowing that Patton's three divisions were fast closing on the city. Between the nineteenth and the twenty-second, Patton had rushed back and forth between his divisions on the road, exhorting them to "drive like hell!" At 0600 on December 22—in a logistical feat never before accomplished in the history of war—Patton's 4th Armored and 80th and 26th Infantry Divisions began attacking south and southeast of Bastogne, as he had promised Ike.

Elsewhere throughout the Ardennes, the German advance was slowed by pockets of Allied troops holding out as long as possible against much larger enemy forces, from Elsenborn in the north to Echternach in the south. The Germans had hoped to press forward on a wide, eighty-mile front. But the northern and southern shoulders of the attack had been narrowed and stabilized by the stout resistance. By December 23, at the center and farthest point of the "bulge" in the American lines, Joachim Peiper's SS spearhead had advanced to positions within six miles from its original goal of the Meuse River. But the Germans had not reached it.

"Word is the Krauts are throwing everything at us but the kitchen sink," said McNeil. "They've pushed forward more than fifty miles and created a kind of bulge in our lines. And it ain't over yet."

"I hear them Germans have committed atrocities up there," said Willie Devore.

McBurney had heard that too, but he was skeptical. He hadn't seen anything like that in Lorraine or the Saar. The Germans had fought hard, but fairly, and the ones that surrendered didn't seem that different from American GIs. In fact, most of them seemed to be scared and uncertain young men just like him.

"There's a lot of rumors flying around. What kind of atrocities are we talking about?" he asked, stomping his feet in the snow to warm himself.

"Well for starters, I heard they stripped captured tankers naked in groups and tied ropes around them before machine-gunning them to death. They also say that some of the SS units have English-speaking soldiers in U.S. Army tanks. They're supposedly wearing American uniforms and are armed with American guns. The bastards have managed to infiltrate our lines and cause havoc all over the place."

"Damn," gasped Smitty.

"I don't know if I believe that," said McBurney, still skeptical. "That sounds like soldier gossip to me."

"Nope, he's telling the truth," he then heard Teddy Windsor say as he came up from behind the group standing in line for their Christmas turkey dinners. "It happened a week ago near the town of Malmedy. SS troops murdered eighty-six U.S. prisoners of war in cold blood. Shot them in an open field. A few lucky ones got away. They were with the 285th Field Artillery Observer Battalion. Those SS bastards just gunned them down like shooting fish in a barrel. Those are the boys we'll be fighting soon enough. There's plenty of SS Panzer divisions up in those woods in the Ardennes. So you fellas better be on your game."

McBurney felt a little shiver. The Black Panthers hadn't tangled yet with Waffen-SS troops, whom he had heard were some of the best-trained and toughest in the German Army. One thing he knew for sure: if he was caught by the SS, he wasn't going to surrender. Now that he knew what the bastards did to their captives, he had no choice but to fight to the death.

A pair of jeeps drove up. With great fanfare, they pulled to a halt before the long line of men waiting in front of the mobile field kitchen for their Christmas dinners. Jumping out of the vehicle with a bullhorn was an officer, who quickly announced that he was sorry but the 761st and the 87th Infantry were being ordered to move out on the double. A huge, collective groan went up from the tankers and infantrymen as today's Christmas meal was to be their first full hot meal in weeks.

"Damn, that's just our luck," grumbled Smitty.

McBurney felt his heart sink and stomach growl. "Man, I was looking forward to that turkey," he lamented.

"Me too," agreed Preston McNeil.

"Ain't nothing we can do about it—mount up," said Windsor, motioning them towards their Shermans.

With heads hanging low, McBurney and Devore began climbing aboard Taffy as Smith and McNeil shuffled off to their M4, Cool Stud. But to McBurney's surprise and delight, even though the turkeys had not finished baking, the cooks and servers began ripping off chunks of steaming, half-done meat from the baking birds and tossing them to the tankers as they mounted their Shermans and Stuarts. Jumping down from their tank, McBurney and Devore managed to snatch practically a whole turkey from the cooks.

But then, as they started to climb back on board, a white sergeant from the 87th brought them up short.

"Why the fuck you niggers even bother to fight?" he snarled. "Y'all ain't gonna change nothing!"

"Merry Christmas to you, too," said McBurney sarcastically, more worried about dropping the turkey breast and wing under his shoulder than defending his honor against some small-minded rabble-rouser.

"You weren't too smart to have joined the Army, boy," the sergeant continued to spew forth, his voice from the Deep South, most likely Alabama or Mississippi McBurney thought. "What are you even fighting for? When y'all get back home, you still won't be able to get a drink of water at a fountain or a meal in a restaurant. Hell, you still won't even grab a seat on a goddamn bus. So, what you doing here? What the fuck you fighting for, boy?"

The North Carolinian Devore, normally a good-natured and easygoing sort, dropped his slab of turkey meat on the tank, and jumped down from Taffy.

"We're fighting for the same reason you would be if you weren't nothing but a dumb cracker," he fired back. "Because we're red-blooded, Grade-A Americans doing our duty, that's why."

The sergeant snickered scornfully. "Hell, you ain't nothing but monkeys. I can't believe the Army actually lets you drive around in them tanks."

"Fuck you, you ignorant cracker!" roared Devore, and the skinny little scrapper started to close in on the bullet-headed sergeant with two closed fists.

Suddenly, Windsor's voice cut through the air as tank engines up and down the line began firing up.

"Get inside the tank now, Willie!" he commanded Devore. The TC had scrambled back down from Taffy to give the order. To the white sergeant, he then said, "You move along now, you hear. You're causing nothing but trouble."

"You fucking niggers—y'all don't deserve to be driving them tanks. You ain't nothing but monkeys. When this war is over, there still ain't gonna be nothing for you back home."

Windsor gave a combative smile. "We'll see who the monkeys are when we get to Belgium. While you're crawling on the ground to hide from the German machine guns, we'll be nice and safe in our armored tanks. Don't even ask to get in our vehicles when the shit hits—we don't take no *Southern* white boys. Now be on your way, cracker."

"Fucking nigger tankers!" snarled the sergeant one last time, and he waved his hand dismissively and stomped off.

Shaking their heads in a mixture of anger, amusement, disgust, and disbelief, the trio climbed down their hatches into Taffy. McBurney and Devore clutched their savory hunks of turkey like precious gems as they settled into their gunner and driver seats. Ten minutes later, the Sherman was rolling down the road.

McBurney was still simmering.

To his dismay, he realized that he truly didn't know what he was fighting for. Two and a half years earlier, he had volunteered to fight, and perhaps die, to preserve rights and privileges that his own fellow American soldiers were still insisting he would not be able to enjoy when he got back home. *How can that be?* he wondered. The white cracker was right. What was the point of fighting if there was no light— no freedom—at the end of the tunnel? He was suddenly angry at himself for allowing his country to use him as cannon fodder when nothing was going to change even after the goddamn war was won. Now he knew why his old man had been reluctant for him to join the Army and why he was so bitter about his experience as a Harlem Hellfighter in France.

The Black Panthers rolled west through the night, stopping for a maintenance check in the city of Bar-le-Due, France, the following afternoon. On December 27, they pivoted and began moving north, driving for two days. They stopped north of Reims, at Rethel, where they camped in the ruins of a WWI battlefield. The weather had turned bitter cold, with temperatures hovering around zero. Here the tankers learned that Patton's Third Army spearhead, the 4th Armored, had relieved Bastogne the day before. The town remained surrounded on three sides and German forces still prowled the area, but an Allied corridor into Bastogne had been opened up, thereby ending the first phase of the most dramatic battle yet of the war.

In the end, Major General Maxwell Taylor and Brigadier General Anthony McAuliffe and their men of the 101st Airborne Division had held out. But they had suffered more than 1,600 casualties. While the relief of Bastogne stood as a victory, the task of securing the huge swath around Bastogne still controlled by the Germans and pushing the enemy back across the Our and Rhine remained.

The 761st stood ready for the mission.

Before dawn on the 29th, as the crews warmed up their engines, the men took turns standing behind their tanks, grabbing a bit of heat from the exhaust fumes. They took off again, advancing in a column through the following night. Drivers strained to keep sight of the taillights of the tank in front of them. On the long drive north into Belgium, McBurney talked by headset to Devore to help keep him focused on his driving. In the grinding push up the steep, narrow Ardennes roads made treacherous by snow and ice, ten of the battalion's tanks were lost to accidents and mechanical breakdowns.

But the dangerous roads and Germans didn't bother McBurney as much as his fellow bigoted white soldiers. To his dismay, on the long journey north into Belgium, white Southern infantrymen being trucked to the front or walking along the road would shout out to him and his crew, "Where the hell you niggers going with them tanks? You ain't got no business in them!"

On December 30, they reached Offagne, Belgium, a small village located in the 87th Infantry Division's assembly area between Bertrix and Libramont. MPs directed the men and their Shermans and Stuarts to the woods two miles north of Offagne. The faint guns the men heard to the east were the sounds of a confused battle underway. Unbeknownst to the 761st, the untested 87th Infantry Division and 11th Armored Division were already engaging German forces. The cold and stiff 87th had stumbled out of their deuce-and-a-half trucks straight into the teeth of a massive German counterattack, a hail of mortar, artillery, and tank fire.

Just before dawn the next day, New Year's Eve, McBurney and the other members of Charlie Company rolled northeast from Offagne to join the 87th Division's 345th Infantry Regiment. What McBurney glimpsed in the white-shrouded woods along the road gave him pause: the remains of a desperately contested battlefield with blasted trees, upended jeeps, and grisly shattered bodies. The corpses, partly covered with snow, were casualties from the fighting ten days earlier, when the German Seventh Army broke through thinly spread elements of the 28th Infantry Division. Scattered among the ruins, farther on, were fresh shell craters and overturned, still-burning American vehicles. The inexperienced 345th had been badly mauled the day before.

The infantrymen had taken severe casualties against an elite German Panzer division, and directly to the east, Combat Command A of the 11th Armored Division, rushed to the front from training in England, had been slaughtered. The unit had suffered more than a hundred killed and wounded in its first twenty minutes of battle outside the village of Remagne. Despite such crushing losses, their presence had succeeded, as Patton had hoped, in turning the flank of the German forces approaching Bastogne.

The 11th Armored's Combat Command A had withdrawn at midnight across the woods to the east; the remnants of the 345th Infantry Regiment and C Company of the 761st were ordered to take over its zone of advance. Their orders were to continue pushing the Germans back from Bastogne. Charlie's tanks were first to attack the German outposts at Nimbermont and Rondu. From there they intended to proceed north, supporting the 345th Regiment's assault on fortified Remagne itself.

As the Germans hurled attack after attack against the Third Army front in sub-zero temperatures, McBurney realized he had never seen the enemy fight with more tenacity. The weather posed problems the Black Panthers had not previously experienced during their lengthy stateside training or in Lorraine and the Saar. The dense, shifting ground fog lent the terrain an unreal and ghoulish aspect. At times, the fog acted in the 761st's favor, neutralizing the superior range of the German guns. But more often than not, it simply helped to conceal the waiting enemy troops. The Germans, outfitted with gray-and-white winter uniforms, snow capes, and whitewashed tanks, were hard to make out until they opened fire. The American soldiers and tanks, lacking such camouflage, stood out like sore thumbs. Consequently, many of the infantrymen resorted to wrapping themselves in white bedsheets to conceal themselves in the snow.

As the Panthers continued to advance, McBurney fired his 76mm cannon at suspected machine-gun nests and antitank posts. His teeth and those of his brothers-in-arms chattered in the frigid cold even with extra blankets draped around them, as Sherman tanks were not equipped with heaters. Though it felt to him as if they were fighting inside an icebox, at least they had cover. The doughs, now comprised of a large number of clerks and supply men reassigned as infantry replacements, were even more exposed to the elements. They couldn't even dig foxholes in the hard, frozen ground and waist-deep snow.

In the fighting, he and the other younger crew members looked to the older and more-experienced Teddy Windsor, whose steady leadership ensured stability in the face of a Nazi enemy determined to blast the 761st out of the war. As a matter of routine, Windsor would receive his orders and he and the crew would move out on their next mission with little said. No fuss, no lengthy discussion, just move on to the next objective. McBurney appreciated the clear-cut simplicity.

Rondu and Nimbermont proved to be lightly defended and were taken easily. The attack on Remagne, however, promised to be more difficult, involving a push across open ground heavily mined and covered by high-velocity guns. C Company attempted to provide covering fire for the infantry before moving in to support the close-in fighting in the town. The Oklahoman Warren Crecy, as had become his custom, stood on his turret directing a constant stream of .50-caliber fire against German ground positions.

As the fighting escalated, McBurney saw the exposed, ragged line of American infantrymen stumbling and taking enemy hits on all sides. Although the footsoldiers were young, many of them only eighteen or nineteen, they somehow kept getting up and pressing forward. While the relationship between the 761st and the 87th Division was still strained—the racial remarks and distrust on the part of some of the infantry had left a bitterness on both sides that never fully disappeared—the two groups were now fighting at least with a grudging respect. Whatever their underlying attitudes, they had no choice but to work together and support each other when the Germans were knocking them down like bowling pins.

The two outfits continued their advance. McBurney and the other Charlie gunners knocked out three machine-gun nests and killed fourteen German gunners. Soon the resistance at Remagne dissolved and, when no enemy troops emerged from the surrounding woods to counterattack, the Americans were able to clear the town. The Germans seemed to have strategically fallen back. By the evening, the infantry and Charlie had succeeded in capturing all three of their assigned towns. But to McBurney, the fight that would become known as the Battle of the Bulge seemed like a desperate yard-by-yard struggle with no clear lines of advance.

On New Year's Eve, McBurney and the other tankers shivered in their tenuous forward positions, teeth chattering as they curled up in the interior compartments of their frosted and snow-covered Shermans. Their eyes were bloodshot from lack of sleep. Their combat fatigues and gloves were threadbare and stained with motor oil and gunpowder. McBurney, huddled against Willie Devore, wore his mackintosh, two pairs of pants, two shirts, and every single piece of clothing he could find along with a pair of wool blankets, but this did little to stave off the biting cold.

New Year's morning brought sleet, snow, and plummeting temperatures as the tank battalion and infantry started towards the primary objective, the Belgian village of Tillet. It was considered by the brass to be a vital town to the Germans because of its east-west road. The order to the company commanders from the 761st's new commander, Major George, who had slipped into the battalion CO slot in place of the indifferent Colonel Hunt with ease, had been unambiguous: "Clear Tillet." The word trickled down through the crews. McBurney and some of the other tankers believed the order had come from the top from Patton himself.

But there was a more immediate and troublesome problem—the weather. Temperatures continued to plummet as the 761st and doughs made their way towards Tillet, pushing through heavy snowdrifts. The worsening conditions worked to the enemy's favor. Visibility deteriorated, negating any possible Allied air support on ground targets, and slippery ice and thick snow made the roads in and around Bastogne hazardous to impassable.

Driver Willie Devore found that the intense cold had one blessing: the ground was frozen so rock solid that it provided him with traction to maneuver off the main roads. Yet, even as the Sherman drivers drove off-road and ploughed their way through the deep snow drifts, the progress was slow. That's when Dog Company's complement of Stuart tanks again proved worth their weight in gold. Their lighter armor allowed them to almost glide over the ice and snow compared to the M4s. The Stuarts sacrificed protection from AP rounds, but they stood a better chance of reaching the fight.

But there was an even tougher obstacle in their path to take Tillet. Though they did not know it, the 761st's tanks were heading straight into awaiting elements of one of Hitler's top armored units. G-2 was reporting that the Panzer Lehr Division was stationed between Bastogne and Tillet. Created around a group of top instructors from the Nazi tank-training schools, the Panzer Lehr held tremendous pride for the Führer and stood as one of his most trusted units. The majority of the soldiers in the unit were decorated veterans of the Russian Front well versed in winter warfare. And the Panzer Lehr stood ready to fight, with more than forty tanks, far exceeding what the hardscrabble 761st could cobble together.

But more importantly, the crack outfit had orders from Hitler to defend the road leading to Bastogne at all costs.

# CHAPTER 38

## LUXEMBOURG CITY TO HOUFFALIZE
## SOUTHEAST BELGIUM

### JANUARY 8, 1945

"GODDAMN MONTY," grumbled Patton. "He just doesn't get it."

Master Sergeant William Meeks, clutching the general's heavy winter parka for him to put on, looked at him sympathetically. "What's he done now, sir?"

"The unspeakable, George, that's what. For tactical purposes, Ike has placed part of Brad's forces—the First and Ninth Armies—under Monty in the north sector of the bulge. But then yesterday, Monty gives a press conference and announces that we Americans have bungled badly in the Ardennes and that he—Sir Bernard of Lancelot—has come to the rescue of the foundering U.S. Army. And not a moment too soon, I might add. He didn't even mention any of our forces involved in the battle. He just praised himself for half an hour. Brad and Ike are furious, of course."

"I'm sorry to hear that, General," said Meeks, helping him slip on his parka.

"The fact is I respect Monty as a military planner—but the son of a bitch just can't move an army. And he has even less of an understanding of politics than me— and that's goddamn saying something. He's been a thorn in Ike's side for the past three months and I'm told it's only getting worse."

"You remember what I said about him back in August, General? When he was holding at Caen while you and General Bradley were carrying the football?"

"As a matter of fact I do, George. But tell it to me again because it was as poetic as Shakespeare."

"I said, sir, that if old Monty didn't get a move on, those British soldiers were going to have grass and limpets growing on their left foot from standing in the water. The man just doesn't know how to get his troops fired up and moving."

"And now he's taken Brad's U.S. First and Ninth Armies. Sir Monty wants to go at the industrial Ruhr with forty divisions, leaving Brad and I with the leftovers to guard his flank. He thinks the good ole US of A is nothing but a bunch of second-stringers here to expand British imperial rule. What do you think of that, George?"

"Why I think it's a shame, sir. Especially with all our men dying."

"Now that's a fact. Look, I love Monty and the British—they're our allies, goddamnit, and that means something to me—but when they tell our officers that we don't know how to lead our men into battle or how to fight, why that just doesn't sit right in my craw. And when the British men—not the women, mind you, because they love our GIs—tell our troops that they are 'overpaid, oversexed and over here' when they're dying by the tens of thousands coming to Great Britain's aid, well that just makes me angry as hell."

"As it should, sir," said the orderly, reaching for the general's self-designed leather gun belt holding a pair of ivory-handled pistols: a Colt .45 and Smith and Wesson .357 magnum. "But when they say those things to us, we know what to say right back. We just tell those British boys that they are 'underpaid, undersexed and *under* Eisenhower.'"

"I couldn't have said it better myself, George. But this whole thing with Monty has been tough on Brad."

"Sounds to me like General Eisenhower has either sidelined him due to a lack of confidence, or he's afraid Monty will 'regroup' again. Maybe he thinks giving Monty two American armies is the only way to keep that boy moving."

"I suspect you're right. But I still feel bad for Brad."

Though Patton still regarded the Missourian as too timid and unimaginative for Army Group command, he still thought highly of him and did his best to protect him from the wolves at SHAEF and from the poaching Monty, who, because the British had tapped out their reserve of replacement troops from Great Britain and the Commonwealth countries, was relying on American manpower for replacements.

"Sometimes, George, I think it's a hell of a lot easier to be a sergeant, like you, than a general. When you get to the top, you become nothing but a target. I've had a bullseye on my chest for the past two years now."

Meeks fastened Patton's leather holster about his waist. "I'll keep those words of wisdom in mind when I'm a general commanding three hundred thousand men."

Patton turned around and grinned his bucktoothed grin at the aide. "Goddamn, that's why I love you, you old Buffalo Soldier—you always know the right thing to say. Now I've got to get on the road."

"No breakfast today, General?"

"Nope, not today—just coffee. I want to get out there and see my boys. It's a fine day to be killing Krauts."

"Yes, sir, I reckon it is," said the black man in his easy Georgia lilt.

With his heavy coat buttoned against the frigid January gusts and his trusty driver Sergeant Mims behind the wheel, Old Blood and Guts set out on the road, darting to and fro amongst his frontline units, checking on progress, barking out commands, joking with the troops, and giving encouragement—in a way that the Brits Montgomery and Dempsey and the Yanks Bradley, Hodges, Devers, Patch, and Eisenhower, who had never tasted battle, never could have. He looked imposing in his down parka, thick helmet, and ivory pistols strapped on for the occasion, a big White Owl dangling from his mouth. He had Mims drive him along the icy, snow-swept roads to each and every division post in his command jeep, its Plexiglas windows and .30-caliber machine gun protecting him against both the Germans and the cruel Belgian wind and snow. At each stop, he told the troops, "I believe that the Bastogne operation is the biggest and best the Third Army has accomplished, and I'm going to make sure you troops get the credit for your great work."

He had made his frontline presence felt in the same manner on Christmas Day. After ordering that every soldier in the Third Army was to have a hot turkey dinner for Christmas, he had ensured that his orders were carried out by driving from one unit to another to make sure the men got their meals. He and Mims drove around from 0600 in the morning until well into the night, stopping at every frontline unit to visit with the troops and make sure their turkey meals had been delivered.

As they drove north into Southeast Belgium, Mims had to work hard to navigate the treacherous roads to keep from slipping off. But Patton wasn't paying attention to the icy roads or foul weather. With Bastogne relieved and the German offensive held in check, he was thinking about how hard he was going to stick it to the Krauts tomorrow when he launched his own counterattack against them.

He had much to be thankful for in the New Year. Since the fall of 1943, he had gone from the doghouse to the top of the heap. He had captured Brittany and Lorraine, bridged the Seine, the Moselle, the Saar, and dozens of other smaller rivers, and had liberated hundreds of towns and cities. But the past three weeks had been his pièce de résistance: his reputation now soared as a result of a battle that gripped the minds of the public like no other since D-Day and the breakout from the hedgerow country in August. It had been a long wait in that grimy Sicilian doghouse, but now that he had turned his army ninety degrees in three days under horrific winter conditions, rescued Bastogne, and was tearing into von Manteuffel and Co. in the Ardennes, Old Blood and Guts's star had risen higher than that of any general in the Allied ranks. His army stood at nearly 350,000 men, seventeen divisions in all, and Bradley had just decorated him with a second Oak Leaf Cluster to his Distinguished Service Medal.

But mostly he was proud of his men. Though he knew the battle was far from over and that far more blood would have to be spilled to push the enemy out of the Ardennes, the German offensive had at least been thwarted in its tracks and the Krauts were on the defensive. And it was all thanks to the American soldier, Patton knew. The average GI was the one who had bought time for his commanders, who had embarrassingly been caught flat-footed, to regroup and bring mobility and airpower into play. It was the American soldier who had halted the German *blitzkrieg* and made the generals look good. And the freezing-cold tankers and doughs out there were not finished. They understood more Germans had to die, and they remained equally aware they would lose more of their own. But they kept on pushing forward in sub-zero temperatures and driving snow and wind.

The war had changed for the tankers and footsloggers of his vaunted Third Army. Until he had turned his army and started north, the fight had been an officers' war—a chessboard war planned by the brass and led by them. But now the winds had shifted. The grunts and NCOs of the Third Army would drive the Germans back first across the Our, then the Rhine, and finally all the way to goddamn Berlin.

But he knew it wasn't going to be easy. His three divisions had broken the back of the siege at Bastogne, but the relief of the important crossroads didn't signify the end of American troubles in the region. Although it was evident by the first week of January that Hitler's strategic aim of splitting the Allies in half was doomed to failure, thus sealing Germany's ultimate fate, no one bothered to inform the soldiers of the German Army who were hungry, frozen, and low on supplies and ammunition but somehow still high in morale. Patton understood only too well that the Allies could still lose the war. The Germans were colder and hungrier, but they were the better fighters in winter warfare in his estimation, having several divisions that had fought on the brutal Eastern Front.

As he and Mims drove on to the next forward command post, his thoughts returned, as they so often did, to the situation with Monty and Ike. Though he loved and respected Ike, it seemed as if his old buddy had gotten too big for his brushed-wool trousers. Consumed with politics, he was forgetting his pals. As hard as Patton had worked to bring glory to the U.S Army—and its supreme commander—he couldn't help but feel Ike had no interest in thanking him. He had long preached to his officers that a pat on the back was worth ten kicks in the ass, and he had spent the past three weeks relentlessly encouraging his officers and men in the Ardennes. Was it too much to ask for a pat on the back from Ike every now and then?

But what Patton was convinced of most of all was that more aggressive leadership at the top would have put the Allies against the Rhine long ago. After Third Army had relieved Bastogne on December 26, Patton and several other generals—including SHAEF Chief of Staff Beetle Smith and Lieutenant General Brian Horrocks, Montgomery's XXX Corps commander—advocated cutting the bulge at its base, rather than at Bastogne. But Ike wanted the safe bet, a coordinated "big picture" attack. Patton fumed. He knew that if Ike would only put Bradley back in command of the First and Ninth Armies and turn himself and Brad loose, the Allies could bag the whole German army. He wished Ike were more of a gambler.

But for all the flaws he found in Ike's command, what he feared and dreaded more than anything else was that Ike—or more likely someone above him—would knuckle under and place Montgomery in command of the ground war. Ike was his friend, Ike had been there for him, and Old Blood and Guts could only imagine how intolerable life would be if "God Almonty," as the Canadians called him, directed the war. As he had on several occasions before, Patton steeled himself to quit in protest if Ike gave in. In his view, if Monty wanted to be deputy ground commander of all troops in Europe, then Patton would ask to be relieved.

In his view, one of the gravest mistakes of the war was that he was not on at least equal footing with Bradley and Monty. He knew it was his own damned fault for self-destructing his career in Sicily, but it still stung to have to play second fiddle to the uninspiring, indecisive Brad on the one hand and the decisive but overly cautious and plodding Monty on the other. The record indisputably showed that the latter was incapable of adapting on the fly and engaging in the type of rapid-movement *blitzkrieg* approach of their enemies. A sense of urgency just wasn't in the man.

Deep down though, Patton knew that the best plan to conquer Nazi Germany would be for him and Monty to be the two primary army group commanders under Ike, as had been the case in Sicily. For all his private complaints about Monty, he was fully capable and willing to work with the British general—but only as an equal. He knew they would both work effectively together for they both respected one another and were often in agreement. Their interests were professional and tied to the operational scene, and their strengths were complementary. The rapid thrust and drive of Patton and the set-battle-piece planning capability and balance of Montgomery would have produced a perfectly matched team, Patton knew. The end result would have been a quicker breakout from Normandy and happier resolution of Overlord, a firm entrapment of the Germans west of the Seine at Falaise, and a swift annihilation of the Germans at the moment at the bulge. The only military drawback he saw with Montgomery was that war required the taking of risks and, for all his strengths in planning large set-piece battles, the British general refused to take them unless he had a massive numerical advantage in men and equipment.

But the biggest problem with Monty, in Patton's mind, was that he didn't respect Ike. He looked down sneeringly at the supreme commander for his humble Kansas upbringing and lack of combat experience, and he didn't want to be subordinate to him any longer. He was using every means in his arsenal—including lobbying Churchill and Brooke, Patton had been informed—to push out Ike and assume control over all ground forces. But Monty appeared to have overreached, and both Patton and Bradley had recently soured on the man. Where previously there had existed a measure of mutual respect for the British general, there was now mostly contempt. Especially when they learned that Ike had recently said to a reporter, "I can work with anyone except that son of a bitch!" Patton doubted that the politically naïve Monty even recognized how deeply resentful most American commanders had become of him in the past two months.

Monty's disrespectful treatment towards their boss and continual pleas to take over command of all ground forces for his "dagger thrust" into the Ruhr—despite his failures at Caen, at Argentan, at Nijmegen, and at Antwerp—had actually pulled Patton and Bradley closer together. With Monty increasingly becoming a thorn in their sides and especially that of Ike, they worked well and joked often to keep up their own spirits and those of their staffs. They even called each other "Brad" and "George" in front of junior officers, instead of the usual "General Bradley" and "General Patton" they used in mixed company. Bradley needed his subordinate to eradicate the bulge and return him to the offensive, and he had given Patton a mission that was the kind the cavalryman dreamed of: riding to the rescue and hitting the enemy in both the flank and rear.

Soon Patton and Mims were heading on the road to Arlon, the headquarters of III Corps, to arrange tomorrow's attack at the village of Houffalize, north of Bastogne. As the road became clogged with vehicles, Mims was forced to bring the command vehicle to a halt. With the temperature six degrees below zero, Patton stepped out to take a look ahead. He quickly saw that the line of trucks and armored vehicles stretched for miles. On one side of the narrow road, he saw a column filled with trucks carrying infantry of the 90th Infantry Division forward for tomorrow's attack; and on the other side, heading in the opposite direction, was a convoy of ambulances bringing the wounded of another division back to the rear.

*I am so damn proud of you boys,* he thought as water vapor steamed from his nostrils. *If you only knew how goddamn much I love you.*

It was then a great and wondrous thing happened.

As the trucks carrying the infantry forward to attack drove by, the troops recognized Patton and, leaning out of their trucks, they cheered wildly and waved their arms. The men, he knew, had been cramped in their icy-cold trucks for several hours, and were undoubtedly thoroughly chilled. And yet, hundreds and hundreds of them broke into rousing cheers, waving and leaning out of their trucks in a glorious salute to their leader—and to the cause of freedom.

Patton broke into a huge smile and stood there, waving back and saluting at them, as the trucks rolled past, one after the other, to the battlefront. He was so moved that he couldn't hold back the tears, which streamed down his face and froze like icicles. Tomorrow many of those now cheering, men who were his direct responsibility, would be dead—because of his orders. And yet, to see them waving and cheering and ready to lay down their lives in the name of freedom was the most heartrending experience of his life, especially knowing what the ambulances on the other side of the road held.

# CHAPTER 39

## TILLET, SOUTHEASTERN BELGIUM

### JANUARY 9, 1945

AS MCBURNEY checked over his main gun and coaxial one last time in the early-morning darkness, he shivered against the bitter cold. The thermometer read six degrees below again. The steel of the tank was so frigid that even wearing his gloves he could scarcely stand to touch the ice-frosted sidewalls.

Thinking of the fight that lay ahead today, he thought, *Man, it's going to be a cold and bloody one.*

The 761st had received orders to take the lead in a renewed assault on Tillet—a small village that had proved a thorn in Third Army's side for several days. The combined force of tankers and 87th Infantry had hit a German wall of resistance on each previous attack, but like Joe Louis coming at Max Schmeling in the ring in 1938, they were taking another run at the stubbornly held objective. Tillet and the surrounding area were of critical strategic importance to the Germans as the road leading to the hamlet was part of a major highway system running southwest from St. Vith through Houffalize, Bastogne, and St. Hubert to the Meuse River. In Patton's mind, control of the roads in the Ardennes equaled control of the battle. To that end, the Black Panthers had been ordered to lead the infantry into Tillet, cut off the Brussels-Bastogne Highway, and link up with the First Army—all with only two tattered, depleted companies of Shermans.

After several days of furious fighting, the 761st and 87th Infantry had been unable to seize the Belgian village, even with the doughs engaging in punishing house-to-house combat. On each attempt, they had been pushed back by the suicidally determined Führer Begleit Brigade, which had relieved the Panzer Lehr Division. Having once served as Hitler's personal palace guard, the Führer Begleit, like the Panzer Lehr, had been created around some of the premier tank soldiers in the German Army, members of the Grossdeutschland Panzer Division that had earned its reputation on the Eastern Front. The brigade was a big outfit, equipped with seventy-one tanks and assault guns and supported by a range of heavy artillery and self-propelled weapons. Its handpicked soldiers fought with a discipline and dedication that Oscar Koch and his Third Army intelligence team called "fanatical."

During the past ten days of intense combat in Belgium, the severe cold and lack of sleep McBurney and the other members of the 761st faced had reduced life to fighting to stay alive and keep warm. Their first thought wasn't about winning the war, but rather about getting food and shelter at the next village. The battle had become what McBurney and GIs everywhere in the Ardennes were calling "the bitter battle for the billets." They fought tenaciously to take the next town for the simple purpose of gaining access to whatever lodgings and food it might afford.

As dawn broke across the frigid wintry landscape, the 761st and 346th Infantry Battalion of the 87th Infantry gathered all along the designated line of departure. The footsoldiers clustered around the massive M4 Shermans as if they were being protected by a herd of elephants. As he prepared to climb aboard Taffy, McBurney was struck by the doughs' youth and their air of bewilderment and vulnerability. He looked at his buddy Leonard Smith—who was joining his crew today as a loader since Cool Stud was down for maintenance—and saw that he had noticed it too. Though McBurney and Smith were only twenty years old, these troops looked to them as if they had been pulled straight from a high school history class. One of the soldiers closest to their tank carried a bazooka so awkwardly that McBurney realized he had likely never even fired the weapon before.

*Damn,* he thought, *are we really going up against crack German outfits with these greenhorns? Third Army must be running out of goddamn bodies.*

After a few final words from the officers, they mounted up and started rolling forward towards Tillet. Though the 761st was depleted of tanks and men from the past ten days of hard fighting, they had prepped well for the attack. They had spent all day yesterday gathering all available firepower. McBurney and the other gunners had made it clear they wanted as much weaponry as possible, and Windsor and the other tank commanders obliged by scavenging what they could find for their gunners. But just as importantly, the round-the-clock maintenance crews had performed the necessary tweaks and repairs on Taffy, Cool Stud, Crecy, and the other tanks to carry them through the 761st's most important attack yet. The depleted battalion was throwing everything it had into the mission—eleven Shermans, two assault guns, the mortar platoon with three 81mm mortars, and one platoon of five reliable Stuart light tanks. The supreme irony was that the battalion had taken so many casualties in the past two months, with only limited replacements, that most tanks were reduced to crews of four, operating without their bow gunners and the firepower of their .30-caliber machine guns.

The tanks ground forward, each one leading its own small group of infantry. There were no clear military guidelines for their mission except to seize the village and take the contested hills and ridges surrounding it. The area they had to cover was wide, divided by ridges and thick stands of trees. Advancing in a clear line was impossible and the Shermans quickly lost sight of one another. As they continued to advance through the early morning fog and snow, their radio transmission was scrambled by German interference.

The voice of Axis Sally came over the airwaves, along with the unexpected and haunting sound of Louis Armstrong's version of *I Can't Give You Anything but Love, Baby.* McBurney and the rest of the crew often listened to the American female propagandist for the Third Reich whose signature line black and white GIs loved to mimic: "Go easy, boys—there's danger ahead." But the sound of the legendary Louis Armstrong in the background made him feel genuinely worried about what the Germans had in store for them today.

"Good morning, Negro soldiers of the 761st," crooned Axis Sally. "I am sorry that you will die today in Tillet. Our fight is not with the Negroes in America, and your fight is not with us. Your fellow Negroes are rioting in Cleveland. Your commander, Captain Williams, is leading you to death and destruction. He is white and not one of you. Your battalion commander, Major George, is also white and not one of you. Leave your tanks now and return home to Cleveland where you are needed and you will not be killed…"

"Captain Williams and Major George?" cried Smitty as Axis Sally continued to drone on. "Man, how does that bitch know all this shit?"

"German intelligence," answered Windsor. "They got G-2s too, you know."

"I think her voice is sexy," said Devore, navigating Taffy with both hands as the upbeat, brassy notes from Armstrong's trumpet echoed in the cold, steel tank.

"You think so?" challenged Smitty. "Why I'd bet you'd have sex with Veronika Dankeschön if you could."

"Who the hell is Veronika Dankeschön?" asked Devore.

Smitty grinned devilishly. "Haven't you seen *Yank* magazine?"

"Yeah, I seen it."

"Well, they got a cartoon reminding us GIs to avoid the temptation of Veronika Dankeschön so we don't get VD."

"Oh, I've seen that cartoon," said Windsor. "And the Veronika I saw was definitely not my type. She was a real porker with braided pigtails and a fondness for sauerkraut."

"Man, that Kraut bitch sounds nasty," sniffed Devore, wrinkling his nose in disapproval. "But I still think Axis Sally's voice is sexy as hell."

"Yeah, she's sexy all right," allowed McBurney. "But I still don't like that girl. She shouldn't be spouting Nazi propaganda to the beat of our boy Satchmo. That's just wrong, man."

There were murmurs of agreement all around. "Don't worry," said Windsor, chuckling. "When the war's over, they'll probably hang her as a war criminal along with Lord Hah-Hah and Goebbels."

"Amen to that," said Smitty. He then sang along with Armstrong, but changing the words: "*I Can't Give You Anything but a Hangman's Noose, Baby!*"

At that moment, the Third Army artillery opened up with a thunderous advance round of fire to soften up the German positions. The battalion was greeted in return with pinpointed artillery fire. The advancing column took heavy casualties, as the Führer Begleit Brigade had concealed forward artillery observers throughout the valley. As the 761st tanks and the infantry pressed forward to near the edge of Tillet, enemy fire tore in from every direction. But with the tanks widely spaced as they moved up the valley, none of the shells hit near Taffy. Still, with the Germans taking out tanks and individual platoons coming under a fury of fire, soon Windsor was ordered to advance on Charlie Company's outside flank to relieve the pressure.

Despite the echo of artillery and machine guns blasting away across the valley, they continued to advance on their lone trek with no enemy resistance. A platoon of infantrymen trudged along stolidly behind the tank, and McBurney thought to himself, *Man, am I glad to be in here and not out there.* Taffy's 400-horsepower gasoline engine throbbed and puffed exhaust into the frigid January air. Devore focused intently on the frozen snow and ice immediately in front of the tracks. He navigated the Sherman with his usual wily confidence despite the frigid temperature, shell craters, and snow-packed terrain all around them.

The intercom twitched with static. As they ground slowly forward with still no sign of the enemy, McBurney couldn't help but feel they might be walking into a trap. Or maybe a minefield.

He could tell the rest of the crew felt it too. There was a tense anticipation in the air. Peering through his horizontal telescopic turret sight, he could see little more than slivers of white. But what was even more frustrating was that, in his enlisted man's perpetual state of need-to-know uncertainty, he didn't know precisely where they were, what German outfit they were up against, or what their ultimate military objective was. Even Windsor had only been told in advance that they were heading to Tillet and that their job was to neutralize any Germans encountered along the way. The limited visibility, frigid cold, and desolate winter landscape made the situation even more eerie and uncertain.

Directly before them, over a slight rise, lay an open field flanked by dense pine woods on the far side. There seemed to be no easy way around it; approaching the big field, they had a moment's choice either to advance or retreat. Peering through his telescopic sight, McBurney could see the clearing was exposed and that they could be taken out by enfilading or defilading fire. Which meant they were seriously fucked if they continued across the field and the enemy was hiding out in the trees or ridges beyond. After two months of fighting, he had no remaining illusions about the protective capabilities of the Sherman tank or its many hazards in combat, particularly when advancing with open flanks and a young, inexperienced, and frightened group of infantrymen.

"Stop!" barked the TC Windsor over his intercom mike, the pork chop, apparently coming to the same conclusion as McBurney that they were too out in the open and exposed.

Devore brought Taffy to a skidding halt. Windsor popped his head out the tank to confer with the infantry sergeant. The two men talked while the doughs urinated on their frozen M-1 rifle bolts to free them in the bitter cold. The sergeant, too, was aware of the threat of ambush, but like Windsor he was doggedly determined to lead his troops forward per their orders. Climbing back into the tank, the TC ordered Devore to continue forward.

"Keep a sharp eye out, Sergeant," he said to McBurney.

For the next few minutes, the two men and accompanying infantry strained to peer ahead through the wintry-white landscape for the enemy they all knew was waiting for them like a pack of predatory wolves.

"Far trees, one o'clock—I think we may have bogeys," said Windsor to his turret gunner over the intercom. "Stand by, Billy."

"I got eyes on 'em." Clearing the frost from his sights, McBurney kept his reticle trained on the far trees and stood ready to fire.

But there was still no sign of the enemy.

They continued forward. As they moved further into the clearing, the tension in the freezing cold tank continued to escalate. They were still too damned exposed, McBurney knew. But they couldn't turn around when their orders were to press forward until they made contact with the enemy. Smith stood anxiously in his loader's compartment where the sightlines were as narrow as archers' slits. Devore took care to negotiate around the shell craters and clumps of frozen bodies from the last several days of fighting. The fallen were captured in death poses like marble statues, with the bitter cold having turned the skin the purplish-red color of wine from the blood in the capillaries freezing swiftly upon death.

Soon, they had advanced far enough without any sign of the enemy that it seemed to McBurney as though they might actually make it. But, once they were halfway across the snow field, they were now so exposed against the sea of white that he couldn't escape the feeling they were in imminent danger. Seconds later, when the first 88-millimeter antitank shell came roaring in, he knew they had been lured into a clever trap.

"I was right…bogeys one o'clock!" cried Windsor over Taffy's intercom as the first shell exploded right in front of them. "Two Mark IVs! Loader, I need AP!"

Leonard Smith rammed an armor-piercing shell into the breech. "Got a little present for you, Fritz!"

"Gunner, traverse right…steady on…eight hundred yards!"

Now McBurney could see them along the treeline: two whitewashed German Mark IV Panzer tanks with their 11-foot, 8-inch long main cannons, a score of infantrymen, and a pair of antitank guns. The turret traversed with an electric whine. He would go for a hull shot; it was the largest target with the least chance of missing.

"Ready!" he shouted into his mike once he lowered the reticle and locked on.

"Fire!" cried Windsor.

Gritting his teeth, McBurney slapped his foot down on the trigger, unloading with the 76mm cannon on one of the tanks, and then with the .30-caliber coaxial on the *Panzerfaust* antitank unit. The main-gun shot on the tank ricocheted off the Panzer, but the coaxial proved lethal for the soft targets. Though the winter-clad enemy was almost indistinguishable from the snow and backdrop of white-capped trees, McBurney managed to knock down several infantrymen and troopers in the German antitank crew.

They fell like dominoes.

Smith yanked another AP shell off the wall, rammed it into the breech, and ducked aside as the breech kicked back after firing, jamming home another and ejecting the spent cartridge in one continuous motion. Now the Germans' machine-gun bullets pinged and ponged against the tank's steel sides and mowed down the infantry like bowling pins.

"Loader, AP again!" cried Windsor frantically. "Traverse a hair right…steady-on…range still eight hundred!"

McBurney turned his handwheels to fine-tune his aim. "Ready!" he said into his mike once he had the target in his sights and Smith had jammed in the AP round.

"Fire!"

This time he scored a hit on the Mark IV on the right with his powerful 76mm cannon. But the shot had struck the thick part of the armor and he wasn't sure if he had completely disabled the Panzer.

"Hit that motherfucker again!" cried Windsor.

Over the next three minutes—which seemed to McBurney like an eternity—the TC called out targets to McBurney in his gunner's chair and gave commands to Devore to drive and turn Taffy any way he could to escape enemy fire. In response, the Germans unleashed a barrage from their two tanks, machine guns, and artillery. Dragon-like tongues of fire burst forth, green lances of tracer crisscrossed the battlefield, and a rain of high-velocity 75- and 88-millimeter shells and machine-gun bullets began pelting the snow all around the Sherman. The whistling 88mm projectiles crashed in first too long and then too short—the German were attempting to bracket them—while Devore shifted gears furiously, fighting to swing the tank around and get Taffy the hell out of trouble. Windsor then called for high-explosive shells instead of armor-piercing rounds to take out the Germans, thinking that maybe a dose of HE would mix things up and keep the enemy off balance.

"Jesus Christ, I think we somehow got behind the Kraut lines!" cried Windsor over the intercom. "Man, are they coming in hot!"

An explosion rippled beneath their feet. The tank coughed and sputtered.

"What the hell?" gasped Devore.

"Shit, was that a land mine?" asked McBurney.

"I don't know!" said Windsor. "But we got hit by something!"

Even without the chaos of motion, neither the infantry nor any of the tankers had had any chance, in the unmarked snow, of spotting the buried Tellermine. But somehow the thirty-three-ton vehicle had set off a full pound of TNT—rocking the Sherman with such force that it seemed to the crew like a "Ripsaw" 88.

Now the M4 shuddered to a complete halt.

"Reverse gear! Quickly now!" cried Windsor.

"I'm trying!" replied Devore.

"Back the fuck up now, Willie!"

"I can't, man! She won't budge!"

McBurney considered his buddy Willie Devore the best tank driver in the entire battalion; if he couldn't get the M4 moving, no one could.

*Come on, Willie, come on!*

But despite the grinding gears, the goddamn Sherman wouldn't move. The tracks had been blown off and the wheels were spinning in the snow. Stuck out in the open in a paralyzed, flammable target, Windsor quickly realized they had no choice but to evacuate.

"Get out now! Abandon tank!"

The crew had been trained on the evacuation procedure when a Sherman was incapacitated by the enemy. Windsor quickly scrambled out the commander's turret hatch with McBurney and Smith close behind, all of them clutching their .45-caliber M3 submachine guns.

Outside of the tank, the whizzing bullets and artillery fire reverberated in a deafening roar. The cold snow scalded McBurney's bare hands and face as he crawled under the blanket of bullets. He glanced back to make sure Devore was right behind them. But while Windsor and Smith had crawled along with him from the tank into the snow, the South Carolinian was still half-inside the tank, standing up in his seat with his head and torso sticking out of the driver's hatch.

"Come on, Willie, let's go!" shouted Smith.

"Jump, Willie, jump!" screamed McBurney.

But he wouldn't budge. To McBurney, it looked as if he was frozen in place, blind to who or where he was.

At that precise moment, an 88 shell came roaring in. The explosion from the incoming shell was as sudden as it was devastating. Nearly decapitated, Willie Devore folded and toppled over like a stringless puppet.

"Noooo!" screamed Smith, lurching back towards the immobilized tank.

McBurney blocked him. From his angle of vision, he now saw that Devore was gone. The 88 strike had taken off half the technician-fifth grade's head.

A second later, the tank exploded as the ammunition stowed on board ignited in a burst of flame and mushroom cloud of smoke.

"Goddamn Willie's dead, man!" cried Smith, weeping openly now as the three tankers stared in awe and disbelief at the inferno blazing from the turret and hatches.

Wailing and half-crazed from shock, Smith clamored through the waist-deep snow towards the crippled Sherman. McBurney again cut off his path and pulled him back from the flames.

"I don't belong here!" screamed Smith. "I don't fucking belong here!"

"None of us do, goddamnit!" shouted McBurney. "But we can't worry about Willie—we've got to tend to ourselves!"

"He's right!" shouted Windsor. "We're both sorry about Willie, Smitty, but this ain't no time to grieve! All we can do now is survive!"

They again came under heavy German fire along with the three infantrymen still alive. But the doughs, unprotected by the tank, went down in a hailstorm of machine-gun bullets. McBurney and Windsor returned fire with their grease guns at the treeline.

Though they took out a pair of the white-clad infantry, McBurney could tell that the smart move would be to retreat from the enemy as fast as possible rather than shoot at them. Their .45-caliber M3 submachine guns had a normal accuracy of less than fifty percent at twenty-five yards, let alone over a hundred yards and while the enemy was moving. But more importantly, they were greatly outnumbered and the Germans were closing in on them.

Windsor realized it too. "We've got to get the hell out of here or we're dead!"

McBurney looked at his buddy Smitty. Seeing that he seemed in a state of shock at witnessing the death of their friend, he grabbed him by the collar to set him in motion. Amid the tumult of falling shells and spitting machine-gun bullets, the three tankers headed south with Windsor in the lead, stumbling over the bodies of the infantrymen that had fallen moments before.

One of the Panzers moved forward from the trees to fire its machine-gun at them. The remaining Germans continued their barrage from the woods: a company of infantrymen, a second Panzer Mark IV, and two antitank guns firing 88s. They had obviously expected to face down a much larger assault force than one single Sherman and platoon of infantrymen.

With bullets whistling past, Smith moved excruciatingly slowly at first. But with prodding from McBurney and Windsor, he seemed to get a grip on himself and moved more rapidly. Soon, they were able to put some distance between themselves and the Germans. But they were still badly exposed and under heavy fire. It was worse than anything McBurney had imagined from the belly of the tank.

They plodded forward through the deep snow with Windsor out front, McBurney behind him, and Smith some distance behind McBurney, all three men freezing cold and struggling in the heavy drifts. McBurney had no idea where Windsor was trying to lead them. After a hundred yards, McBurney looked back to make sure Smith was keeping up. To his relief, he seemed to be doing okay. But then suddenly, a pile of snow gave way without warning and his buddy disappeared into some sort of hole.

McBurney fought his way through the snow back to him. As he reached down to help him out, he saw that his friend was staring into the face of a freshly killed, unusually handsome, white U.S soldier with a pair of blue eyes. There were other bodies too, but they were frozen stiff. It took McBurney a moment to realize that Smitty had stumbled into a trench packed with a recently deceased infantryman and what looked to be more than a dozen dead doughs killed during earlier fighting.

Windsor waved to them and called for them to come on. Green bolts of tracer flared against the wintry backdrop of barren white; swarms of bullets snarled past their ears like angry hornets. Spotting the German infantrymen stalking them from along the edge of the trees, McBurney returned fire, struggling to keep them at bay with his greaser.

"We can't stay here, Smitty! We gotta go, man!"

For a moment, his buddy seemed not to understand and to still be in shock. But with prodding, McBurney got him moving again. They quickly put 10 yards between them and the Germans, then 20 yards, 50 yards, and finally 100 with bullets chasing after them. But as they continued wading through the heavy snow, the adrenaline rush that had accompanied their escape thus far dissipated and they began to tire. Especially McBurney. During the attack, his every muscle had burned with an urge to action, but he began to feel as though he was moving in place. His fingers were so numb, he could no longer find the trigger of his .45 even with his gloves.

The enemy rounds continued to fall all around them. In the early stages of hypothermia, McBurney had trouble believing that they were in fact real bullets and that people were trying to kill him. It seemed unthinkable that he was attempting to make his escape under heavy fire through an open field in a country to whom he was a total stranger.

After another 100 yards of staggering through the snow, he came to a halt. It was so frigid it hurt to breathe. His fingers were now too numb to even pull the trigger of his grease gun. The edge of the woods they were making their way towards was still a mile away—an impossibly far distance in the bitter cold and deep snow. It wasn't hopelessness that made him stop and fall to his knees but a simple dawning realization: he was too cold to go on and it didn't matter what he did or did not do.

His buddy's voice came from behind.

"Come on man, we gotta keep moving," Smith urged the gunner, the roles now reversed. "If we stay here, we're dead men."

McBurney just looked at him dumbly, breathing hard.

"Come on, Billy—think about the Savoy. We're going to get back there and do some serious drinking and dancing. Let's go so we can get back and party."

Bullets and shells continued to whistle past and blast holes in the snowy field. Exhausted and half-frozen, McBurney shook his head and collapsed into the snow.

"I ain't going no further. Go on without me."

Smith tugged his arm. "The Savoy, man! Remember the Savoy!"

"Shit, you're out of your damned mind."

"No, I ain't. We're going back there, you and me, to light that place up. I mean, we're going to drink and dance and carouse with fine-ass ladies all night long!"

McBurney pictured the legendary ballroom in Harlem with Count Basie banging away on his piano and the polished oak dancefloor packed with sweaty men and women having a good old time. It was a beautiful sight, but still he shook his head.

"I can't make it—you go on," he told his friend.

Smith persisted. "No, I ain't leaving you, damnit!"

The Germans unleashed another salvo of gunfire. The bullets kicked up puffs of snow but failed to find human flesh and bone. McBurney couldn't have cared less if they did hit him and wanted only to lay down for awhile.

"The Savoy, man, the Savoy! We've got to see it again! Man alive, just think of all those foxy ladies!"

McBurney was so cold and tired that he couldn't even think about women or drinking and dancing. He was thinking he was going to die here in Belgium, thousands of miles from home. He was thinking that his buddy must he out of his mind and that he was as scared as McBurney had ever seen him. Exhausted past the point of caring, William Haywood McBurney simply wanted to lie there, close his eyes, and go to sleep.

But Smitty refused to leave him.

He again tried to wave his buddy to just move on without him but was jerked to his feet. "We're going right now, motherfucker! One day you're going to tell your grandkids about this! So buck up, damn you!"

His mind suddenly flashed back to Patton in November in Lorraine. *Everyone has their eyes on you and is expecting great things from you. Most of all, your race is looking forward to you. Don't let them down and, damn you, don't let me down!*

He jerked upright as if from a dream. "All right, I'm coming, I'm coming!" he cried with a newfound sense of resolve.

They started off again, treading through the deep snow. Moments later, an incoming shell struck the spot McBurney had just vacated.

*Damn, that was close! What was I thinking? Get a grip on yourself, man!*

They quickened their pace. With his irrepressible spirit, Smitty kept on talking about Harlem, about dancing, about the beautiful girls at the Savoy, anything to get McBurney's mind off their present situation. But they were still three visible targets in an open white field, three miles from any aid or shelter, with bullets falling all around them, sending up puffs and vapors in the snow.

They struggled on but the clearing seemed endless. The unevenness of the ground and mist sent up by the German bullets provided them with obscuring cover. But the odd combination of luck and terrain would surely run out, McBurney was certain. He could hear his own ragged breathing as they fought through the waist-deep snow, but eventually they caught up to Windsor, who was clearing and packing out a trail for them. Unfortunately, the German Panzer rolling towards them showed no sign of stopping.

And then a little miracle happened.

Over the continuing hum and pop of the bullets, McBurney didn't even hear the sound of the airplane engine above. The first he heard of the American P-38 was a thunderous crash as it strafed the German tank, exploding the Panzer's ammunition.

Then the plane flew out of sight.

McBurney, Windsor, and Smith stared in disbelief at the burning tank amid a backdrop of bone-white sky. Overcome with emotion, they waved and cheered wildly. The P-38 returned and zoomed past once more—tipping its wings in tribute to the three lone Americans below—before disappearing to the southwest.

*Damn,* thought McBurney with renewed hope. *We just might make it after all.*

# CHAPTER 40



IT TOOK SIX HOURS for McBurney, Windsor, and Smith to make it back to the safety of their own lines—after three miles of wading through snowdrifts, running, taking periodic cover, and literally crawling through German patrols. When they finally staggered into camp, they were surprised to see hundreds of faces as grim and exhausted as their own.

Darkness quickly fell along with the temperature. They had scarcely dug into their K-rations of greasy meat spread, hard cheese, crackers, and instant coffee, while warming themselves around a steel drum filled with burning timber soaked in gasoline, when the Germans pressed forward in a surprise counterattack. Much of the 761st had withdrawn for resupply and refueling, but the white-clad enemy swarmed in like commandos. The Germans caught the refueling tankers off guard, forcing the battalion and infantry regiments to retreat to the morning's line of departure.

For McBurney and the rest of the Black Panthers, there would be no break. The fighting raged on well into the night, and the next morning at dawn the tankers and 346th Infantry Regiment of the 87th were right back at it, setting out from the new LD and pitching into the German lines. Living to fight another day was once again the only break the tankers and doughs got in the gelid winter apocalypse that would one day be officially known as the Battle of the Bulge.

The task force moved on, grinding and crunching through the heavy snow. But as the line of tanks and infantrymen moved cautiously over the same contested ground they had been grappling to capture for the past week, McBurney was surprised to see that the area had grown eerily quiet and no targets presented themselves. Or was it that he just couldn't see them?

Frozen bodies were everywhere: the stiff limbs sticking up like wax figures, chests and torsos ripped open in a macabre display, the faces that weren't blasted away a deep claret color from the frozen blood in the capillaries. McBurney could see that the enemy had inflicted tremendous damage on the 87th Infantry. Though he and his fellow tankers disparagingly referred to their Shermans as "Iron Coffins" and "Ronsons" like the cigarette lighter due to their susceptibility to armor-piercing rounds, he was damn glad he wasn't an infantryman. Seeing the residual aftereffects of the doughs' assault on Tillet, he saw that in places whole platoons had been wiped out in a lethal combination of enemy gunfire and the harsh cold.

As they pressed on, it soon became apparent from the forward observers of the spearheading column that the enemy had withdrawn from the field. McBurney was stunned. The German resistance seemed to have vanished as if it had never existed. But the wilderness of carnage and devastation left behind left no doubt that there had been a savage battle under horrific conditions—in fact, the coldest winter in nearly two generations. Taking in the burnt-out armored vehicles and slaughter all around, he couldn't believe that all the fighting seemed to have been for nothing.

The enemy had chased them back to where they had started, and now the battle for Tillet had ended as suddenly as it had begun.

In an anticlimactic reversal, the village was now in the hands of General George S. Patton, Jr. and the U.S. Third U.S. Army. Unbeknownst to McBurney, the Führer Begleit Brigade had pulled out hours before dawn. Unable to continue its fierce resistance, the enemy had withdrawn in the direction of Fosset and Roumont—and now the Panthers and doughboys were in pursuit, albeit cautiously given the respect they gave their formidable enemy. Though the Battle of Tillet stood as a crucial victory toward the objective of the St. Hubert-Houffalize road and a huge feather in the cap of the 761st, it had been so savage and costly a fight that for McBurney it failed to bring any real sense of triumph.

For many, it felt like the Black Panthers and 87th Infantry Division had won with more a whimper than a bang. But with possession of the field and the Germans sustaining casualties they could ill-afford to lose, McBurney knew at the same time that they were indisputably the victorious army. Especially when he saw all the barricades being set up on the network of roads in the area, choking off the vital supply arteries leading in and out of Bastogne. In the end, the 761st had done more than its fair share in breaking the back of Hitler's breakthrough in the Ardennes.

Which McBurney thought was only fitting. They were, after all, Patton's Panthers.

With guns now silent, the task force halted briefly east of Tillet. Headquarters officers and company commanders made a tally of the previous day's fighting. Amid the blanket of snow, no precise count of the destruction and carnage on both sides could be made. The engagement had been fought ridge by ridge, each separate tank and squad of infantry waging its own individual and often seemingly futile campaign but continuing to push on. But the officers and NCOs recorded what they could. Able Company was credited, among other successes, with knocking out an 88mm antitank gun and a self-propelled 75mm gun; and Dog Company with destroying an enemy mortar position and ammunition dump as well as killing fifty enemy soldiers and capturing ten. McBurney's Charlie Company—which had assaulted Tillet with all three tank platoons led by Staff Sergeants Windsor, Cochrane, and Dade—took out eight machine gun nests, a Mark IV tank, an ammunition dump, and three antitank guns while eliminating more than a hundred enemy soldiers.

Reflecting on the harrowing events of the previous day, McBurney realized how lucky he was to be alive. He had watched brave men like Windsor, Cochrane, and Dade doing whatever the situation required at the moment. Cochrane's tank had taken three hits in the heavy fighting. With his shattered tank, he and his crew had returned heavy fire and continued to advance with the entire tank platoon. Moses Dade's turret top had been blown some thirty feet in the air after taking a direct hit from a German 88. Dade, too, had continued to lead his platoon while he and his tank crew gave the enemy hell with their remaining weapons.

But for McBurney, Windsor took the prize. He knew he was fortunate to have the older, more experienced Clevelander as his tank commander. As second in command, McBurney always took over as TC whenever Windsor dashed out from the tank to sight the enemy or confer with the infantry commanders, as he often did.

But it always gave him an anxious feeling in the pit of his stomach. Though he and the other crew members continued to work seamlessly whenever Windsor was away, McBurney knew that he was not as good a leader as Windsor, nor did he even want the responsibility of being a tank commander. He saw Windsor as special, possessing qualities that he did not have. For McBurney, his turret gun satisfied him and he felt safe in his gunner's chair. Fighting in the Ardennes in January had come with severe challenges, but life behind his main cannon inside a buttoned-up tank remained close to how "Smooth" Bates had trained the battalion.

During the past week of fighting, the white infantrymen from the 87th Infantry Division had proved nowhere near as solid as those from the 26th "Yankee" Infantry Division of New Englanders. McBurney remembered seeing some of the doughs from the 87th getting so scared when they came upon the Germans that they dropped their rifles, turned tail, and ran away like frightened jackrabbits. Johnnie Stevens had told McBurney about an incident he had had with the green division: "Man, those dudes were getting their hats. When they were running away, I said to them, 'I'm going to turn this tank gun right on you if you don't stay right here!'" In Stevens's estimation, if it wasn't for the 761st, the Germans would have overrun Tillet. It wasn't that the infantrymen were cowards, McBurney believed. It was just that the firing was too heavy for them since they were so damned inexperienced. They didn't know what war was about, whereas after two solid months of combat the 761st consisted only of well-seasoned veterans.

On several occasions in the past week, McBurney had encountered white infantrymen under heavy enemy fire running up to the battalion's tanks begging to get inside to safety. "Please! Please! Let us in the tank!" they would cry. But McBurney and the other crew members had their prejudices too. They would ask, "Where you from, man?" and if the dough would say "I'm out of Atlanta," "I'm from Mobile," or anywhere else in the South, the tankers would reply, "Sorry, man, ain't got no room." A minute later, somebody else would knock on the tank and say, "Hey, you guys got any room in there?" "Where you from?" the tankers would ask, smiling at one another. If the answer was "New Jersey," "Colorado," "Massachusetts," "Chicago," or anywhere else up north or out west, they would answer. "Sure, come on in!" But the answer was always no for the Southerners who had caused them—and continued to cause them—so much trouble with their racial biases.

He thought about his driver and friend Willie Devore that he had lost. He recalled that when they had crossed the Atlantic, the South Carolinian had made it known to anyone who would listen that he would not survive the war. The fatalistic prediction had annoyed the gunner and some of the other tankers—they believed such morbid thoughts would only bring bad luck—but McBurney realized it was only because he and most of the other men tended to keep their vulnerabilities to themselves. Devore's loss made him realize that facing up to one's fears was a good thing. He would miss Little Willie. The easygoing and fun-loving farmer and ladies' man had performed his duty without hesitation. He felt badly having to leave his body behind on a frozen battlefield. He realized that he needed time to grieve for his buddy, and he knew Smitty was even more upset and would need time too.

As he stared into the mercury-colored winter sky, he made a slow sign of the cross and begged for God's forgiveness.

He asked the Good Lord to take good care of his brother Willie.

ΨΨΨ

Three days later, on January 12, the battalion stopped between Amberloupe and Saint-Hubert for emergency maintenance. They refitted their weapons, repaired their tanks, and washed their standard-issue ODs—olive drab uniforms—and their field jackets in gasoline to clean them. McBurney stood around a burning gasoline can warming his hands with Smith, E.G. McConnell, and several other Panthers. Some of the men were eating their K-rations, others were tossing around a football. The whole battalion was still talking about the Battle of Tillet.

"Yo fellas, I just found out those Krauts we fought weren't regulars," said McConnell.

"Who the hell were they then?" asked Leonard Smith.

"Some outfit called the Führer Begleit Brigade."

"I thought they were the Panzer Lehr Division," said McBurney.

"No, it was the Führer Brigade. Those bastards used to serve as Hitler's personal palace guard and are a crack outfit."

"Damn, I guess we're lucky to be alive then," said McBurney.

"Now that is true," said Smitty. "But you're mostly lucky on account of me. I saved your ass when you wanted to call it quits. And one day, your kids and grandkids had better thank their Uncle Smitty."

They all laughed. "Don't worry," McBurney said, "I'm never going to forget what you did. I owe you, that's for damn sure."

"And I ain't never going to forget what you did for me right after Willie bought it. I just couldn't believe my eyes."

"I still can't figure out why he didn't get out of that damn tank," said McBurney, shaking his head. "He just wouldn't move."

"He froze up, man, like a deer in headlights."

McBurney nodded and they fell into silence. Smith had confided to him that he wanted to write a letter to Willie Devore's family in Greenwood, South Carolina. But he confessed he didn't know how to explain to Willie's mother how his good friend had died in a frozen field nearly 4,000 miles from home with a pack of angry Germans bearing down on them. McBurney and Smith, and Windsor as well, still didn't have an answer as to why Willie had hesitated at the end. Had the impact of the Tellermine been more severe in the driver's front compartment than in the turret and he had lost his senses? After two months of combat in Lorraine, the Saar, and the Ardennes, Devore had developed a reputation as one of the battalion's ablest drivers and calmest men under fire. And he had been well-trained. Neither McBurney nor Smith could get their minds around the question of why Willie had seemed so confused and disoriented. Why had he hesitated and died in terror in that clearing? Maybe, they would never know the answer.

A three-quarter-ton field ambulance drove up. Out of the front passenger seat gingerly stepped Captain Dave Williams, commander of Able Company, who had just been awarded the Silver Star days earlier. To McBurney's surprise, the officer looked teary-eyed, and he wondered what the hell was going on. He and several of the men went over to the ambulance.

"I just wanted to say goodbye, fellas," said Williams without preamble as he hobbled towards them, his voice choked with emotion. "They're sending me home."

"What happened, Captain?" asked McBurney.

"Bad case of trench foot. I fought the medical order, but they just won't let me stay. It's a damn shame."

"Able's going to miss you, Captain," said Smith, and there were nods and murmurs of agreement all around. "And so are we."

"You always treated us square, sir," said McConnell. "Just like Colonel Bates."

"I'm going to miss you all, too, and that's why I wanted to say goodbye to each company," said Williams, fresh tears in his eyes. "You guys are better than heroes because you weren't supposed to be able to fight, and you've been goddamn treated worse than lepers. It takes a rare sort of character to go out there and do what you fellas have done. For more than two years now, I've been asking myself, 'Why the hell do you guys fight? Why?' But now after fighting with you in battle, I know the answer. I know what makes you tick."

Here he paused to wipe the tears from his eyes. As he struggled to bring voice to his thoughts, his lower lip trembled.

"It's a ferocious pride that nobody has ever recognized, and I'm honored—honored—to have fought with you."

He stood ramrod straight and saluted, tears pouring down his cheeks in a torrent now. McBurney and the others returned the honor.

"The toughest battles we've all fought have been spiritually," Williams went on, sniffling. "At least over here in Europe we can strike back at an enemy. Back in the States what the hell could we do?"

"Well, you were always there for us, Captain, and especially for your men in A Company," said McBurney. "We're all going to miss you."

"When we first met, I was nothing but a young punk out of Yale. I was a snob who didn't know a damn thing about Negroes. We had two people, a chauffeur and a very fine lady, working for us and I had barely even heard of a ghetto. I was the most unlikely candidate to be with you men. But now I can say that I got my manhood from you. Without you, I would be nothing. I wouldn't know the true meaning of duty and honor. I'm never going to forget you—never. And I'm going to goddamn make sure that Ruben Rivers gets his Medal of Honor. If it's the last thing I do on this earth, I'm going to make sure he gets the award he deserves."

They bid a final farewell and Williams drove off in the ambulance. McBurney felt powerful emotions. The young captain, scarcely older than McBurney himself, had been one of the good guys. He had fought and cried as a commander who loved his men, and McBurney had heard him say on several occasions that he would see the war through to the last man. It was obviously a crushing blow for him to have to be unceremoniously shipped home with a bad case of trench foot. But the gods of war had final say over the fate of any soldier, including Dave Williams, once a boy-of-a-man who had found his place, albeit by a route strewn with agonizing loss. McBurney could see that he was still consumed by guilt over Ruben Rivers's death, and he believed Williams when he said he would not rest until he had gotten Rivers the Medal of Honor everyone in the battalion knew he deserved.

McBurney and the other tankers of Charlie Company continued to stare, a tad bewildered, as the medic drove the young white captain away. Then they returned to their fire to warm themselves and to playing football. McBurney watched Privates Floyd Dade and Steven Reed throwing the pigskin, noting that they were damned good ball players. After ten minutes, Dade said he was getting tired and wanted to quit running and catching passes. But when he came over to the gasoline can, Reed chucked him the football when he wasn't looking. The football hit the can and sprayed gasoline onto Dade, who when he tried to step away somehow managed to catch on fire.

"Damn, put me out, fellas! I don't want to burn like a Coney Island dog!" he cried, knowing not to run.

Someone nearby took off the blanket he was wrapped in and they smothered him with it until they had extinguished the flames. Just then, a GI truck manned by two colored soldiers pulled up. Through the window, the driver said, "I think we got one of your guys here. KIA."

"Who is it?" asked McBurney.

"Devore, William J. We pulled his dog tag."

*Our boy Willie?* gasped McBurney in inward disbelief. He and Smith looked at one another.

The soldiers reached into the back of the truck, hauled out the stiff frozen body which had not been placed in a bag, and set it down in front of the group. McBurney heard the snow crunch as the frozen corpse hit the ground. They all looked down at the grim sight. McBurney could see that the top of his head had been blown off, and all he could think was, *Thank God he died quickly*.

He looked again at Smith. There were tears in his eyes.

"I remember when we steamed out of New York Harbor," said McConnell, his voice laced with emotion. "Little Willie told me he wasn't coming back. We were just passing the Statue of Liberty and I was angry at him for saying it. I thought it was bad luck. And now look here what happened. Poor Willie got his Purple Heart."

"I remember. We were all mad at him," said Smitty.

McBurney looked down at the disfigured face and body, feeling himself choking up. War wasn't like in the moving pictures at all. Not goddamn at all.

"Well, one thing's for sure," he said, his voice cracking.

Smith wiped away his tears and looked at him. "What's that, man?"

"We've got to write his mother and father and tell 'em Willie died bravely. And that he did it so the good people over here in Europe could be free."

"You got that right. Our boy fought for freedom," agreed Smitty.

"That he did," said E.G. McConnell, pulling out his pocket Bible. "If you all don't mind, I'm going to say a few words."

There were solemn nods all around. Artillery crackled in the distance as the men gathered around the frozen body and McConnell thumbed through his Good Book, searching for the right prayer.

"Willie was our brother," said McBurney, fighting back the tears. "So be sure to make it a good one."

# CHAPTER 41

**LUXEMBOURG CITY TO BASTOGNE
SOUTHEASTERN BELGIUM**

**FEBRUARY 5, 1945**

SITTING AT HIS HQ DESK, Patton finished writing his letter to his wife and read it over one last time.

> *February 5, 1945*
> *Darling Beat:*
> *Am going to Bastogne to meet Destiny and the Tent Maker. I am trying to keep the impending Bitburg offensive secret so that the powers that be will not order it stopped. I hope the meeting won't be a stop order as we are doing very nicely.*
> *The weather could not be worse. It is snowing like hell again now. But I doubt if Willie needs a sweater. When I am reading in bed, he gets in with me. But as soon as I start to open the window he hurries into the bathroom where it is warm.*
> *If I have to go on the defensive, I think I will visit the Leicester-Warrens and the Stockdales for a few days. I am not tired but get bored when there is no fighting.*
> *I love you with all my heart.*
> *—Your Loving Georgie*

As Willie snuggled up against his booted feet beneath his desk, Patton tried to picture his wife. He hadn't seen her in such a long time that he wondered if she still looked the same. Then he thought of Jean Gordon, whom he had seen recently with the Red Cross girls handing out donuts to his troops. Beatrice had written him several testy letters about Jean, whom she knew was serving as a nurse attached to Third Army. He had dismissed her concerns and told her not to worry, claiming that he wouldn't engage in any hanky-panky as he was in the midst of complicated battle movements and extremely occupied. But despite his claim of innocence, he had continued to see Jean sporadically since arriving to France in the summer.

All the same, Beatrice was still his rock. She had always been there for him—and he knew he was lucky that she had stood beside him, especially after what he had put her through in Hawaii nine years earlier. He hated himself for giving in to temptation and not ending his lingering affair with his young, socialite mistress whose beautiful blue eyes lit up in the presence of her "Uncle Georgie." But he was so lonely sometimes, especially when the weather was foul and his army was at a standstill and not allowed to advance. He just hadn't been able to give her up.

His thoughts turned to his forthcoming visit with Ike and Bradley—Divine Destiny and Tent Maker—this afternoon. As he had indicated in his letter to Beatrice, he was worried that they might ask him the details of his impending Bitburg offensive and try to stop him in deference to Monty again.

With Ike's blessing, the Combined Chiefs of Staff had decreed that the main thrust to the Rhine would be made by Monty's Twenty-First Army Group, while Patton's Third Army and Devers Sixth Army Group in the south would be restricted to the defensive in a secondary role. In the meantime, Patton had been permitted by

Bradley to launch his planned attack against Bitburg and Prüm "provided the casualties and the ammunition expenditures are not excessive"—which to Old Blood and Guts meant that he had no limits whatsoever unless he wanted to twiddle his thumbs while Monty "regrouped." He expected to move so quickly that casualties would be minimal. He also reasoned that if the attack was successful, he would stand poised to unleash his armored divisions upon the enemy's rear and break the Siegfried Line. If not, he'd still be advancing the goal of putting Monty to the Rhine, since the Germans in the south would be unable to disengage and shift north to fight the British. Either way, he figured, Ike would get what he wanted.

What bothered him most, though, was that, after riding in on a white horse to save the day in the Ardennes, he was being forced to return to beggary and deception to keep Third Army part of the Allied victory strategy. It was Lorraine all over again. After what he and his brave troops had done for the war effort, keeping his Third Army sidelined in the south while the slow-moving Monty got the vast majority of the troops and supplies in the north seemed a waste. Especially now that, after a horrific start, the Ardennes stood as an American triumph. While 19,000 U.S. troops had been killed in the fighting through the end of January, with another 47,500 wounded and 23,000 captured or missing, the end result was an American victory snatched from the jaws of defeat and a crushing blow to Nazi Germany.

An editorial in the *Washington Post*, published under the headline *PATTON OF COURSE*, gushed that "it has become an unwritten rule in this war that when there is a fire to be put out, it is Patton who jumps into his boots, slides down the pole, and starts rolling." Throughout January, Patton and his Third Army were acclaimed by the world for their swift and timely response in thwarting the German thrust. Taking on the German Seventh Army, half the Fifth Panzer Army, and portions of the Sixth Panzer Army, Patton's forces had almost single-handedly returned the front lines to where they were on the eve of battle in mid-December, gaining back virtually all the territory the Allies had lost. In rolling to the rescue and halting the German *blitzkrieg*, Third Army alone had suffered nearly 30,000 casualties.

The Germans sustained losses between 82,000 and 98,000 men, based on German High Command estimates, but the Allies thought the numbers could be as high as 100,000. More than seven hundred armored vehicles were lost, German manpower reserves were exhausted, and the *Reichsbahn* was so badly battered that as of late January all rail freight shipments were banned except for coal and Wehrmacht supplies. The German Army Group B forces in the West had virtually no fuel reserves and only about a third of the ammunition they needed, while the Luftwaffe was so feeble that Hitler likened air warfare to "a rabbit hunt." After more than five years of war, four million German soldiers had been killed, wounded, or captured—and neither they nor their weapons could be replaced fast enough to keep pace with American war production alone.

Patton could feel the Allies were moving in for the kill. "When you catch a carp and put him in the boat," he had recently told reporters, "he flips his tail just before he dies. I think this is the Germans' last flip." Indeed, the final tally revealed that Hitler's Ardennes Offensive was a desperate gamble by a country teetering on the brink of defeat. Old Blood and Guts's vaunted opponent from Lorraine and the Bulge, Hasso von Manteuffel, had come to the same conclusion. Hitler's last-gasp had left the Wehrmacht so eviscerated, he warned, that Germany henceforth would be capable of fighting only "a corporal's war."

Although the Germans managed to begin their offensive with complete surprise and enjoyed initial success, Hitler's desperate gambit had turned into a boon for the Allies. Though they had inflicted heavy casualties, the Wehrmacht had proved unable to seize the initiative on the Western Front and sustained losses they couldn't replace given their severe manpower shortages. Patton knew the enemy had no strength left for anything other than defense. In that sense, Germany had already lost the war, although he knew that Hitler would likely fight until the bitter end. The biggest outcome of the fighting was to delay the Allied invasion of Germany by six weeks. The Allies had planned to resume the offensive by early January 1945, after the wet season rains and severe frosts, but those plans had to be postponed until the coming weeks due to the German offensive.

By saving the day in the Ardennes, Patton emerged as the only senior commander in the battle with his reputation greatly enhanced. Those of Bradley, Hodges, and Montgomery were blemished. Bradley's for the perception that he had been duped and lost control of his men, thus leading to Eisenhower's controversial decision to assign the northern half of the bulge to Monty and hand over the U.S. First and Ninth Armies. Hodges, whose First Army bore the brunt of the German counteroffensive, was consigned to the same fate as Bradley for failing to foresee the German attack. Monty lost credibility and drew joint British and American censure for his ill-advised press conference on January 7, where he had gloated before the cameras and patronizingly belittled the American effort. Many at SHAEF also blamed the field marshal for his lengthy delay in linking up his British divisions with Patton's forces, thereby allowing most of the enemy to escape eastward—a virtual re-enactment of Falaise. It was not until January 16 that the two Allied armies linked up and only by the end of January was the "bulge" eliminated.

When a news reporter asked Patton "Why have the British not attacked?" Old Blood and Guts told him the unvarnished truth. "Why in hell don't they attack? They're just being true to form. More afraid of losing a battle than anxious to win one. Well, that's Montgomery for you." But Patton knew it wasn't all on Monty. The cautious January counterattack had been agreed to by Bradley and Eisenhower, who had favored patiently dislodging the German troops from the bulge rather than cutting them off and killing them in large numbers.

But with the battle now over and the push for the Rhine the new priority, Patton could tell that his battle with Monty over resources was about to heat up. When he had held his press conference after the liberation of Bastogne, he had praised his American troops and celebrated what had turned out to be the largest battle the U.S. Army had ever fought: "The purpose of this operation as far as the Third Army is concerned is to hit this German son of a bitch—pardon me—in the flank, and we did, with the result that he is damn well stopped and going back. To me it is a marvel what our soldiers can do. I know of no equal to it in military history. I take off my hat to them." When Monty held his own press conference—which his staff had desperately tried to stop beforehand knowing he would only insult his allies—he came across as if he had personally won a great victory and singlehandedly thwarted the German attack. Despite the fact the British had contributed only one unit that didn't even start moving until January 3, he exaggerated the Brits part in the battle to the extent that it appeared as if the Americans had been in severe trouble and were saved by the British, or at the very least by Montgomery.

In fact, the opposite was the case: the battle had been primarily an American victory. But Monty had handed the British press a good story and the home-town reporters were not going to give any credit to any bloody Yanks. It was written up as if Monty had intervened personally to save the floundering Americans, and while some papers used words that were not his, the sentiment clearly was.

Across the board, the American generals were not just resentful but furious. Bradley said Monty was "all-out, right-down-to-his-toes mad." Both he and Patton told Ike they could no longer serve with Monty and threatened to resign. Monty tried to extricate himself, telling war correspondents that "I salute the brave fighting men of America" and "I am absolutely devoted to Ike"—but it was too late and the senior commanders on both sides, including Monty's staff officers who had tried to stop him from giving the press conference in the first place, knew it was a shameless lie. His comments proceeded to trigger a crisis that threatened the Anglo-American alliance and Churchill was forced to act quickly to repair the damage.

Speaking in the House of Commons, the British Prime Minister, knowing that he needed the support of an ally that was now contributing nearly three-quarters of the men and war materials in Europe, gave a thinly veiled rebuttal to Montgomery:

*I have seen it suggested that the terrific battle which has been proceeding since December 16 on the American front is an Anglo-American battle. In fact, however, the United States troops have done almost all the fighting and have suffered almost all the losses. They have suffered losses almost equal to those of both sides at the Battle of Gettysburg. Only one single British Army corps has been engaged on this occasion. All the rest of thirty or more divisions which have been fighting continuously for the last month are United States troops. The Americans have engaged thirty or forty men for every one we have engaged and have lost sixty to eighty men to every one of ours. That is a point I wish to make. Care must be taken in telling our proud tale not to claim for the British Army's undue share of what is undoubtedly the greatest American battle of the war and will, I believe, be regarded as an ever-famous American victory.*

Churchill also told those who would listen that there was "no greater exhibition of power in history than that of the American Army fighting the battle of the Ardennes with its left hand and advancing from island to island toward Japan with its right." After being admonished by the PM and others and coming within a hair's breadth of being relieved for insubordination by Eisenhower in mid-January, Monty tried to initiate a charm offensive by writing uncharacteristically courteous notes to Ike and Brad. But the Anglo-American alliance remained fragile. Patton blamed Divine Destiny as much as Monty: "Why isn't Ike a man?" Patton wrote in his diary on January 24. "We will attack and win in spite of Ike and Monty."

Unbeknownst to Patton, even General Hastings Ismay, Churchill's chief military adviser, hoped that someone would "muzzle or better still chloroform Monty. I have come to the conclusion that his love of publicity is a disease, like alcoholism or taking drugs, and that it sends him equally mad." Goebbels and German Intelligence cleverly took Montgomery's words from his condescending speech, rearranged them while still maintaining his preachy schoolmaster's tone, and produced their own broadcast on the radio that sounded uncannily like a real BBC broadcast. When American troops reacted just as badly to the newspaper and radio reports of what Monty actually said as they did to the Germans' doctored version, Goebbels knew that Monty had won the propaganda battle *for* Nazi Germany and was ecstatic. The words and pedantic tone were recognized as pure Monty—even though in this case they had been scripted for the British field marshal in Berlin.

After handing the letter to his wife to Meeks to mail, Patton set out for Bastogne. God, he hoped Bradley and Ike wouldn't ask a lot of questions about his plan to push through Bitburg with Eddy's XII Corps. Even more importantly, he prayed they wouldn't try to stop him. Since his plan involved the movement of a hundred thousand men on the sly, Patton's warning bells had gone off when Brad had called him this morning, a mere two days before the attack, to ask if he could meet him and Ike in Bastogne in the afternoon.

He headed to Bastogne with Mims and Codman, clad in his battle helmet, tall boots, and thick GI parka cinched with his gun belt. When his Willys pulled into the tiny Belgian town that the whole world now knew about, he found Ike and Brad waiting for him along with a Signal Corps photographer. Patton realized that the meeting was a routine staged photo session for the folks back home and historical posterity. Looking at the wilderness of devastation, he noted how drastically different Bastogne was from the last time the three of them had been here, back in early November. Back before the disaster of the Ardennes and before he had rode in on his white horse to save the day.

Ike was effusive. "Hi George," he said with a pleasant smile as the two men shook hands and the photographer snapped away. "Thanks for coming. We're going to take a few pictures and then we can head over to First Army HQ and catch up."

*Catch up?* Patton was relieved the meeting seemed to be a purely social and PR visit. "Sounds swell. I just hope I don't crack the lens," he said with a grin. "Hello, Brad," he then said to Bradley, who stood uncomfortably off to the side—like an underconfident, awkward child.

But his lantern-jawed smile was genuine. "Good to see you, George."

Patton nodded amiably and looked around at the battered buildings and endless piles of rubble where the 101stst Airborne had held out for a week of bombardment during the Siege of Bastogne.

"The town looks a little different than the last time we were here, eh fellas?" he said sportingly.

"It sure does, George. It sure does," said Ike.

They continued to make warm small talk. As they did, the trio were photographed before the carefully selected backdrop of a destroyed commercial building surrounded by piles of rubble. Ike and Bradley were dressed in their pressed general's uniforms and neckties, while in his heavy rain-spotted parka Old Blood and Guts looked as though he had just stepped off the front lines, like Grant at Appomattox. Patton noticed that Ike had on his new five stars, which he thought made a very striking insignia. As the photographer snapped away at the three men, Bradley said little and hovered in the background, beaming at Ike as if to garner the supreme commander's approval. To Patton, the historic photographs being captured accurately reflected how the Bastogne operation had gone down—with him and Ike in the central roles and Bradley, who had never seen the Germans coming and had paid the price for it by having his troops shipped off to Monty, in the background.

With the photo session completed, they drove to First Army headquarters and sat down at a conference table to talk in private.

ΨΨΨ

"Some days, I don't know what I was thinking when I took this thankless job of supreme commander," began Eisenhower with cigarette smoke pouring through his nose like a dragon.

Patton gave a sympathetic smile and thought about lighting up a cigar, but then remembered that he had recently quit. "Is this one of those days, Ike?" he inquired.

"Nope," said the rangy Kansan. "That would be yesterday and the day before— and the day before that. Brooke and the British chiefs of staff have been pushing relentlessly for a single, full-blooded thrust towards Berlin. I'm more worn out from the British than the damned Germans."

"Well, once Monty 'regroups' again, I guess we'll see about this 'dagger thrust' of his. Personally, I'm skeptical," said Patton, his tone more sarcastic than incisive.

"I think it's fair to say we all know that, George. The bottom line is the British are horrified at the notion of fighting major battles west of the Rhine and risking the gutting of their army for the post-war world. They no longer have the manpower to sustain their own armies in the field. Plus Monty just wants total control."

"So that's why the British want us to hand over our divisions?" said Bradley. "So our boys can die instead of the Brits, and Monty can win the war? Is that you're telling us, Ike?"

*There you go, Brad, I wasn't sure you had it in you,* thought Patton. *Now that's telling him. God, I would love a cigar right now.*

Eisenhower held up a hand. "Okay, stop it, you two. I was only filling you in on what's been going on. I don't want to get into a pissing match with you *and* the British. I've got enough to worry about between Churchill, Brooke, and Monty."

"All right, we'll be good boys—or at least we'll try," said Patton. "You know damn well what the problem is, Ike. The British have never liked the broad-front strategy. But a war of attrition will work as long as we can move on at least two fronts at once. You know what the British call it, don't you?"

"Yes, George, of course I know. SHAEF is leakier than a sieve when it comes to military gossip and innuendo."

"Good, then I can come right out and say it: 'Have a go, Joe.'"

Bradley appeared confused. "Have a go, Joe? What's that mean?"

Patton looked at Ike and the two of them smiled. "Uh Brad," said Patton by way of explanation, "it's an expression commonly uttered by London prostitutes seeking business from American GIs. In this case, they think Ike's broad-front strategy is akin to the words of a Piccadilly street-walker. But, of course, you and I don't think that's true. Right, Brad?"

Eisenhower was grinning. "Okay, George, that's enough bullshit for one day." He took a long pull from his half-smoked Lucky Strike. "So in the end, gentlemen,

255

what happened with my little dispute with Brooke is Marshall stepped in and threatened the British by telling them that I would ask to be relieved as supreme commander unless they accepted my broad-front strategy."

Patton's eyes lit up. "Is that true, would you have stepped down?"

"I don't know, most likely. I'm getting awfully tired of Monty, and now Brooke has become equally unbearable."

Patton nodded sympathetically. Despite his differences with Ike over Allied strategy, it bothered him that the British ridiculed his boss behind his back and loathed having to serve under him. The picture of Ike painted by his British critics, led by Brooke and Montgomery, was that of a genial, good-natured "chairman of the board" suddenly snatched from obscurity by Chief of Staff George C. Marshall and placed in a supreme leadership position for which he was ill-suited and with duties he was unable to adequately perform. Patton had once heard that Monty had unflatteringly said of his boss, "Ike is a nice enough chap. But he is *no* general."

"Okay, fellas, that's enough SHAEF gossip for one day," said Ike good-naturedly. "Let's get to the plan for taking the Rhine and Berlin. Here's how it's going to play out."

He quickly laid it all out. His strategy was to unfold in three phases, during which the Allied armies would invade Germany, breach the great obstacle of the Rhine that had proved such a daunting challenge to the Romans, and overrun the Third Reich. While Monty made plans for *Operation Plunder*—a massive airborne and amphibious operation to breach the lowlands of the Rhine in Holland with the First Canadian and Second British Armies and the Ruhr with Simpson's Ninth U.S. Army—Bradley was to clear the Eifel and drive to the Moselle with the Seventh and Third Armies. Once across the Rhine, the armies of Hodges and Simpson would encircle the Ruhr and crush Model's Army Group B in the jaws of a huge Allied pincer. Patton's Third Army and Devers's Sixth Army Group would advance towards Czechoslovakia and Austria and the Elbe River, where Ike intended to halt the Allied advance and link up with the Red Army, which was crushing everything in its path advancing from the east. The overall objective of the plan, maintained the supreme commander, was to effect "a massive double envelopment of the Ruhr to be followed by a great thrust to join up with the Russians."

Once he was finished with his broad-brush overview, they went over the details. In the first phase, Monty's Twenty-First Army Group, with the Ninth U.S. Army under his command, would seize the west bank of the Rhine from Nijmegen to Düsseldorf, while Bradley's Twelfth Army Group was to maintain an aggressive defense. Then, while Monty prepared to cross the lower Rhine, Bradley was to secure the river from Düsseldorf to Cologne, following which Patton's Third Army would "take up the ball" and thrust eastward from Prüm to Koblenz. At the same time, the Third and Seventh U.S. Armies would be responsible for securing crossings over the Rhine between Mainz and Karlsruhe for the forces destined to carry out the thrust south of the Ruhr.

Patton was far from happy to see Monty being given not only the main role, but also a complete U.S. army. With just under three-quarters of the Allied Expeditionary Force now made up of American troops, he, as well as Bradley, wanted the main effort to be made by U.S. forces under American command. Indeed, he envisaged all four U.S. armies driving into central Germany with the British, Canadian, and French armies being relegated to flank protection. The two of them had lobbied Ike for just such a plan, but their pleas had fallen on deaf ears. But what bothered Old Blood and Guts most was that Monty had not only all the muscle and firepower in the north and an entire U.S Army, the Ninth, under his command, but the full authority of decision in the event of disagreement with Bradley on the boundary between the Twelfth and Twenty-First Army Groups. It seemed like a waste for his powerful and successful Third Army to have to adopt a posture of "aggressive defense" while Monty got to launch the major offensive.

But he decided, right there and then, that he was not going to be so easily sidelined. He chose to view the order to adopt a posture of aggressive defense as meaning that he could keep moving towards the Rhine with a low profile. When he returned to his headquarters, the first thing he was going to do was tell his staff that the Third Army was going to carry out an "armored reconnaissance"—but that it would be accomplished with seven divisions and that the initial objectives were Prüm, Bitburg, and the vital city of Trier on the Moselle River. Furthermore, he would also instruct his commanders to make sure that their units were always fully committed so that they could not be removed from his command and placed in SHAEF's theater reserve.

Comparing the master plan to Hannibal's envelopment of the Romans at Cannae, Eisenhower finished off by telling his two subordinates just how powerful their Allied army was at this late stage of the war. But this only reaffirmed to Patton that he was right and Ike and SHAEF wrong. The Western Allies, Ike said, now mustered 3.7 million soldiers in 73 divisions along a 730-mile front, with U.S. forces providing the bulk of that strength. Eisenhower made it clear also that he had at his disposal almost 18,000 combat aircraft—complemented by air fleets in Italy—and overwhelming dominance in artillery, armor, intelligence, supply, transportation, and the other sinews of modern combat.

When he was finished, he lit another cigarette and the three generals sat back and mulled over the plan. Though Patton was impressed with the strength of the Allied forces, he didn't like that, in the blueprint for the final conquest of Nazi Germany, American forces were again relegated to playing a secondary role. He believed Ike's plan was too timid and failed to attack von Rundstedt's defeated armies aggressively. Instead the American units were confined to limited offensive actions, and only then if they conformed to the SHAEF plan. To Patton, Third Army's role would be reduced to the same type of "active defense" he had been forced to undertake in Lorraine. It was certainly no way to win a war. Why only a few days earlier, he had written Beatrice to tell her that if she ever heard he was on the defensive, "It was not the enemy who put me there. I don't see much future for me in this war if that's how we have to fight." He felt it ignoble for the American armies to finish the war on such lame-duck terms. But what irritated him most was that SHAEF was collecting a theater reserve by taking divisions from the hard-fighting, successful front-line armies.

The main problem, as Patton saw it, was that there were too many "safety first" people running the war. Churchill, Ike, Brooke, Bradley, Monty, Beetle Smith—the list went on. At the same time, he knew he would continue to find a way to work around his orders so that he could keep his army fighting and moving forward. He would just have to return to the stealth approach he had employed in Lorraine, taking advantage of whatever he thought Brad or SHAEF would give him, buying time, deliberately remaining out of communication, and taking objectives that would keep his units committed and unavailable to be removed. Thankfully, Bradley felt just as strongly as he did about making sure the U.S. armies weren't consigned to a secondary role. He was, therefore, at least partly complicit in Patton's subterfuge.

As Ike smoked and he and Bradley looked on, Patton wondered if ever before in the history of the war, a winning general had to plead to be allowed to keep on winning. It just seemed like such a misuse of resources for his army to be held back while Monty and the British got all the laurels. But he supposed there was a silver lining. While Ike's grand strategy made Monty's attack north of the Ruhr the main assault, Patton knew that the northern sector would be strongly held by the enemy and that even SHAEF believed no more than thirty-five Allied divisions could be supported above the Ruhr until new rail bridges spanned the Rhine. Given the torpid pace of Monty's advances, this made the need for a second active front all the more necessary. Furthermore, Ike envisioned the bulk of Patton's and Bradley's troops attacking from Mainz and Karlsruhe toward Frankfurt and Kassel—a corridor Patton had long touted as the best southern approach into the Reich.

"George, why don't you tell Ike and me about your forthcoming 'probing' attacks of XII Corps," said Bradley, taking him off guard.

*Uh oh, here we go.*

"Not much to tell, Brad. As you and I have discussed, I am having Eddy's make a determined probe to see what's in front of him." His "determined probe" would, of course, be a full-scale attack, but he wasn't about to tell Ike or Brad that. And he would tell Eddy that once he was prepared to attack, the both of them would be nowhere near a telephone when SHAEF found out about the advance. His operating principle, he told his wife Beatrice and brother-in-law, was, "if I win, no one will say anything, and I am sure I will win."

"That sounds good, George," said Ike pleasantly. "Have at it."

"What are we to do about Middleton?" then asked Bradley about the commander of VIII Corps.

"I want to keep him."

Bradley persisted. "But shouldn't he go back to the First Army? That's where he came from."

"If I have to lose a corps, I had hoped it wouldn't be Middleton's. I prefer to keep Middleton rather than Millikin."

"What's your reasoning, George?" asked Ike.

"Millikin did a damned good job at Bastogne. Don't get me wrong, he's a fine general. But he's a lot more inexperienced compared to Middleton. That's why I'd like to keep the latter."

Blowing out a cloud of cigarette smoke, Ike smiled reassuringly. "I don't see any reason why you shouldn't keep someone you trust. Personally, I feel handicapped by having to keep Devers under me," he added, referring to the commander of the Sixth Army Group south of Patton's forces. "I just don't trust him."

"I feel the same way about Devers," said Patton sympathetically. But he knew the real reason Ike didn't like the man: he viewed Devers as a potential rival, since Devers, too, had criticized his broad-front strategy that had made Bradley's Twelfth Army Group and Devers Sixth Army Group secondary to Monty.

The three generals talked for a few minutes longer. Ike and Bradley made no further mention of his Bitburg offensive. All during the meeting, Patton thought of Lord Nelson the night before his attack on Calvi in Corsica. Nelson had discovered the French were twice as numerous as he thought they were, but didn't report it to his chief for fear the attack would be called off. Whenever he could get away with it, Patton made it a practice to keep Ike and Brad in the dark about his future actions, even though Brad was sympathetic and often subtly aided, abetted, and cooperated with him where he could. He liked to believe that he was putting something over on his superiors, like Huck Finn getting away with mischief. But both Ike and Brad knew exactly what he was up to—in fact, they counted on it. As long as Patton didn't steal the limelight at Monty's expense and threaten the fragile Allied coalition, they tacitly approved of Third Army's stealthy operations.

Ike stood up to indicate the meeting was finished. "Thanks for coming, George," he said pleasantly.

"Good to see you, Ike," said Patton, and the two old friends shook hands. He then tipped his head at Bradley. "Take care, Brad."

"Remember, George," said Ike. "You and Hodges are only permitted to continue attacking until the priority of resupply again reverts to Monty. And only if your casualties and ammunition expenditure are within acceptable bounds. You're clear on that, right?"

"Crystal clear," he said laconically.

The meeting broke up. On his way back from Bastogne, he had Mims drive him to Trois Vierges, the new command post of the VIII Corps. He was excited to discover that its attack was going better than expected, with the 4th Infantry Division only two miles from Prüm. But in the back of his mind, one thing bothered him: Ike hadn't said a word about Third Army's actions in the Ardennes. It surprised him, considering that today's meeting was the first time they had seen one another since late December, when the supreme commander had seemed so pleased that he was taking the lead on the liberation of Bastogne and cutting off the bulge. He was amused more than offended, but it did sting that Ike failed to make any reference at all to the success of Third Army. He had expected at least a pat on the back. If not for him then at least for his brave troops, who had weathered the frigid cold and slugged it out against crack German divisions for more than a month.

He didn't believe it was intentional. But it did seem to signify carelessness and questionable leadership.

He vowed that the next time he met with Walker, Eddy, Middleton, and his other generals, he would make sure to give them some words of encouragement. In his mind, it was the least a commander could do.

# PART 4

# THE RHINE

# CHAPTER 42

## COLOGNE

### FEBRUARY 12, 1945

"WE MUST LEAVE NOW, ANGELA. You must pack your bags."

"But why, Papa? What's happened?"

"Himmler recently ordered the Cologne Gestapo to draw up lists of enemy collaborators for future execution. Your name was on the list."

She felt the breath catch in her throat. "How do you know? Did you see the list?"

"No, my informant at the Gestapo did. Pack your things, we have to hurry."

"But why is my name on the list? I have not collaborated with the enemy."

"You have been connected to the Edelweiss Pirates and that's all the SS cares about. When Himmler learned of the cozy fraternization between Germans and the Americans at Aachen and other towns that have fallen to the Allies near the Belgian border, he went ballistic. The regime is terrified that people will switch sides and aid the enemy. That's why they are arresting anyone they feel could pose a threat. The Nazis have long feared internal collapse, and that is what we are seeing now that the Americans and British are pushing in along our western border and the Russians are pressing in from the east. The Gestapo are pre-emptively rooting out danger as they deport the remaining Rhinelanders to the interior of Germany."

"My God, what has become of our country? How could it have come to this?"

"I don't know. All I know is our beloved Fatherland has become more dangerous than I ever imagined. New special patrols have recently been formed all along the Rhine. Security forces are searching *zwangsarbeiter* camps for Allied leaflets, stolen weapons, and radios in order to head off the uprising they are expecting amongst escaped foreign laborers. Instead of letting these suspects off with warnings, officers are sentencing them to concentration camps or shooting them on the spot. As for German citizens they consider a security risk, they are mostly taking them into custody and shipping them to labor camps. But they are murdering some too. It's all coming apart, *Bärchen*."

"But what triggered all this?"

"The deluge of Allied propaganda raining down from enemy airplanes has frightened the Nazis. Now the Gestapo is in a panic. That's why they've ramped up the arrests and killing of not only escaped foreign laborers, deserters, and criminals, but ordinary Germans citizens they view as defeatists or disloyalists. Security officers believe the majority of Germans and foreign workers arrested west of the Rhine are spies for the Allies. Even though they have no evidence these people have actually assisted the enemy."

She took a deep breath to calm herself. "Okay, I understand the situation now. But where are we going to go?"

"I have made arrangements with General von Manteuffel to join his staff now that the Ardennes Offensive is over. You will serve as my personal nurse as a German Red Cross Wehrmacht auxiliary. That is the best I could do to ensure that you are close to me in an official capacity. My only fear is that if the general is sent back to the Eastern Front, we could be in even more danger. The Russians are as ruthless as the Gestapo."

Having heard the horror stories of widespread German and Russian atrocities in the East, she felt a chill down her spine. *The Russian Front? Good heavens, isn't that just exchanging one bad situation for an even worse one?*

"We have to go now, Angela. Hurry up and pack your things. We must leave Cologne at once."

"I will get ready now."

"Quickly, and just two pairs of spare clothes. Also, don't forget your gun."

"Yes, Papa."

She dashed into her room. Grabbing her valise from her closet, she started packing. Her heart raced frantically knowing that she was being sought by the Gestapo. She couldn't believe how the situation in the Rhineland had deteriorated. She knew that *Sonderkommando Brauweiler* commanded by Kütter and the other security units operating inside the city were still working alongside the Hitler Youth and *Volkssturm* patrols searching the ruins to root out supposed enemies of the state. Jews, Communists, Jehovah's Witnesses, saboteurs, members of resistance movements, enemy agents, asocials, criminals and stockpilers of stolen goods, and foreign workers who left their job sites or refused to work had long been especially targeted. But now, with Germany descending into chaos in Hitler's *Endkampf*, Himmler and the SS were going after ordinary German citizens that had not been previously targeted by the regime—just because they lived west of the Rhine.

She was pleased, though, that more and more people were fighting back. She had heard from Marie Peukert, and two other Edelweiss Pirates friends that had managed to avoid arrest, that the *Einsatzkommandos* sweeping through the charred ruins of the damaged neighborhoods were encountering stiff resistance. In search of "bandit hideouts," the Gestapo was increasingly coming across well-armed groups of German deserters, fugitive Eastern workers, and other gangs, like the group that had killed Hoffman. In the process, they were also encountering regular German civilians that, out of sheer desperation, had been forced to set aside their allegiance to the *Volk* to rob and steal alongside fugitive Eastern workers to survive.

The Gestapo's view of Rhinelanders was worsening by the day as its officers emptied the region of the civilian population, and only those who resisted the orders to leave or who were deemed critical to the war effort like her and her father remained. The Gestapo had ceased referring to civilians as *Flüchtlinge*—refugees— and now referred to them as *Zwangsevakuierten*—deportees—denoting how unsympathetically they viewed those that remained in the area behind the front as a security threat. Disgruntled officers also referred to the *Räumung*—clearance—of the Left Bank Rhineland, rather than the "evacuation" of its residents, as if the German people were partisans on the Eastern Front.

In the past three months, Angela had seen the signs of anger and unrest growing in the streets for the sixty thousand people still living in Cologne. Since the fall, propaganda calling for the end of the war could be seen regularly at prominent landmarks and high traffic areas throughout the ruined city. She had also seen broadsheets encouraging soldiers to desert from the front, proclaiming, "We don't want a blood bath on German soil! We don't want the total destruction of our homeland! We don't want any more terror bombings! We want peace! We want freedom!" She had also noted the recent increase in Allied leaflets and pamphlets targeting both soldiers and civilians. One leaflet she had recently snatched up was titled "*Was kann Mann tun?*"—What Can One Do? Pointing out that "every German knows the war is lost," the flyer asked Germans to do everything they could to shorten the war, in particular by refusing to join the *Volkssturm* or work at the front.

The leaflets showed that the Allies knew all about what was going on inside Germany. They knew about the deportation and mass murder of Jews in the death camps. They knew about the forced-labor roundups and appropriation of the property of Germans who chose not to leave the region. They knew about the escalating tension between civilians and the regime. Capitalizing on the growing rift between *Staat* and *Volk*, one flyer dropped over the Rhineland informed Germans that after their deportation, the Wehrmacht and Gestapo looted the homes of "thousands of Aacheners." The propaganda pointed out that while the regime claimed it conducted the clearances to protect the German people, "security" according to the Gestapo meant deportation or digging fortifications under enemy artillery fire and air attacks. American troops were also said to be distributing newspapers along the front informing civilians and captured German soldiers about the massive defeats the Reich had experienced on both the Eastern and Western Fronts, forcing Rhinelanders to confront the reality that the war was lost.

To counter Allied propaganda, the regime was sending special political officers to the Rhineland. They distributed flyers justifying the deportations, which caused consternation amongst troops who witnessed crying women and children being forced from their homes as their property was seized and carted off. The flyers claimed the clearances were for military reasons to prevent the enemy from using civilian labor against the Reich. While the Nazi counter-propaganda admitted the deportations were a strain on the population, the flyers noted that hardship was necessary if National Socialism was to survive the war. Thus, the regime equated the survival of the Reich with the survival of Germany. Further trying to drive home the notion that the *Volk* was a community of fate, the flyers reminded war-weary citizens that in Hitler's *Endkampf,* everyone was a soldier. Goebbels made it even plainer: "Victory or Siberia!" he spouted from Berlin.

Angela just wanted it all to end.

"Come on, *Bärchen*—we've got to go!"

"All right, Papa, I'm coming!"

She threw an extra pair of cobbled shoes in her valise along with her toiletry kit, closed the bag, and took one last look at her room to make sure she hadn't forgotten anything. A sad feeling overcame her. This was her bedroom, the place where she had played with her dolls, listened to Brothers Grimm fairy tales read by her mother and father, and comfortably slept with her down quilt for the past sixteen years. Tears came to her eyes as she realized she was likely leaving it all behind.

"Angela, please!"

"I'm coming, I'm coming!"

Carrying her valise, she dashed down the partially destroyed hallway from a recent air raid bombing and went into the parlor. Her father, dressed in his Wehrmacht uniform, was waiting for her. He had a suitcase and grocery bag stuffed with food. Despite his many war wounds, he looked reasonably well, dapper even, in his full uniform glittering with war medals. In the past two months his physical health had improved immeasurably, though he was still not fully healed. He still had been getting occasional migraine headaches, and the buried shrapnel in his body caused him constant physical discomfort, but he looked much better, especially since he had cut way back on his drinking.

"To the car—quickly!" he commanded.

But they both stopped in their tracks as they heard the low, distant groan of approaching aircraft. As if on cue, a cacophony of air-raid sirens began shrieking into the night.

"British bombers—we have to hurry!"

Dashing outside into the freezing cold, they threw their belongings inside the Volkswagen *Kübelwagen* and quickly de-iced the vehicle. But as they started to pull away, a pair of Opel Blitz trucks came roaring up in front of their house. Angela's jaw dropped as she saw Kütter in the passenger seat of the lead vehicle. He was wearing his jet-black SS uniform. Glowering at them with alarm, he quickly rolled down his car window.

"*Halt mal! Halt! Halt!*" he cried, leaning out and waving at them to stop in the cold night air.

"I'm not stopping for anyone!" cried her father. "We've got to get across Hohenzollern Bridge or we're done for!"

"*Halt oder wir werden schießen!*" Stop or we will shoot!

"*Nein!*" Slapping his foot down on the gas pedal, her father drove off just before Kütter and his men could cut them off. Heading northeast on Hültzstrasse, they made a quick right-hand turn and headed east on Aachener Strasse towards the bridge with the Gestapo in pursuit. Their route followed the antique Roman road *Via Belgica* that once passed through *Aquae granni* in Roman times—now the West German town of Aachen—when necropolises lined the roads near the city.

Glancing behind her, Angela's eyes bulged wide with fear as she saw the huge Opel trucks gaining on them.

"Hurry, Papa, hurry!" she exclaimed. "They're catching up!"

The *Kübelwagen* surged forward like a racehorse over the gunning of the vehicles' engines, the dull roar of the fast-approaching bombers, and the shrieking air-raid sirens. But even though Aachener Strasse was a main thoroughfare that had been cleared of bomb debris compared to most routes in the city, the road was still littered with concrete rubble, partially infilled bomb craters, and huge natural potholes. It took all of her father's dexterity to navigate through the maze of obstructions, especially since he only had one hand to work the steering wheel. As they roared over the uneven ground and around the chunky obstacles, the Volkswagen churned up snow and mud, which Angela hoped would help mask their escape and throw off their pursuers.

But to her dismay, the lead Opel was hot on their tail.

"Faster, Papa, faster!" she cried.

"I'm trying, damnit!"

Suddenly, they were rammed from behind. Angela felt her neck whiplash violently forward and saw her father get thrown into the steering column. He gave a heavy grunt, shifted gears with his left hand, slammed his foot down on the accelerator, and pulled away from their pursuers. But within seconds, the fleet Opel out front again rammed them from behind and they were jerked hard forward.

"Can I shoot at them, Papa? We have to fight back!"

"Absolutely not! If we shoot, they will definitely kill us if they catch us!"

"Who are you kidding? They're going to kill us anyway!"

"Don't shoot—I will outrun them! You have to trust me, *Bärchen*!"

Now Kütter swept in on their left side, and Angela could see his face up close. He rolled his window down, pulled out a pistol, and, with the wind flapping the collar of his SS uniform, he gritted his teeth and pointed his gun at them. She couldn't believe her eyes: here was a fanatically desperate Nazi willing to take extreme measures just to capture one sixteen-year-old girl!

"Watch out, Papa, he's got a gun!" she cried.

Slapping his foot down on the gas pedal, he started to pull away. But not before a crackle of gunfire filled the air and a slew of bullets blasted out the side window and ricocheted off the side of the *Kübelwagen*. Once again pressing his foot down hard on the accelerator, her father tore off down the road.

But Kütter's Opel quickly caught up and flanked them on the left. This time, instead of shooting at them, the *kriminalkommissar* had the driver swerve at them to knock them off the road. The heavy truck came at them like a Tiger tank. Gripping the wheel tightly, her father swerved hard right to avoid the impact, but it wasn't enough as the massive Opel struck the Volkswagen a hard blow. The air was filled with the sound of scraping metal as the two vehicles ground against one another.

"We have to get off this road! It's too straight!" cried Angela.

"All right, I know what to do! Hold on tight!"

But they were rammed hard on the left side again, and Angela was thrown against the passenger door. Her right arm instantly went numb. Then they were hit from behind by the other vehicle, which had caught up. This time, Angela was thrown forward against the dashboard and hit her forehead. She grimaced in agony.

"Are you okay, *Bärchen*?"

"Yes, but it hurts! Get off this road! Please!"

"All right, I will! Hold on!"

He hit the gas again, pulling ahead of both of the pursuing trucks, and darted hard left onto the next cross street, Habsburgerring. The two heavy trucks missed the turn. But to Angela's dismay, they quickly turned around and started after them. Now she could hear the roar of the enemy bombers drowning out the sound of the car engines on the ground. Her father looked at her and shook his head in disbelief.

"That's just our luck. Now we have the British to contend with too. With all these car lights and the whole city blacked out, we'll stand out to those bombers like a landing strip."

"You're right, it doesn't seem fair."

He gave a fatalistic grin. "It certainly doesn't."

She smiled back at him. "Whatever happens, I love you, Papa."

"And I love you, *Bärchen*. You are everything a father could hope for."

"Don't say that. It sounds like you think we're going to die."

"I'm sorry, I just got emotional. After all, we *are* fighting for our lives."

They drove on. On their right, the blackened spires of the city's magnificent cathedral came into view.

Just then, the front tire hit a bump and they bounded in the air. They came down hard just before a curve in the road and pile of rubble, skirting the western edge of the *Altstadt*. Passing a pair of antiaircraft guns on the right—*Flakvierling* 38s with quadruple barrels—they swung in close to a mountain of rubble. In the process, they scattered a group of civilian refugees bundled up in heavy winter overcoats and head scarves that had started to cross the street.

"Be careful, Papa!" cried Angela. "You don't want to run anyone over!"

"I'm doing the best I—!"

His voice was cut off by a thunderous explosion of gunfire, coming from behind them. Looking over her shoulder out the rear window, she now saw a trio of security officers hanging out of the windows of the Opels firing pistols at them. She saw another flash of gunfire, heard the echoing staccato. Kütter and his men were now aiming low: they were apparently trying to shoot out the tires.

The colonel was forced to slow down to control the skidding vehicle. An instant later, Kütter had caught up to them and rammed them from behind. The impact jerked their heads forward then snapped them back as the suitcases in the back seat smashed violently against their headrests.

At Magnusstrasse, her father took a hard right, but he was again forced to slow down due to the large number of bomb craters. The street was pockmarked with them and he had to carefully pick his way around the blast holes, while at the same time zig-zagging around heavy blocks of concrete rubble. On both sides of the street, rubble rose in front of the ruined buildings like foothills of talus, while support posts, beams, and pipelines jutted uselessly into the sky.

The Gestapo vehicles hugged their rear bumper. When the street widened again, Kütter flanked them on the left while the other truck rammed them from behind. They were slammed forward again. Her father sped up, gunning the engine and pulling away. But though he was able to gain some separation, the massive Opels quickly closed the distance to ten yards behind them.

"*Verdammt*, I can't shake them!" he said in exasperation.

"You've got to do something! They're going to ram us again!"

"I'm going sixty miles an hour on a road cratered like the surface of the moon! What more do you want?"

"Maybe you can force them off the road!"

"And just how am I supposed to do that? They are heavy trucks! And now the British are coming in!"

Through the windshield, Angela could see the planes now, illuminated by the powerful yellow searchlights traversing the dark sky. All around the Queen City, Cologne's flak defenses had sprung to life and were firing at the attacking enemy bombers. There were only eight of the RAF aircraft in this particular raid, but they still looked menacing as they swept in like angry birds of prey.

"It's a squadron of Mosquitos!" said her father. "And they're headed straight for the *Altstadt*!"

He pounded his foot onto the gas pedal, bringing the *Kübelwagen* up to sixty-five miles per hour. A pair of bullets zipped through the rear window, made small holes, and exited through the windshield without shattering the glass.

"Keep your head down!" cried the colonel, and they both ducked down, keeping their heads just below the top of their headrests.

Another spray of bullets struck them, this time smashing into the rear of the car. The Opels were still hot on their tail and showed no sign of letting up.

"Faster, Papa, faster! We have to make that bridge!"

"It's going to be tight! But we're going to make it!"

Up ahead, Angela caught the drab-brown silhouette of El-De Haus in the headlights, its blood-red Nazi flags fluttering from the rooftop. Located just five blocks from the Cologne Cathedral, the notorious, five-story headquarters of the Cologne Gestapo had been reduced in the past two months to a half-ruined shell due to the around-the-clock air raids hammering the city. She felt herself shudder at the sight of the building that continued to double as a holding facility for prisoners and execution site for those sentenced to death. She had heard from her father and surviving witnesses that every Friday since November, shackled prisoners arrested by *Sonderkommando Brauweiler* and *Sonderkommando Mohr* arrived in transports from Brauweiler, Klingelpütz, or one of the other regional prisons for execution. With the Allies fast approaching, the pace of the killings had intensified in the past few weeks. According to her father's informant, an estimated sixty to eighty prisoners were arriving each day to the ruined building, where officers hung them from the gallows in the outdoor courtyard.

Now the RAF bombers screamed past overhead. With the booming flak guns and Kütter's machine guns rattling her ears, she looked up at the racing planes against the backdrop of El-De Haus. As the bomb bay doors to the squadron of de Havilland Mosquito twin-engined light bombers opened up, she realized that the British were targeting the Gestapo headquarters.

"Hold on!" cried her father. "They're dropping their payloads!"

"They're going for El-De Haus!"

"Yes, I see! Now hold on tight! Here we go!"

On the street up ahead, Angela saw a column of German soldiers scrambling for cover in the rubble. But they had barely made it ten yards before the bombs started dropping. Above the roar of the engine, she heard the whistling sounds of the plummeting bombs and the firing of the city's antiaircraft guns. The downtown area was rocked with a series of massive explosions. There were more than a dozen of them in all, one right after another, as the bombs struck in and around the Gestapo headquarters and adjacent buildings along Appellhofplatz. The entire *Altstadt* lit up in a series of yellow-white bursts.

The explosions shook the Gestapo headquarters and surrounding skeleton of a commercial district like an earth tremor. The ensuing flames rose fifty feet into the air. Swelling black fuel clouds spread east like tentacles towards Hohenzollern Bridge. She felt a wave of searing airborne heat through the gunshot windows from the blasts as they passed El-De Haus on their right.

Within seconds, they were enveloped in dense bomb smoke and volcanic-ash-like debris. Her father was forced to slow down. But the cloud of smoke and dust concealed them from their pursuers as her father took a right onto Tunisstrasse. They were now in the once proud financial district, "Cologne's Wall Street," but everywhere the bank buildings were reduced to roofless honeycombs covered in soot and bombed-out windows barren like eye sockets. The *Altstadt* was ground zero of the British RAF bombing campaign.

"I think we may have lost them," said Angela, no longer seeing anyone following in pursuit.

"Let's hope they haven't taken a different route and are going to try and cut us off. They must realize by now that we're headed for the bridge."

"Hurry then! We can't let Kütter catch us!"

As they drove on, smoke, debris, and a great quantity of dust continued to rain down upon them and envelope the Gestapo headquarters and surrounding financial district. Through a gauze-like opening in the smoke and dust, Angela saw the British Mosquito bombers bank left and fly off over the Rhine with their bombing mission completed. She wondered if there might be a second or third wave of bombers, which was sometimes but not always the case during enemy air attacks.

Her father turned left onto the Am Leystapel, heading north along the riverfront road next to the Rhine. It was pockmarked with bomb craters and he was forced to slow down again and zig-zag through the maze of depressions. Up ahead, Angela saw a Wehrmacht checkpoint a hundred yards south of Hohenzollern Bridge and a second checkpoint at the entrance to the bridge. There were three Wehrmacht Phänomen Granit 25 camouflaged trucks filled with troops waiting to pass through the first checkpoint and no vehicles at the second.

"Okay, we've got to make it through those two checkpoints," said her father. "Are the Gestapo still following us?"

She looked back through the battered rear window. "No, I don't see them."

"Good, maybe we've lost them. But even so, we've got to get through quickly."

The air-raid siren stopped and suddenly the night turned quiet. She took a deep breath. In the excitement of the escape and bomber attack, she felt lightheaded. She looked ahead at the red-and-white wooden bar stretching across the road with a yellow barricade light flashing in front of their path. A Wehrmacht sergeant with a submachine gun slung over his shoulder and a flashlight was checking the papers of the second truck now, as a group of heavily armed guards looked on beneath the twin spires of the famous Gothic *Dom*.

"All right, I'll do the talking. Get out your papers. Remember, you are a German Red Cross Wehrmacht auxiliary and my personal nurse. Keep your pistol out of sight and make no sudden movements. We're going to get through this."

He waited until the third heavy Wehrmacht truck drove through the checkpoint before pulling forward and coming to a complete stop before the security post. The full-beam headlights of the *Kübelwagen* now illuminated the guards, who had tensed up at their vehicle's approach and tightly gripped their weapons. Wehrmacht regulations specified that all cars driven at night should have dimmed lights to reduce the danger of aerial attack. But her father apparently wanted his bright lights on to blind and disorient the sentries at the checkpoint.

"I am a Wehrmacht colonel on an important mission for General von Manteuffel! Open the gate—I am in a hurry!"

He held out his Wehrmacht Soldbuch and Angela's Wehrpässe auxiliary papers, both of which were authentic and official. Taking the documents from him, the sergeant raised his flashlight and scrutinized them and their papers closely while the other armed guards pointed their flashlights at them and drew closer to peer inside.

Her father shook his head impatiently. *"Ich sagte, öffne das Tor—ich habe es eilig!"* I said open the gate—I am in a hurry!

The sergeant said nothing and continued to study the papers. Angela felt a bead of sweat trickle down her temple as the moment seemed to drag on forever. She looked back over her shoulder to see if Kütter and his men were coming up from behind, but she didn't anything. Could it be they had been hit during the air raid?

"Did you not hear me?" snorted her father impatiently to the Wehrmacht sergeant. "I am in a hurry, damnit!"

Still, the security man hesitated. The three other guards armed with rifles bearing drawn bayonets continued to peer inside the vehicle with their flashlights. Angela made eye contact with one of the guards. For a split second, she was sure they were going to arrest her and her father. But then, after several excruciating seconds that seemed like a lifetime, the sergeant handed back the papers to her father and motioned to one of his men, who promptly lifted the bar.

"You can go now," he said. "But you must dim those lights or the enemy will shoot them out for you."

The colonel nodded. "Yes, of course." He flicked off his headlights and turned on his driving lights.

The sergeant waved them through. Angela breathed a sigh of relief as her father pressed his foot on the gas pedal and drove forward towards the second checkpoint.

"That's it, we've made it," said the colonel. "No one can stop us now."

"Just get us across that bridge, Papa. Then we can celebrate."

He glanced out his window, to the west in the opposite direction from the Rhine on their right. "Look at our cathedral. More than two hundred air raids and it still stands tall."

She looked up at the twin spires reaching towards the heavens. The Cologne Cathedral truly was an enduring symbol of Germany. It filled her with pride that it had resisted so many aerial attacks and continued to stand as the symbolic guardian of the Queen City along the banks of the Rhine. But the train station to the north hadn't fared as well; only the charred ribs of its arched glass ceiling remained and the lengthy galleria was blanketed with concrete rubble and twisted steel.

"I am going to miss that old church," she said. "When the war is over, I hope we can come back home and—*Papa, look out!*"

As he looked up, a heavy Opel truck seemed to materialize from out of nowhere. It bore down upon her and her father with a vengeance, racing down from the steps leading to the cathedral, and she realized that the truck had been waiting for them to attempt to cross the bridge. The last thing they both saw before the terrible impact was the face of Criminal Commissioner Kütter, who was now behind the wheel. His teeth were bared like a wolf and his eyes were swollen to the size of plums as they locked onto the Volkswagen. The hands gripped the steering wheel tightly, like the tentacles of an octopus, and Angela felt momentarily paralyzed.

Her father turned hard right towards the river to deflect the blow, hoping the huge Opel might sideswipe them instead of crashing into the driver's side head-on, but it wasn't enough. The vehicle drove into the left-front of the car like a freight train, pitching the *Kübelwagen* to the right like a giant shoving aside a luckless child.

The car flipped over once before coming to a halt upside down with the driver's side facing the river and the two of them tangled together in the passenger seat.

For a moment, they both just lay there, too stunned to do anything. But then, realizing that she and her father were trapped inside the vehicle and would not get away from the Gestapo as planned, she felt an overwhelming despondency. She and her father would soon be dead Germans. Just two more anonymous victims of senseless murder, like the hundreds of thousands—or was it, like the BBC said, millions—of Jews that had been exterminated like rats.

It was then she heard the stentorian voice of the dreaded fifty-four-year-old Kütter. He was barking out orders to his men, as well as to the guards who had run over from the security checkpoints to see what all the commotion was about.

"I want them alive! I want them alive!" he was shouting excitedly.

Angela touched her face and body, trying to gauge if she was badly hurt. Blood trickled down her cheek. Pain throbbed in her head and shoulders. But she was all in one piece and seemingly mobile. But to what purpose, if Kütter was just going to have her and her father killed?

She heard a heavy groan. "Papa, are you all right?"

"*Ja*, but we have to get out of here."

"But how? We're trapped inside the car."

"They'll kill us, *Bärchen*. We must steal away somehow before they…"

But his words died out as the legs and jack-booted feet of several Gestapo officers became visible next to the vehicle. Slowly, a figure kneeled down and she came face-to-face with the *kriminalkommissar* in his jet-black SS uniform and pointing a *Schmeisser* machine pistol at her and her father. His eyes blazed with the intensity of a zealot, and she hated him.

"If you can move under your own power, get out of vehicle now!" he commanded. "Slowly, or we will shoot! Can you get out?"

"What should we do?" she whispered to her father. "Should we fight back?"

"No, our best chance is to surrender and buy time," he whispered back. "My Wehrmacht rank and association with General von Manteuffel may very well save us. That's why, once we are under interrogation, we must admit to nothing and constantly remind them of our connection to von Manteuffel."

"Are they going to torture us?"

"Yes, and you can confess nothing, *Bärchen*. They are going to want confessions and we must not give them to them. It is all right for you and me both to admit we knew Bartholomäus Schröder, but that is all. You had a girl's crush on him, but were never an Edelweiss Pirate. Do you understand me?"

"Yes, Papa."

"Good, then stay strong."

"If you can move under your own power, you must come out now!" shouted Kütter again. "Can you both move?"

"Yes," replied the colonel.

"Good, then get out of the damned car! Now!"

He punctuated the command by clicking his *Schmeisser*. Her father took her hand and held it reassuringly, and their eyes met. *Be strong, my daughter, and we will come out all right,* his expression seemed to say. She gripped his hand harder.

"I love you, Papa," she said.

"And I love you, *Bärchen*. As I told you before, you are everything a father could ever ask for."

"You're not supposed to say that, remember?"

"I just wanted you to know how I feel. In case something should happen to me."

"What about me?"

"You are my sweet baby girl. Nothing is going to happen to you."

"Damnit, I've had enough! Seize them!"

"Stop! We're coming! We're coming!" cried her father, but it was too late as Kütter and his men smashed the windows and dragged them from the battered car. Still dazed, they shook away their blurry vision as they were roughly handled and handcuffed. Slowly the *kriminalkommissar*, immaculately dressed in his black-leather SS uniform with a red swastika armband, came into sharper focus along with a pack of Gestapo officers and German soldiers pointing pistols and submachine guns at them. The dreaded Torquemada of Cologne and monster of Brauweiler Prison looked at them with a grotesque curvature of the mouth that made it appear as though the man was smiling when in fact he wasn't at all.

It was the smile of a vulture.

The Gestapo officer then clicked his gleaming, polished boots together with an air of self-importance.

"I must tell you how thrilled I am to be having you two as my guests at Brauweiler Prison—a place that, I regret to say, will most likely be your last residence on earth."

# CHAPTER 43



ONCE REGARDED AS one of the most historic monasteries in all the Rhineland, Brauweiler Abbey had since the last century been transformed into a place of misery and torture. Founded by Count Palatine Ezzo and his wife Mathilde of the Benedictine order in 1024 A.D., the resplendent grounds included the Romanesque St. Nicholas Abbey Church, a medieval cloister, and magnificent baroque abbey buildings from the late 18th century. But since 1803, when Napoleon secularized and converted the abbey into a labor camp for beggars, Brauweiler had become notorious for forced labor, deprivation, and savage mental and physical abuse.

During the *Kaiserreich* from 1871 to 1918, the workhouse grounds were expanded to include a new cell block and a women's prison to house "asocials" such as prostitutes, juvenile delinquents, beggars, and alcoholics. The poor food and physical, monotonous work provided a grim contrast to the lively bustle of the sprawling metropolis of the Queen City. Indeed, parents often resorted to invoking the abbey's name to discipline their wayward children, warning them that if they misbehaved the police would take them away to Brauweiler. But it was the extreme cruelty directed towards alleged enemies of the state during Hitler's sadistic reign that eventually came to define the prison.

Like nearby Klingelpiitz Prison, since the start of the war Brauweiler had served as a regional detainment facility for German political prisoners and escaped foreign laborers before transport to concentration camps deeper inside the Reich. Between March 1933 and March 1943, the site was referred to as the "Brauweiler Concentration Camp." During this period, the *Provinzial* labor camp with its workhouse was used as an auxiliary prison by the Cologne Gestapo and a center for criminal-biological research. The Gestapo also used the prison during large-scale arrest operations, such as the roundup of Jewish men after the 1938 *Kristallnacht* pogroms and the destruction of underground resistance networks of Polish and French prisoners in April 1944.

As the Allied forces closed in on the Reich, the prison transported most of its inmates to Hannover or sent them to the Wehrmacht. Largely emptied by late August 1944, the Gestapo used the site to hold high-profile political prisoners arrested during the roundup of dissidents after the July 20, 1944 bombing attempt on Hitler's life by Colonel Claus von Stauffenberg. The most prominent of these inmates was Konrad Adenauer, the former mayor of Cologne the Nazis forced from office after seizing power in 1933.

At 11:09 p.m., Angela and Colonel Günther Lange—both aware of Brauweiler's dreadful history—were taken to the prison's clothing depot. Here they received their prison uniforms and had to hand in their personal belongings, including their shoelaces so they wouldn't hang themselves. From there, they were shoved, poked, and prodded up the stairs and into a second-floor interrogation room, where they were handcuffed and stuffed into chairs. It was here where even they were shocked to discover the true depths of inhumanity Kütter and his two chief interrogators—

*Kriminalassistents* Josef Hoegen and Walter Hirschfeld—were capable of during "intense interrogation." That was the Gestapo's euphemistic term for the brutal torture of prisoners to force them to confess. If the officers went too far with the torture or decided to exterminate their prisoners, which was often the case for Eastern European inmates but rare for Germans since Himmler wanted a loyal *Volk* to fight on behalf of the Reich, they would carry out *sonderbehandlung*, or "special treatment," the term they used for executions carried out without court judgment.

Beneath powerful electric lamps, Hoegen and Hirschfeld repeatedly struck her and her father in the face and body with truncheons for fifteen solid minutes. From Edelweiss Pirates' survivors, Angela knew that Kütter and his men used the initial beatings as a form of "welcoming" their detainees to Brauweiler and that it was administered to all prisoners, regardless of age or sex, upon their arrival. She also knew the inhumanity had its own twisted logic: it was designed to physically and mentally break the inmates and send them into shock as quickly as possible, making them pliable for future interrogation.

But as bad as the beatings with truncheons were, it was the thick wooden table leg—called the "Clock of the Rhine" because it left prisoners' ears ringing—that terrified Angela the most. Hoegen and Hirschfeld took turns striking her and her father more than half a dozen times with the lethal implement in the head, buttocks, shoulders, and shins. And then, when the two of them lay wrecked on the floor with blood bubbling from their noses and mouths, a smiling Kütter stomped in to deliver a few well-placed kicks to their ribs. Once they were thoroughly bloodied and close to unconscious, the officers tightly handcuffed their mangled arms behind their backs and took them to separate cells in solitary confinement.

"We will talk again soon, young lady," said Kütter, standing in the open doorway to bid her a cruel farewell. "Enjoy your rest."

She scowled at him, doing her best to conceal the terror and overwhelming despair she felt inside. Though she wanted to cry, she held back her tears, not wanting the reprehensible Kütter or his goons to see any sign of weakness. She quickly looked around the cell: it had no bed, a single barred window high up on the wall, and a wooden bucket into which she could relieve herself. The place wasn't fit for the worst criminal on the face of the earth. But she would have to stay strong and gut it out, as her father had told her to do. After all, there was at least some chance—albeit a remote one—they might be able to survive.

The heavy steel door clanged shut. She collapsed onto the cold concrete floor in total darkness, battered and terrified out of her mind. But she knew this was just the beginning and it would get much worse. Crawling to a corner of the cell, she leaned her back against the wall. As she did so, she was nearly overcome by the suffocating, nauseating odors from human excrement, perspiration, and wet moldy dankness.

She tried to sleep but could not. Her whole body ached with pain from being savagely beaten. But it wasn't the physical suffering that kept her awake—it was the screams of terror of those being tortured on the floor above. The shrieks and moans lasted all night long, and she knew her time would soon come for similar "treatment." She waited fretfully for the banging on the door which would tell her that it was her turn to be interrogated. Or, with the Allies so close, to simply be transported eastwards to a labor camp and almost certain death. But she lost all sense of time until dawn when a trickle of diffuse sunlight bled through her small, steel-barred window and she was fed a slice of moldy dark bread and that was all.

They didn't come for her until the following evening. It was again Kütter and his two chief interrogators, Hoegen and Hirschfeld. They brought her to the same interrogation room they had taken her and her father before, stuffing her in the chair in the center of the room with her hands manacled behind her back.

But this time she was all alone.

ΨΨΨ

The interrogation room was spacious and lit up with heated lamps since the curtains were drawn and no natural light could enter. Judging from the screams she had heard throughout the night coming from the interrogation rooms on the floor above, the walls were not sound-proofed at all. In one corner rested a chair like a dentist's next to a tray of sharp medical instruments. In another was a table with an oven and copper wires that were heated to burn beneath the fingernails of victims, and a huge tub of cold water and ice for subjecting the prisoner to the much-feared "water treatment." On the west wall loomed a portrait of a gimlet-eyed Hitler, and on the opposite wall a painting of SS Chief Himmler—in case a prisoner needed to be reminded to whom he or she would ultimately have to answer.

*Stay strong and tell them nothing,* she reminded herself.

"It is time for you to confess your crimes," said Kütter without preamble. "We know you are an Edelweiss Pirate—specifically a Cologne Navajo. We also know that you were the girlfriend of Bartholomäus Schröder with the code name Mucki, and that you took part in crimes against the state with the Steinbrück gang. Just tell us the truth and you will likely survive this war. That is the best I can offer you."

She hated being completely defenseless against these brutes. Somehow, she had to convince them that, though she had known Barthel and they were boyfriend and girlfriend, she had not actually taken part in the Edelweiss Pirate resistance movement or any gang activity.

"Can you please take off these handcuffs?" she asked. "They hurt my hands."

Unused to acting on any humanitarian impulse, the rabid Nazi Kütter hesitated. But after a moment, he relented and gave a little nod to Hoegen. The *kriminalassistent* stepped forward, unlocked the handcuffs, and ripped them off her hands in a violent motion. Angela screamed. The handcuffs had caused her hands to swell so badly that they looked like fat sausages, and when Hoegen tore them off her bound wrists, the skin tore away. She was bleeding and in severe pain.

"Now tell us what we want to know," said Kütter impatiently.

"All right, I will tell you what I know," said Angela, rubbing her bloody wrists to ameliorate the stinging pain. "I did know Barthel Schröder. But I did not know that he was an Edelweiss Pirate. Nor did I take part in any criminal activities with him or anyone else. On that score, I think you have me confused with someone else and this is all a big mistake."

Kütter looked at her sharply. "A mistake?"

"Yes, a case of mistaken identity."

"Let me explain how this is going to work," he said in a calm voice that carried an undercurrent of brutality. "Here at Brauweiler, we do not tolerate liars. In fact, we detest them and enjoy inflicting unspeakable pain upon them, which is fully within our legal right to do."

"How can that be so?"

Kütter's face showed surprise, followed swiftly by irritation; he was not used to his charges questioning him or disrupting his interrogations. But officers abusing inmates for their own entertainment was in clear violation of Himmler's orders to curb violence against Rhinelanders, her father had told her on the way to Brauweiler. He had also told her to remind her interrogators of her rights when being questioned, to hold their violent tendencies in check.

"For your information, which I shall of course repeat to your father for his benefit, the guidelines issued by the Reich Security Main Office in June 1942 specifically call for officers to resort to 'intensified interrogation methods' if they suspect prisoners know about threats to state security. Sleep deprivation, reduced rations, solitary confinement, and physical force are not only allowed but recommended in such situations. You are an Edelweiss Pirate, Angela. You are as much an enemy of the state as a Jew, Bolshevik, or Allied agent. You are a member of a resistance movement, a terrorist, and an asocial who has been in league with foreign criminals and army deserters. Now I am going to ask you questions and you are going to answer them, or you will undergo 'treatment' for days, weeks, perhaps even months. You need to understand that at this moment you are in control of your fate. Just tell the truth and your conscience will be free and you will not be harmed."

"I already told you. I am not nor have I ever been an Edelweiss Pirate. I admit I knew Barthel but he didn't tell me he was in a criminal gang."

"Stop these damned lies. In the end you will talk. Everyone does, even men far more stubborn and brave than you. The only question is how long you can last before I break you and you tell me what I want to know. Now tell me what you did on behalf of the Edelweiss Pirates."

"But I've already told you that I don't know anything about them."

He shook his head in dismay. "Very well, you leave me no choice."

He motioned his two pit bulls.

"Stop, stop, I'm telling you the truth!"

"Shut up, you sow!" snarled Hoegen.

"*Ja*, shut your vile mouth, whore!" bellowed Hirschfeld.

She tried to fight them off, but they quickly clamped the handcuffs back on her, turned her upside down on the chair, lifted her skirt, and took turns beating her with the thick, wooden Clock of the Rhine. When she finally lost consciousness, they poured water over her and Hirschfeld kicked her in the back of her neck with his boot. When she screamed in agony, he gagged her with a towel. When she again fell off the chair unconscious, Hoegen grabbed her by her feet and dragged her across the floor face down, so that blood ran from her nose and mouth.

Unable to resist getting in on the bloodbath, Kütter pushed his way past his two underlings and smacked her in the face with a truncheon, drawing a torrent of blood from her battered nose. He then motioned for his brutal comrades to join in. With malicious smiles, Hoegen and Hirschfeld stepped in and delivered a series of savage blows to her arms and legs while calling her a "sow" and "whore." When he saw they were getting carried away, Kütter ordered the two *kriminalassistents* to stand down. They seated her handcuffed again in the chair and drew away, red-faced and out of breath.

With blood streaming down her face, Angela just stared at them in silent rage, biting her lip and forcing herself not to even utter a moan despite her agony. She found it inconceivable that human beings could abuse a defenseless person like this. Hoegen, in particular, seemed to get a sadistic thrill out of punishing her.

Now Kütter leaned in close, and Angela could smell the schnapps mingled with bratwurst on his breath. "Tell me the names, code names, and whereabouts of everyone you came into contact with from the Edelweiss Pirates and Bomber Hans Steinbrück's Ehrenfeld Group. I know you know them, so it is time to come clean."

Struggling hard not to whimper in pain, she decided that she had to give them something. "I told you I don't know anything. Barthel never told me what he and his friends did. But I must admit I had my suspicions that they were up to no good. Though I couldn't prove anything."

"So, you did know that they were with the Cologne Navajos."

"No, I didn't."

"I think you are lying. I need names, code names, and addresses. We've probably already rounded most of them up already, but I need to know everything you know about Steinbrück and the Pirates, as well as the Committee for a Free Germany. These terrorist groups are all connected and I want you to tell me about them."

"They are not terrorist groups. Or at least, that's what I heard."

"That's what you heard? Who planted these subversive thoughts in that stupid little head of yours? Your father perhaps?"

"No, I suppose it was Barthel."

"Your terrorist boyfriend. How can you expect us to believe that you are innocent in all this when you admit that he was your boyfriend?"

"Because it's the truth."

"No, it's not. You know how I know that? Because I have an instinctive feel for which of my prisoners is telling the truth. And you should know that I have never used enhanced interrogation measures against anyone who wasn't ultimately found to be harboring illegal secrets, or who wasn't working for the underground."

Again, he motioned his brutish cohorts. This time they pounded her all over her body. When she slumped in her chair and lost consciousness, they threw a pail of water on her and she came to again. She looked up groggily at her tormentors; one of her eyes was swollen shut and Kütter's face was distorted, surreal.

"How many Edelweiss Pirates are left and how do you contact one another?"

"I have no idea since I am not a member of the group."

Kütter struck her in the face again with his truncheon.

"Who is the leader of the group? Are they stockpiling weapons with foreign criminals and army deserters?"

This time she remained silent.

Kütter motioned his two goons again. This time Hoegen delivered a hard blow to her shins with his truncheon. The blow made a sickening thud and Angela couldn't help but let out a small groan of agony.

Now the *kriminalkommissar* spoke in a gentle, soothing voice. "I know that one hurt. Just remember, only you can make the pain stop."

Angela scowled defiantly at him through a mask of fresh blood, tired of being a punching bag to these National Socialist monsters. "You are going to wish you had never laid a hand on me and my father. General von Manteuffel is going to intervene on our behalf. You are going to be severely punished. My father is a colonel directly under his command and I myself am a Wehrmacht auxiliary. You have made a serious mistake in arresting and torturing us. We are German patriots, damn you!"

At the mention of the Panzer Baron and her and her father's Wehrmacht service, Kütter's men looked at him. "Commissioner, should we check with higher authority?" asked Hirschfeld timorously.

"No, we do not need any such authority. We are dealing with common criminals who tried to evade capture."

Now even Hoegen looked worried. "But if General von Manteuffel is going to intervene, shouldn't we have all our ducks—?"

"Shut up, you cowards! We are not giving these prisoners up unless ordered to by Gutenberger or Himmler himself! It is simply out of the question! Now go fetch her father from his cell! We'll soon see just how tough these two truly are!"

Hoegen looked confused. "You want me to get the colonel, sir?"

"Fetch him now, the both of you! We'll see if young Angela here—or should I say Mucki—changes her tune once she sees what we've got in store for Herr Lange!"

Hoegen and Hirschfeld left the room and returned five minutes later with the manacled colonel. Seeing him limping in one-armed dressed in his drab and dirty prison uniform instead of his medal-laden Wehrmacht uniform, Angela couldn't help but feel as if all hope was lost.

"I tried to give you a chance, young lady," said Kütter. "But since you continue to lie to us, I'm afraid we're going to have to give your father the water treatment."

"But why?" she gasped. "He has nothing to do with this."

"With all due respect, I think he does."

Her father reached out to her with his captivating blue eyes. "You have done nothing wrong, *Bärchen*, and there is nothing to tell them." Now he turned towards Kütter. "I drove away last night because I refused to continue to be harassed by the Gestapo and am under strict orders to report to General von Manteuffel's at his headquarters near Bonn. What I did was not a crime and you have no right to hold either me or my daughter. I have given you the letter from the general, so you know that he is to be contacted immediately about our whereabouts."

"I don't care about your stupid letter. You are both criminals and are going to pay for your crimes. Give him the water treatment."

She and her father vigorously protested, but their pleas fell on deaf ears. They jerked her father from his wooden chair, carried him to the corner of the room, and placed him before the huge tub of ice-cold water. With his hands handcuffed behind his back, he was powerless to resist.

"*Nun fahren Sie zum Himmel!*" exclaimed Kütter, as if they were about to play a fun children's game. Now you go to heaven!

"*Nein! Nein!*" cried Angela

Hoegen and Hirschfeld thrust him beneath the frigid water and held him under. He jerked and kicked furiously, but to no avail. They were able to keep him pressed beneath the surface so that his head was near the bottom of the water tank. She couldn't believe her eyes and cried out in protest, but Kütter just slapped her and told her to shut up or he would gag her. More than two minutes passed before he was pulled to the surface. He gasped desperately for air.

"Under again!" commanded Kütter.

With brutal force, they shoved her father under over and over again for several minutes, finally yanking him from the freezing water and tossing him to the cold, wet floor like a slab of salmon. Then Kütter, Hoegen, and Hirschfeld proceeded to grill her and her father with questions, whacking them with blunt implements when they didn't receive the answers they sought. When she and her father were slow to respond or evasive, the process was repeated, again and again, sometimes using the Clock of the Rhine. When it was finally over, Kütter was panting—in the way that Angela imagined an ox would be after pulling a heavy load or an overweight, middle-aged man seconds after letting go his seed. She was both revolted and heartbroken. But neither she nor her father were defeated.

"Colonel, you must stop this obfuscation. I know the law—and I know you know the law—so why don't you and your daughter come clean. Just tell us what we want to know so you can return to General Manteuffel's staff. What do you say?"

"I say that you, Commissioner, are everything that is wrong with Germany."

Gritting his teeth like an enraged German shepherd, Kütter gestured towards his subordinates. They came in swinging like windmills. The thrashing continued for several minutes until the interrogators were once again out of breath. Kütter then again took over the questioning—issuing threat after threat when his queries remained unanswered. Hoegen kicked her and her father in the shins with his jackboot, and Hirschfeld struck them both so hard with the Clock of the Rhine that he knocked the wind out of them. When they fainted once more, Hoegen and Hirschfeld threw buckets of water on them until they came to.

"Now, Colonel and Fraülein Lange," said Kütter after letting the pain subside. "The time has come for you to talk. You have established that you are among the bravest we have ever faced. But further resistance is pointless. Now tell me the truth, or I am afraid you will force me to leave you two alone with *Kriminalassistents* Hoegen and Hirschfeld. As you have no doubt gathered, they take their loyalty to our Führer quite seriously."

"We don't know anything," said Angela, not caring any more what happened to her. "You have been wrong all along—and you are going to pay the price."

"Pay the price?"

"When the Allies win, they are going to hunt you and everyone else who worked for the SS down! When they find you, they're going to hang you or lock you up for a very long time!"

Kütter twitched with a combination of rage and fear, but quickly gathered himself. "Well then, young lady, I would have to say that until that day comes we are going to have to get much better acquainted."

And with that, he pulled out a set of worn brass knuckles and a pair of tweezers for ripping out pubic hair.

# CHAPTER 44



## JABEEK, SOUTHERN HOLLAND

### FEBRUARY 17, 1945

STANDING BEFORE the Quartermaster Department supply desk, McBurney glowered at the white clerk who was busy ignoring him while rummaging through army requisitions and bills of lading. He had politely informed the supply clerk that his two-month-old tanker's uniform stunk to high heaven and was falling apart—which was why he needed a new one—but the corporal dismissed him out of hand. He told McBurney that he was fresh out of clean uniforms, though he might get some more in later in the week. The clerk then told him to scram: he was busy and didn't want to have to look at the dirty tanker's miserable black face anymore.

It was only through great effort that McBurney was able to control his temper. But he knew things were about to get ugly. He was determined to get a fresh, clean uniform and new pair of boots—and he was not going to leave the supply depot until he had them. Though affable and cautious by nature, he had been on the front-line for more than one hundred straight days and he was tattered, gunpowder-stained, and exhausted beyond care about the potential consequences of his actions.

The 761st had arrived two weeks earlier to the Netherlands, after having traveled 100 miles north from Bastogne through a battle-torn landscape along narrow roads clogged with army traffic. Their headquarters and supply tents were set up just across the Belgian border in the town of Jabeek, near Sittard. In the relative safety of Holland, the 761st's assignment was to relieve elements of the Twenty-First British Army Group as they prepared for the Rhineland offensive scheduled to begin in late February. The battalion's secondary mission was to perform tank and auxiliary vehicle maintenance and to train the sizable number of replacements who were, at long last, augmenting the battalion's strength.

Standing in front of the supply clerk's desk, McBurney couldn't believe he was pleading his case before some little deskbound prick when only days removed from savage fighting. Supporting the 345th Infantry, Charlie Company had recently met an enemy column moving east from Emierscheid and had killed at least 175 enemy soldiers. As he and his fellow tankers had driven off, McBurney had turned around to see the enemy bodies and weapons ablaze, and the visceral image that would forever be imprinted in his mind came back to him right now. He remembered what a strange sight it had been to see such devastation and carnage on a simple country road. Now, as his mind returned to the present, he leaned forward and placed his hands on the desk, managing to make eye contact again with the desk clerk, who looked up with irritation. A smoking Camel dangled insolently from his mouth.

"What are you still doing here, boy? I thought I told you to get lost."

"I want a new uniform and boots right now."

"Or else what?"

"Or else I'm going to beat your candy ass, that we both know hasn't seen a lick of combat, until it's black-and-blue. Do you understand me?"

"Jesus, are you one uppity fellow or what? You can't talk to me like that. I told you that we're out of uniforms."

"I'm a sergeant and outrank you, you little pecker, so I'll talk to you any damn way I please. Now if I'm not wearing a clean new uniform in the next five minutes, I'm going to break your fucking nose. I'm also going to report you to the MPs."

The clerk scoffed through a haze of cigarette smoke. "*You* report me? For what?"

"I know what you're up to around here. You're a goddamn black marketeer."

"What the hell you talkin' about?"

"I'm talking about you selling off unit supplies to troops and local civilians—and making a handsome profit doing it. That's what I'm fucking talking about."

Suddenly, the clerk's expression changed and he looked nervous. He threw up his hands in protest, but McBurney could tell it was just an act. The bastard was guilty as sin. "Now just wait one second here. I ain't done any such—"

He stopped right there as McBurney leaned over the desk and grabbed him by the collar. "I'm going to tell you one last time. If I am not wearing a brand spanking new uniform and boots in the next…four minutes now…I'm going to break your fucking nose and tear off those wingnut ears of yours. You got it, *boy*?"

The dynamics had swiftly changed. Now the clerk didn't just look nervous but genuinely terrified. McBurney couldn't help but feel a little jolt of satisfaction. But he still needed the little bastard to back down and get him what he wanted.

"Why are you still sitting there, corporal? Now you only have three minutes until I wring your neck like a chicken. Get moving!"

"Okay, okay, I might could be able to scrounge up—"

But McBurney was having none of it. "You ain't scrounging up anything, goddamnit!" he cut him off. "I want a fresh uniform and new boots—and I want them right now! And everything better fit just right!"

"A-All right," stammered the clerk. "I'm fixing to get you what you want. But why do you have to get all bat-shit crazy on me like this?"

"Shut your piehole and get my gear! And make it quick, damnit!"

It took the mulish corporal five minutes but McBurney got everything he asked for—plus two new pairs of socks. Changing right there, he tossed the supply clerk his smelly ragged uniform, dirty socks, and worn-out boots as if discarding a bag of rotten vegetables. Returning to his C Company tent, he had a smile on his face. He had successfully managed to obtain his first change of clothing since being pulled off the line in France and driving north to Bastogne. The new uniform felt so good to him his only regret was that he hadn't done it sooner.

"Well, well, well," said Smitty. "Someone got himself a new set of duds."

"Yeah, but I had to threaten the damned supply clerk to get them. I told him I'd break his nose if he didn't give me a new uniform and boots."

"Man, I didn't know you had it in you. I've got to say you're looking good. Now if you just washed up, you could almost pass for that fellow I used to go dancing with at the Savoy."

"We're going to get back there someday. I want to see Chick Webb play 'Stompin' at the Savoy' and jitterbug to Count Basie out on that dance floor."

"I'm partial to Cootie Williams myself."

"I know you are. And you're going to be dancing to Cootie all night long because we're going to make it, man. We're going to survive this here war, Smitty."

"How do you know?"

"Because I saw it in my dream. I had what you might call an 'epiphany.'"

"An e-pi-phany? That's a mighty big word, Satchmo."

"I know some big words."

"Apparently." His expression turned glum. "But that e-pi-phany of yours didn't save poor Willie, now did it? And neither did it Ruben Rivers, Turley, or Coleman. So why should *we* be the ones to survive?"

"Because we got each other's backs and we're luckier than most. We're like cats—we've got nine lives and we've only used up one or two so far."

"You really believe that?"

"Yep, and I know you do too. I know Willie, Ruben, and the others didn't make it, but we're gonna. We just have to keep on saving each other's asses, man, and we'll come out all right."

Smith grinned. "Okay, I like that. That sounds like a plan to me."

"And then one day, we're going to take that big boat home and march in our uniforms up ole Fifth Avenue. And the folks lining the streets are going to look at us with newfound respect. It'll be a sight to see."

They were both grinning now, their heads filled with dreams of a picture-perfect end to it all. Somehow, they would survive the madness and brutality of both the Germans and their own white troops and return home as conquering heroes. In that moment, McBurney felt the power of their brotherhood and their intertwined destinies.

But they both still missed their buddy Willie Devore and had not gotten over his loss. At night when they sat around with the other men playing cards and swapping stories, McBurney could tell that Smith was still deeply hurting. Something had changed in his brother that sad day Willie had died. The dreams of heroic exploits that had defined his every waking thought since childhood had for the most part been stripped away with Devore's death. McBurney knew that he himself had changed too. He tried his best to find solace in fleeting moments of shared humor around the campfire and in the presence of his friends, and otherwise resigned himself to the daily grind. But the image of easygoing and fun-loving Willie getting half his head blown off still haunted him as well.

McBurney remembered back to the three of them huddling and shivering around a small fire in the encroaching dark before Tillet, listening to Willie talking about long, hot summer days growing up in South Carolina, the shifting and swaying summer dresses of the girls offering tantalizing glimpses of their supple breasts and bare calves. The way Willie described it made it sound like paradise. But right now, McBurney was just glad to see his good buddy Smitty smiling, something he hadn't seen him do much since Devore had fallen under enemy fire.

McBurney knew he owed his life to Smith's refusal to leave him behind at Tillet—and he had saved Smith's bacon in the Lorraine campaign. They had a knack for saving one another. But they would have to continue to lean upon one another and lift each other's spirits, McBurney knew, because with the ferocity the Germans were still showing, the conflict was looking like it wasn't going to end anytime soon.

Since the 761st's arrival in Holland, the war had again shifted. Only a few weeks earlier, the Germans had been on the offensive and stood as strong and formidable as a giant dragon, breathing fire and munching on the bones of the Allied armies.

But by early February, it had become obvious to McBurney that he was facing a fading and overstretched enemy, though the 761st still encountered pockets of heavy resistance. By the middle of the month, the Germans had consolidated their forces and pulled back, and the Black Panthers were up against a solidly entrenched army in a defensive position, a fanatical enemy that was prepared to defend its own soil for its demented Führer until the last bullet. Now the tables had turned and the Germans were waiting for the Americans and British to come to them.

Though the enemy remained unseen along the front lines, McBurney knew the Germans were lurking just over the next ridge. The infantry patrols continued to encounter stiff automatic and small-arms fire from their hidden opponents. After the bloodletting at Tillet, McBurney knew that Nazi Germany still had fierce resolve and that the 761st had to be ready for what would likely prove to be the bloodiest fighting of the war yet.

After more than a hundred days on the line, the Black Panthers were no longer the gung-ho unit of old. McBurney and the battalion's other veterans had given up all illusions about the honor and glory of war. They had seen too much death, destruction, and loss to believe any more that war was anything like Errol Flynn battling the Nazis in *Desperate Journey* or what Spencer Tracy experienced in *Thirty Seconds Over Tokyo*.

What the tankers wanted most of all was to be a strong outfit again. Coming out of the Bulge, the battalion was dangerously understrength and in desperate need of tank commanders, gunners, and drivers due to the crippling losses in the Ardennes. To make matters worse, the 761st had hobbled away from the grueling campaign with less than twenty operational M4 Shermans and M5 Stuarts combined.

In the past two weeks, the battalion had built up the effective strength to 33 officers, three warrant officers, and 680 enlisted men to go along with more than 25 tanks. The men even turned in a number of their Shermans and received brand new tanks in return. But they needed more men and more tanks, and they also needed R and R. After more than a hundred straight days on the line, many were physically spent and at a low point, unable to see any end to the conflict. They needed a well-deserved break. But unlike the all-white outfits they fought beside, they would not get one.

Still, despite the grind of the war and worst European winter in thirty-five years, the men rose to the challenge of repairing and building up their fleet of tanks and training the new combat replacements. McBurney and the other tankers pitched in a helping hand to the overworked maintenance teams to service and repair their vehicles. They trained the replacements in the mechanics of driving, loading, and bracketing targets. In the battalion's two-week crash course, they turned the "fillers" into proficient enough tankers that they could take part in combat missions while learning other skills on-the-job. And when called out to support the infantry in offensive operations and front-line skirmishes, the companies fought tenaciously.

The emergency replacements came from a variety of army units. Completely untrained in tanks, they wanted to join the 761st because of the battalion's fighting reputation. Aching for the chance to see action instead of hauling supplies and digging latrines, the volunteers took reductions in rank for the opportunity to become Panthers and come out fighting. The U.S. Armored Force Replacement

Training Center at Fort Knox continued to train replacement tankers throughout the fighting in Europe, but none of these men were African-American. Unlike white units, the Training Center turned out no replacements for the 761st since the experimental tank battalions had been intended solely to pacify Eleanor Roosevelt and had never been intended for combat. The segregated Army, thus, had no choice but to put out a call among Negro soldiers in service units for volunteers to fight in tanks. Black replacement tankers were called to combat duty only because the heavy fighting in Lorraine, the Saar, and the Ardennes had taken its toll and well-trained separate tank battalions were desperately needed.

Some of the men didn't like the Replacement Command pumping new troops into the 761st. They considered the move ill-timed when they had just lost their brothers and the volunteers too green to make a genuine difference. At first, McBurney and the other veterans cared little about the replacements and actually resented them. Though they knew the battalion needed tankers, somehow replacing the friends and comrades they had lost seemed a sacrilege, and they had little interest in untrained, untested men from what they considered lesser specialties.

But as McBurney worked with the new volunteers, he realized they were just like him and Smitty two years earlier when they had been rejected from the Air Corps and had stumbled upon the idea of joining the 761st. He and the other veteran tankers quickly learned that the replacements had names and more experience than they gave them credit for. Many came from service units, and a number had seen action at the front in the Ardennes and were committed to fighting with the 761st. He and the other trainers made tankers out of them in the two-week crash course, with many of the new volunteers becoming competent machine-gunners and cannoneers within a few days. Some of the more seasoned and mature replacements, McBurney had to admit, might even see tank commander in their future.

For McBurney and the other tankers, the best thing about Holland was the people. The Dutch citizens spoke English fluently and treated them with genuine respect and warmth. They welcomed them not as black men but as Americans, honoring them as liberators from the German occupation forces. McBurney found the simple and sincere kindness of the Dutch people a welcome and pleasant surprise after the treatment he had experienced at the hands of many of the American soldiers, particularly those from the 87th Infantry.

"Hey, what's all that commotion about?" asked Smith.

McBurney had heard it too. "Sounds like cheering to me. Let's take a look."

Stepping out of their tent, they saw a sight that made their jaws drop.

It was Paul Bates!

The colonel climbed down from his jeep before a welcoming crowd of officers and enlisted men. A big smile creased his face. But as he parted his way through the tankers, McBurney saw that he limped with a cane. And yet, he was able to look past his hobble and celebrate the fact that the man who commanded the 761st, their Great White Father who had molded and always believed in them, had returned to lead them.

McBurney's face lit up with a huge grin. "Well I'll be damned, look who's returned to the land of the living," he said joyfully.

"Just in time to cross the Rhine and make the final push into Germany," said

Smith, grinning just as happily. "Now that's what I call perfect timing."

"Let's go welcome our fearless leader home."

They walked quickly over to the jeep. More than a hundred men had gathered around now, with more still spilling in, and they were cheering wildly and throwing their hats and tanker helmets in the air. Then the old Buffalo Soldier Pop Gates said, "Where you been, Colonel? You missed all the damn fighting!"

The glowing reception seemed to take Bates off-guard, and for a moment he appeared choked up with emotion and at a loss for words. But then he regrouped and gathered his composure.

"I've been confined to a damned hospital bed—thinking all day long about you fine men and how badly you're taking it to the Germans!" he fired back with a gleam in his eye.

"We thought you were dead, sir!" cried one soldier.

"No, we thought you were back in the States living it up!" shouted another.

"Have you returned to us for good, Colonel!" asked yet another.

Bates, standing a head taller than most everybody else, smiled. "Yes, I am back for good, men—and no, I have not risen from the dead nor was I ever across the Atlantic in the good ole US of A. For the past three months, I have been stuck at the 104th Evacuation Hospital near Southampton, England. I had a badly broken fibula. But now I've returned to finish what we all started together and take Berlin—with my walking cane, of course!"

That brought laughter and cheers from the men. For even the most battle-weary battalion member, the return of Lieutenant Colonel Paul L. Bates was a magnificent moment. It may have taken days for everyone in the battalion to learn of his loss early on in the Lorraine campaign, but they all knew now that he had returned. The man had shown them the highest degree of respect and honor from the time of their earliest training at Camp Claiborne through their first day of battle—and McBurney would go to hell and back for the colonel just as he would for Patton. In fact, McBurney was thinking of how much he would enjoy knocking down a few Krauts just for the colonel. He and Smitty both felt the considerable lift in morale that the other men, even the new replacements who knew little or nothing about him, were feeling. He looked around at Smith, Pop Gates, Teddy Windsor, Warren Crecy, E.G. McConnell, Preston McNeil, and all the other familiar surviving faces: they were rejuvenated, as if given a new shot in the arm that would give them that extra push to make it to the finish line of the long, bloody war.

Even during his lengthy absence, Bates had still always been their guiding light and reason for existence, though most of the men had already internalized it for themselves. McBurney considered his return to the outfit even more impressive given that his bullet-shattered leg had still not fully healed and he could have had his pick of assignments. He knew that Bates's return would not dramatically change conditions for the men compared to his predecessor, Colonel George, who had filled in adequately enough. But there was clearly a new spark in the tankers: they would see the war through to the bitter end with fierce resolve.

It was a day of celebration and reaffirmation that Sergeant William H. McBurney would remember for the rest of his life.

# CHAPTER 45

## BRAUWEILER PRISON, COLOGNE

## FEBRUARY 28, 1945

"STOP THIS NONSENSE, MUCKI—WE *WILL* BREAK YOU!"

Angela looked at Kütter uncomprehendingly, pretending to be so severely beaten and exhausted from sleep deprivation that she didn't understand. After more than two straight weeks of interrogation and torture, she had still revealed nothing—not a single shred of information, except what she wanted the Gestapo to know to deceive her interrogators and throw them off balance. It didn't matter that two of her fingers were broken, that she had huge gashes on her head, that her close-shaven hair was filled with lice, or that her face and body were covered with bruises—she would not tell the Gestapo a single thing, just as her father had instructed her to do.

But then again, she knew that not even the strongest and most determined person could withstand torture indefinitely.

Red-faced with anger, Kütter stepped forward and swatted her across the face with his truncheon. There was tremendous power in the blow and she felt an excruciating pain, but forced herself not to make the slightest whisper of sound. The *kriminalkommissar* then struck her a second blow. This time she couldn't help but wince in pain as she felt a burning sensation and blood cascaded down her face onto her blood-stained, lice-infested prison uniform. Within seconds, she was soaked with a fresh layer of blood.

Puffing with vitriol, Kütter stood above her in his black leather SS uniform with the red swastika armband like an immovable mountain of vengeance. She was stuffed in a chair in the same second-floor interrogation room they had been bringing her to for the past two weeks, her hands handcuffed behind her back to restrain her. In the room with her and Kütter was Josef Hoegen. Given the fierceness of her rotating team of interrogators—Kütter, Hoegen, and Hirschfeld—she was surprised that she was even still alive, though she suspected that her father's close connection to General von Manteuffel was keeping her and her father from receiving the most heinous tortures. She knew the colonel was still alive because they had been interrogated together on several occasions during the past two weeks, and a sympathetic guard, an older man that had served in her father's company on the Western Front during the Great War, kept her and her father informed of the other's condition under "treatment."

"You will answer my questions, damn you!" snapped Kütter. "Do you understand me? I have had enough of your insolence!"

She said nothing, focusing all her energy on not making a sound or showing any sign of weakness. But deep down, she knew she was close to breaking. After two weeks of enhanced interrogation, she was physically and emotionally spent.

They then blindfolded her and delivered countless blows to her shins, knees, elbows, and other hard parts without striking her face any further or risking harming vital organs. It was a technique they had used often during the past two weeks so that she could be interrogated indefinitely while under extreme agony without risking dislocating her jaw or damaging her brain, which could prevent obtaining any useful information and result in her accidental death. While Kütter liked to give her a good thrashing in the face on occasion with his truncheon or brass knuckles, he knew enough to be careful not to deliver too many head blows. It was the blindfold that made it most terrifying for Angela. With her eyes covered, every blow came as a terrible shock and the dreadful anticipation between blows was agonizing.

After letting the pain subside for a moment, Kütter said, "You are going to tell me the names, or code names, of every Communist pig and Edelweiss Pirate you have come into contact with in the past six months. Do it now or the punishment will continue!"

"I've already told you I don't know anything," she said, struggling not to whimper in pain. "You have the wrong person. You should be trying to hunt down actual *Volksfeinde*, not patriotic Wehrmacht auxiliaries like myself."

"You are no patriot!" cried Hoegen, and he removed her blindfold and spit on her, then whacked her in the stomach with his truncheon.

The blow knocked the wind out of her and she gasped for air. The coal-eyed Hoegen gazed down at her with a fiendish smile, nearly salivating from the perverse excitement. She had seen the look so many times in the past two weeks that she knew the old, hollow-eyed *kriminalassistent* derived a perverse and titillating pleasure from his brutal interrogation work.

At that moment, Hirschfeld stormed into the interrogation room, disrupting the proceedings. Kütter turned around, mildly perturbed.

"Yes, what is it, *Kriminalassistent*?" he demanded to his four-eyed subordinate.

"One of the prisoners has caused a disturbance on the upper floor of the cell block," explained Hirschfeld. "He's a middle-aged and usually quiet man, but he went crazy and attacked us."

"Subdue him at once. That is an order."

"That may be easier said than done, sir."

"Do as I say, damn you!"

"*Jawohl, Herr Kommissar*!" and he left. But five minutes later, he was back, looking like a sickly dog with its tail between its legs.

"Sir, I report to you that the inmate attacked me again and knocked my glasses off!"

"You can't handle an old man? Some Gestapo officer you are!" blurted Angela. As soon as the words left her mouth, she knew she shouldn't have said them, but she was tired of being on the defensive and wanted to shake things up and keep her interrogators off-balance by reversing the roles and being the unpredictable aggressor. Her father had told her as much, reminding her that they would be beaten badly anyway until they talked, so it was not advisable to be uniformly passive.

"How dare you talk to me that way, you sow!" shrieked Hirschfeld, and he quickly stepped towards her with a raised truncheon. But Kütter cut him off and ordered him to come with him to the cell to deal with the unruly prisoner. They left. Five minutes later they were back—but with a pair of the female prison secretaries.

Angela was puzzled. *What are they doing here?* But then, she realized she already knew the answer.

Her body stiffened.

"There's another inmate who won't be making any more mischief," said Kütter, rubbing his hands together with an air of finality.

"What did you do to him?" asked Angela, feeling a sick feeling inside.

"I sent him to his Maker," said Hirschfeld, gloatingly. "Where you'll soon be headed if you give me any more lip!"

This time Angela kept her mouth shut. Now she looked worriedly at the secretaries that Kütter had brought with him. She had heard the horror stories of how violent the interrogations often became in the presence of the women, particularly by Hoegen. From the sympathetic guard who had fought with her father in WWI, she had learned that Kütter's officers routinely summoned the unit's female secretaries to watch them beat German and East European inmates after gang attacks or killings of their Gestapo colleagues during police roundups. The presence of the young secretaries seemed to inflame the brutality of the interrogators. Both younger and older officers alike enjoyed proving their masculinity by practicing boxing techniques during interrogations, competing to see who could impress the secretaries by landing a knockout blow. According to the guard, the women seemed to delight in the violence, laughing as officers beat their victims senseless. Hoegen, she had learned, was the biggest perpetrator of the violence. When he had discovered that a German inmate was a former masseuse, he moved the man to a better cell and provided him with extra food and luxury items such as tobacco in exchange for massages on his aching shoulders. The sessions ensured that he maintained his reputation as one of *Sonderkommando Brauweiler's* most feared interrogators.

"This girl refuses to talk," said Kütter to the two German secretaries. "What should we do with her?"

"Make her eat out of a bowl like a dog!" exclaimed one.

"Hit her in the face with the Clock of the Rhine!" suggested the other.

Kütter nodded approvingly. "Why can't we do both?" he asked, drawing a sadistic smile from the coal-eyed Hoegen.

Hoegen and Hirschfeld jerked her from her chair, threw her on the floor, and forced her to eat from a bowl of watery soup left over from the previous interrogation. Shoving her head down, they made her lap it out of the bowl like a dog, whacking her in the buttocks to the delighted laughter of the secretaries whenever she tried to pull away and stop eating.

When they were finished humiliating her, they set her back in the chair and Hoegen and Hirschfeld took turns punching her with their bare fists to see who could score a knockout blow. With the secretaries cheering them on, all Angela could think during her intervals of consciousness was: *Who are these people? What in the world has happened to my country? Where did it go?*

But once again, she realized that she already knew the answer: her interrogators and the secretaries were the norm, not the exception. For the ugly truth was that every German was ultimately guilty for allowing Hitler and the Nazis to rise to power and hiding their head in the sand and turning their backs when the regime began singling out Communists, Jews, clergymen, and other racial, political, and social enemies of the Reich. The great majority of German citizens, she knew, had not suffered at all from Nazi terror since the advent of Hitler—instead they had been complicit with the Gestapo due to their indifference and passivity. Many Germans had long known that they were living in a vile dictatorship and that there were victims of that dictatorship, but they mistakenly rationalized to themselves that most of the victims were criminals with whom they had little or nothing in common. They somehow convinced themselves that these people had brought their misery upon themselves. That's what the secretaries—ordinary Germans by any measure—were doing right now. That was the real tragedy of her country, in Angela's eyes: her beloved Fatherland had sunk into a morass of indifference and passivity to the point that most of its people were unmoved by a mothers' pleas, a child's tears, or the agonizing moans of innocent men and women being tortured.

The German population, she knew now more than ever before, was and always had been complicit in the Nazi terror. Combining fear and apathy with the traditional Teutonic respect for authority and devotion to duty, she realized, most people still supported the regime, or at least didn't lift a finger to stop it, even with the Allies pushing towards the Rhine. For more than a decade now, the overwhelming majority of the German people had complied willingly with Nazi ideology and policy and suffered little, while the Gestapo punished all nonconformity and disobedience with the utmost severity. Mass silence had led to mass murder—and now, in the closing days of the war in Hitler's *Endkampf*, the killing was escalating like floodwaters spilling over a dam. Only now did even a minority of the sheep-like German people realize that they had long been willing accomplices in the program of state terror.

It was then she saw the door fly open and a senior Wehrmacht officer storm into the room with a prison guard frantically on his heels.

"What the hell?" gasped Kütter.

"I'm sorry, *Kriminalkommissar*, but I couldn't stop him!" cried the guard.

"Let that girl go now!" commanded the Wehrmacht officer. "By the orders of General von Manteuffel, commander of the Fifth Panzer Army, and Higher SS and Polizeführer Karl Gutenberger, she and her father, Colonel Günther Lange, are to be released at once!"

Caught completely off guard, Kütter just stood there, mouth wide open. But he quickly regained his senses and shook his head vigorously.

"You have no authority to take my prisoners!" he bristled.

"Like hell I don't!" The officer produced a sheet of paper. "As this official order states, the colonel and his daughter are to be released into my care immediately. If you do not comply, you will be brought up on formal charges. The prisoners' clothing and possessions are to be returned to them and they are to be discharged in the next fifteen minutes. Read the order—that is your copy. As I said, it has been signed by both General von Manteuffel and your boss *Polizeführer* Gutenberger. It is a matter of the highest importance and military necessity."

Kütter quickly scanned over the document.

"But this cannot be!" he cried. "They are criminals and traitors! Why they tried to escape arrest in their car! Who the hell are you?"

"I am General von Manteuffel's chief of staff, General-Major Reinhardt, and you will obey that order or you will be shot!"

"But these people are *Volksfeinde*! They do not deserve to even live!"

"It is you, *Kriminalkommissar*, who are the criminal, damn you! According to reliable witnesses, you rammed them at a Wehrmacht checkpoint when they were obeying General's von Manteuffel's order for them to join the Fifth Panzer Army near Bonn. And you have been holding them against their will illegally for the past two weeks despite the fact that they informed you verbally and in writing that they are on General von Manteuffel's staff. You, sir, are a disgrace to the Reich!"

"But the girl is not on the general's staff!"

"Yes, she is. She is a Wehrmacht auxiliary and Colonel Lange's official private nurse."

"But this…this is highly irreg—"

"Shut up, you swine!" Swiftly removing his pistol, he swiped it across Kütter's face, opening up a lengthy gash and drawing blood. Then he pointed the pistol at Hoegen. "You there, uncuff Fräulein Lange this instant or I'll blow your fucking brains out!"

The female secretaries—who a moment earlier had been shrieking with delight as Angela was savagely beaten—were now quaking in their cobbled shoes and crying. One of them was so terrified that she wet herself, the urine dribbling down her leg onto the blood-stained concrete floor and forming a puddle.

"All right, all right," relented Kütter finally, "the order appears to be valid and we will do as you say. We will relinquish the colonel and his daughter to your control. Now please put the damned weapon away."

"No, you pig—I don't trust you." He sniffed twice and looked around the interrogation room that was closer to a torture chamber. "What kind of people do things like this to other human beings? You all ought to be ashamed of yourselves."

"Just take the prisoners and go," growled Kütter. "I don't need a lecture from you about right and wrong when I am striving diligently to protect the Fatherland from its mortal enemies."

"A Wehrmacht colonel and decorated veteran of two world wars and a girl nurse? They can hardly be considered enemies of the state. Now where is her father being held?"

"The basement. Solitary confinement."

"Very well. For your sake, you had better hope the colonel can walk under his own power. Or General von Manteuffel and your boss Gutenberger are going to have your fucking head!"

# CHAPTER 46

## HINDENBURG BRIDGE AND EL-DE HAUS
## COLOGNE

### FEBRUARY 28-29, 1945

TWENTY MINUTES LATER, Angela and her father were in the back seat of a Mercedes staff car racing towards the Hindenburg Bridge.

She couldn't believe their swift reversal of fortune. Or, as she gazed out at the chaos and desolation all around her, how dramatically the situation had changed in Cologne since her capture two weeks earlier. There were still the honeycombed buildings, ruined churches, mountains of rubble on the streets and sidewalks, and huge bomb craters. But now there was anarchy and chaos on the streets; piles of rubbish and hastily discarded items everywhere; and, to her shock and dismay, hundreds of corpses that were no longer even being pulled from the rubble, identified, and buried. The overwhelming drain of resources from the evacuation of the Rhineland and the seemingly unstoppable advance of the Americans had rendered Western Germany's oldest and most revered city impotent.

From General-Major Reinhardt, she and her father had learned that on February 23 U.S. forces were already on the western edge of the Rur River and had unleashed a massive artillery barrage, commencing the Allied push to the Rhine. German troops—the Führer's supposedly invincible and fanatical true believers in *feldgrau*—had quickly caved under enemy pressure and now all of Cologne was desperately being evacuated. But despite the orders to abandon the city, some 40,000 to 50,000 civilians still remained behind, unwilling or unable to flee the city.

She couldn't believe her eyes as she gazed out the car window. She saw German troops looting the remaining supply depots. She saw mobs of starving civilians plundering storehouses and picking over ransacked shops, bombed-out buildings, and unburied corpses. She saw streams of refugees in rags, cast-off uniforms, and tattered blankets shambling along the streets, carrying possessions in bundles over their shoulders, weather-beaten rucksacks, and dilapidated suitcases, more than a few hobbling along with crutches or canes. She saw prisoners—many weak from the abuse, malnutrition, and disease they had suffered over several months of confinement—being herded across the Rhine on foot like cattle and riding aboard open trucks in the freezing cold. She saw Hitler Youth and *Volkssturm* units made up of boys no more than fourteen or fifteen armed with submachine guns and disposable, one-shot rocket launchers that were no match for the American tanks that would soon roll into the city's outskirts. She saw packs of wild dogs that had once been family's beloved German Shepherds, Rottweilers, and Doberman pinschers wandering the streets in search of food and being shot down by the police.

Entering the ruined *Altstadt*, they encountered desperate civilians by the hundreds who had spent weeks living without electricity, running water, or sanitation. Angela thought to herself that Robinson Crusoe couldn't have lived a more desolate existence. But she also saw the great cathedral, the tallest building in Europe until the Eiffel Tower was completed in 1889, still standing majestically on the hill overlooking the Rhine. She couldn't believe that after countless Allied bombings and more than a dozen direct hits, it still stood tall and proud.

She felt a great warmth inside.

They started to cross Hindenburg Bridge. It was packed with a procession of civilian vehicles, troop transports, and people on foot, wheeling carts, and driving horse-drawn carriages. But they had not made it a quarter of the way across when a squadron of Allied bombers bombed and strafed the bridge. After three years of aircraft bombing, direct artillery hits, near misses, and deliberate demolition attempts, the bridge was criss-crossed with internal fractures and already on the verge of collapse. But the simultaneous aerial bombardment and heavy load from the escaping column of humanity, motorized vehicles, and overfilled carts was the straw that broke the camel's back. The weight of the traffic and equipment, along with the dead load, was supported by the good downstream truss and it began to buckle under a tonnage which it had not been designed to carry.

The sound of peppering machine-gun bullets, shouting and screaming voices, and wrenching metal filled the air as the bridge began to give way. Angela heard a deep groaning sound, the buckling and bending and snapping of heavy steel, as the center portion of the bridge began to tip into the Rhine and the two end sections slumped off their piers.

She couldn't believe their bad luck as the bridge began to plummet, ineluctably, into the mighty river. Just when she had thought they were in the clear, their hopes for the future and survival were being dashed once again.

"Hold on tight—she's going down!" cried her father, and he took her in an embrace in the backseat.

The corporal driving the Mercedes slammed his foot down on the gas to back up and return to Cologne, but the bridge was packed with traffic and there was no open path to escape. One by one the vehicles, carts, and carriages tumbled into the water along with hundreds of civilians and soldiers, sweeping them into the frigid, fast flowing Rhine swollen by the spring thaw.

"Quick, open your car windows!" cried General-Major Reinhardt from his front seat as the Mercedes' wheels struck the water. "The doors won't open with the water pushing inward, so you must open your windows!"

Angela and her father did as instructed, rolling down their car windows as the ice-cold river water began pouring into the vehicle like a broken dam.

"Go, *Bärchen!* Hold your breath, climb out, and swim to the left bank!"

"But what about you? How are you going to make it with only one arm?"

"I am a good swimmer—I will find a way. Quickly now!"

"Let's go! Let's go!" cried Reinhardt, and he took a deep breath.

All four were able to make it out of the car, but they were momentarily pinned underwater before being swept up in the swift current. As she floated downstream, Angela became separated from her father and the others as a nearby heavy truck was dragged under and she was sucked into a swirling vortex of bubbly foam.

A moment later she was able to break the surface only to be dragged under again. For an instant, she was completely disoriented, unable to tell up from down. Kicking upward, she was able to break the surface. She saw people all around her screaming and shouting in panic and paddling and flailing hysterically against the stiff current.

Looking downstream, she spotted her father.

With several powerful strokes, she closed the gap between them and took hold of him with one arm while using the other to paddle towards shore. But then they hit another vortex, and she went under and spun crazily, losing control of his hand.

When she broke the surface again, she could hear shouting all around her, coming from the river and the near bank. And then she hit another set of fast-moving water and the noise was swallowed in the roar of the river. She felt her shin crash into someone and she turned to see her father, who was upstream behind her now. Backpaddling to slow herself down, she was able to kick and swivel her position so that she was moving feet first with her one-armed father next to her and both of them keeping their heads just above the surface.

They drifted nearly a mile, slowly angling closer to the west bank. The frigid water made them shiver violently and forced them to take short breaths. With a series of desperate kicks and strokes, they were able to make it to the slower water near the bank. They kept swimming until finally the current had slackened enough that they could stand up.

Touching down on the muddy bottom, she looked at her father and gave a sigh of relief: the feel of solid ground beneath her feet was reassuring. They managed to scramble over some rocks and logs along the shoreline downstream of the city, where they collapsed and struggled to catch their breath.

Within minutes, more people began to make it to shore. She and her father looked around for General-Major Reinhardt and their driver, but they were nowhere to be seen. She figured they were stronger swimmers and had made their way to shore further upstream.

With the help of a soldier, she and her father heaved a half-drowned little girl up onto the snowy bank. Rolling her onto her back, they began pushing down on her stomach. No response. They pushed harder. Still nothing. They tried again and this time the little girl shuddered and began coughing up water. A moment later, she looked up at them with a mixture of fear and surprise, her eyes big as plums.

"You're going to be all right," said Angela.

Soon after they had helped several more people ashore and the young girl was reunited with her mother, several trucks of firemen, Gestapo, regular police, and Hitler Youth drove up to help civilians and recapture prisoners who had been in the process of being shipped east into the interior of Germany when the bridge collapsed. Angela realized that someone must have radioed in on the emergency channel when it fell. Cold and shivering, she was grateful for the aid, but she felt badly for the recaptured prisoners. She and her father produced their soaked papers and started to climb into one of the open-topped trucks. But as they did so, one of the Hitler Youth called out to her.

"You there, halt!"

To her shock and horror, it was the beefy, red-haired boy that had tried to rape her last summer. A member of the *HJ-Streifendienst*, he was dressed in a brown uniform with a red Nazi armband and armed with a military rifle. Standing next to a Gestapo officer, he and the officer both appeared to be on the lookout for anyone suspicious amongst the survivors boarding the trucks.

"I know this girl!" he exclaimed to the Gestapo officer. "She is an Edelweiss Pirate, a common criminal!"

He pointed his rifle at her.

The Gestapo officer stepped towards her and clamped his hand around her wrist. "You come with me on another truck!"

"Wait!" cried her father. "I am Colonel Günther Lange and this girl is my daughter as well as a Wehrmacht nurse and auxiliary. She is no criminal. This boy is mistaken." He pulled out his soggy Soldbuch again and handed it to the officer. "You can see my papers for yourself, and I am vouching for daughter as well."

As the officer read through the booklet, Angela pointed an accusing finger at the boy. "He tried to rape me!" she said to the Gestapo officer. "He is the one who should be arrested! He is a sexual deviant!"

The Gestapo officer looked at the boy. "Is this true?"

"No, she is lying!"

"I am not! He is a rapist, but I fought him off and he was unable to finish what he started! He needs to be arrested at once!"

Her father appeared stunned. "Is this true, Angela?"

"Yes, he did it! He is a monster!"

"I did not! This little wretch is trying to save her own skin! She's an Edelweiss Pirate! She and her criminal friends attacked me when I was on patrol!"

"No, you assaulted my daughter, you little bastard!" said her father, and he clocked the boy with his good arm. "I will have you imprisoned for this!"

"Stop this!" shouted the Gestapo officer, and he withdraw his pistol and restrained the colonel. Two more armed policemen quickly stepped in to break up the disturbance. "I've had enough of this craziness. You are all getting in the truck. We'll get this sorted out at El-De Haus."

Her father was livid. "But I am a Wehrmacht colonel and this girl, my daughter, serves on my staff as my nurse and is under my protection! We are not going to Gestapo headquarters! We are expected posthaste at General von Manteuffel's Fifth Panzer Army headquarters! That's why we were crossing the Rhine with General-Major Reinhardt! Check with Reinhardt—he will vouch for us!"

"Where is this Reinhardt?"

"I don't know if he made it to shore. He and his driver were in the car with us when it went down. But we lost them in the current."

"That is not enough, I'm afraid. We are still going to have to get all this sorted out at Gestapo headquarters."

With guns pointed at them, they had no choice but to submit. Wet and freezing cold, they were prodded up onto the open-topped truck and driven to the notorious holding center in the Elisenstrasse. The cold winter wind bit right through their soaked clothes and their lips turned blue. The Gestapo headquarters had been battered from the round-the-clock air raids hammering the city, but like nearby Cologne Cathedral it still stood mostly intact. Angela overheard one of the guards on the bus say the facility had been quarantined and temporarily closed down earlier in the month because of a raging typhus epidemic. She prayed to God she and her father wouldn't catch the disease.

As they drove into the inner courtyard, they saw five men and two women who looked like foreigners being hung from the transportable gallows next to the south wall of the courtyard. Piled again the west wall were more than three dozen bodies, waiting to be trucked off by the Municipal Rubbish Disposal to the *Westfriedhof*—West Cemetery—and dumped in the "Gestapo Field" where the State Secret Police had its own landfill section to entomb its murdered victims. As she and her father disembarked from the truck, the prisoners were hung, choking and gagging with their hands tied behind their backs as they kicked violently in a dance of death.

Angela gasped in horror and covered her mouth so she wouldn't vomit.

Her father turned her head away and squeezed her hand tightly. "Don't worry, that's not going to happen to us," he said to assuage her. "Just keep yourself together and we will soon be on our way eastward again."

"I can't believe we're here. I wish we had Reinhardt with us."

"I do too. But you must not worry. And once again, whatever happens in there you cannot admit to anything except knowing Schröder or they will kill us both. Stay strong, *Bärchen*."

"I will. I won't talk."

"Good. That is the only reason we are still alive."

They were taken inside through the basement stairs by armed Gestapo guards. But this time, instead of being checked in at a desk on the second floor, they were thrown immediately into one of the basement cells—despite her father's vigorous protests. The freezing-cold, poorly ventilated, concrete-floored room was already packed with more than a dozen dirty inmates covered with bruises and lice, some quite possibly infected with typhus. There was barely enough room to sit and not enough to lie down. They were forced at gunpoint to cram into the stench-ridden cell that contained only a single bucket in the corner to relieve themselves. Angela couldn't believe that her own countrymen could subject anyone—German or non-German—to such squalid, overcrowded living conditions.

It was inhuman.

It wasn't until the next day that they were taken to an interrogation room. Forced all day and night to sit on the floor with their heads leaning on the shoulder of the person in front of them, they had been unable to sleep that night and had been fed only watered-down soup and dark bread. What they didn't know as they stepped into the room were two important things. First, that with the Allies fast approaching, Cologne Gestapo officers were sentencing suspects themselves since the region's courts no longer functioned; and second, that El-De Haus had been turned into an extermination camp for Eastern European prisoners and those Germans the Gestapo regarded as the greatest security threats in this, the final purge of the Left Bank Rhineland's prison system. In fact, the pace of the killings in the courtyard had intensified to the point where Counterintelligence Chief Kurt Matschke and his officers were murdering eighty prisoners a day on the poorly constructed scaffold, many immediately upon their arrival to the ruined building.

What Angela and her father also didn't know was that most German and West European inmates were now being transported across the Rhine to the Buchenwald and Ravensbrück concentration camps and to facilities in Siegen, Wipperfürth, Siegburg, and the Hünswinkel work reeducation camp. This was the paradox of the Nazi regime as the enemy closed in on the Rhineland: the indiscriminate, collective punishment of German civilians was tantamount to admitting defeat and that the regime could not abide. As *Volksgenossen*, Angela, her father, and others like them still required careful investigation and sentencing, if the state wanted to avoid undermining civilian support for the continuing struggle. The efforts made by security officers to sentence German and West European prisoners to Buchenwald, Ravensbrück, and other facilities where survival was challenging but still possible reflected their reluctance to serve as both judge and executioner in cases involving German citizens.

As Angela and her father hobbled into the interrogation room, she felt her whole body seize up with panic when she saw who was waiting for them. Seated at the table were two men, one in his late twenties or early thirties that she didn't know, and the other a middle-aged brute she knew only too well: Ferdinand Kütter. She glanced at her father. But to her surprise, he didn't look scared at all—he appeared angry and outraged.

"I demand that you release me and my daughter at once!" he bristled. "We should never have been locked up at Brauweiler or here, damnit, and you two are going to pay for this!"

"Save your breath, Colonel," said the younger, blond-haired man that Angela didn't recognize. "You will be safely leaving El-De Haus within the hour—if you agree to certain conditions."

"Conditions? What conditions? Who the hell are you?"

"I am Richard Foltis, acting chief of the Cologne Gestapo. Now I have some good news for you and I have some bad news."

"This is preposterous! I am a Wehrmacht colonel, damn you, and my daughter and I should never have been arrested in the first place! Commissioner Kütter has overstepped his authority!"

Foltis looked unfazed, and even worse, unimpressed. "Save your speech for someone else, Colonel," he snapped, "for I am in no mood for sanctimonious outbursts. The Americans will be here any day now and you must be evacuated from the city."

"We don't need to be evacuated. We need a car."

"I'm afraid that will be impossible. You and your daughter are being sent by rail to the interior—specifically to the civilian relocation camp at Thuringia. I'm afraid that's the best we can do."

"This is outrageous!"

"I would remind the colonel that he and his daughter are quite fortunate to get off so lightly." He glanced at his colleague seated to his right. "If *Kriminalkommissar* Kütter here had his way, you would be taken down into that courtyard right now and strung up with the Poles and Russians. With that in mind, I'd like to tell you a story about two teenage girls: Vera Suchowerchowa and Nina Sawina. As you might have guessed, they were not German."

"*Were?* I take it they were executed."

"Quite so."

"Who were they?"

"They had the misfortune of assisting the late Hans Steinbrück while he attempted to hide from us after we raided his hideout."

She could see that her father was growing impatient. "I don't understand what this has to do with—"

"It has to do with Commissioner Kütter *and* your daughter here," Foltis cut him off, his tone now brusque and official. "You see, Angela knew Vera Suchowerchowa and Nina Sawina because she attended subversive meetings with the Edelweiss Pirates and Steinbrück's *Ehrenfeld Gruppe*. This has been confirmed beyond any reasonable doubt, so please do not deny it, either of you. That would only insult my intelligence and quite possibly force me to rescind my more than generous offer to you."

Angela licked her lips nervously and looked at Kütter, who was visibly scowling. Somehow, despite what Foltis was saying, she still didn't feel safe with Kütter still in the fold and the Americans still tens of miles from Cologne.

"All right, go on," said her father.

"I have the files of the two girls right here," the Gestapo chief continued. "Upon their arrest, they were to be sent to a labor camp while many of their male East European inmates were sent here for execution. But Commissioner Kütter protested their impending transportation to a labor camp. To even my surprise, he successfully lobbied me to have them executed along with a Ukrainian man accused of murdering a Party official in Ehrenfeld. You see, in this particular instance, you would have to say that *he* had his way. When it comes to protecting the Reich, Herr Kütter is a most persuasive officer. But today, I have decided to grant you two clemency and not execute you, or have you shipped off to Buchenwald or Ravensbrück. This despite the fact that your daughter took part in criminal activities as an Edelweiss Pirate with her boyfriend Bartholomäus Schröder. *Kriminalkommissar* Kütter has been lobbying me all day long to execute you, or send you both to a labor camp. In fact, he has been lobbying me most vehemently. But as I have said, I am not going to do it, provided you agree to certain conditions."

Angela didn't like the sound of that, despite that the arrangement with Foltis obviously bode well for her and her father.

"What do we have to do?" asked her father.

He pushed forward a sheet of paper. "You two must sign this."

"What is it?"

"A statement saying that you were held briefly in our custody, but have been released in good health to the civilian relocation camp at Thuringia."

"But that's a lie," said Angela. "We have both been beaten nearly every day for the past two weeks."

Foltis looked sternly at them both. "Sign it—absolving me and my office for the overreach of my subordinate *Kriminalkommissar* Kütter here—and you both walk out of here under your own power. Refuse to sign it and…well, I wouldn't recommend doing that."

"We have seen what you do in that courtyard downstairs—and I tell you it makes me sick to be a German," said the colonel through gritted teeth. "But we will sign this piece of paper so that we shall be done with you."

"Good, then I believe we have an understanding."

"I will do no such thing," protested Angela, not wanting to be complicit with these Nazi bastards by signing.

Her father looked at her sternly. "No, we have to do this, Angela. We have no choice if we want to walk out of here alive. This is our ticket. You are but sixteen years old and have—"

"Seventeen, I am seventeen."

"What?"

"My birthday was yesterday. I turned seventeen and my birthday gift was torture at the hands of *Kriminalkommissar* Kütter here. He and his thugs Hoegen and Hirschfeld beat me senseless."

"You are a brave girl, I can see that," said Foltis. "But you should watch your tongue and listen to your father. He knows what is best for you."

"That may be true, but I'm still not signing that piece of paper. It is a lie."

"Look here, young lady, there's only one way you and your father are going to survive this war—and that is to sign."

"I cannot."

"You cannot?"

"Neither can I," said her father, suddenly changing his mind. "My daughter's right. It is a sham, a fraud. How can we possibly be expected to sign such a thing?"

"You know the answer. To ensure your own survival."

"I told you the girl would refuse," hissed Kütter. "You should have let me deal with them for their crimes, damnit!"

"*Deal* with us? Is that the word you hide behind when you kill someone?" interjected Angela. "The very idea that you would even think of murdering German patriots like me and my father makes me sick. You are not a man—nor are you merely a lowly brute and coward—you are a monster. An absolute monster!"

Foltis, again, looked unmoved. In the absence of a confession or unequivocal evidence of wrongdoing, the bureaucrat just wanted a signed agreement absolving the Gestapo for exceeding its authority. It was all part of Himmler's decree that German civilians were not to be tortured, executed, or shipped off to labor camps unless they were from the key targeted groups of *Volksfeinde* that were believed to constitute a serious threat to the Reich, or in cases where the evidence of crimes against the state was overwhelming.

"I am only going to tell you this one more time," said Foltis, his patience clearly dwindling. "You will no longer be in existence if you do not sign this. Is that what you want?"

Her father looked at the Gestapo chief. "I don't believe you would do such a thing. Not when you know that my daughter and I are continuing the fight with General von Manteuffel when army deserters are pouring into the Rhineland by the thousands."

Foltis nodded. "You're right, I wouldn't do such a thing," he said, before nodding towards Kütter. "But *he* would, and if you do not sign I can promise you your fate will be in *his* hands."

Kütter looked at her with a rapacious look on his face. Angela stared into her tormentor's agate eyes and felt a chill down her spine at the thought of having to endure another round of "treatment." Here was a man so fanatical and devoid of compassion that he couldn't possibly be human.

Still, there was no way she—or her father—was going to sign.

# CHAPTER 47

## TRIER, WESTERN GERMANY

### MARCH 14, 1945

PATTON DUCKED as mortar shells screeched in from the left and right along the dirt road to Trier. He couldn't remember ever taking mortar fire from opposite directions and regarded it as most unusual.

"Step on it, John!" he shouted to his driver Mims while clutching his terrified dog Willie in his lap. "I don't want to goddamn die until we've taken Berlin!"

"Yessir, General!" The master sergeant slammed his foot down on the gas pedal, spurring on the open-air Willys-Overland jeep with its 60-horsepower L134 "Go Devil" engine and three-star flags over the wheel wells.

In a sudden barrage, a half dozen mortar shells exploded no more than thirty yards away, blowing up an armored car. The concussion of the blasts was enough to knock down part of a column of troops marching along the road and send the rest diving for cover. Patton realized that they would have been killed from the shrapnel if they hadn't been protected by a nearby fleet of armored trucks and radio vehicles that had taken the brunt of the blasts.

"Shouldn't we take cover, sir?" asked General Hobart Gay, Patton's chief of staff, sitting in the back seat of the jeep.

"No, those German units are firing blindly at each other. Must be young boys or old men. We're going to be all right."

"Are you sure, General?" Gay persisted. "This is heating up pretty good and I don't think General Eisenhower would be too happy to see you become a casualty."

"Hell, who knows what Ike might do? He might celebrate. Regardless Hap, in my considered judgment, I believe the thing to do is get the fuck out of here, drive home, and have a drink."

Another volley of mortar fire exploded from the thick forest trees on both sides of the dirt road. It was swiftly followed by several more, the ground shaking from the reverberations. But the mortars were quickly located and silenced by a pack of armored vehicles that let loose with a concentrated fusillade, the white-hot bullets cutting down the pine trees behind the mortar teams with a retching crash. The storm of lead was so intense that the machine guns blew off entire branches.

Patton smiled with satisfaction—*Goddamnit, I love it, Third Army is a machine!*—and they drove on. But they soon came across a traffic jam and he climbed out of his command car to take a look. When he discovered that a 155mm self-propelled gun had become tightly jammed under a rail overpass, he stomped up to the hapless artillery commander with Gay right behind him.

"Colonel," he said testily, "you can blow up the goddamn gun. You can blow up the goddamn bridge. Or you can blow out your goddamn brains, I don't care which. But clear this fucking road!"

He headed back to his jeep. Nearby, he spotted a man in civilian clothes. Knowing instinctively that he was a German officer disguised as a noncombatant, he flagged down a pair of MPs driving up in a jeep and ordered that the man be taken to a POW camp immediately.

"But how do you know he's a German officer, General?" asked one of the MPs.

"Goddammit son, if after all these years of fighting I can't recognize a soldier when I see one, I should turn in my uniform."

Soon the column got moving again and Patton, Gay, Mims, and Willie were heading once again on the road to Trier, Germany's oldest city and a key point on the juncture of the Moselle and Saar Rivers. In the last six weeks of fighting, the Third Army, tasked with destroying the enemy forces west of the Rhine and south of the Moselle, had put nearly 7,000 Wehrmacht soldiers in the ground and bagged over 60,000 prisoners. Along the way, Patton had captured the ancient German fortress of Trier thirteen days earlier on March 1, attacking decisively and suffering few casualties. Now he was taking the opportunity to follow in the footsteps of Julius Caesar, who had conquered the city in 57 BC, and visit the city he and his modern American legions had vanquished. Amusingly, on the day he had taken Trier, he had received a message from Allied headquarters.

"Bypass Trier. It will take four divisions to capture it," read the order.

His irreverent and acerbic response was pure Patton: "Have taken Trier with two divisions. Do you want me to give it back?"

Now, as he approached the fabled city once held by the ancient barbaric hordes of Germania, he felt as if he had been here—two thousand years before. The Roman legions marching on Trier from modern Luxembourg had used the same road he was on that ran through Wasserbillig, and he could almost smell the coppery sweat and see the low dust clouds where those stark fighters had marched forward to give battle. Each night before bed the past week, he had been reading Caesar's *Gallic Wars* recounting the legendary Roman commander's battles in Gaul and Germany from 58 to 51 B.C., and he felt a deeply personal connection to the action.

"I was here, Hap. Two thousand years ago, I was here with Caesar."

"I know you were, General. I can feel it in the air too."

Patton saw that Mims was smiling. "You don't believe me, do you, John?"

"No sir, I believe you. I just find it amazing is all."

"Amazing?"

"That you're doing it all over again—only this time you *are* Caesar. Ain't that something, General?"

He grinned. "I hadn't thought of it that way, but I goddamn like it. You should have been a philosopher, John."

"How do you know I wasn't? In a previous life?"

"A Greek or Roman, or maybe a Carthaginian. Now that would be something."

They chuckled and drove on. He looked out the window of the jeep at the ancient Roman highway ahead and the steep hillside tumbling down into the rain-swollen Moselle River on his right. Yes, he had traveled this road two thousand years earlier. But before that, in other heroic ages, he had hunted for fresh mammoth on the cold steppes, battled in a phalanx against Cyrus the Persian, fought shoulder to shoulder with Alexander the Great during the Siege of Tyre, and crossed the Alps on an elephant with the Carthaginian conqueror Hannibal. And then after fighting with Caesar and his redoubtable Tenth Legion, he had knocked on the gates of Valhalla as a Viking warrior, fought with the Scottish Highlanders for the House of Stuart and as an English knight during the Hundred Years War, and served as a cavalry marshal in the Grand Army of the great Napoleon.

He could feel it in his bones. He had lived and fought alongside Caesar as a Roman legionnaire and in the body of countless other warriors, he was convinced, and he would continue to do so in future lives. His belief in his own reincarnation, over and over again during the course of world history, offered him a means of fulfilling his ultimate and eternal destiny: to lead a great army in battle in an epic conflagration. And now here he was doing just that. He was presently living in the body of a man named Patton, and for him, death merely meant that his soul would once again change bodies. In past lives, he had always been a warrior and in his future reincarnations he would continue in that role to fulfill his destiny.

They drove to the gateway to the ancient Roman amphitheater, which he was surprised was still standing. Most of the city and all the bridges except the one Third Army had captured intact, he had noted on his drive in, were badly ruined. But the entrance to the old Roman amphitheater still stood, and he ordered Mims to stop the car. As he stepped out of the jeep with Willie on his leash, he could feel it all there for him: gladiators grappling with wild beasts; legionnaires and centurions marching down the same road from Wasserbillig to Trier now carrying his own legions; Caesar himself mulling over how best to bound across the Rhine to drive the final stake in the heart of his mortal enemy who, as fate would have it in the present day, was now the reincarnated General Patton's Germanic adversary.

After allowing Willie to relieve himself, he and Gay climbed up onto the second-story of the Roman ruins and stared out at the decimated city. Over the week that it took to force the Wehrmacht to surrender the strategically vital stronghold, the Germans had fought with their usual fierce resolve. But the twenty air raids by Weyland's marauders from the skies and the land-based assaults of the American 10th Armored Division and infantry units had reduced the city to 730,000 cubic yards of rubble, and sent the Germans into headlong eastward retreat into the Palatinate. Gazing out at the desolation, Patton was reminded of a still-life painting frozen in time. The fact that the ancient Roman amphitheater where he now stood was one of the few structures still standing, while all else lay in ruins, was not lost on him.

"After two thousand years it still stands," he said to Gay, pointing at the walls of the *Porta Nigra*—the Black Gate—one of four original city gates built in the time of Christ. "And I was here. Back then, I stood in this exact spot. I don't know how I know that, I just do."

"And now you're off to the Rhine—just like Caesar."

"You and I, Hap, are going to cross that damned river before that cheeky bastard Monty, I can promise you that."

"I can't wait, sir."

Crossing the Rhine as Caesar had done had long inflamed Patton's imagination. As he stared out at the vanquished city of Trier while puffing his cigar—his attempt to quit had not lasted long—he went over in his mind the plan for Third Army he and Bradley had concocted. He hoped it befitting of Caesar. With his big offensive against the Palatinate launched yesterday, his goal was to cross the Rhine before March 24th—D-Day for Monty's massive *Operation Plunder*, a spectacle that was calling for 50,000 tons of high explosive, thirty divisions of 250,000 men, and a fleet of high-speed assault boats to vault across the mighty river. Monty's pageant was to take place in the august presence of Sir Winston Churchill, who had long promised to be the first amongst the Allied war lords to unbutton his trousers and relieve himself in the watercourse to snub Hitler. Patton's much more economical and low-key plan called for Eddy's XII Corps and Walker's XX Corps to wipe out the pockets of enemy resistance south of the Moselle River and west of the Rhine. Then, aided by an attack by Patch's Seventh Army, the two corps would cross the river around Mainz and Worms—without a single assault boat—and dash eastward.

Thus far, Third Army's initial attack had gone splendidly and Patton could already almost smell the Rhine just as he could the Roman legions here at Trier. Walker's infantry and artillery had opened the show with a boisterous demonstration, drawing German reserves to the south, and Eddy's XII Corps had leaped over the Moselle and was speeding towards the Rhine. Patton's spearhead of four armored divisions were already breaking through and, in places, charging behind the vaunted Siegfried Line, destroying and scattering German defenders in their path. Using the combination of fast armor, close air support, and rapid infantry advance, the German First and Seventh Armies would soon be encircled and crushed between Third Army and Patch's Seventh Army. With any luck, Patton believed, the Saar industries would be in Allied hands and he would be pissing in the Rhine a day or two before Churchill or Monty.

He knew this was the final push of the war. Cologne had fallen on March 6, and the one and only bridge that was able to be secured over the Rhine, the Ludendorff railway bridge at Remagen halfway between Cologne and Koblenz, was seized on March 7. Although the bridgehead could only be held and not developed beyond a few miles from the river since Monty had been allocated divisions from Simpson's Ninth U.S. Army for his northern push, the Germans were still on the run. They faced severe manpower shortages, and Patton had heard that the Wehrmacht, SS, and civilian population were all turning against one another in their own internal bickering and bloodbath. Men sixteen and sixty had been thrust into the German Home Guard, the *Volkssturm*, in a last hopeless defense of the Fatherland. Old sailors and crews from the grounded Luftwaffe now served in the ground forces. And battered and war-weary German men, woman, and children were fleeing eastward to get out of the way of the Allied tanks and endless air attacks.

But it was the Rhine that preoccupied the mind of Old Blood and Guts, like a dog gnawing on a bone. The mighty river had stood as a forbidding barrier to invasion since long before the days of Caesar, and with the bridge at Remagen unusable for exploitation, Patton knew he had the opportunity to be the first general across who would be able to take advantage of the crossing and go on a bold offensive. Ike had recently turned him loose again to "carry the football"—and by thunder, that's exactly what he planned to do.

He would beat Monty and everyone else across the Rhine and quickly exploit the gain so that no one and nothing could stop him. And then, it would be only a matter of time before Hitler's Thousand-Year Reich crumpled into the ash heap of history and he would have fulfilled his destiny.

He would be an American Caesar.

# CHAPTER 48

**NIEDERSCHLETTENBACH
SOUTHWESTERN GERMANY**

**MARCH 21, 1945**

AS THE TANK FORMATION moved cautiously forward towards the battered German village of Niederschlettenbach, McBurney surveyed the ground ahead through his horizontal telescopic turret sight. Although target coordinates had been radioed in and fire directed by the approaching Shermans onto the German defenses, there were still a large number of well-entrenched pillboxes and antitank posts that hadn't been knocked out during yesterday's initial attack. Others were so well-hidden that he couldn't even see them. But it was the handful of German Panzer Mark IVs prowling about the town that concerned him most.

*Are they waiting to draw us into a trap?* he wondered. *Or are they just making a show of strength?*

The 761st had rolled into German territory nine days earlier with a full 1,200 men in the battalion, exceeding full combat strength. Following their brief tank maintenance and crew training period in February in Holland, the Black Panthers had initially been told to report to Patton's Third Army for his campaign to break through the Siegfried Line, cross the Rhine, and drive into the enemy's heartland. But while still en route from Holland into France, with the men sleeping beside their tanks in freight cars heading south through the rural landscape, the "bastard" battalion's orders were changed and they were instructed instead to attach to the 103rd "Cactus" Infantry Division of Patch's Seventh Army.

The "Cactus" Division—so-called because of its Saguaro cactus insignia adopted in 1922 when the division had its headquarters out west in Denver, Colorado—was commanded by Major General Anthony McAuliffe. The general had become something of a celebrity after issuing his now-famous "Nuts!" reply to the German forces surrounding Bastogne demanding his surrender. McAuliffe— every bit as colorful as Patton himself—was inheriting a battalion filled with battle-hardened veterans that possessed a certain flair and unconventional esprit de corps that matched their commander, driving masses of steel that packed a punch. McAuliffe and his men in the 101st Airborne Division had survived Bastogne by doing very little by the book, and he was looking for the Black Panthers to open up a corridor through the Siegfried Line as part of Task Force Cactus.

With the 761st and 103rd Infantry Division holding positions along the southern end of the Seventh Army zone, the task force's drive took the units straight into one of the most strongly defended sectors of the line. With the Ardennes but a bloody memory, the Germans were now forced to defend against attack along hundreds of miles of their Westwall—but the defenses along the southern sector where the 761st would advance were particularly stout. The Germans had dug deep tank ditches, erected concrete dragon's teeth, and laced the area with mines. They backed the antitank maze with fortified facilities for command and control and to funnel in reinforcements. But most important of all, the enemy was defending its sacred homeland and many troops would obey their Führer and fight to the last bullet.

While the men of the 761st and Seventh Army battered against German Army Group G at the Siegfried's tough defenses, to their north Patton's Third Army was already catapulting across the rear of the German troops towards the Rhine. Patton's forces were trying to envelop the German rear and cut off the enemy's escape so it couldn't fall back across the river, regroup, and make a stand on the eastern bank.

McBurney's Sherman ground forward, churning through the mud towards its objective to a hiss and crackle of radio static. The sultry, seductive-voiced Axis Sally had signed off minutes earlier—*The secret weapons are coming out, boys! Throw down those little old guns and toddle off home!*—but she drew only snickers from the tank crews these days with Germany's defeat a virtual certainty.

With Charlie Company having lost several of its tanks to mines and enemy fire the day before, Lieutenant Frank Cochrane's and Staff Sergeant Moses Dade's battered platoons had joined forces to create a larger unit and continue the attack on Niederschlettenbach. The inseparable Teddy Windsor and McBurney now had a five man-crew in their tank that included Corporals John Stafford and Mozee Thompson of Texas and Private Robert Thrasher from Atlanta, Georgia. Leonard Smith served as the gunner in the latest incarnation of "Cool Stud," rolling behind McBurney. Sergeant Warren Crecy—the "Iron Man" and "Baddest Man in the 761st"—commanded the next tank in the formation. Technician Fourth Grade Isiah Parks captained the final Sherman of the advancing column.

As the column moved forward with the doughs of the 103rd, McBurney felt the tension in the air. He kept a sharp eye out for the enemy. Over the past few days, just when he had started to believe the end of the war was in sight, he had found himself in the most savage fighting since Tillet. As he took in the rhythmic creaking and grinding of the Sherman's horizontal volute suspension system—HVSS—tracks, McBurney reminded himself that he had seen and done this many times before since being blooded back in November. All the same, he was still wary.

He had once felt Tillet might usher in the end of the war, but now it was clear that only breaching the Siegfried Line would accomplish that goal. And yet, would cracking the line signal an end to the war or the beginning of the struggle for Nazi Germany? That's what the tankers had been debating around the campfires the past week. For the most part, McBurney kept his thoughts to himself. But deep down, he couldn't help but think the seemingly empty and eerily quiet villages Task Force Cactus was supposed to subdue concealed a more desperate and violent enemy than before, now that the Germans were defending their own hallowed soil.

"Incoming!" came the voice of the platoon leader, Lieutenant Frank Cochrane, over the intercom.

Through his gunsight, McBurney caught the flash of a green, comet-like bolt from a German 88 shell streaking across the sky. The shot sailed overhead, and a second round followed quickly after, this one coming up short to dangerously bracket them. The explosion blew out a huge, smoking crater twenty yards in front of the tank and threw up clods of dirt and mud onto the Sherman.

"Driver, hard right! Get us out of here!" cried Windsor to Mozee Thompson.

"Yes, boss! They ain't gonna bracket us! No way, no how!"

"That's what I like to hear!" With gears grinding and explosions rippling the air, the tank dashed right, flanking the piney treeline. "We've got a pill box at three hundred yards! Loader, AP followed by HE! Gunner, penetrate that bunker first then blow 'em up!"

"You got it, my brother!" replied McBurney into his gunner's mike, as Private Robert Thrasher rammed an armor-piercing shell into the breech.

"Traverse right…steady on…three hundred…don't miss!"

"I don't miss!" roared McBurney as he adjusted his main turret gun and sighted the target. "Ready!"

"Fire!" cried Windsor.

McBurney unleashed his 76mm cannon at the pill box, which shuddered upon the impact from the armor-piercing round and erupted with a cloud of smoke and dust at its seams. Seconds later, he followed up with a high-explosive round. This time, the firing ports of the concrete bunker spat out tongues of flame and German soldiers poured out like ants from an anthill, several of them embroiled in flames. The burning figures were swiftly mowed down by the Texan Safford with his Browning M1919A4 bow gun and McBurney with the coaxial machine gun, also chambered in .30-caliber.

"Damn, it's like killing swamp rats!" gushed Windsor, peering through his periscope.

He then barked new commands that crackled over the radio headsets.

"Driver, flank right!"

"Loader, this time just HE! We're going to blow them to kingdom come!"

"Gunner, hit the next pill box over!"

"I thought you'd never ask!" cried McBurney. He quickly made his adjustments and settled the reticle on the target through his gun sight's crosshairs, his booted foot hovering over the trigger button on his footrest. "Ready!"

"Fire!"

McBurney stamped his foot down. A massive flash leapt from the Sherman's barrel as if from the snout of a dragon. The second bunker proved better concealed and harder to take out than the first, but minutes later McBurney had taken out the second enemy pill box and its occupants with three 76mm high-explosive rounds.

"Now that's some fine shooting, Billy!" cried Windsor, and he was echoed by the other tankers.

"Yes well, when it comes to waging war, I take after my pop. He can be one tough son of a bitch."

"And your mama?"

"Sweet as apple pie."

"I heard she's a full-blooded Seminole," said driver Mozee Thompson. "Doesn't that make you a black Injun warrior or something like that?"

"I believe it does. Those Krauts better watch out, or I just might just scalp 'em!"

They all laughed and continued moving forward. During the next hour, the advancing column had taken out several more pillboxes and an antitank gun. The tanks and infantry charged forward, shooting steadily into the ditches and hills beside the road. The tankers fought their way into the village using fire and movement tactics, with two tanks rushing forward while the next two in line stood back to provide covering fire.

As they pressed on, the battle heated up. The sounds of the battle echoed in

McBurney's ears like a crazy symphony: the rattle of the Shermans' engines, the boom of the incoming 88 shells, the crash of their own main guns, the terrible ping of metal on metal from enemy machine-gun bullets, and the radio commands barked over his headset from the platoon leader and Windsor—all of these melded together in his overloaded brain. The unceasing cascade of noise made the violence as palpable as if he was outside the tank dashing forward with the doughs.

On the left, Sergeant Crecy's tank knocked out a pillbox high on a hill with its 76mm cannon. As the Germans fled the burning concrete bunker, the "Baddest Man in the 761st" climbed up through the open hatch of the commander's turret and manned the .50-caliber machine gun. He cut down a half-dozen enemy soldiers within a matter of seconds, the bodies piling up in a bloody mound of shredded cloth and butchered meat. And then, to top it all off, he cheated death yet again by ducking down and closing his hatch the instant before an 88mm shell exploded within spitting distance of his tank.

Witnessing the heroic yet risky feat, McBurney could hardly believe his eyes. Since he and Crecy had been together in C Company before the Bulge, he had seen the Iron Man dispatch literally hundreds of enemy soldiers, more than any other tanker in the battalion, more perhaps than any other tanker in the ETO—and he was still in utter awe every time. But what impressed him and everyone else in the 761st most was that Crecy had not lost a single crew member to enemy action. Other men vied to fight with him because of his combat prowess and because he appeared to live and fight under a protective charm. When Crecy moved over out of Dog Company's light tanks to Charlie Company, turret gunner Billy Burroughs gave up his first sergeant's rank in order to ride and fight with him. Everyone agreed Crecy had unbelievably good luck and seemed to be invincible. The new replacements like Christopher Navarre had all heard the stories of his courage under fire from the other battalion members, but they were always stunned to witness it firsthand for themselves.

McBurney felt a sudden tremor beneath his feet and was jerked forward, his helmeted forehead crashing into his telescopic gun sight.

"Jesus Christ, what the hell was that!"

He had a sudden flashback to Tillet when Taffy had struck the land mine.

"It's a tank ditch!" cried the TC Windsor. "Reverse! Reverse!"

"I'm trying!" cried Mozee Thompson, hauling back on the steering levers but to no avail.

Windsor reacted quickly. "Smitty, Crecy! Cover fire!" he yelled into the pork chop. "We're stuck in a tank trap!"

*Damn,* thought McBurney, realizing from experience how vulnerable they were. His mind flashed an image of poor Willie Devore, frozen in place one moment and nearly headless the next. Windsor continued to call out for cover fire and for Thompson to try to pull their tank out. Crouched inside the turret, McBurney readied himself to dismount on the TC's signal. They would have to try to break out since it was only a matter of time before the nearby artillery zeroed in and blew them to smithereens.

He peered through his periscope at Smith's and Crecy's tanks. To their credit, they were riding in swiftly to bail them out. But still, his heart pounded in his chest as he realized the odds weren't in their favor. Though he couldn't see the full field of battle due to his limited view, he could see enough to know there wasn't much chance all five of them would make it. The enemy positions in the surrounding hills were well-hidden and widely dispersed, and the 88s were already bracketing them.

"Dismount! Abandon tank!" ordered Windsor.

After shutting off the electrical switches to prevent an explosion, Windsor and McBurney were up and out of the tank first, followed quickly by crewmates Safford, Thompson, and Thrasher from the other hatches. When the crew reached daylight, they were bombarded with noise from a swarm of machine-gun nests and 88s. They dove off the tank, hitting the ground hard as the artillery barrage began and bullets snarled overhead and ricocheted off the hull. Smith's tank had already moved forward to deliver covering fire with his own tank now fully exposed.

*Thank you, my brother,* thought McBurney, as he and the crew ducked down and made themselves small. Smith fired his 76mm cannon and .30-caliber coaxial on the enemy posts with fury, refusing to let his good friend and comrades down. Meanwhile, Crecy and Isiah Parks rolled forward to create a crossfire.

A series of violent explosions rocked the earth all around them. The noise was as loud as thunder and the shockwaves sucked all the air from McBurney's lungs.

Again, his mind flashed an image of poor Willie.

"We're dead if we stay here! Let's go!" shouted Windsor.

McBurney scanned the ground immediately around them. The noise was deafening with the sickening, familiar rush of incoming artillery and the ear-splitting reply from his own tanks. Under heavy fire, the five tankers began crawling on their bellies along the road back in the direction they had come. McBurney moved with determination: he had been through too goddamned much to go out this way.

Encouraging one another, the five men had crawled for over a quarter of a mile back towards their own lines when up ahead, McBurney caught sight of a pillbox they had previously cleared. The crew members looked at one another and smiled.

*Home free at last, man,* he thought. *Home free at last.*

Suddenly, the pillbox exploded into concrete dust and smoke.

They were still blinking away concussion and astonishment when a team wearing U.S. uniforms rose up from the nearby woods and strode up to look over the mangled pile of concrete and rebar sticking up like dinosaur ribs. Stunned, McBurney required several seconds to realize that the post had been detonated by a team of American combat engineers.

*We've made it! Those boys are ours!*

"Lordy Lord!" exclaimed Private Robert Thrasher. "I ain't never been so happy to see white motherfuckers as I am right now!"

When they returned to base, Windsor immediately took over another tank and returned to the action. McBurney, without a Sherman to serve as gunner for at the moment, was more than happy to have a brief respite after his second dismounting of a Teddy Windsor tank under enemy fire.

The battle for the Siegfried Line ground on. Task Force Cactus and the combined C Company platoon fought on in a fury of fire throughout the night, clearing the road between Niederschlettenbach and Erlenbach—a narrow corridor overlooked by cliffs containing numerous pillboxes connected by communications tunnels.

Engineers of the 411th Regiment of the 103rd Infantry were able to bridge the Lauter River under heavy fire, and the battalion continued northward until even the town of Erlenbach was pummeled into submission. For six hours, the Black Panthers blasted their way past the pillboxes built into the overhanging cliffs, which towered more than a hundred feet above the thoroughfare.

The battle raged on until dawn. By the time the sun was up and the smoke had cleared, the 761st could tally seven pillboxes destroyed, ten machine-gun nests obliterated, 12 enemy soldiers dead, 64 surrendered, and an unknown but still substantial number of wounded that had to be at least five times more than the number of KIA.

Wolfing down his K-rations the next morning with Smitty and Crecy, McBurney made his own personal tally as the men got ready to set out on the trail again. This time they would spearhead for a new task force commanded by Bates himself: Task Force Rhine. By his reckoning, he had destroyed three enemy gun emplacements and killed or severely wounded close to a dozen of the enemy.

The twenty-year-old—once a cautious, reticent, non-smoking, mild-mannered kid from Harlem—was now a cursing, chain-smoking, battle-hardened tank gunner and expert at killing Germans before they could kill him. Life had become simple for William Haywood McBurney: all he cared about now was doing his job and not letting his buddies down, and maybe one day earning the right to get a meal of hot chow and take a shower.

# CHAPTER 49

## REISDORF TO KLINGENMUNSTER
## SOUTHWESTERN GERMANY

### MARCH 22-23, 1945

AT 1600 HOURS ON MARCH 22, McBurney and Windsor peered out from atop the turret as Task Force Rhine jumped off from the LD. With warming daytime temperatures and a nascent spring feeling in the air, it seemed strange to McBurney that he and his brothers-in-arms were rolling forward yet again to kill other human beings. But he accepted it as something that had to be done in the name of freedom— even if as a black man in a white man's army he wasn't truly free himself.

With engines groaning and coughing and tank tracks churning and grinding, the column traveled single file along the narrow road south of the small village of Reisdorf. Out front was Lieutenant Colonel Paul Bates and Baker Company. The 761st's leader, handpicked by General McAuliffe himself to command the new task force, had elected to remain with the lead platoon for the forthcoming attack. Baker was followed by elements of Able and Charlie Companies. Members of Lieutenant Bruce's platoon of Charlie Company, who had engaged in bitter fighting to reduce the town's approaches, pulled to the side and waved encouragement as McBurney's new Sherman and the other tanks passed.

Task Force Rhine was the spearhead for a new concentrated push to take Klingenmunster and open the way for the 14th Armored Division. Located nine miles to the northeast as the crow flies, just beyond the Siegfried Line and Hardt Mountains, Klingenmunster stood as a gateway to the open plains before the Rhine. Task Force Rhine included the 2nd Battalion of the 409th Infantry Regiment, a recon platoon from the 614th Tank Destroyers, the 103rd Signal Company, and a detachment of combat engineers. But because of the heavy German defenses along the route, the 761st's commander had determined he could commit only a few tanks at a time as the task force drove over the rugged mountains towards its objective.

McBurney understood the stakes. Task Force Rhine, if it could crack the Siegfried Line all the way to Klingenmunster and break through to the Rhine Plain, would set the stage for a leap across the river that would open the way to the final defeat of Nazi Germany. Paul Bates's and the 761st's *blitzkrieg* would be the pinnacle of the battalion's journey. The men had proved themselves in Lorraine and the Saar as well as at the Bulge, but Task Force Rhine stood as their chance to display their true prowess as American tankers.

McBurney believed in Bates and all he had done to train, inveigle, and mold them into a fierce fighting force. All their months of training and combat came down to this opportunity. It stood as the promise Bates had made to him and the other men—and that the Black Panthers had made to one another. If they put their trust in their colonel and in one another, they would carry the football all the way to Prague or Berlin before spring turned to summer, and the 761st would have played a vital role in destroying Hitler's Thousand-Year Reich.

The task force quickly spread out and took up firing positions along the southern perimeter of Reisdorf. "Let 'em have it!" came Bates's voice over the intercom, and for the next hour McBurney and the other tankers battered at the village continuously with 75mm and 76mm shells, while the footsoldiers of the 409th Infantry Regiment fought their way through the high ground on either side of town. Reisdorf quickly fell to the joint attack, and the task force next assaulted and successfully destroyed a series of enemy pillboxes northeast of the town.

"Man, that almost seemed too easy," said Corporal Mozee Thompson from behind his wheel when it was all finished.

"I was thinking the same thing," said McBurney. "That's why I know it's only going to get harder."

"You can bank on it," said Teddy Windsor. "So stay alert."

Continuing on past the town, the task force split into two columns—one headed along the narrow unpaved road towards Birkenhardt, the other along a well-paved road towards Bollenborn. Heading with Bates in the column making for Birkenhardt, McBurney looked watchfully for signs of the entrenched enemy through his periscopic gun sight. At the northeast edge of the town, the advancing column was brought up short by a heavy barrage of antitank fire. Bates wisely pulled them back and called in artillery support from II Corps. The artillery did its work with swift, violent efficiency—reducing the town to rubble in a matter of minutes. The Shermans then rolled through, firing at machine-gun and antitank positions as the 409th's infantrymen fanned out through the smoke-filled streets to solidify their hold. To the south, the Bollenborn column had met stiff resistance, and the two units rejoined at dusk with the objective of pushing on to take the village of Silz, located in the middle of some of the toughest Siegfried defenses in their sector.

With darkness now upon them, the column had to pick its way over dangerous, winding roads notched into the Hardt Mountains. They pressed on without the benefit of headlights, so as not to give the task force away. The Germans had used natural terrain as a barrier and a large portion of the Siegfried Line wound its way through a craggy and heavily forested landscape McBurney considered the most rugged they had encountered since the Bulge. While Windsor and driver Mozee Thompson scanned the ground for mines and bomb craters, McBurney searched for their next targets, aided by stray flares and burning enemy vehicles.

The task force traveled nearly ten miles over the jagged and cratered mountain trail, made all the more harrowing in the uneven shadows cast in the thick stands of trees and waxing gibbous moonlight. But what made McBurney most anxious was knowing the Germans were watching them. In the winter moonlight, the task force was easy prey in enemy-held territory and, even though McBurney didn't see or hear anything suspicious, he couldn't escape the feeling that the Krauts were patiently observing and waiting to move in for the kill.

*Are we walking into a trap?* he wondered.

But as the task force approached the outskirts of Silz and the steep mountains gave way to flatter terrain, it was the advancing American column that spotted the Germans first. A large, mostly horse-drawn convoy was moving enemy artillery and supplies to the rear.

McBurney studied the unsuspecting horse-drawn artillery and supply carts and smattering of enemy trucks through his periscope. The moonlight flickered a silvery color off the majestic animals' smooth coats. He remembered back to the picturesque country farms he had seen last fall in England. For some reason, the handsome creatures were a welcome break from the killing of the past several days.

"Are we going to take 'em, Sarge?" asked the driver, Mozee Thompson.

"I don't know. We'll see what the colonel has in mind," answered Windsor.

"It seems like it would be a shame," said McBurney. "Those horses are so beautiful in the moonlight."

"They sure are," agreed Thompson. "Reminds me of back home in Texas."

"I miss ole Texas," chimed in Corporal John Safford, the tank's bow gunner. "I miss home."

*Don't we all,* thought McBurney wistfully.

The radio squawked with orders to destroy the column. The momentary beauty and tranquility of the night was broken by a sudden wretching explosion of sound and strobing light as the lead tanks rushed forward to attack the enemy convoy. In the time it takes a hungry man to eat, the entire horse-drawn column was wiped out before it could engage the task force in a firefight. It was a slaughter, with the Germans only managing to get off scattered return fire. An indistinguishable mélange of enemy trucks, towed artillery pieces, supplies, splintered wood, and the smoldering remains of German soldiers and the beautiful horses that a moment earlier had captivated McBurney and Thompson blanketed the road as far as the eye could see, rendering the path into the town impassable.

The radio squawked again as Bates gave orders to move the carnage. A tank dozer lumbered forward to push the bloody and broken carcasses, destroyed weapons, and smoking conveyances to the sides of the road.

Like garbage.

Popping up out of the commander's hatch to take a look with Windsor, McBurney watched in mute horror and morbid fascination. He thought to himself: *Man that is just cold.* He had for the most part thought of the Germans the 761st killed in battle as faceless soldiers without an identity, and not as sons and fathers and uncles with women and children who loved them and feared for their safety. But when he saw the piles of limp, smoking bodies being unceremoniously pushed off the sides of the road along with dozens of smoldering horses, he realized that the tentacles of war reached out and touched everyone, and the men being bulldozed into oblivion were not that much different than him. They had mothers and fathers, wives and sweethearts who would deeply miss them.

But he quickly steeled himself. He couldn't be feeling sorry for Hitler and his goddamned Supermen, not when they were the ones who had started the war and taken over most of Europe, killing millions of innocent people in the process.

The task force pressed on towards Silz. To light up their path, several of the lead tanks began firing straight ahead and to the left and right into the brush with high-explosive rounds, instantly changing night into day. The tanks and doughs sped forward in the eerie, flickering light of countless fires. The footsloggers shot steadily into the ditches and hills beside the road to scatter and terrify any German *Panzerfaust* units that might be lurking nearby.

When they came to the edge of the village, Bates gave the command over the designated channel, "Raze it to the ground! Fire for effect!"

The column's Shermans belched salvo after salvo of HE shells from their 75mm and 76mm main guns. McBurney watched round after round pummel the town until it turned into a swirling inferno. The tank rounds continued to burst as they struck a number of homes that exploded like bombs. Many houses and buildings along the Siegfried Line had been converted into munitions and supply warehouses, and several of the shells lobbed at the town struck caches of stockpiled ammunition. In a matter of minutes, the raging fire reduced Silz to ashes. Looking out at the devastation, he tried not to think of the German villages they were conquering as places where people lived.

The task force continued on. Just beyond Silz, the column set off a sprawling enemy ammunition dump with a cataclysmic explosion. It was so big Windsor had the whole crew unbutton their hatches and climb topside to take a look.

"Lord have mercy, will you look at that!" gasped Private Robert Thrasher, the tank's loader. "That's the biggest damn fire I've ever seen!"

"Reminds me of Fourth of July back home," observed Mozee Thompson.

"Yeah, but it sure gives 'fire for effect' new meaning," said Corporal John Safford. "I'm not sure it's my favorite order any more. There's got to be innocent people burning alive down there."

"This is the Siegfried Line, man," said Windsor. "There ain't no *innocents* here."

McBurney agreed, as he continued to watch the explosions fill the air and the fire grow. The towns of Hitler's Westwall stood as armories for the Reich, and the images of fire, destruction, and carnage he had witnessed the past few days, while unsettling, were part of the business of war for him now. But he still didn't like the damned bulldozer pushing aside the burning horses.

The task force pressed onward to the east towards its next objective, the village of Munchweiler. Just outside the town, the 761st's tanks pushed directly into a new enemy force. But the Germans were no match for Paul Bates and his Task Force Rhine. The Black Panthers swiftly unleashed a reign of terror, mowing down Wehrmacht soldiers like a scythe and reducing their armored vehicles to a series of burning metal hulks. Scores of terrified German soldiers dashed towards the Americans weaponless and with their hands up, pleading to surrender.

But the advancing task force and surrendering soldiers quickly came under a heavy barrage of antitank fire. Bates, knocked off his feet by the jolt from an 88mm artillery shell, was rescued by Johnny-on-the-spot Warren Crecy, who dismounted his tank amid a continuous rain of incoming fire and ran forward to carry their commander to safety. The tanks sprayed the German emplacements with machine-gun fire, the enemy crews fled, and the task force overran the positions, killing a large number of Germans and taking scores of prisoners. As the task force pushed eastward again with another town vanquished, the growing number of German prisoners held by the tankers and infantry proved a hindrance. Windsor and the other TCs placed them at the front of their tanks or wherever they had room.

As the column pressed onward towards the Rhine Plain and more and more enemy troops and horses fell and burned before his eyes, McBurney couldn't help but feel that opening the way into Germany seemed a hell of a long way from Harlem. He was pleased that he and his fellow tankers now stood as respected combat veterans entrusted with an important mission, but burning down villages and mowing down men and horses in the dark of night seemed somehow barbaric to him. He thought back to his visit to the army recruiter three years earlier and realized that back then he had had no clue what war was truly like. He had always thought it would be like the moving pictures, but this wasn't like that at all. This was more like the fiery paintings of hell he had seen in a library book back when he was in high school.

But then he reminded himself of why he was here. He and the other members of the 761st had been entrusted with an important mission. Generals in addition to Old Blood and Guts were counting on them to punch through to the Rhine and beyond, and they were anteing up and kicking in by doing their part and helping win the war. Through their deeds on the battlefield, McBurney believed they were already in the process of changing the opinion of their nation. In combat, a black man could think and fight just as good as any white man—and now *Stars and Stripes* and the news sheets conceded as much. Clearing the way for Task Force Rhine offered something in return for the endless training they had endured and all the crap they had been forced to take from bigoted white civilians and doughs, as well as from unsympathetic officers like Major Wingo. McBurney saw a bold future for himself and his brothers-in-arms when the blood stopped flowing and they caught that big boat back home: they might not be on equal footing with the white man, but they would be a damn sight closer after taking it to the Krauts and winning the day in Europe.

The task force continued east from Munchweiler, reaching the outskirts of its final objective—the large, heavily fortified town of Klingenmunster—shortly before 0200. It was bigger and better-defended than McBurney had expected and he suspected that it might be too big for the task force to occupy. His gut instinct proved correct. Having outrun their artillery support, the task force's tanks and infantry were pushed back by intense fire from permanent German artillery and machine-gun installations around the city.

To McBurney's surprise, Bates announced that he had no intention of stopping, and the 761st's tanks and assault guns regrouped, took up positions in the countryside surrounding Klingenmunster, and unleashed a punishing barrage until fires raged throughout the city. The tanks and doughs then moved forward again, meeting this time with only sporadic mortar and sniper fire. The burning city was reduced to an empty, almost apocalyptic landscape. As they advanced, the German defenders broke ranks and ran, retreating into the night, and the remaining resisters were swiftly dispatched with overwhelming firepower.

Shortly after 0430, Klingenmunster was fully cleared and in American hands, and the 761st and the 103rd Infantry had successfully completed their mission. They had blasted a path in their sector leading through some of the stoutest defenses of the Siegfried Line—gashing open a wide hole for the 14th Armored Division and other Allied units to pass onto the Rhine Plain and, from there, across the mighty river itself. In the U.S. Army's final official tally, between March 20 and 23, 1945, the 761st would go on to be credited with clearing seven towns; destroying more than 400 vehicles, 80 heavy weapons, and thousands of machine guns, mortars, and rifles; and inflicting over 4,000 casualties against soldiers of fourteen different German divisions.

When it was all over, Windsor, McBurney, and the rest of the crew climbed out of the tank and quietly shared a smoke. After more than twelve hours of solid fighting, they were hungry and exhausted but still full of crazy combat energy. With perspiration still dripping off his chin, McBurney reflected on Charlie Company's part in the operation. In some ways, it seemed more harrowing than his first engagements in Lorraine and even the five-day siege at Tillet. For McBurney, supporting the task force seemed different from other missions. There was no doubt that Task Force Rhine stood as a major battalion victory, but for some reason he felt a sadness inside, a sense of loss. He couldn't quite put a finger on it. Without question, cracking the Siegfried Line stood as the 761st's most remarkable mission yet, and Bates's return and steady hand had clearly been a blessing for the battalion…and yet, he felt broken somehow, as if something had changed inside of him.

And then he realized what it was.

It was the horses. His mind drew an image of the tank dozer ploughing forward to push the still-smoking bodies of the equines off to the sides of the road, along with the smoldering wreckage of artillery pieces, support vehicles, and badly burnt Germans.

*Why did we have to kill the damned horses?* he wondered, but then he realized he already knew the answer. *We did it so these folks over here in Europe could be free—even though we're not yet free ourselves.*

# CHAPTER 50

## LUCKY FORWARD, LUXEMBOURG CITY,
## AND OPPENHEIM, WESTERN GERMANY

### MARCH 22-26, 1945

STANDING OUTSIDE HIS LUCKY FORWARD COMMAND POST AT Luxembourg City on the evening of March 22, Patton unleashed Willie so he could take a leak, turned to Hap Gay, and said, "I've got to admit I had a good time with Ike the other day. He seems happier of late."

"With the Germans on the run, he's definitely lightened up a bit," agreed Gay.

"He just seemed to be having a good time. He ought to get out to the front more often."

Gay nodded. "The only thing that was kind of odd was his statement to the effect that Third Army isn't cocky enough. How do you explain it?"

"You know my thoughts."

"That before long Ike will be running for president."

"That's right. Third Army represents a lot of votes."

Gay gave a bemused smile. "You really believe that's why he said what he said?"

"I do. What, you think I'm joking? I'm not, Hap. Just you wait and see—Ike is going to run for president someday."

Gay considered this a moment. "I think he'd make a good president. What do you think?"

"I think he would too. After what Monty and SHAEF have put him through, he's certainly learned the art of patience and diplomacy. And being the son of a bitch prima donna that I am, I've given him more than enough headaches to prepare him for the job as well. Personally, I think he's ready and it's just a matter of time."

They stared out at the war-torn landscape as Willie raised his hind leg and pissed in a nearby bush. Ike's visit had been six days earlier with Bedell Smith. He was pleased with the early returns from Patton's Palatinate Campaign to clear the Rhine Plain, predicting that Old Blood and Guts's swift move would save thousands of lives down the line. As a measure of Third Army's success, a beaming Eisenhower granted Patton's request for one of Patch's armored divisions, the 12th Armored, so he could hit the Germans even harder. Patton was ecstatic that for once Third Army was receiving reinforcements instead of shipping them off to another outfit.

Ike spent the night at Third Army headquarters, and the next morning he had paid Patton and his troops a great compliment. At a staff briefing, he declared that the Third Army was such a veteran outfit that its men didn't appreciate their own greatness. As Hap Gay had indicated, Ike had said they should be more cocky and boastful so that people would realize how good American citizen-soldiers truly were. Furthermore, Ike had told Patton that not only was he a damned good general but he was also a lucky one, and he reminded the Third Army commander that Napoleon preferred luck to greatness. With the war going so well, the meeting had been a congenial one and everyone had fallen all over themselves to be friendly.

A week later, Patton had more than justified his old friend's faith in him. His Palatinate Campaign had proven to be every bit as successful as his end run in

Western France and his timely rescue at Bastogne. Like a modern-day Hannibal, he had pushed his divisions across the Moselle and through the Hunsrück, a mountainous area to the east of Trier thought by SHAEF to be too rugged for armor. In the process, he had bagged much of Kesselring's First Army and shattered the Siegfried Line. He had done this all while sweeping around Patch's Seventh Army. By this morning, he had eight divisions on the Rhine from Koblenz to Ludwigshafen at the cost of less than 8,000 casualties. It was shaping up to be perhaps Third Army's finest hour. Other U.S. generals had cabled Patton to congratulate him on his "masterpiece" of surrounding several armies, "including one of our own." Patton had even heard that Twelfth Army Group's chief engineer had called a Seventh Army staffer in mock alarm to warn, "For God's sake, start running for Paris or you'll end up in one of Patton's prison cages!"

Everything was going Old Blood and Guts's way—except one thing. His powerful army still had not crossed the Rhine.

Now, with the Germans shorthanded, ill-equipped, and demoralized, was the time to seize a river crossing, as the legendary Caesar had done, and drive a stake through Hitler's heart. With the smashing success of his Palatinate offensive, Bradley had given him permission to cross the Rhine as soon as possible, and already the pressure was mounting on him to get his army across. To the north, Montgomery was scheduled to cross the Rhine on March 23, with a massive preparation of seventy thousand artillery rounds fired by two thousand guns; an air bombardment utilizing hundreds of heavy bombers and three thousand fighter planes; smoke screens; a multitude of amphibious vehicles, assault craft, and bridging materials; and an airborne landing in support of 80,000 infantry troops. The earth-shattering *Operation Plunder*—the largest military operation since D-Day— was to be reported in a speech by Winston Churchill over the BBC.

Though Patton couldn't help but admire Monty for managing to extract such a huge concession from Ike, he, his staff, and his soldiers of the Third Army were tired of playing second fiddle to the man. But just as important in Patton's mind was the rumor that if he didn't get to the Rhine's east bank soon, he and Patch would lose up to ten divisions to the British field marshal. More was at stake than the prestige of beating Monty across the river, and after taking the Rhine on the run Patton planned to launch a drive so furious that SHAEF wouldn't be able to pull his divisions away and give them to Twenty-First Army Group.

Considering the crossing as an opportunity to score off Monty and steal some of the limelight from Hodges, whose Remagen bridge coup had recently snatched the headlines for First Army, Patton had ordered his engineers forward and stockpiled large quantities of bridging material in anticipation of crossing the Rhine. His commanders would have preferred waiting a few days longer, but Patton had already selected sites for potential crossing and would not allow any further delay. Earlier that morning of March 22, Patton got his break near the winemaking town of Oppenheim. Receiving word from General Eddy that the crossing point was virtually undefended, he had ordered him to carve a bridgehead over the Rhine by nightfall. The first wave, from Eddy's 5th Infantry Division, had crossed an hour earlier at 2200 without opposition. By 0800 the next morning, the 5th Infantry, moving steadily in assault motorboats and rafts, had put six battalions on the east bank of the Rhine.

When Patton awoke on the morning of March 23, the day Monty was scheduled to commence his ballyhooed Rhine crossing, he was informed of the good news.

"God be praised! I am very grateful to the Lord for the great blessings he has heaped on me and the Third Army!" he cried, and he had Meeks quickly help him dress so he could deliver the news to Bradley.

He was able to reach him while he was having his usual breakfast in the elegant dining hall of Chateau de Namur. As the commander of Twelfth Army Group was sipping his second cup of coffee, an aide passed through a telephone call from Third Army.

"Brad, don't tell anyone but I'm across!" announced Patton in a conspiratorial whisper, barely able to control his excitement.

"Well, I'll be damned," exclaimed Bradley. "You mean across the Rhine?"

Patton grinned with the phone to his ear. "Sure am. I sneaked a division over last night. But there are so few Krauts around there they don't know it yet. So don't make any announcement—we'll keep it a secret until we see how it goes."

"Good job, George," said Bradley. "Now I want you to push ten divisions over the Rhine. And make it snappy."

"Oh, you don't have to worry about that, Brad," and he hung up.

Calling together his staff, he told them to pull out all the stops to make sure Eddy kept getting men across all day long. Then he wrote up a special order to the soldiers and airmen of the Third Army and the XIX Tactical Air Command announcing the first Third Army bridgehead over the Rhine. He wanted to make sure his and Opie Weyland's boys knew how proud he was of them, for it was not either general but their men that had taken it to the Germans and crossed the Rhine.

### Third Army General Orders 70, March 23, 1945

*To the officers and men of the Third Army and to our comrades of the XIX TAC:*

*In the period from January 29 to March 22, 1945, you have wrested 6,484 square miles of territory from the enemy. You have taken 3,072 cities, towns, and villages, including Trier, Coblenz, Bingen, Worms, Mainz, Kaiserslautern, and Ludwigshafen.*

*You have captured 140,112 enemy soldiers and have killed or wounded an additional 99,000, thereby eliminating practically all of the German Seventh and First Armies. History records no greater achievement in so limited a time.*

*This great campaign was only made possible by your disciplined valor, unswerving devotion to duty, coupled with the unparalleled audacity and speed of your advance on the ground; while from the air, the peerless fighter-bombers kept up a relentless round-the-clock attack upon the disorganized enemy.*

*The world rings with your praises: better still, General Marshall, General Eisenhower, and General Bradley have all personally commended you. The highest honor I have ever attained is that of having my name coupled with yours in these great events.*

*Please accept my heartfelt admiration and thanks for what you have done, and remember that your assault crossing over the Rhine River at 2200 hours last night assures you of even greater glory to come.*

*G.S. Patton, Jr.*

*Lt. Gen., U.S. Third Army*
*Commanding*

Two hours later, he learned that Third Army's crossing of the Rhine was no longer a secret. The Germans on the east bank had reported the breach, and throughout the morning the Luftwaffe had been attacking Third Army's pontoon bridges relentlessly in a desperate attempt to knock them out. In response, his gunners shot down thirty-three fighters and bombers. By midday, other American units were calling Gay to find out about the rumors that Patton's infantry had crossed the river. After conferring with his chief of staff and realizing that his stealthy crossing was no longer a secret, he called Bradley again just after darkness fell.

"Brad, for God's sake tell the world we're across!" he exclaimed over the phone, his voice squeaky and filled with boyish excitement. "I want the world to know Third Army made it before Monty starts across!"

"Don't worry, I'm on it, George," Bradley reassured him.

He was as good as his word. Extremely pleased by Patton's news, he swiftly gathered his press pool to detail the crossings at Oppenheim. All the reporters knew that Montgomery was on the verge of his long-planned, million-man crossing to the north, a mass migration preceded by a month-long aerial bombardment, heavy naval, air, smoke, and artillery support, even studies of soil samples of the Rhine's banks. Bradley emphasized that Third Army had crossed the famous river without benefit of aerial bombing, ground smoke, artillery preparation, and airborne assistance—in fact, without firing so much as a mortar round—knowing the unfavorable comparisons the press would draw to Monty's showy crossing. After having been humiliated after Bastogne and with a second Rhine bridgehead to crow about, Bradley took great pleasure in stealing Monty's thunder. His statement broadcast over the radio was specifically worded not only as a notice of the Third Army's crossing, but also as a direct slap in the face of Monty. The crossing had, moreover, been made with a minimum of casualties; the 5th Division suffered only twenty-eight killed and wounded. He further announced that American forces could now cross the Rhine at almost any point. And they, too, would do this, as Patton's troops had, without the aid of air bombardments, paratroopers, and heavy artillery.

The announcement came just four hours before the BBC broadcast of a recorded speech in which Churchill bragged to the world that Monty and the British had begun to traverse the Rhine. This, Churchill boasted, constituted the first assault crossing of the Rhine in history and soon the British field marshal would be the first general to cross the river by assault in modern times. The prepared speech by Churchill was erroneous, of course, as Third Army had already crossed the river by boat and seized the eastern bank.

When he awoke the next morning, March 24, to hear about it, Patton had to smile. But not as much he did when he drove to Oppenheim an hour later to celebrate the taking of the Rhine, as he had previously done when crossing the Seine. The 5th Division bridgehead was already five miles deep and two miles wide and growing by the minute. With Mims, Eddy, Codman, and Stiller, he drove to the river and went across on the pontoon bridge built by his engineers.

Halfway across the river, he said to his driver Mims, "Time out for a short halt." When Mims stopped the vehicle, Patton stepped from his command jeep and walked to the edge of the pontoon bridge.

"I've waited a long time to do this," he announced to the assembled crowd of grinning onlookers, who he could tell had a good idea what he was about to do.

With great fanfare, he unzipped his fly, pulled out his pecker, and proceeded to piss into the swirling eddies of the mighty river.

"I didn't even piss this morning when I got up so I would have a really full load," he said when he was finished. "Yes, sir, the pause that refreshes."

He then walked along the bridge to the eastern bank. Reaching it, he deliberately stumbled, fell to one knee, and grabbed two handfuls of clayey silt German soil. Then he stood, and with the dirt wafting earthward through his fingers, exclaimed in a symbolic gesture: "Thus, William the Conqueror!"

His act was a recreation of the victor of the Battle of Hastings in 1066 A.D., when William reputedly stumbled and fell on his face emerging from his boat on the shores of England. "See," the quick-thinking future king had said, "I have taken England with both hands."

Patton wanted to ensure that no one—and especially not the history books—would forget his arrival.

Two days later, he received a letter from his old buddy Ike that he had long dreamed of receiving:

*March 26, 1945*
*Dear George:*
*I have frequently had occasion to state, publicly, my appreciation of the great accomplishments of this Allied force during the past nine months. The purpose of this little note is to express to you personally my deep appreciation of the splendid way in which you have conducted Third Army operations from the moment it entered battle last August 1. You have made your Army a fighting force that is not excelled in effectiveness by any other of equal size in the world, and I am very proud of the fact that you, as one of the fighting commanders who has been with me from the beginning of the African campaign, have performed so brilliantly throughout.*

*We are now fairly started on that phase of the campaign which I hope will be the final one. I know that Third Army will be in at the finish in the same decisive way that it has performed in all the preliminary battles.*

*With warm personal regard,*
*as ever,*

*Dwight D. Eisenhower*

# PART 5

319

# THE RECKONING

# CHAPTER 51

**GUNSKIRCHEN LABOR CAMP**
**NORTHERN AUSTRIA**

**MARCH 26, 1945**

AS EXHAUSTED AND HUNGRY as she was, Angela knew that her poor father was even worse off. They had been force-marched more than forty miles in the past three and a half days, and she wasn't sure how much longer they could go on when the other prisoners had been dropping like flies the past five miles. The brutal SS guards shot stragglers in the back of the head to keep the shambling procession moving towards its new destination, which was still unknown.

*How has it come to this?* she wondered, as she placed one foot in front of the other without thought and therefore without effort, moving slowly but steadily to conserve her energy. *What has happened to our country?*

The thought had been echoing in her mind since she and her father had been released by Foltis and shipped eastward by rail from Cologne to the Thuringia refugee camp north of Nuremberg. When they had reached the camp in early March, they had been shocked to discover that it was severely overcrowded and disease-ridden, and that the local German farmers mistreated the newcomers and refused to share their dwindling resources. After two weeks of excruciating hunger and the breakout of a typhus epidemic, she and her father managed to escape the camp with several other Germans. But they were later rounded up and arrested by the SS along with a group of escaped Russian forced laborers with whom they had stolen potatoes and taken refuge. Deemed political enemies of the state once again despite their vigorous protests, they were shipped by rail south to the Mauthausen camp in the Austrian Alps. After being unloaded from the cramped train, they were thrown in with a larger group of prisoners from Mauthausen and force-marched at gunpoint towards the southwest, presumably to some satellite camp.

The SS guards were calling the death march an "evacuation transport," but Angela doubted that more than two-thirds of the prisoners would make it to their final destination, whatever it might be. Most of the prisoners that had joined them at Mauthausen were Hungarian Jews, though she had learned that there were a smattering of Poles and Ukrainians added to the ranks of the German political prisoners like her and her father in the miserable group.

They walked on. But soon her father grew tired and he was forced to slow his pace. Their health had deteriorated significantly in the past month: he had lost nearly twenty pounds, and she over ten. But her father was falling apart far worse than her. His old war wounds, the severe beatings he had endured at Brauweiler Prison, and nearly drowning in the Rhine had taken a heavy toll on him: he was a shell of the robust staff officer that had served with von Manteuffel on the Eastern Front and in Tunisia. Their only chance was to find a way to rustle up more food so they could hold out until the Allies arrived. From word of mouth, they knew that the American cowboy Patton and his *blitzkrieging* Third Army were drawing nearer every day. When passing through Nuremberg on the train days earlier, they had heard the booming of the guns and roar of aircraft to the west towards the Rhine.

Departing from Mauthausen, they were marched off with only a watery bowl of soup in their stomachs, and they had been given only a half loaf of bread since in three days' walking. She and her father had plucked out grass and herbs, which they boiled at night, and they had managed to dig out a few potatoes, but that was all they had gotten their hands on to supplement their meager rations. The SS guards shot anyone caught stepping off the trail to obtain food, and SS officers rode by on bicycles all along the road and gunned down anybody they found resting. Earlier in the day, when she and her father had stopped to sit down on a boulder to rest, an SS guard riding by on his bicycle pointed his *Schmeisser* at them. But they quickly rose to their feet and he grudgingly spared their lives.

They continued on, passing by large sections of farmland surrounded by emerald green forests and rugged alpine mountains. Soon they entered a thick stand of pine trees and walked along a dirt road through the woods. At a small brook, they were allowed to stop to take a drink of water. Angela cupped her hands into the brook and splashed water onto her face. Numb from exhaustion, the icy cold water revived her instantly. For a blissful moment, she forgot about her terrible predicament, her blistered feet, and the murderous insanity of the war. Instead, she imagined herself back at the Königsforst, walking hand in hand with Barthel and kissing beneath the wind-rustled trees. She wondered if she would ever love another with the same passion as the young Edelweiss Pirate who had changed her world. The first love of her life would always have a special place in her heart.

The peaceful moment was broken as the SS guards came stomping up with their usual belligerence, prodding and poking the prisoners with their guns to get them moving again. They walked on for at least an hour, all the while Angela thinking about all the terrible things she had witnessed since leaving Cologne. Several times during their eastward journey from the city to the Thuringia refugee camp and in their southward trek to Mauthausen, they had fallen victim to enemy shelling or Allied pilots who mistook them for Wehrmacht units. Though she and her father had managed to escape the strafing attacks unscathed, Angela had witnessed innocent civilians getting their arms and legs blown off. The casualties amongst the women, children, and elderly frantically trying to take cover were painful to watch.

But what she found most shocking was just how far her country had fallen and how swiftly it had turned to anarchy. She had seen SS troops lining up men and women against walls and shooting them dead; German soldiers pressganging civilians into helping repair damaged roads and prepare fortifications, robbing them of their shoes to replace their worn-out boots, and appropriating food, livestock, and coal for the war effort; scuffles and arguments between police and angry civilians; farmers firing on approaching patrols in order to protect their property; and civilians heckling and spitting upon security officers and Party officials who forced them to leave their homes and give up their food or property against their will.

In her eyes, the only good thing was that the German people were finally blaming the true culprits—Hitler and the Nazis—for their misfortune. They denounced the Führer as a "scoundrel" and "mass murderer" and castigated security officers and Party officials as "rascals and criminals," warning that "soon all the Brownshirts will be strung up." In one town she passed through, Angela had heard an elderly man snarl, "It's a damned shame Hitler survived the July 20 attempt—the man is a murdering lout!" Others had merely given up all hope. With artillery thundering and flashing on the horizon, she had overheard one woman saying, "The war is lost. Things will soon come to an end and the state will kick the bucket."

Soon they came upon an enclosure consisting of a sturdily made fence approximately 8 feet in height. The fence wire was of a heavy gauge and the openings were 2 by 4 inches. In the middle of the fence was a wide gate with halves formed with wide planks as frames and covered with fencing material. Above the entrance, the gate was inscribed with the words *Arbeit Macht Frei*—Work Makes Freedom. Hundreds of emaciated, bedraggled, and half-clothed people stared blankly back at her and her father through the fencing. Some were crying, others mumbling incoherently, still others speaking in languages she didn't understand. All of them were insane with hunger. It was apparent the camp was already totally overcrowded, sanitary conditions were dreadful, and food was insufficient. It may have been called a "labor" camp—but it was really a death camp.

"My God, what is this place? How can this be?" she heard her father mutter as a line formed to go inside the camp.

Angela felt a shuddering anger; during the past month she and her father had continued to debate who was ultimately responsible for Hitler's rise to power and the state-sanctioned imprisonment, murder, and abuse of specific groups that the Nazis labeled as *Volksfeinde*.

"You know perfectly well what this is," she snapped at him. "Each and every German has known about these kind of camps all along. And now we are about to suffer the same fate as those we have condemned to death—which is better than we deserve."

"No," he said flatly. "I never knew about *this*—or I would never have worn the uniform. Look at these people—they are skeletons. Who can do such a thing?"

"We knew all along, Papa. We all knew—every last German—and yet we did nothing."

He shook his head adamantly. "No, not *this*. I never knew about *this*."

"Yes, you did. You just didn't want to acknowledge it," she said angrily. "And now every German will be guilty in the eyes of God for a thousand years. There will never be redemption for this. Never."

He stood there gaping-mouthed, still unable to believe his eyes. Then he shook his head with resignation. "You're right, after this, there can be no redemption for us. Whatever eternal damnation God sees fit for Germany, whatever ignominious judgment history hands down to our people, is what we deserve. It is our reckoning."

He squeezed her hand and his piercing aquamarine eyes, moist with tears, met hers. She remembered back to the photographs she had seen of him wearing the distinctive desert cap and insignia of the vaunted *Afrika Korps*. He had looked so strong and proud in the photos from Tunisia, standing with his sun-burnished officers in front of a pair of Panzers. Now it all seemed like an eternity ago.

She looked around at the faces of the other prisoners, most of them Hungarian Jews that had tromped along the road with them the past four days. The new arrivals were starving, exhausted, and terrified—and she felt for them.

The gate creaked open.

As the weary group started forward to go inside, they were greeted in the usual way—with vicious snapping dogs and yelling guards wielding truncheons and submachine guns. Officially designated a "labor camp," Gunskirchen was not a death camp like Auschwitz where "undesirables" were sent for extermination, but rather a camp where the standard method of execution was systematically working prisoners until they died from the combined effects of exhaustion and malnutrition.

Angela looked at her father, trying to gauge his reaction to their new surroundings. The Wehrmacht colonel was closely scrutinizing the camp, the guards, and the prisoners with the studied precision of a police detective. He seemed to be already plotting how best to escape. They would have to do so soon, while they still had some strength, she realized, as it was obvious the SS were deliberately starving the prisoners in the camp.

The compound had four guard towers, each manned by a guard and sporting a menacing-looking machine gun, a siren, and a search light. The thousands of prisoners had been crammed into a few low, one-story, frame buildings with sloppy, muddy floors. Those who were able had ventured out of the buildings to see the new arrivals, but Angela knew that there were hundreds left in them—the dead, the near-dead, and those too weak to move. No trees or shrubs grew between the compound buildings or around the perimeter road, ensuring that any escape attempt would be in full view from at least one guard tower. She could tell straight away that it would be no small task to escape from this heavily-guarded place, especially when weak and malnourished. The ground was pulpy throughout the camp, churned to a consistency of warm putty by the milling of thousands of feet. The mud was mixed with feces and urine. Feeling sick to her stomach, she wondered how a benevolent God could allow such inhumanity to exist on the face of the earth.

But it was the smell that revolted her most.

It was made up of several different odors—human excrement, foul body stench, smoldering trash fires, German tobacco—all mixed together in a heavy dank atmosphere in a thick, muddy woods where little breeze could circulate. The smell of whatever place this was nauseated her and she knew she would never forget it. It was completely different from anything she had ever encountered—even the hundreds of dead bodies buried amongst the rubble of Cologne. It hung over the camp like a fog of death.

Taking in her surroundings one last time, she shook her head in dismay. "What is this place?" she asked the group of cadaverous prisoners on the other side of the fence as she and her father began walking inside.

"This is Gunskirchen Lager," said a man from the crowd in the voice of the Fatherland. "We don't see too many Germans here."

"No, I don't expect you do," said her father.

And with that, Angela stepped forward—with tears in her eyes and her father clutching her hand for reassurance—to be registered and given her striped, numbered prison uniform.

# CHAPTER 52

## LUCKY FORWARD, IDAR-OBERSTEIN
## WESTERN GERMANY

### MARCH 27, 1945

"GEORGE, I'M IN TROUBLE AGAIN. This time I've really done it."

Patton looked guiltily at Meeks, who had paused from brushing down his field tunic. The two men were alone in the Lucky Forward trailer.

"What did you do, sir?"

"I sent a task force to liberate a POW camp and only a few of the men have come back. I'm afraid I sent Alex Stiller and those other fine soldiers off to their death for nothing. Goddamn, I am one dumb son of a bitch."

As if to underscore his own self-censure, Patton shook his head in disgust. Failure was his own worst enemy. Knowing this, his African-American personal valet looked at him sympathetically.

"You said Major Stiller was on the task force?" asked Meeks, referring to Patton's junior aide-de-camp.

Patton nodded. "I loved that boy like a son. He looked so hurt when I told him he couldn't go along. And then like a fool, I let him talk me into it. I gave in and told him to go ahead. And now the whole thing has turned into a fiasco."

"What sort of outfit did you send?"

"Basically, a reinforced company. Around three hundred men. I should have sent at least a combat command."

"Maybe they got delayed and will make it back, General."

"Unfortunately, that's not how it turned out. I'm going to be in a lot of trouble. You'd better pour me a stiff one, George."

"Yes, sir. I'll pour you a cognac."

With a heavy sigh, he turned away from Meeks and stared out the open window of his trailer into the darkened night. What he hadn't told his personal aide and confidant was his primary reason for attempting the dangerous mission deep behind enemy lines: to rescue his son-in-law, Lieutenant Colonel John Waters, taken prisoner two years earlier in Tunisia. Patton had first learned that Waters had been moved from a prisoner-of-war camp in central Poland to somewhere in western Germany back in February via Beetle Smith's secretary. G-2 had verified that Oflag XIII-B, a prison camp near Hammelburg, was housing American officers, and Patton believed there was a good chance his son-in-law was being held there. Oflag XIII-B contained some 3,000 Serbs of the Royal Yugoslav Army, around 800 Americans who had arrived in January, most of them captured during the Bulge, and more than 400 additional Americans who arrived from Poland in early March.

The camp lay well outside Third Army's boundaries, in Seventh Army territory, but Patton was determined to rescue Waters and liberate the camp. For all he knew, the prisoners might be moved or even massacred before the camp was freed. Moreover, across the globe MacArthur had garnered headlines by sending a Ranger force to liberate a prison camp in the Philippines, where some 500 American POWs who would have been slaughtered by their Japanese captors were set free. Patton decided to lead a similar raid in Hammelburg to rescue the American prisoners being held at Oflag XIII-B. Task Force Baum—commanded by a young captain named Abraham Baum—had left last night with 53 vehicles in the task force: 10 M4A3 medium tanks, six M5 light tanks, 27 half-tracks, three 105mm self-propelled guns, six jeeps, and one tracked medical vehicle, along with 307 officers and men. Patton and Baum had wanted to send an entire combat command—one-third of a division—but Eddy, the commander of XII Corps, had refused, insisting upon just two motorized companies to allow greater mobility and surprise.

Task Force Baum, which had counted on stealth, was forced to shoot its way into the camp and then surround it. As Waters and another U.S. officer walked out to the camp's gate under a flag of truce, a German sentry fired a Mauser round through the colonel's lower back. Dropping to the ground, Waters had to be dragged back into the compound. Local troops, armed with *Panzerfausts* and small arms, converged on the American raiders and destroyed all fifty-three vehicles. Of the 307 men sent out, only fifteen had thus far made it back to the American lines.

Patton knew he would catch hell for ordering such a reckless mission. He had been frantic all day wondering what fate had befallen his son-in-law and aide Stiller. An hour earlier, when he had first learned that Waters had been wounded and was expected to die, he had burst into tears. Ike's son, John Eisenhower, had been at Lucky Forward visiting at the time and Patton had told him about the incident. Later on, as he was leaving, he told young Eisenhower how much he owed his father before breaking into tears again. For Patton, the guilt was overwhelming.

Meeks handed him a glass of Hennessy four-star cognac. The Old Man tossed it back and handed the glass back to his aide.

"Better make me another, George. I'm in a bad way."

At that moment, a knock was heard on the door to his trailer. Codman poked his head in. "General Bradley is on the line for you, sir."

*Oh shit,* thought Patton, feeling a little flutter in his chest. *Here we go.*

"Did he say what it was about?"

"No, sir," said Codman. "But he did say it was important."

A minute later, Patton took the call in his trailer while Meeks gave him his second cognac and continued tidying up his quarters.

"Brad, what can I do for you," he said without preamble.

"Hello, George. Something's come up and I need to find out what's going on."

Patton held his breath.

"A newspaper reporter asked me today," continued Omar Bradley, "about a mission you apparently ordered to liberate a POW camp behind enemy lines. I must admit I was a bit taken aback. I gave no information about the raid because I had none to give. But I promised the reporter that I would find out. Did you, in fact, order such a raid, George?"

Before answering, he took a moment to work out in his head how much information to reveal and how to present the raid in the best possible light. But he knew there was no excuse for what he had done. He had ordered the rescue mission without Bradley's approval. But even worse, it was going to look as though he had sent the task force for the sole purpose of rescuing Johnny, which wasn't true. Though it was an important reason and he probably wouldn't have ordered the raid if his son-in-law hadn't been there, he had wanted to get all the other Americans trapped in the POW camp out as well and had hoped that the rescue would act as a diversion to cause confusion behind enemy lines.

"Yes, Brad, I ordered the raid. Task Force Baum hit the Oflag POW camp in Hammelburg late last night. The task force consisted of around three hundred men, over fifty armored vehicles, and three self-propelled guns."

"What happened?"

"It was a fiasco. The task force was surrounded by elements of at least three German divisions. They were chopped to pieces in a series of desperate firefights. Dozens of men were apparently wounded, and most were captured and returned to Oflag as POWs. Among them were Baum and Stiller."

"You sent Al Stiller?"

Patton felt himself choking up again. It was only because the short, tough-as-nails, former Texas Ranger from El Paso had badgered him that Stiller had been allowed to join the expedition, and also because he could identify John Waters. But Old Blood and Guts still felt guilty for allowing him to go.

"No, I didn't order Al to go along, Brad—he insisted on going. But it is still my damn fault for agreeing to let him go. Of the three hundred men who began the raid, all but one were listed as missing until a couple of hours ago. Since then, more than a dozen have straggled in. I'm sick about the whole thing."

Bradley said nothing. The silence was acute, and Patton felt the sting of silence more of a rebuke than an actual dressing down.

"I had no idea it was going to fall apart like this," he went on. "I didn't think there was anything in that part of Germany heavy enough to hurt them."

"Well George, as your friend, I can only say that I hope this doesn't play out like Sicily."

Patton felt suddenly as if he had a bad case of indigestion. *God, is it really that bad? You have really done it now. Brad is right, what in the hell were you thinking?*

"Frankly, I can understand why you would want to liberate the camp, George. But there is also a rumor going around that you ordered the operation to free your son-in-law. Please tell me that's not true."

Patton squirmed in his chair. "It isn't, Brad, I swear," he said, his high-pitched voice as squeaky as a protesting child. "I didn't know whether Johnny was interned at the camp or not."

"But you had a pretty good idea he was there, right?"

"I thought it was maybe fifty-fifty. But I didn't know for sure. You've got to believe me."

"I believe you, George. But whether you knew or not is beside the point. This fiasco has put not only you—but me and Ike—in a bad position with the press."

"Unfortunately, it could get worse. Johnny's shot up and might not make it."

"I'm sorry to hear that."

"It's my damned fault. But I honestly didn't think it would turn out like this. I thought it would be a snatch and grab."

"What we've got on our hands now is a public relations nightmare *and* an unnecessary disaster. I'm not trying to rub it, I'm just telling you straight."

"Like I said, I'm sorry, Brad. I don't know what else to say."

"If you had asked me for permission beforehand, I would have vetoed it. You do understand that?"

This time, Patton said nothing. He didn't want to add to his culpability. *Goddamnit, what in the hell have you done? You were supposed to stop this shit. But if you had overruled Eddy and insisted on a full combat command, this would have never happened. Goddamn Eddy! In the end, it's just as much his fault as mine!*

"I realize that it could have been a spectacular stunt. You could have rescued Johnny and all the other American officers and gotten a lot of headlines. But personally, I think it was doomed from the start and it was a foolhardy operation to even attempt. The Germans are far from whipped yet, especially not in their own backyard. They only had a few tanks and two companies to contend with."

"I know that, Brad, and again I'm sorry."

"At the same time, George, I have to say that this Hammelburg raid is about the only lapse of judgment you've made since England. And there's another thing."

"What's that?"

"This story began as a wild goose chase and ended in tragedy due to circumstances that were beyond your control. That's one reason I'm not going to formally rebuke you for it. But the main reason is I, more than anyone else but perhaps Beatrice, know that failure itself is your own worst reprimand."

Patton said nothing. He knew Brad was right. Hammelburg was the least defensible military decision he had ever made, and he could only hope it wouldn't prove to be as self-destructive to his career as the slappings. But the worst thing was that the whole thing had the potential to brand him as a liar and tarnish the very fabric on which his fame rested: that the welfare of his troops came first and he would never squander their lives needlessly. Instead, the press might very well conclude that he had sent a task force on a mission whose sole purpose was to selfishly rescue his own son-in-law. He would, of course, deny it and argue that Task Force Baum had caused havoc behind German lines by forcing the Germans to divert a number of enemy units to the Hammelburg area, thus easing the advance of his Third Army during the last stages of the war. But his detractors would no doubt argue that the camp would have been liberated within a matter of days anyway by forces that would not have been seriously challenged—and thus, all he had done was squander lives for his own selfish interests.

"Brad, I know I screwed up," he said with genuine feeling. "But I promise I'll make it up to you and Ike both. I just wanted to do the right thing and didn't put enough forethought into it. We needed a full combat command and, goddamnit, I let Eddy talk me out of it. But still, the buck stops with me. I'm the one ultimately responsible for this mess."

"I have no doubt that your intentions were good, George. But for God's sake, lay low for awhile. With any luck, this all might blow over."

*I doubt it,* thought Patton worriedly, despite the fact that he had already censored the story so the press couldn't get hold of it.

And with that, the phone clicked and Bradley was gone.

# CHAPTER 53

**SOUTHEAST OF LEISENWALD AND COBURG
CENTRAL GERMANY**

**APRIL 3, 1945**

"HIT THOSE TREES HARD!" McBurney heard Pop Gates roar over the radio intercom. "Fire at will! Fire at will!"

"You heard the man. Let 'em have it, Billy," ordered Teddy Windsor from his tank commander's seat.

"My pleasure," replied McBurney.

As he peered through his gun sight, the intercom squawked again. "Yo mothers, let's come out fighting!" someone shouted over the airwaves. He realized it was Smitty in his nearby tank Cool Stud.

*That's my boy,* he thought, his smile weary but confident.

Other tanks swiftly chimed in with the 761st Black Panther motto. "Come out fighting! Come out fighting!" came the crescendo over the intercom.

From his gunner's chair, McBurney swung his turret into action with an electric whine and let loose with a blast from his main 76mm gun. All along the line, the tanks opened up into the pine forest outside Leisenwald where the remnants of the crack 6th SS Mountain Division Nord were stubbornly holding out. Tongues of flame and smoke leapt from the turrets. Since crossing the Rhine, Charlie Company counted twelve working tanks in its ranks, and every one of them blasted away into the trees where the SS troops were hiding. The 75mm and 76mm shells cut down the thick pine and spruce with a retching crash, knocking down trunks and cleaving off entire limbs. But still the intractable Germans refused to come out and surrender.

*Goddamn SS,* thought McBurney. *Fanatics to the core. We just might have to burn the little Hitlers out.*

"Hit 'em again!" ordered Pop Gates.

For the next five minutes, the sky whistled with fresh rounds of shells, the ground shook, and the forest exploded with fire, smoke, and dust. But still the Germans wouldn't come out.

For the past three days, the 761st's tanks and accompanying infantrymen had spread out over a wide area to complete the encirclement of the SS Mountain Division. A ground force with its own chain of command independent of the Wehrmacht, the unit of Nazi diehards gave no sign of willingness to surrender. Almost completely surrounded by American forces, the Germans were stuck inside the forest and had been making a series of increasingly desperate attempts to break out all along the pocket's perimeter. The Black Panthers—once again reunited with Patton's Third Army and assigned to fight alongside the 71st Infantry Division—had been waiting patiently just beyond the thick woods to kill or capture the last of the holdouts.

McBurney's Charlie Company had taken up strategic positions along the southeastern edge of the remaining pocket of SS Mountain Division troops to prevent their escape. Sighting the imposing line of Sherman tanks, the Germans realized that they'd be slaughtered if they tried to make a mass escape. They had, therefore, broken up into platoon-sized groups and were attempting to break out at various points from the forest, having been cut off from behind by the 66th Infantry Regiment of the 71st. The doughs were pressing forward from the Germans' rear like beaters driving a fox towards an awaiting group of hunters.

"Raise your fire! I want HE in those treetops above the Germans!" Gates commanded McBurney, Smith, and the other tank main gunners. "If fire, shrapnel, and falling branches can't flush them out, then nothing will!"

The tank firing line erupted with fire, smoke, and death. In less than a minute, the flames were roaring through the forest. Through gaps in the smoke, McBurney could see flashes of the SS troops dashing and darting amidst the burning trees, struggling to avoid the licking flames. Some of them seemed to be forming a defensive skirmish line. Charlie's dozen tanks continued to spit HE rounds from their main cannons and tracers every four bullets from the .30-caliber machine guns. The coaxials hammered away with a *rat-tat-tat* staccato and bullets crisscrossed the forest like angry, battling hornets. The tanks kept firing away until the forest turned to an inferno and the smoke roiled as thick and heavy as a full artillery barrage, cutting down available oxygen. Sure enough, Pop Gates's tactic worked and, in groups of two, three, and four, the Germans began staggering out waving white handkerchiefs, underwear, or anything else white they could scrounge up.

"Stay buttoned up inside your tanks with hatches closed tight until those SS troops reach us," ordered Gates. "When they reach our line, we'll direct them back to surrender to the infantry."

McBurney couldn't help but feel it was just another form of humiliation that the Germans had to surrender to white infantrymen rather than to the Negro unit that had actually defeated them, but it was the accepted protocol now that they were deep inside Nazi territory. Since their drive to the Rhine, they had discovered that the Fatherland's troops were utterly terrified of black soldiers, based on the savage reputation of French Senegalese soldiers during World War I. The African soldiers from the French possession were notoriously tall and fierce-looking warriors with black shiny skin and eyes so dark they almost glowed with bellicosity. During the Great War, when they had crossed into enemy territory, the black warriors had shown little mercy to their German foes, delivering punishing raids and returning to their lines bearing grisly trophies such as ears, fingers, and heads. A common question asked by German soldiers relieving their fellow soldiers in the WWI trenches was "Are there any Africans opposite?" The exploits of the fearsome *Schwarze Soldaten*—Black Soldiers—as they came to be known had so terrified the Fatherland during the war that, a generation later, German soldiers and civilians alike looked upon the new interlopers as the second coming of the black invaders. Most Germans had never before seen anybody with dark skin, and they failed to realize that aside from skin color, the African-American tanker or infantryman was not that different from the white American doughboy.

The surrendering troops approached the line of tanks in their grimy, bloodied, and scorched SS uniforms, hands and guns held up to the sky. Some staggered and limped, many coughed from the smoke, and more than a few had tears rolling down their grimy checks.

"*Kameraden!*" they called out, pleading and waving their white cloths in surrender. "*Kameraden!*"

Though Gates had ordered his tank crews to stay buttoned up inside their vehicles until the troops reached them, one of the Charlie tankers mistakenly opened his hatch out of curiosity when the troops were only a short distance away. The nearest Germans saw him and began screaming and yelling in panic.

"*Schwarze Soldaten!*" they shrieked, running and stumbling back towards the woods in mass panic.

"Gunners, I need a warning volley! Fire over their heads!" commanded Pop Gates over the intercom. "They need to be stopped now!"

Bullets tore through the trees overhead of the retreating Germans as they dashed and stumbled towards the treeline. But after a moment, one of the SS officers realized that it was only a warning volley and they weren't being fired upon. Outgunned and with no choice but to surrender, he ordered his men to stop or they would be massacred. In obeyance, the dozens of fleeing soldiers halted, turned around, and threw up their hands again.

"*Kameraden!*" they shouted, more frantically this time, still terrified of their captors but figuring they had better go along with them after all.

"*Komm schon—sie werden nicht verletzt!*" shouted Pop Gates in ragged German, directing them towards him. Come on—you will not be harmed.

Once calm had again been restored, the Germans stepped cautiously back up to the line of tanks. One by one, the tankers emerged from their hatches to take a look at the Aryan Supermen they had been grappling with the past three days and who had stubbornly refused to surrender.

From the turret, McBurney and the rest of the crew watched as one of the captured SS officers who spoke English asked Pop Gates, "How many Negro Panzer divisions are there?"

McBurney looked at Windsor and smiled. Obviously, the Germans had encountered the 761st's widely dispersed tanks in every direction for miles around and the German officer was puzzled over how the black tankers could be in so many different places at once.

The grizzled veteran Buffalo Soldier Gates grinned at the SS officer, saying without skipping a beat, "Oh, maybe twenty or thirty."

The SS man's mouth dropped open with shock.

"Damn, now we're just poking fun at these motherfucking Supermen!" cried Mozee Thompson, and the whole crew had a good laugh.

"These boys are SS—they goddamn deserve it," said Windsor, his jaw set in a stubborn line. "If Colonel Bates had his way, he'd shoot every last Nazi. He hates 'em. Look around this here country at all the death and destruction they've caused. Everything you see is because of these motherfuckers. They brought it all upon themselves and I have no sympathy for them. None at all."

McBurney agreed. Hitler and his Nazis were the ones most responsible for the war, and they should pay the heaviest price when Nazi Germany was defeated.

He wanted to be there at the very end when the bastards surrendered.

# CHAPTER 54

## MERKERS MINE, OHRDRUF LABOR CAMP,
## AND LUCKY FORWARD HERSFELD
## CENTRAL GERMANY

### APRIL 12-13, 1945

AS THE RICKETY WOODEN ELEVATOR CAR descended down the pitch-black mine shaft, Patton felt his throat go dry. He looked at his fellow officers packed into the elevator with him—Ike, Bradley, Weyland, and Colonel Bernard Bernstein, Ike's financial advisor—but he couldn't make out any of their faces in the inky blackness. With a German national operating the creaky elevator, he was feeling anxious about the group's safety. The sound of the elevator's motor reverberated through the dark shaft as they descended with ever-accelerating speed two thousand feet into the abyss of the Merkers industrial salt mine.

It was here, in a huge underground cavern, where the entire German gold bullion reserve of the Third Reich and countless stolen European art treasures had been cached away by the Nazis.

Peering up at the elevator's spindly cable silhouetted against a shrinking dot of daylight, the prankster Patton remarked, "If that clothesline should part, promotions in the United States Army would be considerably stimulated."

From the darkness, a flat, unamused Kansas voice replied, "Okay, George, that's enough. No more wisecracks until we are above ground again."

"Yessir," responded Patton affably, realizing that Ike was just nervous.

The Merkers potassium mine with its concealed Nazi repository had been discovered six days earlier by the Third Army's Manton Eddy, commander of XII Corps, who immediately notified his boss. But when Eddy informed Patton that he still didn't know for certain what lay inside a number of the sealed vaults belonging to the German Reich bank, Old Blood and Guts exploded.

"Goddamnit General Eddy, you blow open those fucking remaining vaults and see what's in them!"

Once he received confirmation of the contents, Patton called Bradley and urged him to get SHAEF to take custody of the gold right away, knowing its ownership might become a contested political issue. He also ordered an embargo on the story from reporters until it could be confirmed. Acting on Patton's suggestion, SHAEF dispatched the Columbia-graduate financier Colonel Bernstein to arrange for the gold's safekeeping. Bernstein selected the Reichsbank at Frankfurt am Main, far to the west, as the storage facility, since the gold reserve had been found in the Red Army's occupation zone. Unbeknownst to Patton, at the Yalta conference in February, the Big Three—FDR, Churchill, and Stalin—had decided that the Erfurt-Ohrdruf portion of Germany, now occupied by Third Army where the mine was located, would be handed over to Stalin and his Soviets once the Germans were defeated. It was, therefore, imperative that the gold and other Nazi loot be moved—and quickly—if the Allies didn't want it to fall into Russian hands.

The elevator with its none-too-secure cable ground to a merciful halt. The German official opened the clinky metal door. Pulling their overcoats tight, the five

American officers stepped from the pitch black into a cool, unventilated tunnel beneath bare lightbulbs. The U.S. Army loot-handler Bernstein led them first into Room Number 8.

Spread before their eyes was the entire reserve of the Berlin Reichsbank—gold, cash, and treasure systematically stolen by the Nazi regime and hidden underground 200 miles from Berlin to protect it from Allied bombing. Grim-faced, they inspected wooden pallets of gold bullion, paper currency tightly baled, Reichsbank currency printing plates, and several tons of coins packed in crates, suitcases, and steamer trunks.

Patton couldn't believe his eyes. This was his first look up close at the sinister underbelly of the Nazi empire and he was flabbergasted. He estimated that the rows upon rows of gold bars and banknotes in Room No. 8 alone were worth hundreds of millions of dollars, and noted that the banknotes were in German, British, and French currency.

They went into the next room, the newspapermen and Signal Corps photographers continuing to document and photograph the inspection. Stacked in the second room were tall wooden crates containing art treasures pillaged from museums across Europe. Ike began flipping through some of the artworks as Patton and Bradley stared wide-eyed over his shoulder. Many of the works, by Manet, Titian, Raphael, and other masters, had been formerly housed at the Kaiser-Friedrich Museum in Berlin and other private and public art galleries throughout the continent.

"I don't know, Opie," Patton whispered to Weyland, out of hearing range of Ike. "These babies may have been painted by the grand masters, but some of them look like they're worth about $2.50 and are best suited for saloons."

"You just don't have good taste in art, George," replied the commander of the XIX Tactical Air Command, who had played a key role in the success of Third Army throughout Occupied Europe with his relentless air support. "For the simple reason that there's no gosh darn war in it."

"Tell that to William Sadler, the painter of the *Battle of Waterloo*. Now there's an artist and one hell of a painting. I've had the pleasure of seeing it in London many times. I believe it was completed in 1815."

"I didn't know that. But didn't you fight at Waterloo? I mean in another lifetime?"

"You bet I did, Opie. But that day I was on the losing side. Unfortunately, I was just a young cavalryman and didn't have you raining down death and destruction from the skies."

The two warriors and good friends—who, though from different branches, had worked so seamlessly together to defeat the Reich—chuckled and moved on to the next room. The mood swiftly turned grim again. With their footsteps echoing in the dungeon-like shaft, Ike, Patton, and the others began poking around a different sort of loot: long, neat rows of suitcases filled with false teeth, wrist watches, cigarette cases, jewelry, silverware, and other personal possessions stolen by the Nazis from the Jews and other innocents they had systematically murdered.

Frowning with disgust, Patton was deeply disturbed by the experience. He couldn't believe how much gold, silver plate, and ornament had been looted from private dwellings throughout Europe. He noticed that the precious metals had been flattened by hammer blows to save storage space before being thrown into the receptacles, apparently pending an opportunity to melt them down later into gold or silver bars. But what vexed him most was that the Nazis were so vile as to pull out the gold-filled teeth of their victims.

*I can't believe how bastardly these Krauts are,* he thought as he opened a battered suitcase and poked around inside at hundreds of blood-stained teeth with gold fillings. *Why did we let them get away with this for so goddamn long?*

Ike began to pose questions to Bernstein. The colonel informed the generals that much of the treasure had come from victims in the labor and murder camps—a visible legacy of Hitler's loathsome Final Solution. He then described how the treasure and loot had been delivered to the mine and provided an estimate as to its value based on his preliminary findings. Patton wasn't surprised to learn that there were more than 4,500 twenty-five-pound gold bars stored in the mine, worth over an estimated $57,000,000, and millions more in currency. He told them he was planning to take a full inventory of the mine and to move the treasures to Frankfurt as soon as possible, to which Eisenhower and the other generals concurred.

Returning to Room No. 8, Bernstein showed the generals the plates the Reichsbank used for the printing of German currency and the paper currency itself once again. While they were looking at bundles of paper, a German interpreter said that they were the last reserves in Germany and the three billion Reichsmarks were badly needed to pay the German Army.

"I doubt," Bradley interjected caustically, "the German Army will be meeting payrolls much longer."

Patton and Ike both nodded their heads in agreement and scowled at the German.

The photographers clicked off more photos. To document evidence of Nazi looting and atrocities, Ike wanted to make sure his blue-ribbon parade of generals, reporters, and photographers would be able to bear uncontestable witness to the despicable conduct of Hitler's "master race." With the inspection finished, they then headed back to the rickety elevator.

"If these were the old free-booting days when a soldier kept his loot, George, you'd be the richest man in the world," Bradley said to Patton as the two stepped towards the elevator.

Patton nodded with amusement. But he knew perfectly well what was going to happen to the loot. Although he would have liked to have some portion of the gold cut up and made into medals for his troops that had fought and bled to vanquish the Germans and liberate the mine from them, he knew the fate of the captured war booty. All of it would be itemized by Bernstein and his team of Army bean-counters, packed up, shipped to Frankfurt, guarded, and eventually returned to the survivors of the Holocaust—the families of the victims and the survivors from whom it had been stolen.

The group took the creaking wooden platform back to the surface. Blinking in the harsh daylight, they piled back into their jeeps and made the short drive through a series of heavily guarded roadblocks to Eddy's headquarters to have lunch.

"George, what would you do with the money if the decision was yours?" asked Eisenhower between bites at the lunch table.

Patton considered a moment. "Well, Ike, there's two schools of thought in the Third Army: Half would like to see the gold made into medallions, one for every son of a bitch in Third Army."

"And the second school of thought?"

"They want the loot hidden until Congress cracks down on peacetime military appropriations. Then Third Army could drag out the money, pay the men a decent living wage, and buy new weapons."

Ike looked at Bradley and Weyland and shook his head in amusement. "He's always got an answer!"

They all laughed.

"Now I know that neither of those options is actually viable," said Patton. "I just like to know what my troops are thinking. And it is their firm belief that Third Army should get something for their efforts. But we all know that's not going to happen."

"That is correct," said Ike with a note of finality. "That stolen loot is going to go back to its proper owners or their surviving families." He shook his head. "God, I hate the Germans."

That afternoon, the gallows humor of the morning and lunchtime was replaced with disgust and horror when the generals boarded a flock of L-5 planes and visited the second destination of Ike's blue-ribbon tour.

The Ohrdruf concentration camp, just liberated by the 4th Armored Division.

ΨΨΨ

The smell of death and decay overwhelmed Patton as they passed through the gates of the eerily quiet camp and dismounted from their jeeps. A part of him didn't even want to come to this horrible place—he knew from reports the shocking inhumanity that was about to confront him—but he realized it was something he had to do. He had to see with his own eyes what the "master race" had done and what the Third Army was fighting for.

As he and the other Allied commanders began walking through the camp, trailed by a bevy of MPs, cameramen, interpreters, and aides, he saw emerging from the wooden barracks former prisoners in striped rags. When they gazed at him and the other generals with dark, sunken eyes, he felt revulsion mingled with pity and despair.

*How the hell,* he wondered, *is such base cruelty towards other human beings even possible? This isn't fucking war, goddamnit. This is mass murder.*

The Ohrdruf camp was the first Nazi concentration camp liberated by American troops. Staring out at the grim scene, Patton was too revolted to utter a syllable. Looking at Ike and Bradley, he could see that they, too, were shocked beyond words at the mind-numbing degradation all around them.

They were led by a German guide to a gallows. Several survivors, shrunken to mere skeletons, pulled themselves up on shriveled legs and saluted the generals as they passed. Patton and the others walked on in sympathetic silence, their lips drawn taut. Old Blood and Guts frowned as he took in the execution post strung with piano wire and wide enough for three humans to be hung simultaneously. He noted that the drop board was about two feet off the ground. The height was low enough to ensure that a victim would not die from a broken neck, but would suffer a slow, terrifying strangulation that would take many agonizing minutes, forcing inmates to witness death up close.

He shook his head in horror and dismay.

The group's next stop was a large wooden whipping table on which prisoners had been strapped and beaten with thick wooden poles. The camp guide explained that the victims' feet were placed in stocks on the ground and the prisoners were pulled over the table, which was slightly hollowed, and held by two guards, while they were beaten across the back and loins. Patton noted that the stick was bigger than the handle of a pick and still had some blood on it.

Just beyond the whipping table he saw the first of many piles of semi-clothed, shriveled bodies in a ragged circle of dried blood. About forty, Patton estimated, each shot through the head at close range. The SS weren't just criminals, they were sadistic monsters. Other piles of cadavers lay just beyond. Some of the naked and emaciated bodies had been flung in shallow graves; others lay on the ground where they had fallen. Patton noticed that lice crawled over the yellow skin of their bony frames. In a nearby shed was another pile of three or four dozen naked bodies in the last stages of starvation. The bodies were sprinkled with a thin layer of quicklime to squelch the smell of rotting flesh.

He gaped out at the heinous scene, utterly speechless. But as his mind struggled to process the gothic horror all around him—a visual tableau far worse than any battle carnage he had witnessed in fighting Pancho Villa and in two world wars— he suddenly felt sick to his stomach. Without warning he bolted from the group, wheeled around the corner of a building, and vomited. Struggling to control his gag reflex, he then decided not to accompany Ike and Bradley into a large holding shed packed with dead bodies. It was all too much for him. He did, however, question two of the survivors about the shed. They informed him that more than three thousand corpses had passed through the building since the beginning of the year.

He shook his head in dismay. *More than three thousand?*

Recovering his composure, he rejoined Ike and the others when they re-emerged from the shed. He could see the pain and revulsion on Ike and Brad's faces. Eisenhower, once a fresh-faced lad from Abilene, just stood there among the dead, his words failing him. He had no stirring oratory about the justness of the Allied cause, no eloquent condemnation of the Nazi menace the Allies had been battling to vanquish. His eyes glowered and his lips were twisted into a tight scowl, while Bradley just shook his head in dismay, as if unable to fully comprehend what he was witnessing. What they were all seeing with their own eyes beggared description— and, however long the war lasted, Patton vowed he would make the Germans pay dearly for what they'd done.

Their barbarism exceeded his wildest nightmares.

They moved on to another part of the camp, where they saw a giant makeshift pyre, hastily built to destroy evidence of the atrocities. The SS guards appeared to have used the inmates to exhume the recently buried bodies and build a fire pit of railway tracks laid on a brick foundation. Corpses were piled in the pit and the guards had attempted to incinerate them to remove evidence of their crimes when Third Army had drawn near the camp. The attempt had proved a failure, however, as the pyramid of skulls, bones, and charred cadavers revealed that the victims had been badly roasted but not destroyed. The whole scene looked to Patton like some sort of gigantic, cannibalistic barbecue. In the pit, arms, legs, and portions of bodies stuck out of the green rainwater which partially filled it. It was one of the most appalling sights he had ever seen, like something out of Dante's *Inferno*.

At the end of the tour, the generals gathered at the entrance. Hardly a word had been spoken in the last two hours. The visual evidence and verbal testimony of starvation, cruelty, and bestiality were so overpowering as to leave them all a bit sick and too revolted to speak. Patton was pleased that his generals, Walker and Middleton, had decided to have as many U.S. soldiers as possible visit the camp. It was important the men see how brutal and inhumane their enemy truly was. Looking at the grim and disgusted faces of his troops that had fought so hard to free the camp, he decided then and there that he would make the local townspeople—who had undoubtedly been aware of the horrors taking place here—come to the camp and see first-hand what Nazism was all about. He would make them dig graves and bury the dead. And he would do the same at every other death camp Third Army liberated.

*I'm going to make these Nazi bastards pay,* he though bitterly. *They're all guilty—every goddamn one of them. No exceptions.*

As he and the other generals stepped towards the waiting jeeps to take them back to the airfield, Ike came up to him. The stony expressions on the faces of the two warriors as a Signals Corps photographer clicked off a photograph of them bore testament to the utter disgust and fury they both felt over the Nazi inhumanity and bestiality they had just witnessed at Ohrdruf. The two generals had seen war in all its brutal forms, but neither of them had ever seen anything like this.

"This right here, my friend, is evil incarnate," said Patton solemnly. "There's no other way to describe it."

Eisenhower put a hand on his old buddy's shoulder. "I'm going to order that every American unit not in the front lines in Germany see this place," he said. "We are told, George, that the American soldier does not know what he is fighting *for*. Now, at least, he will know what he is fighting *against*."

"You're right," said Patton. "You're always goddamn right."

And with that, they climbed back into their jeeps and drove off for the return flight to Lucky Forward. As they boarded the L-5s, Patton realized that the stench of death still clung to him like a burial shroud.

ΨΨΨ

That night, the three generals ate dinner together at Third Army headquarters, where they slowly absorbed the sights of the day with drinks and conversation. Old Blood and Guts had invited Jean Gordon and some of the other Red Cross girls to lighten the atmosphere. The trio sipped champagne confiscated from the Nazi camp commandant as they talked. Trying to keep the mood light after the shocking day, Patton and others told some jokes. But the supreme commander, still steaming from the visit to Ohrdruf, was in no mood for jesting.

"George," he growled once dinner was served, "you had no right to relieve that SHAEF censor who passed the story of the Merkers treasure trove being in Russian territory. That was a crackpot action and you'd better hope it doesn't get any more publicity than it has already gotten."

"I'm sorry, Ike, but I don't see it that way. When a SHAEF censor attached to Third Army permits a leak of a story to pass unchallenged, I have the man relieved. It's as simple as that."

"No, it's not that simple, George, and you goddamn well know it."

Unwilling to back down, Patton defended his judgment call. Defiantly stabbing his steak with a fork, he threw back his head and said, "I knew I was right on that one. I just was."

Eisenhower's face reddened. "For Christ's sake, George, until you said that, maybe you were. But if you're that positive, I *know* you're wrong."

The table snapped silent. Everyone was embarrassed, especially Jean Gordon and the Red Cross girls who seemed to have walked into a hornet's nest. Patton looked at Bradley, who he knew agreed with him in principle, but the Tent Maker's eyes were buried in his plate. He was not about to cross the supreme commander who had zealously promoted him.

Hap Gay quickly changed the subject and the group finished the meal without further disagreement. It had been a hell of a day for everyone, after witnessing the handiwork of the Nazis and their complicit enablers the German people. After dinner, the three men sat together in a sparse room on the second floor of Lucky Forward. As the rumble of army traffic came and went outside, Eisenhower led a discussion about the line where Patton and Bradley would halt their ground force for the east-west linkup with the Russians.

"First and Ninth Armies," explained Ike, "will halt at the Elbe River to await the arrival of the Red Army. The line will run on the other side of the Saale River west of Leipzig."

Patton silently noted that his troops had already reached the line. "What about Third Army?" he asked.

"Third Army will be given a new mission. It will halt its drive east and turn south, towards Bavaria and Czechoslovakia. That's my thinking, at least for now."

Patton frowned. *Are you fucking kidding me? We've got to take Berlin, by thunder! It's the goddamn key, what we've all been fighting for! We've got to stop those mongrel Russians!*

"What about Berlin?" he asked innocently.

"From a tactical point of view," replied Eisenhower, "it is highly inadvisable for the American Army to take Berlin. Personally, I hope political influence won't compel us to take the city. It has no tactical or strategic value. Furthermore, it would place upon our American forces the burden of caring for thousands and thousands of Germans, displaced persons, and Allied prisoners of war."

He shook his head emphatically, incredulous that his boss and old friend would do such a foolhardy thing. "Ike, I don't see how you figure that one," he said to him. "We had better take Berlin, and quick, and then move on to the Oder."

"Come on, George. Berlin is just a city on a map. Another Paris filled with hungry mouths to feed."

"With apologies, I think it's a hell of a lot more than that."

"Taking Berlin is going to cost plenty of American lives before we charge up those Reichstag steps. Better to let the Russians crack that tough nut."

He shook his head again. "No, Ike, we've got to take Berlin. It could be done in forty-eight hours by Ninth Army."

Eisenhower wondered aloud: "Well, who the hell would want it?"

Patton did not reply at once but, placing both hands on his friend's shoulders, he said: "I think history will answer that question for you."

Just before midnight, the group broke up for the evening. Ike and Bradley retired to a nearby house, Patton to his trailer. He suspected the supreme commander hadn't run his plan past Marshall yet, and that he and Bradley were the first senior officers to learn of what he knew would prove to be an extremely controversial decision. Like Churchill and Montgomery, he saw the lion's share of postwar Europe, to say nothing of military glory, entwined with the capture of the German capital. He didn't want to see the Red Army take both just because Ike wanted to avoid another battle. He knew that Monty—with whom he competed furiously but often agreed with on military decisions—would concur with him. It would be of little avail for the Allies to win the war strategically if they lost it politically.

As he turned in for bed, he noticed that his watch had stopped. *I must have forgotten to wind it,* he thought, flipping on his radio tuned to the BBC to obtain the correct time. As he did so, he heard the news that was shaking the world: President Franklin Delano Roosevelt had died earlier that afternoon in Warm Springs, Georgia.

He had loved and greatly admired the man.

Pulling on his boots, he marched over to his guesthouse and gave Bradley the news. Then the two gathered in Eisenhower's room and the three old soldiers grieved the loss of their commander in chief, the leader who had pulled their nation through one of its greatest moments of crisis.

"This has been one hell of a day," said Ike. "And I don't mean in a good way."

"It's a tragedy," said Patton. "I think Roosevelt's going to be sorely missed at a critical moment in American history. That's my humble opinion."

"Come on, George, you don't have a humble bone in your body," needled Ike, returning to the gallows humor of lunchtime.

They all chuckled. But after the laughter died off, they fell into a sober silence. In Patton's view, FDR had been one of a kind, a bold leader in desperate and trying times. He remembered back to how the president had stood by him after the slapping incidents. During his stopover in Sicily, Roosevelt had grabbed Patton's hand in a receiving line, deliberately held it for a long moment, and said, "General Patton, you will have an army command in the great Normandy operation." In that life-altering and world-changing moment, he had been reprieved by his commander in chief.

In a secluded corner away from the president's entourage, Patton had glanced around to be certain he was alone before bursting into sobs. For a full minute he wept, tears of relief, of regret, of gratitude, and of proud defiance running down his cheeks. Wiping his eyes, he gathered himself and strutted back to the jeep to join the president for cocktails at the officers' club. Thanks to Franklin Delano Roosevelt, his destiny had been assured. He owed his fallen leader a debt of gratitude for giving him a second chance, just as he did Ike and Marshall.

"George, am I mistaken or do you look a little teary-eyed?" asked the supreme commander, who Patton now noticed was looking at him.

Patton wiped his eyes; he hadn't meant to tear up—it had just happened. "The president was a good man," he said. "He's done right by us old war horses and I must confess I'm going to miss him terribly."

"Amen to that," said Ike, and they shared a moment of silence.

It was broken a minute later by Bradley. "I wonder what the future holds," he said. "I have to admit I don't know much about our new commander in chief—except that he's from Missouri like me."

"Harry S. Truman," sniffed Patton. "It seems very unfortunate that in order to secure political preference, people are made vice presidents who were intended neither by their party nor by the Lord to be presidents."

"Oh come on, George, give the man a chance," said Ike. "At least he's an old soldier. He served in the Great War. I believe he was an artilleryman and that he fought at the Argonne. Hell, you probably chewed him out once or twice at the battle front. You were at the Argonne, weren't you?"

"Yessir, I was. I led a troop of tanks in an attack on a German machine-gun nest and got my ass nearly shot off. They awarded me the Distinguished Service Cross, but I don't remember chewing out young Harry S. Truman."

"I do wonder, though," said Ike, "if our new commander in chief has the Machiavellian cunning needed to handle Stalin."

"Or even Churchill and de Gaulle," quipped Patton. "Compared to those three ruthless bastards, even I seem like a cuddly little Teddy bear."

"I believe Truman has chaired several Senate committees," said Bradley. "But international diplomacy is going to be quite a new experience for him."

Ike nodded. "Yes well, we'll find out soon enough what President Harry S. Truman is made of."

"Haberdasher Harry is going to want us to take Berlin, Ike, I can guarantee that."

"All right, George, you've made your point. Now if we did take Berlin, who do you think should lead the charge? Did you have anyone special in mind?"

"You know the answer to that. I've been looking forward to punching to Berlin and fighting the climactic battle of the war for three years now. If you give the job to me, I'll have those Krauts defeated in less than a week—and then I'll turn them right around, point them east, and defeat the Russians in less than a month."

Ike gave a bemused sigh. "That's what I was afraid of, and that's precisely why you're headed for Bavaria and Czechoslovakia. Where hopefully you will stay out of trouble."

"I'll do my best. But I will promise you one thing."

"What's that?"

"However much time is left in this goddamn war, I will be kicking Kraut ass with a renewed sense of purpose. After what we saw today, I'm going to make those Nazi bastards wish they had never been born."

"That's what I like to hear, George. Now let's all go to bed and hope that tomorrow is not half as miserable as today. I've never seen anything more abominable in my whole life. Goodnight, gentlemen."

# CHAPTER 55

## GUNSKIRCHEN LABOR CAMP
## NORTHERN AUSTRIA

### APRIL 17, 1945

"YOU'VE GOT TO HOLD IT until you reach the latrine, Papa. If you don't, they'll shoot you."

"But I don't think I can make it."

"You have to, damnit."

"I don't even care anymore. I just want to die."

"No, you don't because you have me, your daughter, to worry about. That's why you are going to hold it. Just a few more minutes."

"This isn't right. How did we end up in this godforsaken place?"

Angela had been wondering the same thing every hour of every day since their forced march into Gunskirchen three weeks earlier. But she already knew the answer: they had ended up at this hellhole on earth because they, like every German, hadn't done enough to stop Hitler and his Nazis from rising to power and had complacently followed him or refused to seriously challenge him once he had seized power. The German people—not Hitler and his Nazis—were ultimately to blame for all the death and inhumanity they saw all around them. The whole nation, she knew, was complicit in the atrocity. The people had actively supported Hitler or stood by and done nothing—and now here she and her father were imprisoned by their own countrymen, captives in a hell of their own making.

They had stood in line to relieve themselves for more than an hour now. The line extended all the way around one of the wooden barracks, with more than a thousand people waiting to do their daily business in the camp's one and only, 20-hole latrine. For the fifteen-thousand-plus prisoners at the labor camp, this was the only toilet, and the rule of the SS guards was to shoot on sight anyone seen relieving himself in any place but the latrine. Many of the persons in the camp had diarrhea, and there were always long lines at the latrine, making it impossible for many to reach it in time because of the hours spent waiting. Twenty to thirty prisoners were shot every day as they could not wait in line. The Germans left the bodies lying on the ground in their own filth or forced the healthier inmates to bury them.

"I can't hold it anymore, damnit," snorted her father. "I'm just going to shit on the ground."

She grabbed him. "No, Papa, they'll shoot you! Please don't—I can't lose you! All we have is each other!"

Her words seemed to bring him to his senses. When their eyes met, his lower lip trembled and he looked down at her with shame.

"You're right," he said. "We have to stay together and never give up. There is always hope. But I still don't understand how this has happened to us."

Used to order and stability, a systematic chain of command, and adhering to the rule of law, Angela realized, her father had not yet come to terms with their predicament. As a lifelong soldier, the current state of self-destruction, violence, and chaos in the Fatherland was utterly beyond his ability to comprehend.

"The Allies will be here soon to free the camp," she said to reassure him. "We just have to hold on a little while longer."

"Yes, you are right." His manner seemed emboldened now, and he appeared to be his old self again. "We just have to hold on. Our survival is our victory."

It took forty more minutes before they made it to the latrine and relieved themselves. During that time, two prisoners were shot before their eyes: one for pissing on the ground, the other for not moving quickly enough to get out of the way of one of the young SS guards. Two other emaciated souls had simply collapsed to the ground and expired. The bodies of all the victims were left where they lay. When she and her father were finished, they walked slowly and methodically a short distance to the north part of the compound near the fence line, sitting down to rest against a pile of lumber.

They stared out numbly at the muddy camp. Typhus had broken out, and hundreds of cadaverous prisoners were dying every day. Dead and half-dead bodies were sprawled and piled everywhere, along with macabre evidence of torture and butchery. The stench was indescribably repugnant. All Angela could think was that she and her father could only have been consigned to such a horrible fate by Lucifer himself. Her father had fought in two world wars and seen death up close on the battlefield in all its gruesome forms, but even he was at a loss to explain what lay around them.

It seemed beyond all human reasoning.

Thousands of starving, half crazed inmates lay dying or wandering aimlessly throughout the prison camp. Virtually all of them had been reduced to hollow-eyed skeletons and looked alike, with the only difference being in their height and the color of their hair. Since their arrival, Angela had learned that the prisoners were mainly Hungarian Jews like the prisoners she and her father had come here with. Most had been force-marched on foot from their Hungarian homeland through the Austrian Alps to Mauthausen or Gunskirchen. The prison population was also sprinkled with a small group of political prisoners like herself from Germany, Austria, Czechoslovakia, and Yugoslavia. The stories were similar only in the hardships and terror thrust upon the victims. One story she heard was about inmates being marched from camp to camp, during which time the SS took random target practice on the prisoners. Those who ran were automatically shot, which the SS seemed to think was amusing sport.

The prisoners' treatment at the hands of their brutal German masters had turned them into a primitive state due to dire hunger. Most were from the intellectual class, for the most part professional people with many distinguished doctors, university professors, lawyers, and other representatives of skilled fields. But these people who would naturally be expected to maintain their sense of values, their human qualities, longer than most, had been reduced to something less than even animals, as had she and her father. The deliberate prolonged starvation, the indiscriminate murder with little or no provocation, and the spartan living conditions had transformed even the strongest among the prisoners in the camp into the dead and almost dead.

Unfortunately, she and her father, who had already lost another ten pounds in only three weeks, would soon transform into the skeletons they saw all around them. Their food ration was only a lump of sugar every other day and one loaf of bread for every ten people per day, hardly enough for them to live on let alone escape into the surrounding countryside and walk a hundred miles to safety. They had been supplementing their meager rations with an occasional mouse they managed to trap amongst the lumber pile, but the past three days they had been too tired to even try.

They had made two escape attempts. Shortly after their arrival when they were still in reasonable shape, they had tried to escape along with several of the other new healthier inmates, but both times they had been thwarted. The first time, four Hungarian prisoners sneaking through the wire before them had been caught and she and her father, coming up behind them, had been fortunate to be able to turn back and return to the barracks before being caught. The second time they had been apprehended in the woods several miles from the camp and savagely beaten, while the three Hungarians and two other Germans with them were lined up and shot in the woods. The only reason they weren't shot was because her father had paid off the guards with the last of the Reichsmarks he had concealed in a metal container in his rectum. Without any more money for bribes and with word that the Allies were drawing nearer every day to liberate the camp, they had not tried to escape since their first two unsuccessful attempts.

In their starvation haze, Angela and her father continued to stare out at their newfound hell on earth. In a nearby copse of cedar trees a ragged group was eating the bark off the trunks. Below the trees, an area of exposed clay-rich soil was visible and people were devouring clumps of the earth while others dug roots and chewed on them. Right next to the fence line was the carcass of a horse that had been killed by an errant Allied bomb. There was a great, gaping wound in its belly and several of the inmates were down on their knees, eating off the carcass, which had been dead for several days.

Further up the fence line were large animal bones—those of a horse or cow the prisoners had found and smuggled into camp. Usually the prizes were eaten raw, the flesh torn from the bones and swallowed in great gulps, as rarely did a prisoner have the strength to curb their hunger long enough to cook what food they managed to scrounge up. Angela and her father had not yet resorted to eating dead animal carcasses, but Angela knew that day was not too far off.

At night, they had been sleeping in one of the low, single-story, frame barracks with sloppy, muddy floors. The structures were no more than crude shacks. Gunskirchen's buildings were so crowded that people slept three-deep on the floor, one on top of the other. Last night, Angela and her father both had awoken in the morning to find the prisoners beneath them dead. It wasn't the first time. Too weak to move even the pathetically light bodies of their comrades, most of the living continued sleeping on their brethren in the shack-like prison barracks. Only those that were physically able to move under their own power like Angela and her father ventured out of the buildings during the day; the others—the near-dead and those too weak to move—remained inside with the rotting corpses.

"You there!" a voice suddenly snapped.

Angela and her father looked up to see a pair of SS guards, approaching from the other side of the lumber pile. Angela's heart instantly sank: the one out front was Sergeant Gustav Klug, a rabid Nazi fanatic and hulking brute of a man in his early thirties. His wide mouth was perpetually creased into a faintly supercilious smile, his nose was flattened like a lumpy pancake, and his eyes were an icy crystalline blue, like a dimly backlit stained-glass window. To Angela, they were the eyes of a cold-blooded killer who was every bit as savage and ruthless as her nemesis back in Cologne, Commissioner Kütter. She had seen him murder nearly a dozen prisoners since their arrival, usually for nothing more than looking at him the wrong way or not moving out of the way quickly enough. It was also rumored that he had raped at least two of the young Hungarian women when they had first arrived to the camp three weeks ago.

The pimply-faced corporal with him was much younger, in his late teens, but Angela didn't know his name. She had seen him severely beating inmates but she hadn't seen him actually murder anyone. Like the other camp guards, he specifically targeted the Hungarian Jews and other East European prisoners, who were viewed as carriers of morally corruptive Judeo-Bolshevism. Though she didn't fear him as she did Klug, all of the SS guards were frightening. Any one of them could turn to swift and unspeakable violence without the slightest provocation, since they thrived on power and control and didn't view any of the prisoners as actual human beings.

"We need you for a burial detail!" snapped the SS sergeant. "Come with us at once!"

"*Ja*, just give us a moment," said Angela, and she started to help her father to his feet.

But he wouldn't budge. "No, I am not going to bury anyone," he said to her in a stubborn voice, just loud enough for the guards to hear. "I am a Wehrmacht officer not a gravedigger."

Klug looked at his partner with a look of astonishment. Then he looked back at the colonel and Angela fiercely. "What did you just say, old man?"

"I said I am a colonel in the Regular Army, a veteran of the Eastern Front and Tunisia. Neither I nor my daughter, who is a nurse auxiliary with the Wehrmacht, are going to dig graves for anyone. We are German soldiers, not gravediggers. I told your commandant that when we first arrived. There has been a mistake and we are not supposed to be here."

"Please, Papa," she pleaded with him. "Don't do this. We just need to dig *one* grave."

"No, I am not going to do the bidding of these pigs who have never even fought in a battle." He spit in the direction of the two guards, who stood there in open-mouthed shock. "You are not soldiers—you are murderers and bullies. We will dig no graves."

"Is that so?" said Klug with mocking sarcasm, and he took his *Schmeisser* submachine gun and rammed the butt end into her father's nose, drawing a cascade of blood. Then he kicked him in the stomach with his jackboot, knocking the wind out of him. Her father writhed on the muddy ground, gasping for air.

"You are no Wehrmacht colonel, you swine!" snarled Klug, standing over him, his jaw jutting out aggressively. "You are a lowly prisoner in my camp! And you will do as I say!"

"Please, let me help him up and we will dig your grave!" pleaded Angela. "He is a one-armed old man who has been wounded in battle so many times he doesn't know what he is saying! He has shrapnel in his brain and it has clouded his mind!"

Klug hesitated. The fact that she and her father were German was probably the only reason they were both still alive. But recovering his breath, her father now only seemed angered and emboldened.

"No, I will not dig!" he snorted defiantly, wiping the blood from his face with his one and only hand, his left hand. "And neither will my daughter!"

"Stop it, Papa! Stop it!" she cried, jumping in between him and Klug to prevent another blow. "He is so hungry he doesn't know what he is saying! Of course, we will dig your grave! Please, Sergeant, please! Don't hurt him! We are Germans!"

"No, you're not—not anymore! Now get on your feet!"

Her father was crimson with rage. "No, we will not dig! You pigs murdered those innocent people—you dig their fucking graves!"

"Papa, stop it!" Then to Klug in desperation. "He doesn't know what he is saying! As I said, he has shrapnel still lodged in his head! He was wounded in Tunisia, Italy, and in Cologne! Please have mercy—we are Germans!"

"Get out of my way!" growled Klug, and he and the corporal grabbed her by her arms and flung her to the side like a rag doll.

Stepping forward, Klug then pointed his *Schmeisser* directly at her father. The April air suddenly seemed to turn savagely hot as his look narrowed hard and straight as a trunk of pine.

"You're going to burn in hell for what you've done," said her father accusingly yet with a tone that was calm and measured, as if he was stating a simple fact. "Your reckoning with God is going to come on Judgment Day."

Klug gritted his teeth. The nose of the submachine gun reached out until it nearly touched her father's chest.

"No, Sergeant, no!" cried Angela, and she again dove between her father and Klug to spare her father's life. "Please, you must spare him! He is a Wehrmacht colonel who has fought bravely for the Fatherland! He is all I've got!"

He smashed her in the face with the butt of the *Schmeisser*. "Get this bitch out of my way, Corporal!"

"*Jawohl! Jawohl!*"

The young man, who looked terrified of Klug, started to forcefully pull her away.

"Please don't hurt him, please! He doesn't know what he's saying!"

But Klug wasn't listening. The remorseless killer of innocents took a step backward, gripped his *Schmeisser* tightly with both hands, and aimed the gun directly at her father's upper body. His face was contorted with werewolf-like rage and intensity; his baleful expression reminded Angela of the Führer in the newsreels of the Nuremberg rallies, spitting out his venomous words to the roaring crowds.

"I'm staring at the face of the devil!" said her father fearlessly. "You and Hitler both will burn soon in hell! When the Americans get here, you and your kind will be finished! Finished!"

"You silly old man! Our beloved Führer and the Reich will never die!"

But her father was no longer even listening; instead he was looking endearingly at her.

"I love you, *Bärchen*. Please remember that. You are everything a father could possibly hope for."

She was frantic. "No, Sergeant, please! Don't shoot him!"

But it was too late—all reason and humanity was lost. The *Schmeisser* erupted with a spray of bullets. Her father, who had straightened up and brought his left hand into a crisp salute in the final seconds, shuddered violently and then toppled to the muddy ground, his chest opened up and head literally pulped like a squashed melon before her eyes.

"No, Papa, no!"

She darted to his prostrate body, kneeled down, and took him in her arms, rocking back and forth. Tears poured from her eyes as the blood poured from what was left of her father's face and his neck and upper chest. Klug stood above her, breathing heavily and blotting out the sun with his hulking frame.

After a moment, she looked up at him. "*Warum?*"

*Why?*

To which the murderous SS guard sternly replied, "*Hier ist kein warum*"—There is no why here.

"Now bury him—or I will shoot you, too, down like a dog!"

Angela looked up at him through narrow eyes. In that moment, she vowed that one day she would kill him. If it took her the rest of her life, she would avenge her father's death and take down SS Sergeant Gustav Klug.

# CHAPTER 56

## NEUHAUS, SOUTHERN GERMANY

### APRIL 18, 1945

"WHAT'S THE FIRST THING you're gonna do when we get back home?"

McBurney pondered a moment, his spoon paused above his C-ration can of frankfurters and beans that the troops disdainfully called "fuckers and beans."

"The first thing?" he asked.

"Yeah, the very first thing," said Leonard Smith. "How about it, you gonna get some sweet-ass pussy?"

McBurney grinned. "No, that would be the second thing. The first is to have myself a real fine meal. I'm thinking a filet mignon steak cooked medium-rare with mashed potatoes and gravy, carrots, and green beans—and a whole apple pie smothered with whipped cream for dessert." He licked his lips. "Man oh man, I can practically taste it."

"That sounds mighty good. But me, I'm going to get me a woman. A real high-class woman with big brown eyes, skin the color of caramel, and an ass that makes you go weak in the knees. We're going to drink and dance at the Savoy, and then I'm gonna take her home. We're going to go at it all night long, like a pair of tomcats. Then the next morning we'll have ourselves a big old champagne breakfast. That's gonna be my first twenty-four hours home."

"What are you going to have besides champagne?"

"Eggs, bacon, and biscuits with gravy. Then we're going to finish it off with piping hot fried chicken, mac and cheese, fried okra and pickles, and a pile of greens. I guess it's gonna be more of a breakfast and lunch."

"Rich folks call that a brunch. Man that sounds good. I might just have to have that instead of my medium-rare steak."

They chuckled and continued eating their insipid C-rations, dreaming of home. They were sitting against a battered wall on the northern edge of Neuhaus an der Pegnitz, a small German village that lay fifty miles from the Czechoslovakian border and a hundred and fifty miles from Austria. As part of Patton's Third Army's southern thrust, the Black Panthers had been rolling rapidly forward day after day, firing in support of the 71st Infantry wherever resistance was encountered. Patton, believing rapidly advancing would bring the fastest end to the war, had ordered his armored divisions simply to smash forward as far and fast as possible, without concern for securing territory or protecting flanks.

The tankers had taken so many German villages—most of them containing tidy, squat stone houses with firewood stacked neatly outside—that McBurney had lost count. Sometimes, he and the other tankers didn't even know their precise location or the names of the villages through which they passed. In their wake, the armored spearheads left a kind of no-man's-land, where McBurney had learned to expect the unexpected even more than he had in France, Belgium, and during Task Force Rhine. Quiet, mild towns alternated unpredictably with scattered snipers and larger pockets of determined SS holdouts that the Panthers' tanks, often moving by ones and twos along with groups of infantry, were forced to fan out to eliminate.

McBurney's Charlie tank was most often assigned to ride beside his fellow New Yorker Leonard Smith's Cool Stud. The two buddies had become even closer friends since Willie Devore's passing, looking forward to bivouacking at night when they could kick back, rib each other, and talk about what they were going to do when the war was over. Neither of them had given serious thought as to what kind of career they were going to pursue after the fighting ended. After five solid months on the front lines, their goals were more basic: specific lists of hot foods that didn't come from C- or K-ration cans, hot showers whenever they wanted them, and the freedom simply to sit somewhere without worrying about snipers or artillery fire.

The Black Panthers gave the retreating enemy no rest, punching through whatever German units blocked their path and racking up the grueling miles, day and night, with little rest themselves. But McBurney was beginning to sense that the end was not too far off. The deeper the 761st pushed into Germany, the more rapid seemed its advance, the farther apart the remaining pockets of resistance, and the greater the number of surrendering prisoners. The soldiers they captured were nothing like the vaunted *Wehrmacht Soldaten* they had earlier faced in Lorraine and the Saar, at Tillet, and in the Rhineland. Rather, they were a testament to how far the Reich had fallen. Most were draftees and a conglomeration of Waffen SS survivors, reservists, and rear-guard types of extremely young or old men drafted to fight a delaying action. McBurney was surprised and relieved to see to his front increasingly makeshift units comprised of gray-haired old timers and boys so young that many of them didn't yet shave.

The advance into the heart of Hitler's Reich seemed to be a new sort of war. Though at this late stage of the conflict they were mostly performing "mop-up" operations against a badly weakened foe on its last legs, the days of quiet and no enemy sightings on the front lines were often punctuated by sudden bursts of violence. As they moved eastward and then southward, the enemy resistance in places stiffened and the engagements were brief but potent, with enemy soldiers vanishing into the woods and rubble as quickly as they appeared. It was clear to McBurney that he and his comrades-in-arms were still up against a fanatical enemy, especially when reconnaissance companies reported small pockets of 100 to 300 enemy entrenched and ready to attack approaching American forces five to ten times their size. He and Smitty called them "Nazi suicide missions."

For the fanatically determined Hitler and millions of his countrymen, unconditional surrender was not an option. The final chapter of the Third Reich, McBurney was beginning to realize from first-hand experience, was being written in blood as the Nazis made a last stand on the soil of their homeland. One day, his platoon was confronted with the disconcerting spectacle of a wounded SS officer slashing his own throat with a razor, gasping and choking to death yards from the Americans' Shermans rather than suffer the ignominy of surrender. Though he knew the war was close to won, McBurney was still wary of this unpredictable enemy who fought like a cornered animal. Charlie's tanks took sporadic small-arms fire from every direction, and heavier attacks often materialized from machine-gun emplacements and mortar platoons. Sometimes German soldiers simply appeared in the road as the Panthers pressed forward, surrendering to the tankers as mysteriously as they had once vanished at Tillet. Though he had witnessed enemy forces melting away during several engagements, the threat of guerilla attacks kept McBurney more on edge than the adrenaline-fueled pace of the Ardennes or Task Force Rhine.

Together with the 71st Infantry Division, the 761st smashed through Bavarian town after town as the battalion drew closer and closer to the Austrian and Czechoslovakian borders. Occasionally, McBurney caught glimpses of the man who had recruited the Black Panthers into the ETO in the first place and put his name behind the outfit. The men of the 761st waved their helmets and cheered as General George S. Patton, Jr. rode by standing up in his jeep, his big helmeted head projecting above his colored driver and machine gun, his pearl-handled pistols and stars gleaming like sunlight on water. He always had a pocketful of medals to pin on soldiers who had earned them, regardless of race. McBurney had learned that many of the other generals were following his example in distributing medals, and he was proud to fight for the Old Man, as he and his fellow tankers called Patton.

All the same, he and his buddies still smarted at being treated like dogs by some of the white units they fought beside or came across on the trail. It irked them that they were one of the best tank units in Germany in terms of enemy kills and tank preservation, but as they moved across the enemy's country Bates constantly had to "sell" their acceptance to white officers whose units weren't half as well-trained or successful. It seemed to McBurney as if they shouldered the blame when something went wrong and received little or no credit for what went right.

When they captured German towns, the white reserve units would sashay up leisurely behind them to occupy them. While they went without sleep, showers, or hot meals, most white outfits were getting their fair share of all three. And when they completed a spearheading mission that opened the door for the doughs to take a town, the newspapermen would roll in with their cameras and glide right past them to interview the white infantrymen. There were so few black faces in the newsreels back home that the average American citizen would have been hard pressed to know that there were more than a million African-American troopers willingly laying down their lives for Uncle Sam.

Despite this overt bigotry, McBurney and the other tankers still took great pride in doing something white Americans continued to claim their colored countrymen could never do. They had said black soldiers couldn't master the necessary skills to fly an airplane, drive a tank, or shoot the enemy from a half-mile off as a skilled sniper. But that's exactly what his brothers were doing by the thousands, McBurney knew, proving black soldiers were every bit as good as white troops. Hell, in his mind, they were even better since they had never even seen R and R like the white outfits. But at least they had been given the chance to fight: men like the late General Leslie McNair, Patton, and Paul Bates had seen to that.

Having had enough of their insipid C-rations, he and Smitty tossed their cans still containing a few scraps of food in a nearby trash bin. The 66th Infantry Regiment of the 71st had already cleared the houses along the outskirts of the town, and two C Company platoons had gone forward to support the 1st and 2nd Battalions while McBurney's and Smith's platoon waited in reserve. The men had climbed down from their tanks to stretch and grab some chow. Suddenly, McBurney saw a flash of movement out of the corner of his eye. When he and Smith looked up, they saw a frightened, hollow-cheeked German boy pulling out the food that they'd just tossed aside from the trash bin. It disturbed McBurney to see a child going through garbage while he and Smitty both had food, even if it did taste like crap.

"Hey there, buddy, you don't have to do that," he called out to the boy. "We got more food right here."

The scrawny child looked him through terrified animal eyes. McBurney reached down into his pack next to him, plucked up a fresh box of C-rations, and held it up for the boy to see.

"*Halt der Junge,*" he commanded the boy to stop. "Look here, we got a box for you right here."

The boy stopped backing away and he and Smith waved him over. With surprising quickness, the skinny little German, who couldn't have been more than ten or eleven, darted in, snatched the C-ration, and ran off like a frightened dog given a treat by a stern master.

"Man, that was strange," said Smitty. "These people really think we are the devil or something."

"Remember, to them we're the terrible *Schwarze Soldaten,*" said McBurney. "Just saying the name aloud sends chills down their spine."

"Who knew when we were training at Camp Hood that we'd be the bogeymen to these Krauts just because of the color of our skin?"

"The difference is over here it ain't such a bad thing to be the bogeyman. It keeps the Germans in line once they've surrendered. They know that if they misbehave, we're going to boil and eat them like cannibals."

"Shit, now you're even scaring me. Still, I can't believe they're so afraid of us."

Gradually, a small group emerged cautiously from the bomb-damaged and seemingly deserted houses around them. McBurney, Smith, Mozee Thompson, and the other tankers handed out whatever C- or K-rations they could spare. As had become customary for the Panthers in Bavaria, the German townspeople had been terrified into hiding upon their initial entry into the area, as much, it seemed, by the rumored fierceness of the *Schwarze Soldaten* as by the assault on their homeland. Over the past month, McBurney had learned that most Germans had still never even seen anyone with dark skin. In town after town, he and Smith found the same pattern: an initial fear and suspicion replaced by surprisingly genuine warmth.

For McBurney, it was odd to see up close a struggling humanity where he had expected to find only brutal, goose-stepping Nazis. It made the reasons behind the battlefield carnage he had witnessed, and the horrors he knew he would continue to experience until the war mercifully ended, an even greater and more troubling mystery. Nazi Germany was proving to be a nation of striking contrasts. A poorly supplied enemy army struggled in the shadows of warehouses stockpiled with weapons, food, and liquor. A Wehrmacht teetering on the brink of defeat, but still quite dangerous, and a nation devastated by war stood against a backdrop of stunning beauty and pristine medieval towns. Though the 761st was in enemy territory, there was incredible natural splendor all around them.

McBurney found that the fine spring weather only added to the region's scenic beauty. Above the medieval castles and villages, fluffy clouds hung suspended in beautiful skies tinctured each day in a different shade of blue. The valleys were drenched in emerald green, filled with blooming flowers, and flanked by thick woods. The lakes, rivers, and creeks were spectacular, and the men had learned to use them to supplement their meager rations. Like many hungry and enterprising GIs, they discovered that a grenade strategically plopped in a lake or stream would serve up large quantities of trout, char, whitling, pike, or perch. By this point, anything beat their staple of C- and K-rations.

All of this beauty presented a paradox for McBurney. Set against the backdrop of budding trees, verdant hillsides, singing birds, and stupendous mountains were ample signs of devastation. Though many towns had been spared from Allied bombing and ground attacks, there were still a large number that lay in blighted ruins all over the country. Thousands of homes and farmhouses were obliterated. Some towns smoldered for days after being bombed or after clashes of opposing ground forces. There were almost no stores or businesses left, nowhere for the average German to obtain food except to steal, beg, or scrounge for it.

The continued shelling and burning of enemy towns where the German troops resisted sometimes seemed overkill to McBurney, and he was often sickened by it. The thing that bothered him most was the smell. The stench of musty houses and burnt animal and human flesh not only filled the tank gunner's nostrils, it permeated his body such that the atrocious acts remained a part of him.

Death and destruction had crossed the Rhine, and the German people were now paying a heavy price for what they had allowed their maniacal Führer and his henchmen to do. Refugees clogged the roads, walking with their heads down and their faces expressionless except for pained and haunted eyes. Some pulled toy wagons or pushed wheelbarrows filled with pots and pans and clothing. There were elderly people, terrified small children, young women with shawls, mothers carrying infants. They were weary and stumbling, fleeing homes to escape invasion and further devastation. McBurney could see everywhere that the German people were suffering immensely, as he had observed with the French in Lorraine and the Belgians around Bastogne from the German Army and SS.

But as bad as it was for the German people, he knew it was far worse for the Eastern European slave laborers the 761st uncovered in virtually every town it liberated. Amid the wreckage of the small villages and larger urban centers, the German people appeared well-dressed and well-fed compared to the stringy Polish, Russian, Czech, Italian, and Hungarian forced laborers. The "slave" population, as he and his fellow tankers called it, had increased and grown more desperate as the battalion had moved east and then south. Behind the picturesque facades of the fairy-tale-like villages were the countless enslaved laborers that revealed the true nature of Hitler's Thousand-Year Reich. Ragged, hungry, and dirty, they often had neglected wounds and skin diseases. To McBurney's surprise, he often saw them scrounging up recently discarded food from the 761st's garbage cans, as he had just seen the German boy do. Bates ensured that they received food, housing, and medical attention. But in some towns, there were so many refugees, and the tankers were under strict orders to press on to their next objective, that they sometimes just handed out boxes of rations and pressed on without stopping.

"All right, let's get moving!" cried Windsor as a crackle of gunfire echoed from the south, coming from the center of the town and surrounding hills.

"Where we headed, Sarge?" asked McBurney.

"We're going to take up a new position on a bluff overlooking the town and remain in reserve. Mount up!"

The tankers chucked aside their ration boxes, climbed aboard their tanks, and the platoon started off. They took up a position on the high ground overlooking Neuhaus an der Pegnitz along with the 3rd Battalion of the 66th Infantry Regiment. McBurney watched the battle unfold from his gunner's position, eager to fire but holding back since his platoon was being held in reserve. In addition to himself and Windsor, the tank's crew still consisted of driver Mozee Thompson, bow gunner John Safford, and main gun loader Robert Thrasher.

Looking down at the town through his 3X telescopic gun sight, McBurney was surprised to see the well-concealed enemy repel the infantry platoons as they moved to take the town.

"Damn, those boys must be SS," said Windsor over the intercom, peering through his binoculars from his tank commander's position sticking out of the turret.

"I think you're right," said McBurney. "This could be a tough one."

"They should take us out of reserve and let us stick it to 'em, man," said Mozee Thompson. "We can't do anything sitting way up here."

"Don't worry," said Windsor. "They'll be calling us up soon enough. The Germans are putting up one hell of a fight."

They watched as Able Company's tanks and Pop Gates' Charlie Company platoons drove forward to support the infantrymen pinned down by machine-gun emplacements. When Gates's platoons came under heavy fire, his tanks attacked. The fighting seesawed between the 761st tankers and 66th Infantry and the Germans for more than two hours.

When it was all over, McBurney thought to himself that many nameless German towns had fallen with far less effort. The enemy seemed unusually determined today. As the engaged units assaulted Neuhaus and cleared portions of the surrounding Veldensteiner Forest, McBurney's Charlie platoon and the 3rd Battalion of the 66th were directed to attack a castle to the west of town.

It happened to be Hermann Göring's five-hundred-year-old redoubt, the platoon leader excitedly announced.

"Holy shit," exclaimed Windsor into the pork chop. "Looks like today's gonna be a little more interesting than usual."

"We talkin' about that fat Nazi son of a bitch in charge of the Luftwaffe, the second or third in line to Hitler?" asked Mozee Thompson. "That Göring?"

"That's the one."

"No shit? I say we blow that fat boy's castle to the goddamn ground!"

McBurney chuckled along with the rest of the crew: he would like to stick it to old Göring too. With the doughs taking cover behind their olive-drab tanks, they drove southward until they came to another high point overlooking Neuhaus, the Pegnitz Valley, and Burg Veldenstein, the centuries-old Bavarian fortress where the commander in chief of the Luftwaffe had grown up as a boy, pretending to be a medieval lord and master. From where McBurney's tank sat, below the bluff that jutted above the town, he could see a soaring stone tower that looked as if it might topple from its foundation. A maze of trees covered the opulent compound.

*There's definitely going to be SS defending that place,* thought McBurney, feeling excitement mingled with a trickle of apprehension.

The attack force moved forward in a coiled formation with the tanks arranged in a half-moon configuration, maintaining a distance of twenty yards between tanks and the infantry hugging close. As they approached to within two hundred yards of the massive structure, they came under furious attack.

"Stay sharp now, these Nazi boys are shooters!" cried Windsor. "Gunner and loader, ready? I want HE on those machine-gun nests!"

"Coming right up!" said McBurney as Thrasher threw a shell into the breech.

"Two hundred yards! Let 'em have it!"

McBurney slapped his foot down on the trigger. A belch of fire leapt from the Sherman's 76mm barrel. He saw a German officer in an SS uniform operating a radio and pack of black-uniformed troops blasted from their feet, while a portion of the castle wall dislodged from the battlement and toppled into the woods below.

"Now that's what I call a kill!" shouted Windsor, as all along the onrushing tank formation 75mm and 76mm cannons opened up, sending fire and smoke leaping from the muzzles. Thrasher yanked another HE shell off the wall and rammed it home. *Ready! Fire!* McBurney held an eye to his telescopic gun sight, settled the reticle, and let loose with another shot.

More dead Nazis. The tank roared in celebration.

"Billy, you are the motherfucking man!" cried Mozee Thompson from his driver's seat.

"Yeah, but I almost feel guilty. Too much like shooting fish in a barrel."

"Come on now," said Windsor. "It's a mighty fine day when you get to kill SS."

*Now that's true,* thought McBurney. But the battle didn't last long. Even with machine guns and mortars, the hundred or so SS troops protecting the fortress were no match for tanks and a swarm of angry infantrymen. With Göring on the run or at least in hiding, the Germans had little incentive to resist to the last bullet for their *Reichsmarschall,* and the Nazi criminal's lair swiftly fell into American hands.

After piecemeal fighting in the surrounding woods, McBurney and several other tankers headed back to tour the castle with some of the infantrymen. The American conquerors tromped behind the thick stone walls and through a maze of air raid tunnels, hoping to find Göring's rumored riches. But they quickly discovered the Germans had already removed the bulk of the castle's treasures. McBurney was, however, able to gaze in wonderment at a series of secret passageways, an impressive dining room, and the marbled walls of a huge master bath.

Then the order came across again, more emphatically this time: The 761st and the infantry had to take Neuhaus.

The fighting picked up. But a stalemate prevailed and carried into the evening hours. In an unusual tactical move, at 2030 hours Gates ordered Frank Cochrane's platoon to attack the town from one side and shifted Moses Dade's platoon to shell from the other. The surprise crossfire proved effective. The tankers were able to pummel the enemy with their main guns, allowing the 1st and 2nd Battalion infantrymen to move in swiftly for the kill and finish off the dazed German force.

Once Neuhaus fell, McBurney got to sleep in a hayloft for the night. It was the first time he had slept in three days.

# CHAPTER 57



AS PATTON DISEMBARKED from his spindly L-5 reconnaissance plane and hopped into a jeep for his meeting with Eisenhower and Bradley, he couldn't help but feel both cursed and blessed. Yesterday, he had experienced the triumph of promotion to full, four-star general—but a mere three days before that he had been chewed out by Ike over his failed rescue attempt at the Oflag XIII-B POW camp. On the one hand, he was a conquering hero, feared by the Germans like no other general; on the other, he was a "problem child" who had made yet another fatal error in judgment, using up another of his nine lives.

After lifting the news blackout of Task Force Baum six days earlier on April 13, he was certain the press would crucify him over the disaster. He was worried that the papers would try to make another slapping incident out of it. But with Roosevelt's death and with no shortage of bloody battles, raids, and skirmishes to be reported each day, it became clear that Hammelburg news did not rank as news at all. The ill-conceived mission—a much more serious incident than any of his previous indiscretions—lacked the high drama of his outbursts in Sicily. The story passed with no comment, and he turned a corner on April 18 when, sitting down to breakfast in Paris while visiting his recently rescued and recovering son-in-law John Waters in the hospital, he read in *Stars and Stripes* that he had been promoted to four-star general. As the congratulations poured in from all quarters and there was still no public outcry over Hammelburg, Patton knew he had dodged a bullet. "With the president's death," he joked to Hap Gay and the rest of his senior staff, "you could execute buggery in the streets and get no farther than the fourth page."

Still, deep down the incident gnawed at him. He knew he had violated his sacred bond to his troops. In attempting to emulate what McArthur had done in the Pacific, he had abused his authority by issuing reckless orders to indulge his personal goal of rescuing his son-in-law and hundreds of other men. As in the slapping incidents in Sicily, his actions were unworthy of the soldiers he was privileged to lead. Yet with victory so near, neither Ike nor Bradley issued public rebukes, though Eisenhower had given Patton an earful over the phone.

"George, you are a great fighting leader in pursuit and exploitation and your troops worship you," he said. "But you, old friend, are a goddamn problem child. You'd better clean up your act or I will have you relieved. And don't think I won't do it!"

When Mims pulled into the Eagle TAC command post, Patton jumped out of the jeep and went with his staff into Bradley's large trailer. His heart beat like a war drum. After cordially greeting Ike and Brad, he had his staff turn on the long fluorescent lamps and tack up a large map showing his recent offensive movements and the positions of his various divisions.

"George," said Eisenhower, dispensing with the small talk after lighting up another Camel, "I'm anxious for you to commence your attack in the direction of

Linz in northern Austria, and also towards Prague east of your current forces."

"That's great news," responded Patton. "My corps commanders have informed me that they are facing only slight opposition and that their armored units can penetrate fifteen to twenty miles a day."

"Now just hold on, George, because there's a catch. I can't authorize you to start just yet because Monty has gotten bogged down again up north and it might be necessary for us to send a corps up there. I don't want our forces to get overextended until his situation is cleared up. Therefore, I want you to be ready to jump off, but you are not to launch your offensive until you receive permission from Brad."

Patton looked at Bradley. "I'm ready to attack as soon as you give me the green light."

Bradley nodded and Ike gave his patented, wide-mouthed grin. Patton could tell they were both in a good mood. With the Germans on their last legs, why shouldn't they be?

"It's nice to have a commander who's always ready for a good, old-fashioned barroom brawl," Ike then said between puffs. "That's why whenever an officer or reporter asks me your present whereabouts, George, I always tell them, 'Hell, I don't know—I haven't heard from him for three hours.'"

They all laughed, Patton the loudest. In that moment, he realized that it was a hell of a lot more fun joking around with the supreme commander and being praised by him than being chewed out by him.

"Linz to the south in Northern Austria and the River Elbe in Czechoslovakia— those are your stopping points," continued Ike as he blew out a cloud of cigarette smoke. "You are not to advance so far that you meet the Soviets marching northwest from Vienna. The Elbe is going to be the stop line for all of our U.S. forces. A rough line through the center of Germany seems to be the logical way to split the remaining German divisions. With Twelfth Army making the main thrust into central and southern Germany, Czechoslovakia, and northern Austria, that will keep you and Brad center stage and relegate Monty and Devers to flank roles."

Old Blood and Guts grinned. "Monty protecting our flanks for once? By God, that's rich. What did his lordship have to say about that?"

"What do you think? He didn't like it—but, of course, I didn't give him any choice in the matter. And then I sent Brad to urge him to push faster along the northern coast and to politely ask if we could help him get a move-on."

"Oh, I'm sure he just loved that," said Patton, his grin widening. He looked at Bradley, whose face was framed by the mahogany wall paneling. He was drinking a bottle of Coca-Cola, his favorite drink. "What did the hero of El Alamein have to say when you two met?"

"To be honest, he looked defeated, almost indifferent. I assured him that Ike was not going to let his Twenty-First Army Group swoop down on Berlin and asked whether Twelfth Army could help him out—once our objectives to the south had been captured, of course. Monty told me that he lacked the strength to cover my flanks. But as I told Ike, I think we'll fare just fine with our own flank protection."

"Goddamn Brad, you sure can be one coolheaded customer. I hope I never get on your shit list."

"Okay, George, that's enough bullshit," said Ike.

"I'm just giving Brad his due credit. And my personal thanks for maintaining an equitable relationship with old Monty. Frankly, this news makes my goddamn day."

Eisenhower allowed himself a little laugh. "Don't gloat, George, it's unbecoming for a four-star general."

"Thanks for that by the way. I know it wouldn't have happened without your pushing for me."

"Yes, but you should know that I did it before Hammelburg and your mishandling of that SHAEF censor. Please tell me that unfortunate lapses such as those are behind you."

It irritated him when Ike picked on him in front of his staff or Bradley. But his skin was as hard as leather, and he was only too well aware of his own personal failings. He knew he almost always deserved the ass-chewings Divine Destiny gave him for the stupid stunts he pulled.

"I promise to stay out of trouble."

"That's music to my ears, George. Now back to the war. If Monty can't or refuses to take his final objective of cutting off Denmark and seizing the port of Lubeck—that's our northernmost meeting point with the Red Army—then we've got a problem. So that's why I need a couple more days before I can turn you loose."

As always, Patton was skeptical of Montgomery's ability to move at anything but a snail's pace. "I wouldn't count on Sir Monty if I were you," he said. "He's slow enough when his heart is in the fight. I can't imagine how slow he'll be when he's been relegated to guarding Brad's flank."

"Yes well, you let me worry about that. The war is as good as over and, as far as I'm concerned, we'll be in fine shape if it ends on SHAEF's terms."

Patton nodded. He was pleased to see the war would end with Monty rendered irrelevant by protecting Twelfth Army Group's flank. Somehow, it seemed only fair that the bombastic British field marshal should get his comeuppance for his long-term ill-treatment and disparagement of his American allies, particularly Ike and Bradley who had by necessity been forced to put up for so long with his antics.

"He's been given his marching orders and that's all that matters," said Ike flatly, stamping out his cigarette in a nearby ashtray.

"And I've got my orders, too, and I intend to follow them," said Patton.

What especially pleased him was that Ike was finally standing up to Monty. From his G-2 Oscar Koch and other sources, he was well-informed about Ike's recent victories over Monty in their acrimonious tussle over power and control over all the Allied armies. Clearly, the strong likelihood of a swift victory over the Germans had finally given Ike the opportunity to carry out the war as he saw fit rather than kow-tow to the Brits that were now only contributing a quarter of the men and matériel to the Allied war effort in Western Europe. The certainty of victory freed him from his role of protector of the alliance. From his G-2, Patton had even managed to get a copy of the supreme commander's recent, curtly worded orders to the British field marshal: "Ninth U.S. Army will revert to Bradley, who will be responsible for occupying the Ruhr and will deliver his main thrust on the axis Erfurt-Leipzig-Dresden to join up hands with the Russians. The mission of your army will be to protect Bradley's northern flank." Monty had attempted in Sicily and on other occasions to relegate American armies to the secondary role of protecting his flank, and Patton knew that Ike's final words were especially meant to rub salt in the wound.

"All right, George, now you have your marching orders just like Monty," said Ike, looking at his watch. "Just remember, we're near the end of the war now, a time when politics prevail, and you're going to have to wait for the go-ahead from Brad."

"When the time comes, you can be sure Third Army will be ready."

"Good, then we're all set. Now what's the story with General Eddy?"

"I'm afraid he's in a bad way. His blood pressure is so high, it's damn close to fatal right now. He's heading home."

"Who's standing in for him?"

"General Canine, chief of staff of XII Corps."

"Who do you think should replace Eddy long-term as the corps commander?"

"I think it should be Gaffey, Harmon, or Irwin."

"I don't think we can afford to spare Gaffey or Harmon at the moment," said Bradley.

"Then its Irwin."

Ike's brow wrinkled. "What about General Wyche?"

"You throwing his hat in the ring?" asked a smirking Patton.

"He's senior to Irwin."

"But wasn't Irwin a classmate of yours at West Point?"

"George, you're irritating me again. Can you please stop?"

*I knew it. He's bending over backwards not to promote a fellow classmate.* "Yes, I'll be a good boy," he said. "But with regard to Irwin, I must say that he has more combat experience. In fact, not only has he fought continuously here on the continent, but he also fought throughout the Tunisian campaign."

"All right, you can have Irwin." Ike took a long pull from his Camel. "I must say though, it's too bad about Eddy."

"He's a fine corps commander and I hate to see him go." He sat back in his seat with a reflective expression on his face, remembering back to Tunisia. "You know he has been with me almost since the initial *Torch* landing in Africa. Hell, he's probably commanded larger units of combat troops longer than any other general. I'm going to fly out and say goodbye to him tomorrow. Like I said, I'm going to miss that old son of a gun."

"Are you going soft on us, George?" said Bradley, good-naturedly poking fun at him. "Why for a second there, you sounded almost human."

"I am almost human, Brad. *Almost.*"

Again, they all laughed. Patton realized that after two and a half years of war he was, indeed, getting a bit soft. He had witnessed firsthand the pathos of civilians left displaced and destitute countless times now from Tunisia to Sicily, from France to Belgium, and now in Germany. The other day he had been particularly moved by three incidents: a woman crying on a hillside with all her worldly goods packed inside a baby carriage; an elderly man with three small children, wringing his hands and cursing God for his destitute condition; and a teary-eyed woman with five children holding out a tin cup for money. He had felt for them—just as he had felt for the enslaved prisoners from the labor and concentration camps.

He was so outraged and incensed after liberating Buchenwald that he had forced more than 1,500 of the leading citizens in the immediate vicinity of the death camp to march through the grounds. He wanted them to see with their own eyes the horrifying spectacle of emaciated skeletons, both dead and living, and the inhumanity they had either outright facilitated or ignored through their own passivity. He wasn't sure if the German people realized to what depths they had sunk, but he hated them for what they had done. In his estimation, it would be an unspeakable stain on their country for hundreds of years.

Lighting up another smoke, Eisenhower said, "Before you go, George, what's this I hear about a Third Army war memorial project?"

"Oh that. It was started by 80th Division. Whenever they approach an unsecured town, they have a unit fire projectiles containing a proclamation to the effect that the town must surrender. The burgermeister is instructed to appear by a certain hour with a white flag, offering his guarantee that there are no German troops inside to resist—or else. The object is to let the Krauts in every town we take have something to show to future generations by way of proof that Third Army passed their way."

"My God, you're always coming up with new stuff. Do you ever think about anything but war, George?"

"No, not really. But I do like to have fun when I fight."

Ike looked at Bradley in mock disbelief. "Fun? Is that what we've been having since Pearl Harbor?"

"I just like to lighten things up sometimes. Why just the other day, General Weyland and I were passing through a German village that had by some miracle been left unscathed. I said to Opie, 'Of course, we may have to come back here and create another Third Army memorial.' But the jocular mood quickly ended a few minutes later when we stumbled upon a German supply column that had been wiped out only minutes before. It was a smoking wreck, with bloody and still-burning soldiers and horses strewn everywhere. Opie and I just stood there for some time viewing it all in silence before I finally said, 'That is the greatest scene of carnage I have ever witnessed.' And it was. In fact, not even Falaise or Bastogne could compare. But a mere five minutes earlier we had been joking around and laughing our asses off. You never know when you're going to buy it in this mean old world."

"That's quite a story, George. I'm just glad I don't have to go up against you. I think I would prefer Genghis Kahn or Attila the Hun."

"My boys are fighters because I trained them that way. I always lecture them to be aggressive. The Germans don't expect such tactics from supposedly complacent and coddled Americans. I tell them to keep running forward and never stop firing their rifles against the enemy because nine times out of ten, the Hun will prove more scared than them. The way most new soldiers use their rifles, I tell them, they are no more use than a pecker is to the Pope."

"George!"

"I'm just telling it like it is, Ike! Oh my God, now I guess I'll have to write a letter of apology to the goddamn Vatican!"

"No, you don't have to do that," said Ike with good humor. "But you do have to stay out of trouble, especially now that your handsome mug is once again on the cover of *Time* Magazine. Can you manage to do that, at least until we win the war?"

"You have my word on it."

"To be perfectly frank, in the past sometimes your word hasn't meant all that much when it comes to trouble."

"Well, I'm trying to turn over a new leaf. Good day, gentlemen—I'm headed back to the front to tell my boys to get their asses ready for one final push."

ΨΨΨ

Early the next morning, tears came to Patton's eyes as he reread the letter he had recently received from his son George, who was set to graduate from the U.S. Military Academy next year. The young man had written him shortly after his Rhine crossing to congratulate him, and Patton had kept the letter along with his other papers on his Lucky Forward headquarters desk.

*Tonight I guess is one of the greatest moments in history and to think that you're the guy that did it. Well I can't express myself. The Rhine bridged—Hot damn! Not a casualty—I know you took a calculated risk, and won again. I'll die happy, so help me God, if I can serve under you in combat for one lonely month. I called up mother last night and she was right-square out-of-this-world with enthusiasm. Damn I don't know how you do it, I really don't. Well just stay healthy so the both of us can go to Asia. Hot damn!*

"Good letter, General?" asked Meeks, having just pulled out his battle jacket and steel helmet with the new four-stars.

Caught off guard, Patton quickly swiped away the dampness from his eyes. "It's from my son. He's going to make a hell of a general someday."

"I know you're awful proud of that boy. He'll be fighting soon, won't he?"

"He has one more year at West Point."

"I guess it will probably be over by then. The Krauts are damned near whipped and the Japs can't be too far off with old MacArthur and Nimitz pounding away at them. Have you heard anything from General Marshall about a Pacific command?"

"There's been no word yet. But I wrote McCarthy, the Secretary of the War Department General Staff, and told him if the question of somebody going to China to fight the Japanese came up, please count me in. But I don't know if the Pacific is big enough for both me and MacArthur. I think maybe Old Mac knows it and that's why he's refusing to give me a place at the dinner table."

"Well, that's his loss, General. Now let's get you ready for today."

Ten minutes later, Patton was fully dressed in his battle jacket, four-star helmet, jodhpurs, and high-topped boots thanks to the master sergeant. An hour after that, he had wolfed down a quick breakfast, conducted his morning briefing, and was flying in his L-5 Cub plane to bid goodbye to Eddy, with Codman trailing behind him in his own Cub. As a gesture of his respect for the outgoing commander of XII Corps, Patton had sent him an Army C-47 to fly him from his headquarters to Paris. The general was headed back to the U.S. for treatment of his high-blood-pressure. After thanking him for his service and seeing him off with great regret, Patton flew to see General Walker at his recently requisitioned XX Corps HQ at Schloss Weissenstein. Amidst spectacular murals, parquet floors, gigantic plaster statues of overfed Teutonic women, and luxurious drawing rooms, he and "Bulldog" went over the plan of attack for the jump-off currently set for April 23. He also presented

Walker with his three-star collar pins since he had been bumped up to brigadier at the same time Patton was promoted to full, four-star general.

From there, Patton and Codman reboarded their L-5s and took off for the headquarters of III Corps at Reidfeld. The afternoon was fine, sunny, and cloudless. Old Blood and Guts found the rural country between Nuremberg and Hersfeld some of the most beautiful he had ever flown over. When he passed over several horse farms with exercise tracks behind the stables, his mind reached back fondly to his many long horse rides with his wife Beatrice before the war. God, what a horsewoman. But the peaceful afternoon was soon broken as the pilot began his preparations to land at the III Corps Reidfeld airstrip.

From out of the sun, a fighter plane screamed over and past the Cub with a clatter of machine-gun fire. Patton was stunned as he saw a stream of green tracers blast past the right side of the plane, just barely missing the aircraft. Near the ground the fighter leveled, then zoomed up and out of sight into the sun, presumably to make another pass.

"Jesus Christ, are we under attack!" he asked the pilot.

"Yes General, and I'm taking evasive action! Hold on!"

The Cub dove for the ground and banked hard left as the radio intercom suddenly crackled with excited voices, coming from Codman's Cub. Patton kept his fingers crossed that the two American pilots knew what they were doing, since the only evasive action an unarmed Cub could take was to get down low and hedge-hop, in the hope that an enemy fighter's excess speed would cause him to overshoot. In the course of the Sicilian campaign, he remembered, one of his Cub pilots had chalked up three enemy kills by luring German fighters into narrow ravines, where each enemy pilot in his overeagerness crashed against a mountainside. But here, unfortunately, there were no ravines—just huge green fields, a few fences, and some wooded areas.

The attacking fighter swooped in again for the kill. In response, the Cub dove towards the ground again, skimming the treetops. But to Patton's mortification, the fighter shooting at them dropped in altitude at precisely the same moment and very nearly collided with them in midair. As the attacking aircraft flew past, almost clipping them, the roar of its engines was as loud as a passing train.

"Wait a second—isn't that a goddamn Spitfire?" cried Patton.

"That's what it looks like, sir!" replied the pilot.

"What the hell is that RAF bastard doing?"

"I don't know, General. But don't you worry, I'm going to get you out of this in one piece!"

"Damnit, I wish we could shoot down the son of a bitch!"

"Brace yourself! He's coming in again!"

The Spitfire screamed towards them again. But this time, Patton could see it was targeting Codman's L-5. With engines gunning, the fighter roared in for a pass on the aide's plane, but missed, and now set its sights on his Cub.

Old Blood and Guts held his breath.

*Rat-tat-tat.* Over and past, another miss, another ear-piercing zoom.

"Damn that was close!" he said with a wave of relief. "He really is trying to shoot us down! Maybe it's Monty and he's angry at me for getting all the headlines!

Why I wouldn't put it past that little limey bastard!"

"Whoever it is he has poor eyesight! He should be able to see that we have U.S. markings!"

"The son of a bitch must have us confused with a Kraut Storch!"

Feeling vulnerable, he pulled out his camera. Both Cubs were racing down low now, contouring the fences, the hollows, and the treetops.

"General, what are you doing?"

"What does it look like I'm doing? I'm going to take a picture of the son of a bitch! I want to know who's flying that RAF plane so I can lop his head off!"

"He's coming in again! Hold on tight!"

Patton pointed the camera at the Spitfire as its nose lurched forward and its propeller spun hypnotically. A terrific whining scream filled the air as shafts of green tracer and a torrent of bullets zipped across the fuselage and tail of the L-5 Cub. But this time the attacker came in so fast and the Cub was so close to the ground that the attacking pilot was unable to pull out of his dive. The Spitfire hit a knoll in the field ahead of them and ricocheted like a flat stone on the surface of a still pond.

Then the plane hit the ground again.

The earth reverberated from the explosion as the RAF fighter burst into flames and a mushroom cloud rose into the sky. Patton clicked away at his camera. *Man, what a way to go,* he thought excitedly. *In a fiery ball of flame.*

"We've got company! Eleven o'clock!" declared the pilot.

Looking up from his camera, Patton now saw four more RAF fighters circling overhead. "I see 'em—goddamn Spitfires! Have the British gone crazy?"

"I'm thinking they're not British at all, sir, but Polish volunteers flying for the RAF. I'm not sure what they're doing out of their sector, but I would wager they haven't seen a Cub before and have mistaken us for a pair of German liaison planes."

"I would wager you're right, Lieutenant." He started photographing the RAF-marked planes with his camera. But he quickly realized that he had been so nervous during the attack, he had forgotten to take off his lens cover. All of his photos would be blank and he had no images of his attacker at all.

"Boy, am I an idiot? I forgot to take the damned lens cover off. I really wanted a picture of that son of a bitch."

"Sorry, sir. But at least we made it. Look—they're flying off."

The four remaining Spitfires banked hard right and tore off to the north, as Codman's Cub swung in behind Patton's aircraft.

"I still don't get it," said Patton. "They should have recognized that we're friendly by our markings."

"I'm awfully sorry about the whole fracas, General. But at least we're going to get you and Major Codman to III Corps in one piece."

"Hell, I was in need of a little excitement. Still, I can't believe that I almost got shot down by one of our own. Now that would be a hell of a way to go."

"Maybe God is looking out for you, General."

"Someone sure as hell is—or I'd be long dead by now." He looked down at his camera with the lens cap fastened tight. "Too bad I didn't get a photo of that son of a bitch. When I pulled my camera out, I figured if I was going to die I might as well take some pictures of my impending demise. But I guess it wasn't my day to die and that's why I forgot to take the damned cap off."

The two men laughed. A minute later they landed. A pair of jeeps and an ambulance came racing over from the nearby III Corps headquarters. Climbing out of the plane, he spoke a moment with Codman, who like him was still high from the adrenaline rush of the attack, and they hitched a ride on one of the jeeps to the headquarters for the planned meeting. Along the way, Patton spied two GIs walking with a pair of women along the side of the road. He called out to them.

"Hey there fellas, don't you know there's a $65 fine for fraternizing with German women?"

The closest soldier looked at him fearfully and saluted. "Yessir, General. But these are liberated Russian women, and we're just trying to learn their language."

"Well then boys, you'd better get behind the bushes. It looks to me like they're teaching you to talk Russian with your hands."

"Roger that, sir," said the dough, giving a crisp salute. "We'll carry on in the bushes."

"Let's go," commanded Patton to the driver. To his senior aide: "My God, Codman, I truly believe I have seen it all today."

"And to think the day's only half over, sir."

"Lord help us," he said, pulling out a fresh cigar. "And Lord help me when this war is over."

"Why's that, sir? I would think you would celebrate."

"No, Codman. With nothing to do, I'm going to be a goddamn wreck and an absolute nuisance to my wife."

ΨΨΨ

The next evening, Patton sat in his Lucky Forward trailer writing a letter to Beatrice with Willie snoring on a chair.

*April 21, 1945*
*Darling Beat:*
*We go all out in the morning for a junction with the Russians near Linz. Willie ate something and got paralyzed but is now better. I would have felt terrible had he died. To him I am always right.*

*The country here is the most beautiful I have ever seen. All the trees are in bloom and there are yellow fields of mustard.*

*There is a big green house where we have our mess. All the plants were dying for water, so I personally watered them. I am not as hard as painted.*

*As usual, the day before an attack there is nothing to do.*

*I miss you.*
*—Your Loving Georgie*

# CHAPTER 58

## INN RIVER TO GUNSKIRCHEN LABOR CAMP
## NORTHERN AUSTRIA

### MAY 4, 1945

AT 0730 HOURS, Charlie Company's Shermans became the first of the 761st Tank Battalion to commence crossing the Inn River, the boundary line between Germany and Austria. McBurney, now commanding his own tank, stood halfway out of the hatch with the turret up to his ribs as he approached the wide, meandering river above Egelfing. Drawing on his fourth cigarette in an hour, the veteran tanker surveyed the bridge spanning the dam in front of him.

He could already see that Egelfing Bridge was going to be one of the diciest of the dozens of bridges the 761st had successfully negotiated from France to Belgium to Germany and now Austria. With Shermans standing 8 feet 7 inches wide, the span of the battalion's tanks' tracks appeared to be wider than the road across the dam. Not only that but there were no guardrails, and the drop into the river's turbulent, icy waters below was at least thirty feet. Would the tanks tip and tumble, as he had seen more than one unlucky M4 from other units do? But McBurney was most worried about the weight. He knew the drivers could safely cross the narrow span as long as they moved cautiously, but could an old, decaying structure hold a thirty-three-ton Sherman?

Pop Gates cleared the first company to cross. He had instructed the tank commanders and drivers to stay inside their vehicles, and the rest to walk behind and then remount once they were across. McBurney watched the first Sherman start to roll, slow and steady, across the rutted span. But after going a short distance, the TC ordered a halt and waved off the battalion in disapproval. The bridge structure was too weak for his liking. A squad of army engineers was rushed in and they quickly reinforced the dam with thick wooden planks. The tanks started rolling across again, creeping one by one and limiting any unnecessary movements.

After two tanks had made it safely across, McBurney's turn came and he started forward. With his hatch open, he could locate the trouble spots on the bridge and anticipate the M4's movements, thereby helping driver Mozee Thompson with steering, breaking, and controlling his speed during the crossing. As they began clanking across the dam, he could feel the sweat trickling down the leather side flaps of his A.G. Spalding & Bros. football-style tanker's helmet. He wondered if perhaps the enemy was concealed in the trees on the other side ready to blow the structure and break up the battalion.

*No,* he thought, *you're just letting your fear get the better of you.*

He and Thompson made it safely across. Smith's Cool Stud, now on its fourth iteration, was next in line. Though Pop Gates had ordered that only the TCs and drivers stay inside their vehicles, Smith remained in his gunner's chair during the crossing. Figuring that he had come this far in a Sherman, he was determined to go all the way to the end buttoned up inside his tank. It made McBurney smile that his friend, though more somber and guarded since the passing of their brother Willie Devore, had gotten his mojo back and was as willful and high-spirited as ever.

Despite several close calls, all of the Charlie tanks made it safely across. Once on Austrian soil, the gunners and loaders who had not defied Pop Gates's command and chosen to walk climbed back on board. McBurney and his crew performed a quick check to make sure ammunition sat ready for the .30- and .50-caliber machine guns, and also checked the rounds for the main gun. With the checks complete, the armored column started off to the southeast again.

The 761st's orders were to advance with the 71st Infantry Division towards Steyr, a small strategic city where the Enns and Steyr rivers converged. The tankers had been waiting anxiously for two days for the go-ahead to cross into Austria and continue their offensive and mop-up operations. Though the Allied soldier's motto had turned from "Win the War in '44" to "Stay Alive in '45," McBurney and his brothers-in-arms were eager to push hard and punish the Germans until the very end. If the drive east towards Berlin, Prague, and Vienna had been the sole defining mission of their lives through some of the war's most brutal moments, then here, when they could all feel that the end drew near, the Black Panthers were not about to be stopped. Like the man who had originally requested them, Patton, they intended to go east as far as they could, making sure to be at the finish line at the very end with all the white outfits of the victorious Allied army.

With his goggles on, McBurney rode head and shoulders above his open hatch, his battered and muddy olive-drab tankers jacket flapping in the wind. To the distinctive slap of metal-and-rubber tank tracks, his thirty-three-ton behemoth churned beneath him, grinding along at a steady 22 miles per hour, following the Salzburg-Vienna autobahn towards the twin Austrian objectives of Linz and Steyr. As they fanned out and pushed forward to support the advancing doughs of the 71st, he kept a sharp eye out through his field glasses. With Hitler and the Nazis calling upon every German to stand and fight until the bitter end, anything that moved in the green fields and woods was a potential sniper and every man, woman, or child who resisted was cannon fodder for their Shermans. Though every swaying tree and shifting shadow seemed to portend hostile intent, they encountered only minimal enemy resistance and swiftly silenced the German machine-gun nests and mortar outposts in their path.

As they approached the woods running between the small Austrian villages of Lambach and Wels, McBurney's Sherman and Smith's Cool Stud broke off from the main pack of Charlie Shermans and accompanied a squad of infantry. Soon the doughs encountered bursts of fire from a concealed enemy machine-gun position in a clearing up ahead. McBurney could see the green tracers zipping past like comets. As the infantry took cover and returned fire, the commander out front, a captain, darted from tree to tree back to McBurney's tank and Smith's tank, commanded by Sergeant Daniel Cardell, to give them new orders.

"Take that son of a bitch out! We'll fall in behind you!"

"Copy that, Captain! We'll clean 'em out!" replied McBurney, and Cardell echoed him from the turret of Cool Stud.

Grabbing the pork chop, he quickly gave orders to his crew: "Time to come out fighting! Advance on that bogey nest…eleven o'clock…seven hundred yards…on my order we'll hit 'em with HE!"

Engaging the gears, Mozee Thompson advanced into the field, grinding forward at a steady four miles per hour. Through his field glasses, McBurney saw a long fence and an enemy machine-gun nest beside a high gate. When they were halfway across the field and he had made out the position of the enemy nest precisely, he called out the coordinates to his gunner, Corporal John Safford, and commanded loader Robert Thrasher to ram a high-explosive shell into the breech.

"Loader, HE! Gunner, traverse a hair left…steady on…four hundred yards!"

The electric motor whined as Safford swung the turret into action. "Ready!" he cried once he had locked on.

"Fire!" cried McBurney.

Safford stepped on the foot trigger and the high-explosive blast leapt from the muzzle. Peering through his field glasses from the turret, McBurney saw an eruption of splintered wood and three dismembered bodies fly in the air.

"That's a kill! Cease fire!" confirmed McBurney into the pork chop, and the crews of both tanks cheered, their voices booming loudly over the intercom along with scratchy static.

He slid down in his commander's seat and slapped Safford on the back of his leather tanker's helmet.

"Nice shot, Corporal!" Then to Thompson: "Advance! Right through that gate!"

Climbing back up his open commander's hatch, he stood exposed from the chest up peering through his field glasses at the destroyed enemy machine-gun post and heavy iron gate next to it. But gate to what? The tanks rolled forward with the infantry right on their heels.

"Knock it down! We're going in!"

Shifting gears, Thompson ground forward and battered down the gate, the heavy iron crunching beneath the tank's treads like twigs underfoot of a giant. McBurney realized they were entering some sort of compound with a collection of barracks. He had seen POW camps before and assumed this must be another. But why were there no German soldiers anywhere to be seen besides the ones he had just taken out?

And then he saw the most bizarre and disturbing thing he had ever seen. A scraggly young girl, maybe sixteen or seventeen, was running for her life from a German SS soldier armed with a submachine gun and bleeding from the throat— and behind them, framed in the backdrop of the wooden barracks, were what looked like hundreds upon hundreds of living skeletons that could not possibly be human. The terrified girl and emaciated people were wearing tattered prison uniforms that looked like striped pajamas.

Rising from his hatch, McBurney reflexively swiveled the roof-mounted .50-caliber machine gun and trained it on the SS man chasing the girl, thinking to himself, *What in the hell is this place?*

ΨΨΨ

Looking at herself in a shard of a broken mirror, Angela just wanted to die. She looked ten years older than her actual age from a combination of malnourishment and torture. Though she was in far better shape than most of the prisoners at Gunskirchen Lager, she knew she was slowly dying and would not last much longer. She could only pray that the Americans would liberate the camp soon. From the

364

whispers of the guards that had not yet abandoned the camp, she knew they had crossed the Inn River in force and were fast approaching.

Sitting with her back against a woodpile along the fence line, she was doing her best not to move a muscle and conserve all her energy. Some 15,000 prisoners were still in the camp, but hundreds were dying by the day and most prisoners were too weak and malnourished to move. Three days earlier, when the SS troops guarding the camp heard the Americans were approaching the Inn, they had suddenly gotten busy burying the bodies of their victims—or rather, having them buried by inmates—and gave the prisoners who were still alive what they considered an extremely liberal food ration: one lump of sugar per person and one loaf of bread for every seven persons per day. But there had been no food today and, fearful of being captured, most of the guards had left the corpse-littered camp. Only a skeleton force, including her hated nemesis Sergeant Klug, remained behind.

With the stench of death overwhelming her nostrils, she stared off listlessly at the hundreds upon hundreds of dead bodies lying on the ground and half-buried in shallow graves. There had to be almost a thousand newly made graves. Most had been buried where they had fallen. Many of the mounds of dirt bore crosses made of tree branches or wooden staves despite the fact that most of the camp's prisoners were Jewish. Knowing the victims were Jews, the Christian crosses were placed by the SS as a final act of disparagement and defiance towards both the approaching American soldiers and the remaining Jewish inmates.

Looking around at the survivors clustered near the barracks, she knew that none of the inmates of Gunskirchen, including herself, would ever be the same again. The scene was like something out of hell that she knew she would never forget. The hundreds of bodies that looked like caricatures of human beings and the putrefactive combination of decomposing flesh and feces sickened her and made her want to give up all hope. That her own countrymen could be responsible for such a nightmare tore her up inside.

She felt a kind of weary anguish work its way into her soul. But more than anything else, the whole situation made her feel angry. It was both traumatic and maddening to see up close, firsthand, what the Nazis had done to those they viewed as a threat. She would never forget the tramping of the SS jackboots, the shouting and cursing and macabre laughter of the guards, the barking of the German shepherd attack dogs, the gunshots casually delivered to the back of the head as if flicking away a fly. But most of all, she would never forget what the one SS bastard she had vowed to kill had done to her father.

"What are you doing out here?" she heard a voice snap, coming from her right.

She felt her entire body shudder with fear as she looked up to see Klug. She had thought she would be left alone out here concealed behind the woodpile and wondered how he had snuck up on her without being seen.

"Nothing—I am doing nothing," she replied, hoping to avoid a confrontation.

"Pull down your pants," commanded Klug. "A week from now, I wouldn't touch you with the commandant's dick, but right now you don't look half bad."

She couldn't let this happen. Somehow, she had to buy herself time.

"I wouldn't come near me if I were you," she said. "I have typhus."

He stopped right there. Germans—and Nazis in particular—were terrified of infectious diseases, and for a moment it looked as though her ploy might work. But after closely scrutinizing her face, he shook his head coldly.

"You little cunt, you're lying to me!"

Stomping towards her, he smashed her in the arm with the butt of his *Schmeisser*. She screamed out in agony, feeling her arm go numb.

"Shut up and get those prison pants off!"

"Please, no, don't!" she cried.

"On all fours now! I'm going to take you like a dog!"

"Please, you can't do this! It's wrong!"

"Shut up and spread your legs, you little whore! I know you want it!"

"Fuck you!" Fueled now by adrenaline, she jumped to her feet. "I'll die before I let you lay a hand on me!"

For a moment he looked stunned. Then his face reddened with violent anger.

He still hadn't seen the shiv in her hand.

He closed the distance quickly and swung his *Schmeisser* like an ancient war club, apparently hoping to knock her in the head with sufficient force to compel her to submit but not so hard as to knock her unconscious.

She knew then that was his mistake.

As he predictably lunged forward to knock her in the head, he left himself vulnerable to attack. With her father the colonel urging her on in her mind, she stepped to the side and drove her shiv into his neck, pulled it out, and then slashed at his throat. Klug emitted a primal scream, dropped his submachine gun, and clutched at his wounded throat. In that same instant, Angela heard shouting German voices and the camp's machine-gun post next to the front gate exploded with gunfire. The firing was answered instantly by the *rat-tat-tat* of heavy machine-gun firing and *pop-pop-pop* of rifles coming from the woods and open fields to the north.

*The Americans are coming! The Americans are coming!* she rejoiced, feeling a sudden burst of energy.

"You little bitch! What have you done?" gasped Klug, blood dribbling down his neck from his slashed throat. "I'm going to kill you!"

Wounded but not incapacitated, he reached down to pick up his *Schmeisser*.

Thinking quickly, she leapt behind the woodpile and darted down the row between the woodpiles. A spray of bullets chased after her, splintering the freshly cut pine. But to her surprise she was not hit.

"You little cunt! You'll never get away with this!"

Angela took cover behind the second woodpile. As long as she kept the thick protective cover of the pine logs between herself and Klug, she would be safe.

But she needed the Americans to hurry.

He sprayed the timber again, the air crackling like a string of firecrackers. She kept moving further away from him, keeping her head down so that she was protected by the woodpile. The clatter of Klug's *Schmeisser* mingled with the roar of machine guns from the fighting near the front camp entrance.

And then suddenly the German machine-gun nest blew up from a big shell and she saw the dismembered bodies of SS troops flying in the air. Looking towards the clearing and woods outside the camp, she could now see two tanks blasting in from the north with swarms of infantrymen in olive-green following behind. The tanks were green with white stars on the sides, and the soldiers on foot seemed to be using the tanks for cover as they approached the camp.

"The Americans are here, you pig!" she cried to Klug. "If I haven't killed you myself, they're going to string you up when they see what you've done here! One way or another, you are a dead man!"

"Shut up, you little whore! I'm going to kill you!"

Again, he let loose with a spray of bullets. This time, she felt splinters of wood drive into her stomach from the gunfire. Letting out a yelp of pain, she ducked down lower and tried to figure out her next move. If she tried to make a dash for the barracks, she would be out in the open and he would gun her down.

"The Americans are here! The Americans are here!" she cried to the walking skeletons now shambling out of the buildings to greet their liberators, as if witnessing the coming of a messiah.

She looked back at the front gate. With the machine-gun post silenced, the two massive tanks were charging forward to bull their way right through the entrance.

*Should I stay here or make a run for it?*

"Now I've got you, you little bitch!"

She turned to see Klug. Blood dribbled down his neck from the open slice across his throat, but though badly wounded he was still strong enough to point his *Schmeisser* at her. She cursed herself for allowing herself to be distracted by the approaching American soldiers and the awakened prisoners coming out of the buildings to catch a glimpse of the newcomers.

"You're a Nazi pig and you're going to die in hell!" she spat at him. "After the Americans hang you!"

"I don't care as long as I kill you, you little bitch!"

"You murdered my father for no reason, you monster! You are everything that is wrong with Germany!"

"No, I am a pure German just like our Führer and one day we shall both return in all our glory!"

"Damn you, you can rot in hell!"

"Maybe, but you will be right there along with me for your crimes against the state. And now you must die!"

Gritting his teeth belligerently, he stepped forward and squeezed the trigger.

Angela braced herself for the impact of the bullets. But nothing happened.

Klug cursed and squeezed the trigger again—but again nothing happened.

*What? Is he out of bullets or did the gun jam?*

It didn't matter, she had to run. She dashed for the main entrance just as the two big tanks smashed through the front gate like a battering ram. Behind her, she could hear Klug cursing and stumbling after her as he struggled to get his submachine gun to fire. With her survival instincts kicking in, she jumped into another gear, her legs churning like pistons. As she drew closer to the tanks and infantrymen pouring through the opening, she saw that the men sticking out of the tanks were black soldiers. She had never seen a Negro before, though she had read about them and seen pictures of them in magazines.

*Would they help her?* she wondered. And then she thought, *That's why they're here. Why should you be afraid of them?*

She ran towards the closest tank. The Negro tanker, a solidly built young man, had climbed higher in the turret and was reaching for the trigger of a machine gun.

She began waving her arms. "Help me! Help me!" she cried in English, her second language, running straight for the tank.

She heard the *Schmeisser* explode behind her, the bullets zipping past her ears and peppering the muddy ground. Somehow, Klug had managed to unjam or reload his weapon. She chanced a glance over her shoulder.

"You little bitch!" he screamed, like a demon possessed. "I'm going to kill you if it's the last thing I do!"

She turned and ran, kicking into yet another gear and zig-zagging to avoid being hit. The *Schmeisser* burped again and this time she felt a burning sensation in her right arm.

*My God, I'm hit!*

But though she was bleeding, she quickly realized that it was just a grazing wound and ran faster. Luckily, Klug's aim seemed was off because he was badly wounded and running after her while firing instead of taking the time to stop and fire his weapon. She continued zig-zagging as more bullets whirled past and blew up clumps of mud.

"Help me! Help me!" she screamed again, waving her bloody right arm at the big black soldier standing behind the roof-mounted machine gun.

Peering down the sight of the weapon, the *Schwarze Soldaten* took aim and fired.

# CHAPTER 59

## GUNSKIRCHEN LABOR CAMP
## NORTHERN AUSTRIA

### MAY 4, 1945

MCBURNEY FIRED WITH ANGER, sweeping the .50-caliber across the upper chest and neck of the SS trooper. The German was knocked back and spasmed violently as the stream of huge bullets tore into him, instantly severing his head from his body. The headless corpse fell to the muddy ground with a sloshing thump and twitched in a final convulsive shudder.

"Come on! I got you!" McBurney then yelled to the terrified girl, waving her to the safety of his tank.

"Thank you! Thank you!" she cried in surprisingly good English as he helped her aboard his Sherman. Tears of relief and joy poured from her eyes as he hoisted her onto the turret and she literally jumped into his arms.

"*Schwarze Soldaten*—you are my savior!"

As she burrowed into him, sobbing uncontrollably and clutching him so tight it seemed she might never let go, he felt powerful emotions.

"There, there. You're gonna be all right," he said reassuringly, holding the girl close. As she sobbed into his chest, he took in the bizarre scene unfolding in front of his eyes.

Everywhere, slowly at first and then in increasing numbers, people in striped prison uniforms emerged from the buildings. Or were they people? McBurney couldn't quite believe what his eyes were seeing; it took him a moment to realize that these impossibly frail figures were actual human beings. They looked more like mummies. But that was only part of the horror. The camp reeked with death and decay and was littered with bodies: the dead, the near-dead, and those too weak to move. He stared incomprehensibly at the shallow graves and decomposing bodies and at the wave of withered humanity moving slowly towards him.

After a moment, he turned his eyes away from the horror and looked around at the faces of his fellow troopers. His crewmates were popping up cautiously from their hatches to take a look, along with Leonard Smith and the crew of Cool Stud beside him and the infantrymen coming up from behind. The tankers stared out in disbelief from their open hatches, as the doughs funnelled through the broken-down gate and gawked with the same look of shock. The gross inhumanity and stench were too much for many of them to handle, and several turned away and vomited.

Gently, the girl pulled away from his embrace and wiped the tears from her eyes. "Thank you again for saving me," she said.

"What is this place?" he asked her, staring incomprehensibly at the interior of the compound.

"Gunskirchen Lager. They call it a labor camp but it is nothing but a death camp. The SS starves us and works us to death. I am a German but there are not many Germans here. Most of the prisoners are Hungarian Jews."

"Is that smell from all the dead?

"Hundreds die every day. The SS has murdered many others. There are too many graves to dig."

*Good Lord,* he though. *I never thought I'd live to see anything like this.*

He looked over at Smitty, standing on the turret of Cool Stud. Their eyes met and they both shook their heads in dismay and shock. McBurney then looked again at the infantrymen. Several nearby doughs were bent over puking; others just stared with their mouths wide open or even covered their eyes. The filth of the compound and the sheer human suffering contained within its walls—as well as the knowledge that the suffering had been deliberately, consciously, inflicted—were horrors beyond words for the unsuspecting American troops.

The shrunken prisoners began surrounding the tanks and incoming M-8 light armored cars and jeeps now driving up from behind the spearheading column. McBurney could see that most of the troops still didn't understand what was going on or what type of camp they had stumbled upon. The prisoners were crying and holding up their arms with joy, speaking in tongues that McBurney did not understand. They touched the ground troops, hugged and kissed them. Some knelt down and held the doughs by the legs, as if to make sure they were real.

"What's your name?" he asked the girl.

"Angela. Angela Lange. And yours?"

"Sergeant William McBurney. U.S. Third Army, 761st Tank Battalion."

"General Patton's Third Army?"

"That's the one."

"Everyone in the camp has been talking about this Patton, especially the guards. The Germans are terrified of him. The prisoners know this and have been hoping for several days that he would get here soon. Is he here?"

"Not today."

"What part of America are you from? I have an uncle in Philadelphia."

"New York City. Harlem, actually." He noticed her arm was bleeding. "Hey, you're hurt. We need to dress that wound."

"*Ich habe hunger. Ich habe hunger,*" the prisoners were chanting.

"Food—do you have food?" she asked.

"Yep, I'll get you some."

"Not just for me. For everyone," she said, tipping her head to the hundreds of people now swarming around the vehicles and infantrymen.

"Of course." He called out to Thompson, Safford, and Thrasher. "Grab every ration we got and hand 'em out to these folks! Quickly man—I don't know how long we'll be here!"

"Coming right up, boss," said Thompson, and they slipped down into the tank.

Lowering himself through the commander's hatch, McBurney grabbed the tank's medical kit, climbed back up, and began dressing the girl's wound. The crowd of prisoners had already grown to hundreds of people. They pleaded pitifully in broken English for food, water, even cigarettes. Up and down the line, the crews of the tanks and infantry vehicles and the doughs were handing their C- and K-rations to the prisoners, unaware that the rations could be dangerous for people in a near-starving condition. The liberators bore solemn faces and tears in their eyes as they handed out the rations, determined to do their utmost to stop the suffering.

"Why did they put you here, Angela, if you're German?" asked McBurney as he wrapped her arm in a white bandage from his kit.

"Because I am an Edelweiss Pirate."

"Edelweiss Pirate?"

"It's the name of our group. We are just kids. We resisted Hitler and the Nazis and the Gestapo set out to destroy us."

"What did you do that made them so mad?"

"We handed out anti-war leaflets. We attacked the Hitler Youth and Party members. We listened to underground radio broadcasts. We wrote things like 'Down with Nazis' and 'Hitler is a Murderer' on walls. And we helped escaped foreign laborers, Jews, and others considered enemies of the state. The Gestapo arrested and killed most of us, or shipped us off to camps to die. Like me."

"I didn't know there was a German resistance?"

"You thought every German was a Nazi?"

"Well, to be perfectly honest, yeah."

She shook her head. "No, there have been some in addition to the Edelweiss Pirates who have resisted. But there have never been enough of us."

Finishing her dressing, he opened a K-ration box and began slowly feeding her the crackers and a can of cheese. There were now more than a thousand starving, half-crazed inmates surrounding the vehicles and lining the roads, begging for food and cigarettes. The mere sight of the American liberators brought cheers and shrieks as the troops handed out their rations. The newly freed prisoners crowded around to touch them, to kiss their arms and touch their vehicles. The inmates did it, McBurney thought, as much to show their gratitude as to make sure what was happening was real.

The people who couldn't walk crawled towards the vehicles. Those who couldn't crawl propped themselves up on an elbow, and somehow, through all their pain and suffering, revealed to McBurney through their eyes the gratitude and joy they felt at the arrival of Americans. Some of them were in such bad shape they were only able to make it a short distance from the gate before they keeled over and died. As weak as they were, the chance to be free and escape the prison was so great they couldn't resist, though it meant staggering only a few yards before death came.

"Look what Hitler has done," she said, her tone wistful and mature beyond her years. "I don't want to be German anymore."

"Where will you go?"

"I would like to go to America. I can't live in Germany anymore. I have no family here, but like I said I do have an uncle in Philadelphia."

"Who was that guard chasing you?"

"Sergeant Klug. He was a butcher and I am glad you killed him. He murdered my father."

"Here in the camp?"

"Yes. My father was a colonel in the Wehrmacht. He was arrested because of me being an Edelweiss Pirate and now he is dead."

"Why was Klug chasing after you and shooting at you?"

"Because I slit his throat when he tried to rape me."

"I'm sorry about all this. But at least you are free now."

"Free? I have no family or country. I don't see how I am free."

She began to cry.

He reached out and hugged her. "Please don't cry. Everything's gonna be okay. At least no one can hurt you anymore."

"Can't you take me with you?"

"I'd like to but I can't. We're soldiers and can't take civilians."

"I hate Germany. I am ashamed to be German and can't live here anymore."

"It's gonna be okay, Angela. I swear, everything's gonna be—"

"What the hell is going on here!" a new voice shouted. "Stop feeding those people!"

McBurney looked up to see the infantry captain and a clump of officers pushing their way through the crowd.

"You can't feed these people, goddamnit!" shouted the captain. "You're going to kill them! Now get these goddamn tanks moving!"

McBurney looked at Smith atop Cool Stud and the other tankers and infantrymen handing out their rations. Their faces evidenced surprise, too, at being admonished by officers to cease performing what they viewed as acts of mercy.

"They're starving, man!" shouted McBurney. "How were we supposed to know that we weren't supposed to feed them? No one told us!"

"Well, now you goddamn know! Medics will be here soon and they will feed these people so they don't die!" His eyes now darted between the commanders and crews of both tanks. "Now I need you two Shermans to come with me. We have orders to pull out. The surrounding area has not yet been fully secured, and I need your platoon to advance against a possible counterattack. Let's go!"

"All right, you heard him! Mount up!" cried McBurney.

With compounds like Gunskirchen likely to be discovered throughout the region and the continuing pockets of German resistance, he knew it made sense for the infantry commanders to use the tanks to clear the area.

He looked down at Angela, who was quietly sobbing again. He reached for one of the K-rations on the turret and handed it to her. "Here, you take this. You're not as far gone as the others and can handle it. Just promise me that you'll only nibble a little bit at a time."

"Thank you. I promise."

"Now I'm sorry but we gotta go. You people haven't given up and there's still fighting to be done."

"They're not *my* people. Not anymore."

"I understand. But what are you gonna do?"

"I don't know. Can't you take me with you?"

He shook his head as the Sherman's engine turned over, sputtering to life. "It's not safe. And besides, we'll be pushing east, away from your homeland and closer to the Russians."

"I told you Germany is not my homeland. Not after this."

She tipped her head towards the foul-smelling camp with its signs of mass death, torture, and inhumanity everywhere. It was a hell on earth. He nodded ruefully, feeling a wellspring of emotion. She seemed to be a strong girl. Germany would need people like her to rebuild the country when the war was over.

"You saved my life William McBurney," she said, as the tank began to slowly grind forward, nudging its way through the swarm of emaciated people. "I shall never forget you. You and your *Schwarze Soldaten* will always have a special place in my heart for what you did here today."

"I'm not going to forget you either, Angela Lange. I'll always remember my strong little German girl who fought against Hitler."

He felt tears coming to his eyes as he helped her down over the side to the grinding of the M4's gears. She was so thin she was as featherlight as a pillow.

"We are alike, you and I, William McBurney," she called up to him over the noise of the engine. "We are both Soldiers of Freedom."

"Soldiers of Freedom. I like that."

"But there is one important difference between us," she said, walking beside the tank.

"What's that?"

"While we are both Soldiers of Freedom fighting against the Nazis, you have won your war—whereas I have lost mine."

"How's that?"

"I lost my fight against the Nazis. But more importantly, I lost my entire family and my country."

"I am sorry. Godspeed, Angela."

"Godspeed, Sergeant McBurney of New York City. As I said, I will never forget you."

He bit his lip. Then, with a heavy heart, he waved goodbye and drove off to the east. Now, more than ever before, he knew what he was fighting for—and what he was fighting against.

# CHAPTER 60

## STEYR, NORTHERN AUSTRIA

### MAY 6, 1945

ON FRIDAY MAY 5, McBurney and his fellow Black Panthers received what would prove to be their final order of the war: "You will advance to the Enns River and you will wait there for the Russians," commanded Old Blood and Guts from his roving Third Army headquarters.

The 761st rolled swiftly east with the 71st Infantry Division, towards Steyr in Upper Austria at the confluence of the Enns and Steyr Rivers, reaching the town late that evening. The same day, Admiral Karl Doenitz, Hitler's successor after the Führer committed suicide on April 30, was already attempting to negotiate the terms of the German surrender. In accordance with FDR's policy of "unconditional surrender" of the Axis powers announced at the Casablanca conference with Churchill in January 1943, Eisenhower informed Doenitz that no "terms" would be acceptable to the Allies. Nazi Germany must surrender unconditionally.

The next day, May 6, with the final surrender by the Germans a mere formality, McBurney and others from Charlie Company sat atop their tanks at the bridge south of Steyr. In fulfillment of Patton's orders, they patiently waited for the vaunted Russians to arrive. But for most of the morning and afternoon, all McBurney saw were tens of thousands of worn-out and hysterical German soldiers and civilians fleeing the pursuing Red Army.

It started as a mere trickle, but then, as the artillery shells began exploding to the east, the stream of German soldiers and civilian refugees attempting to cross the river turned to a tidal wave making for the American lines. As the Soviet mortars and artillery chased after the rear of the German column along the eastern shoreline, McBurney could hear the crackle of machine guns coming from the German rearguard making a fighting retreat to the river.

As they had been instructed to do, McBurney and the other tankers directed the German soldiers back to surrender to the white troops of the 71st Division in Steyr. "*Krieg kaput—geh nach hinten,*" they instructed the fleeing Germans, half of whom were terrified-looking young boys or old men. *The war is over—go to the rear.* When they reached the west bank, the surrendering soldiers tossed their battle kits onto piles of submachine guns, rifles, pistols, and field glasses before making for the cages in long, singing columns.

He was surprised at how terrified the Germans were of the advancing Russian troops. Pop Gates and Warren Crecy had told him the reason why. In their advance across Russia in 1941, the Germans, especially the SS, had engaged in a brutal, organized campaign of rape, torture, and murder. Now many of the Russian troops were seeking retribution and responding in kind as they rolled brashly through German-held territory, mopping up the last of the Axis resistance.

As the traffic on the bridge backed up, pandemonium broke out. The German soldiers were so desperate to get across the river to the safety of the American lines that they were shoving civilians aside. Peering across the river through his field glasses, McBurney saw SS and Wehrmacht soldiers pushing men and women out of carts and boats and seizing them for themselves. Some soldiers were so frantic to cross that they were shinnying across the bridge's catwalks. Others paddled skiffs, fashioned water wings from empty fuel cans, or threw together makeshift plank rafts for baggage and bicycles. As the roar of artillery grew louder, he saw soldiers and refugees leaping in panic into the fast-moving river to swim across. Some kept getting washed back to the eastern shore, but still they would not give up.

"Man, this is turning to bedlam," said Smitty, standing next to him shaking his head. "The Russians must be real badasses for the Krauts to be this goddamn scared."

"I'm kind of afraid of them myself," admitted McBurney. "I've heard the stories of the Eastern Front."

"Yeah, me too," said Smith. "I'm just glad we didn't have to fight in the East."

"I wonder what the Russians are really like. I don't know what to expect."

"I heard newspaper reporters say they're drunks and barbarians. They say that we'll be fighting them as soon as we're finished with the Nazis. One guy told me the Allies are each going to occupy different sectors of Germany. He believes if there is a Russian occupation zone it will destroy that part of Germany. He even predicted that Germans and Americans would fight Russia together in the future."

"I'm not planning on fighting any Russians. I just want to go home."

"Me too. But before I do, I'd like to catch a glimpse of at least one Russian. I want to know what all the fuss is about."

Soon the traffic on the bridge began moving again and Germans poured across by the thousands. The troops marched in good order and were singing. McBurney didn't care much for the Nazi fight songs like *Horst Wessel*, but he did like the way the enemy troops sang *Lili Marlene*. The song about a lovesick German soldier had been adopted by both sides during the war, and as the words rose up in the fading sunlight above the muddy river, he couldn't help but smile. Though he didn't have a sweetheart back home since Sarah had left him, the song still made him long for home.

After six months of virtually constant fighting, he was dog-tired. The battalion had traveled over 450 miles in thirty-six days. Exhaustion had set in and his body ached all over. Colonel Bates had dragged him and seven hundred other men along with forty tanks all across Germany, and now all that had to happen for his war to be over was for the Russians to arrive. Once they showed, Hitler's Thousand-Year-Reich would be nothing but a bad memory and he would earn the right to go home.

From their perch on McBurney's tank overlooking the river, he and Smith continued to watch the great parade of German soldiers marching across the bridge. Slowly but inexorably, the numbers started to dwindle until no more than a hundred or so were crossing the bridge. All day long, they had come by the thousands, some in vehicles, many in horse-drawn carts, but most on foot. Though they had many badly wounded men among them and looked exhausted and bedraggled, McBurney had little sympathy for them after what he had witnessed two days earlier at Gunskirchen.

"I'm glad we wiped out that airstrip," he said to his friend Smitty. "After seeing that camp, it felt good to see those bastards burn."

He was referring to the pitched battle they had fought to capture a German-occupied airstrip shortly after liberating Gunskirchen. He and the others who had witnessed the horror of the camp had fought with increased purpose, destroying a number of hangars and blasting a number of Messerschmitts, Junkers, and Focke-Wulfs from the sky. The planes had been attempting to take off and the Panthers had hit them with a deadly stream of .50-caliber machine-gun fire. After downing a Junkers transport plane, McBurney had taken grim satisfaction in surveying the still-burning wreckage containing the bodies of dozens of German soldiers who'd attempted to escape.

"Yeah, that was like shooting fish in a barrel," agreed Smith.

"I don't think I would feel the same way if it had happened before we hit that camp though."

"I agree, my brother. Seeing that place changed everything for me about why we're fighting this here war."

"Now thankfully it's over."

"Not yet. It ain't over 'til the damn Russians get here."

Looking out across the river, McBurney wondered if the Russians would even reach them. Maybe they would turn north and head for Berlin. He had heard about the Battle of Berlin that had raged for the past two weeks in desperate house-to-house, hand-to-hand fighting. Reportedly, the final epic battle on Hitler's doorstep had cost tens of thousands of Russian and German lives and hundreds of thousands of casualties, including countless civilian losses. The demented Führer—indifferent to the fate of his own people to the bitter end—had not allowed the civilian population to evacuate even as the Soviets, on April 30, had flown the Russian flag over the German parliament at the center of the city. The rumor was that he had committed suicide in his underground bunker the day Stalin's Soviets had marched into the city.

"Wait a second. Do you hear that?"

"Hear what?" asked McBurney.

"The sound of tanks," responded Smith.

They pricked their ears to the east, towards Vienna.

"Don't tell me you don't hear that," said his buddy.

Indeed, McBurney did hear it. And now along the opposing bank, he saw—or thought he saw—a flicker of movement. Raising his field glasses, he spotted the tanks. They were Soviet T-34s and there were a half dozen of the behemoths. The mere cough of a 60-ton German Mark VI Tiger engine was enough to send American and Russian tank crew members diving for cover while praying to God, but the T-34 was every bit as lethal. With its 76.2 mm high-velocity main gun, the Soviet T-34 possessed an unprecedented combination of firepower, mobility, protection, and ruggedness that made it the equal, or at least near-equal, of the German Tiger.

In the fading sunlight, the Russian tanks rolled to a stop on the other side of the river. Crews emerged from the tanks and started walking across the bridge towards them.

"It's them, man. I almost don't believe my eyes," said McBurney, handing his field glasses to his buddy.

"Well, I'll be damned," said Smitty, peering through the binoculars. "They're coming right on over."

"You can bet they're bringing liquid refreshment."

"I think we can count on that."

Stepping down and standing at attention warily beside their American tanks, McBurney and Smith both had no idea what to expect. After all the stories they had heard, they weren't sure how the Russians would react to a face-off with the battalion's tanks and in particular with black soldiers.

As the Red Army tankers neared them, one of them began shouting enthusiastically in broken English: "America! America! We are First Ukrainian Front!"

McBurney looked at Smith and they both did a double-take. The Russian was a heavyset female tanker, and she proceeded to dash forward with surprising agility and scoop Smith into a hug so tight that McBurney was afraid she was going to crush his buddy's rib cage. After two thousand combat miles and 183 straight days on the front lines of France, Belgium, Holland, Germany, and Austria, through almost impassable weather and terrain and the deaths of Willie Devore and other close friends and comrades, William McBurney's and the 761st Tank Battalion's war had come to an end. Accompanying the woman were a dozen rosy-nosed, unshaven male tankers and infantrymen with bottles of vodka firmly grasped in their hands. It was quite plain that they were all snot-slinging drunk, and their clothing appeared to be a hodgepodge collection of anything they had managed to pick up or pilfer in their thousand-mile drive from the Soviet Union into Upper Austria.

He could see now why the Germans were so afraid of these hard-drinking and hard-fighting Slavic and Mongolian raiders. He was certain the stories he had heard about the Soviet Army in Hungary and Poland—where the Russians had committed extreme acts of violence against the local populations, sought revenge and collected booty at every turn, and raped countless women—were true.

*Jesus Christ,* he thought. *What the hell are we doing fighting with these motherfuckers as our allies?*

"I love America and General Patton!" exclaimed the buxom female tanker, her fellow tankers swiftly echoing her sentiments in their alcohol-induced jubilation. "You want see my breasts! They huge!"

With an effort, Smith pulled himself away. "No, I think we're good."

"Long live America! Land of free, home of brave. *Da?*"

"Yep, that's us," said McBurney, though he knew his country was anything but the land of the free and home of the brave when it treated a goodly portion of its citizens no better than dogs. But he wasn't about to tell a big, fat Russian tanker woman that.

Instead, he and Smitty took the bottle the Russians handed to them and made a toast to victory. But deep down, McBurney wasn't in a celebratory mood. After all, he thought, what was there to celebrate? The only clear-cut thing seemed to be that they had actually lived through it all. After Lorraine, Tillet, Task Force Rhine, Bavaria, and now Gunskirchen and Steyr in Austria, the fact that he had survived at all was almost impossible to believe.

But then he thought about what he and the other members of the 761st had accomplished. They had realized their dreams and made a genuine difference in the world. They had lost men they loved, true, but they had achieved what most had deemed impossible. While they had done more than their fair share on the front lines to help defeat Nazi Germany, they had achieved something even more important: they had proved that they were just as good as white men. They had demonstrated that they belonged with all the other units in Uncle Sam's Army because they had done what was expected of them, simply by carrying out orders, fighting, living, celebrating, crying, and being one of the guys. In McBurney's mind, that stood as the 761st's biggest triumph.

That a large number of the white infantry soldiers they had fought with had learned to treat them as they would any other combat soldier superseded what in retrospect stood as the inexorable defeat of Nazi Germany. He thought back to Reisdorf, sitting around with a group of tankers and doughs laughing at their clumsy attempts to make pancakes as some soldier outside the unit snapped photos. At some point they would go home to America as triumphant heroes—but more importantly as ordinary men like everyone else. While McBurney knew that the end of the war would bring change to the world, what was more important in his mind was for him and his brothers-in-arms, once they finally returned home, to have transformed America in a positive way.

William McBurney could not wait to get home to his railroad flat on Madison Avenue and 117th Street and say, "Dad, it sure was hell, but they let me fly. And now here I am, walking tall like a man."

Not a colored man. Just an ordinary man.

# CHAPTER 61

## LUCKY FORWARD REGENSBURG
## SOUTHERN GERMANY

### APRIL 7-9, 1945

LYING IN THE DARKNESS of his Lucky Forward trailer, Patton was fast asleep dreaming of a past battle when he heard the light ringing noise. The year was 1915. He was a twenty-year-old lieutenant under legendary General "Black Jack" Pershing, leading a cavalry charge against Pancho Villa's Mexican forces two years before the trenches, mustard gas, and primitive tanks of the first great world war and long before he had turned the Germans' own *blitzkrieg* tactics against them and crushed them in the second.

As always in his dreams, he was right there in the thick of battle: galloping down a hillside in pursuit of a band of swift-riding *Mexicanos* with rawhide quirts slapping muscled rumps, heads bobbing in the saddle, gunfire and artillery crackling, and young sunburnished warriors who were not quite yet men on both sides screaming wildly. In his mind, it was so visceral that he could practically taste the alkali dust, the sweat, the spilled blood.

With the external sound vaguely registering in his unconscious mind, he blinked away the morning fog and lifted his head off the pillow. It was then he realized what the ringing noise was: the Green Phone—the long, thin wire that connected him to Twelfth Army Group headquarters. With a heavy effort, he craned his arm to the receiver and picked it up.

"Hello?"

"It's all over, George," came a war-weary but excited voice on the other end of the line.

"Brad?"

"Yes George, it's me. Ike has just telephoned from Reims. The Germans have surrendered, effective midnight tomorrow, May 8. As of now, everyone is to stay put in line."

"It's really over?"

"Yes George, and you're supposed to be happy not sad. The surrender document has been signed and we have won a great victory."

"That's good news, Brad, and you did a hell of a job making it all happen."

"As did you, George."

It was all happening too fast. "I'm sorry, but I'm afraid I still have to get my brain wrapped around this whole thing. I always knew this day would come, but I must confess it's still something of a surprise."

"I know, it hasn't quite sunk in yet. In any case, I wanted you to be the first to know, George. That's why I called you first."

"Thanks, Brad. I appreciate that."

"I gotta call the other commanders. Bye, George. I'll be in touch soon with more details on the occupation plan. But for now, sit tight."

As he hung up, Patton gave a heavy sigh. *So that's it, my war is over.* Unless he could somehow get his coveted battle command in the Pacific. But unfortunately, that was looking unlikely. For the past month, he had lobbied Secretary of War Stimson and Marshall for an assignment in China or one of the frontline islands when the war in Europe ended. But the War Department wasn't interested. He was told that his bypass and flank methods were well suited to fighting Germans, but not the Japanese. The tactics wouldn't work on the small islands of the Pacific, where the defenders' positions had to be rooted out with grenade, flamethrower, and shell and could not be bypassed. That was the reason they gave him. But Patton knew the real reason: Marshall would never send him where there was already a prima donna in command. The Pacific was MacArthur's show, and the Napoleon of Luzon and American Caesar didn't want another big hitter in his ballpark any more than Monty wanted one in his.

*Damnit, can this really be the end? Is this all there is or will ever be? Will I truly never taste battle again?*

The next morning, May 8, he assembled Hap Gay and the rest of his staff in the former German barracks for the regular Third Army 0900 morning briefing. At one minute before the appointed hour, a dour-faced Old Blood and Guts strode into the room in full battle regalia, trailed by Willie, Codman, and the recently rescued Al Stiller. He walked briskly to his seat and sat down. Struggling to keep his emotions in check, he listened as his G-2 Oscar Koch and his G-3, Air, and PRO officers presented a picture of the final disposition of Third Army's forces, as well as those of their Russian Allies in Southern Germany, Czechoslovakia, and Austria. Ordinarily, when the morning briefing was finished, General Gay would rise from his seat to make the announcements for the day and adjourn the meeting, but today Patton decided that he would address his team instead.

He felt an instant lump in his throat as he rose from his seat and took three steps to the situation map. Studying it for a long moment, he turned and faced the staff that he had lived, fought, ate, celebrated, laughed, and cried with for two and a half years of the most shockingly violent war that history had ever known. Not wanting to tear up, he let the silence draw out for several seconds before getting to the point.

"It is with regret that I officially announce that this is the last of our operational briefings in Europe. I trust we shall have the privilege of renewing them in another and more distant theater of war," he began, making sure that his staff knew there was at least a possibility they would move on to the Pacific Theater of Operations. "In other words, gentlemen, I hope that we shall have other similar briefings in China, but of course, that is out of my hands to control. One thing I can promise you: if I go, you go. That is my word—and despite all the occasions I have soiled the Patton family name by screwing up—you know my word is good."

Light chuckles navigated through the briefing room. He paused a moment, allowing the words to resonate and laughter to subside.

"You men and the troops that have served under me in Third Army are the greatest thing that has ever happened to me. That is not sanctimonious bullshit. During the entire period since we have served in North Africa together until last night at midnight, we have been practically in continuous battle. There is going to be a tremendous letdown unless we watch ourselves. And you know, being the bloodthirsty son of a bitch I am, I will be the one most let down when there is no fighting. You all know that."

There was a murmur of sympathetic agreement and head nods up and down the staff officers. Looking out at them, he felt a powerful bond of affection and sense of mutual purpose in the winning of the war and defeat of such a loathsome empire as the Nazis.

"Not since Napoleon in 1806 has an army conquered Germany or crossed any large portion of it. Hap Gay and I questioned if anyone, even as late as the beginning of this war or late last year, felt the war would end with American forces having completely overrun Germany and occupying other countries. Quite frankly, I would never have thought such a thing was possible. But our success and triumph has had little to do with me. I thank you officers—who have served with me in Tunisia, Sicily, France, Belgium, Austria, Czechoslovakia, and Germany—for your outstanding performance since we first set foot on North African shores during *Operation Torch* in November of '42."

The crowd remained silent, soberly taking in his words, which pleased him. The knot in his throat tightened. He could see that many of them were deeply moved, as many were nodding and several had tears in their eyes.

"I thank each and every one of you for what you have done, and I assure you that no one man can conduct an army. The success of Third Army has been the results of the harmonious work of its staff and the magnificent fighting ability of the combat officers and enlisted men. Without this teamwork, we would never have been successful. Today, the eighth of May, precisely marks the two and a half years since we landed in North Africa. As I said before, during all that time until midnight tonight, we have been in practically continuous battle. But more importantly, when not in battle, we have been under the strain of continuous criticism, which I believe is harder to bear. I know, I know, most of that is on me. But seriously, probably no military commander in history ever did less work than I because of all the fine work you all did. You are the greatest—and I goddamn mean it. That's all I have to say."

As Gay, Codman, Koch, and the rest of his staff members sprang to their feet, he snapped his fingers and Willie uncurled himself from the chair under which he was gently snoring.

"Let's go, boy," he said to the stocky little English bull terrier. Then, with Willie trotting behind him, he marched to the door, down the steps, and over to his trailer, riding crop in hand and holding his head high. Here he finally let go with his pent-up tears as he finished the General Order he was preparing for his troops and that would be released tomorrow. He wanted to personally thank each and every enlisted man and officer of the six corps and thirty-nine divisions which, since August 1944, had comprised Third Army.

*SOLDIERS OF THE THIRD ARMY, PAST AND PRESENT:*
*During the 281 days of incessant and victorious combat, your penetrations have advanced farther in less time than any other army in history. You have fought your way across 24 major rivers and innumerable lesser streams. You have liberated or conquered more than 82,000 square miles of territory, including 1,500 cities and towns, and some 12,000 inhabited places. Prior to the termination of active hostilities, you had captured in battle 956,000 enemy soldiers and killed or wounded at least 500,000 others. France, Belgium, Luxembourg, Germany, Austria, and Czechoslovakia bear witness to your exploits.*

*All men and women of the six corps and thirty-nine divisions that have at different times been members of this Army have done their duty. Each deserves credit. The enduring valor of the combat troops has been paralleled and made possible by the often unpublicized activities of the supply, administrative, and medical services of this Army and of the Communications Zone troops supporting it. Nor should we forget our comrades of the other armies and of the Air Force, particularly of the XIX Tactical Air Command, by whose side or under whose wings we have had the honor to fight.*

*In proudly contemplating our achievements, let us never forget our heroic dead whose graves mark the course of our victorious advances, nor our wounded whose sacrifices added so much to our success.*

*I should be both ungrateful and wanting in candor if I failed to acknowledge the debt we owe to our Chiefs of Staff, Generals Gaffey and Gay, and to the officers and men of the General and Special Staff Sections of Army Headquarters. Without their loyalty, intelligence, and unremitting labors, success would have been impossible.*

*The termination of fighting in Europe does not remove the opportunities for other outstanding and equally difficult achievements in the days which are to come. In some ways the immediate future will demand of you more fortitude than has the past because, without the inspiration of combat, you must maintain—by your dress, deportment, and efficiency—not only the prestige of the Third Army but also the honor of the United States. I have complete confidence that you will not fail.*

*During the course of this war I have received promotions and decorations far above and beyond my individual merit. You won them; I as your representative wear them. The one honor which is mine and mine alone is that of having commanded such an incomparable group of Americans, the record of whose fortitude, audacity, and valor will endure as long as history lasts.*

*May 9, 1945*
*G.S. PATTON, JR.*
*GENERAL*
*GERMANY*

ѰѰѰ

When he was finished writing out his General Order, he took Willie for a walk to the old Stone Bridge spanning the muddy brown waters of the Danube. Built in the 12th-century, the *Steinerne Brücke* was a masterpiece of medieval engineering with sixteen resplendent arches. As he and Willie padded down the stone walkway, passing gawking German civilians and U.S. military traffic, Patton recalled that Louis VII of France and his army had used the bridge to cross the Danube on their way to the Second Crusade.

Reaching the center of the bridge, he turned and looked in both directions across the mighty river. He had a good view of the original Roman fort that was later turned into the German medieval city of Regensburg. He still found it surprising that the town appeared to have suffered virtually no damage from Allied bombers.

As he gazed in the direction of the Roman ruins and the twin spires of Regensburg Cathedral soaring above the muddy brown river, he felt the powerful sweep of history. But more than that, he felt the warrior spirit of the ancients and knew he had fought here before.

It was in 179 A.D. that Marcus Aurelius had built the Roman rectangular fortified town of *Castra Regina*—Fortress by the River Regen—for the Legio III Italica, and the town quickly became an important location at the most northerly part of the Danube. Yesterday, Patton had toured what remained of the Roman walls and buildings of the fortified town that now made up the Old City or *Altstadt*, where he had smelled and tasted the sweat and blood of the legions as palpably as if it had happened yesterday. But in this sacred warrior's place, he could also feel the presence of his hero Napoleon. The French commander had fought the Battle of Ratisbon or Regensburg in 1809, pushing Archduke Charles and his Austrians out of their last foothold on the southern bank of the Danube. Napoleon had turned a potential disaster into a stunning victory that had turned out to be the final major battle in the initial Bavarian phase of the Franco-Austrian War, opening the road into Austria.

Closing his eyes, Patton felt his historic battles with the ancients sweeping through him like fine Burgundy. As he did so, he remembered back to the poem *Incident of the French Camp* by Robert Browning. He recited the words of the poem from long memory:

*You know, we French stormed Ratisbon:*
*A mile or so away,*
*On a little mound, Napoleon*
*Stood on our storming-day;*
*With neck out-thrust, you fancy how,*
*Legs wide, arms locked behind,*
*As if to balance the prone brow*
*Oppressive with its mind.*

*The chief's eye flashed; but presently*
*Softened itself, as sheathes*
*A film the mother-eagle's eye*
*When her bruised eaglet breathes;*
*"You're wounded!" "Nay," the soldier's pride*
*Touched to the quick, he said:*
*"I'm killed, Sire!" And his chief beside*
*Smiling the boy fell dead.*

Opening his eyes, he wondered if it would not be best if he had died in battle in this war—the bloodiest in American history—just like the young soldier in the poem. What was the point of living if he couldn't fight?

It was hard to believe that what was once unthinkable was now a harsh reality: he had reached the end of his life as a warrior and would likely never taste battle again. His place in history was secure, but suddenly that didn't mean as much to him as he had thought it would. Civil life was no doubt going to be mighty dull. He loved his wife dearly but she would never be able to understand how much waging warfare meant to him; and more than likely, once she had him alone back in the States she would no doubt give him hell over Jean Gordon.

*Goddamnit, everything is going to be different now. Everything!*

The titanic stakes, the commanding of hundreds of thousands of men in intense combat, the fierce competition to outrace the other armies, the adrenaline rush of it all—it made him sad to think he would not feel any of it ever again. He was like a championship heavyweight prizefighter that had fought his last bout. There would be no cheering crowds, no flowers, no private airplanes, no triumphant military processions or reviews as he followed in the footsteps of Caesar and Napoleon. A part of him was convinced it would have been better for him to have taken the last bullet of the war than to have to live on now in the messy, bureaucratic peace. For him, war wasn't about dying—it was about goddamn living!

*Keeraw! Keeraw!*

He looked up into the sky and saw the source of the high-pitched shriek: a golden German eagle. He was reminded of the Nazi emblem of the Third Reich—the *Parteiadler*, an eagle violently clutching a swastika in its claws—and somehow, it seemed only fitting that the great bird of prey he saw circling overhead looked nothing like the violent Nazi emblem. The creature he stared up at was a thing of beauty not a monstrosity, and he couldn't help but think that perhaps Germany might one day become free and democratic nation and purge its ugly, violent past. But first, the country of the "master race" had a heavy debt to pay to the world for its warmongering and unspeakable inhumanity.

In his eyes, every German citizen except children and those brave souls who had actively resisted Hitler was guilty for the rise of Nazism and the atrocity of the death camps it spawned. From BBC broadcasts, Allied and German resistance leaflets, and word-of-mouth, virtually every German had known about the horrors taking place in the Fatherland and the surrounding occupied territories, Patton knew. And yet, like sheep, the vast majority of German people had done nothing to stop any of it. How could they have allowed such inhumanity to happen without lifting a finger? To Patton—the liberator of the Mauthausen–Gusen, Buchenwald, and Ohrdruf concentration camps, who had forced German citizens living nearby to walk through and clean up the camps—it seemed as though they had been in a trance. He was at a loss to explain how a supposedly civilized people could allow such a thing to happen.

He watched as the great feathered eagle glided above the spires of the huge Gothic cathedral. It soared majestically for a time then flapped its enormous wings and shot upwards as it was jostled by a pocket of wind. It nosedived again, following along the edge of the Danube, its wings fully extended, the sunlight shimmering off its plumage as it glided gracefully across the periwinkle sky and backdrop of the twin spires.

Staring up at the magnificent creature, watching it soar with unfettered freedom, he felt the stirring voice of freedom inside along with the voices of the ancients. He and his Third Army had done well. Along with the other Allied forces, they had liberated Europe and made the world a safer and better place. Yes, it was going to take a decade or more to build the entire continent back up again, and the ascendance of the Russians would eventually pose a festering problem, but he could take great pride in what he and his beloved troops had done. They had come through for the world, come through on behalf of humanity and civilization, in its time of infinite crisis. Somehow, the eagle soaring overhead reminded him of all he and his men had accomplished in the name of freedom.

Feeling better now, he kneeled down and stroked Willie on the chest. The bull terrier snorted with delight, which made him feel happy.

"I love you, you little bastard," he said. "You know that, don't you?"

The dog nuzzled up to him and he let Willie lick his face. He then rose to his feet, took the dog by the leash, and started walking along the stone path of the bridge.

"Willie, I want you to know that throughout the campaign in Europe, I know of no error I made except that of failing to send a Combat Command to take Hammelburg. Otherwise, my operations were, to me, strictly satisfactory. In every case, practically throughout the campaign, I was under wraps from the High Command. This may have been a good thing, as perhaps I am too impetuous. However, I do not believe I was and feel that had I been permitted to go all out, the war would have ended sooner and more lives would have been saved. What do you think of that?"

The little English bull terrier gave a little grunt and looked at him with his head askew as they came to a halt on the bridge.

"Okay, I guess that's enough history for one day. Especially since you're a dog and probably only as smart as the average Russian. So here endeth the Lesson. Except I do have to say one more thing. I love war because I love the responsibility and excitement, not because I like killing other human beings. Peace is going to be hell on me—and probably on you too since you won't be able to fly in airplanes anymore. You do understand that, don't you Willie?"

The dog just looked at him with puzzlement.

"Goddamn, I'm going to miss it all—I'm going to miss it so," he said, again feeling the power of the legions and Napoleon's *Grande Armée* as he gazed in the direction of the Roman ruins and the twin spires of Regensburg Cathedral stretching towards the heavens.

And with that, General George S. Patton, Jr.—Old Blood and Guts—escorted by his nearly constant companion of the past year, a little dog named after William the Conqueror, returned to the barracks to hold his farewell conference with the Third Army press corps.

# CHAPTER 62

## HARLEM MEER, NORTHEAST CENTRAL PARK
## HARLEM, NEW YORK, U.S.A.

### MAY 21, 1946

"HAPPY TWENTY-SECOND BIRTHDAY, BILLY."

"Thanks, man," said William McBurney to his buddy Leonard Smith.

"Because of me you're going to probably live to a ripe old age."

"Probably?"

"Definitely."

"You saved my bacon all right. I owe you."

"You're damn right you do."

"Well, here's to us. Tankers and friends for all eternity."

"Amen to that, brother."

The two veteran main gunners clinked their Schaefer beer cans wrapped in brown paper bags, leaned back on their park bench, took long pulls of lager, and stared out at the gently rippled surface of the lake. It was a truly idyllic setting. Known as the Harlem Meer, the large man-made pond conceived by Frederick Law Olmsted and Calvert Vaux, the designers of Central Park, was first constructed in the late 1800s and later improved upon in the 1930s. The late May sun shone down resplendently upon the wooden boathouse with the American flag and the rowboats gliding across the lake. From the granite-lined banks, shrieks of delight came from packs of colored and Italian kids wading into the water and playing with little toy boats. Above the majestic oak, black locust, beech, bald cypress, and ginkgo trees and the green, manicured lawns surrounding the water body soared kites, balloons, and a squadron of red-tailed hawks.

"Man, it is one beautiful day," said McBurney, soaking it all in with a mellow buzz coming on. "So peaceful."

"It sure is," agreed Smitty. "A lot quieter than over there, huh?"

"You can say that again."

Smith had returned to the U.S. just before Christmas, McBurney a few weeks later, after they both had performed several months of occupation duty in Teisendorf, Germany. As two of the 761st's battalion's earliest members, the two New Yorkers had been some of the first in the unit scheduled to depart England for the return journey to Camp Kilmer, New Jersey, in time to surprise their families and friends just before Christmas. But McBurney's return had been unexpectedly delayed when he had been forced to spend his Christmas at an Army hospital in Europe. After the deprivations of wartime, he had eaten one too many donuts fresh out of the hot oil of a Salvation Army mess truck, giving him an upset stomach for the ages. Smith and Preston McNeil had ribbed him endlessly about his overindulgence upon his return to the U.S. on a Liberty ship.

Like the other black members of the 761st and the more than 1.2 million other African-American veterans of the war, the two young men had returned home without ticker-tape parades or fanfare to resume their daily lives in a country that cared little about their contributions and sacrifices overseas. The painful truth was they had not changed a nation. In fact, they found themselves in many ways more at the beginning of a struggle than at the end as returning Negro soldiers. Having served their country with distinction during the largest and most violent conflagration in human history, they returned to second-class status and with expectations that were deemed unacceptable to those of many of their white compatriots. But McBurney knew it was even worse for his repatriated veteran buddies in the South. They still could not vote, use public facilities, sit beside whites in buses or at lunch counters, or find work at anything but the most menial of jobs.

For the returning members of the 761st, it was apparent that America had never really cared for them and now had mostly forgotten them. McBurney was surprised that most people did not even know of African-American service on the battlefields of Europe. In the roar of postwar America, the battalion's service might as well not have happened, so few people knew or even cared. What Willie Devore, Ruben Rivers, Samuel Turley, and dozens of others had given and what they themselves had endured for their country was not acknowledged or even believed.

But even more upsetting to McBurney was that white America expected life in the U.S.—with its racial castes and customs—to go on as if the war had never happened. The majority of whites were still unwilling to look at them in the new light that black leaders had originally sought by insisting that colored men receive the right to fight. He and Smith did not have to deal with the lynchings and beatings their Southern tanker cohorts had to in the Deep South, but they had already experienced employment discrimination despite their veteran status. They couldn't help but feel excluded from the postwar economic prosperity they could see all around them.

"Did you ever talk to Willie's parents and tell them what happened?" asked McBurney.

"Yeah, I called them," said Smith, his voice low and solemn. "But I couldn't bring myself to tell them how he died."

McBurney nodded. He had figured as much. He knew how painful it must have been to even talk to them, let alone to tell the bereaved parents the details of their son's grisly death. The top of Willie's head had been blown off, and McBurney still didn't know why he had frozen up that day in Tillet. The most likely explanation that he could come up with was that, when they had struck the concealed German land mine, he had lost his hearing, sense of balance, and direction from the concussion directly beneath his tank driver's seat.

McBurney decided to change the subject. "You found work yet?"

"Yeah, I got a job cleaning up subway cars," replied Smith.

"Subway cars? How'd you get that job?"

"Well, tank gunners aren't exactly in high demand. I got no skills other than those I learned in the 761st."

"Hey, you got a job. Good on you, man."

"The truth is, when I first got home I was at a loss as to what to do with my life. I talked to this old fellow from the neighborhood and he suggested I go into the civil service. I took his advice and applied for the job."

"You got to start somewhere. I'm sure you'll work your way up."

"What about you?"

"I'm starting mechanical drafting school. I still got my day job and soon will be starting classes at night."

"Good on you, too, man."

They clinked beer cans again, downing the ice-cold lager.

"Pop Gates taught me a lot," said Smith. "I miss that old Buffalo Soldier."

"I miss them all—every last one of 'em," confessed McBurney. Then his voice turned introspective. "You know we're never gonna feel what we felt over there."

"I know."

"And we're never gonna see *anything* like what we saw over there."

"I know that too."

"As long as I live, I'll never forget Tillet—and you saving my ass. The Battle of the Bulge—January 9, 1944—that was one hell of a goddamn day."

"It sure was," said Smith. "We did what Colonel Bates trained us to do. We owe a lot to the old man."

"He always believed in us. Always."

Feeling a deep upwelling of emotion, McBurney snapped silent, his mind reaching back to the Bulge. He remembered the deep snow and ear-splitting clatter of the enemy machine-guns; the thunderous roar of the "Ripsaw" 88s; and the moment when, frigid cold and in a state of shock, he gave up all hope only to be coaxed onward through the heavy snow back to camp by his buddy Smitty, to live on and fight another day, by the tantalizing prospect of a night of drinking, dancing, and debauchery at the legendary Savoy. It was a day—and a war—William Haywood McBurney would never forget.

He pulled out two fresh beers from their six-pack and handed one to his buddy. They popped the tops and started tipping them back in peaceful silence, watching as the last rays of sunlight reflected off the surface of the lake like a shimmering mirage. The original Meer—the Dutch word for "lake"—had been a smaller water body occupying the lowest-lying section of the park at the former confluence of Montayne's Rivulet and Harlem Creek. It was at that point where the two freshwater streams widened into a brackish estuary draining slowly into the East River. Now the Meer was Harlem's biggest swimming pool—and best fishing hole if one was an angler partial to yellow perch, crappie, and northern snakehead.

McBurney was thinking to himself that if his white countrymen had not changed and were not ready to greet the 761st's veterans as returning heroes, there was still one significant change: he and his buddies were no longer the same themselves. They had transformed from green boys to seasoned, worldly men by fighting on foreign soil in the greatest conflict in human history. They knew what they had accomplished. They had exceeded anyone's expectations by grappling in combat on equal footing with white troops, many of whom had come to acknowledge their battlefield prowess. They had succeeded in treacherous terrain and horrific weather conditions against superior German equipment, in vehicles that were mobile death traps and coffins on wheels. They had stood up for one another and on behalf of their country in the name of freedom in the face of terrible losses, and had kept going for six straight months without relief. But most importantly, in England, France, Belgium, Luxembourg, Holland, Germany, and Austria, they had experienced firsthand—and, for most of them for the first time—a more enlightened and unsegregated world, a world in which they were viewed by civilians simply as human beings and not defined by the color of their skin.

"I know we've talked about this before," said McBurney, "but I really did think it was going to be different when we came home."

"We all did."

"Now that I've seen the world, I gotta say I expect a hell of lot more. A hell of a lot more from myself—and from my country. We can do better. 'My country tis of thee, sweet land of bigotry' should be a thing of the past.'"

"You're right, we can do better. That's why sometimes I just feel lost. After all that training and six straight months of fighting, I wonder if it was all just a dream."

"It wasn't no dream."

"I know that. I'm just saying there's never going to be anything like it. I think that's why old Patton was the way he was that day back in Lorraine when he first spoke to us. Remember that intense look in his eyes?"

"Yeah, that day was something else."

"I wanted to make him proud of us, I can tell you that. He's the one who gave us our shot."

"The Old Man had a genius for war. He's dead now, you know."

"I heard about his car wreck. And then two weeks later he up and died."

"Not the way he wanted to go, I'm sure. He would have wanted to die in battle."

He thought back to Austria when the battalion's tanks were lined up beside a bridge for the German surrender ceremonies. A jeep bearing four stars came driving up with the commanding general of the mighty Third U. S. Army standing up tall and straight in the shotgun seat behind a .50-caliber machine gun. He had a Negro driver, McBurney remembered, who slowed down as they came upon the tankers, and Patton was dressed in his trademark riding breeches, shiny riding boots, and pearl-handled revolvers so familiar in *Stars and Stripes* and the newspapers. All down the line, the members of the 761st stood ramrod-straight at attention and saluted. McBurney remembered the black driver slowing down and Patton saluting back, crisply, and then the driver drove on. But what McBurney remembered most of all was the quiet, satisfied expression on the great warrior's face.

His mind then reached back to that first pep talk in Lorraine. Old Blood and Guts had told them that he only accepted the best in his Third Army. *By God, you got the best with us, General. Rest in peace.* Like most members of the battalion, McBurney was damn proud to have fought under the celebrated Patton, and the initial meeting with the legendary general had made a lasting impression on him.

The 761st had truly been *Patton's Panthers.*

"I've got to tell you one thing though," said Smith.

"What's that?"

"I don't think we're ever going to feel as powerful as we did when we were behind those big guns. Or as alive as we felt when we all sat around talking at night after the fighting was done."

"I know what you're saying. We had something special over there."

"It was a connection. I'm just afraid we may never feel anything like it again."

McBurney nodded in agreement. He then took a swig of beer and stared out at the Meer. Along the western bank of the lake, a pair of muskrats frolicked in the water, and a short distance away a family of black-crowned herons were just visible in the reeds. Shifting his gaze, he looked at the boathouse, the old War of 1812 gun emplacements at Nutter's Battery above the granite outcrops, and the backdrop of buildings along Central Park North making up the skyline. Somehow, the dilapidated tenements seemed to stand like army sentinels above the profusion of towering oaks, smaller cherry trees with pink and white blossoms, and clumps of birch and copper beech. The springtime beauty and tranquility all around him made him feel a long way from the fighting in Europe. But deep down, he missed it. Most of all he missed the comradery of his pals.

He kept in touch with Smitty, Preston McNeil, and some of the other men from the outfit, but he knew that soon life, career, and family would overtake them all and they would see less and less of one another with each passing year. The end of the war had dismantled what they had all built together and the 761st as they knew it no longer existed. Sometimes, he wondered how it could all be over.

"It's funny, man," he said. "When you're young, you don't think you're going to die. Bullets don't mean a damned thing. It's a cowboy thing. Then, you see the blood and everything changes. We sacrificed all right. But like you said, it's the camaraderie of the unit that got us all through it. We were the first coloreds to fight in tanks. Most tank units only spent twenty days on the front lines, but we spent 183 days without relief. You can't say what a goddamn person can or can't do."

"Amen to that, brother," said Smith, and he tossed back the rest of his Schaefers. "We were as good as Patton's best spearheading tank division, the 4th Armored. Numbers don't lie."

"And yet, man, we haven't gotten the recognition we deserve."

"It will come one day."

"I think you're right. But I do find myself talking less and less to people outside the unit about what I saw and did over there. They just don't believe me."

"I hear you. Even some of my friends that didn't serve think I'm jiving when I tell them about all the shit we saw."

"Sometimes, man, it seems as if not a single colored fought—let alone fought in a Sherman—during the war. That's how ignorant people are. But there's one person who remembers what we did. In fact, she says she's never going to forget us."

"Who's that?"

"That German girl we rescued at that camp we liberated in Austria. I just got a letter from her."

"You did?"

"I got it right here." He reached into his pocket and pulled it out. "You want to see it?"

"Why don't you read it to me?"

"All right." After taking a moment to collect his thoughts, he began to read.

*4 May 1946*

*Dear Sergeant William McBurney:*

*I wanted to write to thank you and your fellow Schwarze Soldaten for liberating me and the other prisoners at Gunskirchen Lager one year ago to the day. The 761st Tank Battalion—and you in particular—will always have a special place in my heart. You saved my life and I owe you a debt of gratitude. If not for you, I would not be alive today.*

*Since the end of the war, I have learned about your unit, the Black Panthers, and your motto "Come Out Fighting." I tried to track you down when you were stationed in Teisendorf, but by that time you had left the area. I am what your American occupation authorities call a "Displaced Person" and it has not been easy to get information. But I have managed to find out a little bit about you and the other men in your battalion.*

*I know that you fought in France and Belgium as well as in Germany and Austria and that you were an all-Negro outfit. I know that, in your travels and battles across Europe, you were often not treated well by your own white soldiers. I discovered much of this from a Negro newspaper correspondent named Trezzvant Anderson, who has written a book of your unit's exploits. From Mr. Anderson, I know that you all fought bravely in the name of freedom.*

*On the day of liberation when you and I met, I told you that I had been an Edelweiss Pirate and that I, too, had been fighting for freedom. I was in the Cologne Navajos. We were not soldiers like you, but we did what we could. We hid and lent aid to Jews, Allied airmen, and German Army deserters. We attacked Hitler Youth patrols. We handed out anti-Nazi leaflets. We stole and stockpiled weapons. We passed on Allied radio broadcasts. Like you we had our own motto: "Eternal War on the Hitler Youth." In response, Hitler and the Nazis hunted us down and punished us for our resistance. They ruined and bankrupted our country, and I am proud to have stood up in the face of such evil. My father, a colonel in the Wehrmacht, and I were shipped off to Gunskirchen for our beliefs, and he was murdered and I almost died.*

*Though Hitler and the Nazis are the ones most to blame for the war and the death of millions of innocent people in the camps, all of my countrymen, including myself, bear the responsibility for what happened. As I told you that day, I am embarrassed to be a German. We should have risen up and stopped Hitler and his Nazis. We should have spoken out against the mistreatment of the Jews and other supposed "Enemies of the State" long before the concentration camps were built. We Germans—all Germans—failed. At the end, we were killing our own people, anyone who was not a fanatic for National Socialism. But the war is over and now we must rebuild our country, with America's help, and bring the Nazis to justice.*

*I apologize to you, William McBurney, for what my country did. And I thank you for what you did for me. As I said, you will always have a special place in my heart.*

*I told you that day we are both Soldiers of Freedom, but that while you had won your war, I had lost mine. But that is not quite true. It appears that in the end perhaps I have won, as I am to become an American citizen. I will be moving this summer to Philadelphia to live with my uncle, Frederick Lange, a doctor, and his family. Needless to say, I am very excited to be starting a new life as a nurse in America, though a part of me is sad to leave my homeland.*

*If I am in New York, I would like to visit you and thank you in person for saving my life. You and your Negro comrades are heroes, and the whole world should know of your exploits. By the same token, the world should also know of the struggle of the Edelweiss Pirates. Many people in Germany call us criminals because we stole, attacked Hitler Youth members, and killed Nazis. But we are not criminals. Like you and your comrades in the 761st, we fought for freedom not criminal gain. But no one seems to care about our story, just as I am sure that many white Americans, regrettably, are unaware of your important tale. That is what Mr. Anderson told me, and it is the reason he has written his book about the 761st Tank Battalion. You probably already know all about it, but if you don't it is called "Come Out Fighting" in tribute to your unit's motto. The book was published in Austria.*

*I want to end this letter by giving thanks once again. You, William McBurney, are a true Soldier of Freedom.*

*I shall never forget you and what you did on behalf of the cause of freedom.*

*With kindest regards,*

*Angela Lange*
*Cologne, Germany*

When he looked up, he saw that there were tears in his buddy Smitty's eyes. They were silent for a long moment. The only sounds were from the squealing children along the shoreline and the distant rumble of traffic along Central Park North, dampened by the thick buffer of trees and rocky outcrops south of the thoroughfare.

"Now that is something," said Smitty to break the silence, wiping the tears from his eyes. "That is one strong German girl."

"She's American, or soon will be," pointed out McBurney. "We need people like her to set things right in our *own* country. After the blood we spilled and the sacrifices we made, there shouldn't be any room for prejudice. It should be a thing of the past."

"I get what you're saying. But unfortunately, that's not the case."

"I still think one day we're gonna change things. After all, contrary to what my dad told me before we left for Camp Upton back in '42, the Army *did* let us fly. We just happened to do it in tanks."

"You're motherfucking right. We flew, man, we really flew. Behind the tracks and guns of those armored beasts."

"We came out fighting," said McBurney, feeling the power of the moment and his love for his fellow Black Panthers of the 761st Tank Battalion, one of Patton's finest. "But more importantly, we are—and will always be—*Soldiers of Freedom* just like Angie said. One day, people are gonna know our story."

"You really think so?"

McBurney gave a wistful look. "Yeah, I do. The winds of change are coming—and there's gonna be a whole lot more of us coming out fighting in the years ahead. One day, our people are going to get their freedom. They're going to get it because stubborn sons of bitches like us earned it for them on the field of battle."

# AFTERWORD

*Soldiers of Freedom: The WWII Story of Patton's Panthers and the Edelweiss Pirates* was conceived and written by the author as a work of historical fiction. Although the novel takes place during the Second World War and is based upon actual historical figures, events, and locales, the novel is still ultimately a work of the imagination and entertainment and should be read as nothing more. Though I have strived for historical accuracy, the names, characters, places, government entities, armed forces, religious and political groups, and incidents, as portrayed in the novel, are products of the author's imagination and are not to be construed as one-hundred-percent accurate depictions. With that said, the story is based primarily upon known and reasonably well-documented historical events and real people.

With respect to the events portrayed in the novel, I have tried to place the actual historical figures where they physically were during a given event and have used their actual words based on primary references such as journals, autobiographies, case files, contemporary transcripts, military documents, memoirs, and other directly quoted materials. Like Michael Shaara in his Pulitzer-prize-winning historical novel about the Battle of Gettysburg, *The Killer Angels*, I have not "consciously changed any fact" nor have I "knowingly violated the action." Most of the scenes in the book are based on known events with specific historical figures present, but a minority are based on incidents that are generally accepted to have taken place but have unfortunately not been documented by history, or that I believe happened under similar circumstances to those described in the book but for which there is no historical record. In these cases, the interpretations of character and motivation are mine and mine alone. Thus, the book's characters are ultimately a part of my overall imaginative landscape and are, therefore, the fictitious creations of the author, reflecting my personal research interests and biases.

The story of the Edelweiss Pirates in Cologne presented in this book is largely based upon the real-life experiences of Gertrud "Mucki" Koch, Bartholomäus "Barthel" Schink, and Jean Jülich (whom the fictitious Angela Lange, Bartholomäus Schröder, and Jean Hüber, respectively, are loosely based upon). Gertrud Koch and Jean Jülich have written books on their wartime experiences, and I had originally intended to tell their stories through their eyes as I have real-life historical figures William McBurney and George Patton. However, Koch's story did not fit the timeline of the novel or historical arcs of the other characters since most of her resistance activities in Cologne proper took place prior to the principal historical events covered in this book from summer 1944 through spring 1945. Furthermore, Jülich was imprisoned by the Nazis at Brauweiler Prison from October 1944 until February 1945, and at Rockenbach Prison from February 1945 until his liberation by American troops in March 1945. I didn't want to have months upon months of imprisonment and brutal torture at the hands of the Gestapo in the book (the prison scenes I have recreated, based on multiple first-hand accounts at Brauweiler Abbey and El-De Haus, are enough for even the non-squeamish, I believe). This made it impossible to have Koch and Jülich in the book in their historically documented real-life roles as I have done with McBurney and Patton. Instead, Angela Lange acts as a proxy for the major historical events of the Edelweiss Pirates from summer

1944 through spring 1945. In addition, as Angela Lange is a fictionalized character, her interactions with William McBurney in Chapters 58, 59, and 62 are fictionalized, although the liberation of the Gunskirchen Lager labor camp in Austria by McBurney and Leonard Smith portrayed in Chapters 58 and 59 is an accurate recreation of this major historical event on May 4, 1945.

Below I present the legacy and ultimate fate of the key historical figures in the book along with the 761st Tank Battalion and Edelweiss Pirates. The Black Panthers of the 761st and the Edelweiss Pirates were, for a long time after the war, not properly recognized for their heroism and achievements, and they are still largely unknown to most people in the world. The opportunity to tell their courageous and long-neglected stories of freedom was the major motivating factor behind writing this historical work.

## WILLIAM MCBURNEY AND THE 761ST TANK BATTALION

Following the end of the war and still proudly wearing their distinctive Black Panther's *Come Out Fighting* patches, the members of the 761st Tank Battalion continued occupation and training duties in the area of Bissengen, Germany, and later Teisendorf, Bavaria. By the end of the war, soldiers and the Army at large had heard of the 761st Tank Battalion. According to Army historians writing at war's end, black soldiers clamored to join the unit, even if it meant more time abroad, until the 761st's deactivation in June 1946. The 761st was subsequently reactivated (as an integrated unit) and assigned to the regular Army in November 1947 at Fort Knox, Kentucky, where it served until again inactivated in March 1955.

During the war, the Black Panthers' *blitzkrieg* across Europe succeeded in crushing the German opposition that lay in its path, but its victory over the Wehrmacht and SS forces it encountered in its circuitous 2,000-mile journey came at tremendous cost. From the time that the battalion was committed to combat on November 7, 1944, it had spent 183 days in action, its only pauses accounted for by the time needed to move from one mission to another. During the unit's combat actions through May 6, 1945, the 761st destroyed or captured 331 enemy machine-gun nests, 58 pillboxes, and 461 wheeled vehicles; killed 6,246 enemy combatants; and captured more than 15,818 enemy soldiers (the number is considered low by battalion historians since it does not fully reflect those achieved in combined operations with infantry). The unit suffered thirty-six men killed in action, including three officers. Thirty-nine officers and 221 enlisted men fell wounded in action. Nonbattle casualties stood at nine officers and 192 men. The enemy captured four from the unit, but the POWs were returned unharmed. Total casualties pressed towards 50 percent, a disproportionately high number for a comparatively small outfit that fought alongside manpower and equipment behemoths like the 26th Infantry Division and the 4th Armored Division. The battalion lost 71 tanks in battle, more than one and a half times its original allotment.

Though the Army recognized the tankers for their sacrifice, it did not give the battalion the full recognition it deserved based on actual battlefield performance, especially when its combat records are compared to white armored units it clearly outfought. The 761st unit was credited with 183 days of combat in four campaigns—Northern France, Ardennes-Alsace, Rhineland, and Central Europe—and eight enlisted soldiers were elevated to the officer ranks with battlefield commissions. The Army also awarded 11 Silver Star and 70 Bronze Star medals (3 with clusters) to the battalion along with 296 Purple Hearts for combat wounds (8 with clusters). Though the medals acknowledged the contributions of the unit as a whole, Lieutenant Colonel Paul Bates, Captain Ivan Harrison, and the battalion's other officers knew it fell far short of what the 761st deserved. After the unit's statistics were compiled, it was readily apparent that a Distinguished Unit Citation for the battalion was in order along with Medals of Honor for the unit's three bravest and most-deserving tankers: Ruben Rivers, Samuel Turley, and Warren Crecy, the "Baddest Man in the 761st."

The quest for the battalion's recognition began on July 25, 1945, when Captain Harrison, representing the battalion with Bates on service in Holland, submitted to General Eisenhower's Headquarters in Europe, a recommendation that the 761st be awarded the Distinguished Unit Citation. Also known as the Presidential Unit Citation, the award was created during the war to recognize units for a collective display of extraordinary heroism and is the highest honor that can be bestowed upon a military unit. The 761st's request was denied by the Army on August 18, 1945, with a statement reading, in part: "1. Not favorably considered. 2. After a careful study of the 761st Tank Battalion described in basic communication, it is considered that the action, while commendable, was not sufficiently outstanding to meet the requirements for a unit citation." Ike formally denied the request on February 12, 1946. Following the rejection of their submission, the tankers remained undeterred, submitting repeated requests over the years for the original decision to be reviewed, but the denials continued.

After thirty-three years of pressing and with racial tensions in the U.S. subsiding, the battalion was belatedly awarded the Presidential Unit Citation for "Extraordinary Heroism" by President Jimmy Carter on January 24, 1978. Charles "Pop" Gates—the crusty old Buffalo Soldier, then a retired lieutenant colonel— spoke on behalf of the unit. The award became official on April 10, 1978 by the Department of the Army under General Orders Number 5. The final award stood as a single citation for all the 761st's actions from October 31, 1944, to May 6, 1945. Most importantly, the government finally acknowledged that "racial discrimination and inadvertent neglect on the part of those in authority" had played a role in the previous disapprovals and that "the climate created by the Army commanders could only have made it difficult to provide proper recognition for a 'Negro' unit during the period 1944-1947."

In 1978, Captain David Williams, who was greatly encouraged by the awarding of the Presidential Unit Citation, resurrected his original effort for Sergeant Ruben Rivers to be considered for the Medal of Honor. On November 23, 1944, four days after the fierce battle for Guebling and Bourgaltroff, France, Williams had handed paperwork to the battalion's acting commander, Lieutenant Colonel Hollis Hunt, recommending Rivers for a posthumous Medal of Honor. But Hunt failed to act on the request and the paperwork was lost or destroyed. Four hundred and thirty-three Medals of Honor had been awarded to soldiers in World War II—but shockingly and embarrassingly, none of the 1.2 million African-Americans who served had received the honor. Through Williams's tireless efforts, in 1997 the army upgraded

Rivers's second Silver Star to the Medal of Honor—posthumous recognition of the tanker's personal valor and a nod to the men with whom he fought.

All the members of the 761st had ever wanted was simple human dignity, to be recognized for their abilities as soldiers without being judged by the color of their skin. The Presidential Unit Citation and Rivers's Medal of Honor went a long way towards healing the old wounds of racial prejudice inflicted upon them by their white counterparts in the U.S. armed forces and the white civilians at Camps Claiborne and Hood. That the men of the 761st and other segregated African-American combat units like the 92nd Infantry Division and the famous Tuskegee Airmen received a less than warm welcome upon their return home than white units would be a gross understatement. The continued discrimination towards the Black Panthers after willingly giving their lives on the killing fields of Europe was a source of significant disappointment and discouragement for the returning men, as well as their embittered families.

As Platoon Sergeant Johnnie Stevens said: "We were treated better by the civilian German population than we were treated in America. See, in our own country, we could not buy a hot dog when we were in uniform, had to ride in the back of the bus when we were in uniform.... But over there, you were treated like a king. We ate together, slept together. After the war was over and the Germans had dances again, we were invited. That's why a lot of black GIs took their discharges in Europe. They said, 'Look, ain't nothing in America for me. I can't get a decent job when I go back, I know that. I'm not gonna have any privileges. I can't even vote. So what the hell do I want to go back there for?" Though the 761st's vets were disappointed to return home to the same old prejudices, they soon began to put their lives together, start careers, marry, raise children, and lead in countless quiet but nonetheless significant ways. Though some struggled, the bloody battlefields of Europe had trained them to be disciplined, responsible American citizens who understood the true cost of freedom.

William McBurney returned home to America a Bronze Star winner for his courage under enemy fire. Upon his return, he met with the challenges of discrimination but still found a comradery with the other men of the battalion. "We just clicked," he said. He went to mechanical drafting school and was awarded his degree—but found that despite his Bronze Star for valor and other qualifications, no one would hire him. Eventually, he took the test to join the New York Police force, but like most blacks pursuing such jobs in post-war America, he was not put on the list. By then he had married and started a family, and he had no choice but to search for other gainful employment. He managed to secure an entry-level job at a plastics plant in the Bronx. He remained in plastics for thirty-five years, becoming a supervisor and eventually rising to the position of plant manager of a factory in New Jersey.

McBurney remained grateful his whole life towards his mentor and tank commander Teddy Windsor, who had looked after him and the other crew members of "Taffy" and their replacement Shermans with a steady paternal eye. In a twist of irony given the monstrous treatment he had endured at the hands of the Army and white America, his grandson went on to serve honorably in the Gulf War. Said the former tanker: "He had it 100 per cent better than we did. Now the troops are integrated and you have a chance to go somewhere. We were fighting for a better country but it took a long time after that war ended."

The wry-humored, affable, and articulate McBurney is featured in the 2007 independent, feature-length documentary on the 761st Tank Battalion entitled *761st* produced by the unit's historian, Wayne Robinson. It features interviews with McBurney and ten other combat veterans of the 761st. McBurney also plays a prominent role in the fall 1944-spring 1945 episodes of The History Channel series *Patton 360*. The veteran tank main gunner relates his experiences with the battalion in the Lorraine Campaign, the Battle of the Bulge, and in the ultimate conquest of the German homeland. Living well into his nineties, McBurney has also been interviewed for several articles on the battalion. "The camaraderie of the unit— that's what got me through it," he has said, which would be a fitting epitaph for the heroic and easygoing gunner from New York and son of a WWI Harlem Hellfighter.

Upon his return to the Big Apple, McBurney's buddy Private First-Class Leonard Smith—the foster child from Queens who originally volunteered for the Army in pursuit of high adventure and ended up winning a Bronze Star—first took a job cleaning up subway cars. He subsequently worked for the sanitation department and drove a city bus. Figuring he had nothing to lose, he eventually took the exam to join the police force and was accepted by the New York City transit police. Married several times, he held his position with the Transit Police for more than twenty-five years before retiring. During his years as a police officer, Smith became close friends with the father of UCLA and NBA basketball legend and prominent social justice author Kareem Abdul-Jabbar (Lew Alcindor), F.L. "Al" Alcindor, who like Smith was a war veteran and Big Band jazz aficionado. As fate would have it, in 2004 Abdul-Jabbar co-wrote with Anthony Walton an excellent work on the 761st Tank Battalion, featuring stories of McBurney and Smith, entitled *Brothers in Arms: The Epic Story of the 761st Tank Battalion, WWII's Forgotten Heroes*. The book was an important resource for the writing of this novel.

Over the years, McBurney, Smith, and other members of the 761st Tank Battalion still carried memories of what they witnessed at the Gunskirchen Lager labor camp in Austria in the final days of the war. Battalion members have visited Jewish organizations and school groups throughout the country to share these memories and to testify to the horrors they saw. Throughout their lives, McBurney and Smith have remained proud of the important role they played as liberators in bashing down the gate of the Gunskirchen labor camp and helping free the Jewish and non-Jewish prisoners from Nazi tyranny. However, McBurney long felt regret for feeding the starving inmates his rations, though it was no fault of his own since the Army had not given any instructions to the troops prior to the liberation of Nazi concentration or labor camps. "I thought I had come into a prisoner of-war camp," he said quietly of the liberation in which he had played a key role. "It looked like the land of the living dead. They were nothing but walking skeletons. We carried food on the backs of our tanks because our food kitchens couldn't keep up with us. We gave some people food but that was the worst thing we could have done. They just weren't used to real food. Some of them got sick." For most of his life, Leonard Smith had nightmares about the poor survivors: "You could count every bone, every rib," he said. "You dream about it, bad dreams. Just like it happened yesterday."

The battalion's beloved commander—Lieutenant Colonel Paul Bates, the "Great White Father" of the 761st—limped away from the devastation of the war a proud but damaged man. The lanky former All-American football star returned to America to find himself in a period of deep confusion, haunted not only because of what he had witnessed in combat but even more so because of the extreme abuse his outstanding troops had been forced to endure at the hands of their own Army and white America. "I was a very confused person when the war was over. I couldn't put behind me all the contradictions I'd encountered, and how badly my men had been treated. I didn't drink, or anything like that. I was just very confused." He was utterly stunned to witness the true dimensions of the racial divide back home, and began a long campaign to help bring his men their due.

Remaining in the military after the war, Bates worked among other assignments at the Pentagon and at an officers' college at Fort Leavenworth. He was eventually promoted to the rank of full colonel. Bates was helped in his readjustment to life back in the States following World War II by his longtime girlfriend, the "Taffy" after whom his storied tank, adopted by Teddy Windsor and William McBurney after he was wounded, had been named. Her promise pulled him through his darkness following his leg wound in November 1944 to the war's end with a strength and determination that surpassed his own. He married Taffy and raised two sons. Bates and his family established a scholarship at Bates's alma mater, Western Maryland College, for descendants of members of the 761st. He remained beloved by and in constant touch with the veterans of the 761st until his death in 1995 at the age of eighty-six.

According to U.S. Army Major Italia Carson: "Lieutenant Colonel Paul L. Bates was a striking example of leadership and moral courage" who "led from the front by training with the 761st, living on post close to his unit, protecting them from mistreatment from the military and local civilians, and accompanying them into battle. His commitment to stay with the 761st cost him a promotion to colonel." In the Jackie Robinson case, his "actions demonstrated the honor, integrity, and moral courage of a leader who chose the hard, right choice when faced with what surely was intense pressure from his peers and superiors to make the easy, wrong choice."

Perhaps the legacy of Bates is best described by Kareem Abdul-Jabbar and Anthony Walton, who dedicated their book *Brothers in Arms* to "Colonel Paul Levern Bates," as well as the members of the 761st: "He was fundamentally decent, honest, modest, and compassionate. He saw and treated the men of the battalion with a simple, direct humanity, and they responded in kind. Unlike other commanders of the battalion, Bates lived on the post with the soldiers. He went with them on marches and runs, listening to their comments and complaints. There was nothing he could do to alter the underlying attitudes of other white officers, but he did forbid any direct mistreatment of his soldiers, and he insisted they be given nothing but the highest caliber of armored training. He believed in them. The men could never find enough words of praise to describe Paul Bates."

Captain David J. Williams, the winner of the Silver Star and two Purple Hearts, returned to the States to complete his degree at Yale in 1947, which he had deferred in order to enter the military. He married and raised three sons, working as a stockbroker with E. F. Hutton in Florida. His true work and passion, however, was writing about his experiences with the 761st so that the sacrifices of the men would not be forgotten. His book *Hit Hard* published in 1983 by Bantam Books told the story of the battalion and was the first of some 75 "Bantam War Books" to chronicle a black unit. According to Kareem Abdul-Jabbar and Anthony Walton, his "tireless campaigning to this end would be instrumental in the battalion's fight for recognition." To the end of his life, the rich kid from Philly, who at first did not exactly endear himself to the black men with whom he served, had tremendous admiration for them: "These guys were better than heroes because they weren't supposed to be able to fight, and they were treated worse than lepers. I can tell you, it took a rare sort of character to go out there and do what they did. I used to ask myself, why the hell should these guys fight? Why? As you get mature, you start pondering—even an old war—and then we started to fight for the unit citation, and I began to see what made these guys tick. It's a pride that nobody ever recognized."

Throughout his life, Williams was proud to have served with the black troopers of the 761st. The man who waged a ten-year campaign to win recognition for the battalion and Sergeant Ruben Rivers said, "We fought three battles: Fort Claiborne in Louisiana, Fort Hood in Texas, and Europe. The only medal we got without any fuss: Purple Hearts. You have to understand—in battle you fight for each other. The pride in the unit. You have a cohesion. When men fight shoulder to shoulder and bleed and die for a just cause, they become brothers." When President Clinton posthumously awarded Rivers the Medal of Honor in 1997, Williams smiled at the victory and openly wept, proudly declaring himself a Black Panther. "We did win, didn't we? God can't take away this moment because the deed is done."

Following the war, the Black Panther veterans formed the 761st Tank Battalion Veterans Association and gathered for their first reunion at the Carnegie Hotel in Cleveland, Ohio, in 1949. Meeting each year in a different city, they remained close, even when faced with the challenges of segregation to find a suitable facility to host a reunion. One year even Williams had trouble booking a hotel for the mixed-race association. The 761st's reunions reached a peak of several hundred veterans attending during the 1960s. With too few veterans remaining to continue the gatherings, the men and their families held their last reunion in 2011.

Thankfully, after a long and arduous struggle, the legacy of the 761st is secure, though the unit is still not widely known outside U.S. military circles. The white commander of the 17th Airborne Division that fought with the battalion during the Battle of the Bulge said unequivocally that he would rather have five tanks from the 761st Tank Battalion than any larger number from another armored unit. A monument dedicated to the 761st Tank Battalion was unveiled at Fort Hood, Texas, during a ceremony attended by surviving veterans on November 10, 2005, as a permanent tribute to soldiers who had served and continued to serve throughout the world for liberty, honor, and democracy. The monument features four black granite tablets surrounding a life-size marble sculpture of a 761st Tank Battalion fighter, kneeling atop a black granite pedestal engraved with a tank on the front and a panther on the back. The monument is located on 761st Tank Battalion Drive.

After the war ended, the distinguished service of the 761st Tank Battalion, Tuskegee Airmen, and other African-American combat units helped convince President Harry S. Truman and other high-ranking government officials to desegregate the U.S. Armed Forces. But the best tribute to the 761st came with the words in the Presidential Unit Citation: "The 761st Tank Battalion Distinguished itself by extraordinary gallantry, courage, professionalism and high esprit de corps displayed in the accomplishment of unusually difficult and hazardous operations in the European Theater of Operations from 31 October 1944 to 6 May 1945.... Throughout this period of combat, the courageous and professional actions of the members of the 'Black Panther' battalion, coupled with their indomitable fighting spirit and devotion to duty, reflect great credit on the 761st Tank Battalion, and the United States Army, and this Nation." Though the citation should have come thirty-three years earlier, it was ultimately the struggles of the 761st—at home and abroad, within the army and outside it—that led to the construction of a stronger U.S. Army and a greater nation.

## GENERAL GEORGE S. PATTON, JR.

At the end of the war, Patton did not get his wish to command in the Pacific, and over the next seven months of his life he exited the big stage of WWII history with more a whimper than a bang. But his larger-than-life legacy as a genius for war was more than secure despite his many character flaws, contradictions, and controversies. As Pulitzer-Prize winning author Rick Atkinson says: "Few military figures in American history have laid siege to the public imagination more relentlessly than George S. Patton, Jr." After all, who else but Old Blood and Guts would have presented his beloved dog with a bust of Hitler to urinate on at his leisure?

In June 1945, Patton was appointed as military governor of Bavaria in an occupation army assignment, with the job of leading the Third Army in denazification efforts. But by the time the Japanese surrendered in August and with the adrenaline rush of war behind him, he had already become dissatisfied with the tedious bureaucratic position and was depressed by the prospect of never fighting in another major war. He desperately wanted a crack at the Russians while the massive U.S. Army still flexed its muscles in Europe, and his behavior and public statements became increasingly erratic.

Though various explanations beyond his disappointment have been proposed for Patton's extreme mood swings and unpredictable behavior at this low point in his career, it seems likely that a contributing factor may have been some form of chronic traumatic encephalopathy (CTE), the degenerative brain disorder associated with repetitive head trauma, particularly among modern NFL football players. As Carlo D'Este, author of *Patton: A Genius for War*, states, "it seems virtually inevitable...that Patton experienced some type of brain damage from too many head injuries" from a lifetime of football, automobile, and horse-riding accidents, especially one suffered while playing polo in 1936 in Hawaii.

The outspoken Patton swiftly attracted controversy as military governor when it was noted that several former Nazi Party members continued to hold civil servant posts in the Bavarian region. There was nothing remarkable about this: Montgomery and other occupation authorities were similarly employing a large number of National Socialists to run the telephone exchanges, power facilities, and street cars and to rebuild the roads, bridges, train lines, and water and fuel plants. As British military historian Terry Brighton states of Montgomery, "He believed, as did Patton, that civilians who had been members of the Nazi Party should be put back to work in their former civilian jobs.… The crisis was so acute that any command structure that worked, and any worker who could be returned to his job, was preferred to the strict policy of denazification sponsored by Eisenhower."

But with Patton being the naughty boy, only he could turn what was a common Allied practice due to sheer necessity into a major scandal. When goaded by the press about the subject, Patton created negative press stateside and enraged Eisenhower by loosely comparing the Nazis to Democrats and Republicans, noting that most of the people with experience in infrastructure management had been compelled to join the Party in the war. In September 1945, after a heated exchange with Ike over his statements, Patton was relieved of his military governorship. As further embarrassment, he was relieved of command of the Third Army on October 7, and in a somber change of command ceremony, Patton concluded his farewell remarks, "All good things must come to an end. The best thing that has ever happened to me thus far is the honor and privilege of having commanded the Third Army." To take away some of the sting, Ike gave Patton the job of commanding the U.S. 15th Army, based in Bad Nauheim, but this was nothing but an empty job. The 15th Army at this point consisted only of a small headquarters staff working to compile a history of the war in Europe.

Patton had accepted the post because of his love of history, but quickly lost interest. He began traveling, visiting Paris, Rennes, Chartres, Brussels, Metz, Reims, Luxembourg, and Verdun. Then he went to Stockholm, where he reunited with other athletes from the 1912 Olympics. Patton decided that he would leave his post at the 15th Army and not return to Europe once he left on December 10 for Christmas leave. He intended to discuss with his wife Beatrice whether he would continue in a stateside post or retire from the Army.

On December 9, 1945, his chief of staff, Major General Hobart Gay, invited him on a pheasant hunting trip near Mannheim to lift his spirits. With Patton's new driver, nineteen-year-old Horace Woodring, behind the wheel, they set out in Patton's chauffeured limousine, accompanied by a jeep carrying a hunting dog. Observing battle-ravaged vehicles along the side of the road, the normally bellicose Patton quietly observed, "How awful war is. Think of the waste." Continuing on, they were proceeding slowly when their car collided with a two-ton U.S. Army truck. As Martin Blumenson, author of *Patton: The Man Behind the Legend, 1885-1945* describes the event, "The crash and the sudden stop sent Patton, who was in the backseat, hurtling through the air. The top of his head grazed the diamond-shaped interior light on the roof, and a protruding corner ripped off the skin of his skull, which hung down like a flap. His face smashed into the driver's partition. The impact broke his nose and his neck. The damaged vertebrae paralyzed him from the neck down. No one else in this freak accident was so much as scratched."

Taken immediately to a hospital in Heidelberg, he joked about his injuries. "Relax, gentlemen, I'm in no condition to be a terror now." Twelve days later— after receiving countless get-well messages from everyone from President Truman and Ike to the Jewish War Veterans organization and a leading African-American journal—he was dead. He was sixty years old. One of his doctors wrote, "Patton died as he had lived. Bravely." Following a funeral befitting a head of state, he was buried on a foggy December morning among six thousand of his men of the Third Army at the Luxembourg American Cemetery and Memorial in the Hamm district of Luxembourg City, in accordance with his request to be buried with his troops. A rifle squad fired the traditional three-volley salute. He had written his own final prayer, a soldier's requiem: "If it be my lot to die, let me do so with courage and honor in a manner which will bring the greatest harm to the enemy, and please, oh Lord, protect and guide those I shall leave behind."

As one of the most colorful, controversial, and brilliant military commanders in world history, Patton has long had more than his fair share of supporters and detractors. As this book has shown, the inescapable truth about the man is that he was both magnificent yet vile, loving yet inconsiderate, humane yet bellicose, generous yet wretchedly self-centered. One British author unflatteringly but honestly said of him that it was an "undeniable fact that Patton was a fascinating, complex, odious, loveable, highly intelligent, foul-mouthed, courageous and unique monster, who but for the two world wars would have drunk himself to death, broken his neck on the hunting field, or ended up in an insane asylum." Love him or hate him, the fanatically driven and cantankerous Old Blood and Guts was a legend in his own time and showed far more humanity and authenticity than his severest critics gave him credit for. This book has tried to show that lesser known side of Patton.

As his most respected biographers Carlo D'Este and Martin Blumenson have demonstrated, Patton was not the racist, anti-Semite, Anglophobe extremist that his detractors have falsely painted him. "Patton's bombast supposedly proves that he was anti-Semitic," author Michael Howard astutely points out, "but a prominent trusted military aide, the intelligence officer Colonel Oscar Koch, was Jewish and beloved by Patton—as was his official biographer Martin Blumenson. Patton was purportedly racist, but more than most other commanders he admired black units ("I don't give a damn who the man is. He can be a Negro or a Jew, but if he has the stuff and does his duty, he can have anything I've got. By God I love him!"); insisted on the presence of some black officers as judges of military tribunals involving black defendants; and spent more time with his African-American aide, Sergeant Meeks, than with almost anyone else while in Europe, developing a relationship of mutual respect that transcended that of a general and his valet. Patton hated the British, but in fact was more appreciative of Montgomery's organizational talents than was either Bradley or Eisenhower."

Patton stands as the first Allied commander to incorporate African-American tankers into an army in the field—the U.S. 761st Tank Battalion—and he backed up that support by putting his name behind it. He was quoted in *Stars and Stripes* as saying that "the Negro tank battalion attached to my command fought bravely in the critical Battle of Bastogne" and that its black warriors were "damn good soldiers." As Kareem Abdul-Jabber and Anthony Walton state, most of the men in the 761st "were aware that it was on Patton's request that they had first been given the opportunity they had hoped and trained for—the opportunity to fight: Their story remains a part of his, and his of theirs. Patton was, along with Douglas MacArthur, the only Allied general whom the Germans truly feared, and most members of the battalion remain proud to have served in his army." Patton was also the first general in the U.S Army to overturn segregation on his own initiative by integrating his rifle companies, and he showed unusual sympathy towards black soldiers when he suspended courts-martials for several of them during the war. "I believe that you will contribute more to the war effort doing duty than in a PW cage," he told them. "But I want to warn you. The first crooked move you make, that sentence will be re-imposed and you go to jail for five years with dishonorable discharge. You have a chance to rehabilitate yourselves. I expect you to do that and to be good soldiers."

All of this doesn't mean that Old Blood and Guts wasn't still something of a bigot; he was. But so were Ike, Marshall, MacArthur, Nimitz, Brooke, Bradley, Montgomery, and the rest of the top dogs in the Allied forces, all middle-aged white men who in the 1940s still clung to the outdated notion of the primacy of white Anglo-Saxons. The more important thing is Patton's actual actions and treatment of African-Americans. The fact remains that he and his black aide Meeks were unusually close, and Patton interacted regularly and favorably with his African-American troops. One of the great photographs of Patton is the picture of him methodically pinning a Silver Star medal in October 1944 on a starry-eyed Private Ernest A. Jenkins, a black soldier under his command. Most significantly of all, at Patton's request, his wife Beatrice removed Eisenhower's and Bedell Smith's names from the list of his honorary pallbearers for his funeral—and replaced them with Master Sergeant William Meeks. In the photograph of the historic event, Meeks is one of the two lead pallbearers.

Most of his Allied contemporaries attested to Patton's uncanny abilities as a field commander—despite the fact that he had to do most of his fighting constrained by Eisenhower and SHAEF, essentially fighting with one hand tied behind his back. After Patton's death, Ike, the coach who owed his star running back a great deal for his pivotal role in winning the war in Europe that eventually vaulted Eisenhower into the presidency, would write: "He was one of those men born to be a soldier, an ideal combat leader.... It is no exaggeration to say that Patton's name struck terror at the hearts of the enemy." Ike called the brash cavalryman and WWI veteran he had first seen strutting onto the fields at Camp Meade in 1919 "one of my oldest and dearest friends—lovable, colorful, generous, a splendid fellow." In the heat of the war, President Franklin D. Roosevelt said "he is our greatest fighting general, and sheer joy." General Geoffrey Keyes insisted that Patton deserved "more than a lion's share of the credit for the victories of our arms in the bitter European struggle." French General Henri Giraud was incredulous when he heard of Patton's dismissal by Eisenhower in late 1945, and invited him to Paris to be decorated by President Charles de Gaulle at a state banquet. At the banquet, President de Gaulle gave a speech placing Patton's achievements alongside those of Napoleon. Even Soviet leader and mass-murderer Joe Stalin was a secret admirer, stating unequivocally that the Red Army could neither have planned nor executed Patton's rapid armored advance across France.

But it was the Germans Old Blood and Guts soundly whipped on the battlefield that offered the most glowing praise. Hans-Gustav Felber, the Seventh Army commander during the Bulge, wrote after the war, "The German leadership had encountered a particularly determined and daring opponent in the person of the commander of Third U.S. Army, General Patton." Hitler—perhaps in one of his fits of rage—referred to him as "that crazy cowboy general." *Blitzkrieg* master Erwin Rommel credited Patton with executing "the most astonishing achievement in mobile warfare." *Generaloberst* Alfred Jodl, chief of staff of the German Army, stated that Patton "was the American Guderian. He was very bold and preferred large movements. He took big risks and won big successes." Field Marshal Albert Kesselring noted that "Patton had developed tank warfare into an art, and understood how to handle tanks brilliantly in the field. I feel compelled, therefore, to compare him with *Generalfeldmarschall* Rommel, who likewise had mastered the art of tank warfare. Both of them had a kind of second sight in regard to this type of warfare." In an interview conducted for *Stars and Stripes* just after his capture, Field Marshal Gerd von Rundstedt stated simply of Patton, "He is your best."

Perhaps a German senior officer captured by the Allies shortly before war's end summed up best why the Germans had more respect for him than for any other Allied commander: "The greatest threat...was the whereabouts of the feared U.S. Third Army. General Patton is always the main topic of military discussion. Where is he? When will he attack? Where? How? With what? General Patton is the most feared general on all fronts. The successes of the U.S. Third Army are still overshadowing all other events of the war, including the campaign in Russia....The tactics of General Patton are daring and unpredictable....He is the most modern general and the best commander of armored and infantry troops combined."

The supreme irony is that Patton would have been even more successful if he had not been held back by Ike and SHAEF, and if he had been able to work closely with and fight on an equal footing with his rival Montgomery, who held him in high regard. As D'Este states, Monty greatly admired the accomplishments of Patton and his armies. He was in particular impressed by Patton's "mobility, speed...rugged determination, and professionalism." In the spring of 1945, when Monty was relegated to the secondary role of protecting the northern flank of Bradley's Twelfth Army Group in pushing forward into the Ruhr, the British field marshal lamented that he had not had Patton fighting along his southern flank instead of the less competent Bradley. The reality is that Patton and Monty, despite their rivalry, had mutual respect for one another and were generally of a similar mind militarily, whereas Monty did not respect Ike or Bradley. Consequently, Patton and Monty were far less rivals than Hollywood filmmakers and armchair historians have made them out to be and were actually more peas of the same pod, despite Patton's predilection towards the role of hard-charging cavalryman and Monty towards that of methodical master strategist. As D'Este says, "One of the gravest mistakes of the war was the reversal of roles between Patton and Bradley." Had Patton commanded 12th Army Group—as indeed he would have had he not self-destructed his career in Sicily—the war would have been much different and ended much sooner. "Patton and Montgomery might have accomplished together what Bradley and Montgomery did not. For all his private complaints about Montgomery, Patton was fully capable and willing to have worked with the British general."

In *The Battle of the Generals*, Martin Blumenson explains how if Patton had been the top American ground commander from Normandy to the end of the war, he and Monty "would have worked closely and effectively together. For they respected each other. Their interests were professional and tied to the operational scene. Their strengths were complementary. The thrust of Patton and the balance of Montgomery would have produced a perfectly matched team...a less discordant Normandy campaign, a happier resolution of Overlord, a firm entrapment of the Germans west of the Seine, and a much earlier end of the war in Europe."

Despite their quarrels and love-hate relationship during the war, Ike always reserved a special place in his heart for Old Blood and Guts. In his later years, the former president and supreme commander enjoyed sitting by the fireside at his home near Gettysburg, where in an epic struggle 80 years earlier the tide of war had turned in favor of freedom, and tell colorful stories of his old warhorse friend Georgie Patton. Whether one feels a jolt of patriotism or cringes at the mention of his name, what is undeniable is that he was one of a kind and utterly authentic. As Atkinson states with a wry grin on his lips, "It is tempting to say that we shall never see his like again. But given Patton's fixed belief in reincarnation, such an assertion could well be premature."

In the end, the epitaph the hard-swearing and hard-fighting horse soldier would probably treasure most came from one of his troopers before the Allied invasion of France: "Here was a man for whom you would go to hell and back."

## THE EDELWEISS PIRATES

Although historians have traditionally placed the Edelweiss Pirates within the gray area between nonconformity and dissidence, recent research has demonstrated that the group was engaged in courageous resistance against the Nazi regime and has made a meaningful contribution to the historical body of active resistance. While some group members were motivated only by a self-interested desire to survive the war, to take part in acts of juvenile delinquency, or to merely snub their noses at authority for youthful thrills, history has shown that the Edelweiss Pirates, taken as a whole, were *Widerstandskämpfer*—resistance fighters—rather than merely disaffected youngsters and criminals. Many of the actions of the Cologne Navajos and other Edelweiss Pirate groups, especially the attacks directed at Party members, the Hitler Youth, and Nazi-controlled infrastructure, cannot be classified as anything but resistance activities. Most importantly, the Edelweiss Pirates have in recent years been formally recognized for their resistance by the German government, Jewish organizations, and other official entities, thus making it clear that the youth group took an active and decisive stand against Nazi tyranny in the name of freedom.

In 1988, the Edelweiss Pirates were officially recognized as "Righteous Among the Nations" by Jerusalem's Yad Vashem Holocaust Memorial. The honor is given, after thorough documented evidence has been amassed, to non-Jewish individuals and groups that have demonstrated extraordinary bravery, at the risk of their own lives, to help Jews during the Holocaust. Gertrud Koch, Barthel Schink, Jean Jülich, and other German youth who defied Hitler and hid their Jewish friends and neighbors from Nazi persecution are now officially recognized as "Righteous Among the Nations." Today, seventy-five years after their small but courageous deeds, the Edelweiss Pirates are no longer relegated in the history books to the lowly status of a "criminal gang" and now officially recognized as anti-Nazi heroes and resistance fighters, while at the same time recognizing that the level of resistance varied amongst the participants.

It was not until sixty years after the war, at the continued urging of Koch and Jülich, that the Cologne Navajos and other Edelweiss Pirate groups were "politically rehabilitated" in Germany. In 2005, the "criminal" status hung around the neck of the Edelweiss Pirates by the Gestapo was finally dropped and Koch, Schink, Jülich, and two others were officially recognized by Jürgen Roters, Cologne's governing mayor, as "resistance fighters" against the Nazis and "heroes." Regrettably, only five Cologne Pirates lived long enough to see this honor. In tribute, city officials in Cologne erected a memorial plaque next to the Ehrenfeld train station in the Hüttenstraße acknowledging the spot where the Gestapo hung Schink, Hans Steinbrück, and others without trial. Ironically, when I visited this bronze plaque, a group of German schoolchildren were gleefully playing next to it. It reads: "This marks the site where, on October 25, 1944, eleven citizens of Poland and the USSR, kidnapped by the Nazi regime for forced labor in Germany and on November 10, 1944, thirteen Germans, including young Edelweiss Pirates from Ehrenfeld and other fighters against war and terror, were publicly hanged, without trial, by the Gestapo and SS." The bravery of Koch and the other four surviving Edelweiss Pirates was further rewarded, in April 2011, when Roters presented them with the Order of Merit of the Federal Republic of Germany. To the five surviving Edelweiss Pirates, the recognition of their ideological battle with the Nazis was far too long in coming.

Since 2000, the Edelweiss Pirates have inspired countless articles, pieces of music, a stage and radio play, and a feature film. In 2005, the same year that the former Pirates were recognized at the public ceremony, Niko and Kiki von Glasow-Brücher's film *Edelweißpiraten* reached the cinemas. The film, made with the help and approval of Jülich, told the story of Schink, Jülich, and Hans Steinbrück and honored those executed by the Nazis at Ehrenfeld. Despite this rehabilitation of the Edelweiss Pirates, however, the surviving members did not appreciate having to face such a long and grueling battle for official exoneration let alone recognition for their resistance against Hitler and Nazism. Furthermore, the honors they have received long after the guns have fallen silent represent but a tiny fraction of the recognition, study, and celebration received by other well-known German resistance groups, especially those represented by the wealthier social classes such as the White Rose group led by the Munich University students Hans and Sophie Scholl.

Koch believes that their social class and the continuation of Nazis in positions of power following the war were significant factors in their longstanding criminal classification. "We were from the working classes. That is the main reason why we have only now been recognized," Koch, who at 81 still went by her Edelweiss Pirate code name of Mucki, told a reporter in 2005. "After the war there were no judges in Germany so the old Nazi judges were used and they upheld the criminalization of what we did and who we were. There are only five of us left in Cologne. Four of the boys and me." The proletarian make-up of the gang, she and others believe, prevented widespread official recognition of the Edelweiss Pirates' as a resistance movement compared to the White Rose, Swing Youth, and other upper-middle-class social movements opposed to the Nazi regime.

As Hitler's Reich crumbled around him, so did the driving reason the Edelweiss Pirates gathered in resistance against Nazi authority. The Cologne Navajos and majority of other groups voluntarily broke up by the summer of 1945. At this time, Hitler Youth and Nazi insurgents co-opted the Edelweiss Pirate moniker in their attempts to conceal their true identities and continue the fight underground against the Allies. However, the post-war variant of the Edelweiss Pirates bore no relationship to the confederation of youth non-conformists and eventual wartime resistance fighters that existed from the mid-1930s through the surrender of German forces in May 1945. As Perry Biddiscombe states in *The Enemy of Our Enemy: A View of the Edelweiss Piraten from the British and American Archives*, the Edelweiss Pirates "of 1946 were quite distinct from the wartime Edelweiss" and the Edelweiss label was "consciously adopted by neo-Nazi gangs as an initial means of protecting themselves from the inquiries of Allied security agencies." Thus, the re-branded, post-war variant was a pro-Nazi group with nothing in common with the original movement except the adopted name, which was hijacked and led to sixty years of confusion over the true role of the Edelweiss Pirates.

As Allied intelligence officers began to realize shortly after the war, the anti-Nazi reputation of the Edelweiss Pirates provided a safe haven for hardened Nazis who wanted to sneak under the radar of the authorities. "The present Edelweiss Piraten," said a British report, "have no connection with their predecessors, who, in so far as they were genuinely anti-Nazi, will have found a legal outlet for their zeal." But as it turned out, the Allies, especially the British who had endured the Battle of Britain and later V-1 and V-2 rocket attacks, weren't all that interested in separating out the so-called "Good Germans" from the bad. Allied interrogators proved indifferent towards the stories of Germans who resisted Hitler, preferring instead the black-and-white narrative of a fully indoctrinated Teutonic youth marching obediently to the drumbeat of Hitler and his jack-booted thugs. Furthermore, at the end of the war, the Allied occupation authorities frowned upon the contrarian, anti-authoritarian nature of the Edelweiss Pirates. They firmly believed that the group only represented "the enemy of our enemy" and "not our friends," thus contributing to the tainted image of the Edelweiss Pirates for the next sixty years.

While some members of the group were far-from-heroic criminals or antisocials who were only mildly opposed to National Socialism, what defines the Edelweiss Pirates is their resistance to the Hitler Youth and Nazi repression. As one insightful commentator has said, "Under whatever label, their activities were far too much to fly as youthful transgression; Heinrich Himmler himself ordered the Ehrenfeld gang busted up in the autumn of 1944. The discourse parsing the degree of 'criminality' in youth defying a criminal society strikes the author as an all too precious critique from the security of the postwar world. These pirates might make for less congenial martyr figures than the likes of Sophie Scholl, but in the end, they took desperate risks to maintain a sphere of freedom in circumstances of inconceivable peril. Not much adult opposition to Hitlerism with proper manifestos did better than they."

Whether one chooses to view the Edelweiss Pirates as youthful rebels or resistance fighters from central casting, what remains indisputable are the actions taken by the group against the Reich. They handed out pro-Allied, anti-Nazi propaganda leaflets; listened to outlawed foreign broadcasts; wrote anti-Nazi graffiti on the walls of public buildings; committed acts of politically charged vandalism and sabotage of Nazi-controlled munitions factories, trains, and military vehicles;

stockpiled illegal weapons; hid army deserters, escaped foreign slave laborers, and Jews; and attacked Hitler Youth, Gestapo officers, and Nazi officials. They also provided active aid during the final Allied advance, intimidated last-ditch Nazi resistors, and attempted to help the occupation forces develop a clear opinion about the character of the movement. Furthermore, once Germany surrendered, they offered to hunt down war criminals and other law-breakers if the Allies would give their group official sanction, which was unfortunately denied.

But perhaps most important is how they were viewed by the Nazi regime. Certainly, Himmler's Gestapo and the rest of the Nazi security forces considered them political resistance fighters when they subjected the group's members to days, weeks, and sometimes months of agonizing torture. Edelweiss Pirates who were caught could expect to face any number of draconian consequences. At the very least, the captured were threatened, beaten, or subjected to a head shaving, one of the most popular methods of humiliation. But more often than not, they were packed into overcrowded jails; sent to reform schools, psychiatric hospitals, or labor, re-education, or concentration camps; or outright murdered without trial like sixteen-year-old Barthel Schink on November 10, 1944, who now has a street named after him that runs along the very place he died next to the Ehrenfeld train station.

As the Edelweiss Pirates are finally securing their well-deserved place in history, it has become clear that the determination, forcefulness, and strength of the group played an important role in undermining the Nazi regime's attempts to rigidly control the hearts and minds of its youth. As Daniel Horn makes clear in *Youth Resistance in the Third Reich: A Social Portrait*, "As a final testimonial to the amazing effectiveness of the youth opposition, Himmler proclaimed the task of bringing the gangs under control as being 'important to the war effort.' Ordering immediate and stern measures, the SS chief gave additional far-reaching credit to the youth opposition when he warned that 'every omission or delay strengthens the activities of the cliques and undermines the trust of the population in the regime.'"

Several former members of the Edelweiss Pirates, including Gertrud Koch and Jean Jülich, published their recollections beginning in the 1980s. These works have established the facts of the Pirates' resistance to the Nazi regime during the last year of the war when the line between criminality and simple survival on the one hand, and active resistance on the other, were increasingly blurred. Surviving Gestapo files, postwar investigative records, and first-hand accounts have firmly established this redemptive narrative in which "Germans" fought "Nazis" in the streets of Cologne, providing a much-needed corrective to the mythology of the Edelweiss Pirates as degenerate youth committing crimes against legitimate police authority, which, of course, the Gestapo and other German security forces were not. Operating during perhaps the darkest chapter in human history, the *Edelweißpiraten* made a meaningful contribution not only to history but to humanity. They sang for freedom, love, and life; they are the Pirates of the *Edelweiß*.

## FERDINAND KÜTTER AND THE COLOGNE GESTAPO

The spearheading U.S. 3rd Armored Division of the U.S. First Army took Cologne with its still-standing cathedral on March 6, 1945—liberating the half of the city on the Left Bank of the Rhine. Despite the orders by the Nazis to evacuate the city to

Germany's interior, between 40,000 and 50,000 desperate civilians remained trapped inside Cologne or unwilling to leave, many of them having spent the last several weeks living without electricity, running water, or sanitation. Just before the enemy arrived, the gutless Gestapo and other security forces (disparagingly referred to as "Golden Pheasants" by Cologne's civilians) escaped across the Rhine with their remaining German and West European prisoners from the overcrowded and lice-infested El-De Haus, Brauweiler, Klingelpütz, and Müngersdorf AEL prisons. Most of the Russians, Poles, and other Eastern Europeans in their custody had already been murdered by the Gestapo in an orgy of violence throughout the month of February.

During the retreat, Richard Foltis, the Cologne Gestapo office's temporary commander at El-De Haus following the shootout-death of Dr. Max Hoffmann, disappeared. A rumor spread amongst *Kriminalkommissar* Ferdinand Kütter, Josef Hoegen, and Foltis's other officers that the Wehrmacht had executed the acting chief of the Cologne Gestapo for cowardice, although West German authorities later confirmed he died in a British bombing raid. After crossing the Rhine at Hohenzollern Bridge, which was subsequently blown up by the retreating German Army, the Gestapo officers were scattered across locations ranging from Bonn to Marienheide, and points farther east such as Siegen and north inside the Ruhr industrial region.

According to historian Michael McConnell in *Home to the Reich: The Nazi Occupation of Europe's Influence on Life inside Germany, 1941-1945*, Kütter and his Brauweiler unit abandoned the abbey prison as the Americans approached and marched their surviving German inmates, along with the few remaining female inmates of the workhouse, eastwards across the Rhine. During this final purge of the Left Bank Rhineland's prison system, most of the incarcerated were now weak from physical abuse, malnutrition, and disease. As a final insult, the Nazis forced them to ride aboard open trucks in frigid conditions to the German interior. Once transported across the Rhine, the Gestapo sent the prisoners to unsanitary and even more overcrowded prisons and work reeducation camps in the Right Bank Rhineland, including Siegen, Wipperfürth, Siegburg, and the Hünswinkel work reeducation camp, where they murdered many of them in April 1945 as the Ruhr pocket imploded from the swift Allied advance.

As McConnell states, during this period Kütter drove frantically "through the valleys and along the winding roads of the Ruhr with a carload of case files, desperately seeking a judge to review the material and sanction the execution of his remaining prisoners. Court officials, recognizing the personal danger involved in ordering the execution of German civilians now that the end appeared near, repeatedly rejected his pleas." Dodging enemy patrols, Kütter eventually made his way to the rubble-strewn city of Wuppertal to meet with his boss Karl Gutenberger, Higher SS and Police Leader in the western Rhineland, who agreed to liquidate the inmates. However, the despicable Kütter's triumph was short lived as the troops of the U.S. 78th Infantry Division had already overrun most of the prisons in the region and were now advancing on Wuppertal. While his panic-stricken Gestapo colleagues hastily changed into civilian clothes and burned their identification papers, Kütter, recognizing that all hope was lost and he would have to pay for his heinous crimes, locked himself in the bathroom of the police headquarters and committed suicide. The American forces captured Wuppertal against scant resistance on April 16, 1945.

While Kütter followed the same path as Hitler by taking his own life, his two brutal underlings, *Kriminalassistents* Josef Hoegen and Walter Hirschfeld, were arrested by the Allies and turned over to the German authorities that spring. But as post-war fate would have it, the two former members of the Gestapo's anti-Marxist section and Brauweiler Prison's two most infamous torturers after their boss Kütter were considered *Rädchen*—small cogs—in the Nazi's machinery of repression. Consequently, they managed to avoid serious punishment. The West German courts were typically lenient to former assistant officers because they supposedly acted under pressure from their superiors. Only if they acted autonomously, exceeded orders, or behaved in a particularly savage fashion did junior officers receive lengthy prison sentences. The German courts, wanting to put the war behind the country and rebuild it, reserved their most draconian punishment for the Himmlers, Gutenbergers, and other big brass of the SS security leadership.

According to McConnell in *The Situation is Once Again Quiet: Gestapo Crimes in the Rhineland, Fall 1944*, Hoegen was charged with fifty-eight counts of abuse and torture during his post-war trial. It was clearly established through eyewitness accounts that he was "an enthusiastic and often overzealous perpetrator." He, Hirschfeld, and other so-called "interrogators" committed hundreds of beatings in Brauweiler prison, brutalizing prisoners, including adolescent Edelweiss Pirates, elderly men, and a pregnant woman, with not just the "Clock of the Rhine," but metal bars, chairs, clubs, and their fists. They got particular satisfaction from treating their charges like animals; one of their favorites was to make prisoners lap up soup like a dog by slurping it from a bowl on the floor on all fours. Despite his documented brutality, Hoegen received a mere nine year prison sentence, and his accomplice Walter Hirschfeld received only two. Rhinelanders were stunned by the light sentences when they awoke to newspapers headlines declaring "The Accused Have the Last Word." In 1953, Hoegen was pardoned and went on to become a merchant in Cologne. He died in 1973 at the age of 75 without paying for his crimes. Unfortunately, the rabid Nazi torturer was hardly the exception to the rule when it came to evading punishment in post-war Germany. Like Kütter, Josef Hoegen will go down in history as one of the vilest and most notorious Gestapo officers of Hitler's Third Reich, a man known for his unbound cruelty and sadistic barbarism.

Though it is impossible to determine the total number of victims who were executed by the Cologne Gestapo during WWII, historical records have established that, at a minimum, between August 1944 and March 1945, 437 prisoners were executed at the Cologne Gestapo headquarters at El-De-Haus alone, while another 72 were executed at Brauweiler prison. As the National Socialist Documentation Center in Cologne (which I visited while researching for this book and is, ironically, located at El-De Haus) has stated, "Based on findings of French and British investigation officers, they were mainly foreigners (forced laborers and prisoners of war). However, they were not the only victims of the Cologne Gestapo. There is no knowing how many died during arrests or as the consequence of torture. Occasionally, the Gestapo also murdered people in the Klingelpütz prison, in

Brauweiler, and the work education camps.... The marches the Cologne Gestapo prisoners endured walking from the individual camps and detention facilities were particularly brutal and cost the lives of many an exhausted prisoner.... [A] local Gestapo branch was responsible for the deportation and killing of thousands of Cologne Jews and hundreds of resistance fighters and also took part in the deportation and killing of over 1,500 Sinti and Roma, numerous homosexuals and so-called antisocial elements."

The pace of the killings increased dramatically as the Nazis became increasingly paranoid over the U.S. Army's advance on Cologne. As the Allies drew closer in late February and early March 1945, the murder of Eastern European slave laborers and other designated enemies of the regime intensified to the point where Gestapo officers were reduced to executioners. According to McConnell, at this chaotic late *Endkampf* stage, "an estimated sixty to eighty prisoners a day arrived at the ruined building, where officers hanged them at a poorly constructed gallows on the orders of Kurt Matschke." After capturing El-De Haus, American troops discovered several corpses buried underneath a pile of rubble, whom the Gestapo had killed by bludgeoning them with shovels just hours before retreating across the Rhine. Following the war, court officials suspected the Gestapo used other burial sites besides El-De-Haus and Brauweiler, or cremated their victims, and that the number murdered by the Gestapo in late 1944 and early 1945 was as high as 1,800. In the overcrowded prisons and work camps, guards didn't just execute suspected criminals and foreigners; they also murdered sick, handicapped, and so-called "politically unreliable" prisoners whose only crime was to refuse to fight on behalf of Nazism, complying with Himmler's orders to liquidate all *Volksfeinde* before evacuation of the Rhineland.

In the end and as history has shown, the members of the Cologne Gestapo were scarcely policemen at all—they were second-rate bureaucrats, sadistic torturers, and mass murderers who would have been janitors scrubbing toilets if not for the rise of Hitler and National Socialism. Their approach to crime-solving, serving, and protecting can be aptly summarized by the words of Kütter himself: "Here we do hard work," he instructed his new recruits. "When prisoners don't sing we work them over for a long time with our truncheons until they confess."

# SOURCES AND ACKNOWLEDGEMENTS

To develop the story line, characters, and scenes for *Soldiers of Freedom: The WWII Story of Patton's Panthers and the Edelweiss Pirates*, I consulted over a hundred archival materials, non-fiction books, magazine and newspaper articles, blogs, Web sites, films, and numerous individuals, and I visited most of the historical locations in the novel. There are too many resources and locations to name here. However, I would be remiss if I didn't give credit to the key historical references upon which this novel is based, as well as the critical individuals who dramatically improved the quality of the manuscript from its initial to its final stage. Any technical mistakes in the historical facts underpinning the novel, typographical errors, or examples of overreach due to artistic license, however, are the fault of me and me alone.

In addition to the primary reference materials from German and United States archives listed below, I relied heavily upon eighteen reliable primary and secondary sources dealing specifically with Patton's Third Army, the 761st Tank Battalion, the 1944-1945 War in Europe, Nazi Germany and the Edelweiss Pirates, and the major historical figures in the novel. These references were invaluable and included the following for those interested in further reading about the historical events and personalities presented in the book: *Brothers in Arms: The Epic Story of the 761st Tank Battalion, WWII's Forgotten Heroes* (2005) by Kareem Abdul-Jabbar and Anthony Walton; *The Black Panthers: A Story of Race, War, and Courage—the 761st Tank Battalion in World War II* (2017) by Gina M. DiNicolo; *Come Out Fighting, The Epic Tale of the 761st Tank Battalion 1942-1945* (1945) by Trezzvant W. Anderson; *The 761st "Black Panther" Tank Battalion in World War II: An Illustrated History of the First African American Armored Unit to See Combat* (1999) by Joe Wilson, Jr.; *Patton's Panthers: The African-American 761st Tank Battalion In World War II* (2005) and *George S. Patton's Magnificent Panthers: The 761st Tank Battalion* (2016) by Charles W. Sasser; *Patton: A Genius for War* (1996) by Carlo D'Este; *Brothers, Rivals, Victors: Eisenhower, Patton, Bradley and the Partnership that Drove the Allied Conquest in Europe* (2011) by Jonathan W. Jordan; *Patton Papers: 1940-1945* (1974) by Martin Blumenson; *War As I Knew It* (1947) by General George S. Patton, Jr.; *The Guns at Last Light: The War in Western Europe, 1944-1945* (2013) by Rick Atkinson; *The Situation is Once Again Quiet: Gestapo Crimes in the Rhineland, Fall 1944* (2012) and *Home to the Reich: The Nazi Occupation of Europe's Influence on Life inside Germany, 1941-1945* (2015) by Michael P. McConnell; *Cologne During National Socialism: A Short Guide Through El-De House* (2010) by NS Documentation Center of the City of Cologne; *The Edelweiss Pirates: Protest Movement of Young Workers in the Third Reich* (1980) and *Inside Nazi Germany: Conformity, Opposition and Racism in Everyday Life* (1987) by Detlev Peukert; *Flowers in the Gutter: The True Story of the Edelweiss Pirates, Teenagers Who Resisted the Nazis* (2020) by K. R. Gaddy; and *Society in the Disaster: Terror, Illegality, Resistance, Cologne 1944/45* (1989) by Bernd A. Rusinek.

In writing the novel, there were many excellent historical books and articles in addition to those listed above from which I drew facts and inspiration to flesh out the story of the War in Europe in 1944-1945 and the major historical figures presented in the book. The interested reader is referred to the following additional sources used to write the true story presented herein.

U.S. 761st "Black Panther" Tank Battalion and WWII Tanks: *Hit Hard* (1983) by David J. Williams; *A Study in Leadership: The 761st Tank Battalion and the 92d Division* (1995) by Major Lenora A. Ivy; *U.S. Army in World War II, The Employment of Negro Troops* (2001) by Ulysses Lee; *The Black Panthers at War: The 761st Tank Battalion and General Patton's Drive on Germany* (2016) by Gina M. DiNicolo; *The Real-Life Black Panthers Liberated Concentration Camps* (2018) by Susie Davidson; The Army Lawyer Military Book Review of *Brothers in Arms: The Epic Story of the 761st Tank Battalion, WWII's Forgotten Heroes* (2004) by Major Italia A. Carson; *Fighting for America: Black Soldiers—the Unsung Heroes of World War II* (2004) by Christopher Moore; *The Double V Campaign: African Americans and World War II* (1998) by Michael L. Cooper; *The Court Martial of Jackie Robinson* (2011) by Callie Oettinger; *Come Out Fighting: Coronaca Man's Time with Historic Army Unit Going Public for First Time* (2019) by Adam Benson; *The Liberators: Fighting on Two Fronts in World War II* (1992) by Lou Potter, William Miles, and Nina Rosenblum; *A Hero's Story* (2002) by Susannah Bryan; *Black Liberators of the Holocaust* (1992) by New York Newsday; *The Original Black Panthers Fought in the 761st Tank Battalion During WWII* (2018) by Ryan Mattimore; *Doubts Mar PBS Film of Black Army Unit* (1993) by Richard Bernstein; *The Court-Martial of Jackie Robinson* (1984) by Jules Tygiel; *American Tanks & AFVs of World War II* (2018) by Michael Green; *Spearhead: An American Tank Gunner, His Enemy, and a Collision of Lives in World War II* (2019) by Adam Makos; *The Story of "Patton's Panthers," the Black WWII Tank Unit that Crushed Nazi Forces on the Western Front* (2017) by Logan Nye; *Tank Tactics: From Normandy to Lorraine* (2008) by Roman Jarymowycz; *Former Soldier Recalls Days in 761st Tank Battalion* (2012) by Sean Wardwell; *Plight of WWII Black Battalion Brought to Light* (2004) by Paul Zeise; *NY War Stories: 761st Tank Battalion* (2004 Radio Show) by David Ballela; *761st* (2007 Documentary Film) directed by Pete Chatmon; *Patton 360* (2009 Television Series on the History channel), featuring William McBurney in several later episodes; *The Presidential Unit Citation (Army) for Extraordinary Heroism to the 761st Tank Battalion* (1978), Department of the Army; *The Men That Served With Distinction: "The 761st Tank Battalion"* (1997) by Major Craig A. Trice; *761st Tank Battalion Veteran's Website* (http://www.761st.com/18update/2018a/), Association Secretary Ivan Harrison, Jr.

Patton, the U.S. Third Army, and the 1944-1945 War in Europe: *Patton: The Man Behind the Legend, 1885-1945* (1985) and *The Battle of the Generals: The Untold Story of the Falaise Pocket-The Campaign That Should Have Won World War II* (1993) by Martin Blumenson; *General Patton: A Soldier's Life* (2002) by Stanley Hirshson; *Fighting Patton: George S. Patton Jr. Through the Eyes of His Enemies* (2011) by Harry Yeide; *Drive* (1957) by Colonel Charles R. Codman; *Patton's Third Army: A Daily Diary of the United States Third Army Advance Through Europe, August, 1944 to May, 1945* (2008) by Charles M. Province; *The Biography of General George S. Patton* (1983) by Ian V. Hogg; *An Army at Dawn:*

*The War in North Africa, 1942–1943* (2002) and *The Day of Battle: The War in Sicily and Italy, 1943–1944* (2007) by Rick Atkinson; *The Lorraine Campaign: An Overview, September-December 1944* (1985) by Dr. Christopher R. Gabel; *The Lorraine Campaign* (1993) by Hugh M. Cole; *Lorraine 1944: Patton vs. Manteuffel* (2000), *Patton Versus The Panzers: The Battle of Arracourt, September 1944* (2016), and *Smashing Hitler's Panzers: The Defeat of the Hitler Youth Panzer Division in the Battle of the Bulge* (2019) by Steven Zaloga; *The Second World War* (2005) by John Keegan; *Patton, Montgomery, Rommel: Masters of War* (2008) by Terry Brighton; *Patton at the Battle of the Bulge: How the General's Tanks Turned the Tide at Bastogne* (2015) by Leo Barron; *The Generals: Patton, MacArthur, Marshall, and the Winning of World War II* (2015) by Winston Groom; *Battle of the Bulge: Hitler's Ardennes Offensive, 1944-1945* (1999) by Danny S. Parker; *Monty (3 Volumes): Vol. 1 (1981), The Making of a General (1887-1942); Vol. 2 (1983), Master of the Battlefield: Monty's War Years (1942-1944); Vol. 3 (1986), Final Years of the Field Marshal 1944-1976* by Nigel Hamilton; *The Memoirs of Field Marshal The Viscount Montgomery of Alamein* (1959) by Bernard Law Montgomery; *The Allies Strike Back, 1941-1943: The War in the West* (2017) by James Holland; *Deceiving Hitler: Double Cross and Deception in World War II* (2008) by Terry Crowdy; *Monty and Rommel: Parallel Lives* (2012) and *Snow and Steel: The Battle of the Bulge, 1944-45* (2014) by Peter Caddick-Adams; *Patton: Ordeal and Triumph* (2005) by Ladislas Farago; *Eisenhower's Armies: The American-British Alliance during World War II* (2015) by Niall Barr; *Roosevelt's Centurions: FDR and the Commanders He led to Victory in World War II* (2013) by Joseph E. Persico; *The Deceivers: Allied Military Deception in the Second World War* (2007) by Thaddeus Holt; *The Supreme Commander: The War Years of Dwight D. Eisenhower* (2012) by Stephen E. Ambrose; *Wild Bill Donovan: The Spymaster Who Created the OSS and Modern American Espionage* (2011) by Douglas Waller; *Ardennes 1944: The Battle of the Bulge* (2016) by Antony Beevor; *A Soldier's Story* (1978) by Omar N. Bradley; *Forward with Patton: The World War II Diary of Colonel Robert S. Allen* (2017) by Robert S. Allen and John N. Rickard (Ed.); *Hitler's Last Gamble: the Battle of the Bulge, December 1944-January 1945* (1994) by Trevor N. Dupuy; *A Tour of the Bulge Battlefields* (2015) by William C.C. Cavanagh and Karl Cavanagh; *Hitler's Ardennes Offensive: The German View of the Battle of the Bulge* (2016) by Danny S. Parker (Ed.); *Armageddon: The Battle for Germany, 1944-1945* (2005) and *Inferno: The World at War, 1939-1945* (2012) by Max Hastings; *The Monuments Men: Allied Heroes, Nazi Thieves and the Greatest Treasure Hunt in History* (2010) by Robert M. Edsel and Bret Witter; *General Patton's Principles for Life and Leadership* (2009) by Porter B. Williamson; *Eisenhower's Lieutenants: The Campaign of France and Germany, 1944–1945* (1981) by Russell Weigley; *Panzer Baron: The Military Exploits of General Hasso Von Manteuffel* (1976) by Donald Grey Brown; *The Price of Being a Patton: Wrestling With the Legacy of America's Most Famous General* (2017) by Tim Teeman; *Famous Cars: Patton's Willys Jeep* (2019) by Chris Kaiser; *Forward With Patton: WWII Diary Shifts Focus to General's Staff* (2018) by Joseph Craig.

<u>Edelweiss Pirates, Gestapo, and Resistance in Nazi Germany</u>: *The Edelweiss Pirates: An Exploratory Study* (2016) by Ryan Reilly; *Youth Resistance in the Third*

*Reich: A Social Portrait* (1973) by Daniel Horn; *Working-Class Resistance: Problems and Opinions*, in D. C. Large (Ed.), *Contending with Hitler: Varieties of Resistance in the Third Reich* (1991) by Detlev Peukert; *Children During the Holocaust* (2011) by Patricia Heberer; *Defying Hitler: The Germans Who Resisted Nazi Rule* (2019) by Gordon Thomas and Greg Lewis; *The Enemy of Our Enemy: A View of the Edelweiss Piraten from the British and American Archives* (1995) by Perry Biddiscombe; *German Resistance to Hitler* (1988) by Peter Hoffman; *Coal Steam, Jail and Camels* (2003) by Jean Jülich; *Confront!: Resistance in Nazi Germany* (2004) by John J. Michalczyk (Ed.); *Nazi Terror: The Gestapo, Jews, and Ordinary Germans* (2000) by Eric A. Johnson; *Edelweißpiraten: Youthful Rebellion as Legitimate Resistance against the Third Reich* (2010) by John Charles Marsland; *Edelweiß: My Youth as a Resistance Fighter* (2006) by Gertrud Koch and Regina Carstensen; *Inside Hitler's Germany: Life Under the Third Reich* (2000) by M. Hughes and C. Mann; *The Edelweiss Pirates: A Story of Freedom, Love, and Life* (2019) by Katie Kellerman, includes Jean Jülich interview; *Towards a New History of German Resistance to Hitler* (1981) by Leonidas E. Hill; *Resistance and Conformity in the Third Reich* (1995) by Martyn Housden (Ed.); Jean Jülich and Gertrud Koch interviews in *Teenaged Rebels who Fought Nazis are Honoured at Last* (2005) by Hannah Cleaver; *Opposition and Resistance in Nazi Germany* (2001) and *The Gestapo: The Myth and Reality of Hitler's Secret Police* (2017) by Frank McDonough; *Popular Opinion and Political Dissent in the Third Reich, Bavaria 1933-45* (1983) and *The End: The Defiance and Destruction of Hitler's Germany, 1944-1945* (2012) by Ian Kershaw; Walter Meyer interview in *German Resistance to Hitler—Personal History*, U.S. Holocaust Memorial Museum (1996); *Pirates, Swings and Junge Garde: Youth Resistance in the Third Reich* (1991) by Wilfried Breyvogel (Ed.); *Backing Hitler: Consent and Coercion in Nazi Germany* (2002) by Robert Gellately; *Edelweißpiraten in Cologne: Youth Rebellion against the Third Reich* (1983) by Matthias von Hellfeld; *He Was Sixteen When He Was Hanged: The Short Life of the Resistance Fighter Bartholomäus Schink* (1981) by Alexander Goeb; *The German Youth Gangs That Battled the Nazis During World War II* (2018) by Kurt Christopher; *Edelweißpiraten* (1984) by Fritz Theilen; *Teaching the Nazi Dictatorship: Focus on Youth* (2005) by Stephen Pagaard; *Campaigning for Cologne's Maligned Resistance* (2004) by Jennifer Macey; *Catholics Confronting Hitler: The Catholic Church and the Nazis* (2016) by Peter Bartley; *Resistance Fighters or Youth Gang?* (1990) by Joachim H. Knoll; *Gestapo: The Story Behind the Nazis' Machine of Terror* (2016) by Lucas Saul; *Jean Jülich* (2012 Obituary) in *The Telegraph*; *Edelweiss Pirates* (2004 Film produced and directed by Niko von Glasow).

I would also personally like to thank the following for their support and assistance. First and foremost, I would like to thank my wife Christine, an exceptional and highly professional book editor, who painstakingly reviewed and copy-edited the novel. Any mistakes that remain are my fault, of course.

Second, I would like to thank my literary agent, Cherry Weiner of the Cherry Weiner Literary Agency, for thoroughly reviewing, vetting, and copy-editing the manuscript, and for making countless improvements to the finished novel.

Third, I would like to thank Stephen King's former editor, Patrick LoBrutto, for thoroughly copy-editing the various drafts of the novel and providing detailed reviews.

I would also like to thank the late Austin and Anne Marquis, Governor Roy Romer, Ambassador Marc Grossman, Betsy and Steve Hall, Rik Hall, Christian Fuenfhausen, Bill and Doug Eberhart, Fred Taylor, David Boyles, Mo Shafroth, Peter Brooke, Tim and Carey Romer, Peter and Lorrie Frautschi, Deirdre Grant Mercurio, Dawn Ezzo Roseman, Joe Tallman, John Welch, Link Nicoll, Toni Conte Augusta Francis, Brigid Donnelly Hughes, John and Ellen Aisenbrey, Margot Patterson, Cathy and Jon Jenkins, Danny Bilello and Elena Diaz-Bilello, Charlie and Kay Fial, Vincent Bilello, Elizabeth Gardner, Robin McGehee, and the other book reviewers and professional contributors large and small who have given generously of their time over the years, as well as to those who have given me loyal support as I have ventured on this incredible odyssey of historical fiction writing.

Lastly, I want to thank anyone and everyone who bought this book and my loyal fans and supporters who helped promote this work. You know who you are and I salute you.

# ABOUT THE AUTHOR

The ninth great-grandson of legendary privateer Captain William Kidd, Samuel Marquis is the bestselling, award-winning author of a World War Two Series, the Nick Lassiter-Skyler International Espionage Series, and historical American fiction. His novels have been #1 *Denver Post* bestsellers and received multiple national book awards (Kirkus Reviews and Foreword Reviews Book of the Year, American Book Fest and USA Best Book, Readers' Favorite, Beverly Hills, Independent Publisher, National Indie Excellence, Next Generation Indie, and Colorado Book Awards). His books have also garnered glowing reviews from #1 bestseller James Patterson, Kirkus, and Foreword Reviews (5 Stars). Critics and book reviewers have compared the books of his WWII Series to the epic historical novels of Tom Clancy, John le Carré, Ken Follett, Herman Wouk, Daniel Silva, Len Deighton, and Alan Furst.

Below is a list of Samuel Marquis novels along with their release dates and book awards.

**THE WORLD WAR TWO SERIES**
**Bodyguard of Deception** – March 2016 – Winner Foreword Reviews' Book of the Year Awards; Award-Winning Finalist USA Best Book Awards
**Altar of Resistance** – January 2017 – Award-Winning Finalist Foreword Reviews' Book of the Year Awards, American Book Fest Best Book Awards, and Beverly Hills Book Awards
**Spies of the Midnight Sun: A True Story of WWII Heroes** – May 2018 – Winner Independent Publisher Book Awards
**Lions of the Desert: A True Story of WWII Heroes in North Africa** – February 2019 – Winner Readers' Favorite, National Indie Excellence, and Beverly Hills Book Awards; Award-Winning Finalist Foreword Reviews' Book of the Year and American Fiction Best Book Awards
**Soldiers of Freedom: The WWII Story of Patton's Panthers and the Edelweiss Pirates** – March 2020

**THE NICK LASSITER – SKYLER INTERNATIONAL ESPIONAGE SERIES**
**The Devil's Brigade** – September 2015 – #1 Denver Post Bestseller; Award-Winning Finalist Beverly Hills Book Awards
**The Coalition** – January 2016 – Winner Beverly Hills Book Awards; Award-Winning Finalist USA Best Book Awards and Colorado Book Awards
**The Fourth Pularchek** – June 2017 – Winner Independent Publisher Book Awards; Award-Winning Finalist American Book Fest Best Book Awards and Beverly Hills Book Awards

**HISTORICAL PIRATE FICTION**
**Blackbeard: The Birth of America** – February 2018 – Winner Kirkus Reviews Book of the Year and Beverly Hills Book Awards; Award-Winning Finalist American Book Fest Best Book Awards